Two Hearts Entwined
in Passion.
Two Souls Inflamed
with Desire.

"It's much too late, isn't it? We are finally alone and no one will come to your rescue this time, Caitlyn. If you want to get away you will have to tell me that you don't want me."

She was trembling so that she was afraid she might fall, but he held her against him, and she could feel that he was trembling too.

"You've made me wait too long for this moment," he whispered, "and now I want you so badly I'm afraid I'll hurt you."

"You won't hurt me," she told him gently. "I love you, Tanner."

A sudden shyness came over her. But she realized that there was no need for shyness now . . .

Jove Books by Theresa Conway

A PASSION FOR GLORY
SEEDS OF DESTINY

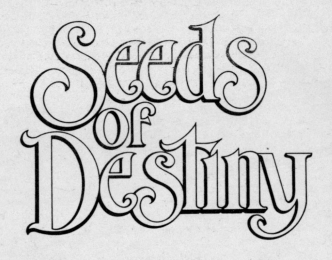

Seeds of Destiny

THERESA CONWAY

JOVE BOOKS, NEW YORK

SEEDS OF DESTINY

A Jove Book/published by arrangement with
the author

PRINTING HISTORY
Jove edition/April 1989

ISBN: 0-515-10008-0

Jove Books are published by The Berkley Publishing Group,
200 Madison Avenue, New York, New York 10016.
The name ''JOVE'' and the ''J'' logo
are trademarks belonging to Jove Publications, Inc.

PRINTED IN THE UNITED STATES OF AMERICA

10 9 8 7 6 5 4 3 2 1

To my older brother, Dan,
and my younger brother, Mark,
with love

1

MARGARET FORRESTER O'ROURKE sat at her escritoire, her slender white hands thumbing distractedly through the sheets of parchment in front of her. They contained the list of guests who were to be invited to the O'Rourkes' annual spring barbecue. At thirty-six, Margaret was a handsome woman with striking auburn hair and soft blue eyes, but her creamy white complexion freckled all too easily in the hot Louisiana sun.

She laid the guest list aside on her smooth satinwood writing desk and tried not to think about what her husband, Timothy, would say when she told him the news she'd received that morning. Heaven knew Timothy had enough on his mind with the spring planting of cotton and the outbreak of measles among the slaves, but now he would have to deal with the dismissal of his elder daughter, Caitlyn, from the Vicksburg Female Academy, the third such establishment she'd attended in the past year. That fifteen-year-old Caitlyn had once again been requested to leave was not as hurtful to Margaret as the additional news that their younger daughter, Constance, had chosen to follow her sister home.

The letter from Vicksburg was dated two days before, so Margaret knew that the Female Academy expected immediate arrangements to be made for the O'Rourke sisters to return home. Timothy would not be pleased to learn that he would have to take a paddle wheeler upriver in order to fetch the girls, but he would never allow his wife to make the journey alone.

She sighed and stood up from her desk, wondering what transgression Caitlyn had committed to warrant her removal from the school. At the Ladies' Academy in New Orleans last fall she had pushed another student into a pond in a fit of temper, later claiming that she thought all young ladies were taught to swim at an early age. She had been amazed to learn that the girl had been fished out half-drowned. They had tried the School for Young Ladies in Natchez after that, but Caitlyn had lasted only two months before taking an intense dislike to one of her deportment teachers and nailing her inside the school's outhouse. Timothy had roared with laughter at that prank, but at his wife's urging,

he had packed the girls off to one more school, this one in Vicksburg, in order to polish off Caitlyn's rough edges.

Fourteen-year-old Constance had always been exemplary in her deportment and her studies, but with unfailing loyalty, she had followed her elder sister to each new establishment, refusing to remain in any school where Caitlyn was not welcome.

Margaret walked thoughtfully to the window of her first-floor office, where she tabulated the household accounts and made up lists of purchases for the running of the huge plantation to which Timothy had brought her after their marriage nearly nineteen years before. She had come from her father's sugar plantation near New Orleans, where the drenching rains and humid soil were perfect for the tall sugarcane but would have been devastating to cotton.

Between the Red River Valley and the Mississippi River, north of Baton Rouge, cotton plantations sprawled across the land. Cotton was king and as long as the planters had their way, it would never be dethroned. She had heard her husband, in the company of other gentlemen, proclaim loudly that cotton would reign as long as it continued to provide nearly half of the value of all American exports, from both the North and the South.

But Margaret did not want to think of cotton now, for her mind was full of other problems: sickness among the slaves; the guest list for the barbecue, which had to be gone over carefully lest anyone be left out, or lest anyone be left in who might be unwelcome in the parish that season. But she was especially anxious about her daughters. She and Timothy would have to make a decision about the girls when he returned from his daily rounds on the plantation. It would be just like Timothy to applaud whatever transgression Caitlyn had committed, and Margaret realized that her husband's levity would cause whatever reproof she might give her willful daughter to be too easily dismissed.

Timothy O'Rourke sat his horse with practiced ease as he paused on a hilltop to gaze out over all of his land. His Irishman's barrel chest swelled with pride as his dark blue eyes swept over the fertile acres of alluvial soil. He scanned the neatly furrowed rows where the plowed earth waited for the cotton seeds. The planting would be done, he calculated, in two days' time. Spring had come a little early this year of 1858, but although it was barely into April, he would not be caught lagging. He looked

out once more over the fertile land and in his mind's eye saw not the naked earth but row upon row of green shoots. In a few months they would grow nearly six feet high, producing creamy white flowers that would turn deep pink before falling off to leave only the small green seedpods. Later, when the seed fibers became tightly packed inside them, the cotton bolls would burst open, revealing the white masses of fiber, which would be harvested by the nearly one hundred slaves Timothy owned.

He smiled to himself, recalling the huge crop they'd harvested last year. It had brought him nearly ten cents a pound at market, enabling him to purchase ten new field hands and make some necessary improvements in the slave quarters. And there were always those expensive fripperies his wife and two daughters demanded, but—and here Timothy's smile widened—no matter what their finery cost him, it was worth every last cent. And so much money was wasted on those worthless schools to which Margaret insisted on sending the girls. She was determined to have their offspring well educated—*too* well, to his way of thinking.

Timothy affectionately patted his horse, a full-blooded hunter that was as barrel-chested as he and nearly the same red as his hair. He wished his daughters were as biddable as the proud steed beneath him. Caitlyn was showing the effects of being given too free a rein; she was as willful and hot-tempered as a mare not yet bred. Timothy knit his brows in consternation. Tonight at dinner he would speak to Margaret about the marriage prospects for his daughters. Lord knew he was spending enough money on those fancy finishing schools to turn out two very eligible young ladies!

Two days later those same two young ladies sat together outside the office of the headmistress of the Vicksburg Female Academy, trying desperately to hear what was being said behind the closed doors. Now and then their father's voice rose to a near bellow, but then it would gradually subside until they had to lean forward to hear anything at all. Finally they realized it was no use and resigned themselves to sitting as still as possible while awaiting their father's reappearance.

Sitting still was not something Caitlyn O'Rourke did well. In her white muslin dress with its embroidered forget-me-nots on the twelve yards of skirt, she tried mightily not to bend one knee and tuck her foot beneath her, knowing the headmistress's sec-

retary would frown sternly at such a posture. But it was impossible to sit with hands demurely folded and eyes downcast when she knew how angry her father would be when he found out what she had done to get herself tossed out of yet another school.

It had all seemed such a lark when she'd first thought of it. Everyone in Vicksburg knew about Mammy Mincy, who had just put up the small canvas-roofed hut across the street from the boarding school. The conjure woman was always hounded by her neighbors, but she would just move her hut over to another vacant lot and set up shop again, charging a few pennies for a palm reading or a quarter for a love potion to catch an errant swain. Women would sneak out to her hut under cover of darkness to procure concoctions designed to rid them of an abusive husband or to cause a miscarriage.

Sheltered for most of her young life, Caitlyn knew very little about people like Mammy Mincy and her clients, but once she saw the hut spring up with the crudely painted sign in front of it, she decided she had to go and see what conjuring was all about. She'd discussed her plan with her sister, but Constance had looked alarmed and had warned her that it was foolish nonsense to even think of doing such a thing.

Caitlyn then stubbornly decided to go by herself. Her fatal mistake had been to confide in a girl who had a grudge against her. Mary Wynch had never liked the vivacious, sparkling-eyed Caitlyn, and when she saw a chance to get back at her, she took it with zest, careful to hide her malice behind an appearance of concerned helpfulness. She offered to wait by the small side door leading out to the alley next to the school, hardly able to keep the spite from her excited face. When she saw Caitlyn cross the street as twilight settled in, she locked the door and went upstairs to prepare for bed with the rest of the students.

One of the teachers, making her rounds of the school before retiring, heard the surreptitious knocks on the side door a half hour later and found Caitlyn waiting to be let inside. After questioning, during which Caitlyn admitted her guilt, the horrified headmistress immediately informed her that such conduct was not fitting for any student enrolled at her school and that Caitlyn O'Rourke would find herself dismissed as soon as a letter was prepared asking her parents to come for her.

Caitlyn refused to implicate anyone else in her escapade and none of the other students volunteered any information, so no one else was punished. Caitlyn had concocted her own scheme

of revenge against Mary Wynch and, even now, as she sat tensely awaiting her father's reappearance, she smiled as she imagined the look on Mary's face when she found her clothes closet completely empty. In an apparent spirit of generosity, Caitlyn had confiscated all of Mary's clothing and added it to the pile destined for the charity hospital of Vicksburg. Only fifteen minutes before, Caitlyn had seen the ragman's cart go by with Mary's clothes on top of his goods and the wrath in her heart had been somewhat appeased.

A thunderous oath ensuing from behind the heavy mahogany doors brought Caitlyn's attention back to her own situation and she dismissed Mary Wynch's betrayal from her mind. She cast an anxious glance at her sister, whose soft blue eyes were rimmed with tears.

"Oh, Constance, don't be a sniveling goose about this," she whispered tartly. "You're not in any trouble, you know!"

"Papa will be so angry at you that it won't matter if I'm in trouble or not," Constance whispered nervously. "He'll yell during the whole trip home and I shall have to listen to it as well as you!"

Their voices were hushed by a severe look from the headmistress's secretary and both turned their attention back to the doors, wondering how much longer they would be obliged to wait for their father. Constance was on the verge of breaking into sobs. Nervously, she brought a hand up to smooth an errant blond curl at her ear. The contrast between her demeanor and Caitlyn's was marked, for the expression on Caitlyn's face could only be described as mutinous. Her dark blue eyes glowered with irritation at all this commotion over a little escapade that hadn't even brought her much satisfaction. After a few mumbled words, a piercing look at Caitlyn's face, and a series of gestures that included rolling her eyes and pointing eerily to the door of the hut, Mammy Mincy had told her nothing out of the ordinary. She would marry well, have numerous children, and live to be ninety.

"Why, you old fake!" Caitlyn had scoffed. "I could have said that!" She'd thrown the pennies on the table, wishing she had the nerve to refuse to pay the old crone.

Remembering how disappointing the conjure woman had been, Caitlyn pursed her lips and tossed her coppery auburn curls. "This is all just a tempest in a teapot!" she whispered indig-

nantly to Constance. "Poor Papa is getting his Irish up over nothing!"

When she beheld her father's high color and flashing blue eyes as he finally retreated from the headmistress's office, Caitlyn knew he was really angry. Was he angry because of her escapade, or because his coming here had delayed the cotton planting, or because of something the headmistress had said?

As Timothy O'Rourke took his leave of the headmistress, he thought he had never received such a reprimand as she had just given him. The old battle-ax had said Caitlyn was headstrong and willful and had told him in no uncertain terms that his daughter's wild schemes were a danger to herself and the rest of the students. She certainly could not have someone with Caitlyn's disposition influencing the daughters of some of the most respectable families in Vicksburg. The implication that *his* family was not as respectable galled Timothy more than anything else.

Finally, when he could no longer trust himself to remain civil, he abruptly donned his hat, turned on his heel, and left the room while the headmistress was in midsentence.

"All right, daughters, we'll be going now," Timothy commanded, gesturing to them to follow him into the adjoining hall, where their bags had been placed.

Both girls followed him, then waited anxiously while he directed two men to load their baggage onto a cart and take it to the riverfront. When one of the bags fell off the cart into the dusty road, Timothy let loose with a stream of oaths that would have done a soldier proud. This outburst only added to the girls' worry about what was in store for them.

Actually, after discharging verbally, Timothy felt much better, although he could not let Caitlyn know that, for the sly puss would find some way to turn her escapade into an innocent prank, giving him a guileless look and assuring him that she didn't think she'd done anything wrong. Hah! That girl could find trouble faster than a hound on the scent of a raccoon!

"Now, Caitlyn Margaret O'Rourke, what put the fool notion into that head of yours to slip away from school at night when you were well aware of the rules?"

"Papa, I didn't see anything wrong in going to see Mammy Mincy," Caitlyn began, choosing her words carefully and keeping her eyes modestly downcast lest they should show the angry turbulence she felt. "I don't think it had anything to do with

rules, Papa," she said. "I think they were all afraid of the conjure woman."

"And so they would be," he remarked, lowering his tone slightly, for he was proud of bravery shown in any human being, especially his own flesh and blood.

Noting her father's train of thought, Caitlyn sought to play it to her own advantage. "But, Papa, *I* wasn't afraid of her! What's there to be afraid of? She's nothing but a fraud! She's just a wrinkled old black woman talking mumbo jumbo because she can make money doing it."

"Well, maybe she's a fraud and maybe she's not," he remarked, "but there's still no excuse for disobeying the rules, missy."

As she heard the conversation going down an unwanted path, Caitlyn tried a new tactic. "Papa, that school had some of the silliest rules I've ever heard. Why, it was practically against the rules for a young lady to think her own thoughts! And you *know* how often you've reminded me that I've got a mind of my own and that I should use it!"

Constance, sitting silently throughout the exchange, noted her sister's neat evasion of the issue and lowered her head to conceal a smile. Caitlyn twisted the truth so easily it could make one's head spin.

"Of course I did!" Timothy said, his bushy red brows lowering slightly as he sensed that he'd been led off the subject. "But these spirited high jinks of yours have got to stop, miss," he continued in a sterner vein. "You're fifteen and it's time you started thinking about your future—your *real* future. I've already told your mother this is to be the last of the schools for you and your sister."

In her excitement at hearing these hoped-for words, Caitlyn missed the look of keen disappointment on her sister's face. No more frosty headmistresses to scowl at her disapprovingly, Caitlyn rejoiced. No more deportment teachers to complain endlessly of poor posture and too much spring in her gait.

"Papa, I'm so happy!" she cried out, springing forward to put her arms around his neck. "I hated to be away from you and Mama!"

After a long squeeze, Timothy gently pushed her back into her seat. Why was it that he felt so absurdly happy that there would be no more schools to take his daughters away from him? he wondered, and he found the answer in the radiant smile Cait-

lyn bestowed on him. That smile could melt the heart of a convict, he thought. He glanced over at his younger daughter with equal fondness. Poor little Connie, he thought benevolently. She was a pretty thing, but when her sister was around she just seemed to fade away. Caitlyn's vibrant personality left no room in a man's sight for her sister's to shine through. But certainly, he told himself, Constance would someday make a man an easier wife than Caitlyn.

2

THE SPLENDOR of Mornhaven plantation was not lost on anyone who beheld its three-storied, balustraded, and columned magnificence, least of all its owner, who had selected the square of ground on which it stood and had seen its completion, from the first brick to the last coat of whitewash. The house was opulent in design, but not burdened by unnecessary architectural frivolities. Its clean white bricks caught the rising sun as it faced east along the Mississippi River, catching the first rose-tinted rays of dawn each morning. The eight massive, smoothly rounded columns were cut from pink-veined marble and stood like tall guardians of the first-floor veranda, where the master of the house would sit on a cushioned, high-backed chair in the late afternoon and watch the sunlight glinting on the mighty river. Above, on the second-floor veranda, with its graceful, ironwork balustrade, twin double doors opened into the bedrooms of the daughters of the house, who would cast proud glances over the front lawn that rolled gently down to the river road.

The gravel drive, laid with crushed oyster shells brought from New Orleans, glistened like a white serpent that uncoiled to meet the dusty brown road that traveled for miles alongside the great river.

Two travelers on horseback, followed by a large dray upon which rested a mountain of luggage and other articles, stopped for a moment to take off their hats and mop their faces, letting their eyes rest on the gleaming house they could see through the arch of trees lining the drive.

"Damn fine sight, isn't it, son?" the elder of the two men commented with a hint of a sigh. "O'Rourke's pride shows right through that house."

"Riverhouse can look just as good once we've had the time to refurbish it," his son commented a trifle sullenly. The hot, dusty ride from New Orleans had been a long affair and the young man was thinking how much he would like to come home to a house in as fine condition as Mornhaven.

"Riverhouse will never be the same again," his father returned with a sad shake of his silvered head. "Not since your mother went, Brant."

Brant Sinclair felt a moment's grief, old and familiar, as he thought of his sweet and pretty mother. His boyhood days had been filled with her gay laughter. He could still recall the way her skirts swayed back and forth as she hurried from one room to another. As a boy he'd been mesmerized by those swaying skirts, running behind his mother, reaching out to touch the soft fabric when she'd hurry off to another part of the house. Christina Sinclair had been a happy woman, secure in the love of her husband and only son.

Why, then, had God seen fit to take her in the prime of her life? Brant had asked himself many times. He had been a young lad of fifteen when she had died. He could remember clearly the fatal trip they'd all made to New Orleans in the summer of 1853. His mother had begged her husband, William, to take her and Brant down to the city that summer. Life at Riverhouse had been too dull that year, the summer oppressively hot, the neighbors all content to stay indoors or in the coolness of shaded verandas. Christina had complained of the lack of social calls and had pressed her husband for a visit to New Orleans, where life was always gay.

William Sinclair had given in, despite a nagging worry that the summer heat would only be intensified in the city. Still, he hadn't wanted his adored wife to go into a sulk because of the lack of gaiety in the parish that summer. He'd taken his family downriver and they'd arrived in New Orleans at the end of June.

Already there had been dark rumors of yellow fever in the city, where the mosquitoes were thick as dust along the river and the very air one breathed seemed tainted. Christina had assured her husband they would stay only a week. She'd said a week of festivity in New Orleans would last her until the social season in the fall. And so they had met friends, attended parties, shopped, and held soirees of their own. Christina had been so happy she had even tried to extend the week into two, but William had been firm. The rumors of cholera and plague had begun

to sound even more ominous and the hospitals had already filled up with yellow-fever patients.

On the way back upriver, Christina had developed a slight headache, more irritating than alarming. But by the time they'd reached Riverhouse she'd had a raging fever. News came from New Orleans that yellow fever, plague, and cholera were rampant in the city and Brant Sinclair had feared for his mother's life. She had held on for a few weeks before she died of yellow fever, leaving a husband who blamed himself bitterly and a son who could not accept the death of such a lively, compassionate woman. The epidemics in New Orleans had raged on from July all the way to November, with the death count reaching a horrific ten thousand.

That was when William Sinclair had turned his back on his house, his acres of cotton, the life he had known from birth. He could no longer live in the house where his beloved Christina had died so unnecessarily. He had taken his son and they had gone up North to Boston, where William had a distant cousin.

Now, five years later, they had come back. Brant watched the sad look on his father's face and wished there were some way he could help him. But there was no easing of the pain for William Sinclair except through the bottle. Many nights he was so drunk he couldn't stand and Brant had put his own father to bed as gently as he might have tucked in a child. The drinking had worsened to the extent that William's cousin in Boston had asked them to leave.

In New Orleans, for the brief time they were there to buy a few supplies and hire a wagon and driver to transport their luggage, it had gotten worse. But to Brant's relief, once they'd started up the river road and gotten past Baton Rouge William had seemed to gain some measure of composure. He'd even been able to sit a horse by himself and had insisted on doing so. Brant had been hopeful at this marked change in his father, but seeing the look of intense pain on his face now, he knew it would not last.

"Well, we'd best be continuing, Pa," he said softly, reaching over to touch his father's arm. "You'll want to be at the house by afternoon so we can make it hospitable." His restless dark eyes looked at his father's face anxiously.

"Yes," William returned. He took up the reins silently and turned his horse upriver once more, averting his gaze from the splendor of his neighbor's house.

They continued a few more miles until another gravel drive angled off the river road. William turned down the drive, seeming to shrink visibly on the horse's back.

They reached the end of the drive and gazed up at Riverhouse, trying not to think of the lilting voice that would never fill those rooms again, of the sparkling eyes that would never look out a window as they returned home in the late afternoon.

Five years of disuse had obviously taken their toll on the house. The whitewashed bricks had browned and become water-stained from the rain. Shutters hung askew and new paint was needed everywhere. Vines and undergrowth had taken over the entire front lawn, where Brant remembered running on an emerald carpet as a boy.

"A lot of work here," his father remarked in a low voice. He coughed suddenly, doubling over on the horse's back.

Brant was used to his father's coughing spells and watched helplessly until William once more gained the use of his voice. When he did he looked at his son almost calmly. "Your mother would have been ashamed of this house and what we've let happen to it," he said. "Riverhouse was her pride and joy. We've got to try, son."

Brant nodded, although the problems of rejuvenating the house depressed him. He was not by nature an energetic young man and the prospect of expending energy on a house that hardly interested him anymore was appalling to him. Much better, he thought, to return to New Orleans or even to Baton Rouge and obtain rooms there. Or perhaps to impose on their neighbors to put them up until the house was made livable again.

He started to say something to his father, but William had already urged his horse forward to the veranda and was dismounting. Brant watched as the older man drew out a huge brass key, fitted it to the lock, and swung open the wide double doors. Hardly a necessary action, Brant thought, when there were at least four windows on the first story whose panes had been broken by wind or rocks.

"Come here," William ordered his son, stepping inside the house. "I want you to be with me now, son. This will be yours someday soon."

Brant dismounted and followed his father into the hall. The inside of the house seemed to be in surprisingly good condition except for dust and cobwebs everywhere. White sheets that had been thrown over the furniture loomed like ghosts, and Brant

couldn't help thinking of the ghost that would haunt these rooms for them.

"Perhaps we should find quarters elsewhere until someone can clean the house," he suggested hopefully. But they had no slaves, for William had sold them all to neighbors before he'd left. Who was going to do all the work?

"We'll make a place for ourselves to sleep," William returned in a tone that brooked no refusal. "If the second story is like this, all we'll have to do is take off the coverings. We've brought enough food for a few days and God knows we have enough to do to keep us busy." He seemed almost to relish the task ahead of him.

"But it's too late to plant cotton, Pa," Brant protested, "so there's no reason to stay here."

"We'll have to hope for the charity of our neighbors," William returned calmly. "I sold twenty slaves to Timothy O'Rourke and at least twice that many to Winfield Cobb. Surely they'll understand if I need them for a few days for the planting. We'll plant only a few acres, of course, just enough to bring in a respectable crop this year. Perhaps we'll make enough to buy back a few slaves for next year."

"But, Pa, O'Rourke and Cobb will need the field hands for their own planting," Brant pointed out.

"We can wait until their cotton has been planted," William returned, unruffled. He turned to his son and fixed him with a level gaze. "Brant, you've got to realize that we must try to bring this plantation back to life. We owe it to the memory of your dear mother."

Brant nodded, though his heart wasn't in it. How could he tell his father that it was all but impossible to revive this plantation, especially without the proper tools and without field hands to work the soil. Everything took money, something they had precious little of right now. The cottonseed alone would cost them a pretty penny and, unless his father intended to beg for plows and mules, they would have to be purchased too.

Brant looked around the house that was part of his birthright and felt no comfort in it now. He wished they had never decided to return to Louisiana. If William hadn't felt so ill this past winter, they wouldn't have come back. But he couldn't let himself die on Northern soil, he'd told his son, and despite the bad memories, he wanted to return to Riverhouse, to the earth he loved. Right now Brant almost hated his home. If he had had

his way, he would have sold the plantation lock, stock, and barrel to O'Rourke or Cobb or one of the other neighbors, who would have paid good money to get another five hundred acres of bottomland. He wished he had had the courage to talk to his father about selling it, but now he realized it was too late. All that loomed ahead of him was years and years of hard work. Any profit that was made would have to be put back into more seed, more slaves, more tools. The house itself would have to wait for all but the most essential repairs.

"Pa, I think I'll take a ride down toward the river," Brant said as his father started up the stairs.

William nodded, already thinking of his land. "Maybe I could buy back some of the slaves I sold to our neighbors," he muttered to himself as he went upstairs. "Have the driver empty the wagon and bring everything inside." Then he added, almost as an afterthought, "And tell him to bring up a bottle of that liquor I have in the carton."

Brant's spirits fell. He hurried out the door, gave the proper instructions to the driver, and then mounted his horse, pushing it to a fast trot down the gravel drive and out to the river road. Just a few yards away the levee sloped down to the river, and he carefully guided his mount through the foliage. He dismounted on the embankment and threw himself to the ground, sitting morosely while he chewed on a long sliver of grass. He tried not to think of the days when his mother was alive and Riverhouse was constantly filled with guests and neighbors. Life had been gay and happy then. He had been a boy approaching adulthood, just beginning to show interest in some of the prettier belles whose mothers brought them to make social calls. And they had been interested in him, he recalled with a little smile.

In exasperation, he threw the piece of grass to the ground. All those belles were probably married by now. How could he boast of Riverhouse and his acreage? Why, he could hardly call it a plantation anymore! Without slaves it was nothing more than a farm, as humble as those of the poor whites who eked out a living in the piedmont districts or other less fertile areas of the tidewater.

The shrill notes of a paddle wheeler's whistle floated over the river and Brant looked up to see the gracefully embellished boat coming downstream. Probably from Vicksburg or Memphis, he thought, standing up and leaning forward to get a better look. He'd always enjoyed watching the big boats churning up and

down the river when he was a small boy and the boat still had the power to lift his spirits a little.

As it came closer he could see people on the deck, some leaning on the railing to look at the shore, others strolling around the promenade enjoying the spring weather as the late afternoon slipped into early dusk. He could almost hear the laughter of the young ladies as they walked arm in arm with young men, one hand tucked into an elbow, the other holding on tightly to a lacy parasol. Somberly dressed businessmen glanced at their pocket watches to make sure the steamer was making good time. Small children ran between the strollers, weaving in and out as they chased one another, causing concerned mothers to call sharply to them if they ventured too near the railing.

The boat passed quite close to Brant and he could make out the faces of passengers on the near side. He smiled to see two young ladies walking together, trailed by an older man who had to be their doting father from the expression on his face. He looked especially proud when young men turned their heads to watch the two females make their way around the deck.

Brant found his own interest stirred by the two girls, who looked quite lovely in their gaily colored afternoon dresses and wide leghorn bonnets. He could just make out the coppery auburn curls of one girl beneath her yellow hat. She was talking animatedly and seemed to have a crackling sort of energy that Brant could almost feel from where he stood. Beside her the other girl, whose strawberry blonde hair curled softly at her cheeks, was listening and laughing, trying to match the other's stride. Brant found himself enchanted by them and leaned forward eagerly without realizing what he was doing.

Watching the boat's passengers, Brant was unaware that the swirling current of the river was just below him, sucking greedily at the muddy bank. When the shrill whistle of the paddle wheeler blew again, he started involuntarily, lost his footing, and plunged headlong into the water.

It took only a moment for the treacherous current to swirl him away from the bank and pull him out toward the middle of the river. As Brant tried to position himself to swim back to shore, a piece of debris hit him solidly on the back of the head and he nearly lost consciousness. Struggling in earnest, he could make out shrill screams coming from the passengers on deck. Several voices called to him, but he was so dazed from the blow on his head that he couldn't be sure of the direction of the boat.

Passengers had begun to line the railing, gazing anxiously at the young man trying to save himself. Timothy O'Rourke called swiftly for someone to cast a lifeline out to the lad and one of the crew immediately did so. When the young man grasped the line, he was pulled slowly toward the boat and finally hauled aboard, coughing and shuddering, trying unsuccessfully to sit up.

Constance tapped her father on the arm. "Who is it, Papa? Do you know him?"

Timothy shook his head, though there was certainly something about the lad that touched his memory. Something familiar about those dark eyes that were just opening as Brant looked around him with a mixture of relief and embarrassment.

"It was lucky we were so close to shore," Caitlyn observed, eyeing the young man with curiosity. "He would have surely drowned had the current taken him farther from the boat."

"Heavens, Caitlyn, don't talk about drowning when the poor young man must feel terrible enough!" Constance intervened. She looked at him sympathetically and blushed to see that he was staring at her.

When Brant had regained his footing and was standing by himself at the railing, Timothy, followed closely by his two daughters, walked up to introduce himself and find out what had happened.

"You're a lucky man, sir," he said kindly, putting his hand out to shake that of the younger man. "I'm Timothy O'Rourke from Mornhaven. It's lucky we were going to be let off shortly or the boat might not have been so close to shore." He turned and gestured to his two companions. "These are my daughters, Caitlyn and Constance."

Caitlyn thought it odd that the young man turned red as a beet and seemed to be searching for words. Something about him was familiar, she realized, if she could just place it.

"Brant Sinclair, in your debt, Mr. O'Rourke," he finally responded.

Timothy's mouth opened in surprise. "By God, not William Sinclair's son?"

Brant nodded weakly. "Yes, sir."

"But—but you've been away these past five years without writing to anyone in the parish," Timothy said, sputtering a little. "The last time we saw you and your father was just after—" He let his words trail off abruptly as he realized that the last time

he'd seen them was at Christina Sinclair's funeral. So that's where he'd seen those lively dark eyes before, he suddenly recalled. "But what's brought you back here?" he asked.

"My father has been ill this past winter," Brant replied, keeping his voice steady but not having as much luck with his eyes, which constantly strayed to Constance's raptly attentive face. Of course she must remember him, he thought ruefully. Hadn't he always been the one to pull her pigtails and drive her close to tears with his teasing? Oh, God, why was youth so unkind, so uncaring? She must think him a villain still!

"Has your father returned with you?" Timothy asked, interrupting the younger man's thoughts.

"Yes, sir. As you may already know, we've been staying with relations in Boston for the last few years. My father was very ill this past winter and decided he wanted to come home," Brant replied, bringing his attention back to Timothy with an effort. He wished it were proper for him to address Constance, but realized what a ridiculous sight he must seem to her, as wet as a fish and stinking of river water.

"How is your father now?" Timothy asked solicitously. "Is he still in poor health?"

"I think he's feeling better just being back home," Brant responded. "We only arrived this afternoon."

"So you've seen Riverhouse?" Timothy questioned.

Brant nodded. "It's not as it once was, sir, but my father and I are making plans to rejuvenate the house and replant the fields."

"Have you brought field hands or house slaves with you?" Timothy asked, eyeing the younger man sharply and noting his slightly defeated look.

"No, sir, we have no slaves. Pa sold them all before we left for Boston. I'm not sure how he plans—"

"Tell your father to come and visit me at Mornhaven," Timothy said briskly. "What are neighbors for if they can't help out a friend in need?"

Seeing a ray of hope in this offer, Brant looked at Timothy with surprise. "Shall—shall I have him call in the morning?" he asked.

Timothy shook his head. "I'll be out in the fields. We'll be planting for the next two or three days. Have him come by Saturday evening for supper—and bring yourself with him," he added with a smile. His attention was diverted by the sound of

the boat's whistle. "Here's our stop, daughters," he said quickly. "And yours too, Brant. Have you a horse to see you home or will you be needing one of my drivers to take you back?"

"I left my horse on the riverbank, sir," Brant answered, embarrassed that he had forgotten about it. "If you'd be kind enough to have someone drive me back to fetch it, I can make my way to Riverhouse from there."

"Good. Come along then and we'll find someone in the stables to accommodate you," Timothy said. "If you'll excuse me for a moment, I've got to see to the unloading of our luggage." He hurried away, leaving his daughters to fend for themselves.

The two girls stood where they were, eyeing the young man with interest. Caitlyn's assessment was frank as her dark blue eyes took in his muddy boots and poorly made clothes, topped by a head that was covered with a shock of sable brown hair badly in need of cutting. The lively dark eyes that kept shifting from her to her sister were appealing though, and she wondered what he might look like in the proper attire of a Southern gentleman.

For her part, Constance thought him nearly perfect. Her romantic nature ignored the state of his clothes and his generally unkempt air. Instead she was thinking how warm and kind his eyes were when they looked at her and was wondering if this could really be the same young man who used to tease her so unmercifully when she was nine years old.

"We'd best go and find Papa," Caitlyn said abruptly, realizing that they couldn't just stand there and gawk at a near stranger like ill-bred hussies. "We shall be looking forward to seeing you on Saturday, Mr. Sinclair," she said, nodding to Brant with a superior air that irked him.

Remembering his manners, Brant bowed as elegantly as he could and took one of Caitlyn's gloved hands in his. "I'm charmed to have renewed our acquaintance, Miss Caitlyn," he said. His dark eyes met hers and he recalled how she had always been able to outdo him at riding horses and climbing trees. It gratified him a little when she was the first to lower her eyes and pull her hand gently from his grasp.

He turned to Constance and bowed over her hand, wishing he could plant a kiss on the knuckles like a true cavalier, but knowing how embarrassed she would be if he did. "It is so nice to see you again, Miss Constance," he said warmly, almost smiling to see the blush suffuse her cheeks. Despite his dripping

clothes and wretched appearance, he knew she thought him a very interesting fellow. Perhaps interesting enough to erase her memories of the high-handed brat he used to be.

"Come along, Constance," Caitlyn put in. She took her sister's arm and followed their father off the boat. An open carriage was waiting to take them up the gravel drive to the house.

After his daughters were seated in the vehicle with all their luggage there was no room for anyone else, so Timothy affably told the driver to go on while he and Brant walked up to the house together, discussing cotton, slaves, and house repairs.

Brant cared little for this practical conversation as his eyes followed the carriage up the drive, catching a last glimpse of two bonneted heads leaning close together in animated conversation. He was arrogant enough to believe they were talking about him and very pleased to think so. A prettier pair of sisters he'd never seen in all his time up North, he assured himself. And what a pleasant prospect that both of them lived only a few miles from where he would be residing from now on.

3

CAITLYN SAT with her face in repose, wondering impatiently how long it would take her father to complete his narration of what had happened in Vicksburg the day before. His voice rose and fell as he enumerated the list of undesirable qualities of the school and more specifically of the headmistress. Beside her Constance was dreamily contemplating her empty plate, and Caitlyn was positive she knew what her sister saw as she looked at the white porcelain. Dear Connie, she thought with unaccustomed generosity toward her younger sister, how sweet she is and how romantic about strange young men, especially those in need of assistance.

Caitlyn saw some promise in Brant Sinclair, but obviously his five years away from Louisiana had not added to his potential. He had been dressed in clothes that an overseer might wear. His unkempt appearance was a disgrace, especially in Southern planter society, which valued appearance more highly than many other aspects of life.

Raised in a time when the Southern planter class viewed itself as landed gentry, Caitlyn had always envisioned the ideal

Southern gentleman as a country squire practicing the arts of gracious living, hospitality, and chivalry toward women. For a young man the ride and the hunt were everything, and a young woman had to know how to hold a fan and dance the waltz with effortless grace if she wanted to make an impression on a young man.

"Caitlyn O'Rourke, you're not listening to me!" accused Timothy, bringing his daughter's attention back to the dinner conversation.

Caitlyn looked at her father and smiled sweetly, showing the dimple in her left cheek. "Papa, I'm afraid I'm too hungry to listen right now," she said pointedly, hoping he might finally call for dinner to be served.

Timothy reddened and eyed his elder daughter with annoyance. "I'll not be calling for dinner until we've straightened out this matter, Caitlyn. Your mother wants to hear why you played such a fool-headed prank in Vicksburg."

"Papa, I told you I was just curious," Caitlyn answered. She turned to her mother, whose soft blue eyes were watching her with an understanding that was heartening. "I just wanted my fortune told; I thought it would be fun."

"One of Caitlyn's high-spirited larks," Constance added timidly, determined to defend her sister's escapade.

"I can't understand the unreasonable attitude the headmistress displayed," Margaret said. She sighed and looked at her husband, who was watching her expectantly. "I suppose you are right, Timothy. The girls shall remain at home now."

A pleased smile broke through Timothy's momentary cloud of displeasure. "I am so glad you agree with me, my dear," he said. Love, respect, and gratitude were written all over his beaming countenance.

Watching her parents as dinner was finally brought in, Caitlyn wondered at how different they were and yet how alike in many ways. They were from such dissimilar backgrounds and yet they seemed to have come together with such a perfect blending, complimenting each other while taking great pains to keep their individuality.

She had heard all the stories about her grandparents many times as a little girl. Her mother often spoke of the old days with fond remembrance, while she had learned about her father's background by listening at keyholes as a precocious youngster.

Her paternal grandfather, Brian O'Rourke, had been born in

County Galway in Ireland. At twenty years of age Brian had come to America to seek his fortune and to escape a prison sentence for participating in an Irish rebel group. He had landed in New York, a thriving city in the new United States of America which had barely won its independence from Britain a few years before. But the work in New York was not to Brian's liking, so he'd sailed southward and found himself in New Orleans, a huge port with much untapped potential. He had found himself a job working on the docks of New Orleans before signing on as first mate on a slave ship bound for Africa.

Through diligence and hard work and a more humane attitude toward the Africans, Brian O'Rourke had been able to bring in cargoes where the mortality rate was much lower than on other ships. He rose quickly through the ranks and was finally made captain of his own ship.

By the time he was thirty-five years old Brian O'Rourke owned five slave ships and was making enormous profits from the slave trade. Three years later it became illegal to import slaves into the United States, but rather than deterring Brian O'Rourke, the ban only spurred him to find new ways of continuing his profitable trade. He had worked with the notorious pirate Jean Lafitte in smuggling slaves into New Orleans for auction in the secluded bayous.

To give himself an aura of respectability, Brian had finally married when he was thirty-nine. Marriage and family had never interested him, for he preferred the solitude of his cabin on board one of his own ships and the familiar sights and sounds of the ocean surrounding him. Yet he knew that in order to gain some regard among the people of New Orleans and to allay any lingering suspicions from the authorities, he must marry—and marry well.

His matrimonial target was Catherine de Poitiers, a young Creole girl from a well-respected family in New Orleans. She was only sixteen and he was nearing forty when he'd made the offer of marriage to her father, but she was considered one of the best catches in the city and Brian would have only the best. Catherine had hoped to marry one of the young Creole blades who added so much to the color of New Orleans; rumor had it that she had fallen in love with the son of one of the great Creole families. But her father, astute businessman that he was, realized that his daughter would never have as comfortable a life with anyone else. He might turn up his nose at the Irishman's lineage,

but he couldn't turn up his nose at the vast fortune he had amassed. And there were two more daughters at home to see wedded. Catherine de Poitiers would marry Brian O'Rourke.

In true daughterly fashion, Catherine had accepted the marriage with as much grace as possible, though she secretly cried into her pillow every night. She feared her husband, who was twenty-three years her senior, but dutifully gave him a son a year after their wedding day. Timothy was born in 1810, and after this gratifying accomplishment Brian had once more sailed away, visiting his young wife only enough to cause two more pregnancies, both of which ended in miscarriages. After a third difficult pregnancy which also took the life of his wife, Brian decided that there would be no more marriages. He had an heir to his fortune and that was enough. When his mother died Timothy was only five, too young to be much good on board a ship, so Brian gave him over to the care of Catherine's sister Marie. She had married a native Virginian, Thomas Boyer, who'd moved to Louisiana and had started a cotton plantation in the Mississippi Valley.

Timothy saw his father infrequently during his formative years and grew to love his aunt and uncle and the land that grew the cotton. By the time he was fifteen he knew everything about growing cotton and nothing about sailing ships across the ocean. As Marie was unable to bear children, Thomas proudly designated Timothy his heir, for he felt toward him as he would toward his own son. Meanwhile Brian had continued his seafaring trade and had actually seen his illegal trade grow into a flourishing legitimate company.

At sixty Brian became ill. Embittered that his only son had no interest in the sea, he had abruptly sold all his ships and dissolved the company. With the enormous wealth from the sale, he began to speculate in land and then give the deeds to old cronies in return for small favors, doing everything he could to punish the son who in his eyes had not fulfilled the heritage of the O'Rourkes. Two years later Brian died, refusing to have his only flesh and blood at his bedside and cursing the fact that he had never had enough time to spend all of the money he had made from the sea. Despite Brian's heavy squandering, Timothy had inherited a vast fortune, enough to make him independently wealthy.

But instead of spending it aimlessly, Timothy had proven himself thrifty as a Scotsman and had used the money to make

needed improvements on his uncle's cotton plantation, expanding far beyond the borders that Thomas Boyer had originally intended. When Timothy was twenty-five his uncle died and his aunt moved back to New Orleans, leaving the plantation to her nephew, who christened it Mornhaven. For four years Timothy played the eligible bachelor while the unwed daughters of New Orleans society were paraded in front of him at balls and soirees. Timothy had dallied with many, but it wasn't until he beheld the seventeen-year-old daughter of James Forrester, a Louisiana sugarcane planter, that he finally fell in love.

Margaret Forrester was polished, refined, and very pretty, with her deep auburn hair and soft blue eyes that always seemed to be crinkled by a smile. Despite her Southern manners, there was a sense of independence in her that had come from her New England mother, Bess Kingston Forrester, who had been born in Boston. Timothy had fallen in love with the pretty airs, the graceful ways, but he had also admired the independent manner of the young woman, which set her apart from most of the Southern belles of her era. He had won her hand in a whirlwind courtship and they had been married a few months later.

Two daughters and two sons had been born to them, but sadly the two boys had not lived beyond infancy. Timothy was more than satisfied with his two daughters. He had named the first Catherine, after the mother he had lost at an early age, but from the beginning she had been called Caitlyn. At the time of the second daughter's birth, Constance had been a fashionable name, signifying fidelity and virtue. As she'd grown older, Constance had been mortified that most of the people she loved called her by the diminutive Connie, but as there was nothing she could do about it, she'd finally accepted it with grace.

As Caitlyn glanced around the table and thought of her varied ancestry, she found herself wondering idly about Brant Sinclair and his parents. She could recall how charming and pretty Brant's mother had been, a small woman who had always seemed to be laughing or talking. His father, on the other hand, had always been more reserved, more restrained, although it was obvious to everyone that he loved his vivacious wife to distraction. She remembered how hot it had been that August when she'd been just ten and had attended Christina Sinclair's funeral, the sweat popping out on her scalp and under her arms. She'd looked over at Brant, whom she'd always despised for being such a dreadful

tease to her little sister, and had suddenly felt sorry for him as he'd stood there, his dark head bowed, trying manfully not to give way to sobs. Privately she'd thought it a horrid thing that men were not allowed to give full vent to their sorrow, while women could wail and scream and cry their eyes out if they wanted to. Poor Brant, she thought unexpectedly, to lose his mother when he was so young. Perhaps he could be forgiven for his appearance, especially when one remembered that for quite some time there had been no female in his life to provide gentle supervision.

Caitlyn brightened considerably. Perhaps that was all he needed. Every woman knew that what every man really needed was a woman's supervision to help him make something of himself. After all, where would her father be without her mother gently, subtly helping him to make decisions? In her deliberations Caitlyn quite dismissed the idea that her father had already possessed the energy, ambition, and determination that made him the man he was today even before he had married Margaret Forrester.

"What are you thinking of, sitting so quietly over there?" Constance asked, her voice breaking in on Caitlyn's thoughts.

"I was just thinking that we should persuade Mama to invite our returning neighbors, the Sinclairs, to the spring barbecue at the end of this month," Caitlyn returned.

"Of course we shall invite them," Margaret put in softly, glancing speculatively at the expectant faces of her two daughters. "William Sinclair was always a good friend to your father, and I think it would be a very proper way of reintroducing him and his son to the parish. I'm sure it will give them both an opportunity to renew old acquaintances."

"Yes!" Constance blurted out, obviously happy at her mother's decision.

Seeing Constance's pleasure at her own inspiration, Caitlyn felt a perverse desire to burst her sister's bubble of happiness. "I'm not sure they'll accept, Mama," she said haughtily. "I mean, you should have seen what the younger Sinclair was wearing when we fished him out of the river today. I wonder if they'll have the proper attire for the barbecue."

"Caitlyn, that's nasty!" Constance interceded quickly. "I daresay they are both still gentlemen no matter what their financial circumstances might be!"

"He didn't look like much of a gentleman with his long hair in his eyes and no heels on his boots," Caitlyn snapped irritably.

"All right, girls!" Timothy interjected. "I don't need your arguments to ruin my dinner. If you insist on quarreling, you'll be doing it upstairs in your rooms and not at the dining table."

"But, Papa, Caitlyn has no right to insult Mr. Sinclair; he certainly couldn't help falling into the river. I'm sure he was terribly embarrassed!" Constance said, staunchly defensive.

"I said that's enough!" Timothy declared. "We'll have no more talk of the Sinclairs for now. They'll both be here for dinner on Saturday and you can judge their clothes at that time." He added the last with sarcasm, his eyes on Caitlyn.

She had the grace to look humbled, although she certainly didn't feel that way. It irritated her that her sister was making such an obvious fool of herself over Brant Sinclair. Goodness knew he would be no great catch for any young woman in the parish!

4

THE ACRID SMELL of smoke drifted lazily in the spring air as Caitlyn sat impatiently at her dressing table, allowing Sara, her personal maid, to brush her long coppery auburn hair until it gleamed. She had not yet dressed for the barbecue, as she had been obliged to help her mother with a few final details this morning.

The barbecue pits had been burning slowly since last night, with slaves carefully tending the long troughs. Hickory logs had burned off to the coal beneath, causing tiny hissing sounds as the juices of roasting pork and beef fell onto them. The barbecue was being held in back of the house, where a gentle slope led away from the house and down toward the flatter land where the barbecue pits were located. Beneath the shade of old oaks and pines, long picnic tables were set up with backless benches on either side of them.

Papa really knew how to do a barbecue right, Caitlyn thought proudly as Sara parted her hair in the middle and pulled it back into a loose bun. Tonight she would wear jewelry for the dance, but for now she would put a bunch of violets into her hair and a bouquet at her waist. Flowers were so fashionable just now,

along with bits of lace and ribbon. Caitlyn was pleased that her mother had all of their dresses made in New Orleans, which certainly kept them in fashion, even here in the country.

She could hear the cantankerous voice of Great-Aunt Marie in the next room. Despite the old woman's bluster and irritability, Caitlyn enjoyed Great-Aunt Marie's visits, for she always said and did exactly as she liked, something Caitlyn wished she could do. It was perfectly fine for a woman of Marie's vast age to be outrageous (although she could sometimes make herself the object of the younger people's laughter), but a young, unmarried woman could never truly relax and be herself in mixed company.

In the room across the hall was Marie's equally elderly sister, Eugenia, a toothless harridan who loved to embarrass everyone by belching loudly after dinner. If she weren't a relative, Caitlyn would have had nothing to do with her.

Grandma Bess and Grandpa James Forrester were here too, staying in Constance's room for their visit.

Besides Grandma and Grandpa and the two great-aunts; Margaret's sister Helen, her husband Paul, their three children, Patricia, Pauline, and James; and Margaret's brother Douglas, his wife Caroline, and their three children, Douglas, Manfred, and Stewart were all staying in the house. Caitlyn didn't mind the crowded quarters, for she enjoyed her cousins, usually seeing them only occasionally throughout the year.

Because of the crowded conditions, Caitlyn had been obliged to share her room with Constance and their two cousins, Patricia and Pauline, two scatterbrained but likable young ladies who were sixteen and seventeen years old, respectively. They had arrived two nights before, full of gossip from New Orleans. Unfortunately, much of their gossip concerned the growing secession fever. The *New Orleans Crescent* was running editorials calling for Louisiana to quit the Union and join with the other cotton-growing states to form a new nation. The girls had all laughed at the outrageousness of such a proposition, but the male guests had been eager to discuss the possibility.

"Goodness, Caitlyn, aren't you dressed yet?" Constance inquired, rushing in through the door, followed closely by her two female cousins. "The first guests should be arriving in fifteen minutes and Mama said to tell you to be on the veranda in ten!"

Caitlyn rose from the vanity and hurried to the bed, where her dress had been laid after being pressed earlier that morning. Quickly, Sara helped her slip the taffeta dress over her head and

fastened it in the back, adding the spray of flowers to the sash, which encircled her waist in dark blue and fell in a large bow at the small of her back.

"You look gorgeous," Pauline sighed, silently wishing her hair were the color of her cousin's instead of the plain brown it was.

"We all look gorgeous," Caitlyn laughed, feeling generous because she knew she was prettier than either of her two cousins. She slipped her feet into blue kid slippers, tied her straw bonnet around her wrist by its blue streamers, and hurried downstairs, her sister and cousins following close behind.

"Well, it's about time you girls made an appearance!" Timothy huffed, pacing back and forth across the veranda from one pillar to the next. He was always nervous before a big gathering, usually settling down only after all the guests had arrived and he was free to discuss current events with the gentlemen.

Margaret gazed proudly at her daughters. "You both do your father and me credit," she said warmly, taking their hands in hers.

Caitlyn glowed under her mother's praise, hoping that someday she would feel and look just as composed as Margaret did. Somehow her mother's mere presence on such an exciting day made it seem as though everything would turn out beautifully. If there were any snags in the proceedings, Margaret's patient efforts would straighten things out.

"Oh, look, here comes the first carriage!" Pauline squealed, dancing with excitement next to her sister, who shaded her eyes with one hand, trying to make out who the occupants were.

Timothy stood at the top of the three steps that led up to the veranda from the gravel drive, checking behind him to make sure the huge double doors were thrown open in warm invitation to all his guests. Margaret stood confidently next to him, a ready smile on her lips as she placed one hand on his arm. He glanced at her as though to draw strength from her for the ordeal ahead.

Caitlyn and Constance stood to the side, Constance brushing at her sleeve distractedly while Caitlyn consciously tried to imitate her mother's composed stance. She could already see that the first carriage contained Winfield Cobb, their immediate neighbor, along with his wife and two daughters. His two young sons were mounted on horseback, their high-spirited steeds kicking up the gravel beside the carriage.

The morning seemed one long succession of people dismount-

ing from horses or stepping out of carriages. All the young women were dressed in their prettiest day dresses, the swirling skirts adding a riot of color to the whitewashed facade of Mornhaven. Pinks, yellows, blues, and greens flitted about the house and the veranda and out to the backyard like bright butterflies in sunshine. Young men were dressed like proud peacocks in moiré or brocade vests of varied hues, sporting silk stovepipe hats or straw hats that protected them against the sun.

Artemas Blair, one of the handsomer young bloods in the parish, bounded up the steps like a lively spaniel, greeting the older O'Rourkes quickly and then taking his time as he stood smiling at the two sisters.

"I swear, you two get prettier every time I see you," he said gallantly, sweeping off his hat to reveal golden blond hair.

"And your tongue gets slicker," Caitlyn laughed, allowing him to take her hand.

"I hear you were kicked out of another school," he whispered, his brown eyes looking into hers and brimming with suppressed mirth. "Ah, a girl after my own heart, for learning always did seem a tedious process to me!"

It was on the tip of Caitlyn's tongue to reply tartly that it wasn't the education that was so tedious but the rules and regulations one had to live by while learning, when she suddenly heard her sister take a deep breath. She looked up quickly and saw Brant Sinclair and his father dismounting from their horses, dressed impeccably in frock coats and matching trousers. For an instant Caitlyn felt a slight stirring in the region of her heart when she saw how handsome Brant looked in the golden sunshine. His dark hair had been cut and his sideburns allowed to broaden beneath his temples. His eyes were dark and lively, flitting about the assembled group on the veranda with unaccustomed energy. Even his clothes were well tailored and Caitlyn silently approved his choice of buff-colored trousers and a chocolate brown vest over a white shirt. He had obviously made an effort to look his best—and Caitlyn was vain enough to think it might be because of her.

"Hello, Miss Caitlyn. I'm so pleased to see you again—under much more pleasant circumstances," he smiled, bowing over her hand and meeting her eyes so that Caitlyn felt she might blush at any moment.

"Mr. Sinclair, it certainly is good to see you again," she answered, hoping her voice was cool despite the sudden warmth

in her chest. She would have liked to trade ripostes with him, but he was already looking toward her sister, his smile broadening unconsciously.

"Miss Constance, you look beautiful this morning," he commented gallantly.

Constance blushed, but smiled back at him. "I'm so glad your father and you were able to come," she told him. "So many of your old friends will be here today."

Caitlyn felt miffed that he had not commented on how well *she* looked. She scrutinized her sister with a sidelong glance, noting that the pink of her dress did indeed make her milky complexion glow and set off her strawberry blonde hair to perfection.

As she absently greeted the last of the guests, Caitlyn was preoccupied with planning how best to show Brant Sinclair that she didn't care one whit about him or his attempts to improve his image. Catching Artemas's tall figure striding along the veranda behind her, Caitlyn turned and waved coyly to him.

"Now do save me a seat next to you, Artemas!" she called out gaily. He bowed in response and soon disappeared behind the house, apparently to do her bidding. Caitlyn felt somewhat mollified that her charms were not lost on everybody.

"I think that's the last of them," Timothy said, trying not to sound utterly relieved as he took his wife by the hand and prepared to retreat to the rear of the house. "Shall we join our guests, my dear?"

Margaret nodded. "Come along, girls. Thank you for your help, but now you must go and enjoy yourselves. After everyone has eaten I'll give the signal for the ladies to retire for the afternoon in preparation for the dance this evening."

Constance strolled with her sister through the long hall, making comments to the older folks who were lolling in easy chairs in the front rooms. Caitlyn would have liked to make a quick escape, but good manners demanded that they chat a bit with each person. By the time they arrived on the back porch to survey the colorful scene spread out beneath the shade trees, it was after twelve and the barbecue was already being served.

Children ran everywhere, dodging each other as well as the adults, who begged them to take their games elsewhere or to settle down and eat something. As usual, most of the men had gathered into a large circle opposite the matrons, discussing everything from secession to the next presidential election. Cotton

was a major topic of discussion too, as well as the rising price of good field hands.

Caitlyn could see Brant in the group of men, listening politely, but hardly aware of how bored he looked. He caught sight of the two sisters making their way toward the tables where the barbecue was being set out and quickly excused himself in order to join them.

"I was wondering if you would have to stay in front forever," he commented with a little laugh. "Did I tell you that you both look splendid today?"

"I believe you've already mentioned it to Constance," Caitlyn snapped irritably. She was pleased to see the happy glow in his eyes replaced by an anxious look.

"You are looking well yourself, Mr. Sinclair," Constance intervened, unhappy that her sister had spoken so unkindly. "You must try the barbecue. Everyone will tell you that our father knows how to make the best sauce in the parish. It's a family secret!" She giggled a little, pleased to see the light return to his eyes.

"If you'll allow me to get you a plate, Miss Constance, I should be most agreeable to sampling it," he returned. And then, as though remembering his manners, he added, "And you too, Miss Caitlyn."

Thoroughly vexed by now, Caitlyn shook her head violently and hurried to where Artemas was awaiting her. His plate was already filled with barbecue, squash, green beans, and salad. She had never been so thankful to see him, she thought, as she resolved not to find herself in the vicinity of Brant Sinclair.

Still, she couldn't help eyeing Brant as he walked with her sister in search of seats. What could Constance possibly be saying to him that would make him laugh so endearingly? she wondered. She was so angry she almost attacked her plate, causing Artemas to stare at her in astonishment. With an effort she calmed her ruffled feelings, remembering how dreadful it would look for a young lady to devour her food in front of a gentleman.

It soothed her a little when Stephen Carter and Darby Howard greeted her and seated themselves on stools close to her bench.

She soon almost forgot Brant Sinclair's slight as she basked in the attention of several of the young blades of the parish. Several young ladies also joined the group. Although some of them were jealous of Caitlyn's looks and vivacity, most of them got along well with her, for she could be quite charming when

she chose to be. Unlike the many pretty young belles who were determined to have all of the eligible young men to themselves, Caitlyn had never been averse to sharing her good fortune. She was so sure of her own powers that she didn't mind other girls being present when men surrounded her.

Conversation dipped and swirled about the group of gay young people as they finished their barbecue and talked about the evening of dancing that was still before them. More than one young man clamored for a waltz with Caitlyn, who shook her head, then smiled, and told them all they must line up that evening and write down their requests on her dance card. The young men laughed good-naturedly, each one promising to elbow ahead of the others in line. Even the other girls, though not half as charming and vivacious as Caitlyn, were the recipients of the boys' good will, for no one could be sullen on such a glorious April day.

Although Caitlyn laughed and chattered as gaily as the rest, she couldn't help casting sidelong glances at her sister and Brant Sinclair now and then. It made her smile widen when she caught Brant looking at her once or twice as if to see why the other boys were making such a fuss over her. He returned her smile, and finally both he and Constance joined the lighthearted circle.

The afternoon wore on and some of the young people paired off to talk or to walk about the grounds of Mornhaven. Caitlyn finally disengaged herself from her more ardent suitors, and seeing her sister occupied with one of their cousins, she strolled over to Brant Sinclair and offered to take him on a quick tour of the grounds. It pleased her when he bowed over her hand and accepted her offer with every appearance of great pleasure.

"I was beginning to think you really didn't like me, Mr. Sinclair," she said coyly, aware of her hand nestled in the crook of his arm. She knew the heat of the afternoon had reddened her cheeks and had made her dress uncomfortably damp in places, but it was all worth it if she was able to keep her composure around this young man who seemed so impervious to her charms.

"Please call me Brant," he responded, evading her indirect question.

"I hardly think that possible on such short notice, Mr. Sinclair," she answered, fluttering her fan in front of her face.

"I've already asked your sister to, and she was most gracious about it," he said pointedly.

The fan abruptly snapped shut as Caitlyn felt irritation sweep

over her. For a moment she had the wild thought of abandoning him on the garden path, but pride stopped her from fleeing and she gritted her teeth determinedly.

"Well, I suppose if my sister has seen fit to address you with such familiarity, than I can do nothing less," she replied, trying unsuccessfully to keep her emotional turmoil from showing in her eyes.

Why was this conversation going down such a tormenting path? she wondered. Did Brant dislike her so much? Or was he just trying to be witty? After all, he *had* been up North for several years—heaven knew what could happen to a man's charm in the company of those cold, stiff-necked Yankee girls. She risked a glance at his face and was mollified to see that his dark eyes were looking down at her with more than a spark of interest.

"You seem to bring out the ungraciousness in me, Brant," she said after a little hesitation.

"Then I should be summarily hanged, Miss Caitlyn, for everyone should be treated to the affable side of such a pretty young lady as yourself."

Now we are on the right path, Caitlyn thought, smiling to show her dimple. "Then see that you don't ruffle my feathers again, sir!" she said sweetly, tapping him lightly on the arm with her fan.

"I shall take great pains not to," he promised lightly.

They continued their walk without any more friction, each uttering the appropriate pleasantries, so that Caitlyn felt quite pleased with herself as they returned to the picnic tables. Brant had been a perfect gentleman and she was sure he was genuinely interested in her. It certainly did wonders for a girl's spirits when a man paid attention to her. She could even afford to be gracious when Brant excused himself to have a word with Constance before the ladies retired inside for naps.

Margaret had stood up, giving the signal to all the ladies to leave the gentlemen to their talk and cigars. Immediately mothers called to their children and groups broke up so the ladies could go inside the house. The young ladies present would nap upstairs in the bedrooms of Mornhaven so their eyes would shine and their cheeks glow tonight while they danced until midnight on the polished oak floor of the ballroom.

As Caitlyn made her way toward the house, several of the young men reminded her they would be first in line for her dance card that evening.

"You must save me a waltz," Artemas said insistently, his brown eyes roving over her possessively, causing Caitlyn to shiver with a delicious little sensation.

"Perhaps I will, Artemas," she half promised, looking at him obliquely. "And perhaps you may even dance the first reel with me." She laughed, then broke away from him and made her way to the back porch. It was much cooler inside the house, she thought, fanning her pink cheeks and watching Artemas wave to her before he joined a group of young men under the oaks. She saw Constance walking with Brant, laughing sweetly at something he said to her.

"Well, you make a cozy pair," Caitlyn said slyly as her sister approached her on the porch.

"Oh, Caitlyn, he really is so nice!" Constance cooed dreamily. "I can't believe he used to tease me so terribly."

"Perhaps he's still teasing you, Connie," Caitlyn said bitingly. She turned and hurried inside the house, leaving her sister to stare after her in confusion.

By the time she was laced tightly into her blue satin ball gown, Caitlyn had decided that she would not let her feelings be turned upside down by Brant Sinclair tonight as they had been at the barbecue this afternoon.

She gazed down speculatively at the tiny square of white that dangled from a silken cord around her wrist. Her dance card would surely be filled with signatures within the first fifteen minutes of the dancing. A smile lit up Caitlyn's face as she remembered the possessive look in Artemas Blair's eyes, for he was the best dancer in the parish. With Artemas as a dancing partner, a girl knew her toes wouldn't ache for two days after the ball!

Caitlyn gazed at herself in the mirror, noting with pleasure her slender waist accentuated by the wide satin sash of the ball gown. The bodice was boned stiffly beneath the soft fabric, pushing her breasts up enticingly, making them appear like small half-moons glowing with the dusting of powder she'd given them. The skirt, with its yards and yards of blue satin overlaid with white lace, covered her slender legs so that only the toes of her satin dancing slippers peeped from beneath the hem with suitable modesty.

"Move over, Caitlyn!" Cousin Patricia's voice broke in irritably. "I've got to see how the back of this dress looks."

Caitlyn obliged after a final pat to her hair, where Sara had cunningly looped pearls whose milky luster seemed to reflect the copper of her curls. After a final dab of toilet water between her breasts and at the wrists of her long white gloves, she would be ready to go downstairs.

Constance, looking radiant in butter yellow taffeta trimmed in bronze satin ribbon, swept by exuding excitement. "Oh, I do love dancing parties!" she sighed to no one in particular. It had only been a year since she'd been allowed to stay up for the dancing.

"Better than stuffy old academies?" Caitlyn inquired slyly, knowing her sister still had regrets that their education was ended.

"Of course, silly!" Constance retorted, refusing to be teased by her sister. "I daresay we're both better educated than most of our friends as it is—and you know how young gentlemen hate to think females know more than *they* do! I suppose Papa is right when he says it never behooves a young lady to be too smart!"

"Papa *would* say that," Caitlyn grumbled. "Still, you don't suppose he would have married Mama had she been as stupid as an ox, do you?"

"Oh, Caitlyn, some of your ideas!" twittered Cousin Pauline with a giggle. "You know very well that if you're too intelligent, then your marriage prospects dwindle accordingly. Why, no man in his prime wants a wife who's got more brains than beauty! Look at all those Yankee bluestockings who never find husbands because they try to impress their beaux with their cleverness!"

Caitlyn would have liked to retort that if so many Yankee girls weren't finding husbands, how come the population of the North kept increasing by leaps and bounds? She held back the words that were on the tip of her tongue, knowing that her retort would only shock her cousin and disappoint her mother should she hear of it. Besides, she'd already promised herself she was going to be her most agreeable tonight. It wouldn't do to get into a silly row with her cousin about something so unimportant as the chances of a Yankee girl getting a marriage proposal! At seventeen Pauline was no doubt more worried about her own chances of snaring a husband!

When the four young women were finally turned out to their satisfaction and that of their maids, they started down the wide hall to the ballroom downstairs. The strains of an orchestra

drifted lazily in the warm evening air. Taking the graceful stairway as slowly as they could to contain their excitement, the girls finally stepped onto the smooth, polished oak of the dance floor, becoming the center of attention as young men hurried to fill their dance cards.

Besieged by flattering males, Caitlyn smiled as provocatively as she dared, letting her long lashes sweep alluringly over her eyes. She was not alone in displaying this behavior, for every girl had been taught by her mammy or by a deportment teacher how to look invitingly at a man so that he would clamor for her attention.

Caitlyn dispensed her favors like a grand duchess, faltering only when Brant Sinclair bowed in front of her requesting her dance card.

"Only three places left," he whispered with a roguish smile. "I shall have to take them all, of course—and be a little speedier in getting to you at the next cotillion." He returned her card, bowing once more and leaving Caitlyn feeling a pleasurable tingling at the masterful tone he had used with her. Surely this was not the same Brant Sinclair they had fished out of the river just a few short weeks ago!

Feeling extremely happy, Caitlyn turned to her first dancing partner and bestowed a dazzling smile on him, causing that young man's heart to beat a rapid tattoo inside his chest. Those blue eyes were the most beguiling he'd ever seen, he assured himself as he placed one hand around the slender waist and grasped her gloved hand in his.

As the evening wore on, Caitlyn found her enjoyment of it increasing. She had already danced one dance with Brant and he had proven himself surprisingly adept. During a short intermission he had escorted her solicitously to one of the chairs placed along the wall and offered to get her a glass of punch.

Fanning the heat from her cheeks, Caitlyn accepted gladly. In a moment he was back, handing her the crystal punch glass, his eyes admiring her becomingly flushed cheeks.

"You are looking very lovely tonight, Miss Caitlyn," he murmured, sitting in the chair next to hers and leaning toward her.

"Oh, for heaven's sake, Brant, you must call me Caitlyn!" she exclaimed, sipping the last of the punch. "All the other boys in the parish do. I practically grew up with you!"

He laughed, pleased that she seemed to be softening in her attitude toward him. "Yes, I recall how you used to outdo me

at climbing trees, even at riding horses! I must admit it sorely wounded my pride when a ten-year-old girl could sit a mount better than I could!''

''I daresay I couldn't do it anymore,'' she replied, feeling a sudden urge to reach up and brush back an errant lock of hair that had fallen over his eyebrow.

''We'll have to find out sometime, won't we?'' he invited, thinking how very pretty she looked. Prettier than her sister, he mused. It was just too bad she couldn't always be as soft and sweet as she was being now. While they were dancing, he had allowed himself a leisurely inspection of her, noting the fine, high cheekbones and the perfectly arched brows that curved like two dark wings on the smooth ivory of her skin. Her lips were parted a little and the edges of her teeth, white and even, caught the tip of her tongue as she contemplated her own thoughts. The smooth column of her neck curved gracefully into her shoulders, bared and gleaming with a fine mist of perspiration. As they sat quietly, he let his eyes delve dangerously along the top of her low-cut bodice to the separation of her breasts, which sloped deliciously into the frothy lace that cupped them.

Caitlyn was quite aware of Brant's inspection, though she tried not to reveal it with a telltale blush. It felt pleasant sitting with him while his dark eyes roved restlessly over her. Her heart was beating quite rapidly in her breast, and it was long after the last dance had ended.

They couldn't sit here forever, and finally it was time for the next dance. Regretfully, Brant took his leave of Caitlyn, explaining that he was promised to her sister for the next dance. She smiled understandingly, although she felt a pang when she saw the eagerness written so plainly on Constance's face as Brant bowed over her hand. The reciprocating pleasure on Brant's face confused Caitlyn a little and deflated her sense of well-being.

''This one's mine, Caitlyn,'' Artemas suddenly whispered in her ear.

With a nod, Caitlyn allowed him to lead her back onto the dance floor, trying hard not to let her eyes stray from his handsome face. Artemas would be a wonderful catch for any girl in the parish, she thought objectively. He was every inch a Southern gentleman, from the top of his blond head to the toes of his brightly polished shoes. And yet he had never stirred her heart, despite all his gallant attempts. She liked him well enough, and he had always responded satisfactorily to her flirtations with him.

Yet Caitlyn realized there was something missing from his games of chivalry. At twenty Artemas was already too interested in cotton and land and horses to pay serious attention to love. She had the feeling that when he married he would be counting the bride's dowry in his head as he walked down the aisle with her. The girl who married Artemas Blair would find herself a poor second to his estates. Caitlyn had long since decided that when she married, it would be to someone to whom she meant everything!

The dancing continued until well after midnight, when some of the chaperones began to stop concealing their yawns behind their hands, hoping the young people would take the hint and act accordingly. Somehow Brant had managed to secure the last dance with Caitlyn, making her feel very happy as she glided about the floor in his arms. Gazing up into his angular face, she saw the look of pleasure in those restless dark eyes. It was a good face, a handsome face, she thought, though not so classically handsome as Artemas Blair's. Brant's jaw was a trifle less square, his mouth a trifle too soft to convey the strength that Artemas's did, and yet there was something so very appealing about that face, especially when he smiled—almost like a little boy so proud of himself for doing something right. Whatever it was, it appealed mightily to Caitlyn's instincts and she was doubly pleased when he insisted on walking her out to the veranda to bid good-bye to the guests.

5

THE LAZY SPRING turned into warm summer as the cotton grew taller, nurtured by ideal weather and perfect rains. Timothy O'Rourke rode his acres every day, never having trusted an overseer to do the job he enjoyed so much. Besides his own healthy crop, he had had much to do with the making of his neighbor's crop. True to his word, Timothy had gladly allowed several of his own field hands to work the crops for William Sinclair. The latter had been so grateful he had not known how to express his thanks, for with even a medium-sized crop of cotton that fall, he would be able to buy back some of his former slaves outright and make much-needed repairs to the outbuildings around Riverhouse.

William Sinclair was pleased that his son seemed to be spending so much of his free time at Mornhaven. He had had a private conversation with Brant, asking him just where his interests lay. Laughing at his father's serious tone, Brant had explained that he was truly interested in *both* the O'Rourke girls and couldn't seem to make up his mind which one to pay serious court to. William had smiled. Surely a marriage with either one of Timothy O'Rourke's daughters would be a nice merging of the two plantations. Despite his pride in Riverhouse, William was astute enough to realize that Mornhaven was the jewel of the parish. If his son could put a foot in its door before any of the other young bloods in the parish did, it would be all to the good.

Although William was pleased by Brant's interest in a possible marriage with the O'Rourke family, he could not find pleasure in Brant's lack of interest in the cotton crop. Instead of staying to listen to his father's glowing reports on the progress of the crop, Brant exhibited boredom and asked to be excused from the discussion. It made William heartsore to think that Brant had not inherited the love for the land that had been in his family for so many generations.

"And what will you do when I'm gone?" he had asked his son before the latter was off on a jaunt with one of the other young men in the parish, or en route to a picnic with the O'Rourke sisters.

"Why, I'll marry a rich young lady, Pa, and I won't have to worry about it! I'll hire an overseer to take care of the crops and leave myself time for other things!" He'd rolled his eyes expressively and left his father feeling at a loss as to how to handle his son's disinterest.

But if Brant would not listen to his father, he had to listen to Caitlyn O'Rourke, who seemed at times to display an unladylike interest in the economics of cotton plantations. Brant felt himself squirming when Caitlyn asked him specific questions about the cotton crop at Riverhouse. How was it that she could be so sweet and feminine one minute, and the next turn around and ask questions he couldn't answer, her dark blue eyes becoming sharper as though she perceived some fatal flaw in him? It was much easier to be in Constance's company, for she obviously thought the world of him. To her, he could talk of his travels in the North or his hunting expeditions with Artemas Blair, and she would hang on his every word as though each were more clever than the last.

But just when he was thinking how sweet and suitable Constance would be as a wife, Caitlyn would flirt beguilingly with him. She easily outdazzled her younger sister when she wanted to, and when she chose to be her most charming, Brant found himself thinking only of how soft and full her mouth was and how much he would enjoy kissing it. But then out of that same soft mouth would come a remark about bettering oneself in order to get ahead and Brant would feel his ardor diminish. It was at those times that he wished to be far away from Caitlyn and instead to be sitting beneath an oak tree beside Constance as she drank in his every word.

He looked forward to embellishing a few of his adventures in Boston for Constance this July day, a day so hot he could feel the sweat popping out beneath his clothes. His father had asked him to stay at Riverhouse in order to go over some accounts, but Brant couldn't be bothered about that today. He'd promised to ride with Caitlyn and Constance to one of the small creeks that jutted out from the great Mississippi where they could picnic in the relative cool under the shade trees.

When he arrived at Mornhaven, he learned to his dismay that Constance would not be accompanying them today.

"Poor Connie, she was out in the garden trimming some flowers for Mama and a hornet had the effrontery to sting her right on the chin!" Caitlyn explained to him, not too unhappy that her sister would not be accompanying them.

"Can I see her?" Brant asked, feeling sorry for Constance.

"I'm afraid she doesn't want you to see her, Brant. Her chin has swelled horribly and Mama is doing everything she can to keep the swelling down and the pain lessened. It's quite nasty looking," she couldn't help adding, noting the look of revulsion on Brant's face.

"Will—will she be all right?"

"Oh, I suppose she will. Goodness, I've had my share of wasp stings and I'm over them the next day! I'm sure Connie will recover under Mama's watchful eyes." Caitlyn matter-of-factly examined Brant's attire and found it most satisfactory. He had adopted the new sporting look of unmatched trousers and coat. Both were made of linen, the coolest fabric one could wear on a hot July day in Louisiana. Before she was through she would mold him into the perfect Southern gentleman, which would only enhance his position as a suitable husband. She

smiled to herself at that last thought before handing him the picnic basket.

"Shall we go?" she asked sweetly, looking up into his eyes with her own limpid pools of blue.

Caitlyn's gaze made Brant forget Constance and he nodded, returning her smile. Outside he helped her into the smart little carriage, sat beside her, and took the reins. Already perched on the rear seat was Caitlyn's maid, Sara, an unfortunate necessity, Brant thought, but she had been sent along to keep her mistress's honor intact should they be late returning home.

He pushed the horse to a dancing trot and guided it out of the stable yard and down the gravel drive to the river road. His companion looked adorable, her hair drawn back in a loose coil at the nape of her neck, her pretty parasol over her head to keep her skin from freckling. Seeing the softness of her throat where the vee of the basque separated, Brant imagined himself feeling that softness beneath his mouth, right on that tiny spot where a blue vein throbbed gently.

He immediately pushed such thoughts from his mind, for Caitlyn was very much a lady despite some of her unladylike traits. He could imagine the horror on her face should he try to take liberties with her. The thought of seeing her blue eyes freeze him into humiliation was sufficient to repress any arousal he felt at the sight of her fresh loveliness. With an effort, he concentrated on the horse and the road in front of him.

"What a lovely place!" Caitlyn exclaimed enthusiastically when they arrived at the spot he had chosen for this picnic. "Brant, how do you know this place?"

"I remember my mother bringing me to it when I was a little boy," he said softly, recalling half-forgotten moments. "She loved the river but was always a little afraid of it. Here she had part of the river but felt safe at the same time."

Caitlyn looked out over the gently moving water that was shallow enough in places to reveal the rocks beneath the surface. Tall river cypresses and oaks grew everywhere, but not so thickly that there wasn't a cool carpet of grass on which to sit. Multi-colored butterflies flitted about, making the whole scene seem idyllic. Caitlyn sighed with pleasure.

"Thank you for bringing me here, Brant," she said, gazing at him happily.

He returned her look, then set about spreading a cloth on the ground so that she could sit without staining her skirts. Sara

obligingly set out the picnic basket, then walked a little away from them, aware that they wanted to be alone.

"Poor Connie doesn't know what she's missing," Caitlyn said half to herself as she sat daintily on the spread, arranging her skirts becomingly around her.

"We'll come again when she's better," Brant promised, stretching out beside her and picking a piece of grass.

"I wanted to talk to you about that, Brant," Caitlyn began seriously, her tone of voice making Brant aware of what was coming. "You know, I do feel rather badly about taking you away from your responsibilities at Riverhouse. I'm sure your father must need you there."

"He manages quite well without me, Caitlyn. Please don't worry yourself about that. I like being here with you more than I like riding those endless cotton fields on a hot day like today."

"Better you than your father," she reprimanded him gently, although her brows had drawn together as she studied him.

"It's his life," he reminded her with a bored air, throwing the piece of grass away and wondering how to get off this unappealing subject. "After he dies I'm not going to ride the fields myself. I'll hire an overseer to do the job and devote more time to the pleasures of life."

"Brant, you're not being very responsible," Caitlyn continued primly, unfolding the towel that covered the contents of the wicker basket. "Any overseer you hire won't do a decent job if he knows the master's heart isn't with the cotton."

Brant crossed his arms and lowered his head onto them as he gazed up at the green canopy over them. "Must we talk about all this today, Caitlyn?" he asked. "I would much rather talk of interesting things."

"Like what?"

"Oh, like how unnecessary it is to keep holding on to that little parasol when there's not going to be enough sun coming through those leaves to put even one freckle on your turned-up nose." He smiled to see her blush in confusion at the compliment.

"You're trying to detour me around the subject of Riverhouse, and the cotton, and—" she reproved him.

"And anything else that lends too serious an air to such a gorgeous day," he added swiftly, boldly letting his hand cover hers. He was elated that she didn't jerk her hand from his grasp. "Perhaps we should eat first and then think about what we're

going to do,'' Caitlyn suggested, breaking the mood with her brisk, practical outlook. ''I'm sure you'll love the deviled eggs Rachel made,'' she added, knowing that the cook at Mornhaven was adept at preparing dishes that would melt a man's heart.

Gratefully, Brant sat up, crossing his legs and biting into one of the proffered eggs. After pronouncing it delicious, he plowed hungrily into the rest of the meal, marveling at how little his companion ate. He didn't realize that she'd been laced so tightly into her stays that she could barely breathe in a seated position, let alone fill her stomach. When he felt replete, he stretched out again, listening lazily to the sounds of Caitlyn repacking the wicker basket. Now if only she would be quiet and just let the sounds of nature lull them into a doze. How perfect it would be!

But it was not to be, for as usual Caitlyn was not one to sit idly in one spot for very long. Immediately after clearing away the food, she got to her feet and walked toward the little inlet that bubbled so merrily over the stones. With a glance at Brant's reclining figure, she seated herself on a large rock and boldly drew up her skirts so that she could roll down her stockings and take off her shoes. Dipping her toes into the cool water felt so refreshing on a hot, humid day, she thought as she watched the water ripple in little pools around her feet. Contentedly, she closed her eyes and leaned back, enjoying the cool sensation, until she heard someone approaching. Looking up, she could see Brant's dark eyes wandering curiously over her feet and the tiny amount of ankle that was exposed.

''It looks refreshing,'' he said slowly, bringing his eyes up to her face.

As she expected, he immediately sat down beside her and took off his shoes and stockings, rolling up his trouser legs so that he could immerse his own feet in the water. Feeling like two guilty children, they nevertheless sat together that way for several minutes, until Caitlyn acknowledged that if she sat any longer with her feet uncovered it would be stretching the limits of propriety. She glanced back to where Sara sat. Seemingly nonchalant, Sara was capable of blabbing Caitlyn's impropriety to Timothy.

With a sigh, Caitlyn drew her feet out of the water and grabbed her shoes and stockings. Of course it wouldn't do for Brant to witness her pulling up her stockings, so she retreated to a more private place to dress, giving him a chance to do the same.

''That was lovely,'' she said as she emerged from behind a tree.

He agreed. "I must say it was more than that. Honestly, Caitlyn, sometimes I feel as though I will never be able to figure you out. Of all the girls I've known, I would have thought you'd be the last one to put her feet in the water like that."

"All the girls you've known?" Caitlyn repeated, arching one elegant brow. "Have there been so many, Brant?"

"Dozens," he replied with an infuriating grin.

"And why didn't you marry any of them?" she demanded.

This was shaky ground. "I—I didn't have anything to offer them," he returned hesitantly, feeling it was the most appropriate answer he could give her.

"Then it would behoove you to make the most of Riverhouse—or you might find yourself an old bachelor!" she retorted flippantly, upset that he had known other girls before her.

Grinning at her feminine sulk, Brant moved closer. "I don't think I'd like the life of a bachelor very much," he admitted, coming close enough so that he could see that little vein throbbing in her neck.

His nearness was arousing to Caitlyn, but despite her apparent boldness, she was still an innocent in matters of the heart. She risked a quick glance at him from beneath lowered lashes, noting how full and soft his lips seemed. Was he going to kiss her? Should she let him? She had been kissed before, she reminded herself, but somehow she felt that should Brant kiss her now, it would be more than those innocent pecks she'd received from other boys.

She could feel his hesitation, see the confusion in his eyes. It was maddening to stand there, poised on the brink, waiting for him to make the first move. Determinedly, she closed her eyes and swayed toward him the tiniest bit as though to give him encouragement. She heard him swallow, the sound seeming inordinately loud to her ears.

"Miss Caitlyn, it be about time to get back to the house." Sara's firm voice interrupted Caitlyn's sweet turmoil, breaking the spell effectively.

Caitlyn opened her eyes, feeling frustration gathering inside of her. Recovering his own composure, Brant shuffled to one side, jamming his hands into his trouser pockets as though to keep them a safe distance from the enchanting little sorceress in front of him.

"I suppose we should be driving back, Caitlyn," Brant said, taking his hands out of his pockets and facing her with regained

composure. "My pa will want me home soon to go over the daily events in the fields." He said the last with a dash of sarcasm.

"You should remember, Brant, that Riverhouse is all you've got," Caitlyn reproved him as he bent to fold the spread and take it and the picnic basket back to the carriage. "If you treat it right and take an interest in the cotton, you'll be paid back a thousandfold."

"Caitlyn, it seems we've already had this argument," he said quickly, helping her into the seat and then jumping up himself. He could still feel the smallness of her waist as he took the reins in his hands. He wondered if she had really been about to let him kiss her a moment before her maid spoke up. He had wanted to in the worst way, but years of upbringing had cautioned him that a young man did not kiss a young lady without having some serious intentions behind that kiss. Were his intentions toward Caitlyn serious? Perhaps so, but there was always the image of Constance in the back of his mind. Both of them could be so much alike and yet both of them were so different. Wouldn't it be grand if he could marry both of them? He smiled to himself at this novel idea, thinking what a satisfactory arrangement it would be.

6

THE HARVEST SEASON arrived with another record crop for the South. Hundreds of thousands of bales of cotton were sent downriver to New Orleans to be sold to supply the demands of the textile mills of the North. In the spirit of generosity, Timothy O'Rourke sold back William Sinclair's slaves at less than what they had cost him. Winfield Cobb was not quite so generous, but though his price was higher, William still managed to buy back half of the slaves he had sold him five years before. Repairs to Riverhouse would have to wait, as would the trip to New Orleans that Brant so wanted to take.

"We just don't have the money," William said, ignoring the sulky look on his son's face. "There's still plenty of work to do to get the fields ready for next spring's planting and you've got to be here to help me with it. Those field hands aren't going to listen to an old man and I haven't the heart to use a whip on

them. Either we'll have to scrape up enough money to hire an overseer, or you're going to have to take over the responsibility, Brant.''

"Damn it, Pa, haven't I worked hard this summer and fall? I deserve a respite from this damned place!''

William looked as though his son had just delivered him a cruel blow. "This *damned place* is your home!'' he roared. "Riverhouse is the only thing that stands between us and the slums of the city, Brant. We're nothing—not planters, not country gentlemen, not even farmers—without it. We've got to make Riverhouse grow and prosper again, and that requires a huge investment of money and time.''

"But, Pa, I didn't mean—''

"It doesn't matter what you meant," William interrupted. "You'll not be going to New Orleans.'' He sat down in his chair and Brant saw that his hands were trembling. "Brant, would you have Josiah bring me a decanter of whiskey?'' he requested urgently.

Brant felt guilty at being the reason his father wanted a drink. William had been doing so well, his pride in his plantation outweighing the need for firewater.

"I'm sorry, Pa,'' Brant said sincerely. "I'll try to do better.''

"Good,'' William returned wearily. "But get me that drink now, won't you, son?''

The late autumn months crawled slowly by at Riverhouse while Brant impatiently awaited the O'Rourkes' return from New Orleans. It wasn't only they who had gone downriver; most of the young people in the parish had gone too. The social season was a time when debutantes attended balls to look for prospective husbands. Bachelors, determined to remain single for as long as they could, attended the notorious quadroon balls and indulged their healthy masculine appetites with beautiful half-caste girls.

Caitlyn and Constance thoroughly enjoyed themselves, now and then sparing a thought for Brant back home. Constance felt sorry that he wasn't able to make the trip downriver. Caitlyn was more practical. Better that Brant stayed at Riverhouse, where there'd be no feminine temptations. There were always more engagements made during the social season than at any other time of the year. Pauline, their cousin, received a proposal from a cotton planter's son from Natchez.

Privately, Caitlyn thought Mr. Edward Winterby a poor catch.

He was over thirty and had a nose that resembled a bird's curved beak. It caused him to speak with a nasal twang, but Pauline could overlook that minor annoyance, especially since he would inherit a two-thousand-acre cotton plantation when his father died.

The O'Rourkes stayed in New Orleans through Christmas, celebrating the holidays with their relatives and toasting the newly engaged couple, whose marriage was set for the following June. It would not be a long engagement, but Pauline preferred it that way, for she was anxious to accompany Edward to his plantation as soon as possible.

As the new year of 1859 arrived, the O'Rourkes returned home to Mornhaven. They immediately received a note from Riverhouse welcoming them back and explaining that the Sinclairs were most anxious to call upon them but would have to delay until William recovered from a nagging cold. Both sisters were concerned, for each considered William Sinclair an ally in her bid for marriage with his son, and he was genuinely liked by the whole O'Rourke family. When William was well enough to sit downstairs and receive company, his first visitors were Timothy and his two daughters.

"Timothy, it's so good to see you!" William exclaimed heartily, rising to shake the Irishman's hand with pleasure. "Come sit by the fire and tell me all the news from New Orleans. I've been hearing reports that some firebrands are saying this year will be the one that sees the South separate from the North. I can hardly give it credence, yet I read in *DeBow's Review* that there are many who are backing such action, especially in South Carolina."

"DeBow is a pompous lout, but he is a leading advocate of Southern economic independence and uses his magazine to espouse his own beliefs," Timothy explained. "No matter how much he professes to hate the North, he still gets three-fourths of his advertising from Northern businesses. Even his *Review* is printed in New York because he has no adequate facilities in New Orleans! I think that's the trouble with secession. I'm for it if the South can stand alone economically, but how can we when so many of our manufactured goods come from the North? I just don't know how it can be done without causing a great deal of economic harm to the South."

"But what of England, of Europe?" William asked. "We can

sell our cotton to them and retain enough profit to buy whatever goods we need.''

"No matter what England does, I think secession is coming,'' Timothy said matter-of-factly. "There's talk of it everywhere in New Orleans. Some want to pull away immediately, but I don't think anything will happen until the presidential election. Many Southerners are being led to believe in the legal and revolutionary rights of secession. The *Crescent* and the *Picayune* are both running editorials for secession.''

"Most of the balls in New Orleans were filled with political talk,'' Caitlyn complained. "Why, a girl couldn't get a word in edgewise unless she was prepared to discuss the merits of slavery over free labor!'' She turned to Brant, who'd been letting his eyes roam between her and Constance. He'd been half certain that one or both of them would return to Mornhaven wearing an engagement ring. "I wish you'd been there, Brant,'' Caitlyn said softly. "At least I could have counted on you to lift my spirits!''

Constance added with a sweet smile, "We missed you.''

Brant smiled at both girls, for he was truly delighted to see them again. Constance, he recalled, would turn fifteen at the end of this month and Caitlyn would be sixteen in March. Not having seen them for over two months, Brant could appreciate the subtle changes in their faces which signaled the new maturity that had replaced the babyish roundness of last summer.

Constance was even prettier than he remembered, with her strawberry blonde hair and those soft blue eyes, round and widely set beneath blonde eyebrows. She had an oval face with a tiny cleft in her chin that fascinated him and teeth as white as delicate porcelain. She was shorter than her sister and a trifle plumper, but pleasantly so, just enough to fit perfectly into a man's arms. Constance reminded Brant of his small, pretty mother, who had always seemed to him to be the perfect wife.

Caitlyn, on the other hand, did not fit Brant's preconceived notions of what a wife should be. Despite its promising curves, her tall, slender body was charged with energy like that of a young colt. Her hair's coppery highlights gleamed and her blue eyes snapped with an inner electricity. She seemed unable to sit still and listen quietly. Caitlyn was always interjecting her own opinions or moving from place to place as if to escape the tedious confines of the room. Sometimes Brant found her boundless energy and healthy vigor tiring. She was a girl with a passion for life. The thought came to him that life with Caitlyn O'Rourke

would never be boring. What kind of wife would that make her? he wondered.

"Brant, you've been staring at the two of us long enough," Caitlyn said, pulling him out of his introspection. "Have we changed so much since you last saw us?"

He smiled. "No," he assured her. "Both of you are so lovely."

"Thank you," Constance replied delightedly. And grown up enough to propose marriage to, she thought with a touch of excitement.

Before Brant had time to bestow more compliments, William and Timothy were drawing him back into their conversation. Their discussion had swerved from secession to the cotton crop. Cotton was their livelihood and their life. Brant had to admit that he was looking forward to a new crop being planted in the spring. Certainly not because of the work involved, but because of the income they would see from the harvest. Enough, perhaps, to allow him to go on a romantic honeymoon with his new bride. He smiled to himself. Would he be a married man by this time next year? He would be twenty-one years old soon, time to be thinking of settling down with one woman and beginning a family.

Soon it was time for the O'Rourkes to leave, the girls waving to Brant as he stood in the doorway. Once he was out of sight, Caitlyn turned around in her seat and let out a long sigh.

"Papa," she said matter-of-factly, "Brant will make someone a fine husband someday when he's polished up a bit more."

Timothy looked at his elder daughter speculatively. "I see," he replied. "And are you proposing to do the polishing, missy?"

"He likes both of us, Papa," Constance added quickly.

"Well, well, now don't tell me *both* my girls are in love with the same man!" Timothy said, rubbing his chin with one hand.

"Oh, Papa, who says we're in love at all?" Caitlyn intervened, annoyed with her sister. "Brant still isn't ready to be a proper husband, but he is entertaining and easy to talk with. I do like him, just as Connie does, but that doesn't mean that either of us is going to marry him."

"You're lying through your teeth, Caitlyn O'Rourke!" Timothy hooted, causing his daughter's cheeks to redden. "You may be able to put out that blather to the young blades of the parish and have them believe it, but you can't fool your father. You've

set your sights on that young man, I'll warrant, and so has your sister!''

"Well, if that's so, Papa, then what are we to do about it?'' Constance demanded. "He can't marry both of us.''

"That he can't,'' Timothy agreed. Privately, he wasn't sure he wanted young Sinclair marrying either one of his girls. Despite his good manners and handsome looks, the boy didn't have his heart in the land or in business. It bothered Timothy, whose love for the land was so fierce, to think that either of his daughters would marry a man without that same love. And what of the lad's business sense? Without his father to guide him, Brant probably wouldn't even have tried to bring in a cotton crop last year. Timothy had the impression that Brant Sinclair would be content to go through life having someone else direct him. He lacked the energy to grasp life by the horns and wrestle with it. Would either of his girls be happy with a man like that?

"Let's not talk of marriage right now,'' Timothy said after a long pause. He noted the looks of disappointment both his daughters gave him. "There'll be time enough for that. You're both young enough to have your choice of any of the young men around here and I know there'll be some who'll be proposing. Artemas Blair is infatuated with you, Caitlyn,'' he said, seeing the rebellious look on her face. "And you've had Jesse Cobb wrapped around your finger since you were twelve!'' he added to Constance.

"Look at your mother and me,'' he continued, warming to the subject. "I was a bachelor for quite a few years before I decided to marry. Lord knows there were many young ladies who seemed perfect at some time or another, but when I met your mother, I knew she was the one woman for me.''

"But that's different!'' Caitlyn protested. "You're a *man*, Papa! We can't remain unmarried until we're twenty-nine! We'd be old maids and no one would want us—except some old widower with ten children!''

Timothy coughed into his hand, realizing that Caitlyn was right. A man could remain unmarried and have a good time and still be considered a great catch for a young miss of seventeen or eighteen. A woman who acted that way would be labeled quite differently.

"Still, I don't want you thinking of marriage right now. You're both young, pretty, and will be going to your husbands with dowries you can be proud of. No sense in taking the first young

man who catches your eye." He glanced at both of his daughters shrewdly. "Young Sinclair hasn't—hasn't tried any—any—liberties with either of you, has he?"

"Papa!" was Constance's shocked response. He was relieved, although he couldn't be sure of Caitlyn, whose face had a mutinous expression.

"Of course Brant hasn't taken any liberties," Caitlyn assured her father. "He's a gentleman, Papa, despite his five years up North with the Yankees."

7

TANNER MALONE stood on the wharf in New Orleans and surveyed the surrounding buildings and warehouses in a brisk, businesslike manner. He was clearly not a tourist from up North come to have a holiday in the Crescent City. He had traveled to the South to do what many Northerners did in that section of the country—make money. As founder of a fledgling import-export business based in Boston, Tanner Malone was constantly seeking to improve his business, spreading tentative feelers to expand his markets. Everyone knew New Orleans was one of the wealthiest ports in the United States, and Tanner had gone there to find out if some of that wealth could be shoveled into his own company.

At twenty-four years of age, Tanner, whose father had come over in steerage from Dublin to America thirty years before, was not the sort of man to let things simply take their course. His father had made a good trade as a shoemaker, but Tanner had no interest in becoming a cobbler. He would have liked to own a fleet of ships and to trade all over the world, but he hadn't the money to start up so expensive a venture. Instead he had found that he had a way with people, a way with words, and a natural talent for buying and selling. With his father's nest egg he had begun the Malone Import-Export Company only four years before and had seen it grow tremendously in Boston. New York was a tougher market, but there was less competition, he'd heard, in the Southern ports. New Orleans was perfect, not only because of its busy commerce, but because Tanner had an acquaintance who lived in Louisiana who might be able to help him find new contacts in the city.

Standing on the docks and eyeing the colorful scenery, Tanner wondered how Brant Sinclair was doing. He hadn't seen Brant in nearly a year, but he remembered the look of misery on his face at the thought of returning home. In Boston Tanner had received one letter from Brant reporting that his father was settling into the life of a Louisiana cotton planter once again. It seemed that what Brant lacked in energy, his father made up in sheer determination.

Tanner recalled that Brant had indulged in a rather hedonistic way of life. The consequences of unplanned actions never seemed to bother him. He would rush headlong into some new adventure without worrying where it might lead him. Brant's irresponsibility had always irked his friend, for Tanner was a man who judged his own actions by their outcome.

Perhaps that had all changed once Brant returned to Riverhouse. Perhaps Brant had finally found out where his own responsibilities lay. If so, he might prove helpful as Tanner tried to gain a foothold in this vast cotton and sugar market. Tanner was well aware that it required an army of middlemen to market those crops and to supply the needs of the producers. Usually there were merchants or brokers to assemble the crops, then warehousemen to grade and store them. Buyers would gather in the market towns to dicker with the sellers until a price could be agreed upon, and then bankers would provide the credit in order to transfer funds from the buyer to the seller. Wagoners, laborers, and transportation workers would move the crops in and out of warehouses and on to distant markets. This was where Tanner had hopes of breaking into the chain. Only three weeks before Tanner arrived in New Orleans, his agent had completed a business transaction for him with one of the largest banks in New Orleans. Some unlucky businessman had defaulted on a loan, losing three of the most conveniently located warehouses on the docks. Despite the burden on his own capital, Tanner had bought the warehouses, relying on his agent's appraisal of their worth. It turned out the agent had been correct and Tanner was more than pleased. The warehouses were located close to the docks and were vast enough to provide storage for thousands of bales of cotton.

All that was needed was to find the planters interested in providing those bales. Tanner had every confidence in himself as a businessman, but he wasn't counting on these clannish Southerners to trust a Yankee right away. That was where Brant Sin-

clair might prove helpful. Tanner had no idea what Brant's position was in the business circles of New Orleans, but surely he must have some contacts in the area around his own plantation. All it would take was a few trusting Southerners to recommend Tanner Malone as a man to deal with, and the rest would come rolling along like a snowball down a mountainside. With New Orleans's commercial networks stretching northward into the Mississippi Valley, the rewards could be immense. The New Orleans levee was the storehouse for the whole Mississippi Valley. All along the wharves lay steamboats and packets two and three deep, and it was obvious the wharfage was insufficient to accommodate all the vessels loading in port. Tanner could imagine the entire levee filled with bales of cotton, hogsheads of tobacco, and sacks of sugar, rye, coffee, and onions after next fall's harvest. Even now in the late winter there stood drums filled with sperm oil; sacks of potatoes and bricks; and crates of ratsbane, spermaceti candles, whiskey, and rum. All around, busy workmen and slaves were constantly loading and unloading, their voices raised in chants to relieve the boredom.

Cargo shipping was a direct link to the planters. Also linked to the planters were the bankers, brokers, and lawyers who dominated the business of New Orleans. Upon them depended the credit, legal negotiations, and facilities for export and import. Those were the people Tanner would have to win over. He smiled broadly to himself, silently accepting the challenge.

Hailing a cab, he instructed the driver to take him to Toulouse Street, where the banks and brokerages made their offices. Tanner hoped that by calling on some of the financial institutions in the city he could get a better idea of the commerce he could expect. After his business calls, he would go to the St. Louis Hotel, at the corner of Royal and St. Louis streets, which had been recommended to him by his business agent. This was the hotel that rich planters frequented, especially when they shipped cotton to New Orleans in the fall. Tanner hoped that by the fall of this year he would be in a position to siphon some of those high commissions on cotton to his own company.

"It's a letter from Tanner Malone!"

Brant studied the crisp, dark handwriting, his eyes sweeping over the page quickly. Standing beside him, fidgeting with impatience to begin their ride, Caitlyn dusted off her gloves one more time and tried not to show her restlessness. The mail had

just arrived and Brant had read this particular piece with an eagerness that surprised her.

"Who is Tanner Malone?" she asked politely.

"An old friend," Brant returned absently, still reading.

Caitlyn sighed and walked over to her horse, who stood saddled and waiting for a gallop in the early March chill. She rubbed the mare's nose and talked to it with soothing promises. In a few moments she heard Brant give a howl of delight and she turned to gaze at him speculatively.

"What is it?" she demanded.

"Tanner's coming to visit—he'll be staying for quite a while according to his letter," Brant replied, a grin stretching his mouth. "Oh, Caitlyn, wait until you meet him! He's been a great friend to me ever since our stay in Boston."

"Boston!" Caitlyn repeated. She was thunderstruck. "You mean he's a *Yankee*!" Her mouth folded itself into a frown. "Brant, you know very well that Louisiana is no longer welcoming Yankees. I'm surprised he had the nerve to travel down South when there's so much tension."

"You don't know Tanner Malone!" Brant replied with twinkling dark eyes. "I've yet to see him back away from any kind of trouble that he thought was just nonsense."

"Well, this isn't just nonsense, Brant," Caitlyn retorted coolly. "The political independence of the South is at stake! I've heard what all the planters are saying. They're practically at the point of breaking with the Union, especially if a Democrat doesn't get elected to the presidency next year."

Brant looked at her in surprise. "My, my, I didn't realize you worried yourself over political issues, Caitlyn," he observed.

"I try not to," Caitlyn admitted dryly. "But if that's the major topic of conversation when guests come for dinner, there's no help for it. Why, only last evening the Blairs were over and Mr. Blair couldn't get off the subject for an hour. Dinner was late and everyone was hungry enough to die! Artemas practically got into a shouting match with his brother over states' rights and I was so bored I would have gladly pleaded a headache and gone upstairs."

"God, you are a heartless wench, Caitlyn O'Rourke!" Brant exclaimed.

"Heartless? I am nothing of the kind, Brant," she replied primly, putting her riding gloves back on, glad that he had forgotten the Yankee's letter and was concentrating on her again.

He started to speak, then thought better of it and closed his mouth firmly. With a noncommittal shrug, he went to check on his horse before helping her to mount hers. Irked by his failure to reveal his feelings for her, Caitlyn settled herself in the sidesaddle and touched her crop to the mare's flank, trotting away from Brant before he had time to mount his own horse.

"Caitlyn, wait!" she heard him call after her, but she paid him no heed. She was furious at him now and needed to distance herself from him before she said something she might later regret. Was he too spineless to admit his growing interest in her? she wondered. The thought infuriated her to the point where she grew careless and was not watching the trail.

The next thing she knew, the low-hanging branch of a tree appeared out of nowhere and hit her in the chest, knocking her backward and off her trotting horse. She lay on the ground stunned, trying to catch her breath, when Brant cantered up, jumped off his horse, and hurried to her.

"Caitlyn! My God! Are you all right?" He knelt down next to her, lifting her head and shoulders gently, peering into her dazed eyes.

With the wind knocked out of her, Caitlyn couldn't speak. She was dimly aware that Brant was holding her against his chest, his arms protectively about her. At any other time she would have felt her spirits soaring at such an affectionate gesture, but now all she could think of was how stupidly she had acted.

"I—I think—I'm all right," she finally gasped, feeling angry and embarrassed at her fall from the horse. She managed to laugh ruefully. "Well, I suppose I can't count myself the best horsewoman in the parish any longer." She tried to get up and felt a pain in her ribs that seemed to suck the breath right out of her.

"Hold on," Brant soothed her. "You've hurt yourself, Caitlyn, maybe broken a rib." His hands were careful as they brushed the sides of her chest, but he could feel nothing beneath the tightly laced stays that encased her. He gently helped her to her feet, watching her stand shakily against his arm. "How does it feel?"

"There's still a pain in my ribs," Caitlyn said. "Every time I breathe in deeply I can feel it."

Worry marked Brant's face. Would it be better to leave her there and get a carriage, or to try to lift her onto his horse and take her home? He could see tears of pain in Caitlyn's eyes and

felt a yearning protectiveness toward her that he had never experienced before.

"I've got to get you home," he said urgently. "You'll have to be put to bed and a doctor fetched at once. Do you think you can sit my horse if I walk it?"

"I think I can, but—oh—this pain! Brant, I'm scared. It hurts—oh—every time I breathe! Brant!" Her eyes were huge now with mingled pain and fear. She thought she was about to faint—she who had never fainted before in her life! What had her impatience done to her?

Making up his mind, Brant started to pick her up in order to put her on his horse, but as soon as his arms closed around her, Caitlyn let out a scream that terrified him.

"Oh—the pain! What is it?"

Quickly, Brant put her down and began unbuttoning her riding habit. Damn it! Something was wrong and he wasn't about to let propriety stand in the way of seeing the full extent of her injuries. He could see how close Caitlyn was to fainting. Supporting her with one arm, he managed to undo the last of the jacket buttons and slipped his hand beneath her jacket, which had bloodstains on it.

"Caitlyn," he said softly, not wishing to alarm her unduly, "let me take off your jacket."

Wordlessly, Caitlyn nodded. She leaned against him, gritting her teeth as he took off her jacket as gingerly as he could. When she pulled one arm out of the sleeve, she thought she would scream with the sudden prick of pain she felt. She heard his low gasp and looked down automatically to see the small bloodstain that was spreading beneath her left arm down almost to the top of her skirt.

"My blouse," she said, feeling nausea rise within her.

Brant stared first at her face, then at the bloodstain on the pristine whiteness of her blouse. He had never undressed a woman before in his life. Hesitantly, his fingers reached for the pearl buttons at her throat. Gradually, he could see the softness of her throat, then the top of her chest. Finally, as he gently separated the two halves of the blouse and began to push it down her arms, he could see the lace-embellished corset cover that housed her stays.

Suddenly, he let out a long, low whistle of relief.

"What—what is it?" Caitlyn asked, fighting her natural embarrassment and the fear that was nearly choking her.

"Your—stays," Brant said weakly, a grin trembling on his lips.

Caitlyn's face turned beet red. She had never been so humiliated in her life! Why was he blathering about her stays when she was bleeding to death with a cracked rib and God knew what else wrong with her? Anger rescued her, but just when she would have pushed away his supportive arm and unleashed a tirade of abuse at him, the pain came again, scaring her further.

"Caitlyn, it seems you haven't broken a rib but one of your stays," Brant explained. He inserted a finger inside the top of the corset cover and pushed out the offending piece of whalebone that was digging into the soft flesh of Caitlyn's side. Caitlyn immediately felt relief.

"You've got to take that thing off," Brant advised matter-of-factly. "You'll never be able to ride a horse. The whalebone will just dig right back in because it's been broken."

Caitlyn blushed once more. "I'm afraid I can't get it off without my maid's help," she confessed. "The laces are in the back—" She trailed off uncertainly.

"I'll undo them and you can take it off," Brant said quickly.

"I don't know, Brant," she said, lowering her eyes in embarrassment. "Wouldn't it—wouldn't it be a rather compromising thing to do?"

Now it was his turn to blush. He hadn't thought of that. Just because he was trying to help her by unlacing her corset, did that mean he would have to marry her? Still, there was absolutely no way she could get home like this.

"Just turn around," he said firmly, "and I'll do the unlacing. Then I'll turn away and you can put your blouse and jacket back on."

After he had unlaced the contraption, but before he could turn away to allow her a moment of privacy, Caitlyn turned back toward him, her eyes pleading. "You—you must promise never to utter a word about what happened today," she said in a breathless voice. It pleased Brant to think that he had the upper hand. And with the pleasure came a sudden surge of desire as he realized that with only one movement of her hand, she would be half-naked in front of him. Despite his good intentions, his dark eyes strayed irresistibly to the half-moons of flesh that were pushed up above the edging of lace. Involuntarily, he swayed toward her, his eyes fastened on the sweet cleavage of her bosom.

Caitlyn saw the direction of his look. Suddenly she felt an odd

sensation within herself as her heartbeat quickened and her breathing grew faster. No one had ever told her about the rush of desire that could obliterate all other feelings. In their careful tutelage, neither her mother nor her mammy had ever warned Caitlyn that someday a yearning would sweep over her so completely that all other considerations would be pushed aside. Involuntarily, the tips of her breasts tightened and a curious tingling began deep down in her belly.

Without speaking, Brant moved closer to Caitlyn and took her in his arms. Her face was turned upward, her eyes closed as she offered her lips to his. The stays she had been holding in front of her dropped out of her nerveless fingers. His mouth came down on hers, tentatively at first, then more strongly as his confidence grew. He was dimly aware that her naked breasts were pressing into the fabric of his shirt and, feeling another surge of desire, he brought his hands around in order to take possession of them.

But as his hand swept her left side, a cry of pain escaped Caitlyn, for he had touched the spot where the whalebone had pierced her skin. Her scream effectively broke the spell of desire. With a little push, Caitlyn broke away from him and snatched her blouse. Brant stepped backward, blood suffusing his cheeks as he realized what he had done.

"Caitlyn," he began, wondering if there was still time to mend the damage, "I'm terribly sorry."

"Please don't say anything," Caitlyn responded, pulling on her riding jacket. "Can we—can we just pretend it never happened, Brant?"

He felt relief flooding through him. She wasn't screaming about her honor, nor was she demanding he speak to her father. He should have realized that practical Caitlyn would not go into hysterics.

"Of course we can," he answered her, although he knew there was really no way he could forget the sweetness of her trembling mouth or the softness of her breasts as they had pushed against him. He watched as she picked up the stays and tucked them beneath her good arm.

"I can't go back to Mornhaven with these hanging from my saddle," she said with a little smile, attempting to lighten the atmosphere.

He almost laughed at her wit. My God, he marveled, what a cool head! Why wasn't his heart stirred by her as it was by her

sister? He enjoyed being with Caitlyn, but there was something missing—something he couldn't put his finger on.

"I'll throw them into the river," he told her, grabbing the stays from her and whistling for his horse. "No telling what some old fisherman will think when he fishes them out of the river." He laughed in a friendly fashion which calmed Caitlyn's nerves considerably.

"Oh, Brant, I do feel rather ridiculous," she confessed. "If I hadn't been so willful and angry, none of this would have happened."

He would have agreed with her, but he kept silent as he helped her onto his horse and then sat behind her so they could ride together until they located her own mount. "Don't worry," he said soothingly. "We'll find your mare and I'll see that you get home to have that wound tended to. Damn thing," he said ruefully, looking down at the offending corset. "I never realized what torture you ladies must go through in these contraptions."

She laughed more confidently, feeling much better as she leaned back against him. "It's the price of fashion," she said as he urged the horse forward.

"Pretty steep price, I'd say," he muttered.

It only occurred to Caitlyn much later, after she managed to slip upstairs to her bedroom and get Sara to tend to her wound without alarming her parents, that she had let a unique opportunity slip through her fingers. Most gentlemen in such circumstances would have asked for her hand as the only decent thing to do. Caitlyn berated herself, realizing that such an opportunity might not come again. And yet her pride would never let her accept a proposal under such circumstances. Good heavens, if Caitlyn O'Rourke had to resort to such trickery to get a husband—then something was mighty wrong!

8

CAITLYN SAT on the veranda at Mornhaven two weeks later dressed prettily in a pink and white striped frock with lace edging on the collar and cuffs, her coppery hair drawn up primly in a snood at the back of her neck. Her hands were folded demurely in her lap, the half-moons of her nails pale pink against the creaminess of her skin. Behind the sweet facade of womanhood,

she was distinctly out of sorts, for she had been sitting there over an hour awaiting Brant's promised arrival.

She was sixteen today, truly a young woman now. Her parents had treated her like a princess and even Sara had stopped grumbling at her. Constance had kissed her warmly as a sister should and presented her with a lovely hand-embroidered shawl. Caitlyn had been very pleased by all the attention, but she told herself that Brant's presence would make her even happier.

Caitlyn was becoming more impatient by the minute as she wondered what excuse Brant would give for being so late. She looked up when she heard Constance come up.

"He's not here yet," Caitlyn grumbled, tucking one foot beneath her voluminous petticoats. "I wonder if he's forgotten."

"He hasn't forgotten, Caitlyn," Constance reassured her, seating herself in a white wicker chair beside her. "He knows how much it means to you for him to be here."

Caitlyn gave her sister an appraising look. "You're in love with Brant, aren't you?"

Constance blushed, then nodded. "Yes, I suppose I am," she said, her eyes meeting her sister's without blinking. "And you?"

Caitlyn shrugged airily. "I'm still not sure," she hedged, thinking it might be unwise to reveal the truth to her sister. "I think he has possibilities, but there are times when I think he will never be the man I want for a husband."

Constance laughed outright. "Caitlyn, you are so funny," she said, her eyes sparkling merrily. "Why don't you just admit that you are hopelessly infatuated with Brant Sinclair?"

Caitlyn turned up her nose. "But I'm not, Constance. I find him terribly handsome and very interesting. But at times I wonder if he has any business sense at all. How will he run Riverhouse when William is gone? Would he be able to provide for a wife and children?"

Constance's eyes grew dreamy. "It hardly matters when you're in love. If Brant's not the businessman Papa is, he's intelligent and can learn as he grows older. My goodness, when he was Brant's age Papa wasn't trying to run a plantation that had been left to weeds for five years! He had his uncle, Thomas Boyer, to help him along. Mornhaven was already a very prosperous plantation when Papa took over after his uncle died."

What she said made sense, but Caitlyn was practical enough to realize that Brant Sinclair would never be the planter that Timothy O'Rourke was. She stared at her sister's dreamy ex-

pression, realizing with a sudden pang that Constance loved Brant Sinclair with an unselfish love that was alien to Caitlyn. How could Constance imagine a future with a man when she couldn't be sure of the outcome? Caitlyn found herself wishing, just for a moment, that her mind could be as uncomplicated as her sister's. Why couldn't she just accept things and trust that they would work out in the end? No, she could never do that. If she could change things to suit her own ends, she would always strive to do just that.

"I think you are an incurable romantic, Connie," she said with a note of tenderness in her voice.

Constance smiled sweetly. "I do hope that whichever of us wins Brant's heart, we will not let it come between us as sisters."

Caitlyn laughed, but her merriment did not ring true even to her own ears. "My goodness, Connie, you make it sound as though we are in a battle!"

"We are," Constance affirmed. "We both love Brant and it's up to him to decide which of us *he* loves."

"You make it sound as though we're two prize chickens for sale in a butcher shop with Brant looking in the window deciding which one he'll purchase!" Caitlyn quipped. "What happens if he catches sight of a pretty goose hanging in the back and decides he'd rather have her than either of us?"

"Then you and I will both have to be graceful losers," Constance replied.

"Graceful losers! Balls of fire, Connie, don't you ever fight for what you want? Must you always let things happen to you? Don't you ever want to mold your own destiny?"

Constance gave her sister a shocked look. "Goodness, Caitlyn, you look so fierce when you get your feathers ruffled! Your eyes are shooting sparks! A young lady can't make things happen the way she wants—she has to wait for the gentleman to make the first move."

"Hogwash!" Caitlyn answered. "Sometimes I think I'll burst my corset cover when I see some young man mincing about me, waiting to see if I notice him or not. Why can't he just come up and ask me to dance? Or better yet, why can't I go up to him and ask him to dance?" Both girls laughed, tickled by the idea of Caitlyn striding purposefully over to a man and asking for the next waltz.

It was this charming picture that met the visitors' eyes as they

rode up the gravel drive to Mornhaven. Brant's eyes roved back and forth between the two young women before glancing at his companion with a little smile.

"Didn't I tell you you were going to meet the two prettiest girls in the parish?" he asked Tanner Malone.

"That you did, my friend," Tanner agreed. "Which one have you claimed for yourself?"

"Both," Brant replied with a grin.

Although Caitlyn was happy that Brant had finally arrived, it still rankled that he was so late. Added to that was a small measure of irritation upon seeing a companion with him. Courtesy would demand that she divide her time between the two men, but that was something she really didn't want to do. Besides, she was not at all sure she liked the look of the stranger with Brant.

Was it that his eyes seemed to be assessing her too frankly? Was it his superior air? Certainly he was dressed more stylishly than Brant this afternoon. Although there was nothing wrong with Brant's casual attire, the stranger was dressed impeccably in buff-colored trousers and a frock coat that matched exactly. His brocade waistcoat was rose-colored, a shade she had never liked on a man before, but which seemed to suit this man perfectly. He was taller than Brant and more heavily muscled; she could see that even from the veranda.

Caitlyn studied the square jaw and strong chin above the deeply tanned throat. His mouth was less full than Brant's, although his lips were formed into a winning smile that revealed even, white teeth. He was clean-shaven except for the broad sideburns that reached down nearly to his jaw. His hair was dark, nearly black. But his eyes drew Caitlyn's—they were as dark blue as her own, but their brows were black and heavier than hers, which accentuated their blueness and extraordinary clarity. His eyes were returning her stare with the tiniest hint of amusement in them.

As the two men neared the veranda, a livery boy hurried to take their horses, grinning at Brant as he did so. Word was out among the house slaves that one of the two young mistresses was going to marry Master Sinclair pretty soon.

"Afternoon, Master Sinclair," the small boy said, still grinning. "Afternoon, sir," he said to Tanner Malone.

"Hello—Franklin, isn't it?" Brant responded good-naturedly.

"Yes, sir," the boy replied delightedly, and he hurried away to the stables with the men's horses.

"You see, Tanner, we don't beat our slaves all the time as Mr. John Brown would have you think," Brant said.

"I never imagined you did," Tanner replied. "Just because John Brown has the moral and financial support of several prominent Boston abolitionists, don't think I would risk money on him. The man's a fanatic and fanatics are never good financial risks."

"Brant, you're late," Caitlyn said accusingly. Her smile softened her words as Brant took her hand.

"I'm sorry, Caitlyn," he responded charmingly, "but I had to wait for the packet at the landing this morning. This is my good friend Tanner Malone of Boston." He saw her angry look and immediately continued, "Now don't get yourself worked up just because there's a Yankee in our midst. He's my friend and a guest at Riverhouse." Brant turned to Tanner. "These are my neighbors, Tanner, Caitlyn and Constance O'Rourke."

"Charmed, ladies," he said, bowing gallantly.

"Since you're a good friend of Brant's, then you're welcome at Mornhaven, Mr. Malone," Constance said as soon as she realized that Caitlyn was going to be belligerent.

"Speak for yourself, Constance," Caitlyn commented sharply, causing her sister to turn red. "Papa won't be happy to see a Yankee here when he returns from Winfield Cobb's house."

"Does he find Northerners so disagreeable, Miss O'Rourke?" Tanner questioned.

"He's not fond of them," Caitlyn admitted.

"Then I shall do my best to change his opinion of us," he responded smoothly. "After all, I confess I thought all Southerners were ogres who mistreated their slaves and did nothing but laze about the veranda with mint juleps in their hands. Fortunately, meeting Brant has changed my opinion."

Caitlyn was positive she should feel insulted, but before she could open her mouth, Constance was asking both men if they would like some refreshments, bringing the subject around to Caitlyn's birthday. Brant was looking at Constance with gratitude and admiration, and Caitlyn felt that she hadn't put her best foot forward. Not wishing to seem churlish, she changed her tactics and smiled prettily at Brant. Out of the corner of her eye, she could see Tanner's amusement deepen as though he could read her mind.

Caitlyn felt her temper rising. What a rude fellow he was! She made an effort to control her sharp tongue though, for Constance

was sending her a pleading look and Brant looked stiff and anxious.

Caitlyn turned to Tanner and smiled so sweetly her jaw ached. "If I offended you before, Mr. Malone, please forgive me." She busied herself cutting the cake while Constance poured fresh lemonade into tall glasses.

Handing a glass to Tanner, Caitlyn said, "I'm sorry it isn't a mint julep, Mr. Malone, but it's the best we can do this afternoon."

Tanner smiled and took the glass from her hand, studying the young lady thoughtfully. She wasn't the most beautiful woman he had ever met nor the most charming. But there was something about her that appealed to him very much—whether it was the energy that emanated from her or the independence he sensed behind the sweet facade of Southern womanhood. Constance he dismissed as a pretty, well-meaning young lady. Ah, but there was definitely something intriguing about Caitlyn that made a man like Tanner Malone want to find out more.

Caitlyn was aware of his scrutiny. Determined not to be upset by it, she turned her charms on Brant. He looked particularly handsome today. She tried to imagine him as full owner of Riverhouse in a few years with power over a hundred slaves and a vast cotton crop that would give him the means to satisfy his wife's desires. Then she realized that the picture seemed alien. She could not imagine him in William's place.

Caitlyn noticed that her sister, outmaneuvered with Brant, was talking pleasantly with the Yankee. Caitlyn thought her papa would probably split his waistcoat when he arrived home and found a Yankee taking his ease on the veranda of Mornhaven. It would serve Tanner Malone right if Papa ordered him off the plantation, although it would be embarrassing for Brant. What had possessed him to bring the stranger along? And on her birthday, too! Surely he could have left him at Riverhouse with William for a few hours.

"I wore this dress just for you, Brant," Caitlyn told him, leaning forward and affording him a view of her cleavage.

The thought suddenly came to Brant that he had once felt her naked breasts against him. And with that thought came a swift, unexpected arousal. He looked away from the pleasing picture she made, concentrating on his glass of lemonade. He tried not to think of how she'd felt pressed up against him.

Instead he thought about her reaction to Tanner Malone. She

had made no secret of her outrage that he was here. The mistress of a great plantation could not behave that way to guests, no matter who they were. A guest was always treated with civility and courtesy. Brant glanced at Constance, who was conversing politely with Tanner. Her manner was cool, polite, almost regal—as befitted the mistress of a plantation.

But then his gaze went back to the volatile expression on Caitlyn's face. If Constance would make a man a befitting wife, Caitlyn would make him a more exciting one. Which did he really want?

Later, after the two men had taken their leave, Brant glanced at Tanner, wondering what his thoughts were. Personally, Brant was relieved that Timothy O'Rourke hadn't come home from Winfield Cobb's before they had taken their leave. Despite his belief that Timothy was a fair and open-minded man, Brant didn't want any trouble.

"Well," he finally said, "what did you think of my neighbors, Tanner?"

"I liked them," came the unexpected reply.

Brant was puzzled. "Even after Caitlyn gave you such a discourteous welcome? Her own grandmother is a Yankee, from Boston too, I believe. There's no reason for her to be so mean-spirited about your place of birth."

Tanner laughed. "I really don't think she gave a damn where I was born, Brant. We just rubbed each other the wrong way."

"But you still like her?"

"I enjoy women, Brant, all kinds," Tanner replied. "I look forward to another visit to Mornhaven. I was never one for ladies who were *too* conventional. A little fire always adds interest, especially when the lady is pretty enough—and rich enough!" He laughed out loud and reached over to slap Brant on the back.

"Don't expect to get anywhere with Caitlyn O'Rourke. She's got a father who'd whip you to within an inch of your life if he thought you were trifling with one of his daughters," Brant warned.

"Are you telling me you *haven't* been trifling with her, Brant?" Tanner asked, his white teeth gleaming.

Brant had the grace to redden. He debated the wisdom of telling Tanner about his experience with Caitlyn the day she'd fallen from her horse. The need to boast won out and, with the air of a worldly man, he confided the details to his friend. He

was unprepared for the look of distaste that appeared on Tanner's face.

"I hope you don't go around bragging about that to the whole parish," he said seriously. "It wouldn't do the young lady's reputation any good, nor would it enhance your own."

"Of course I don't," Brant blustered, feeling more than a little embarrassed. "After all, the whole thing was just an accident. I'm not about to have Timothy O'Rourke pushing me down the aisle at the point of a gun just because his daughter fell from her horse!"

"You sound like you're waiting for someone else to choose a wife for you," Tanner commented quietly. "Maybe you should forget the O'Rourke sisters. I'm sure there are plenty of other young ladies in the parish who would deem it an honor to be your wife."

"I'm not saying they wouldn't," Brant agreed, preening. "But to tell you the truth, Tanner, my pa has his heart set on Riverhouse being joined to Mornhaven in the future."

"Don't marry a girl because of your father's needs," Tanner advised. "My father tried that with a young lady and me and it turned out to be a disaster. There was an understanding between our two families that left both my wishes and hers out of the picture. Thank God she ran away with her true love the night before our nuptials were to be announced. I always admired that young lady—though I didn't love her."

Brant changed the subject. "Speaking of your family, I want to hear what you've been doing since I left Boston. You've been so sketchy about your plans. Knowing you, there's a definite purpose to your travels."

Tanner grinned. "You're absolutely right, my friend. I've come to Louisiana to get a piece of the cotton market. Men are making money hand over fist down here, and I figure there's always room for one more."

"Your business is doing that well?"

"Yes, but I'm always looking for new markets. The business is practically running itself now that I've got some established customers. I've got good men in charge while I'm down here in the South. My younger brother's turning out to be a pretty good manager."

"Morgan Malone a good manager!" Brant chuckled. "I'll be damned! Why I thought he'd spend his life chasing skirts and

tearing up barrooms after he'd drunk everyone else under the table.''

"His skirt-chasing days are over. He's married now with a baby on the way. He's found respectability and responsibility at the same time,'' Tanner told him with a devilish grin.

Brant roared with laughter. "Is that another reason why you've left Boston? Is Morgan trying to persuade you to find respectability?''

Tanner shook his head. "I'm certainly not ready to settle down with *one* woman yet.''

Brant looked at him reflectively. "Neither am I, my friend, neither am I.''

9

"BUT, MAMA, I don't *want* to go to New Orleans!'' Caitlyn protested. She stood in the middle of her bedroom, deliberately ignoring Sara, who was packing her luggage methodically.

"Darling, you have to go,'' Margaret O'Rourke returned calmly, used to her daughter's tirades. "You can't expect to miss Pauline's wedding.''

"But her wedding isn't for three more weeks!'' Caitlyn whined. "Why do Constance and I have to go now?''

"Because your father and I have decided it would be best for you,'' Margaret responded.

"What do you mean by that?'' Caitlyn retorted. "Best for me because Artemas Blair has been over nearly every day for the past two weeks? Do you think he's going to ask for my hand, Mama? I'm not going to accept him even if he does!''

"My dear child, I am not at all worried about you marrying Artemas Blair,'' Margaret cut in.

"Then *why*?'' Caitlyn demanded.

"Because you need to get away from here. I know it's not the social season, but there'll be plenty of parties to go to with your cousin's wedding coming up. Your Aunt Helen is very pleased that you and your sister will be coming early to spend some time with Pauline and Patricia. It would disappoint her if you didn't come. We've already gotten your tickets for the next packet tomorrow morning. I'm afraid I won't listen to any more protests on your part.''

Margaret O'Rourke was not about to reveal to her daughter that Timothy O'Rourke had expressed his misgivings about Brant Sinclair spending so much time at Mornhaven. It saddened Timothy to think that both of his daughters had fallen in love with a man who seemed not to care about the cotton or the land or his duty as a Southerner.

Despite the fact that Tanner Malone was a Yankee, Timothy had grudgingly found himself warming to him. Now there was a man who knew his own mind! He seemed to have damned good business sense, and Timothy was even thinking of letting the Northerner broker this year's cotton crop. He must first consult with his creditors in New Orleans, but Timothy felt sure they would concur with him. Tanner had left for New Orleans a few days before to establish credit and to set up a branch office of his Boston company.

Margaret gazed at Caitlyn's mutinous expression and wondered if she had already guessed that the real reason for her early departure for New Orleans was to keep her away from Brant Sinclair. If Artemas Blair were Caitlyn's choice for a husband, Timothy would have jumped for joy, for Artemas was a planter after his own heart.

Margaret had hoped everything would resolve itself if left to chance, but Caitlyn was stubborn enough to try to bend fate to her own will. She was already trying to change Brant into a suitable husband. Margaret knew that tactics of this kind would never work with a man. Caitlyn's idea of what a husband should be might be totally different from what Brant was capable of being. Better to let him be himself!

Caitlyn seemed not to see the difference between her own brisk determination to mold Brant into the sort of husband deemed worthy by society's standards and Constance's loving acceptance of Brant no matter how he fit into society.

Caitlyn was still grumbling the following morning when she and Constance were driven down to the levee to await the arrival of the packet bound for New Orleans. Sara and Mammy, the girls' chaperones for the trip, were not in much better moods, as they had been listening to her complaints since the night before. Constance was serene despite the ill humor of the others. She always enjoyed going to New Orleans, and being involved in wedding preparations seemed very exciting to her. Privately

she hoped that her own wedding preparations would be coming in the not too distant future.

Margaret was there to bid the girls farewell. She was not surprised to see Brant Sinclair ride up just as the packet came into view.

"I'm sorry I wasn't here sooner to say good-bye," he said breathlessly, dismounting and striding over to where the girls were standing. He greeted Margaret, then smiled at her daughters. "I'm going to miss you both while you're in the city. However, I may have a little surprise for you."

"A surprise, Brant?" Constance inquired. "What is it?"

Margaret felt her hands turn to ice as she saw the expectant looks on both her daughters' faces. Surely Brant would not propose to one of them now!

"Tanner has asked me to meet him in New Orleans in a few days if I can get away. I think I can persuade Pa to let me go down."

Margaret ground her teeth in frustration. They had planned this trip in order to separate the girls from Brant Sinclair! She calmed herself with the knowledge that her sister, Helen, would keep an eye on the girls.

Still, as the packet stopped to pick up its passengers, Margaret saw the happy look that Caitlyn threw back at Brant and she felt misgivings. There was no telling what her elder daughter might do when her temper got the best of her, or when she let her emotions dictate her actions.

As she kissed her daughters good-bye, Margaret held each of them close before releasing them onto the boat. She waved as the boat worked its way back into the middle of the river, and she was actually aware of Brant Sinclair standing just behind her, waving too. When she turned, she was struck by how handsome he really was with his dark hair and those roving dark eyes.

"You're lucky to have two such lovely daughters, Mrs. O'Rourke," he said, looking back at the boat one last time.

"Thank you, Brant." She wished she could think of something else to say, but she felt more inclined to hasten back to Mornhaven, where she could think in private about this unexpected development.

He seemed to sense her awkwardness. "Good morning to you, Mrs. O'Rourke," he said as he mounted his horse.

Margaret went to her carriage, climbing in with the driver's

assistance. "Say hello to your father, Brant," she called out pleasantly. "I do hope he's feeling well today."

He nodded. "He is doing better, thank you." And he touched his heels to his horse, cantering swiftly away as Margaret looked after him.

Two days later Caitlyn and Constance were gazing with pleasure at the crowded New Orleans levee, enjoying the bustle and confusion that were so much a part of the busy port. Their packet had found a space close by the wharves to unload its cargo and passengers. As they disembarked, both young ladies looked around for their aunt and uncle. Disappointed at not seeing them immediately, they resigned themselves to a short wait. Showing their disapproval, Sara and Mammy stood like soldiers next to their charges as though daring anyone to come within a hundred feet of them.

Caitlyn looked into Mammy's wrinkled old face and smiled. "Don't worry, I'm sure they've just been delayed."

"They should be here to meet you," Mammy said in her gravelly voice. Her lower lip stuck out belligerently, making Caitlyn wish her mother had not chosen the old woman to accompany them.

"Do you think we could sit in the shade somewhere?" Constance suggested, fanning herself with her reticule. The sun was directly overhead, making it uncomfortable down by the river. The humidity was high after the last rains, and they could feel the dampness seeping into their clothing.

"I don't reckon we should move from this spot," Mammy offered gruffly. She was suspiciously eyeing the warehouses that crowded the levee. Who knew what kind of man might be lurking behind any one of them like a wolf ready to pounce on her lambs?

"It's hot as July," Sara began, but quickly closed her mouth when she caught Mammy's baleful eye on her.

Caitlyn resigned herself to standing uncomfortably in the sun with her parasol providing the only shade. After a few minutes she felt as though she were beginning to melt into a sticky puddle. Her gloved hand holding the parasol was dark with moisture. Caitlyn wished she hadn't insisted on wearing her new jacketed dress with its long sleeves. She hadn't wanted to appear before that simpering Pauline dressed in anything unfashionable. Now she felt foolish because she was fashionable but miserable.

"Where are they?" she finally whined, losing her polite demeanor in the face of her discomfort. "Surely they knew what time the boat arrived."

Constance shook her head. "I don't know, Caitlyn. Perhaps there was some unforeseen delay."

They were discussing the possibilities when they recognized their uncle's carriage careening toward the levee at breakneck speed. The driver pulled the horses up abruptly. In a moment the door was opened and their uncle hurried out to greet his nieces.

"Children, I'm so sorry you've had to wait," he said, taking their hands in his. Uncle Paul was a short, plump man who reminded Caitlyn of a rooster.

He looked rather muddled and his whole manner was unusually fidgety. "I'm afraid I'm late because your aunt has had a dreadful accident this morning. We were coming downstairs when she slipped and fell. She's broken her leg and will be laid up in bed for at least six weeks."

"But—the wedding!" Caitlyn blurted out.

"I know, I know! She's beside herself; she's been ranting at the doctor and me alternately. She's determined that it won't stop her from attending her daughter's wedding. I'm hoping that in three weeks she'll be able to sit in a wheelchair." He herded them all toward the carriage, directing the driver to load their luggage.

Once inside, he continued his woeful tale. "Of all things to happen! Pauline has been sobbing in her room, refusing to talk to anyone. She keeps wailing that this accident has ruined everything for her."

"She's just upset, Uncle Paul," Caitlyn soothed him, imagining Pauline wailing and secretly tickled at the idea.

"Has Grandma Bess been told?" Constance inquired.

Paul shook his head. "There hasn't been time. As soon as the doctor assured me Helen was all right, I had to get the carriage and come to the wharf to pick you girls up. I'm sure your grandmother will be able to help with the wedding plans."

"Perhaps it's a good thing we arrived early," Constance replied soothingly. "We can help with lots of things, I'm sure." She glanced at her sister for confirmation.

"Oh, yes," Caitlyn chimed in, but without her sister's enthusiasm.

They continued to their uncle's residence in the American sec-

tion of the city, above Canal Street, which was filled with the magnificent mansions of men who had found their fortunes in the Queen City of the Mississippi. Their uncle lived in an imposing four-story brick house with a wide veranda in the front that served as welcome shade for sitting outdoors on hot, humid days. In the back of the house a smaller version of the front veranda was provided with easy chairs for taking one's leisure on lazy afternoons. Aunt Helen's rose garden, her pride and joy, fanned outward from the back veranda, adding its fragrant odor to the idyllic setting of the backyard.

Once inside, with Sara and Mammy sent to unpack their luggage, both girls immediately went upstairs to their aunt's bedchamber, where she was lying unhappily among the pillows, beckoning them with a tear-streaked handkerchief in her hand.

"Ah, girls, what a day this has been! What a terribly black day! I suppose your uncle has informed you of the details?"

"Yes, Aunt Helen, and we are so sorry," Constance answered sympathetically. "If there is anything we can do to help, we would be most happy to oblige." She sat down on an embroidered stool next to the bed and tidied the bedcovers. "I know how dreadful all this is for you."

Helen looked up at her niece gratefully. "You're such a dear, Connie," she said with an exaggerated sigh. She shook her head woefully, her brown ringlets quivering beneath her old-fashioned nightcap. "Do you suppose one of you could go to Pauline's room and soothe her and the other stay with me? I'm so out of sorts, I'm afraid I raged at Patricia and now she refuses to come to my room. I need to have someone with me." She sighed again. "Constance, honey, you stay with me," she said after a pause. "Caitlyn, you be a dear and speak with Pauline. Her sobbing will frazzle my nerves!"

Both girls acquiesced, although Caitlyn wasn't pleased to have to face her cousin after having arrived from the long wait on the levee. Still, she would much prefer tackling Pauline's whining to staying here and babying her aunt. Dishing out heavy doses of sympathy came naturally to Constance, but not to Caitlyn. Caitlyn passed her uncle and managed a comforting smile on her way to Pauline's room. She passed Patricia's closed bedroom door, then determinedly stood in front of Pauline's and knocked firmly.

"Go away!" came the voice from the other side, followed by a series of sobs.

"Pauline, it's Caitlyn," she said loudly, hoping to be heard over the considerable noise her cousin was making. "I've just arrived and found out about your mother's accident."

"She has *ruined* my entire life!" Pauline cried. "I don't want to see *anyone*!"

"Let me in," Caitlyn cajoled. "I just want to talk with you—about the wedding."

"I don't want to see anyone!" Pauline repeated, her voice rising.

At this point Caitlyn would gladly have broken down the door and boxed Pauline's ears. It would have suited her perfectly to have left her cousin in her distraught state and gone to her own room to lie down before luncheon. But she had told her aunt she would speak to Pauline and she supposed she really was obliged to try a little harder.

"Please let me in, Pauline," Caitlyn said. "I've been so anxious to talk with you about Mr. Winterby. You're so lucky to be marrying him!" She tried not to laugh out loud at her own hypocrisy, picturing the beak-nosed Edward Winterby with the nasal twang.

There was silence for a moment and Caitlyn was about to give up when she heard the click of the door being unlocked. She pushed it open and watched Pauline flounce back to her bed, clutching a pillow to her breast in theatrical fashion.

"Oh, Caitlyn, poor Edward! This will be so trying for him too! If Mother can't be at the wedding, how will it look to everyone?"

"Oh, for heaven's sake, Pauline! I'm sure they will all be informed of your mother's accident before the wedding. Besides, you know your mother! She'll make certain she is there no matter what the doctor says." Caitlyn walked briskly into the room and seated herself on a chair, taking a moment to peel off the sticky jacket of her ensemble. She realized that Pauline, in her present state, would hardly notice if the dress was in style or not.

"But *why* did this have to happen now?" Pauline wailed, crying into the pillow.

Caitlyn shrugged. "Fate," she replied. "But that's no reason for you to get yourself into a state. What if Mr. Winterby decides to pay a call today to inquire about your mother when he gets the news? How would you look to him with your nose all red

and your eyes puffed up from crying? You really look terrible, Pauline," she ended with some satisfaction.

Her words had the desired effect, for Pauline stopped clutching the pillow and flew to her mirror to study her reflection. "Oh, you're absolutely right! I look a mess!" she cried. "And Edward is supposed to call this afternoon."

"You can't let Mr. Winterby see you looking like this—he might be tempted to call off the wedding!" Caitlyn added with a devilish chuckle.

"Don't be nasty!" Pauline retorted, grabbing a handkerchief to wipe her eyes. "Oh, I must have Mable come in and brush my hair. And have cold water sent up to splash on my face." She turned to Caitlyn with gratitude. "Everything's been topsy-turvy this morning, but finally someone with a little sense has arrived."

Caitlyn smiled. "You know very well, Pauline, that I would have let you sob yourself sick, but Aunt Helen asked me to come in and stop your caterwauling since it was driving her to a frenzy. Your sister's locked herself in her room and your dear father looks as though at any moment he expects the house to collapse around him!"

"You've never been known for your kindheartedness, Caitlyn," Pauline said sarcastically as she pulled pins out of her rumpled hair. "But just because I've had the good fortune to be proposed to first, you don't have to be nasty about it."

Caitlyn would have laughed derisively, but decided against it. "You are lucky to be getting Mr. Winterby," she said, choosing her words carefully. "After all, think of all the acres of cotton he'll be taking to market this autumn—enough to buy you all the baubles you want!" She eyed her cousin with a sly smile, knowing her weakness for jewelry.

Pauline's face brightened considerably at the reminder. "Oh, yes, you're right, Caitlyn. Edward *is* terribly rich—or at least he *will be* once he takes over the plantation!" She glanced at Caitlyn and smiled. "You don't suppose I'm marrying him for his looks, do you?" she asked archly.

Caitlyn did laugh then. "Oh, Pauline, how like you to admit such a thing so boldly! If the object of your affections could hear you now!"

"Don't be mean, Caitlyn. A young lady knows there's no point in marrying someone without money these days. Why, fortunes can be made in cotton or sugar, and if a man can't

show some business sense and take his share of the pie he's too stupid to bother with! Don't you agree?" She glanced at Caitlyn slyly. "Love really has very little to do with it. Falling head over heels in love is nothing more than a childish fancy."

Pauline's worldly talk grated on Caitlyn's nerves. Was that what her own feelings for Brant Sinclair were? Just childish fancies? Certainly not! She wasn't asking for the moon, wishing for something she could never have. Brant was hers for the taking.

"I don't feel like discussing your philosophy of love," Caitlyn demurred, realizing Pauline was watching her speculatively. "I'm much more concerned with your mother's well-being and your own self-respect. You'll have to tell Mr. Winterby what happened. Perhaps he will agree to postpone the wedding until your mother's leg has healed."

"Oh, no!" Pauline protested. "No postponement! I'm not going to take a chance that Edward might become impatient at the delay. The wedding will go on as scheduled."

"Now you're showing some sense," Caitlyn said approvingly. She went to her cousin and gave her an uncharacteristic hug. "Now get Mable to work on you in a hurry. You do look a fright, my dear." And with that parting shot, she left her cousin to her vanity.

After asking the housekeeper where her room would be, Caitlyn escaped to it gratefully. Heaven knew how long poor Connie would have to stay with Aunt Helen, but at least Pauline was back to her old form and Caitlyn's mission was completed. She stretched out on the bed and gazed up at the ceiling, thinking about what Brant had said on the levee before she had boarded the packet.

Caitlyn sincerely hoped he would be able to get away from Riverhouse and come down to the city for a few days. She realized that with Aunt Helen bedridden, there would be very little she could do about her nieces' comings and goings. How wonderful! It would be heaven to be alone with Brant! She remembered the last time they had been alone, they had kissed so passionately. The memory sent a shiver down her spine. Surely Brant had known what her true feelings were after that. She didn't take the time to wonder why he had not brought up the subject since.

10

CAITLYN LEANED GAILY out her bedroom window as the smell of roses and oleander wafted gently up from Aunt Helen's garden. Brant Sinclair had arrived in New Orleans and she had pleaded with Uncle Paul to include him in a pre-wedding party he was giving for his daughter this evening. Uncle Paul had been like putty in her hands, for he was so grateful for the changes she and Constance had wrought in his household in the last week that he would have been willing to invite the devil himself to please her.

She pulled away from the window and danced a little waltz in front of the full-length mirror. A proposal of marriage from Brant Sinclair! Oh, that would really put smug Pauline out of joint! No matter what she said about Edward Winterby's vast wealth, it still couldn't change the fact that he was a most unattractive man. But Brant was so handsome! And if he weren't as rich as Edward Winterby, who cared? With Caitlyn helping him, he would soon be one of the wealthiest planters in Louisiana, especially with her dowry of several hundred acres of the richest Mornhaven land.

"Well, I must say you look cheery this morning," Constance remarked, coming in from her adjoining bedroom. She yawned and stretched, the dark circles under her eyes a testimony to her late night with Aunt Helen, who had been having difficulty sleeping with her leg immobilized.

For a moment Caitlyn felt sorry for her sister. Connie was such a sweet thing. Caitlyn felt a pang of guilt at planning her strategy for getting a proposal from the same man Constance was in love with. But Connie was certainly pretty, and she was young enough to have many more proposals of marriage. Everyone knew Jesse Cobb, Winfield Cobb's youngest son, was sweet on her and was just waiting until he had made his own small fortune before proposing to her. Jesse was a likable sort, hardworking and boyish, with a sweet appeal that would be so perfect for Connie.

Caitlyn smiled broadly at her sister. "It's a beautiful day, and there's a party tonight. That's enough to raise anybody's spirits

after the turmoil in this house since we arrived. Aren't you looking forward to the party?"

"Oh, yes," Constance assured her. "I'm just hoping Aunt Helen can get along without me this evening."

"It's not fair that you have to be the one at her beck and call all the time. Patricia could do something for her own mother, I would think," suggested Caitlyn.

"Patricia hasn't the patience to tend to an invalid," Constance remarked. "And James is even worse. He won't even set foot in his mother's bedroom because, he told me, sick people make him feel unwell!"

Caitlyn privately agreed with fifteen-year-old James. "Well," she said after a moment, "you simply cannot miss the party tonight, Connie. You'll have to have one of the house slaves sit with her tonight."

"That's the only sensible solution," Constance returned. "But it will break Aunt Helen's heart to miss the party." Then her face took on an eager expression. "I am so looking forward to having some fun tonight. Brant will be there."

Caitlyn could not miss the warmth in her sister's voice, and once again her conscience warred with her heart as she wondered just how much Constance was in love with Brant. Surely it couldn't be more than a girlish infatuation, she assured herself hastily. After all, Brant was so handsome and tall and charming—who wouldn't be in love with him?

"Yes, it will be nice to see Brant again," she said, keeping her voice deliberately cool. "When he sent the message that he'd arrived in town, I took it upon myself to persuade Uncle Paul to invite him to the party. Unfortunately that odious Mr. Malone from Boston will be attending too." Caitlyn's mouth drew down. "I had no idea he was using Uncle Paul's law firm to establish himself in New Orleans. Do you think he picked Uncle Paul on purpose because he's our uncle?"

Constance's eyes widened. "Whatever are you talking about, Caitlyn? I'm sure it's just a coincidence. Why would Mr. Malone want to use *our* uncle as his legal counsel? There can't be any hidden motives to it."

"Oh, I suppose it doesn't really matter," Caitlyn returned, not entirely convinced that Tanner Malone's selection of her uncle was coincidental. "I suppose Brant might have recommended Uncle Paul in passing." She just wished she could trust

that Yankee, but there was something about him that put her on her guard.

"Grandma Bess is coming over today to help with the final details of the party," Constance said as she sat down and picked idly at Caitlyn's untouched breakfast tray. "I think having such a large part in Pauline's wedding has really tickled her. She told me she hasn't been so busy or felt so needed since her children left home to marry."

"I suppose it's part of growing old," Caitlyn said, never imagining herself being as old as her grandmother. "People think you're useless."

"Heavens, don't let Grandma Bess hear you say that or she'll give you a thorough scolding!" Constance warned her with a laugh.

"I'll be good, Connie," Caitlyn promised. "I don't want anything to spoil the party tonight." She walked back to the window and continued her earlier contemplation of the garden below. Tonight colored lamps would be placed strategically among the roses to add a romantic atmosphere for the celebration. Caitlyn allowed herself to imagine what it would be like to receive a marriage proposal in such a setting. She sighed, picturing Brant Sinclair romantically poised on one knee, his heart in his eyes as he looked up at her and spoke the magic words.

Pauline kept giggling, setting Caitlyn's teeth on edge so that she would have liked to slap her. Pauline was sporting a diamond necklace around her throat, a gift from her fiancé, that sparkled in the light. Caitlyn had to admit that her cousin really did look attractive tonight in a yellow satin gown that became her coloring.

Caitlyn herself had chosen a mint green watered silk. It was an elegant gown with a full, deeply ruffled skirt, each ruffle piped with a darker green velvet ribbon. The dress made her coppery hair gleam and her eyes seem to change color subtly, taking on a hint of green in their depths. She had had to beg Aunt Helen to lend her her emeralds, but she knew it had been worth it when she saw them sparkling at her throat and wrists.

As the girls went downstairs to greet the guests, Caitlyn hoped that Brant would be there early. Her hopes were quickly dashed as the guests began to stream through the wide foyer doors and Brant was not among them. She tapped her foot impatiently

beneath the green watered silk, swishing her fan back and forth until she realized that she was blowing her hair out of its pins.

She was standing a little to one side of the doors when she saw a tall, dark-haired figure enter and her heart skipped a beat. But when the gentleman doffed his hat and smiled at Uncle Paul, Caitlyn was disappointed to see that it was Tanner Malone. She could have ripped her fan in frustration. Petulantly, she bit her lower lip until she realized that the Yankee had spotted her and was determinedly making his way toward her.

With a gasp of alarm, Caitlyn turned to escape into the myriad swirl of guests. But in her haste to get away from Mr. Malone, she was careless enough to knock against a potted plant that was standing most inconveniently behind her.

With a crash that sounded like cannon fire, the pot fell sideways and split open on the marble tiles. Immediately all eyes turned to see what had caused the commotion. Caitlyn stood helplessly, feeling her entire face turning a most unbecoming shade of scarlet.

For a hushed moment all attention was focused on the horribly embarrassed girl. Then several people came forward to offer assistance and conversation resumed to near normal.

"Caitlyn, my dear, are you all right?" Uncle Paul asked, hurrying to her side, his face worried. He scarcely glanced at the ruined plant, which was already being attended to by four of the house slaves.

"Yes, I'm quite all right, Uncle Paul," Caitlyn replied, although her cheeks still felt hot and her head was still spinning with embarrassment. She caught a glimpse of a group of young ladies who were looking pointedly at her and whispering behind their fans. With characteristic bravado, she stared back at them until they turned away and began talking about someone else.

"Miss O'Rourke, are you sure you wouldn't like to sit down for a moment?" The smooth, deep voice belonged to Tanner Malone, and Caitlyn ground her teeth upon hearing the Yankee accent with its trace of an Irish lilt.

"I am *quite* sure, Mr. Malone!" she snapped, spreading her fan and waving it back and forth in front of her face, uncaring as to the effect on her coiffure. Blast the man! If she hadn't been trying to avoid him, none of this would have happened. Worse, he insisted on remaining by her side, nodding to her uncle as though taking responsibility for her. "You needn't attend me, Mr. Malone. I'm sufficiently unshaken to take care of myself!"

"I wouldn't be surprised to learn that you planned what happened in order to draw attention to yourself, Miss O'Rourke," he chuckled, continuing to stand beside her. And before she could retort with some scathing remark, he added, "But please let me assure you, there's no need to create a diversion. You look enchanting this evening." His dark blue eyes roved over her attire with a pleased expression. "I must tell you how delighted I was to find out you were related to Paul Savoy, who is representing my legal interests in New Orleans."

Caitlyn nodded, wishing to heaven the man would leave. He only served to remind her what a fool she'd made of herself a few moments before. If only Brant would arrive and rescue her from this odious fellow! Any other man would sense that his presence was most unwelcome and would bow himself away, but this wretch seemed content to stand beside her silent form, studying her quite shamelessly as she was about to make a disaster of the coiffure Sara had worked so hard on.

"Mr. Malone," she finally said, snapping her fan shut and breaking one of the delicate ivory shafts, "I should think it would behoove you to make yourself available to some of the other guests. There are many businessmen here."

"What a practical young lady you are, Miss O'Rourke! I find that most refreshing in a young woman—a female with business sense." He studied her speculatively. "A dangerous combination— brains *and* beauty!"

Caitlyn's exasperation was about to get the better of her when suddenly her sister appeared, a ready smile on her face as she greeted the Northerner.

"Why, Mr. Malone! How nice to see you again," Constance said warmly. For Constance, it was enough that the man was a friend of Brant's.

"Miss O'Rourke, a pleasure to see you again," he answered, bowing formally and taking her hand in his. His movements were as graceful as a dancing master's and Caitlyn couldn't help noticing how elegant his clothes were. "I was just admiring your sister's business sense while working up my courage to ask for her dance card."

Constance laughed sweetly. "You had better ask for it promptly, Mr. Malone, for my sister's card is one of the first that is filled up."

"Heavens, you both needn't talk about me as though I were invisible!" Caitlyn burst in.

Tanner Malone turned to her, his dark brows arching in amusement. "I was beginning to think perhaps you were," he said in an undertone, "or perhaps you were wishing that *I* was!" He gazed pointedly at the card dangling from its ribbon at her wrist. "I think it would be proper for me to sign your dance card now, if I may?"

Oh, how she would like to refuse him! But good manners saved her and she offered her card halfheartedly. He noted her less than eager response and smiled again.

"I can assure you I am an excellent dancer," he remarked. "I don't remember ever having stepped on a young lady's toes."

The orchestra began to warm up and Edward Winterby, leading a blushing Pauline Savoy, began the dancing with a waltz. Regretting that Brant had still not made his appearance, Caitlyn found herself partnered with a dashing young Creole. She had always heard that Creoles were the best dancers. This one was most entertaining as he kept up a steady stream of compliments while he swept her around the room.

After the dance was over she hastily glanced toward the door, hoping against hope that Brant would be there. Instead her eyes met those of Tanner Malone, who'd been lounging against the wall, studying her lazily. In irritation, she turned away from him, glad to accept her next partner for a blood-thumping Virginia reel.

Caught up in the dance steps, Caitlyn momentarily forgot about Tanner Malone, but after a brief intermission he was by her side to claim the next dance. His handsome visage was lost on her as she found herself wishing those dark blue eyes gazing at her so keenly were the dark brown ones of Brant Sinclair. Perhaps if she closed her eyes and tried hard enough, she could imagine herself in Brant's arms dancing the waltz. With a sigh, she felt his arm encircle her waist, and she closed her eyes as he led her in the lilting, dipping steps of the dance.

But her pretense could not last long, for Tanner Malone was not one to lend himself to such fantasies. "I saw you dancing with Bernard de Vincey," he observed, his voice intruding on Caitlyn's make-believe. "I've met him once or twice during my stay in the city."

Caitlyn mumbled an unintelligible response, hoping he noticed her disinterest. Why wouldn't he just hush so she could continue her fantasy that it was Brant holding her and leading her so expertly through the dance?

"De Vincey is a charming rogue," he continued. "I've heard it said of him that he's as quick to kill a man in a duel as he is to seduce a young lady."

"Oh!" Caitlyn's eyes flew open at such improper conversation—even from a Northerner. "I hardly think it acceptable to discuss murder and seduction in the same breath, Mr. Malone," she said primly, realizing he was not going to let her ignore him.

His white teeth gleamed as he smiled. "I've seen them go hand in hand on more than one occasion, Miss O'Rourke," he responded, pulling her closer against him.

She was aware of his maneuver and her eyes flashed upward angrily. "Mr. Malone, you're holding me much too tightly. I assure you I won't run away."

"I can't be positive you won't, Miss O'Rourke," he interjected. "From your expression, I would have surmised that escape was your plan. I only wish you could prove yourself a bit more charming—at least during our dance together."

"I'm not trying to be charming, Mr. Malone," she replied. "I won't be sorry to see you go back up North when your business is concluded here."

He cocked one dark brow as he studied the belligerent expression on her face. "You amaze me with your unmitigated rudeness, Miss O'Rourke," he said, surprising her with his bluntness. "It's too bad you have such atrocious manners, for you really could be a charming young woman. I had never heard that Southern women were so uncivil to strangers. But I suppose you are the exception."

Caitlyn's cheeks burned with the insult, but she stopped herself from releasing her anger, admitting to herself that she had been totally insufferable to Mr. Malone ever since their first meeting. Her anger was quickly replaced by shame at her crass behavior. He was perfectly right in his assessment of her. She'd been unforgivably discourteous toward him.

"Mr. Malone, I must apologize for my behavior," she said in a subdued tone.

If he was taken aback by her apology, his face didn't show it. "Apology accepted, Miss O'Rourke," he returned smoothly.

They continued the dance in relative silence. When it was over he offered to steer her to the refreshment table.

"No thank you, Mr. Malone," she said, glancing once more toward the doors. "I'm hoping to see Brant arrive any moment now."

"He only arrived in town yesterday afternoon," Tanner explained. "In fact I doubt that he will be able to attend tonight. I saw him this morning and, regrettably, he had quite a lot of business to transact. I believe he had meetings this evening with several bank officers."

"He's not coming!" Caitlyn couldn't keep the chagrin out of her voice. Brant not coming! All her careful planning, all her hopes—turned to nothing.

"I'm afraid not, unless he's able to break away early from his meetings." He studied her face, noting the soft fullness of her lips, which were just now pushed outward in a pout. Her lashes were long and dark, unusual for a redhead, he thought. And she was tall for a woman, but he liked that. A tall man could get back strain dancing with a short woman.

"Well, I'm sure Brant will call tomorrow," Caitlyn said, recovering her composure and producing a half-smile.

Tanner Malone felt an intense frustration. Why was this young woman mooning over a fickle scamp like Brant Sinclair who couldn't even make up his mind which of the two sisters he was in love with? It defied all logic that Caitlyn O'Rourke should fall in love with an irresponsible boy. Still, he couldn't help but be intrigued by the girl. He decided he would like to find out more about her while he was in New Orleans.

"Miss O'Rourke, I hope you won't think me too forward if I suggest that I call on you tomorrow. I would enjoy a tour of the city given by one who knows it well."

He was delighted at her sudden blush. "Mr. Malone, I doubt that my uncle would allow me to go out in the company of a virtual stranger."

He shook his head. "Your uncle and I have had several business meetings already and I believe he knows me well enough to assure himself that you would be safe with me." He waited expectantly, seeing her inner conflict reflected in her magnificent blue eyes.

She looked up at him as she considered his proposal. "All right, Mr. Malone," she said softly. "I suppose it's the least I owe you after my earlier discourtesy. I would be happy to act as your guide tomorrow. Of course," she added sweetly, "it wouldn't do to go without a chaperone, so I must insist that my sister accompany us, along with one of our house slaves."

"I understand completely, Miss O'Rourke. I would be the first to agree to whatever you require to assure yourself that your

honor would not be impugned in any way." He smiled devilishly. "For my sake as well as your own," he added.

11

"BUT, CONNIE, you can't propose to let me go off with that Yankee alone!" Caitlyn protested, wondering why her sister refused to accompany them.

"I can't leave Aunt Helen, Caitlyn, you know that," Constance reproved her. "If Uncle Paul gave his permission for you to go with Mr. Malone, there's no need to worry. And Mammy will be more than willing to go along. You know how protective she is."

"I don't want Mammy to go along," Caitlyn groaned. "I'll have Sara go instead; at least I won't feel like I'm having arrows shot into my back from Mammy's cold stare."

Constance laughed. "How can Mammy disapprove when you're only going for a short ride?"

Caitlyn made no reply, as she was unwilling to confide to Constance that she was hoping to persuade Tanner Malone to find out where Brant was and pick him up along the way. She knew she was walking on shaky ground in expecting the Yankee to go along with her plan, but she didn't care what he thought of it. After all, it wasn't as if she *wanted* to be with Mr. Malone—she would a thousand times rather it were Brant who would be calling this morning.

"All right, Connie, I suppose I'll just have to go without you," she said, pulling on her gloves and picking up her parasol to shade her in the open carriage. "I hope Aunt Helen isn't *too* trying today."

"Mr. Malone should prove quite interesting company," Constance remarked with unusual shrewdness. "He *is* a handsome man, Caitlyn. Didn't you notice how all the girls were staring at him last night? If only he weren't a Yankee, I daresay all the girls would be asking their fathers to have him call on them! I heard that Letty Downs and several of her friends are inviting him to parties they are giving for Pauline."

"Letty Downs flirts with anything in trousers!" Caitlyn replied unkindly, looking in the mirror one last time for minor adjustments to her coiffure. "She's nearly twenty and hasn't had

a marriage proposal yet; I'm sure she'd accept one even if it came from a Yankee!''

Caitlyn hurried out the bedroom door to the downstairs foyer. When the brass doorknocker sounded, she felt her heart speed up. Could it possibly be Brant come to rescue her from her commitment just in the nick of time? Her hopes were dashed as the majordomo opened the door to reveal the suave and self-assured Yankee, who swept off his hat in dramatic fashion when he saw her awaiting him in the foyer.

''Good morning, Miss O'Rourke. I must admit to being envious of your ability to look so refreshing on such a hot morning.'' He flashed his white teeth and his blue eyes looked frankly at her person from head to toe, not missing one inch in between.

''Thank you, Mr. Malone,'' she said, trying to avoid his gaze. Instead she busied herself by dusting imaginary lint off her skirt, then by tapping her parasol against the floor and opening it behind her as she passed through the wide front doorway.

''Your sister isn't coming?'' Tanner asked solicitously as he followed his companion to the rented carriage, where Sara was already firmly ensconced in the rear seat.

''Constance will be unable to join us, Mr. Malone,'' she affirmed.

''I see,'' he responded, offering his arm as she ascended the narrow carriage steps. He waited until she'd smoothed her skirts, then climbed in beside her and settled himself comfortably with his long legs in front of him.

Caitlyn had to admit there was something dangerous about the restrained energy she sensed within him. Dangerous, but exciting, she thought; then she stopped herself abruptly. How could she possibly consider this Yankee exciting? He was a devil who stood for everything the South hated. A man who came down from the North to use the South's prosperity for his own gain— only so he could shovel the profits he acquired here back to the North again. She couldn't understand how her own uncle could represent his legal interests—or how her father could be thinking of doing business with him.

Riding was always a pleasure for Caitlyn, even in hot weather, for she much preferred being outdoors to being cooped up inside the house. If anything could spoil the ride for her it was the fact that Tanner Malone was sitting so close to her that she could feel the length of his leg pressed to her skirts. She allowed herself to daydream that it was Brant whose leg was pressed to hers.

"It's a lovely day even if it is a trifle warm," Tanner said after a few moments of silence.

She nodded. "It'll be intolerable by this afternoon," she warned him, adjusting her parasol to keep the sun off her neck. "Oh dear, I do hope this keeps the freckles from popping out." She turned around to look at Sara. "Do you think that buttermilk concoction you made up for me will give me enough protection, Sara?" she asked, hardly aware that as she turned she nearly poked Mr. Malone's eye out with her parasol.

He ducked his head and put up an arm for protection. "That thing might protect you from the sun," he chuckled, "but I don't care for what it's about to do to my vision, Miss O'Rourke. Could you possibly put it over the other shoulder?"

She reddened a little at her thoughtlessness, although she had liked the idea of keeping the parasol as a barrier between them. Reluctantly, she put it over the other shoulder, unable to suppress a smile when she saw him duck again as she transferred the appendage.

Feeling a bit more comfortable, Caitlyn gazed around her with pleasure as the carriage passed several enormous brick mansions that had been erected in the past twenty years to house the recent influx of Americans who had settled in New Orleans. Before that the city had been made up mostly of French and Spanish, the two nationalities mixing often to create the Creoles, who were such a colorful and lively part of New Orleans. Caitlyn loved the city, although her heart was still at Mornhaven. There was always an excitement, a gaiety in the city that added a zest to life, and yet she would always return to Mornhaven for the peace and serenity that even her restless spirit needed at times.

"Have you been enjoying your time here in the city, Mr. Malone?" Caitlyn asked, glancing sideways from beneath her lashes and noting that he was watching her with evident pleasure. His interest made her feel more comfortable, for this was familiar ground for a girl who was used to enthralling all the boys around Mornhaven.

"Yes, I have, Miss O'Rourke," he confirmed. "New Orleans is a lively city, much more flamboyant than Boston."

"I'm sure it is," she replied. God knew *any* Southern city would be livelier than staid old Boston, where everyone must be as stiff-necked as the Puritans! Still, Mr. Malone didn't seem very stiff-necked. "And when will you be obliged to leave New Orleans, Mr. Malone?" she inquired.

"What a leading question, Miss O'Rourke! Are you hinting that you can't wait for me to go?" he asked, leaning toward her.

"I'm sure you must miss your family in Boston," she suggested, skirting his question nicely.

"Yes, I do miss them sometimes," he admitted, surprising her a little.

He offered no further information about his family, and a long silence followed. She looked out the window at the crowds that were peopled with slaves in bright calico, nuns in somber black, and businessmen on their way to make important deals. Caitlyn was glad when they entered Jackson Square, where most of the government buildings stood and she could talk about their history to her companion. When he suggested they leave the carriage and walk a bit, Caitlyn hesitated, realizing she was going to wind up spending most of the day with this man whom she was really only tolerating in the hope that he might provide a clue as to Brant's whereabouts.

"Are you sure you want to walk, Mr. Malone?" she asked. "It is awfully hot today; and besides, I'm sure you have other business to attend to."

He shook his head. "Not at all, Miss O'Rourke. I have no other appointments today. Shall we?" He signaled the driver to stop at St. Louis Cathedral.

It was on the tip of Caitlyn's tongue to refuse him, but there was something in his blue eyes that challenged her and she swallowed her refusal, rising gracefully to take his proffered hand. Muttering something unintelligible, Sara climbed out behind her, wiping her forehead with a kerchief.

"Miss Caitlyn, I be glad to stay here with the driver," Sara offered hopefully. Her big dark eyes gazed imploringly at her mistress, but her hopes were dashed when Caitlyn shook her head sharply. There was no way that Caitlyn was going to have the entire city of New Orleans see her walking with a Yankee unchaperoned!

"Would you like to see the cathedral?" Caitlyn asked, scanning the square to see if there was anyone there whom she knew. The relative darkness of the big church would at least offer some security against gossiping tongues.

"Yes, I'd be pleased to have you show it to me," Tanner answered softly.

Caitlyn couldn't be sure if he recognized her dilemma and was being gentlemanly, or if he simply was expressing pleasure

at touring the city landmark. At any rate, she led him into the cool, dark interior of the cathedral that had been named after Louis IX, the French king. It was quiet and peaceful inside with only a few old nuns saying their prayers in the pews. Caitlyn remembered the many times her mother had brought her here for confession while they were in the city visiting relatives.

Once they were back outside in the brilliant sunshine, Caitlyn couldn't help glancing furtively about in search of society matrons. Gossipmongers were always plentiful in a city like New Orleans, where so much excitement came from rumors and suppositions. Duels were fought because of loose tongues, and reputations ruined.

"I'd enjoy a tour of the French Market," Tanner said amiably, watching the changing expressions on the young woman's face. He too was aware of the power of rumor, but scandal held no terror for him as it would for a young woman of marriageable age. "Are you afraid to be seen with me?" he asked frankly, finding his enjoyment of the outing being spoiled by his companion's furtiveness.

Her head snapped upward sharply. "I am not afraid!" she retorted, wondering how this man always seemed to say the exact words that would challenge her to do the very thing she didn't want to do.

With her head held high and her parasol leveled on her shoulder like a weapon, she walked briskly beside him, skirts swishing on the brick sidewalk as the two made their way toward the levee and the French Market. Afterward they walked to the site of the new French Opera House, which was supposed to be completed by that December. Throughout the tour she kept up a lively and charming conversation, determined that he not detect any anxiety on her part. She supposed it was lucky that the heat kept so many people indoors.

On the way back to Jackson Square, they passed a traveling minstrel show which had stopped on a streetcorner. It was too hot to attract a large audience, but the touring group proceeded with the performance. The show was necessarily brief as the white performers, wearing blackface makeup and imitating black dialect, began to sweat profusely. Even so, they cheerily invited the audience to return that evening for some heartfelt renditions of "Oh! Susannah" and "Old Folks at Home." Tanner obligingly dropped a few coins into one of the performer's hats.

"Why do they dress up as blacks to sing their songs?" he asked.

"It's supposed to be funny, Mr. Malone," she replied.

"What's so funny about slavery, Miss O'Rourke?" he inquired smoothly.

She felt her temper rising in the heat. "I didn't mean that slavery was funny, Mr. Malone. I just meant that—"

"Never mind, Miss O'Rourke, you don't have to defend your peculiar institution to me. I'm afraid the North will never see eye to eye with the South on that particular issue, but I don't want an argument over slavery to ruin our walk. You've been particularly charming, and I suppose I'm too much the coward to confront you now."

For a moment Caitlyn was at a loss for words. Before she could unleash her tirade, a commotion ensued from a nearby building. Two men crashed through a doorway while engaged in fisticuffs, and there were several more men streaming out behind them, urging on one or the other of the adversaries. Each of the two men was sporting an injury, one a bloody nose and the other a swelling eye.

"I think it would be best to slip down this alley," Tanner commanded, grabbing Caitlyn by the elbow and pulling her after him just as she began to watch the fight with rapt attention. Once they were safely away from the commotion, he released her arm.

She leaned against the cool brick of the building, breathing hard from moving so swiftly in the heat. "You didn't have to pull me away like that," she panted. "I've seen fistfights before. That's the way Southern boys always settle arguments."

Tanner raised one dark brow speculatively. "Indeed! Even the gentlemen?" he asked in an insinuating tone of voice.

Caitlyn nodded with bravado. "Especially the gentlemen, Mr. Malone—so I'd suggest you Yankees keep your distance if you don't want to get your heads bashed in a fight!"

"Ah, I see I've unleashed the rebel!" he returned with a devilish smile. "It's amazing how hotheaded you Southerners are—always spoiling for a fight!"

She continued to stare at him belligerently, not troubling to deny his claims. He chuckled and moved closer to her, reaching out suddenly to grasp her arms above the elbows. "Do you know what I do to hotheaded young ladies when they look as charmingly arrogant as you do?" he asked softly. And when she didn't answer, he said, "I kiss them until I wipe that insufferable ar-

rogance right off their faces.'' He leaned forward as she stared up into his blue eyes.

"My papa will shoot you!'' she threatened between clenched teeth, wondering what had happened to Sara.

He hesitated, seemingly taking her threat seriously. Finally he released her arms and moved one step backward, his smile slightly mocking. "In that case, Miss O'Rourke, you're not worth a bellyful of buckshot!''

Caitlyn turned bright red. How dare he make fun of her! She wasn't quite sure how he'd gotten the upper hand, but now that he had, she was furious! She wished she had a gun right now—she'd show him exactly how hotheaded she could be!

"I think we should be returning to the carriage, Mr. Malone,'' she said icily, wishing there were some other way of returning home.

He bowed, but the mockery was still in his eyes, infuriating her all the more. He cocked his arm toward her, but she refused it abruptly and walked ahead briskly, wishing she had the nerve to knock him over the head with her parasol.

"You've managed to prove yourself a true Yankee, Mr. Malone,'' she spat angrily. "A man with no manners and only a thin veneer separating him from the kind of men who were fighting in the street back there.''

"But, Miss O'Rourke, those men were Southerners, if you'll recall, men whom you were proud to call your own.''

"Oh, you are impossible!'' she railed.

"Such passion!'' he said softly. "Miss O'Rourke, I can almost imagine you in a brawl, gouging out eyes and biting off ears and noses with the best of them.''

She stopped dead in her tracks and faced him with the parasol sticking out in front of her like a sword. "Mr. Malone, you insist on bedeviling me, don't you? But I must set you straight on one thing. If I were involved in a fight with you or any other Yankee, I wouldn't lower myself by rolling in the street with you. I'd use a cane or a horsewhip. That's how we Southerners punish our social inferiors!''

He disregarded her insults. "How I'd like to have you rolling in the street with me, Miss O'Rourke!'' he laughed frankly.

For a moment he thought she was going to choke with anger. "Mr. Malone, I will see myself home!'' she said finally, turning and picking up her skirts, intent on reaching the relative safety of the carriage.

Much to her chagrin, he was right behind her as she came up to the carriage, where Sara was already awaiting them, looking a trifle apologetic that she'd deserted her mistress during her stroll with the Yankee. As Tanner was about to assist her into the carriage, Caitlyn shook her head violently and helped herself in, nearly falling backward in her haste. To her disgust, he pulled himself in after her.

"I could never forgive myself if some mishap should befall you, Miss O'Rourke," he commented. "After all, your uncle did entrust me with your welfare and I feel duty-bound to see you safely home."

Caitlyn didn't trust herself to speak and the ride back to her uncle's was made in complete silence. Caitlyn could only think of how eager she was to rid herself of this odious man's company. When she became Mrs. Brant Sinclair, she would make sure Tanner Malone was no longer welcome at Riverhouse.

As they neared her uncle's house, she was surprised to see another rented carriage waiting outside. For a moment she wondered who it might be. Her question was answered as she saw the door to the house open revealing Brant Sinclair tipping his hat good-bye to Constance.

"Brant!" Caitlyn didn't care that her voice was too shrill or that it was unladylike for her to be yelling from a moving carriage. When the carriage stopped and Brant came forward to assist her out, she nearly fell into his arms. "Brant, it's so good to see you!" she said breathlessly. "I was so sorry you weren't able to attend Pauline's party last night."

He smiled. "I was sorry too, Caitlyn. That's why I made a special trip to call today. I'm sorry you were already out when I arrived, but I did spend a pleasant morning with your sister." Brant looked beyond her to Tanner. "I see you've got things well in hand," he laughed. "Trying to steal my girl out from under my nose?"

"She's a hard-hearted girl when it comes to Yankees," Tanner reminded his friend with a smile.

Brant laughed and Caitlyn warmed to that sound like a flower in the sun. She'd been putting up with this ill-mannered Yankee all morning when she could have been in the house with Brant! The irony of it nearly made her weep.

"Can you come back inside and stay a little while?" she asked hopefully.

Brant shook his head. "No. I'm sorry, Caitlyn, but I'm afraid

I've got business meetings this afternoon.'' He looked over at Tanner once more. "Lord, I never did like dealing with bankers and their kind! How do you do it, Tanner?''

"It's all a question of timing, Brant,'' he replied. "You've got to catch them right before they're ready to eat. They'll give you just about anything rather than be late for lunch.''

"I wish it were that easy. Unfortunately no one I've talked to believes that Riverhouse can produce enough cotton in the next five years to justify a loan with the crop as collateral. Bad news travels fast. Everyone seems to know what's happened to Riverhouse in the past five years. Damn! With all the money floating around this city, you'd think one of the bankers could see fit to spare a little.''

Caitlyn was becoming irritated. She hadn't endured Tanner Malone all morning just to listen quietly while the two of them talked business. Still, she found herself drawn into their conversation. Brant's money problems would soon be hers, if all went according to her plans. She bit her lip, wishing there were something she could do. Suddenly she hit upon an idea.

"Brant! What about my father? Maybe he could loan you the money.'' She gazed at him as though she had just found a brilliant solution to all of his problems.

Brant ran a finger around his collar, clearly embarrassed at her offer. He glanced nervously at Tanner, then turned his dark eyes back to Caitlyn. "That's very sweet of you, Caitlyn, but I couldn't ask your father for a loan. He's already done so much for Pa and me.''

"But that's silly!'' Caitlyn retorted, wondering why he was so proud where money was involved. "I'm sure Papa would be happy to loan you the money. Who knows but that in the future our two plantations—''

"Definitely not! I won't ask him,'' Brant interrupted, cutting her off before she could suggest the future merger of the plantations through marriage.

Miffed at his attitude, Caitlyn stamped her foot impatiently. "Brant, you're just being obstinate! I'm sure Papa would loan you whatever amount you needed. After all, you'll be able to pay him back after a few good cotton crops.''

Brant looked to Tanner for help, but none was forthcoming. Tanner seemed to find the situation amusing. Brant opened his hands wide as though pleading for Caitlyn to understand. "Caitlyn, please don't mention this to your father. It would be most

embarrassing for me as well as for my pa. We'll get our money somehow, I assure you."

"But, Brant—"

"No! Caitlyn, I appreciate your offer more than I can say, but the answer is no!" He sighed deeply, glad to end the matter. "I've got an appointment I can't be late for, so I'll have to say good-bye for now."

"You must promise to call tomorrow if you can," Caitlyn said, watching him climb into his carriage and wave to her with his endearingly boyish smile. She waved back, her mind already turning over the problem at hand. She knew perfectly well she had always been able to get anything she wanted from her father. He would not refuse her such an important request, especially when it meant so much to her.

She was so engrossed in her private thoughts, it was a moment before she realized that Tanner Malone was still beside her, his blue eyes studying her.

"Mr. Malone, good day," she said with a dismissive air. "You've succeeded in spoiling my morning; please don't do the same for my afternoon."

"I'm sorry if you feel your time was wasted this morning, Miss O'Rourke. As for me, I found it most refreshing."

"Refreshing, my foot!" she snapped irritably.

He laughed. "I intend to see you again, Miss O'Rourke, before I leave New Orleans. I give you fair warning."

"I doubt it, Mr. Malone. I've no intention of accepting any calls from you, nor do I expect my uncle to receive you after I relate this morning's experience to him."

He laughed again. "You are such a naive child!" he pronounced with a shake of his head. "Your little spat with me will have no effect whatever on your uncle. He's not a shrewd attorney for nothing. I doubt he would wish to give up the fat retainer fee I've been paying him for his services."

She was angry and was obviously searching for something to say that would irritate him. "How vulgar of you to mention money at a time like this!" she finally managed, trying to make her voice sound withering.

"Why, Miss O'Rourke, from your conversation with Brant Sinclair, I assumed that was one topic about which you were quite knowledgeable."

"Sir, you are impertinent!" Caitlyn returned, wishing she could use some of her father's most effective oaths on this man.

"Miss O'Rourke, I am much more than impertinent!" he laughed, finally releasing her.

12

THE FOLLOWING DAYS were filled with so much activity that Caitlyn was unable to formulate a plan to help Brant with his financial problems. There were gala affairs nearly every night for Pauline and her fiancé. Much of the time that was supposed to be spent dancing was spent fervently discussing the events of the day. Relations between North and South were becoming even more strained as heated debates raged in Washington and the dialogues were printed in the New Orleans newspapers.

"It's got to come to a clean break," Brant was saying to Caitlyn one evening after she'd successfully corralled him into a private corner of Letty Downs's ballroom. "It can't continue like this with one side berating and the other retaliating."

"Hush, Brant, please!" Caitlyn said as sweetly as she could, although she felt that any minute she would scream if he didn't stop talking about dull political issues. Why was he so excited about what was happening hundreds of miles away? That wasn't going to affect him as much as the fact that he hadn't been able to secure a loan for Riverhouse. "You gentlemen are always going on and on about the North and how it's determined to keep the South as its own private colony," she observed.

"An interesting theory," Brant murmured. "And it's true. Even though the South has always maintained its self-sufficiency in food production, that self-sufficiency doesn't extend to manufacturing. There are only a few textile mills and iron mills in the South. We constantly have to turn to the North or to Europe for our manufactured goods and for many of our commercial needs."

"Like import-export businesses?" Caitlyn suggested stingingly, her eyes picking out Tanner Malone in the middle of the dance floor, waltzing with Letty Downs. It was sickening the way Letty was making sheep's eyes at that Yankee. Didn't any of these people realize that they were ranting against the Northerners while one was dancing with their womenfolk right in front of their noses?

Brant nodded. "Yes, like Tanner's business. You can't fault

Tanner for being a good businessman. Unfortunately it's become a habit with us Southerners, this reliance on outsiders. Instead of building up our manufacturing capacities, we put our money into cottonseed and slaves every year.''

"And what's wrong with cottonseed and slaves?" Caitlyn inquired. "That's how your father and mine made their fortunes, Brant.'' Why couldn't he see that that was where his fortune lay as well?

Brant shook his head. "I don't think those kinds of fortunes will be made again, Caitlyn," he said with a tinge of sadness in his voice. "Tanner and I have been discussing another way to make money.''

"Don't talk to me about Tanner Malone, Brant!" Caitlyn interrupted vehemently. "I don't trust him. Do you really think he has your welfare at heart? Why, he's just another Yankee trying to make money off the South.''

"Caitlyn, please!" Brant implored, gazing around the room uncomfortably. "Try to remember that Tanner is my friend.''

"And I'm your friend too, aren't I, Brant?" she asked.

She was rewarded by the more than friendly look he gave her with those restless dark eyes she loved so well. "Caitlyn, you know how I feel about you," he said in a low voice.

Caitlyn felt her heart speed up. *Did* she know? She'd hardly had two words with him since he'd arrived. Wishing the entire ballroom could instantly be swept away, leaving just the two of them alone, Caitlyn returned his gaze lovingly. "Oh, Brant, is there more than just friendship between us?''

"Caitlyn, you know you are very special to me—both you and your sister.''

The glow went out of Caitlyn's eyes abruptly. "My sister? Oh, Brant, why do you bring Constance into it now?" Jealousy blinded her to caution. "Can't you make up your mind?" she asked him angrily. "Is it Constance you want or me?''

She jerked her hand out of his grasp. With a withering look, she marched through the double doors that led into the moonlit garden beyond. She knew that if she didn't put some distance between herself and Brant Sinclair she was liable to say something that would destroy whatever relationship there was between them. She was horrified to feel tears gathering in her eyes. Why did she have to be in love with Brant Sinclair? Was he in love with her? Or did he really love Constance?

Caitlyn saw a stone bench a few yards into the garden and sat

down to mop her eyes with her handkerchief, but the thin square of cambric wasn't doing much good.

"Here, use mine."

She was startled by the sound of a masculine voice and looked up to see that damned Yankee standing above her in the moonlight.

"Go away!" she said, embarrassed that Tanner Malone should see her at such a weak moment.

Despite her plea, he continued to stand where he was, holding out his cotton handkerchief. As her anger mingled with frustration, Caitlyn burst into hot tears, snatching at his handkerchief, hating him for being the one to offer it to her. For several moments he allowed her to vent her emotions.

"Are you feeling better now?" he asked after she'd composed herself.

"Yes," she answered, unable to look him in the eyes. And then she added, after a moment's silence, "Thank you."

"You're welcome, Miss O'Rourke. I was never a man to stand by and let a woman cry all by herself."

"Sometimes it's the decent thing to do, Mr. Malone," she sniffled, rolling up his handkerchief in her hand. "A woman isn't usually at her best when she's crying."

"That hardly matters, Miss O'Rourke. It's the reason behind the tears that interests me."

She did look at him then. "Don't worry yourself over me, Mr. Malone. *You* are not the reason for my tears."

He smiled in the darkness and sat beside her on the stone bench without asking her permission to do so. "I'm truly glad," he told her. "Despite your low opinion of me, Miss O'Rourke, I'm not really the villain you think I am. I'm simply down here in New Orleans to extend my business interests. And to see my old friend, Brant Sinclair."

Caitlyn sighed. "I don't want to talk about Brant, Mr. Malone."

"As you wish." He stared at her in the darkness and she wished she could see his expression. "Would you like me to escort you back inside?" he inquired.

"Not yet, Mr. Malone. Could you wait another moment, please? I—I don't want anyone else to see that I was crying. Gossiping tongues, you know." She tried to smile, but the corners of her mouth refused to lift.

"I'm sure they're going to gossip anyway, Miss O'Rourke. You created something of a scene when you left Brant's side."

"I suppose someone will tell Pauline. She'll make sure everyone knows about my quarrel with Brant. They will say I was jilted!" She pressed his sodden handkerchief to her mouth in consternation.

"Ordinarily I wouldn't give one cent for what those mares think of me," she boasted with her usual bravado, "but if Brant—" She stopped suddenly and looked down at her hands.

"You didn't want to talk about Brant," he reminded her.

He bent closer to her. Their faces were inches away from each other's and Caitlyn felt a strange excitement welling up within her. She felt his hand touch her waist and then slide to her back. Closer still he came, slowly, as though waiting for her to stop him with a word. But Caitlyn felt paralyzed. She couldn't move or speak. She couldn't turn her head from him. Her breath was coming faster as her breast rose and fell with an alien intoxication that was spreading throughout her body.

She closed her eyes, feeling him press her forward, urging her toward him. For an instant she felt the touch of his breath against her mouth. Then he was kissing her; kissing her slowly and masterfully with lips that were warm and surprisingly soft. Caitlyn felt herself surrendering to him, felt the pressure of his mouth forcing her head back into the crook of his arm. This, she thought dizzily, was much different from the kisses the boys in the parish had given her, different even from the kiss she had shared with Brant. Only she and Tanner existed with this kiss, their lips meshing to seal out anyone else.

She had no idea how long that kiss would have gone on, but suddenly she felt his body stiffen and an alarm rang throughout her body. He was pushing her away, not violently, but urgently. As their mouths parted, the spell he had woven around her was broken.

Caitlyn opened her eyes and saw Tanner looking not at her, but toward the house. She heard the sound of hesitant footsteps and turned in the direction from which they came.

"Caitlyn?" The voice was tentative, somehow contrite—and it belonged to Brant.

"Brant!" she blurted out, before thinking of the picture she made sitting on the garden bench in the dark with Tanner Malone's arms about her.

Brant appeared out of the shadows and Caitlyn stood up

abruptly, guiltily, wondering why in the world she hadn't thought before she said his name aloud. Now Brant was standing in front of her, his eyes shifting from her to Tanner.

"Caitlyn, I came out to apologize," Brant began. "I didn't want you to be alone—but I see you weren't." He gazed accusingly at both of them.

"Mr. Malone offered me his handkerchief when he saw me crying," Caitlyn said frankly. Then she added softly, "But why are you here, Brant?"

"Caitlyn, I realized how stupid I was and how I'd hurt you, and I—" Brant stopped suddenly, eyeing Tanner. "Would you mind giving us a moment of privacy?" Brant asked him with a hint of irritation.

Tanner bowed and, with a half-smile at Caitlyn, made his way back down the path to the ballroom doors. Caitlyn didn't know whether to feel angry at the liberties he had taken with her or upset that Brant had arrived and interrupted them. She turned her attention back to Brant.

"Caitlyn, can we sit for a moment?" he asked, taking her hand in his and leading her back to the stone bench. She felt guilty sitting with him in the same spot where she had allowed Tanner to kiss her. She tried not to think about the way she had felt during that kiss, but the insidious thoughts remained, taking her attention away from Brant's apology.

"Caitlyn? Caitlyn, aren't you listening? Are you determined to stay angry with me?" Brant was asking, taking both her hands in his.

"Brant? Oh, Brant, of course I forgive you! I know how difficult it is for you with your business problems," she said vaguely, looking into Brant's face. Yes, it was still as handsome as she thought it would be—the mouth still as tender, the eyes still as enticing. And yet Tanner Malone was a handsome man too. Was he as handsome as Brant? She shook her head. Why was she thinking of that Yankee? Why was she comparing Brant to him? She *loved* Brant—didn't she?

"Caitlyn, I'm glad you're not angry with me," Brant continued, unaware of her turbulent emotions. "I have to confess how terrible I felt when you ran outside."

Then why didn't you come right after me? Caitlyn wondered. Why did you give Tanner Malone time to come out and sit beside me and offer me his handkerchief and seduce me into kissing him? "I'm sorry you felt terrible, Brant," she murmured. She

could feel Tanner's rolled-up handkerchief still in her palm even as Brant squeezed her hand.

"Oh, Caitlyn, I like you enormously! Sometimes I think I might even be in love with you."

"You *think* you might be in love with me, Brant," she repeated, looking at him with narrowed eyes. "Don't you know for sure?"

"Don't," he pleaded. "Don't be sarcastic, Caitlyn. It doesn't suit you."

She pulled her hands from his grasp. "Brant, I'm sorry if you find my attitude unsuitable, but I can't help it. I thought—" She took a deep breath and plunged in. "I thought you did love me."

He took her hands again, his expression fervent. "Caitlyn, I do love you!" he blurted out, surprising himself. And yet, after saying it, he knew it was true. He loved her for her strength and her beauty and her determination to help him. "Caitlyn, I love you, but I couldn't ask any woman to marry me now."

He had finally gotten her attention and Tanner Malone was effectively wiped from her mind. Brant had said the magic word *marry*, but not in the way she had hoped.

He pulled her into his arms. "Oh, Caitlyn, I know you think everything is easy, but it just isn't! My father is not well. Riverhouse is in financial trouble, and I can't get a banker to back me."

"Brant, I don't care about that. We can be together and I can help you." Caitlyn beamed, hardly believing that Brant was telling her his problems, confiding in her.

"Honey, I wish we could be together, but you must be patient," Brant sighed. He leaned down and kissed her gently on the lips.

Caitlyn felt a seeping disappointment. There was no passion in his kiss and none in his words. This wasn't what she had hoped and planned for—this talk of being patient. What was the good of that? How long must she be patient? Brant was charming and handsome, but he wasn't being charming now. He wasn't even being entertaining. He was being dull and practical and telling her things she didn't want to hear. She wanted to shout their love from the rooftops.

"Brant, let's go inside and tell my uncle now," she pleaded, taking his hand and standing up. "And we must tell Constance."

He shook his head almost violently. "No! You mustn't tell

anyone anything, Caitlyn! You must promise to keep silent until I feel the time is right to speak to your father.'' He pulled her back down on the bench. ''Riverhouse must come first, Caitlyn. I'm not going to bring a new bride to a house that would have no future.''

''Why can't I tell Constance?'' she demanded, beginning to feel as though the ground were dissolving beneath her.

''Don't tell her, Caitlyn! I know she loves me and I can't bear to break her heart.''

She reared up, anger coursing through her. ''You can't bear to break her heart,'' she repeated. ''I would think not telling her of our intentions would be a more effective way of doing that. It's not fair to let her think you care for her.''

''But I do care for her, Caitlyn,'' he interrupted.

He looked away from her, running his hand through his hair as though tortured by his own emotions. ''Oh, Caitlyn, how can I explain it to you?'' he began helplessly. ''I love you, but I love Constance in a different way.''

''Brant, you're not making sense!'' she told him. ''You can't love two women!''

God help me, but I do! Brant thought, wondering how he had gotten himself into this mess. He had been so sure it was Constance whom he wanted to marry, but when he had seen Tanner and Caitlyn together, everything had gotten mixed up inside him. He'd been horribly jealous. He'd wanted to see Caitlyn look at him the way she had looked at Tanner.

''I have no right to ask anyone to marry me,'' he said sadly. ''I wouldn't make a fit husband for anyone, Caitlyn.''

He looked so utterly miserable that Caitlyn felt herself softening toward him. ''Oh, Brant, you're going to make a fine husband, I know it! And I know how distraught you are about Riverhouse.'' She sat down beside him and held him in her arms comfortingly, feeling very maternal as his dark head pressed against her bosom. This feeling must be love, she thought. It was a protective possessiveness that made her want to fight his battles for him. He couldn't help it if he wasn't as strong as she.

''Brant,'' she finally sighed. ''I promise I won't say anything to anyone.'' She turned his head up so she could look in his face. ''But when can we be together, my dearest? I want to be with you so very much!''

''As soon as I get Riverhouse back on its feet,'' he promised softly, taking her chin in his hand. His face was close to hers

and Caitlyn automatically closed her eyes and tilted her head back for his kiss.

But when he kissed her, it was gentle and sweet with no promise of the passion that Caitlyn could feel inside herself. She wanted more from him. She wanted the fire and excitement she had felt with Tanner Malone. At the thought, she shivered and tried to erase Tanner Malone's kiss from her memory. Determinedly, she pressed her hands around Brant's neck, urging his kiss to deepen.

Surprised at her action, Brant couldn't help his excitement and he responded to her touch with sudden ferocity. His arms went around her waist tightly and he pulled her against his chest, pressing her close. His mouth grew more demanding and he forced her lips open so his tongue could invade the softness inside her mouth. The intimacy startled Caitlyn. She tried to pull back, but his arms were like tight bands around her. And then, strangely, she wasn't afraid, but terribly excited. Her body was like a tightly coiled spring that was tensing, tensing. She felt Brant leaning her backward against his arm so that her breasts, nestled inside the bodice of her gown, were pressed insistently against him.

"Caitlyn, ah, Caitlyn!" Brant whispered urgently, releasing her mouth only to plant a warm trail of kisses down her throat. "God, you are so exciting!" he groaned, pressing his mouth to the top of her low-cut bodice.

Caitlyn's senses thrilled at her power over him. Her blood was pounding in her ears. She knew that no respectable young woman would ever find herself in such a compromising situation, but she didn't care. Brant Sinclair loved her—and wanted her. Lord, how he wanted her! She smiled and threw her head back, caressing his dark hair as his lips kissed the upper swells of her breasts.

It was Brant who came to his senses. Although he was excited by Caitlyn and eager for more of this intimacy, he did not want to be discovered by one of the guests. He had a sneaking suspicion that Caitlyn would like nothing better than to have someone spy them, thereby forcing him to publicly extend a marriage proposal to her.

Something still held him back. Was it the softness of Constance's eyes when they looked up at him on the dance floor? What was wrong with him? How could he sit here with Caitlyn in his arms and think of Constance? He'd made the right choice—

hadn't he? Or had he been pushed into it by jealousy and passion?

"We must go back inside," he began. "Someone might see us."

Caitlyn felt her cheeks burning. She had let two men kiss her tonight, neither of whom was going to make a public proposal to her. If her father knew, he would call her a brazen hussy. She stood up from the bench, shaking a little.

"Yes," she said in a small voice. "I've been out here too long already." She glanced at Brant, and in the moonlight he could see the tears in her eyes.

"Darling, don't cry!" he said swiftly. He stepped toward her, but she shook her head and held her arms up to ward him off.

"No! Please, Brant!" She looked at the handsome face she loved, the tall, elegant figure she was so proud of. Drawing strength from some inner source, she said, "If you will give me your arm, I would appreciate your escorting me back."

Brant extended his arm to her, admiring her composure.

Caitlyn walked beside him, wiping away any trace of tears with Tanner Malone's handkerchief. She stared at the large square of white cotton and smiled ironically. It might be Yankee-made, she thought, but it was Southern cotton. And she was a Southerner and proud of it! She could wear a mask of pretense as well as any of them.

"I'm perfectly all right now, Brant," she assured him as they entered the ballroom. Immediately several young women hurried over to them and asked where they had been, their voices mingling in an unpleasant cacophony.

"Why, Caitlyn, I declare your cheeks are as bright as peonies, honey!" Pauline cried.

"You were outside so long we were all worried," Letty added, poisonously sweet as she eyed Caitlyn's person for any sign of what had transpired in the garden. "I saw Mr. Malone follow you outside and then return without you. I wondered why you didn't come back in, but now I see—Mr. Sinclair was with you."

"Caitlyn, is everything all right?" asked Constance, gazing suspiciously at her sister.

Caitlyn's smile was falsely bright as she remembered her promise to Brant. "I'm all right, Connie," she answered her. "I'm afraid Brant and I had a slight argument about business and I stormed off."

"Business, my foot!" Caitlyn heard Letty whisper loudly into Pauline's ear.

Caitlyn glanced at Brant, who rescued her by asking Letty for the next dance. Letty decided that Caitlyn wasn't worth gossiping about. It was much better to dance with an eligible bachelor. She was led away by Brant, much to Caitlyn's relief.

Gradually the rest of the girls drifted away to dance partners, leaving Caitlyn and Constance together on a settee, watching the dancers quietly.

"Caitlyn, are you sure you're all right?" Constance asked insistently. "You were gone so long I almost went out to look for you."

Caitlyn tried not to imagine the horror of Constance going out to the garden and discovering Brant and her in a passionate grip. She laughed lightly. "I was mad at Brant," she said frankly, "and I just wanted to be alone for a moment."

"I see." Constance eyed her sister, noting the handkerchief rolled up in her hand. "Is that Brant's?"

"No, it's Mr. Malone's," Caitlyn answered, staring at the cloth, then looking out over the dance floor, wondering where he was.

"He's already gone," Constance informed her.

Caitlyn tried to suppress the sense of loss that overcame her. Why should she care if the Yankee was gone? He could very well have ruined her reputation, especially if Brant hadn't come to her rescue. Still—and she looked once more at the cotton square—he had been a comfort when he'd talked with her after her argument with Brant. How could a Yankee have such decent feelings?

"Caitlyn, what has happened?" Constance asked in exasperation. "I can see you're not telling me everything. Was it something Mr. Malone did? Is that why you're so upset?"

"Of course not! Connie, you should know that nothing that Yankee could do would upset me," Caitlyn returned. "He is such an—an irritation, really! I just wish he would go back up North where he belongs. I really don't think he's a good influence on Brant."

"I'm sorry, Caitlyn," Constance said, doubt still in her voice. She looked up to see Brant coming toward them and observed, "Brant has the next dance on my card."

Caitlyn watched Brant take her sister in his arms to dance, recalling how those same arms had only minutes before pressed

her body close to his. She looked down once more to the hand-kerchief in her hand, then let it fall beneath her chair as she stood up to accept her next dance partner.

13

CAITLYN AND CONSTANCE'S PARENTS finally arrived in New Orleans, anxious about the state of affairs in the Savoy household, but overjoyed to see their daughters again.

"It sounds terrible, but I'm so glad that Mama has arrived to take care of Aunt Helen," Constance whispered to Caitlyn as they made their way to Caitlyn's bedroom. "It's only a week until the wedding, you know, and after that we'll be obliged to return to Mornhaven."

"You mean you don't want to go home, Connie?" Caitlyn asked, raising an eyebrow.

Constance smiled and shook her head. "It's not that," she said with a trill of laughter. "It's just that I want to stay here in New Orleans as long as Brant is here. He's promised to take me to the park one day."

As soon as Constance had gone, Caitlyn picked up a brush and threw it viciously across the room. "Damn Brant Sinclair!" she muttered, keeping her voice down with an effort. "Why does he insist on playing up to Connie when it's me he really loves? Why can't he tell her the truth? That he's going to marry *me*!"

She threw herself down on her bed, her chin propped up by her hands. Did Brant truly love her? Caitlyn had never known such frustration in divining a man's feelings. She had always been self-confident around men, sure of her own charms. But she never knew where she stood with Brant Sinclair—even after his declaration of love for her two nights ago. That was one of the reasons she was so challenged by him.

Caitlyn turned over on the bed and stared up at the ceiling, heedless of the dreadful creasing she was giving her gown. She tried to remember the exact moment when she had fallen in love with Brant Sinclair. Surely it wasn't when her father had helped fish him out of the Mississippi. And it wasn't the day of the barbecue, when he had divided his time equally between her and Constance. When had the challenge of gaining a man's attention turned into a contest for love?

Had it been the day he'd taken her on the picnic without Constance? Then she remembered the day they'd gone riding together, when he had taken off her blouse and they had kissed so passionately. The thought caused a thrill of excitement to shiver up her back. She was positive that she was in love with Brant.

She frowned to herself as an unwelcome thought occurred to her. Had Brant ever *really* asked her to marry him? She tried to recall that night in the garden during Letty Downs's party. She remembered him telling her that he loved her, but did he actually make a marriage proposal—or had she just come to that conclusion? She sat up suddenly on the bed, a feeling of panic permeating her breast.

If Brant hadn't actually proposed marriage to her, could it be that he was still undecided? She turned and pounded the pillows in frustration. Brant must come to the decision that Caitlyn was the right woman to marry. How could she show Brant that she would truly be the best wife for him?

She knew that he was still having difficulty getting a loan in New Orleans. Any day now, he would probably give up and return to Riverhouse empty-handed. In his own mind, that would discredit him as a prospective husband. How could she help him?

She could ask her father to loan Brant the money! Caitlyn had conveniently forgotten that Brant had expressly forbidden her to do such a thing. She would be helping him to solve his problems, exactly what a wife should do! Caitlyn must work quickly to convince Brant of her love. She would talk to her father tomorrow morning. She smiled to herself, remembering the loving look on her father's face when he'd embraced her in the foyer upon arriving in New Orleans. Her father loved her very much. Certainly taking advantage of that love was a daughter's prerogative.

"Daughter, have you taken leave of your senses?" Timothy O'Rourke stared at Caitlyn. "You're asking me to lend the Sinclairs *more* money!" Timothy stood in the middle of Paul Savoy's small study, his bright blue eyes on his eldest daughter, who looked very earnest and sure of herself in her gown of spring green.

"Papa, please! It would mean so much to me, and Brant is so desperate. He's been to all the bankers in New Orleans and they've all turned him down." Caitlyn scanned her father's face

for any sign of softening. When she saw none, she squeezed a few tears to the surface, hoping the sight of them would change his mind in her favor.

Caitlyn had cornered her father after breakfast and confided that she needed to speak with him about a very urgent matter. She'd been surprised by the look of worry on his face.

Relief replaced worry when Timothy found out what his daughter wanted to talk with him about. He'd been thinking she would tell him Brant Sinclair had proposed marriage to her. But still, this talk about money! Why in God's name was Caitlyn coming to him about the Sinclairs' financial problems? That was no concern of hers.

"Caitlyn, I'm in no position to loan Brant money. I've got to buy new plows, more mules, and have repairs done on Mornhaven this year."

"But, Papa, you have more money than you need!"

"Do I, now?" he roared, perturbed that his own daughter should be judging his financial situation. "What about the new fashions you and your sister will be wanting this year? What about that trip to Europe? I was thinking this might be the year we could go."

"Papa, all that isn't important. Brant is fighting to keep Riverhouse from going under!"

"*Brant* is fighting! You mean William is fighting. I've seen Brant's disinterest in the cotton crops. If the plantation went under, he'd be the first to sell it to the highest bidder!" He waved away her protests. "Don't pretend not to know what I'm talking about, daughter! The man's not interested in carrying on his father's legacy. Oh, he'll work the plantation as long as he can because that's his only source of income. But when the going gets rough, he'll desert rather than stand and fight. The lad hasn't got the stomach for that!"

"Papa, how can you be so cruel!" Caitlyn demanded, aghast. "I thought you liked Brant."

"I'm not saying I don't like him," Timothy explained, settling down a little. "What I'm saying is that I'm not going to send good money after bad. My obligation's done."

There was silence in the room for a minute while Caitlyn digested the import of her father's words. "I'll bet if it were William asking you for the money—" she began.

Her father interrupted her. "William would never ask me for the money. He's got too high a sense of honor for that."

"But he's desperate! William is a proud man, but if we don't help him, he's going to lose Riverhouse." She played what she hoped would be her trump card. "Papa, would you want your own daughter to become the wife of a man who was about to lose everything he had?"

"Constance doesn't care about Riverhouse," Timothy muttered absently. At Caitlyn's gasp, he looked up.

"I'm not talking about Constance, Papa, I'm talking about *me*!" she cried, feeling as though her father had just betrayed her.

"Caitlyn! Child, has Brant asked you to marry him?" Timothy demanded.

Caitlyn wished with all her heart that she could tell him that he had, but she shook her head miserably. "No, Papa, he hasn't asked me to marry him," she admitted in a low voice.

"I don't think he's going to," Timothy returned, relieved that Brant had more sense than he'd originally given him credit for. "And to tell you the truth, I'm glad of it. He's not the man for you, Caitlyn. He's not interested in being a planter." He shook his head sadly.

"Well, and what if he isn't?" she challenged him. "That doesn't mean he can't change, Papa. All he needs is some help from the people he trusts," she ended accusingly.

Timothy sighed. Where in God's name had Caitlyn acquired that streak of stubbornness that wouldn't let her see the core of a thing if it stared her in the face?

"Caitlyn, he's not worthy of all your tender attention. I'm afraid you can't change my mind, any more than you can change Brant's nature. No matter how you argue for him, my dear, Brant Sinclair is not a good risk. That's why the bankers have refused him a loan." He moved toward his daughter to lay a sympathetic hand on her shoulder, but she jerked away from him angrily.

"You're not being fair, Papa! How can Brant keep Riverhouse going without money? You're just being mean! You don't care about him or his father—or me!"

"Daughter, I love you more than I love my own life! That's why I'm not about to see you throw your future away with both hands. Why do you agonize over a man who's not worthy of you?"

"I know he loves me, Papa!" Caitlyn insisted.

"How can you know he loves you when the poor boy doesn't know himself?" Timothy snapped, crossing the room to his

brother-in-law's desk and drumming his fingers on its smooth surface. He picked up a pencil, then broke it. "Daughter, I cannot help you. I'm not going to lend Brant Sinclair money. I doubt he would expect me to give him a loan. It's true that cotton prices are high now, but we've had huge crops these last few years and the market won't stand much more. Prices will be starting to drop. In Washington there are rumblings of war, and people in the South are spoiling for a fight. How do you think that's going to affect our income?"

"I don't want to hear your practical reasons, Papa!" Caitlyn protested. "If you loved me, if you truly wanted to see me happy, then you would do as I ask and loan Brant the money." She delivered the ultimatum with head held high.

Timothy restrained his anger with difficulty. "It would seem to me," he began, choosing his words carefully, "that if Brant needs money, he would do better asking his friend Tanner Malone for it. There's a man with some business sense. Mr. Malone probably has plenty of money safely tucked away in some of our finer banking institutions."

"Money made from Southerners!" Caitlyn spat out in disgust. "Money he'll send back to Boston, Papa!"

"That's hardly the point," Timothy returned reasonably.

"Oh, Papa, you must know that Brant would never ask Tanner Malone for money!" Caitlyn sighed. She would have said more, but suddenly the thought came to her that perhaps *she* could find a way to induce a loan from Mr. Malone.

For the moment she was deaf to her father's continued arguments. Would asking Mr. Malone be too brazen of her? She felt a touch of excitement at the thought of seeing the Yankee again. With the self-confidence of a girl who had always known men were interested in her, she felt positive she could charm her way into the Yankee's good graces.

Of course, she assured herself, she would be doing it for Brant. Certainly Tanner Malone had money to spare. Why, he had bragged about how well his stupid little business was doing up in Boston! She tried to picture the look on Brant's face when he found out his financial woes would be over thanks to a generous loan from his friend.

She must make the Yankee promise not to divulge her part in getting the loan. Instinctively, she knew that Brant would not appreciate her involvement in such a scheme. But she must do something to help Brant! It was the best way to prove her love

for him. She glanced warily at her father, relieved that he was still engrossed in the economics of cotton planting in the event of war.

"Papa," she interrupted him with false sweetness, "I'm sorry. You're absolutely right."

Timothy was not so easily deceived. "I can't believe you're capitulating so easily, Caitlyn," he said, cocking an eyebrow at her. "It's not like you to give up. What plan are you busy hatching now?" he asked bluntly.

"Papa, you make me sound like a stubborn mule," Caitlyn replied with a coaxing little laugh. "No, I've come to my senses. I realize that even if you offer the loan to Brant, he'll never accept it."

Timothy felt relieved that she'd come round to his way of thinking, but he had the nagging suspicion he hadn't heard the last of this yet. "So you've decided to keep your nose out of the Sinclairs' business?"

She smiled. "I promise not to bother you about it again," she returned, evading his question. Her dress made a swishing sound as she crossed the room. She paused with her hand on the doorknob and turned back to throw a cunning look at her father. "But, Papa, don't think for one minute that Brant can't be helped by the love of a good woman. I intend to show you just how it can be done." And she hurried out the door before her father could protest.

All that day she planned her approach to Tanner Malone. It must be done with care and much charm. She knew he liked her, but she also knew she didn't completely understand him the way she thought she understood most of the boys in the parish.

For a moment Caitlyn felt doubt enter her mind—doubt about Brant's true prospects as a cotton planter, doubt about her own role as his wife. But she briskly swept these feelings aside. She had believed for so long in her future as Mrs. Brant Sinclair that there was nothing else she could think about. She only knew that she wanted Brant with all her heart, and her experience had never taught her that wanting something and getting it were two entirely different matters.

14

THERE WAS LITTLE TIME before the wedding in which Caitlyn could ask for Tanner Malone's help. She barely got to see Brant, who made it a routine to call at the Savoy house. Caitlyn knew he had given up hope of obtaining the money he needed. He was just cooling his heels before returning to Riverhouse to tell his father the disheartening news.

When the day of the wedding arrived, Caitlyn could hardly contain her excitement. Tanner Malone had been avoiding her, and she could only surmise it was because he was discomfited by the memory of their kiss. This supposition made Caitlyn feel supremely powerful, for she had had boys in such a quandary before. She giggled nervously as she checked her appearance in the mirror before joining the others downstairs on the way to the church.

Sara had swept Caitlyn's hair up into a glistening pile on top of her head, secured by pins so the heavy mass wouldn't tumble down during the ceremony. Caitlyn's dress was pink satin, which suited her complexion and made her coppery hair shine, and her wide straw bonnet had a satin band that was the exact shade of her dress. She wore gloves buttoned to the elbow and carried a charming bouquet of flowers, mostly roses from Aunt Helen's garden.

She hurried downstairs and squeezed into the last carriage with her sister, her mother, and Aunt Helen. Pauline and Patricia were in another carriage with Grandma Bess and Aunt Caroline, and the men were all mounted on horses. At the signal from Pauline's coachman, the wedding procession started for St. Louis Cathedral.

Caitlyn looked ahead as the cathedral towered over the wedding party. She was eager to go inside and get the ceremony over with. Pauline's marital happiness hardly concerned her, for it was her own happiness she was worried about. Her spirits rose when she spied Brant conversing with several other gentlemen at the entrance to the church. How handsome he looked in his dark suit! she thought proudly.

"Caitlyn, I feel as though I'm going to faint!" Pauline whispered, pulling her inside the vestibule of the church by a side

door and into a room especially outfitted for the bride. "I think Mable has laced my stays too tightly; I swear I can barely breathe!" Her brown eyes looked into her cousin's with fright.

"Don't be silly, Pauline," Caitlyn returned practically, disappointed that she hadn't been able to greet Brant before the wedding. "You're just nervous and excited."

The rest of the female half of the wedding party hurried into the room, exclaiming over the heat and helping one another to patch up falling coiffures. Suddenly Uncle Paul, looking a little dazed himself, knocked on the door and told Pauline it was time to go.

The ceremony was long, but Caitlyn barely noticed it, standing behind Pauline and Edward Winterby as their lives were irrevocably joined together. Oh, how she wished it were she and Brant who were kneeling together receiving the priest's blessing!

Finally Pauline and her husband turned to the assembly and made their way down the long aisle to where their carriage awaited to take them back to Pauline's parents' house for the reception. Caitlyn was obliged to sit beside Mr. Winterby's younger brother in his carriage on the way back. As she chatted reluctantly with him, she thought only of Brant. She told herself that somehow everything was going to be all right. Brant would soon have the money he needed to keep Riverhouse—and *she* would soon have the marriage proposal she was craving.

The scent of roses and magnolias permeated the Savoy house. The ballroom had been festooned with ribbons and flowers and a dais had been set up at one end for the orchestra. Chairs lined the walls, giving the dancers plenty of room on the polished oak floor. In the dining room and the music room (temporarily converted to an extra eating area), long tables had been set up and laden with food. Beef and veal, pigeon pie, cream soups, vegetables and fruits, and fancifully decorated cakes and pies were all spread enticingly on snow-white tablecloths.

Guests could choose from a variety of liquors that were graciously served by liveried house slaves whose silent, expressionless faces betrayed nothing. Whiskey, rye, bourbon, and brandy flowed freely from bottles that afternoon as everyone imbibed. More than one of the younger gentlemen, including the bride's brother, James, became falling-down drunk. Aunt Helen, seated in a makeshift wheelchair, delivered a scolding to her son, but he barely heard her before he slipped off his seat and fell to the

floor. One of the house slaves hurried to help the young master upstairs to his room to sleep off the effects of the whiskey.

Caitlyn watched in amazement as Pauline was brought to blushes by some of the intimate comments made by the males in the wedding party. Mr. Winterby stood protectively by, his arm held possessively around his new bride's shoulders. Even he was not immune to the teasing, and his thin cheeks flushed a bright red as some of the boys speculated about the events of the wedding night.

"Dance with me, Caitlyn!" said a masculine voice. It was Brant, his dark eyes merry from the drinks he'd already imbibed. He looked so endearing with his dark hair falling over his forehead that Caitlyn could forgive him anything.

"Of course, Brant," she sighed happily as his arms closed around her.

"Caitlyn, you are beautiful tonight!" Brant declared, gazing at her as though he were personally responsible for the glow in her cheeks and the sparkle in her eyes.

"Thank you, Brant, and you look particularly handsome," she replied, realizing how devastating he could be when he was dressed in formal attire. Caitlyn couldn't help feeling proud that this man was hers. She glanced around inconspicuously, convinced that everyone else on the dance floor must be watching them. Surely they were the handsomest couple on the floor, she thought arrogantly.

But despite her pride in their appearance, she couldn't deny that Brant had just tripped on her feet for the second time. "Goodness, Brant, you've had too much brandy!" she scolded him fondly. "Perhaps we ought to sit out the rest of this dance."

"If a gentleman is supposed to hold his liquor, then I suppose I'm no gentleman!" Brant hiccupped, stepping on her toe once again.

Caitlyn winced, both from the pain in her toe and from her embarrassment as his voice grew louder, causing some of the other guests to stare at them. "Brant, I feel a little faint," she said under her breath, gazing at him with pleading eyes. "Could you take me to a seat?"

He hesitated, his face wearing the belligerent expression of one who is drunk, but denies it until he has passed out under a chair. To Caitlyn's relief, he finally did as she wished, escorting her to a bench where he could sit down next to her. Immediately, she opened her fan and waved it beneath her nose, very much

aware of the smell of liquor on Brant's breath as he leaned toward her.

They sat in silence for a few moments until Brant grew weary of her cool attitude. "I'm going to get another glass of that excellent stuff your uncle has put out," he informed her.

"Brant, I don't think it would be wise for you to have any more to drink. After all, there are several influential businessmen here, and it wouldn't do for them to see you drunk. You'd find yourself with a terrible headache in the morning and the business community's opinion of you lowered."

"It's already hit bottom," Brant hiccupped. He laughed sarcastically. "I don't think they'd give a damn how drunk I got," he told her. "They've no intention of having any business dealings with me. Some of those fat-bellied, balding bankers would like nothing better than to see Riverhouse go on the auction block. I imagine they'd be interested in such a prime piece of real estate then."

"Brant, hush!" Caitlyn whispered furiously. "Whatever you think of them personally, they're the power behind everything in this city. You can't afford to insult them. You're going to need them someday," she said practically.

Brant stared at her for a while, then laughed once again. "Caitlyn, you astound me!" he told her. "You try so hard to help me, don't you?" He leaned closer so that his hot breath hit her cheek. "Would it surprise you to learn that I don't want your help?"

She looked at him in mild surprise, attributing his statements to drink. "Brant, you're not being logical about this. You need all the help you can get to save Riverhouse. What will you do if you lose it?"

He shrugged. "Don't know." He pushed himself even closer. "But what does it matter if I lose Riverhouse? You'll still love me, won't you, Caitlyn?"

"Brant, this is hardly the place to talk about our feelings for each other," she reminded him, looking out at the crowd in front of her and desperately hoping that no one could hear their conversation. "Besides, love has nothing to do with what we're talking about. You've got to be practical! How would you live without some sort of income?"

"Don't know," he repeated. "I suppose I'd have to exist on my wife's generosity."

Caitlyn turned to stare at him sharply. "Brant, you don't really

mean that, do you?'' She sighed, realizing that he was probably drunker than she'd first surmised. "I know you don't," she added, answering her own question. "If only someone could be found who would help you," she said, half to herself. Her eyes unconsciously scanned the dancers until they found Tanner Malone, obviously enjoying himself with Maureen McQuillen. There, she thought grimly, lay their last hope.

"Has anyone ever told you you talk about business too much?" Brant asked, not bothering to hide an enormous yawn. "Why can't you be more like Constance? She never bothers herself about business matters."

Caitlyn's attention was effectively caught by that statement. "Of course she never bothers herself about business matters!" she retorted. "Connie doesn't *understand* business! Goodness, Brant, if you are saying you'd rather I were *stupid*—"

"Not stupid," he interrupted with a knowing smile, "just less interested in things that don't become a lady."

Caitlyn swallowed hard. She was speechless for a moment, caught between anger and tears.

If he noticed her dilemma, Brant was too drunk to wonder about it. He looked out over the dance floor, eyeing the pleasing picture Constance made. So what if she wasn't as beautiful as her sister? She had a sweet, feminine quality that was positively endearing and made Brant feel protective toward her.

"Brant?"

He turned back to Caitlyn with some surprise, having forgotten that she was still sitting beside him. To him, it seemed as if her face had blurred. Her mouth was trembling the tiniest bit and he found himself wondering what was wrong with her.

"Brant, you—you really do love me, don't you?" Caitlyn whispered, reddening at her debasement, but unable not to ask. She longed for a measure of assurance from him.

He smiled. "You're so lovely, Caitlyn," he told her, disregarding her question as the whiskey continued to work on him. "I would go so far as to say you are the loveliest woman here. Tell me why I'm not dancing with the loveliest woman in the room."

"Because you're drunk, Brant Sinclair!" she spat back at him, letting her anger win out over her embarrassment. She had begged him for assurance and he had callously disregarded her plea. "Brant, I think you should excuse yourself from the party," she told him.

"Why should I leave?" he asked her. "It's the first good time I've had since I arrived in New Orleans. I'm sick of stony bankers' faces and disapproving attorneys, Caitlyn. I'm sick of all these people who think of themselves as Southern aristocrats while I'm nothing more than a parvenu, an upstart trying to fit in. They're not going to open the door to me, so why should I continue to grovel?"

Caitlyn realized now what was eating at him. It had nothing to do with her, she told herself. It was his extreme disappointment at his failure to get the money he needed for Riverhouse. The whiskey had only brought this out. Her temper dissolved as she laid a gentle hand against his cheek. Poor darling! Little did he know how much she wanted to help him—how much she was going to help him.

"Brant, I'm sorry if I was sharp with you a few minutes ago," she said softly. "I didn't understand."

"And now you do?" he asked, his eyes searching her face. He was pleased by the hand on his cheek and hoped it might mean a few kisses later on. He remembered, even through his whiskey-fogged brain, how potent Caitlyn's kisses could be. Despite the time and place, he felt himself becoming aroused.

"Yes, I do," she reaffirmed. "And now, my dearest, I think it's time you ate something." She took his hand like a child's, feeling very strong and motherly.

Bemused by her control of the situation, Brant let himself be led out to the rooms where the tables had been set up. As he walked, he felt a turmoil inside his stomach and a pounding in his head. Coupled with a dizzying feeling, it made him feel as though he were walking the deck of a ship on the high seas. As they neared the tables, heavily laden with food, the smells of the sumptuous repast hit him with devastating effect. He staggered and bent forward, clutching his stomach with an uncontrollable urge to vomit.

"Caitlyn," he groaned.

She turned, appalled to see his white face. Before she could think what to do, he was running toward the open door, holding a hand in front of his mouth in desperation. Caitlyn would have followed him, but a hand on her arm stopped her. She turned to see her father standing beside her, his face a mask of sympathy.

"That boy's being sick all over your aunt's best roses," he said calmly. "I don't think he'd want you out there as a witness to that, Caitlyn."

Caitlyn passed over her father's remark and glanced anxiously at the door, hoping to see Brant reappear. Obviously, he was too sick to come back in, and she turned to her father. "Would you go out and check on him, Papa?" she pleaded. "He may have passed out."

Timothy stared at his daughter for a while. He finally shrugged his shoulders in defeat and nodded. "All right, Caitlyn, I'll go look after the lad. I've a mind to send him back to his hotel in a carriage. Go and dance with some of those young blades who've been eyeing you all night! Enjoy yourself!"

Caitlyn stood irresolute for a moment, needing to assure herself that Brant was all right. But when she realized that her father would not move until she promised to go back to the party, she agreed. "You win, Papa," she said, not without reproach in her voice. "But please look after him for me, won't you?"

Timothy snorted. "For God's sake, Caitlyn, you're sounding like a mother to the lad! It's not mothering he needs, but some common sense drummed into him. Any gentleman knows you don't drink hard liquor on any empty stomach. Now go back to the dancing before I lose my temper completely! I don't want to be soured on my own niece's wedding day."

Caitlyn nodded, outwardly meek, although she still yearned to take care of Brant. She had visions of helping him to his room, tucking him gently into his bed with a cold cloth over his aching head. Yes, she admitted to herself, she did feel motherly toward him, but that was only because she loved him so much. He *needed* her!

She made her way to Tanner Malone, who, much to her pique, seemed content to ignore her in favor of several other young ladies. He smiled and talked with practiced ease, fielding questions with an innate charm that irritated Caitlyn. His suaveness made Brant's earlier ineptitude seem even worse. Caitlyn hated to admit that Tanner Malone, despite being a Yankee, knew how to conduct himself in a mixed gathering to his best advantage. When he continued to ignore her, she laid a hand on his arm, then quickly withdrew it when he turned to her with a questioning look.

"Miss O'Rourke, good evening," he said with a smile. "Where have you been all evening?"

"I have been at your elbow for five minutes," she retorted.

"Forgive me," he said, and she could see the amusement in his smile. "I thought perhaps you were busy elsewhere. I recall

seeing you disappear in the direction of the dining room with Brant Sinclair.''

So he had been watching her! Caitlyn thought with secret pleasure. No matter how he pretended, she was sure he was not immune to her charms. Perhaps this whole matter would prove easier than she had thought.

"Mr. Malone, I would like to speak to you this evening,'' she said, feeling as though she had the upper hand now. "It's a matter of some importance."

He smiled once more. "I'm sorry, Miss O'Rourke, but I'm afraid each of these young ladies has promised me one of the next several dances."

Caitlyn looked astounded, her blue eyes sweeping haughtily over the other girls in the circle. Did he think she was asking him to dance with her? Why, the conceited scamp! "Mr. Malone, I think you misunderstand me,'' she began, making an effort to be charming, especially with the eager faces of the other young women watching her maliciously.

"Mr. Malone, the orchestra is beginning the next waltz!'' squealed a young woman with a cloud of dark hair and enormous brown eyes. "This is our dance.'' The girl gave Caitlyn a perfunctory glance to dismiss her.

Caitlyn felt her blood beginning to boil. She'd known Barbara Cordero since they were both ten years old. They had never been friends, each one too sure of her own charms. She felt like stepping on the dainty satin slippers beneath Barbara's flounced skirt, but curbed her temper with an effort.

"Mr. Malone,'' she said in a lowered voice, uncaring that Barbara was showing her impatience, "I'm afraid I *must* speak with you tonight.''

"Miss O'Rourke, I will make an effort to find time for you,'' he promised, leading her rival out to the dance floor.

Caitlyn flushed to the roots of her hair. How dare he dismiss her so pompously! And in front of all those eager-eyed girls who hated her because she'd always been the center of attention. Caitlyn turned abruptly and made her way blindly to the side of the room, where velvet-backed chairs had been set out for those not dancing. She settled herself into one and fanned her face vigorously, determined that she would pay that uncouth Yankee back for his insults. But how could she when she was going to ask him to help Brant? She clenched her teeth in frustration. What a miserable mess this was! She was determined to help

Brant, but the only person who had enough money to do so was that despicable cad!

"Caitlyn, you look as mad as a hornet!" Constance whispered anxiously, taking a seat beside her sister.

"I am furious!" Caitlyn agreed, not bothering to lie to her sister.

"Is it Mr. Malone?"

Caitlyn turned to her in surprise. "How did you know?"

Constance chuckled. "He always seems to have that effect on you."

The two sisters sat silently for a few minutes, each lost in her own thoughts. Suddenly Caitlyn was aware of Mr. Malone bowing in front of her, his dark blue eyes giving her a mocking look that made her hate him all the more.

"Miss O'Rourke, I believe you expressed a desire to see me this evening. I've taken a moment to speak with you, but if you've changed your mind—" He was smiling at her in a way that set Caitlyn's teeth on edge. She reminded herself that she must carry out her plan to help Brant.

"Yes, Mr. Malone, I did wish to speak to you," she answered.

"I am listening, Miss O'Rourke," he smiled, seating himself beside her.

She laughed a little nervously. "I'm afraid what I wish to speak to you about, Mr. Malone, is better done in private," she continued, aware that Constance was eavesdropping. She wondered if they should drift toward the garden and talk there, but she wasn't sure she wanted to be alone with Mr. Malone in a garden again, remembering how he had kissed her at Letty Downs's party.

He was watching her, and she was positive he was thinking the same thing as she. Then he smiled knowingly and leaned forward intimately. "Miss O'Rourke, if you would like to discuss this out in your aunt's garden, I would be most agreeable, but I'm afraid I've promised my time to others, as I told you earlier. Still, if you are determined, I could make arrangements."

"Oh!" The exclamation popped out of Caitlyn's mouth. Did he actually think she wanted to be alone with him so he could kiss her again? What a conceited oaf! She felt anger coursing through her veins, and for a moment she was tempted to tell him her real feelings.

He surmised the change in her attitude and cocked an eyebrow at her quizzically. "But if that is not agreeable to you, Miss O'Rourke, perhaps we could meet elsewhere."

Constance was still sitting on the other side of Caitlyn, straining to hear every word. If she heard Caitlyn and Mr. Malone arranging an assignation, what would she think?

"Mr. Malone, if you would just take me to the punch bowl, we can conclude our arrangements in private," she said pointedly, glancing sharply at her sister, who had the grace to look chastened.

He offered his arm and she laid her hand on it, swishing her skirts angrily as he led her to the refreshment table.

"And now, Miss O'Rourke, may I be so bold as to demand an explanation?" he inquired in an even voice.

"I must speak with you about a matter of great importance to me," she replied vaguely.

"Is it about Brant Sinclair?" he asked bluntly.

Without hesitation, Caitlyn shook her head. "No," she lied.

"I see. Are you saying you want to speak with me in private about something concerning yourself and me?"

She nodded, assuring herself that if she could only have a chance to work her wiles on him, he wouldn't care that she had deceived him.

"In that case," he said, lowering his voice, "I would be happy to meet with you in my hotel room, Miss O'Rourke."

"Your hotel room!" she gasped, wondering at his boldness. "But, Mr. Malone, I can't possibly be alone with you there!"

He gazed at her with a slight frown. "If there is no need for secrecy, we could speak right now." He glanced out toward the dance floor. "But I must warn you, if I give you more than five more minutes I will have grossly insulted one of the prettiest young ladies in New Orleans."

Caitlyn swallowed hard, trying to think, but pressured by his impatience. She couldn't blurt out her wishes right here in front of the punch bowl!

She bit her lip. "What about tomorrow morning, very early, in your hotel room?" she proposed, feeling better meeting him in daylight rather than in the intimacy of darkness. "I could be there by six o'clock, if you think you would be awake and presentable by then."

His grin was devilish. "I'll be awake, although how presentable I'll be, I don't know."

She nodded coolly. "I'll be there, Mr. Malone."

"The room number is 16, Miss O'Rourke, just so you won't have to check at the front desk."

15

CAITLYN LOOKED BLEARILY out the window at the silent world below. She glanced at the clock on the night table and saw that it was not yet six o'clock. Her eyes wandered to the gently snoring form of her sister, who had been obliged to share her bed because of all the guests. Constance would surely sleep until noon, unless someone woke her before then. Caitlyn must have a good explanation of where she had been this morning, just in case someone missed her or saw her returning. She would say that she had gone for a morning walk to the cathedral so the priest could hear her confession. Her mother would be pleased with that.

Caitlyn stretched and rubbed her eyes. They felt like sandpaper from lack of sleep. She would have to get dressed without help, and she was glad she'd purposely gone to bed with her corset on, although it made her ribs ache.

She quickly pulled off her nightdress and slipped on two petticoats. She would have to do without her stiff horsehair crinoline. It was too heavy and would make too much noise. She pulled on the simple dress of pale blue muslin that she'd left on the chair after Constance had fallen asleep and tied the sash awkwardly.

Tiptoeing to the dressing table, she washed her face in last night's water, splashing as quietly as possible. She gazed into the mirror and shuddered, wondering how on earth she was going to charm Mr. Malone with her hair sticking out like a banshee's and her red eyes with lilac shadows under them. Well, she thought philosophically, there was no alternative now but to brave the challenge ahead. She brushed her hair into some order, then pulled it into a snood, securing it with pins at the crown of her head and behind her ears. She smoothed her dark brows with a damp forefinger and coaxed some color into her pale cheeks with a few pinches.

Now she was ready. She glanced out the window once more, noting that the rain which had threatened yesterday looked as

though it were going to start any minute. Dismal clouds had darkened the sky so that only a little gray light brightened the outdoors, and Caitlyn realized she would need her umbrella and shawl. Unfortunately both were in the downstairs armoire, whose doors creaked dreadfully every time they were opened. She dared not risk opening them. If she could get to the hotel soon, she might be lucky enough to escape the first downpour. For her trip home, she would have to impose on Mr. Malone to order her a carriage. If she was charming enough to him, he would be willing to pay for the carriage.

Quietly, she made her way to the bedroom door and opened it a crack to make sure no one was up yet. The hall was completely silent except for the loud snores of the gentlemen, one of them probably Papa, she thought with a smile. She slipped out the door, closing it gently behind her, and made her way to the stairs.

She was relieved that the kitchen was deserted, with remnants of last night's feast lying on the large wooden tables. She picked up an abandoned pastry and bit into it. It was dry, but at least it would quiet the rumbling in her stomach. As she reached the kitchen door, she realized she'd forgotten her hat. There was no time to go back upstairs, so she whisked one of the house slaves' poke bonnets from its place by the door and tied it tightly under her chin, trying not to smell the grease on its brim.

Once outside in the garden, she breathed a huge sigh of relief. Walking purposefully, she made her way to the front and started down the banquette. She was glad to be wearing the poke bonnet, whose deep brim would effectively hide her face and protect it from rain.

Caitlyn hurried her steps at the rumble of thunder. She walked briskly down Canal Street and toward the heart of the French Quarter, where the St. Louis Hotel stood. It took her no more than a half hour to get there, as living in the country had made her used to walking.

Tentatively, she walked in to the large hotel lobby, with its wide staircase and magnificent dome. She'd been here with her father when she was a little girl. Timothy O'Rourke had concocted many a business deal within these walls adorned with beautiful frescoes.

"You there! What you doing, gal?" The suspicious voice came from an old black man who was sweeping the floor. "You, get on out of here!"

"I'm here to see someone. I've a message for him," Caitlyn returned with bravado. "I've come from Canal Street and my mistress will beat me good if I don't come back with an answer!"

The grizzled old man reflected for a moment. What did he care if the girl was lying? And sure enough, he wouldn't want to be the cause of a servant girl's getting a beating! Lord knew he'd gotten plenty of beatings himself in all his days! "Get on with you, then!" he growled.

Caitlyn hurried toward the wide staircase.

"Not that way!" the old slave called after her. "You take the back stairs, child, like all of us in service here!"

When she finally made her way to Mr. Malone's room, she knocked softly. She was relieved when the door opened and a hand whisked her inside, but not so relieved when the door was closed to reveal Mr. Malone only half-dressed and looking as though he didn't relish having to wake up this early after last night's revelry.

"Good morning, Mr. Malone," Caitlyn began primly, her eyes avoiding the broad expanse of naked chest he was exhibiting so carelessly.

"Morning," he answered briefly, stretching his arms with a huge yawn. He shook his head as though to clear it of the last vestiges of sleep.

Caitlyn waited a few minutes, her patience wearing thin as he splashed water on his face and combed his wet hair.

"Mr. Malone, if you don't mind," she began, as he brushed his teeth vigorously and then gargled noisily so that she thought he must be deliberately trying to repel her. Was he doing all this as some sort of performance, letting her know he was in no mood for a visit? "Is all this really necessary?" she finally sighed.

He turned, cocked an eyebrow at her, and smiled over the edge of the towel he was using to wipe his face. "Among civilized people such niceties are always necessary, Miss O'Rourke," he reproved her. "If I had more time, I would shave, but I can see you are not about to stand by patiently while I do so. May I order some coffee?" Before she could answer, he stepped out into the hall—still without his shirt, she noted—and bawled loudly for one of the hotel slaves. It took only a moment before someone came, and he ordered a pot of fresh coffee and two cups.

"Goodness, Mr. Malone, you could have awakened the entire establishment!" Caitlyn exclaimed crossly. "I would appreciate as much secrecy as possible, if you don't mind. After all, this is not the sort of thing a girl does if she wants to keep her good reputation."

"No one will know you are here, Miss O'Rourke—unless someone can see through walls." He turned back to the mirror for a moment to finish combing his hair. It was beginning to curl slightly at the back of his neck as it dried. "Please sit, Miss O'Rourke," he said from the washstand.

Caitlyn, undecided whether she was pleased by his brisk and detached attitude, did as he instructed, sitting in one of the two chairs brought up to a circular table that was laid prettily with a hand-embroidered tablecloth. There were fresh flowers on the table, a sign of the St. Louis Hotel's impeccable service and reputation for making its guests feel at home. Covertly, she glanced around the good-sized room, noting the large mahogany four-poster and matching armoire, the brightly colored rugs on the polished hardwood floor, and the lace-edged curtains on the two windows that fronted the street. A well-appointed room, she decided. Then with a glance at Mr. Malone, she realized his half-naked maleness looked incongruous in such a room—except for the fact that the bed was still unmade and mussed from sleep. Her own thoughts made her blush.

Before she could speak, someone knocked on the door, making her half rise from her chair in panic. She was relieved when it proved to be one of the hotel slaves, carrying a silver tray from which the smell of coffee issued deliciously.

The slave, well trained to look on impassively while the hotel guests did as they pleased, hardly seemed to notice the impropriety of a male standing half-naked in front of a female. He merely poured the coffee, then stood silently as he awaited further orders. After pressing a coin into the man's palm, Tanner dismissed him and sat down next to Caitlyn to enjoy the coffee.

"You're not supposed to tip slaves, Mr. Malone," Caitlyn reproved, sipping the hot liquid tentatively. "It's just not done here in the South."

"Why?" he demanded, looking directly at her. "Are you Southerners afraid to give slaves their own money? Afraid they'll be able to buy train tickets to go up North?" He leaned toward her as though spoiling for a fight. "What if they all bought

tickets, Miss O'Rourke? What would your proud planters do without them?''

Caitlyn smiled devilishly at him. "Why, I suppose we would just hire immigrants at wages so low they'd practically starve to death, Mr. Malone—just as you folks up North do!'' She sipped her coffee, watching him over the rim of her cup.

He grinned at her quip. "You win! You seem to have all your wits about you, even at this ungodly hour, Miss O'Rourke.'' He rubbed his temples with the palms of his hands. "I must have drunk a quart of rum last night,'' he muttered. He shook his head, sprinkling her with tiny drops of water from his still-wet hair.

"Mr. Malone, perhaps we had better get to the reason I came to see you,'' Caitlyn said, finishing her coffee and pushing it aside. She leaned forward with an eagerness that made him wary.

"I hope you are not going to ask me some impossible favor,'' he returned, pushing his own cup away. "Somehow I don't feel very accommodating this morning. Besides, I have an appointment with your father at eleven.''

"My father is coming here!'' Caitlyn gasped.

He put a hand on her shoulder to reassure her. "Relax, Miss O'Rourke, your father isn't due for almost four hours. I don't think our business will take that long—will it?'' He looked at her sharply and she was taken aback by the blueness of his eyes, in such startling contrast to the darkness of his hair.

"No,'' she admitted, "it shouldn't take long at all.'' Just a simple yes would do nicely—but how to broach the subject? She took a deep breath. But that unwavering blue stare shook her courage and she dropped her eyes.

"Well?''

"It's—it's difficult to express myself, Mr. Malone, especially when you're sitting there without your shirt on,'' she hedged.

He waved away her words. "Forgive me, Miss O'Rourke. Unfortunately all my shirts are in the hotel laundry except for the one I wore last night, which positively reeks of rum. The laundress should be returning soon with my clean shirts. Until then, I'm afraid you will have to endure my half-primitive state, Miss O'Rourke.''

"Mr. Malone—''

"I wish you would call me Tanner,'' he interrupted.

The intimate tone of his voice encouraged her. Despite his words and actions to the contrary, he seemed to be falling under

her spell. In no time at all she would be able to open the delicate subject of a loan to save Riverhouse.

"Of course, and you must call me Caitlyn," she responded with some warmth. After a long silence, she continued. "So you and my father will be conducting some business today. I suppose he's decided to name you as his factor."

He smiled and leaned back in his chair. "For now, your father wants our dealings kept confidential, Caitlyn." She almost winced when his voice said her name caressingly. "Your father is a very shrewd businessman. Financial ties are strained between the North and the South. One never knows what's going to happen in the future."

"After you talk with my father, will your business here in New Orleans be done?" she asked. "I mean, will you be returning to Riverhouse with Brant, or will you be going directly back to Boston?"

"That depends," he answered enigmatically.

She caught him staring at her and felt her heart speed up. Things were working out exactly as she had hoped, she thought with hidden glee. She had seen that look before on the faces of dozens of men.

"Speaking of business matters," she said, finally plunging in, "Brant is in desperate financial trouble."

"I know," he confirmed.

"I worry about him. He and his father have worked so hard to revive Riverhouse. William's health is not good, you know. It's frightening for Brant to anticipate running his plantation alone. I'm sure he will gain confidence after he's begun to feel more comfortable in the role of planter."

"I would think so," Tanner agreed, although his tone had cooled.

Unmindful of the change, Caitlyn continued. "You, on the other hand, seem to have a vast knowledge of business matters. In fact, my papa was saying how very much he respects your business sense."

"I thank him for the compliment. I'm glad of his confidence in me; with your father's backing, I plan to set up a wide network of planters. My price for factoring their cotton will be cheaper than anyone else's and the business will find new customers each year."

"Yes, yes," Caitlyn cut in, not interested in *his* plans for the

future, but only in her own. "I'm sure your business will do beautifully, but it's Brant that I'm worried about."

"Why?" he asked bluntly.

She gazed up at him, her eyes narrowed a bit. "Well—you must know my—feelings—for Brant," she stammered. "I want to see him succeed. It's important for his self-esteem as well as for the future of Riverhouse."

"Do you really give a damn about Riverhouse, Caitlyn?" he asked bluntly.

She reddened. "There's no reason for you to bully me," she returned. "Of course I care about Riverhouse. I plan to be mistress of it one day," she added boldly.

"I must say you don't set your sights very high, Caitlyn. There are many plantations in this state with much higher values on them than Riverhouse. Why don't you follow the example of your cousin and marry a man who will inherit a fortune someday?"

"Whom I plan to marry is none of your concern!" she snapped. But when she saw the mask of amusement settle over his features, she realized she had tried the wrong tack with him. Better to change course while there was still some hope left. "I'm sorry, Tanner," she said slowly. "It's just that I really am worried about Brant. It upsets me to think you don't believe in my sincerity."

"I believe you, Caitlyn," he said simply. "I believe you think Brant Sinclair is going to propose marriage to you. That would give you the right to concern yourself with his financial affairs."

The words sounded right, Caitlyn thought, but his tone of voice worried her. It was as though he were saying what she wanted him to say just so she would stop bothering him. But she mustn't give up yet. She could afford to swallow her pride for Brant's sake. And tears couldn't hurt her cause.

"Tanner, you understand perfectly," she began, allowing the moisture to seep through her lashes. "I am deeply interested in Brant's future because I plan to be sharing it. I'll make no secret of the fact that I love him." There, she'd admitted her love out loud! She glowed happily for a moment, but the glow abruptly left her when she looked at Tanner and saw pity in his face. Why must he continue to watch her like a cat that felt sorry for the mouse it was about to pounce on?

Despite her dismay at the turn of events, she pushed on, determined to finish. "And because you are one of his closest

friends, Tanner, I know you must be concerned about Brant's future too. I'm positive you are a man who would help a friend in need.''

"You think so?'' he asked her slowly, rubbing his chin with the back of his hand. "Then you really don't know me, Caitlyn O'Rourke. I never waste money, sympathy, or time on someone who neither asks for my help nor presents himself as a good risk.''

Caitlyn felt the beginnings of dread. "What do you mean? You wouldn't help a friend? What does risk have to do with a person's future?''

"More than you seem to understand," he answered her firmly. "I haven't come this far in business by helping all of my acquaintances who either didn't have the sense or the nerve to make their own way. I've always made it a habit to bet on the winning horse, Caitlyn.''

"But—Brant is trying!" she argued, feeling as though it were essential for her to convince this man of Brant's true worth. "It's so difficult for him with his father's illness and the condition of Riverhouse! You can't fault a man for that!''

"I don't fault Brant for things beyond his control," Tanner returned. "But, Caitlyn, it's been over a year since Brant has returned to his plantation. He should begin to show some pride of ownership, some drive in trying to improve the place. I just don't see that Brant *cares* that much about what he's got. I think he is only hanging on because of pressure from others, yourself included.''

Caitlyn wrung her hands in agitation and sprang to her feet, pacing the floor as she spoke. "I don't think you know what you're talking about," she said firmly. She stared at Tanner Malone, who was watching her from his chair. "You think that without Riverhouse, Brant won't be anything but a—a sponger, a person who lives off others. But I won't let that happen!''

"Caitlyn, don't you see?" Tanner had stood up and was facing her with his hands palm upwards. "Don't you see that your fine strength and determination are wasted on Brant? Brant once told me that you have such a—how did he put it?—a *passion* for life that it scares him sometimes. You think if you want something badly enough it's going to happen. And if it doesn't happen in due course, you'll *make* it happen! Things just don't work that way, my dear.''

Caitlyn shook her head and put her hands over her ears as

though to shut out his words. "No! You're wrong! I only want what will make Brant happy!" She felt a twisting, aching tension in her neck and the back of her head as if there were a huge boulder on her shoulders. Real tears threatened to flow as she realized that her last hope was not going to give her what she wanted. The sleepness night after the late wedding reception was making itself felt.

"Let Brant decide on his own future, Caitlyn," Tanner said in a gentler tone. "You can't map out the rest of his life for him."

"Please spare me your advice!" she countered sarcastically. "You, of all people, aren't fit to be handing out pearls of wisdom."

His silence was more goading to Caitlyn than anything he might have said. "You are a despicable man, sir! You pretend to be a friend to Brant, when all the time you are just using him for your own business purposes. Oh, don't think I'm stupid! You are a man who uses people!"

"My dear young lady, we all use people to one extent or another in life," he said with a touch of mockery that inflamed her. "Wasn't that *your* intention this morning, after all? To use me to save Brant?"

The pressure in her head was tightening and Caitlyn felt dizzy. "You loathsome cad!" she stormed, wishing she could let loose with a string of her father's choicest oaths. "At least my intentions were honorable! What can you say about your own actions when you took advantage of me at Letty Downs's party?"

His smile was maddening. "My intentions were quite honorable. I had only come to comfort you after your tiff with the *very honorable* Brant Sinclair," he said in a sarcastic tone that grated further on Caitlyn's nerves. "You can't blame me for the passion of the moment, Caitlyn. From my experience in such things, I'd say you were definitely enjoying it, before we were so rudely interrupted."

She gasped and her eyes narrowed threateningly. "How dare you! You conceited—" She sputtered ineffectually, trying to think of something vile enough to call him. "Yankee!" she finally spat as though that were the lowest thing on earth.

He laughed outright. "I suggest we bring this discussion to a close, my dear, before you burst your corset cover. You don't want to make a spectacle of yourself, Caitlyn."

"I'll do it as I please!" she shouted. "And don't ever call me Caitlyn again!"

"Hush, you silly girl!" he returned, more sternly this time. "You were so worried about being found in my room, but the way you're shouting you'll have the hotel management up here any minute. They will certainly wonder what you are doing here."

"Let them wonder!" she cried, heedless of his warning. "And let the bankers and the other businessmen you're so anxious to impress wonder! They'll find out you had a young woman in your hotel room against her will, Mr. Malone! I'll scream my head off!"

"Quiet!" he commanded, even more sharply. "You don't know what you're saying! It would prove much worse for your reputation than for mine!" He lowered his voice a trifle, trying to bring back some semblance of calm. "What would that do for your future?"

"I don't care!" she screamed. "I don't have a future without Brant—and he has no future without Riverhouse!"

"Damn it, girl, you are nothing more than a spoiled brat having a temper tantrum!" Tanner said, feeling anger beginning to boil. Did she think she was going to get him to hand over a lump sum of money because he'd fallen for her wiles? Did she think a kiss in the garden with her was equal to the thousands of dollars that Brant was in need of? "You price yourself too highly!" he muttered.

He saw her cheeks grow beet red and then whiten to the color of chalk. With all her strength, she took a deep breath and opened her mouth, preparing to scream at the top of her lungs. With a snarled oath, he was next to her in two strides. Before she could let a sound escape from her throat, he had clamped one hand over her mouth, stepping behind her so that he could press her back against him with his other hand.

Enraged, Caitlyn struggled against him. More angry than she had ever been in her life, she kicked her feet and tried to bring her hands back to claw him. He dragged her backward, lifting her off the ground and throwing her down on the bed.

Drawing an agonized breath, Caitlyn felt tears of rage streaming from her eyes. But before she could try to scream again, he was on top of her, holding her down with his body while one hand ground into her mouth and the other held her hands together over her head.

"I'm sorry to have to treat you this way, Caitlyn, but you give me no choice! For your own sake, you must be quiet!"

For answer, she sank her teeth into his hand, tasting blood in her mouth. She had never been treated this way in her life! No one had ever physically punished her or treated her roughly. She would not endure this from a damned Yankee, of all people!

"Damn it!" he cursed in response to her bite. His blue eyes flashed lightning as they stared into hers, just inches away. "I ought to give you a good spanking, you little brat! At the very least, I ought to slap you silly—that would shut you up! But if you promise to behave yourself, I'll let you go and you can get back home before anyone notices you're gone."

Caitlyn stared back at him, her eyes poisonous with hatred. For answer, she pulled one of her hands from his grasp and raked her nails across his cheek, gratified to see tiny drops of blood against his skin.

Tanner winced from the pain and he heartily wished he could beat the hell out of her. Common sense stopped him and he merely grabbed her hand to keep it from doing any more damage. She was a wild thing when her plans were thwarted! He wondered if anyone had ever spanked her; perhaps the lack of punishment was why she was so cantankerous. He felt sorry for Brant Sinclair should he ever actually marry this little hornet.

Caitlyn was trying to bite the hand at her mouth again. In self-defense, Tanner pressed down harder on her mouth so that she couldn't get another grip with her teeth. Her eyes seemed to widen as she fought for breath. When she didn't get any, they rolled backward and she went limp. Suspicious at her sudden capitulation, Tanner kept her hands in one of his while he pulled his other hand away from her mouth. Her eyelids fluttered a little, but didn't open, and he presumed she'd fainted. He released her hands, then stood up from the bed. He could see the rise and fall of her bosom, which assured him that she was breathing.

"Caitlyn O'Rourke, you are definitely a handful!" he said aloud to himself, feeling his cheek ruefully. "A veritable demon when you are thwarted!" Between the rum he'd consumed last night, the lack of sleep, and his struggle with this she-wolf, he felt drained. Slowly, he walked back to the table and slumped into a chair, pouring himself another cup of coffee.

16

CAITLYN FELT HERSELF SWIMMING slowly back to wakefulness. What an awful nightmare she'd just had! She opened her eyes slowly, staring up at the ceiling for a moment before trying to move her head, which felt like it was stuffed with cotton. For some reason, her mouth felt sore, and she brought up a hand to press her fingertips gingerly against her lips. She winced from the contact.

"Oh-h-h," she murmured, bringing a hand to her head when it started to spin as she struggled to sit up. Outside she could hear rain splashing heavily against the windows, punctuated by loud cracks of thunder—probably what had awakened her, she thought wearily.

A movement in the room caught her attention. She leaned up on her elbows, her legs outspread beneath her skirt in the position that sleep had taken her. As her bleary eyes focused, her breath caught in her throat. Balls of fire! It *hadn't* been a nightmare at all, for sitting at the table was that damned Yankee!

Tanner Malone heard her movements and turned around from the papers spread in front of him. "So you've finally decided to open your eyes," he commented.

"No thanks to you!" she returned, remembering the reason for her present state. With embarrassment, she drew her legs together and looked down at the front of her basque, which had been unbuttoned to her breasts. Hastily, she fumbled at the buttons. "How long have I been like this?" she asked, her voice not quite as demanding as she would have liked.

"For about three hours I have been witness to your *charmingly quiet* self," he emphasized, laying his pen down and standing up. "Except for an occasional snore, you've been the perfect guest." He laughed loudly at the hateful glance she bestowed on him. "Oh, come now, Caitlyn, don't be nasty again! It really doesn't suit you."

"I don't care about your opinion of what suits me," she said, her voice becoming brisker now as she swung her legs over the bed and sat on the edge, looking for her shoes. "I've found out what kind of man you are, Mr. Malone! The kind who would

physically abuse a female and then leave her defenseless on your bed to—to—" She stopped, reddening at her own inference.

He laughed again. "If you are suggesting that I might have tried to take advantage of you while you were unconscious, Caitlyn, then you really don't know me. I admit that you are an attractive young woman, but your lack of social graces appalls me. Yankee or not, I'm not used to young ladies of your breeding screaming like banshees. I don't like insufferable brats, Caitlyn."

He watched her take several deep breaths and braced himself for an onslaught of verbal abuse delivered in a screeching tone of voice. But to his surprise, she closed her mouth and looked away from him. "Such ungentlemanly comments don't warrant a reply," she said stiffly, busying herself scanning the floor for her shoes.

Tanner walked obligingly to the armoire, from where he produced the shoes. "Thank you," she said woodenly.

He watched her put them on, then continued to watch as she stood up to smooth her hair and the bodice of her dress. She spoke to him without looking at him. "I can see that my coming here was a waste of time and energy. You probably knew exactly why I wanted to see you from the beginning, didn't you?"

"I entertained the improbable notion that perhaps you had had a change of heart about Yankees—and about me in particular."

"Hardly likely, Mr. Malone, especially after your abhorrent treatment of me this morning." This morning! She tensed as she realized how long she had been here. "What—what time did you say it was?" she asked, her eyes rounding as they looked at him.

"Nearly ten," he said, confirming her fears.

"Ten! Good heavens, when is my papa due here?" Her eyes jumped about the room like those of a hunted animal looking for a place to hide.

"In an hour." He moved closer to her to lay a comforting hand on her shoulder, but she recoiled from him. "I can call a carriage for you. It's raining and you don't want to get soaked."

Caitlyn realized she had no choice. She nodded stiffly. "I certainly wouldn't want my father seeing me here with you," she snapped.

"Believe me, Caitlyn, I would much rather he remain ignorant of our meeting this morning, for I'm not one to be forced into a marriage proposal at the point of a gun!"

"Oh! As if I would accept any such proposal!" she yelped, her cheeks gaining color again.

"As if I would ever extend one to you under any circumstances!" he shot back, tired of her barbs. "No, young lady, I'll leave you to Brant. The poor bastard probably has no idea what he'd be getting into if he takes you as a wife."

A knock on the door made them both freeze. Motioning for Caitlyn to remain quiet, Tanner went to the door and opened it a bit. "The laundress," he said tartly and opened the door to let her in. After laying his freshly laundered shirts on the bed, the laundress took the coins that Tanner gave her and went out.

"Finally I won't be subjected to the sight of you half-naked!" Caitlyn said bitingly as Tanner selected a shirt and pulled it on.

His sharp blue eyes glanced at her from beneath arched black brows and he smiled with amusement. Without buttoning his shirt, he moved forward, making her back up so that the backs of her knees felt the mattress.

He caught her in his arms, pulling her against him so that she could feel the solid smoothness of his chest. "Just a little something to remember me by," he murmured, "so you won't feel the whole morning was a total waste!"

He reached down to capture her mouth, still sore from his hand, which made Caitlyn all the more furious. He kissed her slowly, deliberately, despite her efforts to push away from him, as though he had all the time in the world. Caitlyn felt a faint stirring deep inside her, but stifled it ruthlessly. When he finally released her, she brought a hand up to wipe her mouth.

"I'm afraid I don't relish the taste of Yankee!" she said haughtily, her dark blue eyes meeting his without flinching.

Shaking his head, he stepped away from her to button his shirt. "God help Brant if he does marry you!" he said aloud to himself.

"It will be no concern of yours, Mr. Malone. And now, if you would have a carriage sent round for me—"

Another knock on the door interrupted her.

"Maybe the laundress thought you cheated her," she said spitefully.

Tanner ignored her and went to open the door.

"Tanner, my friend! God, how my blasted head is aching from last night!" Brant Sinclair stood in the doorway, his dark eyes showing the aftereffects of drunkenness. "I've called to see if you're going upriver with me this afternoon." As he stepped

inside the room, his eyes fell on Caitlyn, standing in a state of shock by the rumpled bed. For a moment no one said anything. Brant's eyes went from the bed to Caitlyn's mussed hair to Tanner's shirt, which was still untucked and only half-buttoned. "What in hell is going on?"

"Oh, Brant!" Caitlyn moved toward him, but he stepped backward as though loath to have her touch him.

Instead he looked to Tanner for an explanation. Tanner said nothing and calmly finished buttoning his shirt.

"Don't be alarmed, Brant," he finally said as he adjusted his collar and cuffs, then moved in front of the mirror to put on his cravat. "Miss O'Rourke has done nothing to tarnish her reputation."

"Nothing!" Brant shouted. "How do you explain her being in your hotel room?"

"Look, Brant, Miss O'Rourke came here this morning to ask me for a favor—a favor to help you."

Brant reddened, for he could imagine what the favor was. He turned accusingly to Caitlyn. "I can't believe it, Caitlyn—even of you! Why would you try to humiliate me like this? Were you actually asking Tanner for money?"

Caitlyn took a step backward, unused to the angry stare he was bestowing on her. "Brant, I—I was trying to *help* you— help *us*!"

"Help me! You meddling little idiot!" he exploded, so angry he could have shaken her. "What right have you to take it upon yourself to do me any favors? *What right?* You have *never* had my permission to stick your nose into my affairs! You've done nothing but embarrass me in front of my friend!"

Caitlyn's face crumpled and she burst into tears. She was completely humiliated, unable to face Brant's righteous anger or Tanner's detachment. More than anything she wished she had never met Tanner Malone or agreed to come here to see him. She wished she had never tried to help Brant, who was proving worse than ungrateful. The damage was done, and she wondered if she had driven him away from her permanently.

Before Brant could further express his indignation, Tanner intervened, feeling Caitlyn had been chastised enough, although he agreed with everything Brant had said. "I'm sure she realizes her mistake," he said calmly.

"If you could just get me a carriage home!" Caitlyn sniffled.

Brant rubbed his temple with one hand. "Does anyone know you're here? *Anyone? * Your maid? *Constance?*"

Caitlyn shook her head.

Brant breathed a sigh of relief, but his brow puckered as he tried to think how to get her home without putting himself in a compromising position. She may have meant well, but no decent young woman would have gone to the lengths that she had!

"Her father is due here to discuss business," Tanner stated matter of factly. "I think it would prove beneficial, Brant, if you would conduct Caitlyn home and think of some plausible excuse for having her out with you this morning."

Brant's headache felt like a vise around his temples. What a mess this little chit had gotten him into! It was raining like hell outside; no one would believe they'd just gone for a drive.

"We have to think of a plausible lie," he said quickly. "What plan did you have to get back home without anyone being suspicious?"

"I was going to say that I had gone to confession," she muttered.

Tanner nodded. "It'll have to do. Hurry up now, or you'll meet Timothy O'Rourke in the hotel lobby!" he cautioned.

Obligingly, Caitlyn picked up the poke bonnet she had worn and tied it under her chin, making sure the brim was low over her face. She glanced up at Brant, who was watching her curiously. She realized how dreadful she must look with the house slave's bonnet, no crinoline beneath her skirt, and no shawl. She looked away from him in renewed embarrassment.

"No time to worry about how you look, I'm afraid," Tanner said briskly.

Caitlyn was surprised that he could read her emotions so well, but she quickly dismissed that thought. "I'm ready, Brant," she said quietly, having regained some of her composure.

"You go ahead and order the carriage," Tanner suggested to Brant, "while I escort Miss O'Rourke out the back way." He had the effrontery to joke about the situation. "This reminds me of when I used to play hide-and-seek with my brother and sister." He took her elbow and guided her down the servants' staircase. "Poor Brant doesn't realize what he has!"

She did not respond, for they were on the first floor and she was straining ahead to catch sight of the carriage. They walked quickly through the lobby, which at this hour was filled with

people. Hoping her disguise would enable her to pass unrecognized, Caitlyn bent her head to keep her face shielded.

"Don't worry," Tanner said in a low voice, "everyone will think you're just a hired girl I had in my room last night."

"I could kill you!" she whispered, just loud enough for him to hear.

"Perhaps you should thank me," he said reflectively. "After all, the noble Brant may decide not to marry you. After he makes your sister miserable, you'll realize how lucky you were that all this happened."

When they got outside, Caitlyn saw Brant waiting next to a hired carriage. She bundled herself into it quickly without a good-bye to Tanner Malone, sure that she had seen the very last of him.

Once Brant was inside and the carriage had started, she risked a glance at him, wondering what he was feeling now that his first burst of temper had left him. He did not seem as angry as before.

Thus encouraged, Caitlyn asked quietly, "Will you ever forgive me, Brant?"

He started at the sound of her voice against the steady driving of the rain on the carriage roof. "I don't know, Caitlyn," he replied. He turned his head to look at her, then looked away as though unable to bear the sincerity of her gaze. "It's one hell of a way for a man to start the morning after a drinking binge the night before!" Then he added, as an afterthought, "I've a mind to extend the binge through today!"

"Brant," Caitlyn continued, putting her hand lightly on the sleeve of his coat, glad when he didn't pull away, "I'm truly sorry. I admit I had no right to talk with Mr. Malone about your business affairs. I was stupid to have thought I could solve your problems for you." Though it galled her to say that, she knew Brant wanted to hear her admit her guilt and stupidity.

She heard him sigh deeply. To her relief, he laid a tentative hand on hers and squeezed it gently. "Ah, Caitlyn, I know you were trying to help me, but I have to be my own man. Don't you see? It already hurts badly enough that I have to go home and face my pa without the money to save Riverhouse." Suddenly he took his hand away and smashed it into his other hand. "Damn! Without money, you're worth nothing in this city! You might as well be pushing a broom like those slaves in the hotel lobby!"

He looked at her and she could see his despair. He was sure there was nothing he could do to better his situation. "I'm going to give up, Caitlyn!" he said in a burst of anger. "To hell with New Orleans and Riverhouse!"

His words brought an icy fear into her heart. This outburst frightened her more than his angry tirade at the hotel. He was giving up! He couldn't do that! If he abandoned Riverhouse, what would happen to *her*? Even in her misery, her thoughts were for her own welfare. She was not about to lose everything because of Brant's bitterness. She struggled to think of something comforting to say, but her mind was too fearful for her own future to think of anything constructive.

The carriage stopped and Caitlyn peered out to see that they had arrived at the Savoy house. She shuddered to think what her father would say if he saw her come in, but she remembered with relief that he had probably already left for his meeting with Tanner Malone. The thought of her father doing business with him made her mouth turn sour. It sickened her to think that that Yankee could make money in New Orleans, while poor Brant had come up against a brick wall.

She looked at Brant, but he was lost in his own bitter thoughts. Patting his arm, she said softly, "We're leaving for Mornhaven tomorrow, Brant. Will you be going back with us?"

He seemed to have forgotten her presence. "What? What did you say?" He stared at her. "Go back? God, I don't want to!"

He sounded like a small boy and Caitlyn's heart was touched, although a cool voice inside her head was whispering that this was not the kind of attitude that was going to save Riverhouse.

"Perhaps you had best go back to the hotel and rest," she suggested.

He laughed recklessly. "Hell, no! I'm going down to the wharf to drink until I drop!" He turned to her, his dark eyes bitter. "I suppose I could always follow in my pa's footsteps and drink away my problems!"

"Brant, please don't talk foolishly," Caitlyn begged. "I know there's a way to solve your problems. Just hang on, my dearest." She pronounced the endearment softly, hoping to change his mood, but he acted as though he hadn't heard.

"I'll do as I please, Caitlyn!" he warned her.

His belligerence was returning and Caitlyn realized it was time for her to make an exit. Nothing she could say was going

to make any difference. With a dull feeling of dread, she said good-bye to him.

17

IT WAS ALL Caitlyn could do to convince her mother that she had gone to confession that morning. But finally she was able to assuage her suspicions.

Constance was still asleep when Caitlyn crawled out of her dress and into a nightgown to lie down beside her. Listening to her sister's steady breathing, Caitlyn envied her her innocent sleep. Why, she wondered, couldn't she be as trusting and uncomplicated as her sister? Why was she always scheming to get what she wanted? Was it because she was afraid that, if left to the whims of chance, Brant would choose Constance over her? Caitlyn shook her head at the thought. Of course Brant would propose to her eventually. It didn't matter that he felt kindly toward Constance. After all, everyone felt kindly toward Constance!

Still, when she got up later that afternoon and listened to the unceasing rain pelting the windows, her depression deepened. Would Brant truly forgive her for what she'd done? Did he still love her? The questions seemed to pound against her skull with the same rhythm as the rain outside. Developing a horrific headache, Caitlyn returned to her room.

"Poor dear, I'll have the cook make you some hot lemon tea," Margaret clucked sympathetically as she tucked her daughter back into bed. "Perhaps you're coming down with something, Caitlyn. You shouldn't have gone out so early this morning."

"You're probably right, Mama," Caitlyn murmured, happy to be babied. It felt wonderful to have someone speaking soft words to her after the morning she'd had.

Caitlyn awoke the next morning, surprised that she had slept soundly through the afternoon and into the night. Her headache was gone and she was pleased to see that the rain had finally gone away, leaving a sunny world that beckoned to her. She pushed off the covers and stretched, looking down at Constance, who was just opening her eyes.

"Oh, Connie, I do feel so much better this morning!" Caitlyn said brightly.

"I'm glad," Constance grumbled, "but I'm still tired from last night."

"What happened?" Caitlyn demanded, unmindful that her sister might want to go back to sleep.

"Pauline and Mr. Winterby came for dinner. She looked quite attractive in her second-day dress. I think marriage agrees with her." Constance giggled as she thought of something. "It certainly agrees with Mr. Winterby; he blushed a most unbecoming shade of red when James asked him how he'd slept the night before!"

Caitlyn chuckled, pushing her knees up and hugging them to her body. "James is such a terror! I daresay poor Aunt Helen can hardly wait for him to grow up and get married himself!"

"He'd rather be shot, I heard him say," Constance told her. "He was telling Mr. Malone that he hopes war comes before any woman can—"

"Mr. Malone!" Caitlyn's cheeks immediately lost their color as she turned toward her sister with widened eyes. "What was *he* doing here?"

"Papa brought him back from the meeting. It lasted all day. They went to the bank and to Uncle Paul's office, and then all three came here for dinner. Papa and Uncle Paul couldn't very well leave Mr. Malone out, could they?" Constance studied her sister's face. "Are you sorry you missed him?"

"Sorry!" Caitlyn nearly choked on the word. Thank heaven she had been asleep last night! she thought, wondering why God had seen fit to deliver her from the Yankee after the whopping lie she'd told her mother. "I abhor that man!"

Constance was cool as she noted the agitation in her sister's face. "He asked about you."

"What—what did he say?" Caitlyn demanded.

"He asked where you were, and when Mama told him you weren't feeling well, he sort of smiled and then said he hoped you would be feeling better today. He said to tell you he was sorry he missed you." Constance smiled a little. "Really, Caitlyn, I do think he's interested in you! And for the life of me I can't understand why you aren't nicer to him. I know he's a Yankee, but he's so polite and cordial you'd almost think he was a Southerner born and bred."

"Don't talk rubbish, Connie!" Caitlyn said petulantly. "That

man can't be trusted. I'll bet he wouldn't even lift a finger to help a friend in need." She knew that for a fact! And having spoken of a friend, she asked, "Did you hear from Brant last night?"

Constance shook her head. "No. I think Mr. Malone said something about meeting him later in the evening."

Caitlyn's voice became gentler. "Poor Brant! He's not having any luck with the bankers here. I know he dreads going back to Riverhouse to tell his father."

"It is a shame," Constance agreed, her voice sympathetic. "But I'm sure Brant will think of a way to make everything right."

Caitlyn gazed at her sister in surprise. How little she really knew Brant! To think naively that he would be able to solve such a monumental problem on his own was inconceivable to Caitlyn.

Caitlyn got out of bed and went to the window to look out at the rose garden. She could see the glistening raindrops on the rose petals. The sunlight was caught and reflected a thousand times in each rose so that the whole garden seemed like a fairyland. It felt so much better to enjoy the wonders of nature than to bang her head against the wall of Brant's bitterness and Tanner's detachment.

In no time at all, she got dressed and went down to the breakfast table, where her parents and uncle were already eating. Her mother and father were discussing the trip back to Mornhaven. Uncle Paul was trying to persuade them to stay a few more days, but Timothy was shaking his head firmly. All three looked up when Caitlyn entered.

"Good morning, Papa, Mama," Caitlyn said as sweetly as possible, kissing each parent on the cheek. "Good morning, Uncle Paul."

"How did you sleep, my dear?" Margaret asked, glad to see the pain gone from her daughter's expression.

"Wonderfully!" Caitlyn answered with a bright smile. She glanced contritely at her uncle. "I'm sorry I missed Pauline last night."

Uncle Paul smiled reassuringly. "She'll be calling this afternoon before you leave. She and Edward plan to stay in the city a few more days, then they are off to Edward's plantation in Natchez. I don't blame them for wanting to get their life started there. After all, Pauline will be mistress of the plantation one day."

Caitlyn felt her heart twisting with an insidious pain. Mistress of a great plantation! For all her insistence that she was not jealous of her cousin, Caitlyn couldn't help feeling pangs of envy now. Oh, how she would love to be mistress of Riverhouse!

"We did miss you at dinner last night," Timothy said as his daughter accepted eggs and fried potatoes from one of the house slaves. He smiled to himself. "You missed Tanner Malone. He asked about you, my dear."

"Papa, you know I don't like him!" Caitlyn protested.

Timothy gave her a sharp look. "It doesn't matter if you like him or not. I do! I know he's a Boston Yankee born and bred, but I trust him with my cotton! We set up a brokering arrangement yesterday whereby one of the agents down here will be working for him. No sense in having Malone stay here too long—we all know the feelings between North and South these days. His agent can do the factoring by means of correspondence between here and Boston."

"It seems a lot of trouble to go to just to put your cotton in the hands of a Yankee," Caitlyn observed.

"Ah, but I'm getting a better price," Timothy explained with a twinkle in his eyes. "There's a lot to be done in factoring cotton. There are contracts for transportation and arrangements for insurance and credit, not to mention the ultimate sale to the buyer. The factor charges a commission for each service. My brokerage firm was bleeding me dry, taking as much as twenty percent of the value of my crops. Factoring provides a necessary service, but I'm sick of the drain on my wealth. Mr. Malone's fees aren't more than ten percent the first year."

"What about the second year?" Caitlyn asked.

Timothy laughed. "I get to negotiate with him again for that. If the price of cotton drops, his commission will drop too, you can be sure of that!" He winked at Paul. "And Malone is so well established in Boston, he'll be getting us goods from the North and from Europe much more cheaply than the traders here in New Orleans. Why, I'm betting that you and your sister and mother can have a whole new wardrobe made from the finest imported fabrics this year!" Timothy chuckled again and looked fondly at his wife.

"I'm glad it has worked out so well for you, Papa," Caitlyn said grudgingly. Knowing that scoundrel Yankee, she had no doubt that he had some trick up his sleeve to get that twenty percent eventually. It would serve Papa right! He would finally

realize what a snake Tanner Malone was! Instead of trusting him, Papa should have put more faith in Brant and loaned him the money he needed. "I suppose Mr. Malone will be leaving New Orleans soon," she hinted.

Timothy nodded. "He's hoping I can persuade Winfield Cobb to use his services, but I told him Winfield can be a crusty old fogy. He's not one to accept change, and I doubt that he'd give up that old shark who's been factoring for him for years." He shrugged. "But there are plenty of others who'd be interested."

He would have gone on, but the majordomo appeared in the doorway, carrying a message. "From Mr. Malone, sir," he said solemnly, handing it to Paul Savoy.

With a mystified air, Paul broke the seal of the envelope and unfolded the piece of parchment. His eyes scanned the contents rapidly, and then he sat back in his seat exhaling a loud breath of air.

"It seems Brant Sinclair has gotten himself into some trouble," he began ominously.

Caitlyn felt her heart beat faster and her hands tighten involuntarily on her eating utensils. Her eyes were fastened on her uncle as though held there by invisible strings.

"What's happened to the boy?" Timothy demanded.

"He was arrested last night for taking part in a drunken brawl down by the river wharf. This note is from Mr. Malone. It seems someone was killed in the fight and the authorities are holding Sinclair pending an investigation into the matter."

"Oh, my God!" Caitlyn felt the blood drain from her face as she stood up. Her eyes searched the faces of the others frantically. Surely they knew that Brant could not possibly have been involved in a murder!

"Sit down, Caitlyn," Timothy ordered her gently. "What is it Malone wants us to do?"

"Since I'm a lawyer, Mr. Malone thought Sinclair could use my services. I'll have to go down to the jail." Paul stood up and wiped the breakfast crumbs from his lap. "I'll just look in on Helen and then go down."

"I'll go with you," Timothy offered, also standing. He glanced sharply at his daughter, who'd been about to open her mouth. "There's no need for anyone else to go, missy."

It was late evening when Timothy O'Rourke finally returned. He sat in the parlor while his wife and daughters gathered around him silently.

"Well, they've found the murderer," he said. Everyone in the room released long sighs of relief. "But they're still holding Sinclair for public drunkenness and disorder. He'll have to stay in jail for a couple of nights. Tanner Malone thinks he can get him out early with a few well-placed bribes."

"When do you think Brant will be released?" Constance asked quietly.

Timothy shrugged. "I'm not sure, my dear, but Tanner has promised to see that he gets out of jail as soon as possible. He's delayed his own departure to stand by him." With this, Timothy looked pointedly at Caitlyn. "At any rate, we'll not be going back to Mornhaven until tomorrow. I've booked passage first thing in the morning, so I think we should all be seeing to our belongings." He looked at his wife wearily. "I'm famished, my dear. Could you possibly get the cook to fix me something to eat?"

Margaret smiled gently and hurried out of the room to the kitchen. Timothy eyed both his daughters and was about to speak, then rubbed his eyes wearily as he realized he was too tired to argue now. All he wanted was a hot meal, his wife's soothing ministrations, and a good night's sleep before their packet left in the morning. God willing, he'd be on Mornhaven's sweet soil two days later—and he swore he'd not be coming back to New Orleans until he absolutely had to!

A week later, back at Mornhaven, the O'Rourkes received word from Brant Sinclair. The note was short, most of it an apology for the way he had conducted himself in New Orleans and for his shortcomings in general. "He says he is leaving for Boston with Tanner Malone," Timothy announced after reading the note.

"Oh!" Constance exclaimed, her lips trembling. Her hand flew to her mouth and her soft blue eyes were swimming with tears. For a moment Caitlyn thought her sister might faint, and she hurried to her side to help her into a chair.

For herself, Caitlyn felt a terrible loss, a lurching sense of betrayal that enveloped her and made the room seem to sway alarmingly. Then anger and bitterness replaced fear and she clenched her fist against her skirt. But instead of raging against the man she loved, she raged against Tanner Malone.

"What possible reason would there be for Tanner to want Brant Sinclair with him on his trip back to Boston?" asked Tim-

othy. Then his voice became stern and uncompromising. "I don't think Brant was capable of facing up to his responsibilities, Caitlyn."

"Papa, don't say that!" Everyone looked at Constance, who had spoken up vehemently. "Brant is a good man. He's just not as strong as everyone thinks he should be. I don't think he could face his father after his time in jail, especially after his failure to obtain the loans he needed."

"How do you know about that, daughter?" Timothy demanded.

"While we were in New Orleans Brant told me all about it himself." Constance gazed calmly at her father.

Now it was Caitlyn's turn to feel faint, and she sat down on the nearest chair. No wonder Constance hadn't sounded surprised when Caitlyn had told her the bankers had refused Brant a loan! Brant had been confiding in Constance! When? Where? How much time had they spent alone with each other? While Caitlyn had been doing everything possible to help Brant save Riverhouse, he had been enjoying a flirtation with Constance!

Through a mist of anger, she heard her father ask, "Did he declare any intentions toward you, Constance? I'm not letting either of my daughters marry a man too cowardly to stay and face public opinion after he has acted irresponsibly! What does he think William is going to do without him? Does the boy have no feelings for anyone but himself?"

Constance returned, "Brant never spoke of marriage to me."

Caitlyn felt relief flood through her. The pounding in her ears began to subside and she began to think rationally about Brant's departure. Leaving was probably the worst thing he could have done to himself. In a few years, with good crops and steady business experience, Brant would have been able to command loans as easily as her father did. But to run away, to shirk all his responsibilities—that was shameful indeed!

Caitlyn's real fear now was that Tanner Malone might try to turn Brant against her. She knew he didn't think a marriage to her would be in Brant's best interest. He had never really liked her and probably had only been amusing himself at her expense. For all his business sense, Tanner Malone was a scoundrel.

"After Brant gets his fill of the false companionship Tanner Malone has to offer, surely he'll come to his senses and return home," she proposed confidently. "Mr. Malone had no busi-

ness coming here from Boston in the first place, expecting Southerners to do business with a no-account Yankee!''

''That no-account Yankee is in business with me now, missy, and I'll thank you to keep your opinion of him to yourself!'' Timothy cut in irritably.

''Let's not argue about Mr. Malone when it's Brant we're really concerned about,'' Constance sniffled, dabbing her eyes with her already damp handkerchief. ''Poor William will be devastated when he finds out what has happened. Papa, you really should ride over to Riverhouse and speak to him.''

''Yes, yes, you're right, Constance. I'll ride over there immediately.'' Timothy hurried out of the sitting room to look for Margaret, feeling relieved that Brant Sinclair was out of the lives of his daughters. With luck, he might be able to get them married off before Sinclair eventually returned to Louisiana.

18

THE SUMMER OF 1859 passed swiftly for Caitlyn and Constance with a gay round of barbecues and cotillions. Artemas Blair renewed his attentions to Caitlyn now that his chief rival for her affections was gone. Jesse Cobb shyly squired Constance to several afternoon gatherings, his growing interest in her obvious to everyone but Constance, who continued to pine secretly for Brant Sinclair.

Caitlyn also continued to love Brant, and her humiliation at his hands still rankled. She fought her love for Brant by flirting outrageously with Artemas, letting him kiss her on the veranda as he was leaving for home.

She closed her eyes and waited expectantly for her body to feel something, but was keenly disappointed. Although Artemas kissed pleasantly enough, Caitlyn could not feel intensely about it. She tried to remember how she had felt when Brant had kissed her, but the memories had faded. These faded memories only served Brant better. She recalled Brant's kisses as being much more passionate, more romantic, than they actually had been. As the days and weeks went by and no news came from Brant, her fantasies about him expanded so that she was sure she would never feel such passion with anyone else. It appealed to her to feel like one of the tragic heroines in the romantic novels she

liked to read—lovely, loyal, and pining for a great love lost. She went about Mornhaven, cherishing her secret identity and wondering what wonderful explosion of feeling would occur when Brant finally returned. By then he would have made his fortune in some grand way in Boston and would be ready to ask her to marry him.

Timothy O'Rourke watched his two daughters with a keen eye, wondering why Artemas and Jesse didn't make their intentions plain. Both young whelps must be interested in marriage. Artemas was twenty and Jesse was nearly nineteen. Timothy thought his girls were old enough to take on the responsibility of marriage. He refused to consider that both of them might still be besotted by that Sinclair boy. He was doing the best he could to help William, even riding to Baton Rouge to get an overseer for him. It was easy to see that William could no longer ride cotton fields himself.

These early days of September were hot and dry after the rains of August and the cotton was thriving, growing taller every day. At dusk Timothy would sit on the veranda and listen to the chanting of the field hands as they returned to their cabins after a day's work. It was a soothing sound that made him rest easy in his chair, feeling some of the day's burdens fall away from him.

Hearing him sigh contentedly, Margaret smiled one evening as she sat next to him on the veranda. "Are you happier now that you've got an overseer to do some of the chores in the fields?" she asked, leaning toward him.

Timothy nodded his assent, then blustered, "But I won't turn soft and sit on this veranda for the rest of my life! I'll ride the fields until I drop dead, my dear!"

Margaret laughed. "I know, dear." Then she added seriously, "I suppose you and William have that much in common."

"William is trying so hard to do everything himself, Margaret. It's hard for him not to show bitterness when he speaks about Brant. William told me Brant's last letter was full of the wonders of the North." Timothy shook his head. "Hah! The boy should realize he'll never be happy away from his roots!"

"Perhaps he feels closer to the North, Timothy," she answered gently. "After all, he spent five years up there after his mother's death."

"His roots are still here!" Timothy maintained stubbornly.

"Here comes Caitlyn back from her ride with Artemas,"

Margaret observed, seeing a pale form atop a horse cantering up the drive.

Timothy smiled appreciatively, seeing his daughter with her hat askew and tendrils of coppery auburn hair flying out from beneath it. "She sits that horse like a champion," he proclaimed proudly. "Damn! Maybe if I promise her a new stallion, she'll consent to accept Artemas's proposal when he finally decides to ask her."

"Timothy, you can't bribe her," Margaret intervened.

"Well, it's practically the only thing I haven't tried," Timothy admitted sheepishly. "I think the girl's making a mistake not taking Artemas's attention more seriously, my dear. It's plain to see he's smitten with her."

"She'll make up her mind in due course," Margaret remarked wisely.

"She'd best make it up soon," Timothy growled, "and I'm hoping it's before Brant Sinclair realizes how foolish he was to have left here."

Brant Sinclair awoke to a bright stream of sunlight stabbing him in the face. With an oath, he threw his pillow at the open window, then turned onto his stomach and buried his face in the covers. Christ, how his head hurt! How much rum had he drunk last night? He'd lost count after the first few rounds, especially after the little red-haired barmaid had hopped onto his lap and tilted the bottle against his mouth. Lord, if he could just stop his head from pounding so damnably!

After a moment he realized that some of the pounding was coming from the door. With a groan, Brant got to his feet, then padded stark naked across the room to unlock the door.

Immediately Tanner Malone pushed his way in, an air of excitement about him that Brant hadn't seen since they'd left New Orleans together nearly three months ago. Tanner eyed him and let out a hoot of laughter that seemed to clash inside Brant's head like a cymbal.

"For God's sake, Tanner, how can you be so cheerful this morning when you downed as much rum as I did last night?" Brant grumbled, stumbling back to the bed and crashing into it.

"Brant, you're becoming a veteran at these drinking bouts. I'm surprised your head isn't more used to it by now."

"I doubt it ever will be," he moaned from under the covers.

Tanner frowned as he pulled up a chair and sat down. Brant

was lucky today was Sunday and he didn't have to be at the office. Tanner had gotten him a job with his import-export business so that Brant could pay his bills. Brant was spending so much on drink, he was going to wind up with none left over to pay his rent.

"Listen, Brant, I've come to see you because I've been making some plans," Tanner began.

Brant chuckled. "Don't tell me. You're going to marry that— what's her name? The girl with those splendid violet eyes whose father owns half of Boston."

Tanner shook his head and smiled. "No. Nothing like that. Actually I am about to embark on quite an adventure, my friend. I'm leaving for Australia in three days."

"What!" Despite his pounding headache, that was enough to get Brant's full attention. He scrambled up to a sitting position and stared at his friend. "What do you mean you're going to Australia? Where the hell is that?"

"It's half a world away, Brant," Tanner said, standing and pacing back and forth in his excitement. "New deposits of gold have been found, richer than the ones found a few years ago." He looked at Brant frankly. "I'm tired of Boston. I've grown restless lately and I want to be off to a new adventure."

"That doesn't sound like you, Tanner," Brant commented. "The responsible businessman who runs a thriving company here in Boston, whose business sense was enough to cut through regional barriers in Louisiana. Has it all come too easily for you, Tanner?" There was a naked, bitter jealousy in Brant's words that was not lost on Tanner.

"It's never easy," Tanner said bluntly. "America may be the land of opportunity, Brant, but you have to work for what you get." His piercing gaze made Brant self-conscious. "I'm not leaving forever. My business can do very well in my brother Morgan's capable hands. And my agent in New Orleans has already impressed me with his business acumen. His reports are very encouraging."

"So you're leaving Boston for Australia," Brant murmured.

Tanner nodded. "I've been thinking about it for some time. News takes time to get here from the South Pacific." He stepped to the window and looked out at Boston, a teeming, bustling, industrial city that was getting more populated every month with new immigrants from Ireland and England. "I want to see what

opportunities lie ahead for me. You know I'm not one to sit and wait for things to happen.''

"I know. Your energy has always astounded me,'' Brant admitted. "It reminds me of Caitlyn sometimes when she—'' He stopped short, lowering his eyes and reddening at the memory of how he had treated Caitlyn O'Rourke, how he had left her hanging with half a marriage proposal. He had behaved like a cad toward her.

"Don't worry about your little Southern belle,'' Tanner said, his voice harsher than he had expected. "I'm sure she's found someone else to take your place.''

"I treated her badly,'' Brant sighed. "God knows I thought I was in love with her, but I suppose it was Constance—oh, hell! What does it matter now?'' He looked at Tanner with sudden eagerness. "Why don't I go to Australia too, Tanner?'' His eyes grew excited as the idea took hold.

"You can't keep running away from problems, Brant,'' Tanner said seriously. He wasn't anxious to have Sinclair at his heels again. Although Brant was a good friend, he was a poor businessman. His lack of energy drove Tanner crazy. The man always seemed to be content to ride the wave of someone else's success.

Brant stood up and pulled on a pair of trousers. He paced for a moment before eyeing Tanner again. "Oh, hell, Tanner, we both know I hate office work! If I don't go with you, I guess I'll just have to go back to Riverhouse.''

Tanner walked to the window again and gazed out thoughtfully. Back to Riverhouse—and to Caitlyn O'Rourke. She and Brant would make an interesting couple: Caitlyn sure of herself, with boundless energy and a will to match; Brant a true Southern gentleman, romantic, gallant, and lazy.

Tanner sighed. The romantic Southerners might soon be at war with the practical Northerners. Modern war was not a joust between gallant knights—it was dirt, sweat, and dysentery. He shuddered to think of Brant trying to fight a war like that. Should he save Brant, he wondered, or should he send him back to the South?

"I guess I'll pack my things and take the next train south,'' Brant said dejectedly. Already the thought of facing his father and the O'Rourkes was making him shrink with fear. He would be returning without honor—to a place where a man's honor was everything.

Tanner stared at his friend as he turned over the possibilities in his mind. "Come with me, Brant," he finally said. "Damn it, there's room for one more on the ship to Australia, and it'll be nice to have a friend along!"

Brant looked at Tanner in silence. Then a peal of laughter escaped from him and he grinned widely. "Hell, Tanner—you won't regret it, my friend! I'll work hard and we'll make a fortune together! I promise you!"

"No promises necessary, Brant," Tanner said briskly. "Just be ready to leave in three days. If you want to write any letters to Louisiana, you'd best do it now." He donned his hat and hurried out the door, trying not to think of what he had gotten himself into.

It was the middle of September, a lazy time of year when the days were still hot as summer but the nights were getting cooler. It had been dry for several days, but last night a thunderstorm had drenched the cotton fields of Mornhaven, giving them the moisture they needed. This morning the field hands had had a hard time getting through the mud and water to do their work in the fields.

Looking out her window at the rain-soaked lawn and the river road that was rutted from carriage wheels churning through the mud, Caitlyn sighed deeply and leaned her elbows on the windowsill. She knew that Artemas Blair was working himself up to a marriage proposal. No doubt he would have asked her weeks ago had she given him any encouragement.

"If only Brant would come home," she said to herself aloud. How she loved him! She was positive that he was the only man she would ever love. If he never returned to her, or worse, if he married some horrible Northern woman and brought her back to Riverhouse someday, Caitlyn was sure she would go into a convent. Her mouth quirked at the idea of becoming a nun.

"Good morning, Caitlyn." It was Constance, her eyes shining mysteriously as she sailed into Caitlyn's room without knocking.

She looked so happy that Caitlyn knew something exciting had happened. Perhaps Constance had finally come to her senses and recognized how right Jesse Cobb would be for her. Balls of fire! Had Jesse asked for her hand already? How embarrassing it would be if her little sister had a marriage proposal before she herself did, Caitlyn thought, dismissing any notion of cloistering herself in a convent.

"A letter came from Brant Sinclair this morning," Constance burst out, unable to keep the secret. "I was at breakfast with Mama when the messenger brought it."

Caitlyn stood up and clasped her hands in front of her. Brant had sent a letter! What could it mean? Was he coming home? "What did it say, Connie?" she half whispered.

"It was addressed to Papa, of course, so we'll have to wait until he comes home from the fields," Constance returned. "But, Caitlyn, it must be good news. He hasn't written in so long! Do you think he's going to come home?"

"I hope so, Connie," she said. Why was her sister still so infatuated with Brant? Why couldn't she see that Jesse was the man for her? Honestly, Caitlyn thought to herself, some girls just couldn't see love staring them in the face. She herself would never be so stupid!

"Another message was delivered today—from Blair House," Constance added. "Artemas will be here this afternoon." Constance gave her sister a sly look, for she was positive that this would be the day when Artemas would propose. Once Caitlyn was persuaded what a wonderful husband Artemas would make, she would give up dreaming of Brant. And then Constance would be able to marry him. Constance was sure that Brant loved her as much as she loved him—and why Caitlyn refused to see it was beyond her.

Both sisters scrutinized each other, each sure that she knew the inner workings of a man's heart.

"Then I suppose I'd best get dressed," Caitlyn said briskly. Like her sister, she was positive that Artemas was going to propose to her today. She was also positive that she was going to refuse him, but she didn't want to hurt his feelings unduly. Dressed in her prettiest clothes, she would persuade Artemas gently that she was in love with another man and couldn't possibly consider marrying him. They must always remain friends, of course, but no more than that. "Send Sara up to help me dress," she told her sister, who was leaving the room.

Caitlyn returned to the window and smiled when she looked outside. She could imagine herself under the shade of the old oaks, looking pretty and sweet as she confronted Artemas with just the proper combination of sadness and wistful innocence. He would be charmed, and despite his disappointment that her answer would be no, he would go away thinking what a wonderful wife she would make for that lucky man whom she loved.

From a very early age, Caitlyn had been taught the subtleties of emotional manipulation and, like most Southern belles, she had taken the lessons to heart. A pretty pout and a promising glance were usually enough to get a girl whatever she wanted.

For a moment she thought of one disappointing exception. Tanner Malone had not fallen for her wiles and flirtations. But after all, he was only a no-account Yankee who hadn't the sense to appreciate a pretty girl. Doubtless he was unused to the subtle machinations of decent young women.

When Sara appeared in the doorway, she found her young mistress humming softly to herself and staring out the window dreamily. With a shake of her head, Sara went to the armoire and brought out the afternoon dress that she had carefully pressed earlier that morning.

It took nearly two hours for Caitlyn to be turned out exactly the way she wanted. The dress of green sprigged muslin was flounced twice around the skirt and decorated with wide ribbon sashes that were drawn together in the front. The bodice had a stiffly boned point in front and full sleeves that were split from elbow to shoulder to reveal the white sleeves of the blouse underneath. Sara had added a white collar, giving the dress a demure look that was just the effect Caitlyn wanted to achieve.

Downstairs she ate a bit, hoping to calm her stomach, which was nervous from the combination of Artemas's anticipated proposal and Brant's unopened letter, which was lying on a silver tray in the hall. She glanced at the white envelope, wishing she could see through it to what was written inside.

There was no use thinking about it now. She would do better to calm herself before Artemas's arrival. Escaping to the library, she settled into a cozy chair with a romantic novel, trying to imagine herself as the heroine.

It was not long before Margaret found her there. "Artemas has just arrived, Caitlyn," she said to her daughter, noting the flush in her cheeks and wondering if perhaps Caitlyn's feelings had changed toward him. "Is there—is there something you would like to discuss with me before you see him, my dear?"

"No, Mama." Caitlyn didn't want her mother to know how important this day was. Better to let her think Artemas had not proposed than to have her tell Papa she had refused him. "I think I'll ask Artemas to walk with me outside."

"It looks like rain, dear. You'd best remember your hat and umbrella," Margaret cautioned.

Caitlyn hurried to the hall, where Artemas was waiting. He looked splendid, Caitlyn thought, noting the tall, lithe body attired in riding clothes. The blond hair was like a shining crown on his head and the profile was one of the handsomest she'd ever seen. Still, all of that didn't make her heart beat any faster, and she knew she could never marry Artemas and be happy.

"Hello, Artemas," she greeted him, holding out her hands to him.

He took both of them in his warmly. "Hello, Caitlyn. I wanted to see you," he said simply, his brown eyes looking earnestly into hers.

Caitlyn knew she was not in love with Artemas, but she had to admit that when he looked at her like that, it was hard not to fall into his arms. He could be devastatingly charming when he wanted to be and, especially with Brant gone, Caitlyn now found Artemas quite enticing.

"Shall we walk outside, Artemas?" Caitlyn asked breathlessly. She was heady with the thrill of wielding power over a man.

He looked doubtful for a moment, then nodded. "It might rain, so we'd best not go far," he told her.

She nodded and retrieved her hat from the armoire, grabbing her umbrella at the same time. She took Artemas's proffered arm and smiled up at him.

As they walked away from the house, Caitlyn had the feeling everyone at Mornhaven was watching them. That made her feel uncomfortable, and she gently steered Artemas down the gravel drive and into the copse of old oaks that separated the drive from the river road. They walked companionably, thinking their own thoughts, with glances at the sky in case of rain.

When they were under the trees, both started to speak, then both stopped self-consciously, laughing a little.

"Excuse me, Caitlyn," Artemas began. He seemed terribly shy and unlike his usual self, and Caitlyn thought him all the more charming.

"You look so handsome this afternoon," she said sweetly, letting her lashes half cover her eyes to look even more alluring. "I declare, Artemas, it's a wonder no girl has snatched you into marriage yet." It was a very bold thing to say, but boldness was better than beating around the bush, she thought with satisfaction. Besides, she'd known Artemas almost since birth, and they had always been good friends.

He looked at the ground and shuffled nervously. "Speaking of marriage, Caitlyn—" he began after a long breath.

"Artemas, why are you so nervous?" Caitlyn laughed, her own self-confidence growing as his waned. "I've never seen you this way!" She tucked her arm into his and pressed herself against him. She knew she would have to disappoint him, but it was a great balm to know that a man was about to ask for her hand in marriage.

"Caitlyn, you are so beautiful," he sighed.

She laughed again, feeling her power growing. Should she let him kiss her? Just once before she had to tell him no? She felt nervous, wanting him to get on with it, yet wanting the moment to last. It wasn't often a girl was put in such a lofty position.

"Caitlyn, I must tell you something," he broke in earnestly. "You know how much I've always liked you, admired you. We've grown up together and it seems we've always played this little game between us. I was always there for you when you'd get mad at one of the other boys, and you were always your most charming to me, even when I knew you didn't mean it."

He was so close to her he would only have to move a little to press his mouth against hers. Caitlyn pursed her lips encouragingly and tilted her chin. Goodness, if he didn't get the message now, he hadn't the sense of a goat!

"Caitlyn, ah, Caitlyn," he sighed. "You're making it so difficult for me."

She knew he was going to kiss her. She knew it! But, to her surprise, he took her chin in his hand and merely brushed it with his thumb. Was that it? She frowned. "What is it, Artemas?"

He took another gulp of air, then plunged in. "I'm going to marry Marcella Cobb, Caitlyn."

For a moment she thought she'd misheard him. "What did you say, Artemas?" she asked. Her dark blue eyes gazed into his, but what she saw there told her she'd heard him correctly.

"I'm going to marry Marcella Cobb," he repeated in a stronger voice, as though having said it once, it was much easier to say it the second time. "We became engaged yesterday. The wedding will be next May. Winfield Cobb is anxious for the marriage to take place before war comes."

"Marcella Cobb!" Caitlyn echoed, feeling as though she'd just been doused with a bucket of cold water. "Why, Marcella and I have been friends forever! But, Artemas, *you* are going to marry *her*!" Unwarranted jealousy pricked her. Moments ago

she had wanted to be kissed by Artemas just before turning down his marriage proposal, but now she desperately wanted to hurt him, to show him how little she cared. "I would think your ambitions would have been higher," she snickered. Marcella was pretty enough, but as devoid of intelligence and spirit as a piece of wood, in Caitlyn's opinion.

Artemas eyed her testily as she stepped back from him with a contemptuous look. "Perhaps my ambitions were higher," he acknowledged, "but I'm not one to beat my head against a brick wall day after day, Caitlyn. Marcella has loved me for a long time and I—well—I have always liked her. She'll be all the things I want in a wife."

"No doubt," Caitlyn said sarcastically. "You can stay out in your precious cotton fields until midnight and it won't bother sweet Marcella. Perhaps she'll devise some entertainment of her own," she added waspishly.

Artemas reared like a spurred horse. "Spite doesn't become you, Caitlyn," he told her. "Hell, you know my feelings for you, but you're so caught up with that coward Sinclair!"

"He is not a coward!"

"Damn if he isn't!" Artemas confronted her with a pugnacious look on his handsome face. "Why else would he turn tail and run when his father is in poor health and Riverhouse is going under? My father finally convinced me that any girl who'd pine for a shirker like that wouldn't make the kind of wife I want."

"I'm glad your father got through that thick skull of yours, Artemas Blair!" Caitlyn shouted back. "He saved you from a cold refusal! A man who cares only about how much cotton he grows wouldn't make the kind of husband I want!"

"Then we're both agreed," Artemas returned.

"I just don't understand why you felt the need to tell me in person; I'm sure Marcella will call on us to announce it soon enough," Caitlyn added, still angry, but calming down a bit in the face of the plain facts. She didn't love Artemas and he didn't love her. She had no intention of marrying him, so there was no reason to be hurt that he was marrying another. Still, it rankled that he hadn't given her a chance to turn him down.

Artemas was quiet for a moment, giving his own anger a chance to cool. "I wanted to tell you myself. Caitlyn, if I had thought there was a chance that you and I—" He stopped, then shook his head. "We've been friends too long for me not to tell you," he ended simply.

Caitlyn took a deep breath. "I suppose," she said haughtily, "that our friendship won't last beyond your wedding day. Marcella wouldn't stand for it."

"We both will always welcome you to Blair House," he said firmly, although she could see by the way his eyes slid away from hers that things were definitely going to change between them. A girl in her position couldn't be caught flirting with a married man. For a moment Caitlyn felt her heart sink at the loss of a childhood friend. But then she straightened her back and smiled at him regally.

"Congratulations, Artemas. I hope you and Marcella will be very happy—and I thank you for telling me yourself." She would have said more, but felt unexpected tears welling up in her eyes. "And now, if you'll excuse me, I'll be going back inside."

She heard him call to her, but she picked up her skirts and ran pell-mell into the house, feeling the tears dropping onto her cheeks as she sped by a surprised Sara. She heard her mother call to her from the foyer, but hurried upstairs and flung herself on her bed. Her mother was not far behind.

"My darling, what has happened?" Margaret looked at her daughter worriedly, wondering what had put her in this mood. Caitlyn was crying uncontrollably now and punching one fist into the palm of the other hand.

"Mama, I *hate* men!" Caitlyn yelled, not caring who heard her. "Especially Artemas Blair!"

"Caitlyn, what has he done?"

"He's marrying Marcella Cobb!"

Margaret sighed. So Artemas had given up on a cause he knew was lost to him. "My dearest, don't carry on so. Perhaps he wasn't meant for you anyway."

"I wouldn't have him on a silver platter," Caitlyn sniffled, grabbing the handkerchief her mother offered her.

"Then why are you crying?"

"I just hate him!" Caitlyn railed. How could her mother understand her feelings? She and her father had found each other and fallen in love. They had married with the blessings of both families. Why was it so difficult for Caitlyn to marry the man she loved? Why did everything seem to conspire to keep them apart? Then she recalled the letter downstairs—the precious letter that would set everything right. Surely Brant would ask for her hand. Would he send for her to come to Boston? No, that would be much too bold, she thought. She couldn't possibly

travel up North. No, he would have to come back home and marry her properly. He would have to take up his rightful responsibilities. She smiled bitterly as she thought of Artemas's betrayal. How dare he jilt her for Marcella Cobb! When he received the news of her engagement to Brant Sinclair, it would show him how little his upcoming nuptials to Marcella meant to her. Let Artemas marry the empty-headed Marcella—and when he saw how happy Caitlyn and Brant were together, let him suffer for it!

Timothy waited until after dinner to open the letter. He scanned it hurriedly, then settled back in his chair with a mixture of relief and curiosity on his face. He even had the temerity to smile at the questioning faces of his wife and daughters. "Sinclair's written that he's bound for Australia."

"Australia? Where is that?" Constance blurted out.

"It's somewhere in the South Pacific," Caitlyn returned, glad now for those boring geography lessons in school. She felt dread settling over her as she realized how very far away it was.

"What else does he say?" Margaret asked, catching her husband's eye.

Timothy cleared his throat and continued. "He says he intends to return to Riverhouse someday as a rich and respected man able to present himself as a suitable husband. It seems Tanner Malone has taken it into his head to travel to Australia and Brant convinced him to take him along. Sinclair mentions something about gold strikes in Australia. He's convinced he'll strike it rich there. He compares it to California in '49."

"Australia!" Caitlyn repeated. "Papa, it's so far away." She was remembering Brant's words about becoming rich enough to present himself as a suitable husband. To whom? she wondered. She wished he'd been more specific. Why didn't he mention her name? A girl couldn't wait forever for a man to decide he wanted to marry her! She would be seventeen next March, a scant six months away. She had to be careful not to end up as an old maid! Goodness, when she thought of it that way, Artemas Blair looked mighty attractive—but he was taken now!

19

WHILE CAITLYN AND CONSTANCE worried about Brant's whereabouts and whether he would ever return to Louisiana, the North and South seemed to be pulling further apart. In October 1859 the abolitionist John Brown and twenty-one of his followers launched an attack from a rented farmhouse and took the Federal arsenal at Harpers Ferry, Virginia. He rounded up sixty prominent men as hostages and stood off the United States Marines until he finally surrendered after heavy losses. He was convicted and hanged in December. But his death only served to illustrate the vast differences between the slave states and the antislavery states. The Northern abolitionists revered him as a saint and martyr, while the Southern slaveholders saw him as nothing more than a common murderer, a fanatic who had served to deepen divisions.

There were meetings among the planters of Louisiana, meetings that grew more heated as each faction tried to push its opinions on the majority.

Timothy O'Rourke was offered a delegate's seat at the 1860 Democratic National Convention, but refused. Instead of talking over his future plans for Mornhaven with the family after dinner, Timothy was now obliged to preside over small groups who would meet at his house to discuss the political future of Louisiana. Everyone agreed that should the Republicans win the White House, revolt must follow.

During the 1860 presidential campaign, a wave of mass hysteria swept through the South and John Brown's ghost haunted the Southern imagination. The prospect of a Republican president provoked fears that the North would let loose dozens of John Browns on the South. Southern newspapers reported hundreds of cases of arson, poisoning, and murder attributed to slaves. Most of these stories were made up or grossly exaggerated, but Southerners believed that such things could happen in their own communities. Several suspects, black and white, were lynched and scores were whipped, or tarred and feathered. Hundreds of Northern whites were ordered to leave the South on pain of death.

No more letters had come from Brant and Caitlyn had begun

to lose hope. Many of her friends were married by now, or at least engaged. It was mighty embarrassing when she had to stand as bridesmaid for Betsy Warrington, who was not yet seventeen! Caitlyn imagined people staring at her, wondering why she was not yet wed. It was humiliating! At such times she silently cursed Brant for running off to Australia.

Her father was unsympathetic to her plight. The summer of 1860 brought a severe drought which was affecting the cotton crop. Timothy had enough to do to keep Mornhaven prosperous and his political cronies appeased. It was maddening to the Democrats that the Republicans refused to take the Southern threats of secession seriously. Southern newspapers ran head-lines proclaiming that the South would never submit to the in-auguration of Abraham Lincoln, yet the North flocked to his party.

"The supercilious fools!" Timothy exploded one day after reading a St. Louis pro-Union newspaper that had come down-river. "Don't they think we know what we're doing?"

"Timothy, don't get yourself worked up," Margaret advised. "We both know the newspapers exaggerate everything."

"Everyone in this infernal country seems to want war!" Tim-othy continued, running his hands through his red hair, silvered now at the temples. "Don't they know that war isn't just medals and derring-do? It's bone-deep fatigue, gut-tearing pain from dysentery, and the delirious ravings of men suffering from ty-phoid. I saw a little of it when I fought with the Yanks against Mexico." He settled back in his chair for a moment and closed his eyes. "Sean Flynn and I were lucky to get out of that alive."

"I haven't heard you speak of Sean for a long time," Margaret observed, continuing her stitching as she peered over her em-broidery hoop at her husband's face.

Timothy laughed. "The old vagabond's been in Texas for the past few years. He's always been an adventurous one. No settling down for him."

"He has plenty of time, Timothy. He is a little younger than you," Margaret pointed out.

Timothy appeared to rally against that, then chuckled at his wife. "You're a good woman, Margaret Forrester O'Rourke. And you've a way of turning a man's mind away from the work at hand. I'd like to spend the afternoon recalling old times, but there are other things more pressing. Winfield Cobb and his cohort will be over tonight for another meeting. I don't know if

I've got the head for it tonight. It seems these meetings are one big excuse for emptying bottles of scotch.''

Margaret had to smile, although she didn't approve of the long sessions that were yelling debates combined with drinking bouts. There'd been many nights when she'd waited up for Timothy until nearly dawn, only to see him go out to the fields again a few hours later. She knew her husband enjoyed robust health, but it still worried her to see the dark circles under his eyes and the pouches around his jowls.

''I haven't had much time to spend with my daughters,'' Timothy continued reflectively. ''I remember when I half promised them a trip to Europe this summer. Summer's nearly over and it looks like there'll be no trip.'' He looked inquisitively at his wife. ''Has Caitlyn come to you with any news about marriage prospects?''

Margaret shook her head and pursed her lips. ''She throws herself into the whirl of parties, but she flirts with all the young men there. Even some that are married now,'' she added, eyeing her husband.

''What! I'll not have my daughter making a spectacle of herself!'' Timothy burst out. ''Damn it, the girl's got to learn she can't be gallivanting with other women's husbands! What of Connie?''

''Jesse Cobb is still calling, though Connie acts like he's not there half the time. I'm afraid both our girls are still smitten with Brant Sinclair.''

''It's been nearly a year now and they're still pining for him,'' Timothy pointed out. ''Their devotion is wasted on the boy. His father could have used him here this summer to help with the cotton. William is barely hanging on, you know. If his crop is meager this year, Riverhouse will go on the auction block, despite my best efforts.'' He stopped pacing and gazed at his wife. ''The South is pulling farther away from the North. I think war will come soon, Margaret.''

She was quiet, staring down at her embroidery, her hands lying still in her lap. ''What will happen, Timothy?''

He shrugged. ''I don't know, Margaret. Some believe the North will let us secede peaceably after some debating in Washington. There would have to be some concessions, of course. The North would have first chance at our cotton. But others think the North won't give up without a fight. They're sure that war is inevitable and that it won't end until one side is completely vic-

torious. The damnable thing is that most people *want* war.'' He snorted in disgust. "The pack of fools!"

"My dear, you won't have to fight, will you?'' Margaret asked.

Timothy shook his head. "I couldn't fire a pistol well enough, Margaret. You know that old injury to my hand in the Mexican War.''

"Now I'm glad you got it,'' Margaret said without reservation.

Timothy smiled. "I'll do my best to try to talk sense into the firebrands tonight. But South Carolina is where most of the rabid warmongers are. I think Louisiana will just wait to see what happens there before making any controversial moves.''

20

BRANT SINCLAIR drew a hand across his forehead, wiping off the sweat that had accumulated despite the wintry air. Damn! He'd never get used to the topsy-turvy seasons in this country. Here it was the middle of August and the Australian winter had descended with chilly winds and cold nights. For a moment he let himself think about home—about the drowsy heat and humidity that would be wafting from the river. There'd be the singsong chanting of husky male voices as the field hands trudged back to their cabins after a long day in the cotton fields. One of the house slaves would fetch him a cool drink and he'd sit on the veranda at Riverhouse, watching the sun setting.

Brant shut his eyes tightly, willing the picture to disappear. No sense in thinking about home now. He opened his eyes and gazed at the mining camp around him. It looked the same as the others he'd seen in the last six months. Thousands of tents of every possible shape and size contrasted strongly with the dark, thickly wooded hills in the background. In front of the tents, people were occupied at the fires, preparing supper.

Brant stirred the contents of the iron pot that were bubbling appetizingly. Today was his day to be cook while his partners were out working the goldfields. He didn't mind it, for the task of looking for gold, removing the dirt and rocks, and carting them back several miles to wash in a stream was a long and arduous process. For six months he'd been doing it. He had

found a few ounces of dust and one or two small nuggets. But the money he'd gotten for those he had used to survive.

Brant smiled ironically to himself. He knew Tanner was making more money than he—and the son of a bitch hadn't even taken a hand to a pickax! With his natural instinct for buying and selling, Tanner had smelled profits as soon as he'd stepped off the ship in Melbourne. He'd made the right contacts and arranged to sell tools, supplies, food, and clothing in several mining towns, and now his business was flourishing. Brant supposed he should be thankful, for at least he was able to buy most of his essentials from Tanner's agents for less than the exorbitant prices the other merchants were asking.

As the thickening stew boiled in front of him, Brant recalled how disheartening the last six months had been—nothing like what he had expected. First he'd gone to Ballarat, seventy miles west of Melbourne. It had been a small farming community before gold had been found near its cemetery some nine years ago. Ballarat had quickly changed as men of all sorts streamed out to the goldfields. Almost a decade after gold was first struck, there were still fantastic stories of nuggets as big as pigeons' eggs being found, especially in the Red Hill Gully diggings, near the town.

But after two months of wasted effort, Brant and two other men with whom he'd struck up a partnership had decided to move on. They'd heard about the gold strikes at Bendigo, farther to the north, where the gold was rumored to be finer and purer than any of the gold that had been struck in Victoria before, certainly better than any gold from New South Wales. Brant had worked the Bendigo goldfields for six weeks before finding the nuggets that had kept him going for another six weeks. But there had been no more. In disgust, he'd parted from his comrades and had gone to Maldon, a small mining town a few miles to the south.

Located on the slopes of Mount Tarrangower, the town appealed to Brant right away, for it actually had a small high street where merchants had set up shops and services for the miners. Jesus, it had been heaven to have a real bath in a wooden tub with heated water! It had practically cost him an arm and a leg, but it had been worth it. He'd met up with Tanner there and it had been one hell of a reunion!

The next morning reality had set in and Brant had stared bleakly at Tanner, surprised to feel envy at the other's good

fortune. He'd shaken off the feeling quickly. Tanner had always had an abundance of energy—the energy to make things happen. He was not one to go running after a pot of gold at the end of a rainbow.

Tanner had introduced Brant to two new mining partners. Dan Walker was in his forties and had been around the mining towns for five years, trying his luck first in New South Wales and coming up a winner. Unfortunately claim jumpers had grabbed his claim while he'd been gone. Cursing his own stupidity at not having gone in with a partner or two, Dan had tried again in Ballarat, but had had no luck. He'd met Tanner Malone in Maldon and the two had immediately liked each other, striking up a conversation while nursing beers in a pub. Dan was shrewd enough to recognize an honest man when he saw one. He was doubly glad to meet another American, especially another Northerner like himself. Dan was the son of a coal miner in Pennsylvania, so he'd figured he'd been born with an affinity for digging in earth. Along with Dan there was a young man not yet twenty, Jimmy Lang, a Missouri farm boy who'd run away to make his fortune. Jimmy liked to say he was the impartial one between Dan's North and Brant's South. Dan and Jimmy had been working the goldfields outside Maldon and living in the mining camp nearby when Brant had joined them.

Brant smiled when he thought of Dan and Jimmy, feeling a friendship toward each that went deeper than mere companionship. Dan was almost like a father to him and Jimmy like a brother, despite the relatively short time they'd known each other. In a mining camp time seemed distorted and even a month could seem like an eternity.

Knowing how hungry his partners would be after working all day, Brant went into the tent and collected the bowls and tin cups for supper. He knew Jimmy's enormous appetite, evidenced by the strength and girth of the lad, who was six feet five inches tall. Beside him Dan looked like a small man, although he was nearly six feet tall and square-shouldered. Brant peered out into the waning sunlight and caught a glimpse of them walking slowly toward their campsite.

"No luck today, Brant," Dan said, squatting by the fire to warm his hands. Despite his sunburned countenance, with its large whiskers and bushy mustache, Dan had the kindliest gray eyes Brant had ever seen. Their expression was dejected today.

Beside him Jimmy hunkered down, folding his huge frame awkwardly over the heels of his enormous boots.

"Anybody have any luck?" Brant asked hopefully, beginning to dish out the stew. There were no preliminaries to eating—no washing of hands, no taking a moment to say grace.

Taking the proffered bowl from Brant, Dan shook his head. "Nothing." He sighed and sat on the ground, cutting a chunk of bread with a long knife. "Smells damn good, Brant! Hell, it shames me to think you're a better cook than I am! When it's my turn, we can barely get it past our teeth!"

"I learned to cook when my pa and I lived in Boston for five years," Brant returned, his expression sober.

"Sorry, son, I didn't mean to bring back painful memories," Dan said kindly.

"It's not your fault," Brant said, blowing on the hot stew. "I should have written Pa a long time ago. But I hadn't the courage to tell him what a failure I am here—as bad as I was in Louisiana."

"There's a man in Maldon that'll take a letter and see that it gets carried to Melbourne to catch one of the ships to the States," Jimmy offered. He looked sheepish. "I just sent a letter to my folks in Springfield; I lied and told them everything was great."

Dan guffawed, breaking the momentary sadness. "And here I thought I was dealing with an honest man!"

Jimmy reddened to his ears. "I *am* honest with you two. I just lie to my folks!"

"Don't we all?" Brant murmured, then shook off his mood and smiled at his partners. "Well, tomorrow's got to be better than today." He looked up at the darkening sky, knowing how clear it would be, the stars taking on a crystalline quality that was sublime. "It'll be cold tonight. Jesus, I'll be glad to see the spring weather!"

"That's a fact," Jimmy added, between huge gulps of stew. He poured hot coffee into his tin cup and blew on it. "I hate these damned cold nights. Hell, we had our cold nights in Missouri, we even had snow, but at least it was always in December and January, not in the middle of August!"

Dan chuckled. "You'll get used to it after you've been here five years as I have, Jimmy boy."

The thought of being here five more years left Brant with a feeling of emptiness. Despite his earlier resolve not to think of home, he let his mind wander for a moment. By concentrating

hard, he could bring to mind a woman's face. Sweet Constance, he thought. In the year that he hadn't seen her, he'd gotten her and her sister mixed up. Sometimes he remembered Constance having a dimple in her left cheek, but then he would recall that it was Caitlyn who had the dimple. And was it Caitlyn whose auburn hair had smelled so fragrant on the night of that New Orleans party? Or was it Constance who had laughed so enchantingly when he had told stories of his life in Boston? Both sisters merged in his memory, creating the perfect whole that he yearned for. Was it because they were reminders of that golden time of parties and cotillions and lazy summer picnics? He sighed. No doubt the O'Rourke sisters had changed too.

"Hey, you're off somewhere, boy!" Dan's voice interrupted good-naturedly. "Thinking of how you're going to spend all that gold we're going to find someday?"

Brant nodded. "Yes," he said softly. "That's right, Dan."

Tanner Malone leaned back in his chair and rested his legs on the wooden desk in front of him. Behind him, from the open window of his office, he could hear the ships entering the docks, the swearing of sailors too long at sea, and the bumping of crates and boxes being unloaded from the ships anchored in Melbourne harbor. Melbourne lay at the head of Port Phillip Bay, which brought a great influx of goods and passengers into the city, the largest in the colony of Victoria. It was becoming the commercial rival of Sydney, the largest city in the colony of New South Wales. Melbourne was nothing like the great city of Boston yet, but its newness and youthful zeal were precisely what had drawn Tanner to it. There were fortunes to be made, not from the goldfields elsewhere in Victoria, but from commerce and banking in Melbourne itself. Tanner was no stranger to successful moneymaking endeavors. With the right contacts among the authorities and among some prominent citizens and large sheep farmers, it had only taken him six months to establish himself in this place where millionaires were being made weekly.

His business was running smoothly. He had hired several agents to sell imported goods in the mining towns. The miners were hungry for merchandise and were willing to part with their hard-won gold for a clean pair of trousers or a new shirt. Tanner was an honest businessman, but he knew where the money was. He told his agents to use their best selling techniques to persuade

the miners that clean clothes, decent victuals, and a comfortable tent were more important than the gold they found.

Tanner leaned forward to pick up the newspapers that he'd flung onto his desk when he'd come in this morning. A clipper from the States had anchored last night and he'd gone down to the docks, hungry for news. Perusing one paper from Washington, he saw that it was dated May 1860. This paper reported extensively on political events and its editorials praised the attributes of one Abraham Lincoln, who'd just been designated the Republican presidential candidate. Now it was already November and the presidential elections were over; Tanner found it maddening not to know the outcome.

His thoughts turned unwillingly to Louisiana and to a certain family in particular. If Brant sometimes had trouble distinguishing between the two O'Rourke sisters, Tanner did not. That coppery auburn hair and those flashing blue eyes would be memorable under any circumstances, he thought. Along with the strong temper, the indomitable will, and the zest for life, they made Caitlyn O'Rourke a girl impossible for any man to forget.

A knock on his office door was followed by the appearance of Patrick Talbot, his clerk. At sixty-five Patrick was too old to be panning for gold, but he'd come to Australia convinced he'd find his fortune in a week and return triumphant to his native New Orleans. His wife had been dead several years and his two daughters were both married with their own families. Patrick had caught the gold fever, but had found nothing. A bout with influenza had nearly killed him and he'd been more than glad when Tanner had impulsively offered him a job one evening after talking with him in a local pub. Whether it was the Louisiana accent or just a feeling of sympathy for the old man, Tanner had hired him. Despite his age, Patrick had an affinity for numbers and could add up an entire column of figures in his head. Unfortunately his talents did not include recalling names and faces. Patrick would shake his head and joke that there wasn't any more room in his old brain for anything else after the numbers filled it up. Tanner knew that Patrick was really only biding his time, waiting for the day when he'd saved enough money for ship's passage back to New Orleans.

"Good morning, Mr. Malone," Patrick said respectfully, moving into the room with his shoulders hunched.

"I've asked you to call me Tanner, Patrick. Good morning to you," Tanner returned.

"Oh, yes—yes, sir," Patrick said, looking puzzled for a moment. Then he smiled. "I've got these columns of figures finished, sir. Seems you'd be making a damn decent profit if you decided to start exporting Australian wool to England. Rumors of war in the States are making the cotton brokers in London nervous."

"I figured as much," Tanner said, standing up to take the neatly written balance sheets from the older man. He perused them briefly, wondering if he really wanted to get into this any deeper. He was doing well selling goods to the miners. Did he really want to start exporting wool?

"How much have you heard about Seth Wickham?" Tanner asked Patrick. He'd been trying to learn something about the owner of one of the biggest sheep stations in Victoria since he'd met him at a social evening in Melbourne. Seth Wickham had impressed him with his knowledge of world markets for wool and also with his shrewdness. Wickham's sheep station had grown dramatically over the years. Now he needed a middleman to take over the marketing of his wool to foreign ports. He'd already discussed the matter with several businessmen.

"He's a hard man to deal with," Patrick replied. "Rumor has it he came over as a lad on a penal ship from England."

"Thank you, Patrick. You've done an excellent job."

Patrick nodded and shuffled out of the office, inordinately pleased with the praise from his employer. Tanner looked at the balance sheets again. There was definitely good money to be made in wool these days. One of Wickham's problems, though, was lack of labor. For every two men he hired as shepherds, one eventually ran off to the mines as soon as a new gold strike was announced. Without enough men to care for the flocks, dingoes, the wild dogs of Australia, could kill thirty or forty sheep a day, depleting a flock within a week. Tanner would have to think it over, although he was sure Wickham was already hard at work, figuring out the possibilities himself.

Tanner stared at the newspapers. He wasn't really thinking about them, though, for he was recalling the occasion of his introduction to Seth Wickham's daughter, Deborah.

Deborah Wickham was a very interesting woman. Tall and fair with a robust healthiness that lent a blush to her cheeks and a shine to her hair, she was the kind of woman Tanner had always been attracted to. She was an oddity in Australia because she was unmarried at the advanced age of thirty, older than Tan-

ner by five years. In Australia there were so few women in comparison to men that most unattached females were quickly snatched up and made wives and mothers. Deborah seemed not to care for marriage.

At their first meeting Tanner had noticed how knowledgeable Deborah was about the flocks, how her entire face had become animated when she spoke about the sheep station. She was a dedicated woman and was uninterested in Tanner Malone as anything other than a business associate. This attitude effectively spurred Tanner's interest. Still, if he got involved in a business proposition with Seth Wickham, it wouldn't be a good idea to get intimately involved with his daughter.

He ran his hand through his hair. Was he just giving attributes to Deborah Wickham because she reminded him of a certain little chit back in Louisiana? Impossible! Caitlyn O'Rourke was spoiled, rude, and downright nasty when things didn't go her way. Deborah was nothing like her. She was a mature woman with a good head for business. How could he compare the two of them? Damn, maybe he'd just been too long without a steady woman! He'd been so engrossed in his new business and the enormous profits he was making that he'd neglected his private life. A paid woman a couple of times a week didn't take the place of a regular companion. Like many men in Australia, he was experiencing the frustration resulting from the comparatively small number of women in the population. He laughed out loud when he thought of what this country really needed to import—more women! He wondered if Seth Wickham would object to trading his wool for a few stunners from the States!

21

IT WAS CHRISTMAS at Mornhaven, but there was a false gaiety to the festivities, as the O'Rourkes found it difficult to put aside the political turmoil even during the holidays. The usual round of Christmas parties and balls was dominated by talk of war. Lincoln had been elected in November, and Southerners were sure the Republicans wanted nothing less than the destruction of their entire way of life.

While entertaining friends a few days after Christmas, Timothy O'Rourke listened to various opinions about the political

future of the South, much to the dismay of his daughter Caitlyn, who was hoping to lure Darby Howard away from the conversation.

"Papa, must you men talk about politics again?" she whispered in his ear before following the rest of the ladies into the smaller drawing room.

Timothy winked at her and promised that the gentlemen would join the ladies shortly. But even after they did, the gentlemen were not dissuaded from continuing their discussion.

"If war is declared, I doubt they'd have enough volunteers up North!" Winfield Cobb declared in his loud voice, pulling at his mustache determinedly. "We Southerners are better fighters than those Yankees, and we've always relied on personal action rather than law to avenge insult! If the Northerners think they can legislate us out of the right to secession, they're crazy!"

"I agree, Pa, but if we can avoid war, I think it would be in our best interest as well as that of the North," added his son Jesse.

Caitlyn glanced up at Darby Howard and wished he would look at her the way Jesse looked at Constance. She knew Darby had always liked her, but it was understood that he and Mary Bedford, whose father's plantation was on the other side of the parish, were going to be married. Still, a man could change his mind, couldn't he? After all, there had never been a formal announcement. It wasn't too late to get Darby interested in her.

She caught his eye and smiled enticingly. With a bow to the other men, Darby sauntered over to her chair and sat down beside her.

"You're being mighty friendly tonight," he observed, looking appreciatively at the curve of her bosom beneath the silk of her gown.

Caitlyn nodded, smiling in her most flirtatious manner. "You've not been around much lately, Darby. I've missed you."

"Seems to me you've had enough beaux at your feet," he drawled lazily, "without adding me to the crowd."

"The truth is, Darby, I don't have any beaux at my feet," Caitlyn sighed, batting her eyelashes at him. She was pleased by the sparks of interest that flared in his eyes. "It's been quite dull here since Papa decided to cut short our trip to New Orleans this year."

"Darby! Get over here! We need your opinion." It was Artemas calling good-naturedly to his friend. But when Artemas

saw him sitting with Caitlyn, he couldn't help running his eyes appreciatively over her trim figure.

Caitlyn caught the look and it pleased her inordinately. She glanced sideways, hoping Marcella had also noticed the look, and felt quite smug when she saw that she had. Marcella was nearly six months along with child and looked as big as a house. She was one of those unlucky women who do not bear the physical changes of pregnancy well. She had been a trifle plump before the middle stages of her pregnancy, but now she was almost grotesque, her belly swollen like an inflated balloon, while her face was round as a full moon. It was unfortunate for Marcella, but Caitlyn delighted in these changes, wickedly glad to think that Artemas might be having second thoughts about his marriage now.

Still, as Darby left her to join the other males, Caitlyn's momentary pleasure vanished. No matter how much Artemas might hate the changes pregnancy had brought about in his wife's figure, he was still her husband. He could content himself with his cotton and horses until the baby was born. What did Caitlyn have to content herself with? The memory of a kiss or two and a half promise from a man who was too far away now to do her any good.

The rainy winter weather continued through January of 1861 while the political turmoil in the South increased. In quick succession, several states in the Deep South adopted the Ordinance of Secession by wide margins. On January 20 the Louisiana convention assembled in Baton Rouge and voted for secession.

In the next few months a provisional government was established for the Confederacy, Jefferson Davis was selected as its president, and its constitution was drafted and adopted. Meanwhile Abraham Lincoln was inaugurated President of the United States on March 4, under a cold, gray sky that hung low over the skeletal scaffolding on the unfinished Capitol building. The South did not care that his beginning was inauspicious, for it did not consider him its president.

Political events were happening too fast for Caitlyn. Her father talked constantly at dinner about what was taking place in Montgomery, Alabama, the first capital of the Confederacy, but Caitlyn couldn't understand what these events would mean to her. She was more concerned about her eighteenth birthday at the end of March, which passed nearly unnoticed by everyone else.

Caitlyn had convinced herself to be realistic, and had long since given up on the notion that Brant was coming back to rescue her from spinsterhood. It bothered her terribly to wonder what others were saying behind her back about her lack of a marriage proposal. She had wasted her time and love on Brant Sinclair when she should have been cultivating the affections of some of the other local boys. Now most of the boys she'd grown up with were becoming married men. Darby Howard, whom she'd briefly pinned her hopes on, had announced his engagement to Mary Bedford the week before.

To make matters more galling, Marcella delivered twin sons three days after Caitlyn's birthday. Artemas was a proud husband—and a prouder father. How that man liked to fuss over his babies! Caitlyn thought with disgust. Why you'd think he'd had them himself! When he found out he was the father of twin sons, Artemas had immediately forgiven Marcella for her weight gain and the loss of her figure. She had given him not one, but two healthy sons! What more could a man ask from his wife?

During her obligatory visit to the beaming new mother, Caitlyn felt her heart twisting jealously. Why had it been ordained that Marcella should be so happy when Caitlyn was so miserable? Feeling like an intruder, Caitlyn left the room. Most of the women stayed upstairs, cooing over the twins, but Caitlyn wanted to get away from the women. She was positive they all pitied her, and pity was something her proud nature found difficult to endure.

Caitlyn went downstairs to the drawing room, where the men had gathered to discuss their usual topics of secession and war. When she caught her father's attention and asked him when their family would be leaving, Timothy replied, "Not now, puss, I'm discussing important matters with the gentlemen. You run along upstairs and join the ladies. This political talk will only bore you, honey." He turned back to the group of men who were discussing the confrontation at Fort Sumter, in Charleston harbor, a crisis which threatened to explode into war as mid-April approached.

Dejectedly, Caitlyn started back toward the staircase, when she suddenly heard her name spoken by a female voice. Instinctively, she slid beneath the staircase. She placed the voice as that of Mary Bedford.

"Caitlyn O'Rourke doesn't fool anyone!"

"What do you mean?" asked Sally Cobb, Marcella's younger sister.

"I mean the way she goes about as though nothing in the world were bothering her," Mary continued snidely. "Everyone knows she's in danger of becoming an old maid!"

"Caitlyn O'Rourke an old maid! I wouldn't have believed it only two years ago!" Sally exclaimed, shock in her voice.

"Hah! She's been desperate ever since Artemas decided to marry your sister instead of her. And then she tried to take my Darby away from me. Why, she was practically throwing herself at him! Poor Darby was almost taken in. But he told me he knew her heart wasn't in it. She's still pining for that Brant Sinclair!"

"But I thought her sister was in love with Mr. Sinclair," Sally said perplexedly.

Mary's laugh grated so on Caitlyn's nerves that she felt like running out and pulling every hair from her head. That sharp-tongued miss could also use a few nicely placed scratches near her eyes, Caitlyn thought, unaware that tears of mortification were filling her own eyes.

"That's the odd part, Sally. They're *both* still infatuated with him! And neither one with a marriage proposal to show for it! You know the story of how Brant Sinclair just up and ran away. Everyone says he's nothing more than a coward and a Yankee-lover! Look whom he ran away with—that two-faced Boston Yankee, Tanner Malone!"

I can remember how you squealed for a dance with that same Boston Yankee! Caitlyn thought, clenching her teeth to keep from screaming at Mary.

"I recall Mr. Malone as being quite charming," Sally remarked.

"Oh, don't be silly!" Mary returned airily. "*I* never liked the man. I'm only glad I've got Darby now. You know we're supposed to get married in September, but if war comes before that, I'll be Mrs. Darby Howard even sooner!"

The two girls on the staircase started talking about planning the wedding, while Caitlyn stood beneath them, thinking how she would like to put both of them under her carriage wheels and blithely guide her horses to pull the carriage over them.

She had always known how malicious all the girls were around here, but at least she hadn't had it thrown in her face before! Two years ago she had had every boy in the parish at her feet. But look what loving Brant had cost her! What a fool she'd been!

Outraged, but helpless to release her anger, she rubbed her eyes with clenched fists.

Caitlyn was rescued from her situation by the arrival of a horseman who rode up to the house at a gallop. The front door was thrown open and Stephen Carter, who'd been in Baton Rouge that morning awaiting news from Fort Sumter, rushed in, his eyes fiery with excitement.

"It's come! It's come!" he shouted to the men in the drawing room.

Immediately all the men spilled out into the long hall, demanding to hear the news.

"Yesterday the guns of Charleston began firing on Fort Sumter!" Stephen yelled excitedly. "Today Major Anderson surrendered the garrison! The Confederacy is triumphant!"

All the men started talking at once, each one yelling louder than the next in order to be heard. The women were rushing downstairs, demanding to know what was happening.

"Does this mean war?" someone shouted.

"Hell, yes, it means war!" Winfield Cobb shouted back, snorting like a horse who'd been galloping too hard. "War has come and there's no turning back now!"

Caitlyn stood close to her father while the clamor continued. She glanced at Mary Bedford's face, seeing it whiten as Mary realized that *her Darby* would be going off to war soon. Spitefully, Caitlyn felt glad that Mary was frightened and that all the nasty talk about Caitlyn's marriage prospects had flown from her stupid head. Let's see how desperate Mary will be when she finds out Darby won't have time to marry her before going off to join his regiment! Caitlyn thought with malicious pleasure.

These spiteful thoughts vanished from Caitlyn's mind as she suddenly realized what war really meant. It meant all the eligible young men would be going away soon. There'd be no one left to flirt with, to dance with, to entice into a marriage proposal. She looked around her, seeing the excitement in the faces of the men. How stupid they all are! she thought. Do they think war means having afternoon tea with the Yankees? Some of them would get wounded or sick, and some would even die. Even if the war lasted only a few months, there would be casualties. If the men were smart, they'd decide against war and stay at home. She cared little about the cotton, the slaves, and the fighting. War only meant one thing to her—next year she might find herself turning nineteen with nary a prospective bridegroom in sight!

22

BRANT SINCLAIR squatted over the rock and dirt, squinting into the hollowed-out depression that was grown over with scrubby, low-lying plants. It looked promising, he thought.

"Let's try here," he shouted back to Dan, who was carrying most of the mining equipment on his back.

Dan came up to Brant and hunkered down beside him, shrewdly checking out the ground. The depression would be just large enough for a man to go through once it had been dug out. "All right," he agreed. "Let's hope this is it, Brant, my boy." He leaned closer to his friend. "I think Jimmy's about to quit. He hasn't said anything, but I know he's just about out of money."

"Aren't we all?" Brant agreed grimly. He wiped his forehead with the back of a dirty hand. "Hell, if it weren't for Tanner's help, I'd be in Melbourne working to earn ship's passage back to the States."

"Tanner's a good friend," Dan commented.

"Damn right he is—although why he bothers with me, I'll never know. I'll probably never be able to pay him back."

"He doesn't need the money," Dan reminded him.

Brant nodded. Tanner had the magic touch when it came to business. After a year of growing rich selling to the miners, he'd decided to go into the wool-exporting business. Brant wished him luck.

But right now he could use a little luck of his own. He stared at the basin below him. "This is it; let's stake our claim." They proceeded to place a marker on the site, then brought out their shovels and pickaxes. The tunneling would begin today. The basin would be widened and the resulting dirt and rocks carted nearly three miles to be washed in the tributary close to the mining camp.

Wordlessly, both men started to dig. It was June, the beginning of winter in Australia, and the clouds were already gathering, signaling another rainy night.

After two hours of digging, both men paused to wipe their sweating faces and catch their breaths. Brant gave Dan a grim

look. "This might all be a waste of time," he said in a cautionary tone.

"Hell, nothing's a waste of time out here, boy!" Dan returned with fierce determination. "Gold could be behind the next rock!"

Brant was amazed at the enthusiasm Dan could still muster after six years in the mines. Brant wouldn't be able to stay here much longer. His money was nearly gone and he'd established credit wherever he could to get the items he needed. Credit was a dangerous practice out here. If a creditor thought you might not pay him in time, he'd take it out on your hide. It wasn't uncommon for men to find themselves looking at the wrong end of a gun if their accounts weren't settled when the shopkeeper decided to collect. Brant wiped his hands on the thighs of his thick moleskin trousers and rolled up the sleeves of his dark red shirt.

The two men went back to the dirt and rock, scooping up loose dirt and letting it fall through their fingers as they searched for the telltale glint of gold. Larger rocks were put into sacks and would be carried back, pounded, and washed in search of veins of gold within the ore itself.

When night began closing in, both men sank to their knees exhausted.

"Damn! This rock is the hardest we've hit!" Dan exclaimed, mopping his brow with a faded handkerchief. "Do you think it's a wasted effort, Brant?"

Brant shrugged. "Might be, Dan, but I've got to keep going until we decide whether or not there's anything down there." He gestured to the sacks of rocks they'd already collected. "Let's get that stuff back now. We won't have to trek to the stream because it's definitely going to rain tonight. We'll have Jimmy help us crush the rocks and then we'll set them outside."

"All right, I'm all for getting back to camp," Dan said eagerly. "My stomach's so empty now, I've a mind to eat anything Jimmy can dish out, no matter how bad it is!" He guffawed and stood up.

Both men concealed the shoveled area with the plants they'd dug up. Then each took a sack of rocks over his shoulders. Carrying the sacks and the valuable tools, they made their way back to the camp.

Jimmy was awaiting them expectantly, stirring absentmindedly at the concoction he'd made in the iron pot.

"Christ, something smells like a dead horse!" Dan groaned loudly, sniffing the pungent aroma coming from the pot. "Don't tell me we're down to that now!"

Jimmy grinned, not at all hurt by the slight on his cooking abilities. "It's supposed to be lamb stew. I traded one of the shovels for some lamb from one of the other miners. I thought it was a pretty good deal."

"Lordy, if that's lamb, I'm a New York debutante!" Dan joked, sitting down in front of the pot despite his misgivings. "We'll be lucky if we don't wake up with cramps tonight, Jimmy."

"It's better than nothing," Jimmy replied cheerfully. "And who knows, we might really be eating horse meat before we leave this place."

"Which won't be long now," Brant added sourly. He eyed the sacks of rocks grimly. "This stuff had better show something!" He glanced up at the lowering sky. "We'd better eat before it starts to rain," he warned, sitting down beside Jimmy and grabbing a bowl. Absently, he heard his stomach rumble and tightened his belt around his waist. He knew, even without looking in a mirror, that he'd lost weight in the last year.

After dinner all three men took time to lean back on their elbows and relax. There was still rock crushing to be done, but that could wait. Right now they had a good fire, a short pipe, and some long stories to tell. Dan started reminiscing about the first woman he'd ever had. Brant heard his companions, but his eyes were half closed and his mind wandered back to Louisiana, back to his home.

He was sorry Dan had brought up the subject of women. Dan's recollections only reminded Brant of what he had left in Louisiana. It had been a long time since he'd seen the O'Rourke sisters, but that only made them both dearer to him. Surely his memory had been failing him when he'd recalled Caitlyn as greedy and spoiled. Why, she was one of the loveliest and most charming young women in Louisiana! And Constance! The length of time since he'd seen her only endowed her with charms she'd never really had. Brant thought he could remember her vivacious laugh, her seductive looks, the way she'd pressed her body against his when they'd danced together. Was it just his mind playing tricks on him? Had it been Constance or Caitlyn who'd kissed him in the garden with such passion? Brant felt himself becoming physically aroused by these memories. Bru-

tally, he pushed them out of his mind. What good did they do him now? Maldon was too far away for him to go there for the night and hire one of the girls who worked in rooms over the variety shop. Worse still, they wouldn't even hold his hand without seeing the glint of money in it, and he had none to spare for such activities.

A sudden drop of rain splashed on his face, followed by another. He shook himself out of his reverie and sat up, gazing around at his comrades, who'd been lost in their own private thoughts as well.

"We'd better get those rocks broken," he advised with a deep sigh. He was tired now and ready for bed. The idea of breaking rocks hardly appealed to him.

Dan grunted in agreement, and Jimmy stood up and tended to the cookpot and the fire before joining the other two. The rock crushing was hard work and Brant's muscles were aching by the time he was through. He placed his rocks in a long pan just outside the opening of the tent so that no one would steal them during the night. Not that there was much theft these days, but he wasn't taking any chances. Dan and Jimmy did the same with their rocks and it was finally time for bed. The rain had slackened a bit, but all three men were thoroughly soaked.

"Damn, I'm too tired to change," Brant yawned. "I'll get the lantern." He walked out to the cookfire, which had already been put out by the rain, and grabbed the lantern that Jimmy had hung on a long pole. Wearily, he walked back toward the tent, passing the rocks as he did so.

Suddenly Brant stopped in his tracks, all his senses becoming sharply alert. Was that a glint of something he'd seen in those rocks? The dim light of the lantern had hit on *something*—he was sure of it! Squatting despite the screaming pain in his knees, he peered more closely at the rocks, waving the lantern to and fro in an attempt to catch that glint once again. There! It had come again.

"Holy Lord! It can't be!" he whispered to himself. He peered into the opening of the tent, where Dan and Jimmy were nearly asleep. In a shaky voice, he called to them, afraid he was mistaken, but almost sure he had seen something.

"What is it?" Dan's voice was irritable with fatigue.

"Dan, I think I've found something in these rocks!" Brant whispered.

Instantly the other man was awake along with Jimmy, who

didn't even bother to get out of his warm nest of blankets. He simply drew the blankets along with him in his excitement, not caring whether they got wet from the rain.

"Christ Almighty, something's glinting in there!" Dan whispered, watching closely as Brant waved the lantern back and forth over the rocks.

Jimmy put his big paw in among the crushed rocks and picked out a larger stone, holding it up close to the light. There, glinting and sparkling in the lantern's weak glimmer, was a vein of gold neatly bisecting the ore.

"This is it!" Brant said aloud, his excitement growing.

"Keep your voice down!" Dan whispered urgently. "We don't want a crowd following us in the morning or we'll lose it!"

Jimmy's eyes had popped out. "Look here, Dan! See how the vein widens at the end! It's just the beginning!"

"God damn! You're right!" Dan responded, an astonished grin covering his face. "He's right, Brant! Look here!" His gnarled finger pointed along the vein.

Brant looked at the other two men. He could barely contain himself from jumping up and hollering at the top of his lungs, "We've finally struck gold!"

Dan laughed quietly. "No more lamb stew," he said with a wink.

For the next few days the three comrades were kept busy widening the tunnel and bringing out pounds and pounds of rock, much of which continued the vein of gold, widening into small deposits. The gold had to be separated from the ore, washed in a cradle, and then put in a tin dish. It was dried by pouring it into a spade and placing the spade over a fire. Then any dust was blown away and any iron particles were removed by passing a magnet over the gold. The remaining substance was pure gold. It was put into small sacks for easy storage.

Despite the men's efforts to be secretive about their discovery, word soon spread around the camp that gold had been found and other miners hurried close to the claim. Nearly every day shots were fired into the air, indicating that someone else had hit it lucky. It was all Brant, Dan, and Jimmy could do to keep anyone else from digging on their claim. Finally Jimmy was designated as guard to watch over the claim while Dan and Brant went through the tedious process of extracting the gold.

Every day they found more gold within the tunnel, even some

large nuggets lying among the rocks. Brant's excitement built as he envisioned his triumphant return to Louisiana. How eager the New Orleans businessmen would be to do business with him now! he thought vengefully. How avidly the dowagers of New Orleans high society would press their daughters into his arms! How proud his father would be to realize that Brant had become a success after all! And those who had gossiped behind his back and talked about his worthlessness—how they would now smile in his face and tell him how much faith they had always had in him!

Those dreams were quickly buried when one day he heard the news that war had been declared in the States. All around the goldfields, American miners discussed such possibilities as whether the South might be able to bring England into the war or whether the war might already be over. It was maddening not to know. And once more Brant thought of his father and of the O'Rourkes, wondering what was happening to them in Louisiana. Surely the Yankees would never break through to them. Louisiana lay too far west and south. From the first reports that reached Australia, it seemed most of the battles had taken place in the southeast.

One effect of the war news was to cause fights between miners who only days before had been the best of friends. Northerners avowed their hatred of the South, and Southerners proclaimed that their countrymen back home would whip the Yankees before the next year.

Between Brant and Dan there was some initial strain. Neither of them was foolish enough to jeopardize the cooperation that had brought them the riches they'd worked so long for. Comments about the war were kept to a minimum, although Brant, Dan, and Jimmy were all anxious to hear more news.

As the gold piled up in the hollowed-out space beneath the tent, the men realized it was imperative that one of them get the gold to Melbourne. It was safer traded for British pounds than staying here with the risk that some unscrupulous miner might steal it. Straws were drawn and Brant won. Some of the precious gold was traded outright for a decent horse so that Brant could make the eighty-mile trip in good time.

"Don't trust those damned bankers, Brant!" Dan warned him in a low voice. "It'd be better if you took your business to Tanner Malone. At least he'd know where to get you the best price for the gold. I've heard it's up to three pounds sterling for

an ounce now. You be careful while you're in Melbourne, hear?" His weather-beaten face looked up at Brant kindly. "Stay away from loose women."

"They'll go through your money quicker than a Kansas tornado!" Jimmy added.

"I can't promise I'll stay away from them," Brant responded with a grin, "but I won't go near them until I've got the money safely put away."

"Good thinking, boy." Dan stepped back from the horse and saluted Brant.

"Just remember the particulars to tell us when you get back," Jimmy pleaded. He turned bright red when the other two men laughed at him. "Well, damn it, I'm hoping to draw the long straw myself next time!" he added.

"I'll be back as soon as I can," Brant promised, urging his horse forward. He waved at his partners until he saw them disappear into the tent. He chuckled to himself, realizing that he would miss them dearly while he was gone.

"Brant!" Tanner came around from behind his desk to shake his friend's hand. "Damn, it's good to see you! What brings you to Melbourne?"

"Gold, Tanner!" Brant proudly opened his saddlebag and let the sacks of gold fall onto Tanner's desk.

"Holy Lord, how much have you got there?" Tanner demanded, staring at the amount before his eyes. "I'd say you're filthy rich!"

"There's more where that came from," Brant said confidently. "I've come to get your help. I don't know another soul in Melbourne and Dan charged me with getting you to help me turn this gold dust into money. No matter how much I detest those damned bankers, I suppose I'm going to have to use one of their banks."

Tanner was struck by the common sense that Brant had acquired during his days in the goldfields. Dan was obviously having a good effect on the young man, who a year ago would have blown every last cent in a wild orgy of spending in the city. Tanner slapped him on the back and asked him to sit down while they discussed the possibilities.

Privately, Brant felt stupid in the face of Tanner's business know-how, the broad network of business acquaintances he had cultivated in Melbourne, and his commercial contacts reaching

all the way to Sydney. Brant, who had never had a good head for business, felt out of his league as Tanner blithely discussed the merits and demerits of certain banking institutions.

"So what do you think?" Tanner asked, eyeing Brant with interest.

Brant was at a loss. "Whatever you say is fine with me," he answered after a moment's hesitation.

Tanner noticed the perplexed look on his friend's face and nodded. "All right, I'll send a message to Miles Binghamton. I'll ask him to meet with us in the morning. He owes me a favor or two. Meanwhile we'll store your gold in my safe here." He gestured to a formidable-looking iron box behind his desk that was secured to the floor. "And we'll celebrate tonight!" He smiled at Brant. "We'll go back to my rooms at the hotel and you can have a good hot bath and borrow some decent clothes." He laughed as Brant's brows rose indignantly. "Frankly, my friend, you stink to high heaven and I don't think one of the young ladies I have in mind will want to have a drink with you, much less sex, if you don't do something about it!"

Brant felt himself blushing. In over a year in the goldfields, his sexual contacts had been limited to a few encounters in small, airless rooms over the variety shop in Maldon. The women who serviced him there were just as dirty and smelly as he was, but it hadn't bothered him. Why should they take the trouble to wash and spend precious money on expensive perfumes, when none of the men bothered to bathe?

True to his promise, Tanner took Brant to one of the most expensive brothels in Melbourne. Bankers, attorneys, even judges were known to visit Mrs. Wellington's on Bourke Street, which was located conveniently close to where the new Victoria House of Parliament would be. Mrs. Wellington liked to say that some of her best clients came from the government and she intended that they should not have to go far to get to her establishment.

Upon seeing Tanner Malone arrive with his guest, Mrs. Wellington came out of the main parlor to greet Brant. She was dressed in subdued shades of purple, from her silk dress to the lavender-dyed ostrich feathers in her graying hair. As regal as a queen and as sedate as if she'd just come from a Parliamentary meeting herself, she put her hand out to Brant and he took it in his, brushing a kiss on the knuckles.

"Good evening, Mr. Sinclair. I would like to extend my

warmest hospitality to you. On behalf of my entire staff, may I say that we all hope you will find your stay with us quite hospitable. Any friend of Mr. Malone's is most welcome here. However, I would like to point out the rules of the house, if you will be so kind as to lend me your attention."

She came forth with a list that would have drawn a chuckle from Brant had he not been distracted by the array of lovely young women who were staring at him frankly from the interior of the main parlor. He felt as green as Jimmy Lang. One of the young ladies came out to the foyer and led him back into the parlor. Turning around to look for Tanner, Brant saw him heading up the gracefully curving staircase with a stunning brunette on his arm.

Unable to keep himself from gulping loudly, Brant stared at the bevy of beauties before him. Each was lovelier than the last. And to think that he could have any one of them! He could smell their perfume, hear the gentle murmuring of their voices as they talked quietly with other guests. It could have been a dinner party in Louisiana, he told himself in surprise. And, imagining that it was, he looked around for one particular type of young lady. He saw a young strawberry blonde with demure features who was sweetly plump and not too tall. She looked away from his gaze as though she really were sitting in the parlor back home, pleasantly excited at his gentlemanly attention. Feeling his boldness returning, Brant ignored the others and made a beeline for the one woman who reminded him of Constance O'Rourke.

"Good evening." He was the first to speak, bowing formally in front of the girl as though he were about to ask her to dance.

"Good evening, sir." Even though she spoke with the cockney accent of London's slums, that could not break the spell for Brant. Obviously she'd been some fallen blossom plucked from certain drudgery or death by Mrs. Wellington upon her arrival in Melbourne. If Brant concentrated hard enough, he might be able to believe that he really was back home and that the young lady who was smiling so prettily at him was Constance O'Rourke. Knowing that she was his to command gave him a pleasant sense of anticipation that only whetted his appetite to see this fantasy through.

"You are free?" he asked her, and when she nodded demurely, he inquired, "What is your name?"

"I am whomever you want me to be, sir," she returned, delighting him further.

"Then I'll call you Constance, and you may call me Brant."

"Have you supped, Brant?" she asked, standing up to take his hand.

He shook his head and allowed her to lead him into another room, where food had been set out on tables. He saw cold roast beef, ham, meat pies, beautifully decorated pastries, and desserts. Everything looked mouthwatering and, with only the slightest feeling of guilt that his comrades at the mine were still making do with Jimmy's lamb stew, Brant filled a porcelain plate with as much as it would hold. The girl laughed softly, commenting on what a fine appetite he had and that she hoped his appetite for other things would prove as large.

After they'd eaten with a minimum of small talk, the girl tilted her head to one side and smiled mischievously. "Something to drink now?" she suggested.

Brant looked into her eyes, noticing that they were really nothing like Constance's soft blue ones. Instead they were a light yellowish green like the eyes of some nocturnal animal. Their expression was that of a creature smelling prey in the distance.

"Whiskey," he said brusquely. He was sorry he'd picked this girl now. Perhaps the petite blonde would have been a better choice, or one of the taller girls—the one with coppery hair who had looked at him with a boldness that had made his groin tighten. But, no, she looked too much like—

"Here's your whiskey, Brant," came the girl's voice, soft and demure once again. She batted her eyelashes at him appealingly.

Brant took the drink. And another. He kept drinking steadily until Mrs. Wellington came in at a signal from the girl, her lavender ostrich feathers waving gracefully.

"Mr. Sinclair, Tricia tells me you've been neglecting her sorely this evening. Don't you think it's time to go upstairs and show her how much you've enjoyed her company?" Her smile was gracious, but there was a hint of steel in her eyes. She knew that if all her customers drank so much before bedding down one of the ladies, there'd be no liquor left—and it was damned expensive stuff!

"All right, then. Which way?" he mumbled.

Mrs. Wellington patted him on the head like an obedient dog. "That's very good, Mr. Sinclair. Tricia will show you the way now."

"Her name is Constance!" he said loudly. "Or is it Caitlyn?" He stared drunkenly at the girl, who seemed to waver in front of him. She looked demure enough standing there with her hand extended to assist him from the chair, but was she secretly laughing at him? "Don't laugh at me, Caitlyn!"

"I'm not laughing at you, Brant. I'm Constance, remember? I would never laugh at you!" Despite the money she knew she would get from this one, Tricia was fast becoming irritated with his manner. She had endured her share of drunken sots in the London flat she'd shared with her two sisters before she'd been shipped to Australia for petty theft. Once here, she'd served out her eighteen months and had been lucky to find Mrs. Wellington, who'd been willing to forgive her past and to train her to be a well-bred courtesan.

"Constance," he was saying morosely. "You're sure you're Constance, not Caitlyn?"

"Come along with me," Tricia coaxed. She took his arm and pulled him out of the chair, leading him toward the stairs. She would just as soon have left him in his seat, but she knew her reputation was on the line if she couldn't win this battle. Mrs. Wellington was watching her like a hawk.

Brant was becoming more docile and finally consented to have her lead him upstairs to the hall above. Gently, she took him into one of the rooms and shut the door. The room was almost virginal with its white dimity curtains at the window and the white satin coverlet on the bed. Besides the large four-poster, there was a small writing desk with a quill pen and stationery laid out.

Noticing his interest, Tricia smiled prettily. "Sometimes my customers ask me to write letters for them. Mrs. Wellington taught me beautiful penmanship. It's one of the services we offer."

"You write letters?" Brant was surprised. He laughed unkindly. "I've never known a well-educated whore before." He was thinking of the ones in Maldon who could barely write their own names.

His careless insult infuriated Tricia. "We are human beings with other talents besides the ones we practice in bed!" she exclaimed, losing her temper for a moment.

He blinked drunkenly at her. Who was this strident young woman? Why was he here with her? She was nothing like Constance. He had never seen Constance angry, had never heard her

raise her voice to yell at a friend or scold a slave. "Who are you?" he asked. "You're not Constance." He looked at her suspiciously, his brain befogged with drink. "I've never been to bed with Constance."

"That's too bad, dear. Come to bed with me and you can pretend it's Constance." Slowly, Tricia began to undress, pulling off her clothing in a practiced ritual of seduction that heightened Brant's foggy senses. When she came to her underclothing, he held up his hand to stop her.

"You aren't Constance!" he said. Backing away from her, he sat down heavily on the bed, his head in his hands, crying drunkenly. "You aren't Constance! God, if only you really could be her! If only she could be here now!"

Tricia gazed down dispassionately at the man before her. He was wasting her time and God knew time was something Mrs. Wellington heartily disapproved of wasting. He was caught up in memories of some sweetheart back home. She suddenly thought of an idea.

"Dear, why don't I write a letter to Constance for you?" she suggested, kneeling in front of him and pulling his hands away from his face. She gestured to the desk. "Come on now, love. If it'll make you feel better, I don't mind."

"Write to Constance?" He looked blearily at her. "Could you really do that for me?"

"Of course, dear. Just give me the address and tell me what to say. I can even post it for you," she purred, pleased that she'd finally hit on something that had brought him out of his drunken fog.

"She lives near Baton Rouge, in Louisiana."

"In the States, is it?" Tricia smiled and walked over to the desk to pick up the pen. "And what would you have me say, love? I'll tell her how much you love her and how very much you want to see her again soon."

"Yes, yes," Brant said, excitement coursing through him. "Tell her how much I love her—how I'm going to make her my bride as soon as I can—how much I need her with me now! And tell her I've struck gold!" His eyes were bright with drunken excitement. Oh, God, how he needed her! He needed her warmth and her sweetness and her passion—God, yes, her passion! "Caitlyn!" he sighed, involuntarily reminded of the passion in her kisses.

"Caitlyn, is it?" Tricia cocked her head, wondering about the switch in names. "I thought you said her name was Constance."

"Caitlyn? No, no, not Caitlyn. She's—she's nothing like her sister Constance. Send it to Miss Constance O'Rourke."

Tricia labored over the love letter for a few more minutes, embellishing it with some original flourishes of her own. When she was satisfied, she folded it neatly and laid it on the desk. "Now, Brant," she said softly, standing up and eyeing him as he sat on the bed, his cheeks flushed with a combination of drink, excitement, and crying. "You're a right handsome lad, you know, and I've a mind to see what's waiting for me beneath your trousers." She walked slowly toward him. She had played his game long enough, and now it was time to earn her money and get him out so that she could grab another paying customer before quitting time.

"You—you're not really Constance, are you?" he asked plaintively.

Tricia shook her head slowly and let her wet tongue play around her lips as she came nearer to him. "No, I'm not Constance, Brant. But I'll be Caitlyn for you. Come on now. I'm Caitlyn and I'm waiting for you to love me, Brant. Come close, my love, and feel how soft and smooth my skin is." She held out her white arms, smiling confidently when he rose to stand in front of her. "Hold me, Brant," she pleaded.

"Caitlyn—yes, that's better," he murmured, burying his mouth in her fragrant neck. "Constance was all wrong." He laughed drunkenly. "I always knew you were a whore, Caitlyn. That's why I could never bring myself to marry you, my poor darling. Your passion for living—I could never really understand it."

She was probably too damn good for you, you bloody sot! Tricia thought with disgust. Here he was mewling about what a whore she was, and what was he going to do but take advantage of it. Tricia's mouth turned down sourly, even as she clasped Brant against her ample bosom and felt his mouth groping drunkenly down the front of her corset cover.

"God, but you are sweet—sweet!" he was murmuring, his hands automatically seeking to push down the undergarments that were keeping him from his prize. "My poor Caitlyn—how could you know that I was lying to you?"

He continued to mumble drunkenly until Tricia was able to extricate herself from his arms and peel off her undergarments.

"Come along, duck, let's get your clothes off now," she murmured, her hands working quickly and expertly among the buttons and fastenings of his clothing. Male clothing had long since lost its mystery for her and she could have undressed him blindfolded. When he was naked, she stepped back to see what she'd caught this evening. Cocking her head, she let her eyes roam deliberately over him. Quite a looker, she thought, even though he was only at half-mast.

Brant was blinking at her, swaying a little on the balls of his feet. When he tried to catch her in his arms again, she slipped away from him, laughing tormentingly. "Catch me, Brant!" she sang out huskily.

Brant lumbered awkwardly after her, but she continued to elude him, pirouetting gracefully while he nearly went mad trying to catch her. The excitement of the chase was having an effect on his sexual arousal too, for as Tricia had hoped, he was now fully ready to perform.

"Stop playing games!" he pleaded, raising both hands to his head. "Come here, you little minx!"

"Oh, but you must catch me, love! Come and catch Caitlyn!" Tricia laughed. After all his insults, she wasn't going to make it easy for the bastard. Spinning artlessly around the room, she laughed as Brant called to her to stop. He put his hands to his head, feeling dizzy watching her.

"What's the matter, love, don't you want to play games anymore?" she asked sweetly, coming close to brush his face with her hands.

More swiftly than she thought possible in his state, he grabbed her hands and pushed her backward onto the bed. She slapped him playfully, trying to arouse him further, but it only served to make his head hurt even more.

"I'm—not very good—at—holding my liquor," he warned her.

She saw his face whiten suddenly. With a cry of alarm, she tried to get out from under him, but before she could push his weight off her, he was sick all over the bed, emptying his stomach of the rich food it wasn't used to.

"Jesus Christ, you bloody sot!" she screamed, trying to avoid the wet mess next to her. "You've ruined my new coverlet. Get off me, you bloody bastard!" She pushed him with all her strength and he fell away from her weakly, sliding to the floor in a drunken daze. "You stupid lout! Look what you've done!" she continued. "Damn, old Wellington will take this out of my

pay!'' She was so mad she would have killed him had there been some instrument at hand. Furious, she threw open the door and yelled for one of the maids.

When one finally arrived, Tricia was still fuming, glaring murderously at the man on the floor.

''It smells bloody awful in here!'' the maid observed. ''What in God's name have you done to the bloke?''

''Nothing!'' Tricia said through clenched teeth. ''Not one damn thing, but he's done plenty! I only wish there were some way—'' Her eyes darted about the room for something to spend her rage on and lit upon the folded letter on the escritoire. She had intended to throw it away the next morning, but now she saw the means to take revenge on him for what he had done to her.

''Clean up this mess,'' she directed the maid, ''and then get his friend to cart him out of here—but give me a minute. There's something I've got to do.'' Smiling wrathfully, Tricia went to the desk and selected a clean sheet of paper. She copied her first letter exactly, but changed the name of the woman to Caitlyn. Signing the second letter simply Brant, she perused it quickly, then folded it and put it into an envelope, which she sealed and addressed to Miss C. O'Rourke.

23

BRANT AWAKENED the next morning, his head aching and his mouth feeling like it was full of sand. How he'd gotten to a hotel room he had no recollection, but he did remember someone screaming at him in a rage. After that everything had gone blank. Sitting up shakily, he peered about the room. He noticed the clothes Tanner had lent him, newly cleaned and pressed and lying on a chair; then a white rectangle caught his eye, and when he leaned over he saw it was a sealed envelope addressed to Miss C. O'Rourke. Yes, now he recalled that cockney whore writing a letter for him. For a moment Brant was tempted to tear up the letter. He wasn't worthy of asking Constance to be his wife. Better that she think him dead!

But then, thinking of the bleakness of life in the mining camp and of the monotony of tunneling and crushing rock to extract the gold, he felt nausea returning for a moment. He lay down

on the bed, clasping the envelope tightly against him as though it were a talisman to ward off his desolation. Would Constance be able to lighten the arduous days and dreary nights here in Australia while he made his fortune? Could he ask her to go such a great distance to be with him? Would her father even let her go? He doubted it—and yet he felt compelled to tell her how much he loved her and needed her.

A knock on the door interrupted his thoughts and he sat up once more. "Who is it?"

"It's Tanner, Brant. You up yet?"

"Hello, Tanner." Brant got up and opened the door, never so glad to see a familiar face. He returned to bed as Tanner walked into the hotel room.

Tanner was dressed impeccably in a dove gray coat and cream-colored trousers. With his sun-browned complexion and his startling blue eyes beneath dark brows, Tanner Malone looked fit and prosperous this morning, Brant thought, envying his friend's self-assured air. He couldn't imagine Tanner ever getting sick all over a woman's bed. He couldn't even imagine Tanner in bad health. Brant felt a flash of jealousy, but then he thought of Constance. At least Constance was his. He leaned back on the pillows, smiling weakly as he clutched the envelope tightly again.

"God, what a fool I made of myself last night!" he said, sitting up in bed.

"It was almost funny the way poor Tricia was carrying on, screaming her head off and cursing you out in her best cockney," Tanner replied, sitting in a chair and crossing his legs comfortably. He glanced at Brant, who didn't seem to think it funny at all. "Look," he said, leaning forward in the chair, "don't worry about it. You could go back there tonight and wave a hundred-pound note in her face and she'd take you back with open arms. It's just a business to them, nothing personal."

"I know. But I need something more, Tanner. I need Constance here with me. The mine is going to be bringing in more gold every week. Why do I have to wait until I get back to the States to have her with me?"

"You forget there's a war going on there," Tanner reminded him earnestly. "You don't even know the entire situation. The latest news I've been able to glean is already three months old. At that time Lincoln had every intention of bottling up New Orleans harbor. Everyone there is probably landlocked by now."

"Maybe," Brant returned thoughtfully. "But maybe the South's proving more tenacious than you'd suspect, Tanner."

"Tenacity is one thing, Brant, but superior arms are quite another. You know as well as I do that the North has more ships than the South. And more weapons and troops. The South may have more arrogance, but that's not going to win battles, my friend."

"But, Tanner, there might still be a way to get Constance out. There are bound to be plenty of private vessels running through the blockade to bring in necessities from England and France. Lincoln can't possibly have plugged up all the holes with his gunboats."

"Would you want Constance to take that kind of risk?" Tanner asked reasonably.

"But I need her!" Brant protested selfishly. "Maybe you can go on visiting a whorehouse every night, but I can't afford to, nor would I want to! I should have married Constance when I had the chance and taken her with me to Australia. But I had half promised Caitlyn—well, that is, I had led her to believe—"

"What had you led her to believe?" Tanner demanded.

Brant couldn't quite meet his friend's eyes. "Caitlyn thought I was going to ask her to marry me once I got Riverhouse on its feet. I should never have let her believe that."

"Did you actually propose to her?" Tanner couldn't help thinking of the blow it would be to that proud and headstrong girl if she found out it was Constance whom Brant really wanted to marry. She had always been so sure of Brant's love for her, so positive that it was she who would make him the proper wife. He remembered how she'd swallowed her pride to ask him for a loan to help Brant keep Riverhouse going.

Brant shook his head. "Not in so many words, but the circumstances were such that she may have thought—"

"She only thought what you allowed her to think," Tanner said acidly. He folded his arms and looked at Brant, trying to keep his temper in check.

"Damn it, don't sit in judgment of me, Tanner!" Brant burst out. "You can't tell me you haven't used women for your own purposes. I suppose your visits to Mrs. Wellington's are just in the interests of charity!"

Tanner got up from the chair and walked to the window to look out at the cloudy sky above and the busy streets below. Off in the distance, he could see the tall masts of the clipper ships

in the harbor. How could he bother himself about Brant and his problems with women? He had enough of his own, for he'd made absolutely no headway with Deborah Wickham. And a fling in bed with one of Mrs. Wellington's girls was not food for a man's soul.

"Well, at least I can send Constance a letter," Brant said reflectively. He eyed the envelope, then swiftly looked up to face Tanner's back. Damn! He'd send the letter despite Tanner's reservations. Let Constance make up her own mind! At least she'd know how he felt about her! And she'd be waiting for him when he returned to Louisiana a rich man! "I've got to write my father and tell him I've finally struck gold! I can get a letter off to the O'Rourkes at the same time."

"I hope overseas mail is getting through," Tanner said.

Brant looked crestfallen. "Yes, I hadn't thought of that. Perhaps I could pay someone to carry the letters for me."

"Patrick!" Tanner swung around from his perusal of the cityscape. "I'd almost forgotten that my clerk, Patrick Talbot, is sailing home to New Orleans shortly. As soon as he heard about the war, nothing I could do would induce him to stay here. It seems he's determined to be with what's left of his family now that war has come. He'll carry the letters back with him and deliver them to Paul Savoy's house." Tanner smiled to himself. "I'll have him carry some business letters to my agent in New Orleans. The business is probably all but shut down, but at least my agent may be able to save some of it. If the North takes New Orleans, he'll assure the soldiers there's a Yankee behind the business."

As Tanner hurried from the room, Brant was overtaken by a sudden excitement. No matter which way the war was going, at least Constance would know how much he loved her, how much he wanted her. He'd send her letter as is—he may have been drunk last night, but he remembered the heartfelt words of love he had spoken while thinking of his bride-to-be. Picking up the envelope, he kissed the front of it, then laughed at his own foolish action and got out of bed to put on the clothes that Tanner had lent him.

Caitlyn O'Rourke stood with her sister and her parents, singing one more chorus of "Rally Round the Flag," feeling as though her throat would turn to sandpaper if she had to sing another thing. The group at Winfield Cobb's house had already

been obliged, at old Winfield's urging, to sing "Dixie" and "The Bonnie Blue Flag," interspersed with rebel yells at appropriate intervals. Letting her eyes slide around the gathering, she could see Marcella Cobb Blair, toting a twin on each hip, her face sincere as she sang from the heart. Her husband, Artemas, was in a Louisiana regiment that had been sent to Virginia, where most of the fighting was. She worried every day that something would happen to him. Already, the parish had lost seven of its sons to the Yankees and the reality of this war was beginning to sink in. Even Winfield no longer spoke of licking the Yankees in a few months. It was just after New Year's 1862 and the war was dragging on with many losses on both sides. Captain David G. Farragut, the commander of the Union expedition against New Orleans, was mounting an attack on Ship Island below the city. His aim was to control the Mississippi River and cut the Confederacy in half. Already, the Union ship U.S.S. *Brooklyn* was anchored off the mouth of the Mississippi inaugurating the blockade that prevented ocean vessels from reaching New Orleans, the largest Confederate port. Because of the blockade, basic commodities had become scarce and prices had soared accordingly. A box of soap had jumped from five dollars to nineteen and flour was twenty dollars a barrel.

Looking out the window of the large drawing room, Caitlyn could see Winfield Cobb's distant acres of cotton, tended by field hands. What good was cotton now? she thought in disgust. They couldn't eat cotton and the Confederacy had put an embargo on selling it to European countries, hoping that Europe would become desperate enough to come to the aid of the Confederacy.

"My fellow Confederates!" It was Winfield Cobb's voice ringing out among the assemblage as it had so often in these past months. "It is good of you to come and show your support for our cause. You must forgive my wife the meager refreshments. As you all know, we must all make sacrifices for the cause."

"I'm sick of making sacrifices for the cause!" Caitlyn whispered to her sister behind her hand. "The worst sacrifice is the lack of young men around here! They're all off fighting in this stupid war—most of them getting themselves killed. Can you imagine Jesse Cobb shooting a Yankee between the eyes?"

"Sh!" Constance looked at her sister gravely. "Don't mock them," she rebuked her softly.

"Balls of fire, Connie! Don't you start spouting off like old

Winfield up there on his podium!'' Caitlyn fumed. She caught several pairs of eyes staring at her and glared back at them. She was sick of war talk and sacrifices and boys coming back in wooden boxes. Maybe she should be glad she wasn't married— at least she wouldn't wind up a widow. When the war was over, the men coming home would want women who had never been married, not sorrowing widows with kids hanging onto their skirts!

Finally, when the speechmaking was over, the assemblage moved en masse to the dining room where a meager repast was laid out. Polite conversation was interspersed with eager suggestions about how to win the war and heated debates over when the Yankees were likely to surrender.

''Surrender!'' Timothy O'Rourke's mouth turned down sourly as he repeated the word in an undertone. ''Lincoln's not going to surrender! He wouldn't want to go down in history as the last president of the whole United States! No, he'll try to keep the South glued to the North no matter what it takes!''

William Sinclair, who had ridden over with the O'Rourkes, was looking exceptionally frail, but he was still alive, determined that nothing would take Riverhouse away from him while he had breath in his body. He'd had to sell most of his slaves again and had only been able to plant a few acres of cotton. He still clung to the belief that Brant would return someday with the money to save Riverhouse. Unfortunately there was now another threat—from the Yankees. ''Maybe we can work out a peaceful settlement to the war, Timothy,'' he suggested hopefully.

Timothy shook his head. ''Blood's been drawn. I'm afraid it's a fight to the death, William. I can't imagine Winfield Cobb signing an armistice, nor any of the other regional leaders in the South.''

William murmured sadly, ''It's shameful to waste human lives like this. Strong sons of the South are being killed and maimed every day! If all our strongest are killed, who will be left to continue our Southern legacy?''

Margaret nodded toward Marcella's twin boys, who were crawling around on the floor, endearing themselves to the ladies in the group. ''There is the South's legacy, William,'' she said softly.

William looked at the babies and moisture filled his eyes for a moment. ''I wish I had grandsons,'' he said. Catching himself, he wiped his eyes and changed the subject. ''I'm only glad Brant

isn't here to be sent off to some senseless battle. Better to be alive and labeled a coward than to be a dead hero!''

Caitlyn gazed at him in surprise. It was the first time William had mentioned Brant in a long time. Constance went over to him and patted his arm affectionately.

''I'm sure we'll hear from Brant soon, Mr. Sinclair,'' she said sincerely.

William looked at her gratefully. Caitlyn, unconsciously jealous of the affection between her sister and the father of the man she herself had once thought she loved, turned away to talk to Mary Bedford Howard. Mary had married Darby pell-mell when Darby had received orders from his regiment. Caitlyn didn't like Mary and would never forgive her for insulting her that day at Blair House, but it was better to talk to her than to see William and Constance conversing gently together.

After a few minutes, she turned away from Mary and made her way through the crowd to the veranda outside. God, it was so hard, she thought, and so unfair! Why was she all alone, without anyone? At least Marcella had her twins and Mary would have her baby soon enough. She had no one! She and Constance were the sole misfits of the parish, she thought—and Constance didn't even care! It was sickening the way she clung to the absurd belief that Brant would come back. If he hadn't come back by now, he wasn't going to come back with the war in full swing! Brant was a coward! Caitlyn enjoyed saying it to herself; she only wished she were brave enough to shout it out loud to William and Constance as they huddled together in their shared loyalties.

Petulantly, Caitlyn flopped unceremoniously into a chair on the veranda, feeling the unusually warm January day close around her. Moodily, she stared out at the front lawn, hating Brant for running away to Australia and leaving her behind. Hating him for not marrying her before he left. At least she would have had *something*! Now she had nothing. Nothing but the snide whispers of the girls who had married before their boys went off to war and the pitying stares of the older women.

''*Why* did you leave me, Brant?'' she whispered softly, closing her eyes as tears wet her lashes.

She dried her eyes, ashamed of her momentary weakness. She couldn't let herself love Brant anymore. He had abandoned her shamefully. Not even one letter in all these months! Even William hadn't heard from him!

"Caitlyn, there you are!" It was Margaret looking for her, concern showing on her face. "Is there something wrong, my dear? Are you all right?" She sat down in a chair next to her daughter, looking at her with an affection that would continue even if Caitlyn reached forty and had never had a marriage proposal.

"I was such a fool, Mama! Why didn't I listen to you and Papa? I wasted everything on Brant when I could have found someone else."

Margaret looked reflective. "Call it fate or destiny, my dear, but many things happen in our lives that we don't wish to happen. This war is something no one really wanted except the rabid secessionists, and yet they have dragged us all in with them." Margaret looked out over the green lawn of the Cobb plantation with a faraway look in her eyes.

"If we win the war, everything will be like it was before," Caitlyn said hopefully.

"No, Caitlyn, we'll have to become more self-sufficient. We must build factories and develop industry in our cities. We'll become more like the North, more like those people we profess to hate."

"But don't you hate the Yankees, Mama?"

Margaret stared levelly at her daughter. "You forget that my mother—your grandmother—is a Yankee from Boston," she told her. "I have cousins who are fighting in this war on the side of the North." She looked away and sighed, "The world is surely turned upside down."

Caitlyn nodded, her thoughts returning to her personal dilemma. "It certainly *is* upside down when Marcella Cobb can be married with twins and I'm without a husband!" she sniffed haughtily.

24

LATER IN JANUARY the O'Rourkes received unexpected company in the person of Sean Flynn, an old friend of Timothy's from the Mexican War. His arrival was an excuse to relive, if only for a little while, those happier times before the War between the States. But Sean was in the Confederate army now, and the news

he brought was far from happy as he sat and talked with Timothy on the veranda.

"The South's doing well now," Sean said, "but that's only because the North has idiots running its army. The South's got better officers and better tactics, but the North has more men. All they have to do is keep throwing more troops at us until we have no one left to stand them off. It's a war of attrition."

Caitlyn, who'd brought out cold drinks for the men, set her pitcher down and then seated herself in an old wicker chair, leaning forward to listen to the conversation. She never tired of listening to Sean, who was a wonderful storyteller. On his rare visits to Mornhaven, he'd always delighted her with thrilling tales of Indian fights and scouting expeditions into northern Mexico. With his height and burliness, he'd reminded her of a mountain man, and she'd always felt that with Sean around, her loved ones would be well protected.

Seeing the avid interest on her face, Sean reached over with a sun-browned hand and chucked her affectionately under the chin. "Honey, you're a sight for sore eyes," he said with a quick grin.

"Do you think the South will win?" Timothy asked bluntly.

Sean shook his head. "The South would win easily if it had the proper weapons to fight with and an arms industry to keep manufacturing them. As it is, this war has both North and South rushing pell-mell into the European arms market. Both sides are falling prey to international speculators. We've been able to purchase some new English and French rifles, but the majority are cast-off Belgian, Austrian, and Prussian muskets in such poor repair they're proving inaccurate." He gestured to his own sleek rifle leaning against the doorway. "I took this off a dead Union officer."

"You can't win a war without proper weapons," Timothy muttered.

"The Confederacy will be dependent on imports and captured Union arms for quite some time," Sean continued. "We should all be grateful that there are blockade-runners out there who are able to get through. Unless the South can break the blockade at some point, it'll keep getting tighter and tighter until only a few of the fastest ships will be able to get through."

"You've heard about Farragut laying siege to Ship Island?" Timothy asked.

Sean nodded. "That's something else I want to discuss with you, Tim," he said earnestly. "I'm hoping to convince you to

take your wife and the girls down to New Orleans. I know there's a lot of talk about the Yankees coming up the Mississippi, but believe me, you'd be safer in the city than isolated here at Mornhaven. Union deserters are breaking into plantations along the river.''

"But what if the Yankees reach New Orleans?" Caitlyn gasped, trying not to think of such a possibility.

"You'd still be safer," Sean insisted. "There's always safety in numbers, and with all the young men off to join the war effort, there aren't enough men left out here on the plantations to provide adequate safety. And what if a regiment of Union soldiers reached Mornhaven and told all the slaves they were free?"

"Why, none of them would leave us!" Caitlyn returned stoutly.

Sean shook his head. "Maybe the house slaves would stay, but the field hands would go. You'd be virtually alone and at the mercy of the Yankees."

Timothy frowned and rubbed his chin. "But I can't just leave Mornhaven! I've put my whole life into it!"

"Then send your girls, Tim," Sean admonished him. "It would be for their own sakes."

"Papa, I won't go!" Caitlyn protested. "I couldn't leave you and Mama here by yourselves!"

"Your mother won't leave without me," Timothy said wearily, "but I'm sure she'll agree with Sean that getting you girls to New Orleans would be your best protection. Sean can escort you there."

"I'd be privileged," Sean affirmed heartily.

Caitlyn felt depressed at the thought of leaving her parents during this troubled time. If there was danger, then they should all go to New Orleans.

The next morning dawned all too soon, and there was a sorrowful farewell on the levee as the packet stopped at a signal from Sean. Most of the passengers on board were Confederate soldiers on their way to New Orleans to help shore up its defenses. Their eyes lit upon the two young women with considerable interest, but one stony stare from the massive Sean Flynn and they quickly backed away from introducing themselves.

When they reached New Orleans without incident, Sean saw Caitlyn and Constance safely to the Savoys' house and promised he would try to visit them when he was in the city. Caitlyn waved good-bye to him sadly, worried about her parents and anxious

because of the panic that was in evidence everywhere in the city. Uncle Paul tried to provide reassurance, but Caitlyn could see through his ruse. Everyone was concerned that Captain Farragut would break through their defenses and sail his fleet right up to the city itself. To add insult to injury, one of the Confederate generals had ordered eight gunboats to Memphis to fight the Union navy there, leaving New Orleans with only three thousand troops to defend the city.

In mid-February Farragut's fleet reached Ship Island. Nervous citizens demanded that General Mansfield Lovell provide more troops to defend New Orleans. They complained bitterly that the city had been stripped of most of its protection. General Lovell threatened to impose martial law, which only made the people angrier. Many left the city while they were still able to. Others went from store to store, stocking up on essential items. Aunt Helen, accompanied by Constance and Patricia, went out in the family carriage and bought up everything they might need.

Caitlyn had chosen not to go, preferring to pace restlessly, planning how to make her way back to Mornhaven. One of the Savoys' house slaves came in unexpectedly, holding a packet of letters and announcing a Mr. Patrick Talbot to see Miss O'Rourke.

Curious, Caitlyn took the letters and laid them carelessly on the table. "Please send Mr. Talbot into the small parlor," she instructed the maid. She had hoped to see some fine young man come striding into the parlor, but she was sorely disappointed when a feeble-looking old man made his way into the room and took a seat at her invitation.

"Miss O'Rourke?" he inquired, adjusting his spectacles and peering nearsightedly through them. "Do I have the honor of addressing Miss Constance O'Rourke?"

"You have the honor of addressing Miss Caitlyn O'Rourke."

"Caitlyn O'Rourke? My, my—let me think now! I was almost sure the name was something else, but I suppose—"

"Perhaps you mean my sister?" Caitlyn asked, wondering where this old man had come from.

"You—you have a sister?" he asked, taking out a large white handkerchief to mop his forehead. "My, now I am confused! I confess, Miss O'Rourke, I don't remember anything said about a sister. Mr. Malone gave me the letters and—"

"*Who?*" Caitlyn stood up, whitening at the mention of his name. *Malone!* Did that mean the letters contained information

about Brant? Hurriedly, she snatched the letters that were on the table. One envelope was addressed to William Sinclair and one to her father—but the last! She stared at the unfamiliar hand-writing which had penned the name Miss C. O'Rourke.

"Oh, God!" She dropped into the chair and stared at the envelope, shaking at the thought of what it might contain. Was it news of Brant? Her hands shook so that she couldn't open it. Staring at the old man opposite her, she asked in a trembling voice, "Are these letters from Brant Sinclair?"

"Mr. Malone gave them to me to deliver," he answered. "I do believe there were some letters of a personal nature written by someone else. Perhaps the name was Sinclair." He scratched his balding head perplexedly. "You must forgive me, Miss O'Rourke, my memory—" He opened his hands expressively.

After staring from him back to the envelope, Caitlyn closed her eyes. "Mr.—Talbot, is it? I assume you've come from Australia?" She opened her eyes and leaned forward in her chair.

"Oh, yes, yes, Miss O'Rourke. I've come from Australia, you can be sure. By way of England, of course."

"And how did you come to New Orleans? How did you get past Farragut's fleet at the mouth of the river? How did you know where to find me?"

"Just one moment, if you please," he said, putting his hands up to silence her while he attempted to digest her questions. "In England I was lucky enough to chance upon a clipper ship bound for New Orleans and I booked passage. When we got near land, we sailed somewhere along the coast of Mississippi—or was it Texas?" He shrugged. "At any rate, we were able to anchor offshore and go across in dinghies. I believe there were Union troops quite close because we were hastened ashore with the cargo. In the morning there were wagons to take the cargo to New Orleans and I went along with the rest of the passengers. Quite a jolting ride, I must tell you."

"And how did you know to come here, Mr. Talbot?"

He seemed to think for a moment, then pulled out a piece of paper from his coat pocket. "Mr. Malone—that is, my em-ployer—gave me the address of a Mr. Paul Savoy here in New Orleans. He told me that any letters to the O'Rourkes and their friends would find their way through him."

Of course! Tanner Malone remembered that her uncle lived in New Orleans because he had done business with him. She looked up at the man. "Forgive me for cross-examining you, Mr. Tal-

bot. I've completely forgotten my manners. Would you care for something to drink?''

He shook his head. ''I'm on my way to see my own family, Miss O'Rourke. Would it be possible for you to see that Mr. Malone's correspondence to his agent is delivered? You'll forgive me for imposing on you, but my memory has been quite faulty for some time now. I only want to find my daughter before the Yankees close in on New Orleans.''

''I understand, Mr. Talbot. Can I be of some help in putting you in the right direction? I'll have the majordomo call you a carriage and give your daughter's address to the driver.''

He brightened at the thought. ''That would be nice of you, Miss O'Rourke. And I wish you good news in your letter.''

She smiled at him, all the while feeling her heart beating like a drum. She could barely wait until he was gone to rush up to her bedroom. Throwing herself on the bed, she stared at the envelope, wondering why the writing was so unfamiliar. Unable to contain her excitement any longer, she tore open the envelope and read the letter.

Dear Caitlyn,
My dearest love, I am writing this letter to let you know how much I love you! I have missed you terribly since our last meeting too many months ago. Please forgive me for not writing sooner, my love, but I didn't feel the time was right. Now I have finally found my fortune here in Australia. I've struck gold, Caitlyn! And I want to make you my wife, as I should have done much earlier. Please come to me, my dearest! I miss you! I love you! I know you will find a way!
Brant

Caitlyn continued to stare at the letter long after she'd finished reading it for the tenth time. She couldn't believe it! She hugged the letter to her breast.

''Oh, Brant,'' she sighed, tears falling from her eyes, ''how I love you!'' In her state of excitement, transported by thoughts of Brant's love for her, Caitlyn conveniently forgot how she had sworn to hate him only a short time ago. She forgot her disgust at his leaving her, her derision at his determination to find his fortune in a faraway land. She forgot that he had ever showed affection towards her sister or that she had wondered too many

times if he really loved Constance instead of her. What did it matter now? The letter was proof that he loved *her*!

She sat bolt upright in bed, her mind a whirl of plans. "I'm going to Australia!" she said aloud to herself. "I'm going as soon as I can get out of this city! And those Yankees aren't going to stop me!"

The Savoy household was in a veritable uproar that evening after Caitlyn announced her plans to leave New Orleans and sail to Australia to marry Brant Sinclair. Uncle Paul could only sputter that her father would never forgive him if he let her sail through dangerous waters. Aunt Helen went into one of her tirades, spouting off about the impropriety of a young lady going off to join a young man who had left Louisiana in disgrace. Patricia could only stare openmouthed at her cousin's bold scheme, and Constance tried bravely to conceal her tears.

Constance felt physically ill. She couldn't understand why Brant had asked for her sister's hand in marriage. How could he do that when he had told *her*—in secret—that someday he would prove his love by making her his wife? She had waited faithfully for him for over two years, secure in the knowledge that he loved her. Constance had never felt such devastation in her life. She had never hated anyone as much as she hated Caitlyn when she saw the radiant smile on her face. She had never realized she was capable of such hatred.

Caitlyn was surprised at her sister's reaction. Did Constance think that the slight affection Brant had for her meant so much to him? Brant wanted Caitlyn for his bride, not Constance! Now that he had struck gold, Caitlyn would be better prepared to guide him in his future plans. Riverhouse would come first, of course, but—oh! She tried not to let visions of beautiful jewelry and clothes crowd out her excitement about Brant himself, but it was impossible not to imagine what his fortune would mean. All the humiliation, embarrassment, and pity she had endured for the last two years fell away from her as though it were nothing. She was an engaged woman now! She wanted to make Brant proud of her! And she would certainly see that everyone who knew them looked at them with respect!

"I've got to send a message to your father immediately," Uncle Paul said distractedly. "I can't be responsible for some silly scheme you've thought up to get out of the city when God knows how many Union soldiers are hiding in the bayous! Holy Lord,

with martial law about to be imposed on New Orleans, there is no way you'll get permission to leave the city!"

"Then I'll have to leave before martial law goes into effect!" Caitlyn returned steadfastly. "I'm sorry, Uncle Paul, but my mind is made up. I'm going to join Brant as soon as I can. I'm not going to wait for this stupid war to end!"

Five days later Timothy O'Rourke's voice could be heard from Paul Savoy's downstairs office all the way up to the third floor. His strident tones rang throughout the house as he alternately implored and commanded his daughter to stay in New Orleans and forget about her foolish idea of running off to Australia.

"Daughter, don't be an idiot!" he said bluntly. "You can't just go sailing off! The Yankees are at the mouth of the Mississippi with fifteen thousand troops and twenty mortar schooners. You wouldn't make it to the gulf, Caitlyn. Your ship would be stopped and you'd be captured and God knows what would happen to you then!"

"Papa, I don't have to go down the river. Mr. Talbot told me there are ships dropping anchor off the coast of Mississippi. I could go overland to Biloxi and wait for a ship there."

"The Yankees are close to Biloxi too, Caitlyn. It's just as risky there. Be sensible, child! Even if you were lucky enough to get a blockade-runner to wait in dangerous waters for you to get on board, then what? You'd be sailing with a rough crew to England, where you'd have to change ships. That might require several days' wait in Bristol or Liverpool. You'd be a young woman unprotected! Don't you know you'd be easy prey for any knave that took a fancy to you?"

"Papa, I don't care!" Caitlyn insisted stubbornly. "I want to be with Brant!"

"Brant would wait if he really loved you," Timothy said angrily. He rubbed his eyes with his hands. He hadn't gotten a good night's sleep since the girls had gone to New Orleans—and now to get the news that that irresponsible Brant Sinclair had the audacity to ask Caitlyn to join him in Australia! My God, didn't the man have any idea of the situation in the States?

"Caitlyn, please reconsider," Margaret spoke up cajolingly. "I'm sure that Brant couldn't have known the situation in New Orleans or he would never have asked you to come to him under such circumstances."

"But, Mama, I *want* to go to him!" Caitlyn reminded her.

"I'm not about to lose this marriage proposal because of a little complication."

"A little complication!" Timothy nearly choked. "Daughter, you've lost your mind! That's all there is to it! I'll take you home to Mornhaven and lock you in your room with a guard at the door before I let you set foot on a blockade-runner's boat!"

Caitlyn stood her ground. "Papa, I'll never forgive you if you cause me to miss this chance at happiness!"

"Happiness! My poor darling, do you have any idea of what's awaiting you in Australia? I read Brant's letter to me. He wrote of the primitive conditions in the mining camps and the rough sort of men who inhabit them. What would you have in Australia? You would be alone in the bush!"

"I would be with Brant!" Caitlyn declared, although her father's bleak picture did shake her a bit. By the time she got to Australia, Brant would surely have a fine house in Melbourne or Sydney and she would set up housekeeping immediately. She would make friends easily with other cultured women. And she would have a baby right away, of course.

"Caitlyn, don't you care that you would be leaving us?" Margaret asked softly. "I would be out of my mind with worry over you, my dearest. And how would we know if you had arrived safely? The mails are so uncertain now; in six months' time they could be worse!"

"Mama, I'm sorry, but how can you ask me to give up my chance at happiness?" Caitlyn asked her in return. "All the people I've grown up with in the parish are getting married. I've felt left out, alone. There's no one for me at home!"

"So you're going because you don't want to end up an old maid, is that it?" Timothy growled. "You'll go to be with a man who proposes marriage from thousands of miles away, rather than stay in Louisiana with those who truly love you."

"Papa, no! That's not fair! I only meant that there's no man for me in the parish! Please let me go to Brant! He loves me and he wants me with him. Perhaps he didn't understand the danger, but I'll gladly risk it to be with him. He would never have asked me to come if he hadn't known how much I would want to join him."

Timothy sighed loudly and sat down in a chair. Caitlyn gazed at him with compassion, but could not find it in her heart to give in to him. He must understand her commitment to go to Brant. How could her father expect her to wait in Louisiana for what

might be years? And each year would see her grow older, more undesirable. What if the war continued to drag on and on? Then what? She would be stuck in Louisiana with no options. This was her way to save face. Everyone would think she'd been waiting patiently, faithfully for Brant to ask her to come to him. Despite her love for her family, Caitlyn's love for herself was infinitely greater. This was the only way to redeem her wounded pride—and she would take it! She would!

25

CAITLYN HAD NEVER BEEN so glad to see land as she stood on the crowded wharf in Melbourne, Australia. She gazed around her, tightly clutching her dilapidated valise, which had been considerably lightened since leaving her homeland. All her money was gone except for a ten-dollar gold piece that she had managed to hang on to in case of any emergencies. She tried not to think of that awful six-week voyage she had endured from Biloxi to Liverpool, England. And worse were the memories of her leave-taking from her family. Her mother's eyes had been haunted with concern for her, and there had been such a strange look in Constance's eyes. Was it jealousy? Envy? Their softness was newly hardened by sullenness as she stiffly embraced Caitlyn good-bye.

Papa had taken it well, only because he had gotten Sean Flynn to escort her to Biloxi, where they had arranged to meet a blockade-runner who had agreed to take her to England. An elderly gentlewoman, Mrs. Eudora Lowell, had agreed to act as Caitlyn's chaperone to England. It had been a terrible voyage with Mrs. Lowell's snoring and constant complaining, the rats scurrying about their cabin, and the dreadful food they'd been forced to eat. She was only glad that Mrs. Lowell had seen her settled on board a ship bound for Australia before abandoning her. She had directed Caitlyn to the offices of the White Star Line of Liverpool, where Caitlyn had booked passage on the *Eagle*. The ship would sail to Australia by way of Cape Town, and the entire voyage would take approximately eighty days. Despite her bad experience on the blockade-runner, Caitlyn had looked forward eagerly to starting the voyage, which would be the last leg of her journey.

In Liverpool the news from the States was that martial law had been declared in New Orleans and that the city was in danger of falling to Union troops immediately. Caitlyn was afraid her parents and sister were trapped in the city and hoped they were safe. She had sent a letter to her parents, hoping they would receive it. She had also sent a brief but enthusiastic letter to Brant, telling him how excited she was to have finally arrived in Liverpool and that she would be with him in less than three months. She had included the *Eagle*'s estimated date of arrival in Melbourne, hoping he would be there to meet her.

Once safely on board the *Eagle*, Caitlyn had been delighted to see that sailing on this ship would definitely be a different experience than sailing on the blockade-runner. She had found her cabin quite comfortable and roomy and, best of all, clean. The *Eagle* was a first-class ship almost two hundred feet in length with three decks. Thanks to her father's gold pieces, Caitlyn had been able to secure a private cabin. She had been determined to sail in comfort this time. It would never do to arrive in Melbourne tired and pale. She wanted Brant to see her at her best. After all, they would be married soon after her arrival.

Now, as she stood among the bales and crates on the wharf, she looked around anxiously, hoping to see Brant coming towards her. Surely he would recognize her, she thought, giggling a little nervously. Her first impression of Melbourne was favorable, for the hustle and bustle along the waterfront reminded her of New Orleans. The tall spars of masts and furled sails dotted the sky as she looked out towards Port Phillip Bay, beyond which lay the Bass Strait, which separated Australia from the island of Tasmania. She looked back toward the sprawling city of Melbourne and could see many buildings in various stages of development. Obviously gold fever had made this a growing city.

As she stood alone among the crowd, the only person without a clear idea of where she was going, Caitlyn became aware of someone's slow stare. Her heart beat a little faster as she imagined Brant assessing her with those lazy dark eyes and she turned quickly to search for him among the crowd.

But it was not Brant whose eyes were frankly appraising her. Tanner Malone stood out among the other men in his tan linen suit, a wide-brimmed hat pulled low over his eyes. When he started to walk confidently toward her, she had the wild urge to run away. But steeling herself, she straightened her back and narrowed her dark blue eyes.

"Miss Caitlyn O'Rourke," said that detestable Yankee voice softened only by an Irish lilt. "Who would have thought we would ever meet again? And in Australia of all places!"

"Life is full of surprises," she returned sarcastically, already jumping to engage him in battle. "Certainly I would have hoped not to see you, Mr. Malone!"

"Come now, don't you think we are past calling each other by our surnames? After all, I can still remember your heartfelt plea to me on the morning you came to my hotel room in New Orleans."

"When you almost ruined my chances of becoming Mrs. Brant Sinclair!" she spat, remembering that occasion with emotions far different from his own. "No, Mr. Malone, I truly doubt if we shall ever be on more than the most formal of terms."

"Then you have a lot to learn about Australia, about Melbourne— and about me," he promised with a twinkle in his blue eyes that unnerved her.

After a moment of consideration, Caitlyn looked around. "Where is Brant? I can't imagine him sending *you* to meet me at the pier," she remarked quickly.

"Brant didn't send me. And you should count yourself lucky that I'm here at all. Otherwise you'd be standing here until doomsday! Your letter to Brant with your estimated date of arrival only reached my office this morning. Since I had no pressing business engagements, I came down to the pier to see if your ship had arrived. Once again, fate seems to enjoy throwing us together, Caitlyn." He bowed and smiled with gentle mockery.

Caitlyn was about to reprimand him for using her first name, but realized he was going to do as he pleased. "Then Brant doesn't know I've arrived?"

He shook his dark head. "I'm afraid he has no idea. Why have you come?" he asked her bluntly.

"Since you were so presumptuous as to read Brant's personal mail, then surely he must have told you why I've come," she returned tartly. "Brant wrote to me asking me to come to Australia to marry him."

"He wrote—to you," Tanner repeated slowly. Something was definitely wrong here! Caitlyn O'Rourke was not the name that had been on Brant's lips the morning after the debacle at Mrs. Wellington's. What had happened to bring Caitlyn here instead of Constance? Perhaps Patrick had given Brant's letter to the wrong Miss O'Rourke. Tanner was irritated with himself for

trusting the senile old man with such a delicate mission. Still, the letter itself would have been addressed to Constance.

But here, as he could plainly see, was not the Constance of Brant's dreams, but Caitlyn in the flesh, and she was staring at him with clear frustration. What in hell was going to happen when Brant saw her? Tanner knew that Brant would be unable to hide his confusion. What would Caitlyn think? She was so self-centered that perhaps she wouldn't see the disappointment on Brant's face. Perhaps she would only see what she wanted to see, just as she always had where Brant was concerned.

"Brant is out in the goldfields, Caitlyn," he explained smoothly. "It will take some time to send a message and locate him among the thousands of miners out there. I think it would be best to put you up in a hotel here in Melbourne while we get word to Brant that you've arrived. He will be quite surprised," he ended.

"Surprised, Mr. Malone?"

"I'm not sure he expected you so soon. It's only July. You must have left immediately upon getting his letter. Did Patrick Talbot deliver it in person then?"

"He did. I was at the Savoys' house when Mr. Talbot arrived. Rather a dotty old gentleman, but nice enough," Caitlyn added disdainfully. "He was anxious to find his daughter before the Yankees came upriver. If you don't mind, I would really like to get to my room. I dislike standing out here on the pier."

"I see the long sea voyage hasn't improved your manners, nor your temperament," Tanner observed, his dark brows arching wickedly. "I'm afraid you will find Australia quite different from America, Caitlyn. People don't like young ladies who expect everyone to wait on them hand and foot. You have to make your own way here."

"*I* don't have to do anything of the kind, Mr. Malone," she said primly as he reached down to take her luggage. "I'm sure that once Brant and I are married, we'll be able to afford servants to take care of our needs. I assume he's got property somewhere for the purpose of building a house."

Tanner gazed at her in amazement. "Caitlyn, you truly astonish me! I don't think I've ever met a young woman as arrogant as you!"

"I consider that a compliment, Mr. Malone. Perhaps you aren't used to assertiveness in women, but I assure you that Brant is quite comfortable with it."

Tanner chuckled and shook his head. The girl was full of self-importance. The three years since he'd last seen her had not improved that aspect of her one bit. What she needed badly was someone to teach her a lesson in manners—and he very much doubted that Brant was the man to do it.

Once ensconced in a comfortable hotel room, paid for by Tanner Malone—a fact which irked Caitlyn more than she wanted to admit—she got ready to face the Yankee once again. As she freshened up and changed, she realized that her wardrobe was woefully inadequate now that she'd arrived in Melbourne. Once she and Brant were married, she would have to order a complete trousseau from the dressmaker.

At Tanner's knock, Caitlyn unlocked the door, then called for him to come in as she resumed checking her appearance in the mirror. For a moment Tanner was at leisure to study her. The woman might not have changed emotionally, but she had changed physically. She was taller than he remembered and perhaps a trifle thinner. Her waist seemed slender as a reed, but that may have been because her breasts had grown fuller, straining subtly against the fabric of her basque. He had to admit she was quite a stunner with her coppery red hair and those dark blue eyes that owed a lot to the unusual presence of thick dark eyelashes, quite rare in redheads. What Mrs. Wellington wouldn't give to add Caitlyn O'Rourke to her bevy of beauties! he thought with a chuckle.

"Well, Mr. Malone? I have endured rats, bugs, sea storms, and poor food during my voyages. Must I now endure your silent scrutiny on top of all that?" she asked, turning and finding him eyeing her.

He frowned. "I would have thought you'd enjoy a man's scrutiny," he answered boldly.

"Only if the man is going to be my husband—which you definitely are not, Mr. Malone!" she retorted quickly.

"And I thank heaven for that!" he retorted in kind, enjoying the piqued look she favored him with. "I seem to remember the women in New Orleans as having something called Southern charm. It seems you've lost yours on the voyage to Australia."

"I can assure you, Mr. Malone, my charm is completely intact. But I don't wish to waste it on the likes of you!"

"As I am your dinner partner for the evening, I'd suggest you bring out that charm immediately, Caitlyn, or you will find your-

self feeling very hungry by morning!'' he warned, tired of her haughtiness. His hands itched to give her the spanking she so deserved. Instead he bowed, lending his arm to her as they made their way to the hotel dining room.

Once seated, Caitlyn looked eagerly at the menu. Heavens, it had been ages since she'd eaten a real meal! she thought as she eyed the list of entrees. Even with Tanner Malone as her dining partner, her appetite was healthy and she ordered with gusto. It was the first time she could remember not having to worry about what she ate. There was no Mammy to reprimand her for eating like a hog in front of a gentleman. Not that Mr. Malone even qualified as a gentleman. Why was it that he always seemed to bring out the worst in her? She could be quite charming—and she would be with Brant and the friends they would make together.

After they'd finished their repast in silence, Caitlyn was ready to retire to her room, but Tanner Malone had other plans for her. He ordered brandy for both of them.

''Tell me what news you have of the war in the States,'' he requested. ''All the information we get is three or four months old.''

''Then you probably know more than I do,'' she said. ''When I left New Orleans the *Yankees*''—she stressed the word as she eyed him in derogatory fashion—''had started up the Mississippi to try to take New Orleans. I was lucky enough to find a blockade-runner willing to take me out of Biloxi.''

''The city fell in April,'' he said bluntly, watching the rush of emotion that came over her. She took a drink of brandy, coughing at the unexpected burning in her throat.

''Tell me,'' she said simply, tears glistening in her eyes, both from the brandy she was unaccustomed to and the news that the city she loved had fallen.

''On April 18th Farragut ordered mortar bombardment to begin on forts Jackson and St. Philip seventy miles below the city,'' Tanner began. ''There were five days of heavy fighting on the river and one night of spectacular fireworks from all the shelling. When word came that the Union vessels had passed the forts, New Orleans became a city in panic. Shops and businesses closed. The torch was put to cotton, sugar, corn—everything that had been warehoused on the levee. It was lucky my agent had his wits about him and made sure my property wasn't damaged.''

"How very convenient for you," she interrupted sarcastically, hating him at that moment. He was a *Yankee* and it was his compatriots that had caused all the destruction, yet his business hadn't been touched! She longed to fly at him with all her strength. She took another drink of brandy, feeling the burning in her throat once again.

"Farragut dropped anchor in New Orleans on April 25th," he continued, ignoring her outburst. "He demanded an immediate surrender, but the mayor of New Orleans refused outright."

"Good for Mayor John T. Monroe!" Caitlyn half shouted, lifting her glass in a toast and gulping down another dose.

Some of the other people in the dining room turned to look at her in amazement, but Caitlyn didn't care. Didn't they realize that the city she loved was lost and here she sat with a damned Yankee?

"Go on!" she commanded, downing the last of the brandy. Amazing how it no longer burned! she thought.

"Unfortunately General Lovell evacuated his troops from the city and New Orleans was forced to surrender three days later. It's now an occupied city." He watched her quietly, a touch of sympathy in his eyes. "I'm sure your parents and your sister are all right," he added, hoping to offer some comfort. "General Benjamin Butler was appointed military governor of the city. At least New Orleans may be spared the destruction that other Southern cities will face once the Union army breaks through the Confederate lines."

"Once the *Union army* breaks through!" she repeated incredulously. "Do you think, Mr. Malone, that just because your stupid Yankee soldiers were able to take New Orleans that the rest of the Confederacy is going to fall so easily? Don't count on it!" She reached over and boldly took his glass of brandy, draining it defiantly. "We have superior minds in our military, Mr. Malone! Our Southern men are born fighters, don't forget that! All you blue-bellied Yankees really know is *business*!" She sneered the last word, casting a slur on his own business.

"That might be true, Caitlyn, but we Yankees also know how to manufacture guns and cannons and how to use our diplomatic skills to keep England from coming to the aid of the Confederacy!"

"Not for long!" she retorted. "England must have cotton. Cotton is king!" she half shouted, then hiccupped loudly.

Aware of several pairs of eyes focused on their table, Tanner

decided it was time to get Miss Caitlyn O'Rourke to bed. He soon realized that might prove more difficult than he'd first surmised.

"Don't touch me, Mr. Malone, or I shall scream for assistance!" she threatened, waving him away. "Surely a man is not allowed to accost a young woman alone, even in Australia!"

"Believe me, I would be more than glad to leave you here at this table. You could make a total fool of yourself before you finally found your way to your own room. But unfortunately I live here too. I can't allow my reputation to be sullied when the management sees what an ill-mannered hoyden I've brought here with me." So saying, he stood up and went behind her chair to pull it out so that she could stand.

"I don't need your help," she growled, standing up on wobbly knees. "I'm not drunk! I have never been drunk in my life!"

"If you're not drunk, you're giving a damned good imitation of it, my dear," he said under his breath. Grasping her a trifle roughly under the elbow, he steered her around the tables and out of the dining room. "You and Brant will make a fine pair," he said between clenched teeth. "Neither of you can hold your liquor!"

"I can hold it well enough to get to my room on my own, Mr. Malone!" she said, jerking her arm from his grasp once they'd reached the hotel lobby. The desk clerk looked at them with raised brows, then nodded as he recognized Tanner Malone.

Caitlyn was sure her head would stop spinning as soon as she walked up the stairs, but instead the spinning only seemed to increase, and she clasped the banister tightly to keep from falling. Trying to focus on each step, she moved slowly up the stairs, unaware that Tanner was just below her, making sure that should she fall, he would catch her before she broke her neck. He was amazed when she reached the first landing and then wove down the hall.

Hurrying up to her, he guided her wordlessly to her room and opened the door. "Shall I call for a maid?" he asked.

"You may go to hell!" she said with a little laugh and then a hiccup. "*Good night*, Mr. Malone," she said, pushing him away as she proceeded to close the door.

"I'll be damned!" He stood for a moment, undecided, then boldly pushed the door open, causing her to trip backward and nearly lose her footing. Closing the door tightly behind him, he

stood staring at her, knowing that this time he was going to do what should have been done to her a long time ago.

"Get out of my room, Mr. Malone!" she commanded, pressing a hand to her head and turning away from him with a dismissive look. "After your disclosure about New Orleans, did you really think I would sit quietly and make demure conversation? You really don't know me, Mr. Malone."

"I'm afraid I know you very well, Caitlyn. You are a spoiled, arrogant, insufferable brat who badly needs to be taught some manners!"

"Hah! And I suppose *you* think you're the one to teach me?" she laughed. She was really too drunk to feel threatened despite the black look he was giving her. It all seemed so comical. Was he hurt that she hadn't flirted with him at dinner? Was he angry that she hadn't been glad to see him? Well, he had better get used to it! "I don't like you, Mr. Malone. I never did. You thought you could charm and lie your way through New Orleans society, but I was never taken in by any of it. You're nothing but a two-faced Yankee who persuaded Brant to go with you to Boston so that everyone in the parish would think him a coward!"

"That's all behind us now, Caitlyn," he said, walking toward her slowly. "I don't give a damn what you think about my charm or the reasons why I left New Orleans or why Brant came with me. What I don't like is to be publicly ridiculed in front of people who have come to respect me and my business acumen in the last three years. I'm not about to let some little brat who doesn't think before she opens her mouth make a fool of me!" He moved closer. "You seem to forget that your precious Brant was not there to meet you at the pier, Caitlyn, but I was! I would expect at least a little thanks for that, and for the fact that I'm paying for your hotel room and your dinner! But no! Since I'm a blue-bellied Yankee, you don't think I'm worthy of your thanks, do you?"

She didn't answer. He didn't deserve an answer. He was being boorish and ungentlemanly. She just wished he would get his tirade over with so she could go to sleep. She really had drunk too much brandy and it was difficult to even think of getting herself ready for bed.

His hand was on her arm and he was turning her around to face him. "Why is it that you are the only woman who can make me act like a cad?" he wondered out loud.

"Because you are a cad, Mr. Malone!" she said with an in-

furiating smile of superiority. "And a Yankee! I'm afraid there's nothing you can do to change that. And now would you mind leaving so I can go to bed?"

"You'll go to bed all right, but I'm going to give you something to think about while you're in it!" he vowed, pulling her toward the bed and sitting down on it. With a swift twist of his arm, he pulled her down and placed her across his lap. "I am sick and tired of your bratty ways!" So saying, he reached down and lifted the hem of her dress up over her head.

At first Caitlyn was so disoriented from the brandy she had no idea what he was doing. As she felt his fingers on the waistband of her pantalets, she tried to reach back to stop him. But her chest was squashed against his knees and there was no way to suck in enough breath to scream at him to stop. When she felt air touch her naked bottom as he pulled her pantalets down to her knees, she thought she would die of shame. She would kill him! Or she would tell Brant what he had done and he would shoot him!

"Oh!" The word was jerked from her as she felt the palm of his hand come down harshly on her flesh. Again it came down and she squirmed desperately. "Ouch, that hurts!" she yelled as loudly as she could.

"You're damn right it hurts!" he said through clenched teeth. "It's something I've been threatening to do—something your father should have done when you first started exhibiting this kind of behavior—something I will instruct Brant to do if you continue acting this way!" he threatened.

"You—you let me up this minute!" she cried, real tears falling from her eyes as he continued to smack her with the palm of one hand while the other hand was pressed into her back, effectively keeping her across his knees.

When he was satisfied that her bottom was hurting more than the palm of his hand, he let her slide to the ground, where she tumbled onto her back, struggling to cover herself with her hoopskirt. Glaring up at him, she scrambled to her feet, her dark blue eyes flashing fire and her bosom heaving.

"Mr. Malone—"

"Be careful what you say, Caitlyn," he warned her, not about to be subjected to any outbursts from her. "I've still got another good hand, but I doubt your bottom could stand another spanking at this moment."

She went beet red at his reference to her private part and

closed her mouth abruptly. Fuming inwardly, she nevertheless held back her rage, not wanting to be subjected to any further punishment.

"That's much better. If you have nothing nice to say, it's always better to remain silent, Caitlyn. That's one lesson you should pay heed to. It will keep you from getting yourself into trouble." He watched the rage in her eyes slowly come under control. "And now I will say good night."

He got up from the bed and walked to the door. With a bow he opened it and was gone, shutting the door quietly behind him.

"I hate you!" she whispered, crying in earnest not only from the hurt but from the humiliation he had put her through. How dare he treat her like some ill-mannered child! Oh, if she were a man she'd sneak up on him in his hotel room and stab him through the heart! For a moment thoughts of his gory demise made her smile, but then she realized such fantasies would do her very little good.

She struggled out of her dress and slipped on her nightgown, testing the bed gingerly with her still-smarting bottom. Oh, that man was a devil! Tears gathered in her eyes as she cautiously lowered herself onto the bed, trying to make herself comfortable after what she'd been put through. She comforted herself with the thought that she would repay him for this ignominy if it was the last thing she did!

26

"GOOD MORNING, Caitlyn."

She cringed at the sound of Tanner's cheery voice the next morning as she went down to breakfast. Still, she supposed if she was going to avoid a repeat of his performance last night, she had best be polite this morning.

"Good morning, Mr. Malone," she responded.

He stood up to pull out her chair and she sat down gingerly, her bottom still very sore from the torture he'd inflicted on it. He noticed her flinch and smiled to himself. He'd been so angry at her last night, he hadn't taken the time to appreciate the twin globes of smooth alabaster that had been presented to him. Thinking back on it, he realized he had missed a prime opportunity.

Seating himself opposite her, he watched her eyes flit about the room. She was wondering if any of the people seated for breakfast had witnessed her drunken embarrassment last night. At the thought, she pressed her fingers to her temples, where a headache was steadily drumming. That would teach her not to drink brandy when she was angry! she thought with a sigh.

"I'm surprised you had the nerve to invite me to breakfast with you after your—your treatment of me last night," she sniffed, spreading her napkin in her lap busily.

"Oh, that," he said, trying unsuccessfully to hide his smile. "I would never have done it had I not thought it was absolutely necessary."

Her eyes flew upward and her dark brows drew down. "Necessary, Mr. Malone? It doesn't change anything between us."

He shook his head. "You can't continue with the charade, Caitlyn. Why don't you admit that I'm the only friend you've got right now. You don't know anyone else in Melbourne. If you want to see Brant as soon as possible, you're going to have to trust me to find him for you." He leaned over the table. "Those miners sometimes don't come in from the goldfields for months, you know! How would it look if everyone saw you and me together all the time? Don't you think they might become suspicious as to my intentions?" His eyes mocked her, but she was able to hold her temper, perhaps because the memory of his assault on her the night before was still fresh in her mind.

"You're absolutely right, Mr. Malone," she said unexpectedly. "I suppose I must trust you to get word to Brant for me. When do you think you might be able to do it?"

"Tomorrow at the earliest," he replied, leaning back in his chair. He smiled again. "I like you this way, Caitlyn," he admitted. "Oh, not that I don't like a little willfulness, but you have to admit you were downright obnoxious last night."

"I won't admit anything of the kind," she said, biting her lower lip as a waiter served her tea and biscuits. "Besides," she added, fixing him with a look from beneath her lashes, "what do I care which way you like me? As soon as Brant arrives to marry me, I expect I won't be seeing much of you, Mr. Malone."

He raised one brow. "I'm not so sure of that, Caitlyn. Life in a mining camp can be very rough for a woman."

"No rougher than in a hotel room with you, Mr. Malone," she reminded him tartly.

He laughed at her wit. "Ah, Caitlyn, it really is too bad you continue to see me as a Yankee and yourself as a Southerner! Wouldn't it be easier if we were just friends?"

"Easier for whom, Mr. Malone?" she inquired, buttering a biscuit with little interest.

"For both of us," he replied, his look warming a little.

She bit into the biscuit, seemingly thinking over his recommendation. "I don't know, Mr. Malone. You really are a blackguard. I've never had a blackguard for a friend," she said archly.

"Then perhaps you should try it," he proposed with a knowing smile. "We blackguards have our good sides too, you know. I can show you the theater, the parks, the city of Melbourne."

She looked up and met his eyes, then lowered her own hastily. "I'll be happy when I see Brant," she returned stubbornly. "I'll be happier when we are married."

"I see." Tanner leaned back in his seat. Caitlyn bit into another biscuit, wondering why she suddenly felt shy with this man. Was it because of what he'd done last night? She reminded herself that he *had* come to her rescue in a strange land.

Caitlyn laughed a little. "I was just trying to picture you as a knight in shining armor, Mr. Malone."

"Black armor, no doubt," he added jocularly.

"And visibly tarnished," she added impudently, making him smile.

He leaned across the table and touched her hand gently. "You really can be charming when you want to be."

Blushing at the directness of his stare, she pulled her hand away and felt her heart fluttering busily. How odd that this man should suddenly have this effect on her!

"And you, Mr. Malone, can be charming when you choose to be," she told him, sipping from her teacup and eyeing him over the rim. "Not as charming as a Southern gentleman, of course, but charming in a Yankee sort of way."

"A what?" He laughed and eyed her quizzically. "You will never stop reminding me of our different backgrounds, will you, Caitlyn?"

"Those differences are very real, aren't they, Mr. Malone?"

He shook his head. "Not here in Australia, Caitlyn. Everyone is out for himself in this raw new land. You'll find Englishmen and Irishmen, Scotsmen, American Southerners and American Northerners, even a few Chinese. They're all here because they don't care about the rest of the world. They've come to make

their fortunes or make their homes here. Don't bring your petty prejudices from home, Caitlyn, because they won't endear you to anyone.''

She was silent, considering his words as she ate the last of her breakfast. ''Everyone has to believe in something, Mr. Malone,'' she finally said with a note of reproach in her voice.

''Here the only thing you have to believe in, Caitlyn, is yourself,'' he returned seriously.

For a moment she was mesmerized by his blue gaze. Her eyes were held by his and she could almost feel the force of his will bearing down on her. With an effort, she tore her eyes away. ''Perhaps I'd best go upstairs to my room.''

''You don't want to go back to your room,'' he advised her. ''Come along and I'll give you a tour of Melbourne. I seem to recall you being my cordial guide to New Orleans. Now I shall return the favor.''

''But I wouldn't want to take time away from your business endeavors, Mr. Malone,'' she replied. ''Besides, shouldn't you be searching for Brant's whereabouts?''

''There's time enough for that,'' he told her smoothly. ''Come along. It's not raining this morning and that's unusual for winter in Melbourne. We may as well take advantage of it.'' He stood up and waited expectantly for her answer.

For a moment Caitlyn hesitated, not sure how proper it would be for her to be escorted around the city by Tanner Malone without a chaperone. But, as he said, this was not New Orleans or Savannah or even Boston. This was Australia. Besides, she really didn't want to stay cooped up in her room, waiting to hear from Brant. It might take several days and she simply had too much energy for that.

''Yes, Mr. Malone, I will go with you,'' she finally said.

He seemed genuinely pleased. ''I'll hire a carriage—no, let's walk,'' he decided. ''I'm sure you'll enjoy walking on land after so many months at sea.''

She laughed. ''Oh, yes!'' Then she hesitated. ''Oh, but I really don't have the proper walking dress or even a good hat!'' She looked stricken for a moment. ''I had so very little room to pack things in my valise. The blockade-runner—''

''I understand, Caitlyn. But don't worry,'' he said, winking at her, ''we'll buy you a hat if we have to!'' He pushed her out in front of him gently, leaving her no time to fuss.

''But, Mr. Malone, a lady can't be seen without a hat.''

"Hush!" He stopped her on the veranda of the hotel, turned her around by the shoulders, and laid a bold finger on her lips. "Quit going on about such trivial things. I promise you our first stop will be a milliner's shop and you can pick a hat from the window."

Caitlyn felt his finger against her mouth with an electric shock and found herself remembering that time he had kissed her in the garden in New Orleans. Her cheeks warmed. With an effort, she pulled away from him, wondering at the effect he was having on her.

"Forgive me for being so skittish this morning," she said quickly, seeking to cover up her embarrassment. "I—didn't sleep very well last night." She was telling the truth about that! When she thought of the reason for her sleeplessness, she remembered her sore bottom once more and felt a spurt of resentment toward Tanner. That was better, she thought with pleasure. Much better to feel anger and resentment toward this Yankee cad than to feel anything else. She mustn't let herself fall victim to his insincere charm and handsome looks.

He smiled, much to her chagrin. "Don't be angry today, Caitlyn," he said simply. "Why don't we both make a bargain to behave ourselves?"

"Can I trust you to keep *your* end of the bargain, Mr. Malone?" she asked, gazing at him with her lips pursed primly.

His smile was boyish. "On a day like today, Caitlyn, I'm not sure I can promise anything. But I do want us to stop bickering, if only for a few hours. After that, you can change back into the arrogant Miss O'Rourke and I can change back into the terrible, two-faced Yankee!" He rolled his eyes theatrically and, much to Caitlyn's dismay, she couldn't keep herself from laughing out loud at his dramatics.

Tanner directed her down the street, which was little more than a muddy track that housed several shops and businesses on either side. As he had promised, their first stop was a milliner's. A rather sorry-looking shop, Caitlyn thought, but she kept her criticism to herself. A young woman whose eyes continually slid over Tanner Malone helped her to try on the pitiful array of wares in the shop window. Caitlyn chose the best of the lot, a small, flat-crowned bonnet with a wide brim done in cheap straw with a simple ribbon around the crown to tie under the chin.

"What do you think?" she asked anxiously as they left the shop. Her feminine vanity made her ask the question. After all,

even in a place as provincial as this she wanted to be dressed appropriately.

He studied her for several minutes, then walked around and checked out the view from the back and sides. When she was about to fume at him for taking so long, he finally reached a decision. "It suits you," he said.

She breathed a long sigh. "Honestly, Mr. Malone, you can be so terribly annoying sometimes that I don't wonder you're still a bachelor!"

He laughed, taking her arm. "If I'm still a bachelor, Caitlyn, it's not because I am annoying."

"Then pray tell, what is it?" she asked, feeling her curiosity stirred by this enigmatic man.

"I haven't fallen in love yet," he answered.

She stopped and stared at him. "Why, Mr. Malone! I never would have guessed you were a romantic at heart!" she teased him. "Isn't falling in love much too soft an emotion for a hard-bitten Yankee like yourself?"

"Not at all, Caitlyn. You see, even we Yankees have human hearts beating above our blue bellies. It's just that you Southerners refuse to admit it."

"I think we had better concentrate on the scenery, Mr. Malone," she said, deliberately changing the subject before any heated arguments could begin.

As they walked down Bourke Street, past Swanston, he pointed out shops and offices that had been springing up almost overnight since gold fever had taken Melbourne by storm. The tree-lined streets would have reminded Caitlyn of home, except that the trees were totally different from those she was used to seeing. Tanner explained that they were eucalyptus trees.

"In spring these trees blossom scarlet, white, and coral," he told her. "By October they will be in bloom and you'll be able to smell the pungent blossoms."

"It's so mixed up, having the spring in autumn," Caitlyn said perplexedly.

He nodded and continued with his tour, taking her down to Spring Street, where the Exchequer had just been completed. Its architecture was Italian Renaissance, and Caitlyn held her breath at the unexpected beauty of it in this rough land. Tanner told her that millions of pounds worth of gold would be stored in the underground vaults that had been especially built to house the

precious metal. Up from the Exchequer was the new Victoria House of Parliament, with its Doric columns.

"So many people are flocking in every day," Tanner commented. "Most of them hurry out to the goldfields, but more and more are staying in the cities, and the cities are starting to accommodate the growing population. Someday Melbourne will probably be as urban as New Orleans or Boston."

"And there's still plenty of good land to be bought," Caitlyn said dreamily. She glanced northward, where rolling hills met tall mountains in the distance. "Brant and I could build a beautiful home here, just like Mornhaven!" she said, excitement tingeing her voice. Barbecues on the back lawn, cotillions in the big ballroom, flirtations out on the wide veranda. She closed her eyes and let herself be swept away for a moment.

Watching her, Tanner felt a sudden urge to kiss her. It surprised him, for she really could be quite disagreeable at times. But there was something about her that intrigued him. He sensed that under the surface of a spoiled brat there was a very interesting woman waiting to be released. But that woman was waiting for Brant, not for him.

"Those days of cotillions and parties are gone, Caitlyn," he said, his voice harsher than he wanted it to be.

She opened her eyes and stared at him, her brow drawing into a frown. "Yes," she said, her tone just as harsh. "And all because of the *Yankees*!"

He caught her elbow. "Not just because of the Yankees, Caitlyn," he said. "You forget, it was the Southerners who fired first!"

"Hah!" She pulled her arm from his grasp. "You Yankees drove us to it. What did you expect? Always treating us like second-class citizens just because our way of life was different from your own! You're just pigheaded!"

"That's like the pot calling the kettle black, don't you think?" he said. "Anyway, it seems we've already forgotten our little truce, doesn't it?" Damn it! He could have been at his office going over business correspondence. Or better yet, he could have ridden out to Seth Wickham's sheep station and had a decent conversation with Deborah Wickham about the merits of shipping wool directly to the States. Instead he'd wasted the morning on this little chit!

"I want you to hire someone as soon as possible to take me

to Brant,'' she said as they walked at a more sedate pace down Bourke Street.

He looked at her as though she'd lost her mind. "You want to go to Brant? Don't you listen to anything I tell you? He's in a mining camp with thousands of other prospectors. Many of them haven't had a woman in months. I couldn't even guarantee that your guide wouldn't rape you before you got halfway to Maldon!''

She colored brightly. "Then, *you'll* have to take me, Mr. Malone!''

He looked at her almost scornfully. "You couldn't be sure that *I* wouldn't rape you before we got to Maldon.''

For a moment, she was speechless in the face of his bold masculinity. "That's true,'' she said. "You are a Yankee after all, and Yankees do rape innocent women, don't they?''

"No more than Confederates do,'' he replied coolly.

She was infuriated at her own helplessness. She had no idea where Brant was or how to contact him. She had to rely on this villain—and he knew it! Taking several deep breaths, she calmed herself and tried to be reasonable. "I'm sorry, Mr. Malone. My remarks were uncalled-for,'' she began. "But you must realize how important it is for me to be with Brant.''

"And you must realize that down here everyone isn't at your beck and call,'' he reminded her. "You're not at Mornhaven anymore, Caitlyn. You're not the belle of the ball here.''

"Why won't you help me?'' she wondered aloud. "You always make it so difficult for me.''

"All right, Caitlyn, I'll take you to Brant if you're so determined to go to him. Hell, I suspect there's someone in Maldon who'll be able to marry you!''

"Yes,'' she said, eager now, her confidence returning. "Brant and I can be married right in the mining town.'' She had romantic visions of a cozy tent with the two of them sharing his excitement about new gold discoveries. How perfect it would be!

Tanner was creating quite a different scenario as he envisioned the stunned look on Brant's face when he saw whom Tanner had brought with him. Christ, Brant couldn't turn the girl away no matter how much she deserved it! He might have toyed with the favors of both sisters while he was in Louisiana, but only a complete bastard would send the one home who had come to marry him. No, Brant would have to swallow his disappointment

and marry Caitlyn. Perhaps destiny had sent her here. Somehow Caitlyn had come instead of Constance. Brant would have to accept that.

"When can we leave?" Caitlyn asked anxiously.

"I do have a business to run," he reminded her. "I'll have to have a few days to make sure things will run smoothly while I'm gone."

"How many days?"

He sighed in exasperation. "At least three." He looked at her doubtfully. "How good are you at riding a horse?"

She straightened up proudly. "I was the best horsewoman in the parish!"

"Yes, but Australian terrain is a bit different from the alluvial fields of Louisiana," he said sarcastically. "Can you ride astride?"

She nodded, feeling a little deflated at his lack of appreciation of her talents.

"Good! Then I'll round up some gear and a couple of good horses. Some packhorses and—" He eyed her mockingly. "Do we need a chaperone?"

For a moment she was taken aback at the thought that she would be alone with him for several days on this trip. "What would you do if I said yes?" she asked.

"Oh, I'll find someone," he told her with that mocking glint still in his cool blue eyes.

"Then find someone," she said on a challenging note and smiled with that Southern arrogance that set his teeth on edge.

Three days later Caitlyn met Tanner on the veranda of the hotel. His attire was quite different from the business suit he'd been in earlier. Today he was wearing a pair of buff buckskin trousers, a dark blue shirt, and a dark suede vest. He looked like Sean Flynn fresh off the ranges of Texas, she thought.

Beside him was a grizzled man of indeterminate age. His long whiskers betrayed his aversion to razors, and his long, stringy hair proclaimed that he didn't much cotton to scissors either. Around his leathery neck he had tied a dark kerchief that knotted beneath his prominent Adam's apple. He wore a dark shirt and tan trousers with a pair of animal-skin leggings pulled up above his knees. His boots were dusty and looked as though they'd seen a lot of service. His mouth was a thin line, and his eyes were set deep inside his face beneath bushy gray brows. Caitlyn

could not make out their exact expression, but they seemed to be sizing her up.

"Caitlyn, I want you to meet Radford Hayes," Tanner said.

"How do you do?" Caitlyn extended her hand, but the stranger stared at it a moment, chewed the wad of tobacco in his mouth, and spat sideways. She looked uncertainly at Tanner.

"Your chaperone," he added with an inscrutable smile.

27

THE NEXT MORNING Caitlyn sat her horse impatiently as Tanner made some final adjustments to their packhorses. Because she was too stubborn to ask him for money, she was obliged to ride in one of the day dresses she had brought from home. She hadn't even thought to pack a riding habit, never dreaming she'd be going on a journey on horseback as soon as she arrived in Australia.

Radford Hayes—or Hayes, as he liked to be called—sat looking at her with some curiosity, and she knew she must look foolish in her green sprigged muslin with the tight basque. At least she had the straw bonnet to protect her head, although the sun had disappeared behind the clouds this morning, promising rain later in the day.

Caitlyn had been obliged to leave her hoops in her hotel room and felt odd without them. Her pantalets would protect her legs from being chafed against the sides of the horse, but she had no riding boots and would be damned if she was going to remind Tanner Malone of that fact. Surely he could see for himself that she was wearing only flat-heeled Moroccan leather slippers that were most unsuitable for riding. But he was obviously choosing to ignore it, only concerning himself with the packhorses and the distance to be traveled today.

"We'll go slowly, Hayes," Tanner advised his male companion. He gestured silently toward Caitlyn. "We'll have to see how much she can take before we push her too hard. Tomorrow night I want to be in Sunbury."

Hayes nodded, chewing and spitting at frequent intervals so that Caitlyn was careful to keep her horse behind his.

"Don't worry about me, Mr. Malone," she said crossly. "I'm sure I'll be able to keep up!"

"Don't tempt me, Caitlyn," he said, walking over to stand by her horse, his dark blue eyes looking at her ruthlessly. "We'll go at the pace I set or we'll turn back and let you rot in your hotel room until Brant comes to Melbourne! Do you understand?"

She nodded, feeling hot words bubbling to her lips, but swallowing them. As she watched him mount his horse, she unconsciously took in the difference in his attire. She was used to seeing him in the cool linens he had worn in New Orleans or the business suit he had worn in Melbourne. But this morning, like the day before, he was dressed in Western attire.

"Just think, Caitlyn," he said conversationally, trotting his horse back to ride beside hers, "in a few days you'll be reunited with Brant. Any hardship endured on this journey is nothing when you think of it as a means to a glorious end!"

"You may insult me all you please, Mr. Malone. No doubt it makes you feel good to vent your spleen on me. I suppose if I try to reply in kind, you'll make good on your threat to take me back to Melbourne and wash your hands of me."

"I admit that the idea appeals to me. There's still time for you to change your mind. I can go alone and let Hayes take you back to the hotel. You can be assured I will get your message to Brant."

"I shudder to think what terms it would be couched in, Mr. Malone," she retorted flippantly. "I know you don't like me and you're positive I'm not going to survive out in the mining camp. Well, I'm going to show you how wrong you are!" She eyed him challengingly. "We Southern women are of strong mettle, Mr. Malone. You won't find us sitting at home like those bluestockings in the North!"

"Indeed not," he agreed. "I doubt that any self-respecting young woman from Boston would have gone through what you have gone through, Caitlyn."

She suspected he was ridiculing her, but chose to ignore him. "When you love someone as much as I love Brant," she said briskly, "you can disregard some of the proprieties."

"I'll remember that," he said enigmatically. They were passing the outskirts of the city and entering a rolling grassland that would be prime grazing for sheep and cattle. Tanner spurred his horse forward on the trail, leaving Caitlyn behind with Hayes, who was bringing up the rear with the two packhorses.

Hours later they stopped for lunch beneath a spread of euca-

lyptus trees, which had a pungent, medicinal smell. The clouds had thickened and it looked as though rain were imminent. Caitlyn sighed and looked out over the rolling grassland, wondering what Brant might be doing at this very moment. She hugged her knees beneath her skirt, feeling her thighs already beginning to ache from the unaccustomed ride. Her hands were sore from holding the reins and she was glad her mount wasn't difficult to control. She was sure Tanner had seen to it that her steed was the gentlest in the stables. The animal had absolutely no spirit for galloping or even going beyond a sedate walk. At this rate it would take forever to reach Brant, she thought impatiently.

Looking without interest at the simple fare that Tanner handed out for the midday meal, Caitlyn asked him how much longer they would ride today before camping for the night.

"We'll go as far as we can," he answered. "I want to get to Sunbury by tomorrow night."

"What's in Sunbury?" she asked.

He smiled. "A place to spend the night."

Their rest was too short for Caitlyn. She hated to think how she would feel the next morning, but told herself she was not about to turn back. She eyed Tanner suspiciously. If she knew him at all, she was positive he wanted her to give this up. Well, she would show him! As he helped her onto her mount, she smiled down at him.

"Don't worry about me, Mr. Malone. I'm quite all right. Please go as long as possible this afternoon."

He returned her smile. "As you wish, Caitlyn." He touched the brim of his hat, swung onto his horse, and spurred on ahead just as the first raindrops started to fall.

Caitlyn looked up at the sky and caught a raindrop in her eye. Balls of fire! Why was everything conspiring against her? Soon the rain was coming down steadily and her dress was soaked. Hayes had brought out a canvas coat. Tanner had pulled his hat down over his ears and seemed oblivious to the water running from its brim onto his back. Caitlyn was miserable after only a few hours of travel and sorely wished for the comfortable room with its comfortable bed back at the hotel in Melbourne.

When Tanner trotted back to see how she was doing, she wished she could slap the smirk off his face.

"I'm soaked through," she admitted through clenched teeth.

He eyed the terrain. "We can camp out under any of these trees. Of course there's always the danger of being flooded if the

rain continues. When the rivers run high the water spreads out over the countryside into marshes and dry lakes. You do swim, don't you, Caitlyn?''

She had had enough of his sarcasm. ''I want to stop right now!'' she spat. ''I'm wet and cold and tired. Are you happy, Mr. Malone?''

He looked surprised. ''Why should I be happy? I don't want a sick woman on my hands. We'll stop, Caitlyn, at your request.'' He trotted back to where Hayes was stoically leading the packhorses. ''Hayes, Miss O'Rourke says she can't go any farther. We'll have to stop for the day.''

Caitlyn clenched her teeth and felt like she could have spit nails. If it weren't for this rain she would have ridden until she dropped from her horse.

Dismounting was harder than she'd imagined. Her thighs were shaking, her knees wobbly, and her wet dress was plastered to her legs. When she hit the ground she staggered backward into Tanner's accommodating arms, finding herself pressed up against him. His breath felt warm on her neck where her cold, wet hair had been pasted to it, and for one weak moment she leaned against him.

But when she felt his arms tighten around her, she pulled away abruptly. ''Where do I sleep?'' she asked him, turning around to face him.

''If you want to stay warm, you'll have to sleep next to me or Hayes.'' His eyes traveled over her almost insultingly. ''Take your pick, Caitlyn.''

She stared after him as he walked away to help Hayes put up a lean-to to shelter them from the worst of the rain. In a few minutes Hayes started a fire and looked toward her expectantly.

''I—I don't know how to cook,'' she said.

Hayes gave her an incredulous look, then shook his head and spat into the fire. ''Appears to me a woman's got no right to go off into the wilderness without the skills it takes to stay alive,'' he commented in a rough, gravelly voice.

Caitlyn was almost relieved to hear him talk. At least he seemed more human now. ''I'm sorry. I—I could try, if you'd teach me.''

''I'm no damned teacher!'' he said, spitting again. He let out a few choice oaths and proceeded to heat the coffee.

Caitlyn realized how unprepared she was for this adventure. She had absolutely no domestic skills. She had been born into a

way of life where everything was done for her by slaves. Her mother had never thought to teach her how to cook or make a fire or how to sew more than the simplest embroidery stitches. Margaret O'Rourke had always assumed that her daughters' lives would be much like hers. Who would have thought that war would come and bring changes with it—or that one of her daughters would go to Australia, where the idea of a woman with no domestic skills was laughable? Even those women whose husbands had made gold fortunes and who could now afford servants were able to wash their own clothes, diaper their own babies, and make a good pot of stew.

Caitlyn felt helpless and lost as she watched Hayes busy himself with the cooking while Tanner saw to the horses. The rain was still coming down; she was sodden and cold and miserable. What she would have liked more than anything at that moment was for old Mammy to undress her like a baby and massage her sore muscles. Then Sara would draw a bath for her and she would sink into it blissfully, only to come out an hour later and slip into a freshly scented nightgown. From there she would fall into bed, and on hot nights a small black child would stand over her bed and wave a palmetto leaf to keep away the mosquitoes until she fell asleep.

She stared resentfully at Hayes as he fried sausages and potatoes in an old skillet. She knew what he must think of her. And Tanner—was he thinking the same thing? Had he planned all this just to prove to her that she didn't belong out here?

She sat down on the ground, fighting the urge to cry like a baby. Maybe she didn't belong out here. Maybe Tanner was right and she should never have come. She had thought there would be a house and servants; she and Brant would have children and she could amuse herself with them, but when she grew tired of the children's tantrums, she would give them over to a mammy. But out here, away from real civilization, everything seemed topsy-turvy. Women weren't expected to be just beautiful ornaments in a man's home. They were expected to be real women who could cook and sew and clean.

"What's wrong, Caitlyn?"

She looked up to see Tanner standing over her. She hated for him to think she was defeated and, steeling herself, she replied briskly, "Nothing is wrong, Mr. Malone."

He eyed her wet dress and her generally woebegone look and tried not to smile. "I'm glad. For a moment I thought maybe

you doubted that it was a good idea to come out here into the bush to look for Brant.''

"I would never doubt it,'' she said quickly. "What do you mean by *bush*?'' she asked, looking around in the fading light. "Is that what they call this part of the country?''

"Technically, I suppose we really haven't hit the bush yet,'' Tanner explained. "It's what the Australians call the land that's beyond civilization and beyond the grazing belt. It's really beautiful country, especially in the spring when all the wildflowers start to bloom.'' He eyed her quizzically. "Maybe you won't like the bush, Caitlyn. It's not prim and proper; it's wild and a little dangerous sometimes.''

"If you two are all done with your little tiff, it's time to eat,'' Hayes intervened roughly. Silently, he laid out the tin plates and cups and filled them.

Caitlyn was ravenous and ate everything on her plate, despite the fact that Hayes could have learned a thing or two about cooking from old Rachel back at Mornhaven. But she wasn't going to cast aspersions on his culinary skills, for she couldn't do any better herself. When she was finished she looked longingly at the lean-to, wanting nothing more than to crawl inside and go to sleep. But Hayes had other plans for her.

"Malone saw to the horses, I was cook, you clean up,'' he informed her curtly. "Everyone's got chores.''

For a moment Caitlyn looked to Tanner, hoping for a reprieve. "It's still raining! And we've come a long way since this morning.'' When both men seemed in no mood to soften, her temper started to flare. "I'm too tired to clean up tonight. I'll do it in the morning!''

"Everyone's got chores,'' Hayes repeated implacably.

"Mr. Malone!'' Caitlyn appealed to him. "Surely you can't expect me to go down to the nearest puddle and wash the dishes!''

"You can wash them in the rain,'' Hayes told her calmly. He pushed a dishcloth toward her and indicated the dishes.

"But I—''

"Sooner done, sooner you can get to sleep,'' Hayes interrupted. He sat quietly by the fire, watching her. Tanner, who had lit up a cheroot, was leaning back to enjoy his smoke and watching her with an amused expression.

"I'm sure you're enjoying this, aren't you, Mr. Malone?'' she grumbled, taking the dishes and gathering them in the skirt of

her dress. She snatched the dishcloth away from Hayes and stomped out from under the trees into the rain. As she grumbled and seethed and scrubbed the dishes, she was unaware that the two men were watching her and talking.

"Seems to me she's got no chance to make it out here," Hayes said reflectively.

Tanner shrugged. "She's made of pretty stout stuff, my friend. Just give her a chance."

Hayes looked closely at the younger man. "Appears to me you might be willing to give her a good many chances."

Tanner laughed and ground out his cheroot. "Caitlyn O'Rourke is one of the most cantankerous, stubborn, spoiled females I've ever met. But you're right, I do give her more chances than she's entitled to."

"Trouble is, she doesn't seem to appreciate you for it," Hayes observed.

Tanner nodded absently, his eyes on Caitlyn as she trudged back under the trees. The rain had slowed down and was hardly more than a fine mist, but it was still cold enough to make one miserable. And she did look miserable. Even though she would never admit it, he could see that she was exhausted. From the way she walked, her legs must be really sore. He almost pitied her, but reminded himself that she could have avoided all this if she hadn't been so damned stubborn about going to Maldon herself.

"You'll be lucky if you don't catch cold," he commented when she squatted close to the fire to warm her shaking hands.

"No thanks to you!" she retorted swiftly.

"You wanted to come," he reminded her softly.

She had no answer for that. The three of them sat around the fire for a few more minutes, listening to the rain dripping off the leaves of the eucalyptus trees. After a time, Caitlyn felt that her clothes had dried sufficiently to allow her to sleep in some comfort. She took off her straw hat and felt her damp hair plastered to her scalp and neck.

"I don't suppose you packed a comb for me?" she inquired, looking at Tanner.

He shook his head. "Didn't think of it." He glanced questioningly at Hayes.

"I've got a razor in my bag. You could cut it all off and then you wouldn't have to worry about it," Hayes chuckled, seeing her irritated expression.

"No thank you; I'll make do," she huffed. She made her way to the lean-to and sat down inside, unbraiding her hair so that it fell in dark red loops down her back. She combed it out with her fingers, then fluffed it with her hands, hoping to dry it a little before replaiting it. When she was too tired to fool with it anymore, she rebraided it into one thick tail down her back and wriggled under the blankets to go to sleep.

She could hear the two men talking softly to each other and the sound of their low voices soon lulled her to sleep. Turning on her side, she pulled her knees up and tried not to think of tomorrow.

Sometime in the night, Caitlyn awoke with a start. She'd had a nightmare. She was on the blockade-runner's ship, looking back onto the beach where Yankees were everywhere. She could see their blue-uniformed figures on the beach, pistols leveled to fire at anything that looked suspicious. Hidden in the scrub beyond the sand were the faces of her mother and father and sister. They were white and strained, watching her sorrowfully. When Caitlyn would have jumped off the boat to go back, something held her where she was. She tried to pull away, but it felt as though bands of steel were wrapped around her. She began to cry, for as the ship moved away from shore, she could see that the Yankees were getting closer and closer to the spot where her family was hidden. Turning around to try to free herself from what held her, she saw that it was a man binding her tightly against him. It was Brant, his dark eyes gazing at her with love and longing, begging her to stay with him. She turned toward the shore, but her family had disappeared. Then she turned toward Brant, but he was no longer there. Instead Tanner Malone's face looked back at her. She woke up, frightened, feeling sudden terror at being alone.

As she tried to sit up, she felt those same bands holding her. Disoriented from her dream, she imagined she was truly back on the ship. She half expected Mrs. Lowell to be snoring beside her, but instead she turned her head to feel warm breath on her cheek.

"Sh, go back to sleep." It was Tanner Malone's voice, rough with sleep. One of his hands came up from where it had been encircling her waist and touched her cheek gently. He felt the wetness on her skin and gently wiped it off with his fingers. "It was only a nightmare, Caitlyn. Go back to sleep."

It seemed extraordinary that she could be sleeping with Tanner Malone next to her, but Caitlyn was too exhausted to worry about it. She would worry about it tomorrow when she had the strength to chastise him. Without a word of protest, she snuggled deeper into the blankets and fell back to sleep.

28

IT SEEMED as though she'd only slept an hour when she heard Tanner Malone's voice calling her name, rousing her from sleep. She opened her bleary eyes to see him standing outside the lean-to, preparing the coffee while Hayes busied himself with the packhorses. She blinked and tried to remember what it was about her dream last night that had troubled her, but it was lost to her memory.

"Time to get moving," Tanner called to her. "We'll have coffee and biscuits, but that's about it. We've got to make Sunbury by tonight."

"Sunbury," she repeated stupidly, sitting up and trying to think why she should feel argumentative toward Tanner Malone this morning. Something. What was it he'd done last night?

"Yes, you'll be overjoyed to know we won't have to sleep outdoors tonight. That is, *if* you hurry up so we can get going." Tanner glanced at her. "How do you feel?"

"Tired," she admitted, yawning widely to prove it. "I could sleep for another day."

"You can sleep on the horse. Old Merribelle won't break into a trot and unseat you. She's the gentlest nag I could find for you," he told her.

"I suspected as much," she said sharply. She got to her feet, refusing Tanner's offer of assistance. Her legs felt weak and she wasn't sure if she could walk. Adding to her misery was the musty odor of her damp clothes. She wrinkled her nose in disgust.

He noted her reaction and smiled. "None of us smells all that good," he observed, making her blush. "But don't worry about it. If the horses don't mind, I don't mind."

"Thank you for telling me," she said sarcastically. She reached back to find her long braid and wrapped it tightly around

her head, shoving her hat over it to keep it off her neck. "Is the coffee ready?" she asked.

"No coffee till we get the horses packed," Hayes replied. He leveled a squinty stare at her. "Since you can't cook, I don't suppose you know how to roll bedding, do you?"

She opened her mouth to deliver a sarcastic retort, then closed it as both men looked at her as though expecting the worst. "I can help you," she offered, jerking her chin up stubbornly. "I know how to fold a blanket."

"Jesus, she knows how to fold a blanket!" Hayes said in mock amazement.

Tanner laughed to himself. "Let her help," he told Hayes. "We can get a quicker start."

Hayes gave him a sidelong glance. "You sure about that, Malone?"

Grumbling, the older man showed Caitlyn how to fold the blankets and tie them with leather straps. Caitlyn did her best, fumbling a little because her fingers were sore from riding without the proper gloves and because she was slow from fatigue. But finally everything was packed except the coffeepot and cups, and the three of them enjoyed a few quick sips of coffee and bites of biscuit before they were ready to go.

As they traveled the sun began to break through the thinning clouds. By noon it was providing a welcome warmth to Caitlyn, whose very bones seemed to be frozen from the night before. She gazed forward at Tanner's back and tried to remember what it was that she had wanted to talk to him about, but the memory kept eluding her.

They were traveling through the bush now and Caitlyn could hear birdcalls as they passed the tall white gum trees that appeared between grassy patches of scrub. Flocks of pink and white birds rose up from a small pond created by the rain, making Caitlyn's horse shy away. She watched in amazement as the birds settled down a few minutes later, covering the water with a rosy hue. She could hear magpies chattering, and Tanner pointed out their black and white bodies in the branches overhead. There were wedge-tailed eagles spiraling on air currents high in the sky while red-rumped parrots with bright green bodies squawked at the passersby.

Totally engrossed in the richness of wildlife around her, Caitlyn hardly noticed her aching muscles or the rumbling in her stomach. Gum trees, tree ferns, and lively creeks made the area

they were traveling through seem quite different from the place where they had camped last night. Yet it seemed only a few hours had gone by when there were grasslands once more. In the distance she could see fluffy white dots.

"Sheep," Tanner told her when she questioned him.

Caitlyn wondered what the sheep were doing so far from town.

"There are sheep farms all around this area," Tanner explained. "It's good grazing land and they do very well. The Australians call their farms sheep stations. They raise a good quality of wool here; it's doing well in England and helping to take the place of the cotton that isn't being exported by the South because of the war. They're hoping that exported Australian merino wool will reach America by next year, bringing the price of raw wool to reasonable levels. Since the Confederacy has imposed a cotton embargo, wool should flourish."

"I suppose you enjoy that, don't you, Mr. Malone?" she said coolly.

"You're damned right I do!" he said bluntly. "I'm exporting that wool for some of the biggest sheep stations."

Caitlyn was silent, hating him for being so damned smug about his good fortune. She only wished his business would fail—just once! Oh, to see his face then! But as long as the war was being waged in the States, she knew he was right about cotton. President Jefferson Davis had ordered the embargo and, as her father had predicted, it had only hurt the South.

Beyond the grazing lands, she could see a line of mountains which Tanner told her were the Grampians, stark sandstone ridges that lay along the western edge of the Great Dividing Range, a mountain range that ran through all of eastern Australia. Caitlyn was awestruck as the sun shone on the red sandstone. Closer by, she could see forested foothills and wondered how far into them they would have to go to find Brant. Feeling safe here in the pastoral fields of the sheep stations that were edged with stands of pine and gum trees, she couldn't imagine setting foot in the wilderness of the forests ahead.

Toward late afternoon, as she was growing tired again from the day's long ride, she realized they were following a clearly marked trail that showed the deep ruts of carriage and wagon wheels. Curious, she wondered if Tanner would enlighten her. He remained silent, and they kept to the trail until Caitlyn could see in the distance a large, rather imposing two-story house with a twin-peaked roof and a veranda running along the front and

around the sides of the house. The house had clapboard siding and glass windowpanes and a regal look that impressed Caitlyn. She wondered who its owners might be, and she wasn't surprised when Tanner led their party through the front gate of the fence surrounding the property.

A man stood on the veranda, masked by its shade. Beside him stood a woman, probably his wife, she thought. As the riders approached, the woman walked to the veranda steps, shading her eyes. Caitlyn could see that she was tall and strongly built, with very blonde hair that was swept up in a careless coiffure.

"Who owns this place?" Caitlyn asked, bringing her horse up to Tanner's.

"This is Wickham Station, Caitlyn, one of the largest sheep stations around here. The man on the veranda is Seth Wickham and that is his daughter, Deborah."

His daughter! Caitlyn looked with renewed interest at the woman. Even from this distance, she could see that the woman was handsome and had a healthy flush, although she was not as young as Caitlyn. As Caitlyn rode nearer, she could see that the woman was even older than she had first thought, perhaps over thirty. And where was her husband? Caitlyn wondered automatically.

But she had little time to wonder, for now they were in the front yard and Tanner was dismounting. With a welcoming smile, the woman was hurrying over to be clasped in his arms.

"Welcome back, Tanner!" she told him warmly in a husky voice that Caitlyn thought too mannish for gentility. Instead of greeting Caitlyn or Hayes, the woman waved to her father, who made his way to where his daughter stood, encircled in Tanner's arms.

"Wondered when you were going to get here!" the man snorted, his accent heavily English. "Deborah was so bloody sure you'd be here for supper, we haven't eaten yet, lucky for you!"

"I appreciate your hospitality as always, Seth," Tanner smiled, releasing his hold on the daughter in order to shake the hand of the father. "I've brought company. Radford Hayes you already know. And this is Caitlyn O'Rourke from Louisiana—she's come to find a husband." He winked at Deborah, who let out a hearty laugh.

Feeling affronted, Caitlyn nodded stiffly to the woman. Deborah Wickham's light blue eyes were more curious than com-

petitive as she assessed the young stranger. "Welcome to Wickham Station," she said. "You'll have to excuse our manners; we have so few guests at our house."

"They're more comfortable talking to sheep!" Hayes said, spitting as he dismounted from his horse.

Caitlyn stayed on her horse, awaiting some help in dismounting. After a few awkward moments, Tanner remembered himself and hurried over to help Caitlyn off the horse.

Deborah ushered everyone into the house, where the appetizing smell of food was enough to make one put other thoughts aside. Stepping into the kitchen, Caitlyn saw that the heavy wooden table was already set for supper. The pot over the fireplace was emitting heavenly smells that made her salivate appreciatively. Deborah worked easily and efficiently as she ladled out stew and made sure everyone had something to drink before she seated herself.

This household reminded Caitlyn of a well-oiled machine. Everything seemed to work just so and to come together at the appropriate time. Surely there must be servants somewhere! Were they hidden in the woodwork? Supper conversation was light and Caitlyn was too hungry to talk much. She kept looking over her shoulder, wondering when some silent servant would come to take her plate away. But at the end of the meal, it was Deborah who cleared away the plates, dumping them into a large sink where water had already been poured.

The men were ushered into a comfortable-looking sitting room with upholstered chairs and low footstools. Braided rugs covered the gleaming oak floors and a cheery fire was crackling in the hearth. Seth Wickham lit his pipe, and he and Tanner soon became involved in talk of sheep and wool prices and shipping costs.

Deborah turned to Caitlyn and signaled for her to come back into the kitchen. Once they were there, Deborah handed Caitlyn a dry towel and proceeded to wash the dishes. Caitlyn stood, towel in hand, wondering what was required of her.

"Would you dry the dishes?" Deborah requested, looking at the girl curiously. "The sooner we're finished in here, the sooner we can join the others. I hate to miss out on business talk and Tanner knows it. I think he does this just to annoy me sometimes."

"He can be very annoying," Caitlyn added, feeling a trifle annoyed herself. No guest at Mornhaven would be expected to

help with the dishes! She had to remind herself that she wasn't at Mornhaven. This was Australia and things were different here.

"Have you known Tanner very long?" Deborah asked.

"Too long," Caitlyn retorted. She eyed Deborah closely. "How long have you known him?"

"About two years," Deborah replied, concentrating on the dishes. "He and my father met through business acquaintances in Melbourne. I met Tanner when my father decided he was the man to do business with. He's an honest man and he says what he thinks. I like that in a man."

"We must be talking about two different men," Caitlyn said. She cared little about Tanner Malone's honesty, but something made her want to challenge this woman. "I've seen Mr. Malone do some dirty business in New Orleans," she continued. "He's a Yankee, so of course I wasn't surprised."

"A Yankee? Oh, you mean because he's from Boston and you're from . . . Louisiana, wasn't it?"

"Yes," Caitlyn replied. "You must know about the war that's being fought between the Southerners and the Yankees."

"We hear of it in the newspapers now and then. There are quite a lot of Americans here because of the gold."

"Yes!" Caitlyn's eyes shone with excitement. "That's why I'm here. My fiancé is in the goldfields near Maldon. That's where I'm going—to marry him."

"I see." The dishes were finished and Deborah invited Caitlyn to sit at the table with her for a moment before joining the others. "You must be very much in love to have come all this way to be with him," she said softly.

Caitlyn was embarrassed at such frank talk from a virtual stranger. "Yes," she said proudly, pushing her embarrassment aside. "I've loved Brant Sinclair for a long time. We've been separated for three years and I'm quite anxious to be with him, as you can imagine."

"How lucky that you have Tanner to take you to your fiancé," Deborah pointed out.

Caitlyn shrugged. "I suppose so. Mr. Malone didn't want me to come."

"But why not? There are some wives in the mining camps. It isn't the easiest life though." Deborah looked around the kitchen proudly. "I'd much rather have a roof over my head and four solid walls surrounding me than a canvas tent."

"We'll have a home soon," Caitlyn said defensively. "It takes

time. I expect that as soon as I arrive, Brant will want to begin work on a house somewhere."

"In Melbourne?"

"I suppose so."

For a moment both females were silent, watching each other with a combination of curiosity and competitiveness that was familiar territory for Caitlyn. Just what was this woman's link to Tanner Malone? Was she his mistress? Was she actually in love with that blackguard? How like Tanner Malone to be involved with this amazon who obviously didn't need the security of marriage to cement her relationship with a man! Perhaps their relationship was built more on their mutual business interests. Caitlyn's mercenary nature could understand that kind of love.

"May I call you Caitlyn?"

The question startled her out of her thoughts. "Yes, of course."

"And you must call me Deborah," the other woman replied with a wide smile. "I should hope we will become friends during your time here."

"Me too," Caitlyn returned, reflecting that she had never had any real female friends at home. There had been too much malice, too much underlying competitiveness for two girls to be friendly.

"Is there anything you need before we join the men?" Deborah asked briskly as she stood up from the table. "The water-closet is outside in the back. I'll freshen up one of the bedrooms for you. Do you need a nightgown?"

Caitlyn shook her head. "No, but I would love a bath. I must look terrible! I've had these clothes on for two days and my hair—" She touched the top of her head where her braid felt like it had been pasted.

Deborah nodded in understanding. She explained that the only tub large enough for a bath was the one they used for the sheep-dip, but it was clean. With some hot water and soap, Caitlyn would find it just what she needed. Once the men had unloaded the horses, they went back inside to continue their discussion, and Caitlyn was assured privacy in the backyard. In the tidy bedroom that Deborah had shown her to, she took a quick look in the mirror, almost screaming in alarm at what she saw. Was that sunburned, wild-haired woman really her? Turning away from the glass, she stripped herself of her dress and underclothing, which were in sad shape. She put on a wrapper that Deborah

had given her and, armed with a towel, soap, and a comb, she went downstairs and ventured outside the house.

It was a little after dusk and she could just make out the metal tub with the steam curling above the hot water. She slipped into the water, feeling the welcome heat begin to seep into her sore muscles. Ah, this was heaven! Never had she enjoyed a bath so much!

When she finished washing her hair and soaping her body, she rinsed and then stepped out of the tub to dry herself. It was dark and the lights at the back of the house cast a warm yellow glow on the backyard. Crickets chirped incessantly and a slight breeze stirred the branches of the eucalyptus trees by the stream. Her ears caught the sound of water splashing. She wondered if Tanner had availed himself of the chance for a swim. She covered herself protectively in the dressing gown and wrapped the towel around her wet hair like a turban. She hurried into the house, relieved to see that there was no one in the parlor, where the fire looked quite inviting.

She blew out the candles so that only the fire crackling in the grate gave the room its light. She sat down in front of it on one of the braided rugs and folded her knees to the side so that she could lean towards the fire. Taking the towel from her head, she shook out her hair, then rubbed it vigorously with the towel before taking the comb out of her pocket. She used the comb to fluff out her hair, hoping to dry it before going to bed.

When her hair was nearly dry, Caitlyn stood up and stretched, her ears catching the sounds of laughter coming from the backyard. It was a soft, intimate kind of laughter. Feeling like an eavesdropper, Caitlyn realized she'd dallied too long and now she would be forced to wait here in the parlor until Tanner and Deborah went upstairs. She knew instinctively that Deborah had been with Tanner in the stream, and the thought shocked her.

Unfortunately Tanner stopped to put out the parlor fire. He saw Caitlyn standing there, looking red-faced and guilty. With casual aplomb, Tanner turned to say something to Deborah, who brushed his shoulder softly with her hand before going past him and up the stairs.

"I'd have thought you'd be sound asleep by now," he said quietly, his eyes, dark in the firelight, going over Caitlyn with interest. "You've certainly improved your looks since this morning," he added with a smile.

Caitlyn could think of no light repartee. She wished Tanner

wouldn't stand there in the firelight, wearing nothing but a pair of trousers, his dark hair still wet and curling at the back of his neck. It was strange how she felt her senses sharpened by the sight and sound of Tanner Malone.

"What is it, Caitlyn?" Tanner asked softly, stepping farther into the room.

"Nothing," Caitlyn answered, her voice barely above a whisper. And yet there was *something*, she thought, feeling a stirring deep inside her that seemed to be awakening to the tension in the room. "Good night, Mr. Malone," she said deliberately.

He hesitated, his male instincts telling him that this woman was ready—ready in some strange way that surprised him, even as it stirred a response in him. Was she ready for *him*, or was it for any man? Oh, God, he'd best get her to Brant quickly, for she was like a ripe peach, trembling on the branch and waiting to be picked!

Moving closer, he came within arm's length of her before she jerked her head up and peered at him through coppery tendrils turned fiery from the blaze in the hearth. Her eyes widened. "No," she whispered.

But if he heard her, he gave no sign. Suddenly, he pulled her into his arms and his mouth swooped down to claim hers. She leaned against him, feeling the solid strength of his bare chest. His mouth was warm against hers, heating her lips to a fire. His teeth clicked against hers for a moment before his tongue pressured her teeth open and invaded the inside of her mouth.

Caitlyn felt her head spinning from the fierceness of his kiss. She tried to remember who had kissed her like this before. No one, she thought, no one but *him*! He was kissing her with passion, but with a slow completeness that made her tremble in a growing frenzy of emotions. Her knees were shaking and her arms were trembling as though she were in a strong wind. Slowly, her arms came up to encircle his neck, to hold his lips against hers as his tongue touched hers and fenced delicately with it before pulling away.

She could feel his hands in the rich texture of her hair, weaving themselves into it so that he was caught as though by a spider's web. Against her breast, she could feel the steady drumming of his heart—or was that her heart? His hands were on her back, pressing her closer, closer.

A little cry was torn from her throat, a cry of frustration, of wonder. She heard her voice with a sense of surprise, then re-

alized what she was doing, what Tanner Malone was making her feel. With an effort, she pulled away from him—pulled away before it was too late.

Tears of frustration glistened in her eyes. She was ashamed to look at him, but he drew her chin up with his hand and his eyes met hers fully, shocking her with their intensity. She knew, with a woman's intuition, that this man wanted her! The knowledge shocked her to the core of her being. She was not yet woman enough to handle it.

"Please go away," she whispered.

For a moment they were both silent, and the only sound was the crackling of the logs in the fireplace. It seemed to bring him to his senses, for he walked to the hearth to smother the fire, a necessary task that helped him to think rationally once more.

"I'm sorry," he said, turning to look at her, his eyebrows slanting over his eyes. "You just looked so—enticing—that I couldn't help myself. A man's wild urges, you know."

No, Caitlyn thought, she *didn't* know. Would Brant have such wild urges? Would *she*? "Mr. Malone, I—"

"Go to bed, Caitlyn," he said harshly. "I wish you a good night's sleep. We're leaving early in the morning." He turned abruptly and went upstairs to the darkness above. She followed soon after, trying not to recall the sweet emotions that had made her forget for a moment who he was.

29

THE NEXT MORNING Caitlyn went down to breakfast wearing a riding habit that Deborah had thoughtfully set out for her. Its skirt and jacket were a trifle long, but it would do much better than her day dress, and the divided skirt would help protect her legs from chafing. There were also riding boots and gloves, for which Caitlyn thanked Deborah profusely. Once she dared to look directly at Tanner, but he was engrossed in conversation and seemed unaware of her discomfort. Despite her wish that he leave her alone, her female vanity was piqued and she wondered how he could be so cavalier about the way he had kissed her the night before. Maybe that was the only way he knew to treat a woman, she thought. Why should she care if he thought of last

night with tenderness or not? Better that it be forgotten, for she would soon be a married woman.

Later, while Tanner and Hayes got the horses ready, she helped Deborah pack food for the remainder of the trip. As she worked, her thoughts turned to Brant. Dear Brant, waiting faithfully for her, loving her for so long, wanting her with him! She felt a deep yearning to be safe within his arms. He was the man who would be with her for the rest of her life. If there was an attraction between herself and Tanner Malone, she would have to push it firmly away, for there was no future in having tender feelings for such a man. It was Brant whose honorable intentions she truly craved.

Working herself into high-handed resentment over the way Tanner Malone had treated her last night, Caitlyn told herself she had been correct in her first judgment of him. His attitude toward women was selfish and disrespectful, treating them as though they were there only for his pleasure. She sniffed disdainfully at the notion. Did he imagine she was panting after him the way Deborah Wickham must be?

By the time she and Deborah were finished in the kitchen and Tanner had come inside, Caitlyn's eyes were sparkling with renewed energy. If Tanner challenged her again, she would put him in his place.

"Caitlyn, I would like to speak to you outside, if you don't mind." Tanner was watching her closely, his blue eyes enigmatic in his sun-browned face.

Caitlyn nodded stiffly, and they walked through the backyard towards the stream. They passed acacias that had not yet flowered and then strolled under huge gum trees. There was a nip in the air and Caitlyn was glad to be wearing the warm riding habit. Miles away the mountains were veiled in mist as dawn sent out fingers of pink and cream to lighten the day. She thought how beautiful everything looked, but her attention turned to Tanner as she found him gazing at her with an inscrutable expression.

"Caitlyn, I think you should stay here and wait for me to bring Brant back to you," he said bluntly. "I don't think it's a good idea for you to go on to Maldon. It's still several days away and the journey won't be a comfortable one. The foothills can be rugged and conditions quite primitive."

"I think I'm old enough to be the judge of my own abilities,

Mr. Malone," she said primly. "I can assure you that you won't have to worry about me."

He sighed and leaned back against one of the gum trees. "Caitlyn, can we be honest for a moment? Last night, we—"

She jerked her head up and fixed him with a haughty stare. "I would rather not talk about last night, Mr. Malone. I would hope you would be gentleman enough to forget about it."

He eyed her with amusement now. "It's not an easy thing for a man to forget when a woman kisses him the way you were kissing me."

She flushed bright scarlet at his bold words. "Mr. Malone, I was certainly not kissing you! I believe it was the other way around. You took unfair advantage—"

"Why do you refuse to admit that there is an attraction between us, Caitlyn?"

"Mr. Malone," she began angrily, "there is nothing between us. You are sadly mistaken if you think there is something about your charms that appeals to me. I am going to be a happily married woman in a few days."

"Do you think the fact that you are going to be married can change someone's feelings, Caitlyn?" he asked scornfully.

She looked at him crossly. Was he saying that he felt more than an attraction toward her? Was he in love with her? The notion tickled her immensely and she smiled to herself. How perfect it would be to have this Yankee varmint at her beck and call! She lowered her lashes, giving him the same glance she had used on the boys on the veranda at Mornhaven. "Mr. Malone," she began in her sweetest drawl, "surely you realize that you cannot entertain thoughts of tenderness with me. My heart is already firmly promised to Brant." Her smile widened further. "I'm afraid you shall have to behave like a gentleman, no matter how much of a hardship that might be."

He cocked a dark brow at her. "What in God's name are you talking about?"

"Why—your feelings toward me, Mr. Malone," she replied softly. "I've always known that you've been interested in me, and I'm ashamed to think that I might have encouraged it the tiniest bit."

He stared at her a moment, then laughed out loud as though she'd lost her mind. "Are you trying to say you think I'm in love with you?"

She was stung. "You needn't laugh about it. You aren't the first man who's been—"

"Smitten with your considerable charm? Is that it?" he guessed, still laughing. "Ah, Caitlyn, you astound me with your selfishness, your massive self-importance! Do you think that every man you meet is hungering for a kiss from you?"

"You're just jealous!" she sniffed haughtily. "Jealous because Brant and I have something you'll never have!"

He continued to berate her. "You really believe the whole world revolves around you and your concerns, don't you, Caitlyn? You're still the belle of the ball, the daughter of Mornhaven, with every boy in the parish clamoring for a dance. You're nineteen years old, but you may as well still be that sixteen-year-old I met when I first came to Louisiana."

"You're a fine one to talk, Mr. Malone!" she exploded. "You think life is a game to be played at *your* whim, with *your* rules!"

He smiled. "I admit to my faults," he said unexpectedly. "But one thing I am good at, Caitlyn, is adapting to my surroundings. You've got to start doing the same or you're doomed to fail here. You can't pretend that this is Louisiana and we're on the veranda of Mornhaven. You can't pretend that the most pressing thing on your mind is what dress you're going to wear to next month's barbecue. Don't you understand anything I'm trying to say? Brant has changed; he's not the same man who left Louisiana three years ago."

"But he *is* the same to me!" Caitlyn returned passionately. "He loves me, and these last three years can't have changed that!"

Tanner turned away from her and angrily pressed his fist into the trunk of a gum tree. He was wasting his time trying to make her understand. Brant didn't love her; he'd never really loved her. He would rather Constance had come than Caitlyn. Could Brant carry the charade through? Could he carry it all the way to the marriage altar? Tanner looked at the girl who was watching him, her eyes aglow with belief in the reality of her own dreams. He hadn't the heart to say anything more to her.

"All right," he conceded, throwing up his hands. "You've won, Caitlyn. I'll take you to Brant." He saw the look of triumph on her face. "But only on one condition," he added.

She eyed him warily. "What is it?"

"That you get off your high horse for the rest of this trip and

forget that I'm a blue-bellied Yankee and you're a Southern rebel.''

She was startled at his reminder of the war raging back home. Gradually, in the last few days, she had almost forgotten about their political differences. He was right about one thing. They were at opposite ends politically, yet it hardly seemed to matter out here.

''All right, Mr. Malone,'' she agreed.

''And for God's sake, call me Tanner!'' he added as he started walking back toward the house.

For a moment she watched him walk away and thought about what he had said. Then she followed him into the house to thank Seth and Deborah Wickham for their hospitality.

Hayes was waiting outside with the horses, and their party left shortly, heading towards the mountains that loomed mysteriously in the distance. They passed through more grazing lands interspersed with forested areas of gum and pine trees until they reached the foothills of the mountains, which were carpeted in scrub. The going was slower as they ascended into the thick forests in the valleys between the mountains. Caitlyn could hear various birdcalls, which Tanner tried to identify for her as they rode beneath the trees. The loud, plaintive call of the giant black cockatoo caught her ear more than once, and Tanner explained that the bird was greatly appreciated because its diet consisted mainly of the grubs and caterpillars that infested the bark of the gum tree. As twilight settled over the forest, the undergrowth seemed to come alive with little animals scurrying for food. Brush-tailed phalangers, as big as house cats, and bandicoots, as big as large rats, but with shrewlike faces, ran about the vines and mossy logs, startling Caitlyn with their quickness.

Despite her interest in the land and its animals, she was glad when Tanner called a halt for the day. They camped in a small clearing that was near a good-sized stream. Caitlyn dismounted from her horse and stretched her arms, hearing the satisfying sound of her back cracking.

When Hayes looked expectantly at her after getting the fire started, she stepped towards him hesitantly. ''I'll try to make the coffee,'' she offered.

For some reason she felt glad when Hayes gave her a squinty look without spitting this time. ''It's not hard,'' he said. ''By the time you find your fiancé, maybe you'll be able to cook his dinner.''

Caitlyn smiled and hunkered down beside him to get the necessary implements out of the pack. She hurried to the stream to get water for the coffee while the men saw to other chores. In no time at all, she had the coffee on and was watching diligently as Hayes fried ham and beans in the skillet. It didn't look too hard, she thought, and she told herself that the next night she would offer to do all the cooking herself.

After supper she relaxed with her companions, sipping the last of the coffee and staring up at the evening sky.

"It appears there's some hope for you yet," Hayes said grudgingly.

"Thank you, Hayes," she said. It felt good to be honest and simple and not have to play the games of youth anymore. She was reminded of Tanner's accusation that she still thought she was the belle of the ball. She supposed she had acted that way. Old habits were hard to break. She was determined to prove to Tanner that she could grow up, that she could mature into the kind of woman that was needed here in Australia.

Without being ordered, she stood up after the last cup of coffee was drunk and gathered the eating utensils in a large cloth to take them to the stream. She told herself if she proved useful, the men would continue to be as pleasant as they'd been today.

As she leaned over the stream to wash the coffeepot, she heard Tanner's boots crunching through the underbrush. She knew it would be him and not Hayes. A little smile curved her lips at the thought that he was seeking her out despite what he'd said that morning.

"Hello, Tanner," she said lightly.

"The lean-to's been made up and the blankets are ready whenever you are," he told her, hunkering down next to her. "Are you tired?"

She nodded. "Not like I was the first night, but in a good way. This evening I feel better about the journey."

"Do you think it's because we've called a truce?" he asked cheerfully.

"Oh, I don't know," she replied airily, putting everything back into the cloth and tying its corners up into a knot. "Hayes seemed friendlier today; maybe that was the difference." She glanced up at him. "And maybe I feel more positive that you aren't going to do something conniving when my back is turned," she added impudently.

"Conniving? Me? You wound me to the quick," he said sadly.

"You aren't accusing me of trying to take advantage of you under the circumstances, are you, Caitlyn?"

"Taking advantage of women seems to be a specialty of yours, Tanner Malone," she replied.

They walked back to the camp and she set the eating utensils out on the cloth to dry in front of the fire.

"I suppose you must be right, Caitlyn. I'm a first-class reprobate. And you know what reprobates do when they find themselves alone in the dark with an attractive young woman?"

She shook her head, smiling and feeling comfortable with him. "No, Tanner, what do they do?"

He leaned toward her and brushed her lips softly with his. "They try to steal a kiss."

Instinctively, she pulled back. Staring at him in the firelight, she felt her heart beating a trifle faster than a mere kiss should warrant. "That wasn't the way you kissed me last night," she said, and then wondered why she'd said such a thing.

He stared back at her, scanning her expression for the emotions beneath the surface. "No," he admitted simply.

They were both quiet, listening to the deep snoring of Hayes, who'd already retired inside the lean-to. Caitlyn felt a quivering sensation somewhere in her belly. She wished now that he hadn't kissed her just then.

"I want to kiss you again, Caitlyn," she heard him say in a husky voice.

"No!" She was afraid of what another kiss might lead to. "Brant wouldn't like that," she whispered.

"Would you like it?" he demanded.

"No," she said slowly, deliberately, "I wouldn't like it."

There was disappointment in his expression and she could see the struggle in his face as emotion warred with reason. Finally he stood up and rubbed his arms to ward off the nighttime chill. "Time for bed, Caitlyn," he said as though their earlier conversation had never existed. "I'll put a little more wood on the fire. I might have a smoke, but you go on ahead. I know you're tired."

She nodded and made her way back to the lean-to. As she pulled the blankets tightly about her head, she felt something tugging inside of her, something alien—an unknown emotion that, if she allowed it, would draw her closer to Tanner Malone. Brutally, she pushed the emotion away, telling herself she was just lonesome for her family and Brant. She couldn't rely on

Tanner for a deeper friendship. To him that was only the doorway to a different kind of relationship—the kind he had with Deborah Wickham. And she didn't want any part of that, she told herself firmly. Once she was reunited with Brant, she was certain that these odd, mixed-up feelings about Tanner Malone would go away.

30

CAITLYN LOOKED OUT over a sea of canvas tents in the glow of the afternoon sun as it began to dip behind the nearby mountains. In one of those tents was Brant. If he was not there now, he would be coming in from the goldfields shortly, tired and dusty. When he saw her, he would be as glad as she. Anticipating the happy reunion, she smiled and turned to Hayes and Tanner.

"Where do we start?" she asked.

"We could ride into Maldon and ask around. It'll take forever to go through all the rows of tents," Hayes observed thoughtfully. "You should wait in town."

"Hayes is right, Caitlyn," Tanner insisted. No telling what Brant might blurt out when he saw Caitlyn riding up to him. Whatever Tanner thought of Caitlyn O'Rourke, he didn't want her hurt by the one man she seemed to love with her entire being. "Maldon's right over the ridge there. Hayes can take you while I search for Brant. Maybe Hayes will find out something in town."

She wanted to refuse, but nodded sulkily. She didn't see why Tanner kept insisting she wait to see Brant. She wanted to see him *now*! She'd been waiting forever for this moment and she was positive Brant must feel the same way. Feeling the prize being snatched from her grasp yet again, she turned her horse to follow Hayes, waving good-bye to Tanner, who promised to bring Brant to her as soon as he could find him.

When she rode into the hastily erected mining town of Maldon, Caitlyn was surprised at the number of people, all of whom seemed busily occupied with commerce of one sort or another. There was a variety shop, a pub, a blacksmith's, a barbershop, a feed shop that also sold saddles and harnesses, and a livery barn that had horses and wagons for hire and stables for rent.

Among these commercial enterprises were several small private houses sporting signs that read, ROOMS FOR RENT or PHYSICIAN'S SERVICES WITHIN. Caitlyn was impressed, having expected nothing more than a few crude shanties put up to provide the necessary commodities.

Hayes and Caitlyn dismounted and Hayes saw to their mounts and the packhorses. Then he headed for the pub and she followed him with a bemused smile, wondering if he noticed that ladies were not allowed inside. When she reminded him of that fact, he looked disgruntled for a moment. She told him she would wait outside on the veranda, where chairs had been set up for men to sit and watch the action out on the street while chewing their tobacco. Taking a seat despite the shocked reproach on the face of the old man next to her, Caitlyn waited calmly for Hayes to have his whiskey.

As her eyes flitted about the street and wandered down the boardwalks that served as sidewalks on either side of it, she could see that there were a variety of human beings congregated in this small area. There were men in shabby boots and dusty corduroys who had obviously not struck it rich yet. There were men who wore new boots and laughed loudly as they smoked long cigars; these must be the men who'd made their fortunes already.

She would have been fascinated to watch the parade of humanity all day, until one particular human being caught her eye. He was tall with dark hair and a bushy dark beard. He wore moleskin trousers and a dark red shirt and a long gray coat over them. His hat was pushed down over his head, the brim turned up to reveal the face beneath shaggy hair that badly needed cutting. Caitlyn stood up, her breath stopping for a moment.

"Brant!" It couldn't be him—but it was! She watched him for a few moments, noticing the changes in him, and yet seeing many of the familiar things that she had kept so dear in her memory. Without regard for how it must look, she jumped down from the veranda and ran across the street to where he was about to go into the variety shop.

"Brant! Brant!"

Brant Sinclair heard his name called by a voice that sounded familiar. Cautiously, he turned around to see a tall, slender woman running toward him. As she ran, the wind caught her hat and blew it off so that it hung from its ribbon around her neck, exposing her coppery auburn hair to the setting sun.

"Constance!" he whispered to himself, thinking his mind must be playing tricks on him. Was he dreaming? He saw his mistake as she came nearer. It wasn't Constance, but someone else, someone who looked like—

"Caitlyn!" Her name burst from his lips at the very moment she launched herself at him, uncaring as to who was gaping at them from the boardwalk.

"Yes, yes, it's me! Oh, Brant, I've come to be with you! I've come!" she was saying, laughing and crying and hugging his broad chest. "Brant! Brant!" she kept repeating over and over as though reassuring herself that it was really him.

Stunned, unable to speak or move, Brant felt her arms on his shoulders and her lithe body pressed against him. He was stirred as though in a dream. This couldn't be real. It was an apparition. But why wasn't it an apparition of Constance?

Caitlyn, excited and overwhelmed that she had finally found him, continued to cry against his chest. Tears of joy and relief streamed down her cheeks as she looked up into those dark eyes and saw her own image reflected in them. "Oh, Brant," she said between sobs, "it really is you, isn't it? I've waited so long for this moment! When your letter came, I never dreamed it would take so long to be with you!"

"My—letter?" he gasped out, his voice strained.

She nodded. "Yes, the letter you sent me when you—you asked me to marry you," she said, lowering her voice, suddenly becoming shy. She gazed up at him, seeing the familiar dark eyes that she remembered as merry and lazy and appreciative. Now they were none of these things. They were confused, his dark brows arching downward as he struggled to sort out the meaning of what she was saying.

"How did you get here, Caitlyn?" he demanded. "Did—did Constance come with you?"

She shook her head. "Constance is in Louisiana. Oh, Brant, I don't want to talk about all that now! Just let me hold you and look at you!" Her dark blue eyes were shining up at him and he felt a stirring deep within him at her nearness. There was an emptiness too, a confusion that stopped him from feeling glad to see her.

"How did you get here?" he demanded again.

"Tanner Malone brought me from Melbourne. Oh, Brant, it was terrible what I had to endure on the blockade-runner and—"

"Tanner Malone brought you?" Brant let his breath out in an explosion. He felt as though he'd been holding it for some time.

"Yes. I had sent you a letter from Liverpool, telling you of my estimated date of arrival. I had to forward it through Tanner's business address, as I had no idea how else to get it to you. Before he could forward it, I arrived. Luckily he was there to help me get situated in Melbourne before coming here." She took a deep breath. "But now I finally am here, my dearest. And I'm so happy."

"Caitlyn, I—you must excuse me—I'm amazed, stunned that you're actually here right now," he said. He told himself that something must have gone terribly wrong. Why was Caitlyn babbling about his letter when he knew he hadn't sent her any letter? What had happened to the letter he'd sent to Constance? Why wasn't Constance here instead? And what did Caitlyn expect of him now that she was here?

"Darling, of course you're stunned!" she laughed brightly, holding on to his arm and leaning against it. "But you knew that I would come, didn't you? Did you really believe that anything would stop me from coming once I knew how much you wanted me here?"

"I—I don't know," he said, feeling very stupid. "How long do you plan to stay, Caitlyn?"

She laughed again, pressing her cheek against his shoulder and smelling the scent of metal and tobacco. "Darling, I'm here to stay. You didn't think I would come all this way just to tell you yes, did you?"

"Tell me yes?"

"Yes, yes, yes! Yes, I'll marry you, Brant Sinclair!" she cried out.

Brant felt like he was sinking in a quagmire. Why was Caitlyn talking about marriage? Certainly she hadn't come all this way to hold him to that old, forgotten promise he'd made her so long ago. Why had she really come? And why hadn't Constance come? "Caitlyn, we—we must go somewhere and talk," he said, trying to gather his wits about him. "Where is Tanner?"

"He's out among the miners' tents looking for you, darling," she said.

Brant frowned. Why had Tanner brought her out here? Certainly he had known that it was Constance he'd written to, not Caitlyn! "I'd like to talk to Tanner," he said aloud to himself. "He's got a bit of explaining to do."

"Don't be angry with him for bringing me out here, Brant," Caitlyn pleaded, her eyes going over his face hungrily. "I practically forced him to. I told him if he didn't, I'd come myself! He wanted me to wait in Melbourne, but I wouldn't, Brant. You know me better than that."

How well he did know her! he thought, remembering the strong and willful girl he'd known back in Louisiana. She hadn't changed; she was still doing things her own way. For a moment he allowed himself to really look at her. She was even more beautiful than he remembered and, despite his confusion, he felt aroused by her beauty and by her nearness. She had come to him. She was his to do with as he chose. The thought came to him, dark and lusty, that he would have her all to himself for as long as he wanted her. And when he grew tired of her, he would send her away. After all, he wasn't obligated to her. He had never asked for her hand in marriage. She must have come on her own, knowing that she was giving herself to him without reservation. The idea took on greater appeal as he walked her past the variety shop and he could see the ladies of the evening beginning to ply their trade outside on the veranda.

"I would have thought you'd be married by now," he said jokingly, feeling the shock of seeing her gradually wearing off. "Or at least engaged."

She looked up at him swiftly in some confusion and laughed nervously. "Why, I am engaged, Brant—to you, my dearest! And I'm hoping we can be married as soon as possible. I don't want to go back to Melbourne without you."

He frowned. Why did she insist on talking about marriage? He was going to ask her about Constance again when both of them looked up at the sound of a horse being ridden towards them in a fury. Caitlyn could see Tanner's face beneath his hat and it had the oddest expression she'd ever seen. Fear and worry were written on it, mingled with irritation.

Stopping his horse, Tanner jumped off its back and broke into a run. He halted abruptly, trying to assess the situation.

"Tanner! Christ, I'm glad to see you!" Brant exclaimed. "I don't understand—"

"Brant, I've got to talk to you," Tanner said, giving him a warning look.

"You two don't have to talk about me behind my back," Caitlyn laughed. "I know you're going to say I have no right to stay here, Tanner, and Brant will probably agree with you. But I *want*

to be here with Brant. Surely there's a priest around here, or someone who will marry us!'' She laughed again and hugged Brant once more.

Brant's eyes met Tanner's in confusion, and once again Tanner silently warned him not to say anything.

"I've got a need for a drink!'' Tanner said urgently. Hell, he had a need for two drinks, maybe even three! He could see by the expression on Brant's face that he was not pleased to see Caitlyn here. Something had gone wrong—something had begun to go wrong many months before when Brant had written that damned letter.

"I'll have a drink with you,'' Brant said.

"Caitlyn, I think it would be best if you waited under those trees,'' Tanner advised firmly. "I'll send Hayes out to stay with you.''

"But I don't understand!'' she said, her eyes clouding with confusion. "You don't really mean you're going to have a drink, *now*!''

"Caitlyn, for once just be quiet!'' Tanner commanded.

Caitlyn looked at Brant and saw the confusion still evident in his expression. He looked relieved that Tanner was here, but his face showed none of the overwhelming joy she had expected to see in it when he finally beheld her. Where was the happiness, the excitement? He didn't seem fully to comprehend that she was actually here in Australia, in Maldon.

"All right,'' she acquiesced resentfully, "but please don't be too long. I feel foolish having to wait for you outside a pub, Brant, when I've already waited so long to be with you.'' Reaching up, she kissed him sweetly on the cheek and waited outside. Hayes had come out of the pub and saw to Tanner's horse and then escorted Caitlyn to a grove of scrubby trees next to one of the buildings.

Tanner and Brant walked silently into the pub, each anxiously awaiting an explanation from the other. Once they'd ordered their first drinks, Brant turned swiftly to Tanner, his dark eyes showing emotional strain.

"What in hell is *she* doing out here?'' he demanded in an undertone. "Why in God's name have you brought Caitlyn to Maldon?''

Tanner took a long sip from his drink and fixed his gaze on Brant. "She arrived in Australia with the firm conviction that you had sent for her in order to be married,'' he said bluntly.

"*I* had sent for *her*!" Brant echoed. "That's ludicrous, Tanner! I wouldn't send for her!"

"You told me you were sending a letter to the O'Rourkes about your gold strike," Tanner reminded him.

"Yes, I remember. I sent one to Timothy, and one to Constance, telling her how much I loved her and wanted her to be with me."

"Did you write in the letter that you wanted her to come to Australia to marry you?" Tanner asked.

Brant bit his lip and took a swallow from his drink. "Oh, hell, maybe I did, but I never really thought that Constance would come to Australia! God help me, I wanted her to! I was selfish enough to think that she might want to come, but I had no idea that Timothy O'Rourke would be foolish enough to let a daughter of his travel all those thousands of miles to a strange land."

"Foolish or not, why is *Caitlyn* here, instead of Constance?" Tanner demanded.

Brant shrugged. "Something must have gone wrong. Could Patrick Talbot have given the letter to the wrong girl?"

"It's possible, Brant, but surely you must have written Constance's name in the letter!"

"Well, of course I did—I—" Brant hesitated, trying to recall the exact contents of the letter he'd written. He couldn't actually remember what he had written. He searched his memory for the exact circumstances under which he'd written the letter.

"Can't you remember writing the letter?" Tanner asked impatiently. "For God's sake, Brant, surely you must remember asking a woman to marry you!"

"I'm trying to remember," Brant began. He downed the rest of his drink in one gulp. He wiped his mouth on the back of his hand, then rubbed his beard and concentrated. "Damn! I can't even remember writing the letter!" he said irritably.

"What are you talking about? If you didn't write it, who did?"

"That's it!" Brant exclaimed with sudden comprehension. "I didn't write it! It was that little whore at Mrs. Wellington's!"

"You let a prostitute write a letter to the woman you loved!" Tanner said in amazement. "Well, that's a first, Brant!" He gazed at his friend, shaking his head in astonishment. "If I remember correctly, you didn't leave her with fond memories of your visit."

Brant looked down at his empty glass in embarrassment as he

recalled what a fiasco his visit to Mrs. Wellington's had been. He tried to remember exactly how it had come about that he'd asked the prostitute to write to Constance for him. "I remember feeling depressed because I was with a tart instead of the woman I really wanted to be with," he admitted to Tanner, then ordered another drink. "You know how much I wanted to be with Constance. And now that I'd struck gold, I felt the time was right to ask her to marry me. I didn't want her to marry anyone else. I wanted to tell her that it was her that I really loved."

"And not Caitlyn," Tanner added grimly, trying not to think of how Caitlyn's face had seemed transformed by love when she'd gazed up at Brant as they'd stood together on the boardwalk.

"For God's sake, I wrote the letter to *Constance*!" Brant said indignantly.

"You didn't write the letter," Tanner reminded him. "You left that up to the discretion of a whore. In her state of mind, after you'd vomited your guts all over her bed, she couldn't be trusted to put the right name in. Did you ever mention Caitlyn's name in the course of the evening?"

Brant hung his head. "Yes, I did. I guess she *could* have substituted Caitlyn's name for Constance's. I never thought to check. I just mailed the letter."

"You are the sorriest idiot I've ever known!" Tanner exploded. "With something so delicate as a marriage proposal hanging in the balance, you didn't even think to open the letter to check it! Damn it, Brant! You're a complete fool!"

"Damn it, Tanner! I was drunk that night, and the next morning I wasn't feeling much like checking anything, if you'll recall! All right, so I was stupid not to check the letter! With the war going on and New Orleans blockaded, who in hell would have thought Caitlyn would actually come to Australia?"

"Then you don't know Caitlyn very goddamned well, do you, Brant?" Tanner said caustically. "Caitlyn would risk everything to get to you. You forget—she's in love with you!"

"She just thinks she's in love with me," Brant objected. "When I explain—"

"You're not going to explain anything!" Tanner interrupted, his blue eyes narrowing.

"What—what do you mean, Tanner? I can't let her think I actually wrote to her asking her to marry me."

"You damn well can, my friend," Tanner returned calmly. "You're not going to tell her any different."

"But what about Constance? She's the one—"

"Constance is lost to you, Brant. Don't you realize how many months have gone by since that damned letter was received by Caitlyn? By now Constance has resigned herself to the fact that you chose her sister over her."

"But she must still love me—I know it!"

"It doesn't matter. Caitlyn is *here* and she loves you too!"

Brant gazed in disbelief at Tanner. "But you—you can't be saying that you think I should *marry* Caitlyn!"

"If there's a gentlemanly bone in your body, you will marry her, Brant," Tanner advised. He ordered another drink and downed it immediately.

For a moment Brant considered his options. He could marry Caitlyn. But life would be hell for him. He didn't love Caitlyn the way a man should love the woman he wanted to spend the rest of his life with. Caitlyn would always be trying to run his life for him. She was too domineering and too temperamental. He didn't want that in a wife. He eyed Tanner warily.

"Why should you care if I marry Caitlyn or not?" he asked bluntly.

"Because, despite all my faults, Brant, I don't enjoy seeing anyone humiliated in the way that you would be humiliating that girl," Tanner explained. "Don't you understand what she's gone through to get to you? You *can't* send her back home! Home to what? To parents disgraced by a daughter who went off unchaperoned to be with a man who was supposedly going to marry her and didn't? To an unforgiving parish? She couldn't hold her head up outside of Mornhaven. There'd be no marriage prospects for her and she'd be ostracized from polite society. You know damn well how it feels to be ostracized, Brant! You don't even know if she'd be able to get back into New Orleans. It's an occupied city now. You'd be sending her back to a very real danger."

Brant pounded his fist on the wooden tabletop. "Damn it! I didn't ask for her to come here! I didn't want her to come here! Why should I marry a woman I don't love just to save her honor?" He gazed at Tanner, his dark eyes blazing angrily. "I don't *love* Caitlyn. Don't you think she's bound to find out? Won't she wonder why I asked her to come here and marry me if I never really loved her?"

"That's the chance you'll have to take," Tanner said firmly. "From a woman's viewpoint, it's better to be married to a man who doesn't love her than to be ostracized by society for the rest of her life. You can't do that to her, Brant!"

Brant hunched over his drink and stared moodily into the pale amber liquid. He was silent for so long that Tanner was about to say something, when Brant spoke in a surly voice. "All right, damn it, I'll marry the bitch!"

"Couched in such terms of love!" Tanner said sarcastically, although he breathed a sigh of relief.

"I'll marry her in the morning. Hell, I'll marry her tonight!" Brant said morosely, finishing his drink and wiping the back of his hand across his mouth. He laughed resentfully. "She's finally got me; I suppose she can be happy she had you to champion her cause."

"Don't tell her about my part in it," Tanner warned him. "Just go through with it as though you had always intended it to happen this way."

"I don't want her to stay out here though. She'll only get in the way," Brant said pugnaciously. "Damn it, if I have to marry her, I don't have to live with her! There's a lot more gold coming out of the mine." He looked around the room as though just recalling his original reason for being here. "I'd come into town for more equipment. Jimmy and Dan are expecting me back in the morning." He eyed Tanner. "It'll surprise the hell out of them to find out I've gone and gotten myself married while I was away!"

"We'll have to find somebody to marry you," Tanner said practically. "You know anyone in town?"

"There's a priest—no, I think he's a minister," Brant said.

"He'll have to do." Tanner stood up from his stool and looked down at Brant. "Who knows, my friend, this marriage might turn out better than you think. After all, I can't imagine Constance traveling thousands of miles over high seas and then through the Australian bush. At least you can be sure that Caitlyn really *wanted* to be with you. Hell, there aren't too many men who can boast of that kind of love from a woman! You're a lucky son of a bitch, Brant!"

"Until she takes charge of my life," Brant added morosely.

"You want a piece of advice?" Tanner offered. Brant looked up at him curiously. "Don't let her!" Tanner smiled wickedly before searching in his pocket for the money to pay the bill.

Waiting outside, Caitlyn was relieved when she saw the two men come out. The sun was almost gone and it was getting dark.

"Brant?" she questioned tentatively. Suddenly she felt shy, a little hesitant, as Brant stood in front of her, looking at her as though he hardly knew her. She had hoped he would enfold her in his arms so that whatever fears or reservations she might have about coming would all disappear. But for some reason he only stood there with his arms hanging at his sides.

"Brant thinks there's a minister down the street," Tanner said briskly when the silence grew too long.

"But what about a priest?" Caitlyn asked.

"There is no priest," Brant replied quickly. "If you want a priest, you're going to have to wait to get married."

"Oh. Then I suppose a minister will do, as long as everything is legal," Caitlyn said practically. She certainly didn't want to wait. She wanted to be Brant's wife as soon as possible. Still, she would have liked to have had a real church wedding, wearing a beautiful wedding gown and having hundreds of guests the way Cousin Pauline had had. She remembered the country weddings of Artemas and Marcella Blair and Darby and Mary Howard and how beautiful everything had been. Darby had been dressed in his Confederate uniform and had looked quite dashing with his saber on his hip. Caitlyn couldn't help eyeing Brant. She loved him, but she wished he could have been dressed in a Confederate uniform instead of the dusty moleskin trousers and the gray coat that needed mending at the shoulder. She looked at his shaggy hair beneath his hat and smiled.

Brant noticed her smile. "What is it?" he asked.

"I was remembering how you looked when I first met you after you'd come back from Boston with your father," she said softly. "Your hair was nearly the same length it is now and I told you how badly it needed cutting."

Brant smiled too for a moment. "I remember. You and your sister were walking along the promenade deck of the paddle wheeler and I could see you from the riverbank. You were both so lovely and I slipped into the water because I wasn't watching my footing." His smile faded a little. "I remember how disapproving you were and how Constance was so willing to defend my bedraggled appearance." He stopped and turned away for a moment, wondering if he could find the strength to go through with this marriage. He couldn't help himself from asking softly, "Did you say that Constance is married now?"

Caitlyn shrugged. "She could very well be. There was an understanding between her and Jesse Cobb. Jesse is away fighting, but when the war is over—"

"She'll marry him?"

"Yes, I expect she will," Caitlyn replied, looking at Brant curiously. "Why do you ask?"

Before he could answer, Tanner intervened. "Brant, why don't you go find that minister? I'll take Caitlyn over to the courthouse and you can meet us there afterward."

"It's late, but a few officials should still be there," Brant said hastily. Then he was off, leaving Caitlyn wondering why he hadn't kissed her. She supposed he didn't want to display affection in front of Hayes and Tanner. Still, she thought wistfully, she would have liked the display of affection for her own peace of mind.

The next few hours were a whirlwind of confusion for Caitlyn. First she was taken to the courthouse, where an official was sitting at a desk going through papers on mining claims. He was kind enough to suggest that she retire to his house, where his wife would be happy to extend their hospitality so that Caitlyn might freshen up a bit. Caitlyn was very grateful, and she let Tanner handle the legal papers for her marriage while she prepared herself for her wedding. The official's wife was very nice, but there was no tub to take a bath, so Caitlyn made do with a bowl and pitcher of springwater. She washed the grime and dust from her neck and chest before putting on her last good dress, a simple cotton gown with a tight-fitting basque and embroidery on the long sleeves and at the hem of the skirt. She took her mother's pearls out of her valise and clasped them around her neck, tears coming to her eyes at the thought that her mother would be with her in spirit. She brushed her hair and, with the other woman's help, she wound it into a simple coiffure at the back of her neck, held by a snood. She pinched her cheeks and bit her lips to bring some color into them.

It seemed only minutes before Brant was at the door calling for her, and she went out into the darkness to meet him.

"Hello," she said shyly. If she was disappointed that he'd made no attempt to freshen up himself, she said nothing. After all, she couldn't expect him to find the minister and meet Tanner at the courthouse and still have time to tidy up, she told herself. It bothered her, though, that when he leaned down to kiss her, she could smell the whiskey on his breath.

"Are you ready?" he asked her politely, bending his elbow so that she could put her hand through his arm.

She nodded. "I can't believe this is really happening, Brant," she said softly. "In a few minutes I shall be Mrs. Brant Sinclair."

"It's what you've always wanted, isn't it?" he said with a note of resentment. "Unfortunately you won't get Riverhouse with it—at least not for now."

"Oh, Brant, I didn't want to marry you to be mistress of Riverhouse!" Caitlyn chided him gently. "I love you, darling, you know that!"

He nodded grimly. "Yes, I know that, Caitlyn."

They walked together to the little church, the papers held tightly in Brant's hands. The marriage ceremony was simple, with Tanner Malone and Radford Hayes signing the papers as witnesses. After the ceremony Caitlyn marveled at how quickly it had been accomplished, recalling the hours of church service involved in Pauline's Catholic ceremony. Brant had found a ring somewhere, probably at the variety shop, and she gazed at it proudly. If it had been a huge diamond sparkling on her finger instead of the simple gold band, she wouldn't have been any prouder of it.

Laughing nervously, she accepted a congratulatory peck on the cheek from Hayes, who had actually given up his usual cheekful of tobacco for the occasion. Tanner, his blue eyes enigmatic, came up and kissed her softly on the lips, holding her for an extra second before releasing her back to her husband. His eyes slid back and forth between bride and groom.

"Is there a hotel in town fit for a wedding night?" he asked, smiling at Brant.

"There are rooms for rent," Brant returned casually. "We'll get one of those for the night."

"I'm off to one of the rooms over the variety shop!" Hayes said with a sly wink. "I'm not letting you lovebirds have all the fun!"

Caitlyn flushed at his inference and smiled nervously. Tanner stood a moment longer with them. As he was about to follow Hayes, Brant held him back.

"When will you be coming by in the morning?" he asked. "I've got to get back to the tent. Jimmy and Dan will be waiting."

"There's no need for Tanner to come back," Caitlyn intervened swiftly. "I'm coming with you, darling."

"No!" The word was quick and sharp.

Caitlyn looked confused. "But I've come out here to be with you," she said.

"You came out here to get married, Caitlyn," Brant replied with a touch of sarcasm. "Well, you've accomplished that. Now you have to go back to Melbourne with Tanner. He'll see that you're put up in the hotel."

"But when will you come for me?"

"I usually go to Melbourne every two months," he replied sternly. When she began to protest, he snapped, "Caitlyn, for God's sake, don't spoil everything tonight!"

Caitlyn was quiet, embarrassed that Brant had scolded her like a child in front of Tanner.

They bade farewell to Tanner and walked silently to a small building where a sign proclaimed that there were rooms for rent. After a discussion with the proprietor, Brant got them a room.

"Maybe we'd best get ready for bed," Brant said briskly. "You've a long ride ahead of you tomorrow. You'll need your rest." He took off his hat and coat and for the first time she noticed the revolver he wore underneath his coat.

She watched curiously as he began to unbutton his shirt. When he pulled down his suspenders, she turned around in confusion and embarrassment. This was the time when she should be waiting for him comfortably in bed already. But she was still dressed and he was nearly naked. Hastily, she walked to her valise and knelt beside it to look for her nightgown.

When she heard the bedsprings creak, she turned her head and saw him already under the covers. He suddenly looked alien to her with his bushy beard and long dark hair. She found herself wondering how long it had been since he'd taken a bath, then immediately rebuked herself for thinking such a thing. Certainly when one loved a person, one shouldn't worry about such things. She tried to remember him in Louisiana, dressed so fashionably, his dark hair combed tidily, and his lazy, endearing eyes following her as she danced around the ballroom in the arms of another partner. Oh, yes, that look had been one of restless passion, she told herself, of sweet longing that someday she would be his bride. And now she was.

She stood up and began to unbutton her basque, her fingers slower than usual. She found herself wishing for Sara, or even

old Mammy, to help her prepare herself for this night, but they weren't here. No one was here but Brant, who was waiting with clear impatience for her to join him in bed.

"Do you need help?" he asked.

"No thank you," she said, finally managing to pull off her basque and step out of her skirt. She folded the dress and laid it on a chair. Then she reached behind her waist to untie the strings of her petticoat and took it off. She hadn't worn a corset since setting out from Wickham Station. Although she'd felt half-naked without her stays, Caitlyn had told herself that for comfort's sake, she would have to relinquish them out here. Stays, like ballrooms and perfumed gowns, had no place in the Australian bush. She hesitated over the tiny buttons of her camisole, aware of Brant watching her curiously. Feeling like a coward, she turned her back to him for a moment.

"Could you—would you please blow out the candles?" she requested quietly.

He grumbled softly to himself, and she heard him pad to the shelf where candles had been placed to light the room. In a moment it was dark in the room, the only light coming through the curtains on the window. Caitlyn shivered, then took off her camisole and untied her pantalets so that they could slide down her legs. She wore no stockings and her boots had already been placed beneath the washstand. She quickly donned her night-gown.

Tiptoeing cautiously to the bed, she stood next to it for a moment. "Brant?" she whispered anxiously.

"I'm here," he said. "Are you ready to come to bed now?"

She swallowed nervously, then pulled back the covers to slide in next to him. The bed wasn't very wide and she could feel that he was naked next to her. Her face felt hot in the darkness as she waited, with rapidly beating heart, for what he might do next.

Despite his resentment that he had married the wrong woman, Brant was looking forward to this part of the wedding night. Caitlyn had always remained a mystery to him, and tonight he was going to unveil that mystery. He sensed that she would be more responsive in bed than Constance. In this he was absolutely wrong. For all Caitlyn's passionate nature, she was as scared as any new bride and needed the care and loving of a compassionate husband. Brant had no time for that. He was ready for her now, his male member tumescent and standing

stiffly against his abdomen. He assumed that she, like the whores he'd been with before, would be ready for him.

Turning toward her, he gathered her in his arms. His mouth came down to capture hers in a demanding kiss that sparked excitement deep within her, in spite of her fear. As his lips ground against hers and his hands pulled at the pins that held her hair in place, Caitlyn felt a yearning growing inside of her and she knew that she loved Brant with her entire being. She drew his mouth closer as her fingers tangled in his hair. When his hands came around to clasp her breasts through the nightgown, she gasped, but did not try to pull away from him. She was his wife and this was the way it should be between them now.

Frustrated by the nightgown between them, Brant reached down for the hem and pulled it up above her waist. His hand groped downward, passing over the curve of her waist and hip, sliding along her thigh before delving inward. Caitlyn gasped again, for she hadn't expected him to touch her there. Still, his mouth remained on hers and she continued to return his kiss, telling herself that this was Brant beside her, Brant whom she'd loved for such a very long time. She wanted everything to be right for him.

Meanwhile Brant was fast becoming impatient. He moved his mouth from hers so that he could turn her on her back. Caitlyn felt his manhood nudging impatiently at that part of her that no one had seen since she was a baby. Her passion gave way to sudden, inexplicable terror and she stiffened automatically, trying to close her thighs against him.

"Don't!" he commanded in frustration. "Spread your legs, Caitlyn!"

Tears welled up in her eyes at his brusque manner, but she obliged him quickly, not wanting to anger him further. He pushed her nightgown up higher, wadding it uncomfortably around her neck so that he could kiss and fondle her breasts. Caitlyn tried to concentrate on the wondrous sensations he aroused by doing so, but she was too wary about what he was doing lower down to relax completely.

"Brant, I'm not sure—"

"Hush!" he begged her. "Just one more minute, Caitlyn. Ah!" He abruptly pushed himself between her legs.

Caitlyn caught her breath at the pain she felt, the sudden slice of hurt that resulted from his unexpected entry. To her dismay,

he continued to push forward so that she felt as though she might split in two. She wished he would kiss her again, but he seemed incapable of lifting his head from her bosom as his hips worked back and forth. She waited curiously, seeking some intensity of feeling to explain why this might be such a wonderful part of marriage. The pain had lessened considerably from that initial hurt, but there was still discomfort. Certainly this wasn't what Deborah Wickham had been thinking about when she'd looked so happily at Tanner Malone.

Caitlyn caught herself sharply. She shouldn't be thinking of Tanner Malone. Feeling as though she had betrayed her husband, she concentrated on what he was doing, trying to do what she thought he wanted her to.

"Move—move your hips, Caitlyn!" he commanded, breathing loudly, lifting his head and digging his chin into her breastbone.

Caitlyn obliged, although it was no easy task with his weight on top of her. As she moved back and forth, she realized there was a trick to this that involved matching Brant's rhythm. Surprised at how much easier it was when she moved with him, she tried even harder, instinctively bringing her knees up so that her feet were flat against the mattress.

"Ah, God, Caitlyn! God, yes!" Brant seemed to be going into a transport of delight and Caitlyn, pleased that she had accommodated him so well, redoubled her efforts.

In the course of trying to please her husband, it dawned on her that she was beginning to feel a pleasant sensation herself. "Oh!" The exclamation popped from her mouth as she concentrated on the wondrous feelings that were rippling like waves through her abdomen and thighs. She caught her breath as one exquisite shiver went through her body and she hugged her knees tightly against Brant's hips.

"Jesus! Oh, Christ, you are wonderful!" Brant cried. He moved his mouth to try to suck on her breast, but the sensations he was feeling were so powerful he couldn't do more than lave the underside weakly with his tongue.

As he felt his culmination coming quickly, he went up on his hands to make it easier to drive deeply inside. Looking up at his face in the semidarkness, Caitlyn could see the half-closed eyes, the set determination in his mouth. Suddenly he threw back his head and let out a long, slow moan of ecstasy.

"Holy Mother of God!" he cried, breathing heavily before collapsing on top of her.

Caitlyn waited for her own release, but when he'd stopped, all sensations had stopped for her too, except for a curious building inside that cried for release. She felt a lump in her throat as she tried to catch her breath. God, she wanted, needed, something more! But she could tell that Brant was finished. He had already rolled off her and was lying on his back next to her, one hand playing ineffectually with her breast. They were both silent, awash in their own private thoughts.

Finally Brant turned toward her and kissed her on the mouth, thrusting his tongue inside. It was, Caitlyn thought ruefully, a little too late for that. He ran his hand possessively down her flank, stopping to finger the tight curls that bloomed where he had just violated her.

He was just about asleep when she leaned over to question him. "Brant? You—you haven't told me you love me yet," she reminded him softly.

He reached over to pat her shoulder. "God, I'm exhausted," he mumbled. "Go to sleep, Caitlyn."

She lay back beside him, wondering why he hadn't told her he loved her. She bit her lip and glanced at his back as he turned on his side. She could hear his breathing, loud and even. She pulled her nightgown down from around her neck, wondering how he'd managed not to strangle her during their lovemaking. She pressed her fingers softly against that part of her that he seemed to find so interesting, and felt a slight tingle of soreness. Certainly it wouldn't be like this always, she thought with confidence. Of course there wouldn't be any more times like this if she listened to Brant and went back to Melbourne.

She didn't want to go back to Melbourne. She wanted to be with Brant. She wanted to help him. Just as it had been when she'd first decided she loved him, Caitlyn's protective instinct was aroused by the man beside her. He needed her, she was sure of it. She sighed. It all would be perfect, she was positive, if only Brant would see things her way.

31

"Good morning!"

Caitlyn opened her eyes to see Brant leaning over her, his dark eyes restless with longing as his hand moved beneath the covers to pull up her nightgown. She blushed, and with the sun shining in the window, there was no protection of darkness to hide her embarrassment. Brant's need was clear from his expression and she shied away, feeling that such blatancy was out of place on the morning after the wedding night.

"Good morning, Brant," she said softly, letting her fingers touch the edge of his hair as she pushed it off his forehead.

"I'm hungry for you," he said boldly. With a sweeping motion of his hand, he pulled the covers off her, causing her to squeal in alarm.

Reaching in vain for the bedclothes, she felt him pull her nightgown all the way up and over her head, and the searing look on his face as his eyes traveled over her body was nearly more than she could endure. He leaned down and nuzzled at her breasts, his tongue warm and wet, eliciting an immediate response from their rosy pink points. In spite of her embarrassment, Caitlyn felt a faint tingling between her legs that had nothing to do with any lingering soreness from the night before.

"Brant," she whispered softly.

He took it for an invitation and immediately moved on top of her. Without much preamble, he lodged himself inside of her. Caitlyn gasped, for it hurt more than she would have expected, but after a few moments of steady rhythmic movements, she felt herself accepting him. She wanted him to kiss her breasts again, but his head was lying on her shoulder, his face turned in to bite gently at her neck.

After a few moments Brant got off her shoulder and went up on his hands and knees, speeding up his movements. Caitlyn strove to keep up with him, arching her back and increasing her own tempo to match his. With one deep and throaty groan, Brant reached his pinnacle and spilled his seed inside of her, leaving Caitlyn feeling frustrated, missing her own fulfillment by a heartbeat.

"Ah, Caitlyn, you are a wonderful woman!" he saluted her, rolling to the side as she felt liquid pooling between her legs.

Struggling to sit up, she looked for something to staunch the flow, but as there was nothing she could use, she just lay back. It was embarrassing to think of the proprietor having to change the sheets later on, but there was nothing she could do about it. She snuggled against her new husband, feeling the strength in his arms from his long days using a pickax and shovel. She wished she had the courage to look at every part of him, but it was all still so new. She told herself there would be plenty of time to look at him later on. But now she sensed his impatience to be on his way back to the goldfields.

"Brant, I want to go back with you," she said bluntly, feeling this was not the time to be roundabout. "I don't want to return to Melbourne without you."

She heard him sigh deeply. "Caitlyn, the mining camp is no place for you. There are women there, wives of some of the miners, but they aren't like you. Most of them came to Australia after being convicted of theft or forgery or prostitution. You wouldn't like it there, my dear."

He turned away from her, throwing his legs over the bed and shaking his head to clear it of any vestiges of sleep. Caitlyn gazed at the long, rippled lines of his back, the width of his shoulders, and the tapering of his waist. She was so proud of him. Once she saw to it that his hair was cut and his beard was shaved off, he would look like his old self again, the handsome man she had fallen in love with.

"Caitlyn," he began, "I just don't want to take you back with me. I've got two partners, men who live with me in the same tent. How would you feel, having to share space with two strangers? We—we couldn't be like we are here."

She blushed. "We could get another tent for you and me to share," she suggested sensibly. "Please let me come, Brant. Won't you miss me if I go to Melbourne?"

He thought about that—thought about how unbelievably good he had felt last night and this morning. Not like he'd felt with the hussies over the variety shop. Caitlyn had smelled clean and felt soft. She'd been sweet and responsive. And best of all she was his, his to do whatever he liked with. Visions of sexual variations spun through his head as lust claimed him once more. Hell, why should he send her back to Melbourne? Why shouldn't he keep her with him? She was his wife. He didn't have to pay

for her favors. He smiled bitterly. He had already paid for them: he had given up his freedom and his dream of marrying another woman.

He turned around and gazed at her as she half reclined on the bed, looking more sensual than she could have imagined, with her hair falling down over her breasts so that only one rosy nipple showed through with impudence. He knew she was capable of gnawing at him continuously until he finally gave in. Why not give in now? At the mining camp, she could prove useful for more than just sex. None of the men would have to stay at the campsite and cook. All three could dig in the mine, and Caitlyn could keep watch over the tent and have supper waiting for them when they returned. She could mend their trousers and keep things tidy at the campsite. Brant turned the idea over in his mind. Why not bring her back with him?

"All right, Caitlyn," he said finally. "You can come with me."

"Oh, Brant!" She reached for him, wrapping her arms around his shoulders as she pressed her cheek to the back of his neck. "You've made me so happy, my dearest."

"Well, you made me very happy last night and this morning," he said pointedly. Then, with a derisive laugh, he added, "If you keep that up, you can have whatever you want!"

She hugged him once more, then held her nightgown around her to shield her body as she got out of bed. It would be awkward, having to dress like this, but she was still too bound by old habits and reservations to boldly prance around naked in front of him. She giggled at the thought.

"So you're happy now. You got what you wanted, didn't you?" Brant asked as he got up from the bed to pull on his trousers. There was resentment in his voice, but Caitlyn chose not to hear it. "I'm going to find Tanner and tell him of your decision so he can make his own plans for his return." He dressed quickly and took only a moment to splash his face with water from the washstand.

Caitlyn told herself she would have to improve his hygiene. However primitive the conditions at the mining camp, there must be a stream somewhere near it. Already, she was anticipating the changes that would have to be made to accommodate her sense of decorum, forgetting that she was the intruder here.

* * *

Later that morning Caitlyn stood quietly while Brant saddled the two horses he'd brought with him and packed the new mule with some equipment he'd bought at the variety shop.

Tanner and Hayes were with him. Hayes waited impatiently, chewing and spitting tobacco. He'd already said good-bye to Caitlyn and was in a hurry to leave. Tanner was talking about the gold Brant had brought to Melbourne and entrusted to Tanner's care.

Brant scanned Tanner's face attentively. "You don't approve of her staying here, do you?" he asked bluntly.

"No," Tanner answered in kind. "But she's your wife now, and what I approve of or disapprove of is not going to hold much weight with her. I only hope you know what you're doing."

"She'll be useful around camp," Brant said with a slight smirk, "in many ways, my friend."

Tanner let this tactless comment pass, although it irked him. "Well, I suppose I'd best say good-bye to her." He walked over to where Caitlyn stood. She looked fresh and dewy this morning despite the dust and dirt everywhere. Tanner looked at the coppery auburn hair, the dark blue eyes, and the sunburned skin and hoped she would survive in the Australian bush. He wondered what she would look like when he saw her next.

"I've got to be going, Caitlyn," he said, coming close so that she looked up to meet his eyes.

"Yes. I wanted to thank you for bringing me out here, Tanner. If you hadn't met me in Melbourne, I don't know what I would have done," she told him honestly. "I resented you at first because Brant wasn't waiting there for me. I hope you understand. I know you think I'm spoiled, but now that I'm married, I'm going to change. You'll see." She smiled at him and held out her hand.

Surprised at her admission, Tanner clasped her hand in his, then pulled her gently toward him and leaned down to kiss her. For a moment he could feel her softness against him as she yielded just a little. But the next instant she pulled away, looking embarrassed and glancing over at Brant. "I'm sorry," Tanner whispered, "I just couldn't resist one more kiss to the new bride. I hope you're happy here, Caitlyn." With a quick salute, he mounted his horse and he and Hayes trotted off without a backward glance.

For a moment Caitlyn watched them go, her eyes on Tanner Malone's back as he rode off. That Yankee had angered her so

many times, but she had forgiven him everything for bringing her to Brant. She was Caitlyn Sinclair now. Mrs. Brant Sinclair. She glanced at the gold band on her finger and smiled with satisfaction. It occurred to her that she should have written a letter telling her parents of her marriage and sent it off with Tanner. She would have to write one later and have it posted in Maldon. She only hoped her letter from Liverpool had gotten through to them. She hoped that the next time she saw her parents she would have grandchildren for them.

"Caitlyn? Are you ready?" It was Brant, anxious to be off.

"Yes, Brant, I'm ready," she said quickly, striding to where he waited for her.

As they rode out of Maldon and over the ridge toward the goldfields, Caitlyn looked around her, realizing that she would soon become very familiar with this terrain. Everything seemed dusty and dirty despite the winter rains that had been falling. September would signal the beginning of spring, and Brant told her that all the hills would be ablaze with wildflowers then. This was a wild and different kind of place. The Australian bush was craggy and rocky, filled with unusual plants and animals. Seasons were reversed here, and sometimes there were no clear demarcations. She wondered if she would get used to it. Then she told herself that as long as she was with Brant, she would grow to love it.

As they descended from the ridge into the mining camp, she could see miles and miles of canvas tents stretching in every direction. At this hour most of the men were away from camp, working out in the mines, looking for the gold that would make them millionaires. Here and there Caitlyn saw women boiling clothes in a big iron pot or stirring food over a fire or nursing a baby. Dogs ran about, gnawing at bones or playing with small children. Caitlyn smiled at some of the women. Some smiled back, others just stared in dull misery or acute fatigue. It was not easy being the wife of a gold miner, she realized. Certainly she had never envisioned such a future for herself when she'd left New Orleans to be with Brant.

Where was the big house she'd always wanted? Where were the servants? It came to her in a flash of inspiration that *she* would be the servant here. She would be expected to wash the clothes, cook the meals, and keep the campsite tidy. The thought struck her with deadening force as she realized that all her training at schools and by her mother and Mammy had never pre-

pared her for this kind of work. Her hands had been taught to embroider dainty little samplers or to finger the keys of a piano. They were not used to the steaming hot water necessary to clean clothes of this kind of dirt. Her feet had been taught the intricate steps of a waltz or the rousing steps of the Virginia reel. They were not used to the miles of hard ground she would have to walk going back and forth from the tent to the stream to do the myriad chores required in a camp. Her culinary skills were negligible, as she had already found out during her journey with Tanner and Hayes. She glanced at Brant and wondered if he expected her to take over all the domestic duties immediately. Didn't he see the worn-out women at the other tents and realize that she would look like them someday?

In no time they were at his campsite. Caitlyn wrinkled up her nose at the smelly remnants of three or four meals strewn about the camp. A mongrel dog nosed into one of the pots and barked menacingly when Brant shouted at it. Caitlyn dismounted gingerly with Brant's help, standing in the circle of his arms for a moment before he released her.

"Welcome home, Caitlyn," he said sardonically, watching keenly for her reaction.

"Well, it certainly does need a woman's touch," she said with a little laugh. "Apparently I came just in time."

"I'd say at least a year too late," he said, relaxing a little when he realized she wasn't going to give him a scolding for the untidy state of things. Still, he could see by the look on her face that she was disappointed. "You can't expect much out here, Caitlyn," he reminded her roughly. "People out here don't give a damn what they eat. Gold is everything."

"If that's the case, I won't worry overmuch about my cooking skills," she replied a trifle tartly. Immediately she was contrite. "I'm sorry, Brant, I didn't really mean it that way, but it seems you must have lived without amenities for quite some time."

"Amenities?" He laughed overbearingly. "You won't find any of those here, Caitlyn. You left them all behind in New Orleans and Melbourne. If it's amenities you want, you should have gone back with Tanner."

She flushed, hurt by his stinging criticism. "I only meant—"

"Why don't you stay here and clean things up?" he said derisively, remounting his horse and jerking the mule. "I'll be back by nightfall. Have supper ready, will you?" He looked at her a moment, then left without kissing her good-bye.

Caitlyn watched him for a while, waiting for him to turn back so that they could reconcile before tonight. But he went on without looking back, his shoulders hunched and his hat pulled low over his forehead. Caitlyn walked back toward the tent, feeling dejected.

"Bit of a bastard, isn't he?"

Caitlyn looked up and beheld a woman of indeterminate age staring at her in neighborly fashion. The woman was dressed in a plain skirt of a dark material, an unadorned cotton blouse that had seen better days, and a man's coat with the sleeves ripped out so that it looked like a jerkin. Her hair was black and pulled back severely in a bun at her nape. But despite the plainness of her clothing, she was not an unattractive woman, with a generous mouth and lively brown eyes.

"He's my husband," Caitlyn replied quickly.

"Oh, no need to get upset about it. Most men here act like that. They don't give a damn about their women. Just use 'em to cook and clean and spread their legs when the urge comes." The woman winked conspiratorially. "Sometimes you just hope they're too tired from all the digging to dig at *you*!" She laughed loudly and robustly, her hands on her ample hips.

Caitlyn's eyes widened. Surely here was a fallen woman, some reject from society who had made her way to the goldfields and gotten herself married to an unsuspecting male. There was a definite British twang to her speech.

Caitlyn eyed her crosswise, then stepped closer. "Perhaps you'd best introduce yourself so that I can get on with my work," she suggested. "I really shouldn't be chatting when my husband expects supper on the fire when he gets back and I haven't the slightest idea what to cook or where the supplies are."

"Oh, chatting, are we?" the woman laughed. "Well, that does sound neighborly, doesn't it?" She came closer and put her hand out forthrightly. "I'm Peg Dudley. My husband's name is Robin. And you?"

"Caitlyn O'Rourke—I mean Caitlyn Sinclair," she corrected herself. "My husband, Brant, and I were only married last night."

"Married last night and he goes off and leaves you in the morning! Now that *is* a bad case of gold fever!" Peg laughed. She gestured at the pots and pans stacked unsteadily around the fire. "I'll give you a hand with those, Caitlyn, if you'd like. I'm finished cleaning up for now."

Amazed, Caitlyn accepted her help gratefully. "What do I do first?"

"Gather everything in a cloth and take it down to the stream. You have to elbow your way in between the rest of the ladies and the gold miners panning in the water. Most days it's crowded down by the stream, but you just have to make your place. Don't stand on ceremony or you'll never get to your washing."

Caitlyn started gathering every dirty pot and pan she could find. She hadn't quite gotten up the courage to look inside the tent, but Peg cheerfully offered to go in ahead of her, telling her she'd been watching the three men for about five months since she and her husband had pitched camp a few tents away. "They're a messy lot, especially your husband. I got the idea he was used to someone else picking up after him, either a wife or servants. I worked in the textile mills in Lancaster, England," Peg said dully, "and we were treated worse than slaves. I was only fifteen, but they worked me eighteen hours a day for a pittance. When the foreman decided he wanted to take my virginity, I swore I'd get at him. I would have killed him too, but they caught me. That's why I was sent to Australia. Of course that was fifteen years ago. They don't transport convicts anymore."

"You were a convict?" Caitlyn involuntarily backed up a step or two.

Peg laughed cynically. "No need to be scared, Caitlyn. I've got no quarrel with you. I served ten years of my sentence indentured to a bastard who thought it was fun to corner servant girls in their attic rooms and use them for his own purposes. It was just lucky that Robin came along and rescued me. We've been in the bush ever since, roaming from field to field, hoping to find our fortune."

"Have you had any luck?"

Peg shook her head. "Not yet. I swear if we don't find something soon—" She stopped, stared at Caitlyn, and then said, "We'll find something, I'm sure of it."

Caitlyn followed her cautiously into the tent, where the stink that hit her nearly knocked her over. Trousers, shirts, and socks were everywhere, mixed with remnants of tobacco and spilled coffee. It was disgusting! She couldn't possibly be expected to wash all of that! But it would be impossible to pick out Brant's clothes from the others. They were all equally dirty and malodorous. For a moment she was tempted to sit down in the middle

of everything and weep, but Peg briskly began picking things up and throwing them in a pile.

"Jesus, those men are pigs!" Peg said under her breath.

Caitlyn, feeling as though she might faint from the stale air in the tent, was relieved to make her way back outside as soon as possible. The stinking pile of clothes was hauled out onto the ground.

"You'll need a big iron pot to boil these in," Peg advised. "If you haven't got one, I'll loan you mine, but you'd best get your husband to buy you one in Maldon. They're cheap enough—cheaper than buying new clothes every two or three months."

"I'll be sure to tell him," Caitlyn agreed.

She went to Peg's campsite, which was neat and tidy, to help her haul out the pot. Caitlyn would have to go down to the stream to scrub the clothes and fill the pot with water. Then she would return to the campsite to heat the water and dump the clothes into it. It would take several hours of boiling, Peg advised, to get all the clay off the clothes and to take the stench away. Peg gave her some strong lye soap to speed up the process.

Once the washpot was full of water, Caitlyn dumped the clothes in and started the fire beneath it. Leaving it to boil, she trudged once more to the stream to wash the cooking utensils. Elbowing her way through taciturn gold panners and scowling women, she managed to scrub off the worst of the caked-on food.

Hours later she sat numbly in front of the boiling water, stirring it with a long tree branch she'd collected on her way back from the stream. Glancing up at the sky, she could see it was twilight. Her back ached from hauling water and bending over the stream. Her feet were sore and her hands were already cracked and bleeding from the strong lye soap she'd used on the clothes. Peg had gone to prepare her own supper, leaving Caitlyn feeling alone and tired and cranky. She hadn't even had time to clean up inside the tent. She supposed that could wait one more day. She wearily brushed her hair, which had fallen out of its net. Her armpits felt sticky and she had spilled water all over the front of her divided skirt. She had never wished so badly for her mother or Mammy to come take care of her.

But a few minutes later she was faced with three tired and hungry men who looked at her blankly when, instead of the stew they had expected to find boiling on the fire, they found their clothes boiling instead.

"I'm not supposed to eat that, am I?" Jimmy Lang asked plaintively. At first sight he'd been impressed by the pretty features of his partner's new wife, but now he wondered if she was all looks and no brains. Had Brant gone and married some silly creature who would be totally useless in camp?

"Where's supper?" Brant demanded harshly. "For God's sake, Caitlyn, we're starving!"

Caitlyn looked up distractedly. "I—I've been cleaning up, Brant, as you asked me to do. I forgot about supper." She was on the verge of tears.

"Well, hell!" he burst out angrily. "What damn good are you if you can't cook a man his supper?"

Caitlyn's lip trembled. She was so tired she couldn't even muster enough anger to argue with him. Above all, she wished there were someone else who would bring the men's supper to them so that they would leave her alone.

Dan Walker looked at her and turned to Brant. "She's exhausted, Brant. She'll do better tomorrow," he said quietly.

"We'll have some bread and cheese," Dan said, frowning at Brant, "and we've got that smoked ham in the sack waiting to be eaten. It'll just rot if we don't use it—tonight's as good a time as any. We can celebrate your wedding."

Brant turned around, his face surly, but upon seeing the stricken look on Caitlyn's face, he relented. "All right, I guess you're right, Dan." He eyed the clothes in the pot with sudden interest. "You have done quite a bit today, Caitlyn. The clothes needed to be washed."

All four sat on overturned crates around the fire as bread, cheese, and ham were brought out. Washed down with lukewarm ale, it wasn't too bad a supper for the men. Caitlyn ate very little. She was too tired to feel hungry. She kept glancing at Brant, hoping he would make formal introductions as she smiled tentatively at the other two men.

Finally, when the meal was eaten and the men were able to settle back and relax for a while, Brant remembered his manners. He leaned toward his wife and put a possessive hand on her shoulder, looking over at the two men with a grin.

"I'd like you both to meet my wife, Caitlyn, from Louisiana. Caitlyn, this is Dan Walker from Pennsylvania and Jimmy Lang from Missouri."

Caitlyn nodded, surprised to see that one of her husband's partners was a Yankee. She shook hands stiffly with Dan, won-

dering what propaganda he might have been spouting to Brant all these months. Dan noticed her stiffness and smiled sternly.

"You have something against people from Pennsylvania?" he asked.

Caitlyn straightened her back and her dark blue eyes were unconsciously haughty despite her exhaustion. "You are a Yankee, aren't you, sir?" she asked.

"If that means I'm from Pennsylvania, yes," he answered her seriously. "Look, little lady, you may be a dyed-in-the-wool Confederate in Louisiana, but there's no place for that here. There's no war between North and South here. Everyone works together in the mines. So unless you want to make your life miserable, you'd best keep your nose out of people's political opinions."

"Brant! Are you going to let him talk to me like that?"

Brant grinned at Dan. "Yes, my dear, I think I am," he told her. "How many times do I have to remind you that I didn't want you to come here? If you can't get along with both of my partners, I'm sending you back to Melbourne."

For a moment Caitlyn felt anger bubbling up inside of her. This was *not* how it was supposed to be at all! First of all, Brant expected too much from her. Secondly, she had had no idea that he had a Yankee for a mining partner. How did he know he could trust Dan? And thirdly, she was obliged to sit here and be insulted, not only by a Yankee, but by her own husband too!

"I think we ought to call a truce before this thing gets out of hand," Dan said quietly. "Mrs. Sinclair, you're going to have enough problems to face without adding to them."

"I agree," said Jimmy staunchly. He wasn't as sensitive to the political tensions as Dan was, but he did know that when he came back to camp tomorrow, he wouldn't want to find a petulant, irritable woman who hadn't fixed supper.

"Caitlyn?" Brant was watching her, his dark eyes demanding her acquiescence.

She nodded stiffly. "No more talk of politics," she said tightly.

As they sat and the three men talked about their production that day, Caitlyn closed her eyes and let their talk drift lazily about her. She could hear Dan Walker tamping his pipe and Jimmy Lang scraping the soles of his boots with a dry twig. Somehow she didn't mind them being here. As uncomfortable as they might be with her at first, they kept her from being alone with Brant. And suddenly she didn't want to be alone with her

husband, didn't want to see the disappointment in his face, the censure in those dark eyes she loved. She knew he would only tell her again that she should have gone back with Tanner. Why, she wondered, had his attitude changed so drastically from the words of love he'd written in his letter? She had thought he wanted her with him so badly that he would be able to overlook her mistakes. But he seemed resentful, almost churlish towards her, as though he never really wanted her here. Had he written the letter in a moment of weakness and then wished he hadn't sent it?

"Brant," she said at a pause in the men's conversation, "I will do better tomorrow."

Brant was silent, moodily staring into the fire. He was thinking that Caitlyn really didn't belong here. This was not the kind of place where a woman like Caitlyn could thrive. After a time the dirt and dust and long hours of work would change her into the kind of woman he saw in front of the tents every day. Her hair would grow lank, her skin dry and peeling. When it came time for him to take the gold and return to Riverhouse, she would be useless to him as an ornament for his plantation. He tried not to think of Constance, of her sweetness, her gentle smile, but he couldn't help himself. She would have known that this camp was not for her; she would have waited for him so that she could take her rightful place as the mistress of Riverhouse one day.

"What?" he asked Caitlyn, aware that she had said something to him.

"I—I said I'll do better tomorrow," she repeated. "You'll have to show me where you keep your supplies."

He nodded, his mind on other things. They'd already dragged the iron washpot away from the fire and the water had cooled. He wondered how she proposed to dry the clothes now that it was dark and the evening mist had begun to settle on everything. Hell, why should he worry about that? Let her worry about it.

Everyone was tired. Caitlyn dreaded bedtime, for she realized that she was going to be obliged to sleep in a tent with Brant and the two other men. The prospect was not a comforting one, and she pleaded silently for Brant to think of some other arrangement. When the other men stood up to go to bed, Brant ignored her, stretching his arms and kicking dirt over the fire.

Dan Walker looked first at Brant, then at Caitlyn. "You want

us to sleep outside, I guess," he said quietly. "One of us will have to go to Maldon tomorrow and buy another tent."

Caitlyn was grateful and realized she may have been too hasty in judging this man. He seemed more sensitive to her needs than her own husband was.

When they were alone in the tent, Brant looked at her in the light of a lamp he had lit. "You're going to have to learn to be a little less haughty to other people," he advised her seriously. "There was no call for you to get after Dan like that."

"I know," she agreed, surprising him. After a moment she asked, "What will you do tomorrow?"

"Go to the goldfields," he answered. "That's all we ever do, Caitlyn, except for an occasional trip to Maldon. We don't have a social season here, you know. Everyone's too busy staying alive and looking for gold." His mouth twisted ironically. "I hope it doesn't get too boring for you, my dear."

She stiffened automatically. "I won't be bored. There's enough to do."

He nodded. "Just have supper waiting for us tomorrow."

Once she had slipped on her nightgown and gotten under the covers beside him, she was surprised to feel his hands reaching for her beneath her nightgown. She had hoped he would be satisfied with just an embrace, but it seemed he had other things in mind.

"I thought you were tired," she reminded him, not in the mood for playfulness after the way he'd treated her.

"I am tired," he affirmed. "Turn on your side, Caitlyn, and I'll go in from the back."

"What?" She wondered what in the world he was talking about.

"Turn on your side," he repeated, using his hands to force her to face away from him. When she had turned away, he pulled up the back of her nightgown and she felt his hardness against her buttocks.

For a moment she struggled, wondering what he was proposing to do.

"For Christ's sake, woman, would you stop squirming!" he said angrily. "Just stick your bottom out so I can get between your legs!"

Caitlyn had never been so glad for darkness. Never had she felt so embarrassed, so used, like nothing more than a vessel for him to deposit his seed. She was unprepared for him, but he

only took the most casual interest in her pleasure, squeezing her breasts in halfhearted fashion while his manhood rooted for the opening it sought. When he found it, he moved forward quickly. Caitlyn bit her lip, for she was still sore. She was still new at this, her body struggling to absorb all that was happening to her. Dully, she waited for his release so that she could go to sleep, telling herself that it would be better when she wasn't so tired and so reluctant.

Brant didn't seem to notice her indifference. He moaned loudly, and she wondered if the other two men outside could hear him and knew what he was up to. The thought made her cringe with shame. This was a private act between a man and his wife, not a performance for the benefit of others. When he was finished, she felt him withdraw quickly. In five minutes he was snoring.

Despite her resolve, tears ran slowly down Caitlyn's cheeks. This was not what marriage was all about, she told herself.

A lesser woman might have broken down, given up, and run away—run to Melbourne, even to New Orleans. But Caitlyn was not going to run away from her marriage. She was determined that things would be better. She was too proud to admit defeat or that she had been wrong, even when the proof of it seemed to be staring her in the face.

32

THE DAYS stretched out into one long, monotonous expanse of time. Caitlyn muddled through, although she could see by the grimaces on the faces of the men that her cooking left much to be desired. Unwilling to take all the blame on herself, she explained to Brant that she needed more spices to make the cooking more flavorful. He agreed to take her with him when he went to the variety shop in Maldon to buy some essential items. While he was purchasing a new tent and a large iron pot and making a deposit of gold in the safe, Caitlyn sorted through the shelves of cooking utensils and food items. There wasn't much variety, but it was enough to dazzle Caitlyn. She wished she could remember the special touches that Rachel, the cook at Mornhaven, had always added to dishes to make them taste so

good. She supposed even Rachel had started out learning by trial and error.

Back at camp, armed with renewed determination and enough canned goods and spices to last a month, Caitlyn waved gaily to Brant as he went off to the mine. It had been a week since she'd first come to join him and, although Brant was still not exactly as she'd remembered him, there were times when he was humorous and attentive. Other times he looked at her as though he'd forgotten who she was and Caitlyn would feel dejected.

Now, as she swept the ground under the new tent, she heard Peg's rich voice behind her. "New quarters there?" Peg inquired.

Caitlyn turned around. She liked Peg well enough, but sometimes she felt she shouldn't trust her. Considering her background, she might be capable of anything. Peg's husband, Robin, was a small, sly-looking man whom Caitlyn had seen a few times and instinctively disliked.

"Yes, Brant finally bought a new tent so that Mr. Walker and Mr. Lang can sleep inside again."

"And a new washpot too," Peg murmured. "Your husband and his partners must be doing quite well."

Caitlyn smiled, deciding it was better not to say too much about Brant's luck at the gold mine. Although Dan had persuaded Brant to take out a license for their claim in order to have the protection of the police, there were still plenty of claim jumpers and bushrangers around to steal the gold. Claim jumpers dug on miners' claims in their absence. Bushrangers were like the highwaymen of old. They lurked along the hilly roads, waiting for prospectors to come by with sacks of gold bound for Melbourne. It was easy for the bushrangers to steal the gold from miners who were foolish enough to travel alone, so now many of the miners made the long trip in groups.

Peg offered to lend a hand as Caitlyn arranged boxes and crates to make a crude sort of furniture. Caitlyn wished she had thought to ask Brant to buy a mirror, but she supposed he would have thought her frivolous. He never mentioned if she looked pretty or not. She supposed he didn't have time to think about what she looked like. Most nights he was too tired to do anything more than drop a heavy arm across her shoulder and fall asleep.

It took most of the day to arrange the new tent to Caitlyn's satisfaction. She bade good-bye to Peg and started to prepare

stew for supper. She added peeled potatoes and carrots to the meat and a little thickening to make gravy. After adding generous amounts of spices, she smelled the hearty aroma, her mouth watering.

When the men returned, loaded down with equipment and sacks of ore, they sniffed the air appreciatively. Caitlyn knew better than to ask them to wash their hands. Silently and efficiently, she ladled out portions of stew to each of them, waiting apprehensively for their comments.

"I think I've died and gone to heaven!" Jimmy exclaimed happily.

Dan nodded his agreement. "It's a damn sight better than we've had in a long time, Mrs. Sinclair."

That night Caitlyn was feeling very happy. Once she felt more comfortable with her cooking skills, she would have more time to do other things. She imagined herself as an efficient machine who could keep everything clean and neat, have meals ready whenever the men were hungry, and still be sweet and feminine to a husband she loved. Having a private tent for Brant and herself was a large step in making her feel more comfortable.

"Brant?" she questioned softly as she dressed for bed. "Do you think we might make love tonight?"

He looked surprised. "I thought you'd be too tired," he mumbled, feeling a trifle uncomfortable at such boldness from his wife.

She shook her head and smiled, reaching up to put out the lamp. Alone with him in the darkness, Caitlyn felt a sudden desire for Brant that quenched any feelings of exhaustion. Softly, her hand stole out to touch his flesh. She felt him jump when she made contact with his skin.

"Caitlyn, what are you doing?" he demanded. He'd never had a woman take the initiative like this, not even one who made sex her living. Suddenly, as her hand stroked his chest and dipped boldly down to where dark hair curled against his abdomen, he sucked in his breath and felt himself responding.

Caitlyn could hardly believe her own boldness, but somehow she felt that it was right for her to be doing this. Taking the initiative in making love with Brant was only a further extension of taking control. Breathlessly, she let her hand caress his body. His intake of breath delighted her and she grew bolder still, letting her hand explore that area of *his* body that he found so interesting in *hers*.

"My God! Caitlyn!" Brant whispered as her hand ran the length of his manhood and caressed it lightly. He could feel it responding to her touch and lay back with a little moan, letting the enjoyable sensations roll over him.

Continuing her exploration, Caitlyn let her fingers wander to the twin glands in the curiously made sac that was suspended beneath his hardness. They too were responding as they tightened involuntarily at her whisper-soft touch.

She wondered if she could ask him to caress her in the same way. He never touched her between her legs, except to insert his hard length into her. She sensed that there was much more to it than that, but he seemed disinclined to touch her there. Now she groped for his hand with hers and brought it to where she wanted him to touch her.

He immediately pulled it away as though she had made him touch a hot fire. "Caitlyn, what are you doing?" he demanded, rising on one elbow to look at her in the darkness.

She was glad he couldn't see her blush. "I—I was only doing what I thought—"

"Don't you think I know how to make love to a woman?" he asked.

He was angry with her, but he was also embarrassed that she might think him incapable of loving her the way she should be loved.

"I'm sorry," she mumbled. Softly, she tilted her face up to his and kissed him on the lips. The kiss deepened.

Brant realized it would be stupid to remain angry with her. It had never occurred to him that a woman might want to have certain things done to her in the act of love.

Telling himself that he wouldn't be found lacking as a husband, he deepened their kiss further, opening her mouth so that he could run his tongue inside. At the same time he reached down to fondle her breasts, feeling her nipples harden with swift desire. While increasing the movement of his mouth on hers, he squeezed the points of her breasts, hearing the ragged little groan that escaped from her mouth.

He pulled up the bottom of her nightgown, which she had only half buttoned to accommodate him, and quickly rolled on top of her. Beneath him, Caitlyn rolled her head and wished desperately that he would give some attention to that area between her legs that was raging as though lit by some inner fire. As he continued to nuzzle on her breasts and squeeze them with

his hands, she thought she would go mad if he didn't give equal time to the seat of her arousal.

But because he was now too aroused himself to accommodate her silent wish, Brant ignored anything but his own desire for fulfillment. Quickly, he spread her legs and pushed himself inside her. Caitlyn groaned, partly because she was still not ready for him, but also because she realized he was not going to assuage her needs.

As always, he came quickly to climax, moving back and forth for only a few minutes before emptying himself. When he rolled away from her, Caitlyn sighed deeply, still throbbing, still yearning for more.

They lay together so long without words that she thought he must have gone to sleep. He surprised her when he asked tentatively, "Are you happy here with me, Caitlyn? Are you still glad that you came all the way to Australia?"

She snuggled against his chest. "I'm here because I want to be here."

That was certainly the truth, he thought. "You must forgive me, Caitlyn, when I get angry at you. I suppose most of the time I'm really angry at myself. This kind of life isn't for either of us. But if I have to live through this to get what I want, then I'll do it. If there's anyone who can get through it in one piece, it's you." He realized that Caitlyn was the only woman he'd ever known who could have placed herself in such a situation and adjusted as well as she had. He had to admit he was proud of her for that.

"Don't worry, Brant, I'll be the best wife you could have wished for," Caitlyn promised him softly. "I belong with you, my love. I always knew that."

He was silent, feeling suddenly guilty for the thoughts he still had of Constance. Maybe it was just hard to let go of a dream, he told himself. And Constance was only that—a dream. A sweet dream that he remembered from the old days of lemonade on the veranda and barbecues in the backyard. Caitlyn was no dream; she was flesh and blood. There was no turning back.

"Brant?" Caitlyn's voice roused him as he was drifting off to sleep.

"Yes?"

"Are *you* glad that I'm here?" she asked softly. "You do love me, don't you?"

"I married you, didn't I?" he returned, avoiding using the words she so longed to hear. "Go to sleep, Caitlyn, I'm tired."

It was September before Caitlyn realized it. Spring began with early wildflowers spreading over the landscape, bringing a welcome respite from the clay and dirt that normally covered it. The banks of the stream were covered with tiny purple creepers that Caitlyn picked whenever she went down there to scrub clothes and fill the washpot. She and Peg Dudley grew closer. One needed friends in this remote place, or one would simply go mad.

Several miners were making the trip to Melbourne and Dan would be leaving with them. Caitlyn would have loved to go back to the city for a few days. It would have been heaven to take a real bath in a real tub! Here she had to make do with sponging parts of her body when she was alone in the tent. And she was hungry for news from home. She wondered how the war was going and if she'd received any letters from her parents. She'd instructed her family to write her care of Tanner Malone, feeling it would be safer to have him forward the letters to her than to risk losing them in the mail somewhere on the way to Maldon.

As she saw Dan off, she couldn't help the tears that sprang to her eyes. How she would have loved to accompany him!

Sometimes she hated this place. The tedium was hard when she remembered how much fun she used to have. She and the few other wives in the camp were treated with respect by most of the miners, but along with that respect came a reluctance to engage in conversation.

Although she liked Jimmy, Caitlyn was still a bit uncomfortable with Dan. Sometimes he seemed to look at her with pity. She couldn't understand why he should. She had Brant, didn't she? But Dan would persist in his pitying looks until she would get angry and shout at him for no particular reason, goading him about his Yankee background. At such times Dan would simply walk away from her, lighting his pipe and puffing briskly as though afraid that if he replied in kind, he might say something he'd regret.

It was a little easier with Dan gone to Melbourne, although without him to talk with, Jimmy looked to Brant for conversation at the end of the day. Caitlyn felt resentment that, instead of talking with her, Brant would oblige Jimmy by conversing about

the day's work. She knew her cooking skills were improving. She expected the men to congratulate her and rave about the meals she served them. But after the first few days they had come to expect good cooking as one of the services that Caitlyn was expected to perform in the camp.

As spring blossomed in the bush, the craggy slopes and dusty grasslands were becoming covered with more flowers. By October, lilies, buttercups, field daisies, and wild violets were springing up everywhere, and the gum trees had begun to blossom. Caitlyn would pick bunches of sweet-smelling flowers to adorn the crates that served as a supper table. Peg would come over and she and Caitlyn would gossip idly and exchange tales from bygone days as they stared dreamily into the fire.

The two women had very different kinds of tales to tell. Caitlyn's stories were filled with idle flirtations, picnics by the river, and glamorous balls. Peg's stories were not so refreshing, for they opened up a world that was alien to Caitlyn. They were filled with the horrors of children begging in the streets for bread, of employers working their laborers until they dropped, of mothers separated from their children because they couldn't afford to care for them anymore. Peg had lost her own mother when she was ten and had been virtually on her own since then.

In mid-October, Peg was bursting with news. "I'm going to have a baby, Caitlyn! My very own little baby that I can love and nourish and give a better life than I ever had!"

Caitlyn's excitement was tempered with concern. "I'm happy that you're going to have a baby, Peg, but this is no place to bring a child into the world. Maybe you should ask Robin to take you to Melbourne until the baby is born."

Peg shook her head. "No, I couldn't ask him to do that. He's not happy about the news as it is. He knows it's going to be hard until he finds gold."

"He will find gold, I'm sure of it!" Caitlyn said brightly. "You mustn't give up hope, Peg!"

That evening, as she and Brant lay comfortably in their tent and she felt his hand go tentatively to her breast, she turned to him questioningly.

"Brant, what would happen if I were to have a child now?"

Immediately his whole body recoiled and he withdrew his hand. She could feel his hardness go soft and marveled at how easily it was accomplished. "What do you mean?" he asked,

clearing his throat. "Are you—are you going to have a child, Caitlyn?"

"No, I don't think so," she answered. "I was just thinking about Peg Dudley. I know she's worried about having a baby, although she doesn't let on. Is it very dangerous?"

He let out his breath in an irritated sigh. "How the hell should I know? Women have babies. Don't you remember your friends at home having babies?"

"Marcella had twins. She seemed quite happy when everyone went over on a congratulatory visit."

"There, you see. I'm sure it's not as difficult as some people say."

"But out here, Brant! Out here in the bush is so different from back home. Wouldn't you rather I not have a baby for a while?"

He laughed harshly. "I don't think there's anything we can do about that, Caitlyn. As much as we make love, you're bound to get pregnant."

"Then perhaps we shouldn't make love so often, Brant," she said quietly.

Immediately he sucked in his breath. "Why? Don't you like making love with me, Caitlyn?"

"No, that isn't it, Brant!" she returned, angry that he had jumped to the wrong conclusion. "Why must you continually question my love for you?" she asked him. "How many ways do I have to prove that I love you before you'll believe me? I want to make love with you, but if it means that I might get pregnant, maybe we should be more careful." She wasn't sure what being careful meant, but she was hoping Brant would enlighten her. After all, didn't men always know about these things?

33

DAN WALKER returned from Melbourne and things took on a predictable pattern for Caitlyn. She was up at dawn every morning to give the men breakfast before they went off to the mine. After they left she tidied both tents and began cleaning the worst of the clay and mud off the clothes they'd worn the day before. She had found that if she didn't get to the clothes immediately, it was impossible to get them clean, even with boiling. While the clothes boiled, she sat and talked with Peg for an hour or

two, and then she cooked and prepared the campsite for the men's return. Lately Brant had been leaving ore with Caitlyn and had showed her how to process it. It saved time for them and Caitlyn didn't mind it. In fact, she welcomed being able to help.

Brant had taught her how to dry the gold by pouring it into a shovel and laying it over the fire. She'd learned how to pass a magnet over the dried gold and rock to take out any iron particles. She would gently sift the gold from the rest of the rock and put it in small sacks. After a couple of weeks she had quite a store hidden in a small depression beneath the bed where Brant and she slept.

Caitlyn felt proud that she was helping her husband to make his fortune. If she grew nervous sometimes at the thought that all that gold was lying beneath her bed, she told herself that many of the other women probably did the same thing. When the gold piled up too high, Brant would take it to the safe in Maldon. He'd promised to take Caitlyn with him to buy her a new dress.

She was woefully aware that the few dresses she'd been able to bring with her were becoming threadbare from the harsh washing methods she was forced to use on them. The original dyes had faded so that they all were beginning to look one color. She needed new boots too. The rough terrain ruined leather after only a few months.

One afternoon at the beginning of November she was sitting on an overturned crate by the cookfire, feeling disconsolate, when she heard a horse stop at her campsite. Shading her eyes from the sun, she squinted up.

There, leaning over the pommel of his saddle, was Tanner Malone, his dark blue eyes scanning her with his usual cool amusement. Scrambling to her feet, Caitlyn pressed her hands against her skirt, wishing she'd been able to get out the worst of the grease that she'd spilled on it while making supper last night. Self-conscious about her appearance, she smoothed back tendrils of hair that had escaped from the long braid that hung down her back and wondered if she had anything smeared on her face. How like Tanner Malone to see her at her absolute worst! she thought with quick resentment, forgetting that her husband saw her that way everyday.

"Caitlyn O'Rourke," he murmured.

"Caitlyn Sinclair," she reminded him.

"You've changed, Caitlyn," he said, dismounting and tying his horse to a hitching post near the tent. He walked up to her in his clean buckskins and gleaming riding boots, making her feel terribly shabby. A flat-crowned hat was pushed down over his hair, hair that had been newly cut, she noted, trying not to compare it to Brant's shaggy growth. Tanner was clean-shaven except for a small mustache, while Brant's face was half covered by the bushy beard he'd adopted since he'd been out here.

"Changed?" she questioned, her voice rising. "I should hope so, Tanner Malone. Did you expect me to exist without changing?"

He shook his head. "I'm amazed. You're not the belle of the ball anymore. Could it be that you've become as ordinary as every other woman in this mining camp?"

She flushed, wishing to God she had a mirror so that she might glance in it. Self-conscious, she pressed a hand to where her chest was exposed now that her bodice had lost three of its top buttons in the boiling process. Was it her imagination, or were her bones more prominent than before?

"You don't have to be nasty," she said quickly.

"I'm sorry, Caitlyn," he added hastily. "It's just that I hadn't expected you to adapt so well. I'd pictured you in a proper gown, sitting stiff as a ramrod with your ankles crossed just so and your hair done up in a proper chignon."

"That would be hard to do," she said sarcastically, "even for the belle of the ball, Tanner."

He smiled. "You're right." He strode over to her purposefully, his dark blue eyes playful. "Forgive me, Caitlyn, and greet me, not as the belle of the ball, but as the grateful young woman who has me to thank for bringing her out here to all this wedded bliss."

Her brows arched upward. "I'm wondering how much thanks all this warrants," she said.

"Can it be that the glow has worn off this place already? I seem to recall the day when you would have fought me tooth and nail rather than let me drag you back to Melbourne."

"I remember," she said, her lower lip stuck out belligerently.

"But that hasn't changed, has it?" he asked, cocking his head to one side as his eyes assessed her boldly. "It's still worth all the hardship, isn't it, just so you can be with the man you love?"

"Stop it!" Her eyes narrowed and she raised her hand as if to strike him.

Deftly, he caught her hand in his and held her against him for a moment. She didn't struggle for very long. She was too tired to struggle. Besides, she had to admit that he was right about her stubbornness in wanting to stay. If anything, she was mad at him because he seemed to know her so well. It was unnerving to think that he could read her motives so clearly.

Catching her chin in one hand, Tanner tilted it up and pressed his mouth to hers. He lingered for a moment before releasing her with a smile. "Now that's the proper way to greet a long-lost friend," he informed her seriously, although his eyes still twinkled.

Caitlyn was embarrassed, wondering who might have seen him greeting her so indecently. "Don't you ever worry about proprieties?" she grumbled. "You forget that I have to live here and face these people everyday."

"Then come take a walk with me, Caitlyn, for I want to talk with you. I've ridden a long way to see you and I don't want you looking over your shoulder every minute to see who's watching us. Besides, I might take it into my head to kiss you again." He winked at her.

Although she knew she should be affronted at his boldness, Caitlyn found herself smiling back at him and nodding. He was like a breath of fresh air, and being with him seemed so much better than sitting dully by that stupid fire and watching the stew bubble.

With a feeling of gay abandon, she accepted his arm and walked with him over the rocky ground to the knolls and hills that surrounded the camp. Everywhere a riot of wildflowers greeted their eyes, and Caitlyn found herself wondering why Brant had never walked up here with her. Of course, she told herself loyally, he had so little time to do such things.

"What has been going on in Melbourne?" she asked as they walked through the fields of flowers. The blossoms brushed against the hem of her skirt, and from time to time she would lean down and pick a flower, smelling it appreciatively before going on.

Watching her, Tanner was amazed at the change in her. It wasn't just that she was married. When he'd told her she wasn't the belle of the ball anymore, he'd been truthful. She'd matured; she'd become concerned with something and someone other than herself. Coming upon her sitting beside the fire with her hair falling out of its braid and her cheeks flushed with sunburn and

the heat of the fire, he'd thought she'd looked beautiful, much prettier than the spoiled brat he'd brought to Maldon almost three months before.

"Melbourne is growing," Tanner finally said as they came to a place where gum trees formed an enclosure, their branches sticking out to form a canopy that provided shade from the afternoon sun. "It's trying to become more genteel, more sophisticated. There's a rivalry between Melbourne and Sydney. Each city is determined to be the cultural center of Australia. Melbourne is even talking of bringing opera singers from abroad and of putting on plays."

"It sounds wonderful," Caitlyn sighed wistfully. On, how she would love to attend a play in Melbourne and wear a beautiful dress with wide hoops and a dozen petticoats!

"Oh, Tanner, how good you are to come and see me!" she said.

He sat down beside her and took both her hands in his. "I was worried about you," he said seriously.

"Thank you for your concern," she said, pulling her hands away and letting them fall to her lap. "I probably don't deserve it after the way I've treated you."

"Well, I haven't treated you entirely in the proper manner either," he admitted, making them both recall the night he had spanked her in her hotel room.

She flushed and looked away, wondering why she should feel so shy with this man whom she'd known for so long. He'd seen her at her worst, yet he didn't mind letting her know that he cared about her. It warmed her heart, and she realized that she felt better sitting here with him than she had felt being intimate with Brant. The knowledge made her feel guilty again.

"I also had another reason for coming to see you," he said, reaching into his shirt pocket to pull out two envelopes. He handed them to her. "They're from New Orleans," he added simply.

Caitlyn's hand shook as she took the precious papers from him. Letters from home! She was trembling so, she wasn't sure she could open the envelopes. She carefully opened the first and read it slowly. "It's from Mama," she said softly, looking up at Tanner tearfully.

Caitlyn looked back at the letter, noting that her mother said they were all safe and well and were staying with the Savoys in New Orleans. Tanner was glad to hear it. She opened the second

letter, which was from Constance. Constance reiterated some of what her mother had said and also wrote that her father was fearful for Mornhaven. Union troops had captured Baton Rouge and had spilled over into the region around that city and northward. He hoped that Mornhaven would not be destroyed by Union soldiers, but was prevented from seeing to it himself because of the difficulty of leaving New Orleans.

"Poor Papa!" Caitlyn said. "He must be mad with worry about Mornhaven." She looked at Tanner. "Do you think the Yankee troops will destroy it?"

"I don't know," he answered honestly. "I can't imagine anyone wanting to destroy such a beautiful home. Perhaps by now your father has gotten permission to go upriver to see to the plantation. Once Butler feels the area is secured, it might be easier for people to come and go. I'm only glad that your family is well."

Caitlyn scanned the last few lines of Constance's letter. "She says that Darby Howard was wounded in one of the battles in the East," she said, her voice wavering. "He's in a Union prison hospital and Mary is hoping they'll let him return home soon. She also says—" Suddenly Caitlyn dropped the letter with a cry and her face turned white. She closed her eyes and Tanner thought she was going to faint.

He moved quickly toward her, catching her in his arms as she was about to fall backward. Her eyes fluttered open and he could see the tears in them.

"Oh, Tanner!" she gasped, leaning against him, hardly able to speak. "Artemas was killed in the fighting in Virginia!"

For a moment Tanner couldn't think whom she was talking about. Then he recalled a young blond man with a handsome face. He gazed down at her stricken face and felt sympathy for her loss. Damn, if he'd known what news the letters had contained, he would never have brought them out to her! She had been doing so well, trying so hard—and now this!

"I—I can't believe Artemas is d-dead!" she was sobbing, tears running down her cheeks. "I—I behaved so badly toward him! I was s-so mean to him because he married Marcella instead of m-me!" She cried wrenchingly, clinging to Tanner in her misery.

Seeking only to comfort, he leaned toward her, whispering words of solace, feeling the helplessness of a man at a woman's tears. He rocked her against his chest, unaware of the sun be-

ginning to sink lower on the horizon. Caitlyn cried for a long time, emptying herself until there were no more tears left. Tanner leaned down and kissed her forehead, her cheeks, comforting her in the only way he knew how.

And then suddenly the kisses changed from gentle ones of comfort to dark, passionate ones. As his mouth touched hers, Caitlyn instinctively reached up to deepen the kiss, her arms going around his neck. At news of death, she reached out for life with a passion, with a tenacity that was overwhelming.

Tanner was aware of her change of mood and, despite some qualms, he kissed her back, opening her lips to his tongue and searing her mouth with his. Caitlyn pressed upward, straining her breasts to meet his chest and arching her back against his arm. Breathlessly, she met his kiss, seeking more. Her hands entangled themselves in the hair at the back of his neck. Her mouth grew more fierce as she possessed his mouth until neither was sure who was the aggressor.

Dark passions were lit, and once lit, it was impossible to put them out. Clinging to him, letting her thoughts grow lusty with yearning, Caitlyn continued to press her mouth to his, even when she felt his hands leave her face and move downward to where her bodice opened above her breasts. Before she knew what he was doing, he had unbuttoned her dress to the waist and was seeking the warmth of her breasts beneath her camisole. Already weakened from too much rough washing, it ripped in his hands and he pushed the material away impatiently so that he could cup the fullness of her breasts.

Dizzy with the emotions that were bombarding her, Caitlyn was hardly aware when he laid her back in the flowers and moved his mouth from hers. Traveling slowly down her neck, he reached the pointed tips of her breasts, enclosing each of them in turn with the warm wetness of his mouth. His tongue laved her flesh and his fingers pinched the rosebuds, making her moan softly from the feelings that were rushing through her body, centering in that part of her that was forbidden to anyone but her husband.

Caitlyn arched her hips against him, feeling a fierce need growing ever more fierce as she craved the release she knew must come. Never had Brant brought her to this feverish pitch. She would not be denied, not now, not with this man! So excited was she that she nipped his ear with her teeth, drawing blood.

Her own excitement fed Tanner's so that he was pushing up the skirt of her dress before he was quite sure what he was doing.

Instinctively, his hand reached up her leg for the opening in her pantalets, his fingers gentle despite his own urgency. He heard her sharp intake of breath when he touched her there, then heard the breath turn into a moan of delight when he played gently with the swollen flesh so that she was arching her hips in a spasm of passion.

Beneath his hand, Caitlyn was experiencing something wonderful. Her breath caught in her throat as she sought the feeling she had craved ever since she had been initiated into lovemaking by her husband. With little cries of excitement, she felt wave after wave of some inexplicable feeling roll over her, giving her the sought-after release that shocked her with its intensity.

"Oh!" she cried out one last time, before the feeling subsided and she settled back against the man who was holding her. Lost in the contentment of her own satisfied needs, she smiled lazily, and Tanner, glad that he had pleased her, leaned down again to take her lips. This time the kiss was soft, less urgent, as Caitlyn gloried in the heavenly feeling of release she had just experienced. She felt heavy, almost lethargic, as she looked up into the dark blue eyes above her and wondered what had happened to her.

Then, as she saw the longing, the questioning in those eyes, she realized what she had done. Hastily, she scrambled to her feet, trying to distance herself from this man who had been witness to her shameful need—shameful indeed that Tanner Malone and not her own husband had been the one to satisfy it.

"Don't run away, Caitlyn," he said softly, standing up too after grabbing the letters that had fallen when she'd stood up.

"I—I—my God, what have I done?" she said, afraid to look him in the face.

"Caitlyn!"

"I—I'm married to Brant and I—how could I have done that with you?" She put her face in her hands. "I'm worse than the whores above the variety shop in Maldon. At least they do it for money, in order to live. But I—"

"You did it for yourself, for your own pleasure," he interrupted her, his voice harsh with his own unfulfilled need that was making things a bit painful for him. "Don't be too upset with yourself, Caitlyn," he added. "You weren't technically unfaithful to Brant."

She looked up. "I know what happened, Tanner! I've wanted that, I've needed that for so long, but Brant—" She stopped,

horrified at revealing any intimate details of her married life. "I should have stopped it."

"Hush, Caitlyn, don't torment yourself! It happened and it's over with. Brant is never going to know anything unless you tell him." He looked at her. "And you won't tell him, Caitlyn, because you love him."

"But how can you expect me to—"

"You love him, don't you?" he asked harshly. "You do love him?"

She hung her head. Of course she loved Brant! She'd loved him for so long she couldn't imagine loving anyone else! She had to be honest with herself: what had happened, what Tanner had caused to happen, had never happened with Brant. Hadn't she longed for something like that to happen? Brant had turned away from her and she'd felt wrong even to ask it. But with Tanner—he had done it so naturally. She risked a look at him, although her cheeks still burned when she met his gaze.

"Caitlyn, I'm not going to tell you I'm sorry for what happened," he said. "I'm glad I helped you realize something all women should realize. You have every right—"

"I have *no* right to ask Brant to do anything for me!" she interrupted with sudden ferocity. Her eyes narrowed. "You must never tell him what happened between us! Tanner, you must promise me!"

He shrugged. Why would he want to tell Brant what had happened? Hell, he'd kept quiet all this time about Brant's stupid mistake in sending that letter to Caitlyn in the first place! Damn, he was good at keeping quiet about things! he thought bitterly.

But when she continued to look at him, he said simply, "I promise, Caitlyn."

She seemed relieved until she realized that twilight was already upon them. He saw fear in her face—fear that they would be discovered, fear that what had happened would show in her face. She looked at him desperately.

"We must get back to camp! We've been gone too long! Brant and the others will be home!" She was already running, still clutching the letters in her hand.

Tanner hurried to catch up with her, then pulled her arm to slow her down. "What's the matter, Caitlyn? Are you scared of Brant?"

"No, I'm not scared of him," she snapped. "But he works hard with the others and they expect their supper to be ready

when they come back from the mine. Brant will be furious, and when he sees you, he might think—"

"Caitlyn, don't be foolish! Brant's not going to think anything. He'll be so surprised to see me that he won't be angry that you haven't gotten supper ready," he told her reasonably.

But she wouldn't listen to him. Guilt warred with shame in her mind as she hurried back to camp. She knew that what she had done with Tanner was wrong, terribly wrong. She must never let Brant know what had happened, never let him think she was dissatisfied with him as a lover. It would hurt him terribly. He had sent for her, he had written to her to come to him; and now that she had come, she had betrayed him with another man!

When she arrived at the campsite, her spirits fell as she saw Brant, Dan, and Jimmy looking around in exasperation, noting the empty cookpot, the fire that had been allowed to die down. She slowed her pace, willing her face to show no traces of the passion she had just experienced. She kept repeating to herself, over and over, that she had not really been unfaithful.

"Caitlyn! Where have you been?" It was Brant, his voice irritated but worried too, afraid that something had happened to her. He opened his arms to her and she hurried into them, pressing herself against him, telling herself that she loved him too much to ever hurt him again.

Before she could explain where she had been, Brant looked up to see Tanner. Immediately his arms fell away from Caitlyn and he went up to his friend, shaking his hand and patting him on the back, glad to see him.

"Tanner! Christ, man, it's good to see you! I was wondering if you would ever make the trip again. I thought perhaps you'd gone back home without me."

Tanner returned the handshake, but his eyes followed Caitlyn for a moment. There was a look of desolation on her face. He wished he'd stayed in Melbourne. But then Dan and Jimmy were crowding in, wanting to know the latest news. Tanner's attention was diverted from Caitlyn.

Watching four men together, Caitlyn felt more desolate than ever. She had betrayed her husband with one of those men, and now she wanted to be comforted, to feel that everything was all right. For a moment she'd felt Brant's arms around her and she'd felt safe, comforted, but then he'd been torn away and she felt alone once more. She slowly went to the fire to start supper.

As the men talked and joked among themselves, Brant looked

at Caitlyn, noting how quiet she seemed tonight. He slipped away from the others and squatted beside her, giving her a brief kiss on the cheek while laying a possessive hand on her arm.

"What were you doing with Tanner?" he demanded.

Caitlyn gazed up at him, scanning his expression swiftly. Did he guess at something between them? Did he think they had been alone too long? Was he jealous?

"We went for a walk," she answered simply, turning her attention back to the stew. "He brought me letters from home."

She saw the sudden eagerness on Brant's face, the excitement that lit up his dark eyes. "From your parents? From Constance? What did she say?"

Caitlyn gave him the letters wordlessly, glad that something else had taken his mind off her walk with Tanner Malone. She concentrated on cooking and missed the wistful look on his face as his finger traced Constance's signature on her letter.

"It must be horrible for her—for your sister," Brant commented.

"Yes," Caitlyn agreed. "So much brutality happening around her. Constance was never very strong when it came to such things. I'm sure it's harder on her than on either of my parents. I can only hope that she'll find someone to take care of her soon."

"It's odd that she hasn't married yet," Brant continued.

"I told you before that she and Jesse have an understanding, Brant. I pray that Jesse comes back from the war alive and well." Tears came to the surface as Caitlyn thought of Artemas Blair who was never coming back. "Oh, Brant," she said passionately, "I'm so glad that you're not back home, that you came to Australia! I couldn't bear the thought of anything happening to you! I don't think I could live if I found out you'd been killed in the war!" For a moment she gazed at him, wanting desperately to throw her arms around him and hug him close, but knowing how he would disapprove of such an action in front of the other men.

To her surprise, he leaned over and kissed her lightly on the mouth. "I know, Caitlyn," he told her softly. "Believe me, I know how much you think of me. I just wish I deserved all of your affection."

Later, after they'd all eaten supper, the men sat around the fire talking and Caitlyn washed the dishes. When she was done, she sat wearily next to Brant, feeling the comfort of his knee

pressing against hers. She tried not to look at Tanner, but now and then her eyes would slip over to his face, watching it in the firelight. He would catch her watching him and would smile at her in a way that made her blush.

She realized how wrong she had been to let Tanner have his way with her. He would never forget it. She had the uncomfortable feeling he might use it to his advantage one day. She had inadvertently given him power over her. She couldn't deny he was handsome. Once she'd stopped hating him as a Yankee, she had seen that he was one of those men whom many women found irresistible. She supposed she was now one of them. It galled her, for she'd told herself she would never betray Brant. The comfort she could gather from the fact that he hadn't actually performed intercourse with her was negligible. The pleasure she had felt from his caress had been as damning as if she'd lain with him naked.

When it came time for bed, for a horrific instant Caitlyn thought Brant was going to offer Tanner the hospitality of their tent, but Dan quickly invited Tanner to share the tent with him and Jimmy. She breathed easier knowing that Tanner would be gone in the morning, taking with him the sacks of gold that had accumulated.

Before going to bed, Brant reached under the bed, his hand searching for the depression where the sacks were stored. Puzzled, he reached in deeper. Then he pushed the bed aside and stared at the depression. It was empty.

"Caitlyn! Where the hell is the gold?" He glared at her, his face reddening in anger and accusation. "What have you done with it?"

"I haven't done anything with it," she said, shocked at his accusing look. "You always put it under the bed at night and every morning I make the bed over it!"

"But it isn't there!" he pointed out. He stood up and began searching through the tent, throwing boxes and cans about and generally making a mess of all Caitlyn's hard work.

She watched him numbly. "Brant, I'm sure the gold is somewhere."

"How would you know where it is?" he said, sneering viciously. "You weren't even in camp today, were you? Instead you were out gallivanting with Tanner!"

Caitlyn's heart froze. Be careful, she told herself, be very

careful. The lost gold was nothing compared to the hatred Brant would feel if he found out what had happened.

"Didn't you stop to think that *anyone* could have come into the tent while you were away and taken the gold? Didn't you bother to worry about the safety of the gold that we've all worked so hard for? Do you think everybody in this godforsaken hole is trustworthy, Caitlyn? Do you think it's like home, where you can leave your door unlocked and no one will come in without knocking?" As he shot the questions at her, he was stepping closer until he bumped up against her, pushing her outside the tent. His face, red with outrage, was pushed toward hers, and she backed away, wishing he would keep his voice down.

Tanner looked out from the other tent and, seeing the altercation, swiftly came out. Dan came after him, his face concerned. Tanner, thinking perhaps that Caitlyn had foolishly confessed to what had happened, stepped between her and Brant.

"Brant, what's happened? For God's sake, your shouting isn't going to solve anything!" he said reasonably. He glanced at Caitlyn, seeing the turmoil in her eyes. "What's happened?" he asked again, lowering his voice.

"She's lost the gold!" Brant spat out angrily.

"What?"

"The gold, the gold! I keep it hidden so I don't have to take it to Maldon every morning. I figured she could at least stay near the campsite and keep an eye on it. It wasn't much to ask of her," Brant said resentfully.

"Have you looked everywhere?" Dan questioned.

"I know where I put it!" Brant replied angrily. "It can't just have disappeared! Someone stole it!"

"But how?" Dan asked. "Caitlyn's here every day. Surely she would have seen anyone—"

"She wasn't here today," Brant said. "Someone was watching her, someone who knew we kept gold hidden in the tent." He turned to Caitlyn. "How long were you gone with Tanner? Where did you go? Didn't you think to keep in sight of the tent?"

"Stop badgering her," Tanner said protectively. "For God's sake, Brant, she was distraught when she learned about her friend's death. Haven't you any compassion at all?"

For a moment Brant glared at Tanner and Caitlyn thought he was going to punch him. Then, with an effort, he cooled off. "Someone has stolen the gold," he said to everyone, his voice

calmer. "It was stolen while Caitlyn was away from camp. Caitlyn, surely you have some idea who might be behind this, don't you?"

Caitlyn shook her head. Then a suspicion formed. Peg Dudley! Involuntarily, she glanced over at Peg's tent, but all looked innocent enough. Could she have stolen it? She was over so much, she could have looked in the tents and found out where the gold was stored. Maybe she was waiting for just the right moment to take it. After all, she had admitted that she and her husband were getting desperate, and with the baby coming—

"Well?" Brant was watching her, waiting for her to say something.

"I don't have any idea who could have taken it," she said simply. "I'm sorry, Brant."

He turned away from her with a vile oath that made her shrink back. Tanner stepped up as if to say something, but at the look Caitlyn gave him, he stayed quiet. Dan scratched his head and wondered aloud whether it would do any good to inform the police in Maldon. Brant snarled something unintelligible.

"Well," Dan said finally, "there's no sense in all of us standing out here in the open. There's nothing to be done about it now. The gold's gone and there's no way we're likely to get any of it back."

"Weeks of effort wasted," Brant mumbled. He turned away and stalked back into the tent.

"Wait, Caitlyn, don't go in right away," Tanner advised. "Let him cool off first."

"I can't stay out here in my nightgown," Caitlyn said practically. What she didn't say was that she couldn't stay out here with Tanner. She was afraid of what might happen. She was feeling so lonely, so depressed, that she would be vulnerable to the kind of comforting Tanner was likely to offer. "I suppose," she whispered softly so that only he could hear, "that this is God's way of punishing me for what happened earlier."

"Damn it, no!" Tanner whispered, catching her arm as she passed him. "Don't ever think that, Caitlyn! If anyone should be punished it's Brant! He's expecting too damn much of you! My God, it took him a long time to acclimate himself to life in the goldfields, yet he expects you to be the perfect miner's wife in less than three months!"

"But I was the one who forced him to let me stay," Caitlyn reminded him.

"Then come back to Melbourne with me tomorrow," Tanner said. "No, I'm not suggesting anything that would shock your sensibilities, Caitlyn. Just come back and stay at the hotel. Let Brant see how much he would miss you!"

For a moment she was tempted to leave this humiliating place. But then she realized she couldn't go back with Tanner. Despite his remarks to the contrary, she knew very well that the spark between them could all too easily be ignited again. She suspected he knew it too.

"No, thank you, Tanner," she said softly. "I can't leave him. I know he would miss me terribly, but for some reason he won't admit it. I do love him," she said, looking into his eyes.

"Are you saying that to convince me," he asked, "or to convince yourself?"

34

TANNER LEFT early the next morning with a stiff farewell to Brant and an equally awkward one to Caitlyn.

Tanner would have liked to kiss her good-bye, to tell her not to worry, to remind her that he would be there for her if she should ever need him. But Brant was watching them with suspicion and Tanner didn't want to cause any more trouble for Caitlyn. Quickly, he pressed her hand and mounted his horse. Then he was gone, galloping away, leaving Caitlyn watching him before Brant's voice caught her attention.

"Now that he's gone, do you think you might come and kiss your husband off to work?" he asked sardonically.

Caitlyn hurried to kiss him on the cheek. She was surprised when Brant put his arms around her and held her tight against him. He kissed her heavily on the mouth, so that she had to fight for breath.

"Now," he said with some satisfaction, "maybe that will help to remind you where your loyalties lie. The next time Tanner Malone comes here and wants you to walk with him, remember who your husband is, Caitlyn."

She nodded, still out of breath. Did he suspect anything? Was he still angry at her about the gold? She would never know, for Brant was so closed to her these days. She wished he would talk to her about what he was feeling, but he didn't seem inclined to

do so. She waved to him as he rode off, telling herself she wouldn't let him down again.

Sighing, she turned back towards the tent, girding herself for the work she had to do to straighten up the mess Brant's search had made of it last night. She continued to wonder if Peg Dudley had played a part in the disappearance of the gold. As she cleaned inside the tent, she tried to think if there had ever been a time when Peg could have nosed around the campsite alone. There were so many times! Caitlyn remembered when she'd forgotten her soap at the tent and Peg had obliged her by going back to get it so Caitlyn wouldn't lose her place in the stream.

Caitlyn continued to mull over the problem as she cleaned out her tent. When it was finished, she went to the other tent, pulling out dirty clothes from between the bedcovers, marveling at the lack of consideration the other men gave her. As she grumbled, she came upon something that must have fallen beneath the covers.

Reaching down, Caitlyn picked up a crumpled piece of paper, wadded together as though it had been squeezed by a man's fist. Curious, she opened it, realizing that it was a bill of lading from Tanner's export company. What caught her attention was the piece of jewelry that was inside. She extracted it from the paper, catching her breath at how lovely it was. It had a thin gold chain, on the end of which was suspended a golden locket with enameled inlay. Marveling at the locket's delicacy, Caitlyn fingered it gently. It was a fashionable piece of jewelry, and she knew it must have cost quite a bit. She wondered why Tanner had had it with him. The thought came to her that he might have intended it as a present to her. Quickly, she shook her head. No, he wouldn't have done that.

But then her fingers turned the locket over and she beheld the inscription To THE BELLE OF THE BALL and the initials TM. She caught her breath and squeezed the locket between her fingers.

She carried the locket outside and stared at it for a long time. It was much too fine a thing for a man to give to a woman who lived in a tent in the Australian bush. She couldn't possibly wear it out here where it would be scratched or broken or stolen. Perhaps Tanner had meant it as a peace offering. He couldn't have expected her to accept such a gift. It was quite improper.

"Why, Tanner?" she questioned softly. She knew the answer. It was because he cared for her. Caitlyn pressed the locket into her hand and placed it close to her breast for a moment. Had he

left it intentionally for her to find? Had he realized that she would be too embarrassed to take it from him if he'd presented it to her himself?

She smiled suddenly. She would never have guessed Tanner to be so sensitive. Jewelry always brightened a woman's spirits, and he had wanted to brighten hers. She thanked him silently for his thoughtfulness. Holding the locket up to the light, she smiled at the way the sun caught it, making it gleam.

"A new bauble from your husband?"

Caitlyn automatically clutched the locket in her hand, shielding it from a stranger's eyes. She turned swiftly to behold Peg Dudley smiling as though this were an ordinary day.

"Oh, it's you," Caitlyn said softly.

"Well, don't look so spooked, Caitlyn," Peg laughed. "You don't think I'd steal it, do you?"

Caitlyn couldn't help the flush that suffused her cheeks. Yes, she did think Peg would steal it. She'd stolen the gold, hadn't she? Yet she still wasn't sure. Even Peg wouldn't be so bold as to come over today and act as though nothing had happened. Her face seemed open and honest. She was smiling into Caitlyn's eyes as though nothing had changed between them.

"I don't know, Peg. I'm sure there are many around here who would steal whatever was necessary to stay alive," she answered slowly, "whether it was this locket or anything else." She watched the expression on Peg's face change.

"Well, don't look at me as though I'd do something so low," she said quickly. "I'm not a thief, Caitlyn! Besides, Robin told me last night that he feels his luck will change pretty soon. There's a spot he found yesterday that's likely to yield something. He says the baby has brought us luck."

Caitlyn frowned. She wanted to believe Peg, she truly did. Yet she just couldn't bring herself to dismiss everything so conveniently. What if Robin said he'd discovered gold only to cover himself for the sacks he'd stolen from Brant? She remembered a girl back in New Orleans who could tell lies with the sweetest expression on her face. The girl had half the men in the city at each other's throats because each one swore she'd accepted his marriage proposal. But she would only shake her head sweetly and say she hadn't done any such thing.

"I'm glad he's accepted the baby, Peg," Caitlyn said quickly. "But I must tell you what happened last night."

"Oh, I know what happened," Peg said, her eyes wise. "I

saw you and that handsome man go off together in the late afternoon. And when you came back you looked very guilty, my dear. I don't think your husband was too pleased about it, was he?''

Caitlyn colored again. ''That's hardly any of your business, Peg! That man was an old friend of mine, and of Brant's. He brought me letters from New Orleans, from my family.''

''Really? And so what's that locket for, remembering old times?''

Caitlyn held the locket tighter. ''I found the locket in the tent, Peg,'' she explained simply, not wanting to say anything else about it.

Peg nodded, though her eyes seemed knowing. Caitlyn automatically dropped the locket into the pocket of her apron. It was better if she forgot about it for now. She must return it to Tanner, of course, even if he had given it to her for all the right reasons. It would hurt Brant terribly if she accepted such an expensive gift from Tanner, when Brant had never given her anything. The thought made her shake her head. It sounded disloyal. Brant would buy her lots of presents once they were finished here and settled in Melbourne.

''Let's not talk about it anymore, Peg,'' she said firmly. As they walked down to the stream to do their wash, Caitlyn realized that she had forgotten to bring up the subject of the missing gold. Had Peg intentionally steered her away from the subject?

As they knelt together and pounded the clothes against the rocks, she glanced over at Peg curiously. Odd, how they had become friends. They had nothing in common in their backgrounds, but everything in common now.

''The stream's getting shallower,'' Peg commented, wiping her forehead with the back of her hand. ''Once summer comes it'll all but dry up. I've seen it happen before out here in the bush. The streams swell up in the winter with the rains, but with the dry season there's nothing left. It'll be hard.'' She was obviously thinking about her baby. It was due in May, which was late fall in Australia.

''Maybe by then Robin will have found gold and you'll be able to afford to stay in Maldon with the baby,'' Caitlyn said soothingly.

''And who would take care of Robin?'' Peg asked. ''He wouldn't let me leave him alone to take care of himself. He needs me, Caitlyn!''

Caitlyn sat back on her heels and stared at Peg as she leaned over the stream. Would Brant feel the same way when she was pregnant? she wondered. He came from a different world than the Dudleys. She remembered that when Marcella had the twins she was told to stay in bed for at least six weeks of recuperation. She didn't have to lift a finger, even to take care of her own children. There were wet nurses to feed the babies and slaves to take care of them. All that had been required of Marcella was to look pretty and proud and to receive the guests who cooed over the babies and congratulated the mother.

Later that day, after Peg had gone back to her tent to take a brief nap, Caitlyn sat thinking in front of the fire. Would the gold keep coming forever? If it was that good a strike, it was conceivable that Brant would remain out here for a good many more months, perhaps even years. How long would it be before they could go home to Riverhouse?

When the men returned that evening, she voiced her fears to Brant after supper.

"How much longer will we stay here, Brant?" She was sitting next to him companionably, her head on his shoulder as he smoked a cheroot that Tanner had brought him from the city.

"What do you mean, Caitlyn? We'll stay as long as the gold continues to come," he told her.

She took her head off his shoulder and met his dark eyes questioningly. "Do you mean we could be here for years?"

He laughed. "What a wonderful dream! Years of bringing out gold! Do you realize how rich we would all be if that was the case, my dear? We'd be rich enough to tell every one of those bankers in New Orleans to go to hell. Rich enough to thumb our noses at the social set of the city."

"But why would we want to do that, Brant?" she asked reasonably. "I thought you wanted to be a part of that social set. I thought you wanted to be welcomed into the business community in New Orleans."

He shrugged. "I don't know what I want, Caitlyn," he said, his voice becoming softer, almost dreamy. "I thought I knew what I wanted once. I wanted enough money to make Riverhouse a great cotton plantation. I wanted to look the part of a successful planter, to make my father proud. I wanted a wife who would make me proud, who would preside over Riverhouse and make it renowned for its hospitality and grandeur."

She snuggled up to him, holding her cheek against his shoul-

der. "But you already have part of that dream," she reminded him. "You have me, Brant."

He looked down at the top of her head as her hair gleamed in the firelight. For a moment he felt a crushing numbness inside of him that this was not the woman he had wanted to be mistress of Riverhouse. Resentment threatened to bubble up inside of him, but he thrust it back. What good was there in reminding himself of old dreams? Caitlyn was his wife now. Constance was lost to him.

"Yes, I have you," he said softly, putting his arm around her shoulders and holding her close against him. "But I may not have Riverhouse to bring you home to, Caitlyn. It could all be gone by now—lost to the Yankees or crumbling in decay because there's no money to keep it going. I should write my father again, but I just don't have the heart. I'm afraid of what he'll write me in return. All this, everything I'm doing here, may be too late."

"But it's not too late, Brant!" she said fiercely, meeting his eyes in the glow of the fire. "You can start over, you can rebuild Riverhouse! You can have your dream, my love, if you just keep believing in it!"

He laughed gently and kissed the tip of her nose. "God, you are a passionate little hoyden, aren't you?" he said affectionately. "You'll never be defeated, will you, Caitlyn? You just won't allow it."

She smiled, her heart gladdened by his unusual lightness. "I won't allow anything to defeat you either, Brant, not as long as I'm with you."

He kissed her again, this time on the mouth, tasting the sweetness of her lips, feeling himself grow hard with wanting her. Yes, he really wanted her tonight. He wanted her with more than just that physical part of him, he wanted her emotionally and spiritually. He wanted to please her as much as he wanted to find his own pleasure.

Silently, he stood up and put out his cheroot with his boot. Without looking at the others, he took Caitlyn's hand, his dark eyes conveying to her his intent.

Blushing a little, Caitlyn felt his hand squeeze hers as he led her back to the tent. Once inside, he didn't light the lamp overhead, but pushed her gently back onto the bedcovers. Kissing her lightly on the cheeks, the forehead, the eyes, he unbuttoned her bodice, sliding it down her arms and pushing it

past her hips. He kissed her neck and shoulders, making her shiver with the imprint of his mouth on her skin.

"Oh, Brant!" she whispered, her breath catching a little in her throat. She put her arms around his neck when he brought his mouth up to claim hers. In wonder, she felt the caring in his hands as they divested her of the rest of her clothing so that she was naked against him. He quickly undressed so they could lie beside each other, feeling the texture of each other's skin and the intimacy of pressing it close.

"Caitlyn, I'm such a fool!" he murmured as he kissed her mouth while his hands teased the points of her breasts.

She wasn't sure what he meant and hardly cared as he brought his mouth down to kiss and suck the tips of her breasts. Her thighs shifted restlessly and she couldn't help remembering the wonderful feeling she had had when Tanner had touched her between her legs. Such thoughts seemed wicked, lustful, but only served to increase her passion as she moaned softly while her hands pressed his head to her breasts.

Determined to give her pleasure, Brant let his fingers caress the sides of her waist, the softness of her belly. Tentatively, he brushed the tight curls that grew at the juncture of her thighs, then touched the swollen flesh below. He felt her jump and stiffen beneath his touch and it pleased him to think he held power over her. Encouraged, he explored further, delving deeply so that she let out a cry of delight. Never had he heard her react like this. It made him feel even more lustful. So lustful that he couldn't help himself from climbing on top of her and thrusting himself in that place where his fingers had lingered all too briefly for Caitlyn's happiness.

Caitlyn bit her lip, feeling like screaming. She had been close, so close to that release she had felt with Tanner. For a moment she had thought Brant was going to take his time, to see to her pleasure first. But no! Her disappointment was all the greater because he had begun to give her what she craved. Still, the feel of him inside of her, thrusting slowly, deliberately increased her passion to the point where she clasped him to her, squeezing her eyes shut tight as she tried to concentrate on pleasuring him. But as her eyes closed, she conjured up, not the face of her husband, but the face of Tanner Malone, his dark blue eyes watching her face as he pleasured her with his hand. Caitlyn tried to dismiss the apparition, but it persisted. Finally she gave herself up to the fantasy and imagined Tanner holding her again, his hand be-

tween her thighs assuaging that inner need that demanded to be released. As she felt Brant's own passion reaching its peak, she arched upward against him, reliving that exquisite moment of ecstasy that she had reached with Tanner. With a sharp cry, she felt the same release, the same wave of feeling roll over her, even as Brant reached his climax.

Lying beneath him, Caitlyn shivered and squeezed her knees against his hips, unwilling to let the feeling pass. She felt herself smiling with an idiot's delight in the sensations that were running through her body. Oh God, this was truly heaven! she thought. She opened her eyes and saw Brant's face over hers. In the semidarkness she could see his surprised expression.

"My God, Caitlyn, you are one hell of a woman!" he sighed, pressing his lips against hers in an outburst of feeling. "I can't believe how good that felt!"

She smiled sweetly, refusing to feel guilty for thinking of Tanner while she reached that wonderful pinnacle.

The next morning, as Caitlyn tied her apron around her waist to begin the day's chores, she automatically pushed her hand into the pocket. To her dismay, the pocket was empty. Feeling a rush of panic, she searched it with her fingers, refusing to believe she'd lost the precious locket. Kneeling inside the tent, she ran her hand over the ground, between the covers, anywhere it might have dropped without her knowing it.

Kneeling on the ground, she hung her head, letting tears of frustration fall unheeded down her cheeks. How could she have lost something so beautiful? Pounding the ground with her fist, she berated herself for being so clumsy, so stupid as to have lost the locket.

Several minutes later she got to her feet, wiping her eyes with the corner of her apron. She realized it would do no good to continue crying. The locket was lost as surely as the gold was lost and there was nothing she could do to bring it back. Maybe it was better that it was gone. Gone so that it wouldn't remind her of Tanner.

35

DECEMBER CAME to the bush with bluebells dotting the landscape and a plague of grasshoppers that seemed to be everywhere, from beneath the bedclothes in the tent, to the stew that Caitlyn made for supper. By January they were still around, but less of a nuisance as they moved from the crowded mining camp to the wilder areas of the bush. In January pink orchids bloomed, causing Caitlyn supreme delight as she sniffed their powerful fragrance and used them to keep the mustiness from inside the tents.

With the dryness of summer came the cessation of rain, and the stream, as Peg had forecast earlier, began to dry up until only a thin trickle provided the only water around for miles. Life became more difficult as the acute water shortage lasted throughout the summer, making cleanliness impossible. Along with the lack of water came more insects, including stinging March flies, which were bigger than Caitlyn's thumb and caused her to shriek in constant alarm when they buzzed around her head. The fleas too were bad, and Caitlyn thought she would scratch off every bit of skin from her legs if the pests didn't go away soon.

In January Caitlyn began to suspect that she'd conceived a child. She couldn't be sure, for her menses had been disrupted ever since she'd first come to this alien land. But along with that sign had come episodes of dizziness and mornings when she could hold nothing in her stomach. She was worried by these signs, recalling that Peg had exhibited none of them during her first few months of pregnancy. She longed to tell Brant, but he seemed in no mood for such news. The heat and dust of the summer were harder on him and the other men than on Caitlyn, for they were forced to work beneath the ground, where the closeness of the earth was almost strangulating. Some days they returned before noon, unable to work under the stifling conditions. Caitlyn hadn't the heart to give Brant the news about the baby. She suspected he wouldn't be happy to hear about it, for it would only add one more worry to an already overlong list.

Dan Walker caught a fever, possibly from the flies that seemed to bite continuously throughout the night. Caitlyn was forced to sit by his bed for hours at a time, sponging his face and neck,

trying to make him as comfortable as possible. Sometimes he was delirious, speaking of home and of people lost to him. She blushed to hear him recall a young woman who'd married another man. And he would speak of his brother and his fears for him as he fought in the Union army.

Such human fears helped Caitlyn to realize how foolish she had been to show hostility to a man who had only shown kindness to her. She felt ashamed of herself, guilty for resenting his presence in camp. She was gradually beginning to realize that political differences meant very little.

Some days she would feel so blue, she would weep quietly as she sponged Dan's face, telling herself she was sorry she'd found out these new insights so late. Perhaps she wouldn't have treated Tanner so unfairly all those years, blaming him for taking Brant away from his responsibilities. She realized now that it was all Brant's own doing, that *he* had been the one to run from his duties. It had not been Tanner who'd had to coerce him into doing so.

Caitlyn took extra care with Dan, trying not to mind when he cursed her out in his delirium or when he threw up his food onto his bedcovers so that she would have to do extra work to clean him up again. She patiently nursed him through the fever, wearing herself down so that she could barely respond to Brant when he turned to her at night. Thank heaven Brant understood and didn't press her.

As the days passed and Dan grew stronger, they talked quietly together, telling each other about their families, about their lives back home. Dan even brought out his letters from his family, showing her another side of the North. Pennsylvania was not all that different from Louisiana. Its people were concerned with the economy, the earning power of their wages, the outcome of the war and what it would mean to them directly. Caitlyn grew more gentle with Dan and he with her. She felt she had made a real friend, and that knowledge helped her to cope more easily with Brant's disappointments.

Caitlyn realized a few days after Dan returned to the goldfields that she was not feeling very well herself. Determined not to succumb to a fever, she rested during the hottest part of the day, glad when Peg would come over to sit quietly and keep her company.

Peg was now in her fifth month of pregnancy and was beginning to feel very uncomfortable. Caitlyn had confided to her that

she might be pregnant herself, and despite the glad look Peg gave her, she knew the other woman was concerned.

"You have to tell your husband soon," Peg scolded her. "You can't go on pretending there's nothing different. Now that you've nursed Dan Walker back to health, your husband'll be expecting you to cater to his needs again."

Caitlyn was embarrassed that Peg would talk freely about such intimate things, but realized that she was right. Still, Brant looked so worried and tired all the time, she just couldn't bring herself to tell him.

One evening in February when Caitlyn was tiredly washing the supper dishes in preparation for bed, she saw Robin Dudley scooting toward her in more of a hurry than she'd ever seen him. His thin, sly face was worried, his eyes bulging with excitement.

"Mrs. Sinclair, I'm sorry to be bothering you, but you've got to come quick. Peg's bad, Mrs. Sinclair. She's—she's having some trouble with the baby."

Caitlyn couldn't move yet. It's not fair! she thought. She was tired, her back hurt, she hadn't been feeling well herself. She'd nursed Dan through his illness; she couldn't go through that again. But despite her inner pleas, she realized her feet were moving. She was following Robin dully, turning only once when Brant called after her.

"Caitlyn, where are you going?" he demanded, coming out of the tent where he'd gone to take off his boots.

"Peg Dudley—she's having some trouble," Caitlyn returned numbly. "I've got to go and help her."

"Help her! My God, you look exhausted yourself!" Brant protested.

"I won't be long," Caitlyn said, turning back to Robin.

"Damn it, I'm going to send for the doctor. You can't be expected—"

"Caitlyn, do you need help?" It was Dan at her side, his concern for her evident in his face. "Let me come with you. I might be able to help."

For a moment Caitlyn clung to him, feeling appreciative of his offer. Then she shook her head, her sense of propriety still strong. "No, you can't be helping with this woman's thing, Dan," she said quickly. "Stay with Brant and calm him down, please. I'll try to be back as soon as I can."

She saw Dan's protesting look, but she shook her head once

more and followed Robin to his campsite. Inside the tent, Peg looked terrible indeed. Her face was dead white, her hands clasped together over her belly as she writhed beneath the covers. Her hair was plastered to her head with sweat and her eyes were closed, the lids squeezed together in pain.

"Mr. Dudley, you've got to get a doctor!" Caitlyn said urgently. "I—I have no experience in this. Peg's losing the baby, and I don't know how to prevent it."

"My God, Mrs. Sinclair, you can't be expecting me to send for the doctor! He'll charge me five pounds just to come and tell me the same thing you're telling me."

"Mr. Dudley, you don't understand," Caitlyn said sternly. "Peg could die. I—I can't be responsible."

When it seemed he would continue to protest, Peg opened her eyes, her pain evident in them. "Do as Caitlyn tells you, Robin!" she urged him. "You know you can pay for the doctor. You've got the gold."

"Shut up, woman!" Robin's voice was ugly as he glared at his wife, then moved his eyes toward Caitlyn. "Now you just do as Mrs. Sinclair tells you and you'll be all right." He stood up and his eyes slid over Caitlyn's face. "I'll be back with the doctor," he said and then was out the tent flap, leaving Caitlyn to wonder at his strange behavior.

"Caitlyn, ah, God, but it hurts!" Peg groaned, reaching out blindly to clasp Caitlyn's hand. "It hurts!" she repeated.

Peg thrashed from side to side, holding her belly and howling from the pain. She brought her knees up and closed her eyes as though trying to bring the baby out. Caitlyn looked around in distress. Couldn't anyone else hear the woman's screams? Surely there was some other woman out there who would be more help than Caitlyn! She looked at the tent flap, but it remained closed.

"Peg, I don't know what to do," she said truthfully. "I think— I'm afraid you're losing your baby."

"God, no! Oh, no!" Peg burst out, rolling her eyes upward as another spasm of pain shook her.

Caitlyn continued to sponge her face as the minutes went by slowly. Soon she was sweating herself in the close atmosphere of the tent.

"Where is the pain?" she asked when Peg seemed to collapse and was quiet for a few moments.

"Ah, my God, it's tearing at my guts!" Peg screamed.

As the minutes crawled by, Caitlyn continued to sponge Peg's

face until the water ran out. Her own back was killing her, her legs felt cramped, and she would have liked to go to sleep more than anything else in the world. But Peg was still thrashing, though weaker now. Hesitantly, Caitlyn lifted the covers from her body and gasped. Between Peg's legs, spreading in a widening pool on her nightgown, was a red bloodstain.

Quickly, without regard for modesty, Caitlyn pulled back Peg's nightgown and tried to staunch the flow with some clothing. Pressing the cloth tightly between her legs, she watched in horror as it soaked up the blood and became scarlet in an alarmingly short time. Something was terribly wrong.

Peg continued to move about weakly, although she was no longer screaming. Caitlyn hoped she would lose consciousness, but the pain was too strong and Peg stayed awake. Her eyes rolled back and forth in terror, and her mouth opened, but no sound came out.

Caitlyn continued to talk to her, meaningless blather, only to keep her own wits about her. She talked about England, about Peg's youth, about the gold that Robin would find soon, and about how all their troubles would be over.

She felt Peg's hand clasping her own. "Caitlyn?" she croaked.

"Yes, Peg, I'm here. I won't leave you," she returned. "I'm sure Robin will be back soon with the doctor. Just hold on."

Peg shook her head. "I'm done for, Caitlyn. Maybe I was too old to be having my first baby. Maybe this is God's way of punishing me for being wicked."

"Don't talk nonsense!" Caitlyn said quickly. "You're not wicked. And God would never cause something like this to happen. It's just something that can't be helped. We must concentrate on saving you now."

Peg shook her head weakly. "No, I am wicked, Caitlyn. You're being so good to me now and I don't deserve it." Before Caitlyn could protest, she pointed to a knapsack in the corner of the tent and indicated that she wanted Caitlyn to get it.

Puzzled, Caitlyn tried to lift it. But it was so heavy that she ended up dragging it over to where Peg lay, still moving weakly as the pool of blood widened menacingly.

"Open it," Peg commanded softly.

Caitlyn did. She gasped, for inside was the gold that Brant had hidden under their bed. It must be the same gold, she thought, for she could see Peg nodding. "Yes, that's yours, Caitlyn. I knew where it was and I told Robin. When you went for

a walk with your friend that day, Robin went inside and stole it. I lied to you, Caitlyn. I lied to you about everything.''

"Peg, I—I don't understand,'' Caitlyn said helplessly.

"I had to do it, Caitlyn,'' she said weakly. "Robin was so desperate, I was afraid he might leave me. I was afraid he'd go away some night and I'd be all alone. He didn't want this baby! He didn't want it! Ah-h-h!'' She brought her knees up against her belly as she pushed ineffectually, trying to bring out the fetus that was costing her her life. She ran out of breath and her legs fell awkwardly to the bed. Slowly, she reached inside the pocket of her nightgown, closing her fist around something inside, but before she could bring it out, she let out a terrible scream that shook Caitlyn to the marrow of her bones.

"Help me, Caitlyn! God help me!'' Peg screamed. Then she was suddenly quiet, her breath coming slowly and painfully. Her whole body seemed to be shaking uncontrollably and Caitlyn could do nothing but hold her hand and stroke her forehead.

"It—doesn't hurt—so much—now,'' Peg whispered. In truth, she looked as though she had found some peace. Her face, though twisted from the pain, had a kind of contentment. "You'll tell Robin that I'm sorry about the gold. He—he shouldn't have taken it. And here—'' She pulled her hand out of her pocket, but it fell heavily against her.

"Peg?'' Caitlyn looked at her cautiously. Peg seemed to be staring back at her with a gaze so intense her eyes seemed to look directly into Caitlyn's soul. And then they clouded over and the life went out of them. "Peg! No, you can't let go!'' Caitlyn whispered frantically. She patted Peg's cheeks, trying to bring the color back into them. But the color was all gone, drained from her body and staining her nightgown a bright red.

For a moment Caitlyn couldn't believe she was dead. Peg was the only friend she had out here in the bush. "I don't care if you stole the damned gold!'' she said fiercely. "I forgive you, Peg!'' But it was too late. She was truly gone. Caitlyn reached to bring Peg's hands together and as she opened her fist she saw the bright gleam of gold fall onto the stained nightgown. Caitlyn picked up the object. It was the locket that Tanner had meant to give her.

"Oh, Peg!'' she sighed, clutching the jewelry in her hand.

"Peg! Peg!'' It was Robin Dudley standing by the tent flap, his eyes bulging with horror as he perceived his wife lying so still. His eyes looked from her to Caitlyn and then lit upon the

open knapsack. "That's mine!" he said fiercely, determined not to lose everything in one night.

As he hurried inside to claim the knapsack, Caitlyn shook her head wearily. "It's yours, Mr. Dudley. I'm not going to say anything. Your wife is dead. Doesn't that matter more to you than the gold?"

His eyes were sly, narrow like a ferret's as he looked around the tent as though to reassure himself that no one else was about. "Did she say anything?" he demanded.

"I told you the gold was yours!" Caitlyn said, her voice rising in anger. "Your wife is *dead*, Mr. Dudley! Can you stop clutching that knapsack long enough to embrace her one last time?"

Realizing that she was not going to contest the ownership of the gold, he let go of it and went to kneel beside his wife.

"What happened to the doctor, Mr. Dudley? Couldn't you part with some of your precious gold in order to save a human life?"

Stung, Robin looked up. "I told him to come," he protested. "He said he wasn't about to make a call at this hour for a woman giving birth. He said to find her a midwife." He looked at Caitlyn accusingly. "*You* let her die, Mrs. Sinclair! You should have done something to save her!"

Caitlyn stepped backward. How dare this little runt tell her she let Peg die! "You little rat-faced thief!" she yelled. "Her death is all your doing! If you thought she shouldn't have a child, you should have seen to it that she didn't! Don't kneel there and pretend to be a pious, God-fearing man, so concerned over his wife! You make me sick, Mr. Dudley! You used Peg as surely as those other men used her in England!" She started to walk out of the tent, then turned back with a sneer. "If you can part with some of your ill-gotten gains, I would suggest having the funeral tomorrow, and then you can be on your way that much sooner. If you don't leave tomorrow, Mr. Dudley, I can assure you I will tell my husband just what happened to our gold."

He scanned her face, his eyes looking murderous for a moment. Then he shrank back in a cowardly fashion and nodded meekly, hardly able to believe that she was going to keep her word. "Yes, Mrs. Sinclair. I'll make all the arrangements in the morning. You won't be seeing me anymore."

She stepped out of the fetid air of the tent, breathing in huge gulps of the warm summer air outside. Her head felt as though it were held in a vise and her legs still felt cramped from sitting

so long. She had no idea what time it was; it seemed hours had passed since she'd gone to watch Peg die. She was only glad that she had been there with her instead of that slug who dared to call himself a husband. She walked slowly back to her campsite, her leaden legs refusing to walk correctly. There was a tightness in her chest and she was afraid she might fall to the ground.

In front of her she saw the figure of a man sitting by the fire. He stood up when she came close.

"Oh, Brant!" she gasped before she crumpled at his feet.

Leaning down, Dan Walker picked up the unconscious woman in his arms.

Caitlyn was hardly aware of the days passing. She felt nauseous one moment and ravenous the next. Her head hurt terribly as though someone were pounding on it constantly. She rolled it weakly against the pillow beneath it, wishing it would stop hurting.

Above her, a man leaned over, a stranger. For a moment she thought it was Tanner Malone. Had he come back to get his locket? She clasped her fist tightly, imagining that the locket was still inside it.

But the voice was not Tanner Malone's. As she became more lucid, she could see the black clothing and the bag that belonged to a physician. She wondered why he'd come. He'd refused to come to Peg Dudley's side as she lay dying—or had Robin Dudley been lying then too? Had he even tried to reach the doctor?

She felt someone pinching her chin to make her open her mouth. She coughed and sputtered as some concoction was poured down her throat. She heard men talking quietly close by and wondered if they were talking about her. Was she going to die too? The thought made her panic and she called out for Brant. Where was he? She needed him desperately.

"Caitlyn, I'm here, I'm here!" It *was* Brant, close beside her, holding her hand and talking to her anxiously. She felt his hand on her hair, combing it back gently with his fingers. "You're going to be all right, Caitlyn. My poor, poor girl! You're going to be fine!"

"Brant?" she croaked. "What—what happened to me?"

She could see his face smiling down at her reassuringly. "You collapsed. The doctor seems to think you caught the fever from

Dan. You were just pushed to the edge by the night you spent with Peg Dudley.''

"Peg! Poor Peg!" she whispered with a sigh.

"She was buried three days ago, Caitlyn," he told her softly.

"Three days! Have I been like this for so long?" she asked.

"I'm afraid so. The doctor's been to see you twice and he seems to think you'll be all right in a few more days." Brant leaned over and kissed her on the mouth gently. "You must hurry and get well, my dear! We all are so worried about you!"

She felt a tear escape, but smiled through it. "I'm so happy you are!" she whispered huskily. She held his hand tightly, smiling at him and feeling unreasonably happy. She was about to tell him that she might be pregnant, when the doctor returned with a bottle of medicine and made her swallow a spoonful of the vile-tasting liquid.

"Keep giving her this medicine for another three or four days," the doctor commanded with an air of importance. "Let her rest until then."

"Of course," Brant said, following the doctor outside.

For a moment Caitlyn felt bereft and reached out instinctively for him. But instead of Brant returning, Dan Walker came through the tent flap, looking extremely happy that she was going to be all right.

"Excuse me, Mrs. Sinclair," he said quickly. "I don't mean to be disturbing you, but I—well, I felt pretty bad when I heard you probably got the fever from me. I just wanted to let you know how sorry I am about it."

Caitlyn smiled wanly. "It's not your fault, Mr. Walker. And I think," she added with a shy grin, "that you might start calling me Caitlyn now. It seems silly to stand on ceremony after all we've been through."

He looked relieved. "I'm glad to hear you say it, Caitlyn. Damn, if you haven't surprised me in these past few weeks, little lady. I admit that I had my doubts at first, but now—well, I'm just glad you're here." He hesitated a moment, then reached into the pocket of his trousers to bring out the locket. "It's none of my business, of course, but this dropped out of your hand on the night you fainted. I picked it up and kept it for you. I just happened to look at it and I noticed the inscription. I didn't mean to be prying."

She smiled again, clutching the locket in her hand. "Thank you, Dan. I'm glad we're friends." She watched him as he

walked out of the tent, wondering what her father would think of her being friends with a Yankee from Pennsylvania. If he knew Dan as well as she did, he'd probably be friends with him too, she thought to herself.

In a few more days she felt well enough to cook supper. All three men were relieved. Jimmy complained that he'd lost too much weight from having to eat Dan's cooking and his own, causing Caitlyn to go into a fit of laughter.

"And to think," she said with affection, "that I was the world's worst cook when I first came out here. Trial and error, Jimmy, that's all it takes! Even *you* could make meals fit for a king!" she teased him.

He smiled. "Maybe so, but I'd probably give everyone dysentery before my trial and error period was over," he told her. "It would be *my* error causing *their* trials!"

Caitlyn laughed and felt pleased that she was so welcome in this group. It was her family now. Without Peg to talk to anymore, she had only the men to rely on for conversation. It didn't take long before her vocabulary was liberally sprinkled with curse words. Dan commented that they'd ruined her for high society, and Brant warned her that she'd have to be careful when they visited Melbourne. Caitlyn would promise to reform, but then she would get angry at something and a few choice oaths would color her language, relieving her considerably.

As the summer waned, making way for March, Caitlyn knew without a doubt that she was pregnant. She calculated that she was about four months along. She knew she wouldn't be able to hide it much longer, but she still balked at telling Brant. He seemed so happy now. The mine was bringing forth an unbelievable amount of gold, and with the summer turning into fall, the weather was cooling a bit. They'd had rain the last two days and she'd kept a barrel out to collect the rainwater. She was afraid that telling Brant about her pregnancy would spoil his happiness.

She couldn't keep him ignorant of the baby's existence for long. One night at the end of March he was caressing her softly as he held her to him with her buttocks snuggling close against his groin. His hand moved over her belly, then stopped and cupped it.

She could hear the surprise in his voice. "You're gaining

weight, wife!" he said teasingly. "Don't tell me this life agrees with you so much!"

She laughed too, but nervously, as she realized that this would be the time to tell him. "Brant," she said, swallowing a mouthful of air, "I've been waiting for the right time to tell you." She squirmed around in his arms so that she was facing him. "I'm going to have a baby," she admitted softly.

For a moment he could only stare at her in the darkness. "A baby," he repeated stupidly. Then he held her close and kissed her gently on the mouth. "Caitlyn, how far along are you?" he questioned.

She admitted to being nearly five months pregnant.

"Why didn't you tell me sooner?" he asked in astonishment.

"I was afraid you'd be angry or worried or upset," she told him truthfully. "I didn't know what your reaction would be, Brant. I didn't want to change the way things were. Everything has been so wonderful in the past few weeks."

"But you shouldn't be here if you're going to have a baby."

Those were the words she'd been dreading to hear. "Brant, no! I don't want you to say I can't stay here and have the baby here."

"But Peg Dudley—" he began anxiously. "Caitlyn, I don't want anything to happen to you," he said firmly. As the words left his mouth, he was almost surprised to hear them. A few months ago he wouldn't have worried about her like this. If she'd died, he would have been free to ask for Constance's hand. Now he no longer felt that way. Constance was just a dream to him. Caitlyn was a reality. She was here with him and she had proven herself capable and strong. He had come to appreciate her strength and he couldn't think of losing her.

"Brant, I won't leave you!" she said stubbornly.

He kissed her into silence. "Caitlyn, I'm not saying it has to be right away," he told her. "But when you get further along, I'm going to have to send you to Melbourne."

"Will you stay with me in Melbourne until the baby's born?" she asked petulantly.

"Caitlyn, you've got to be sensible about this," Brant said, trying to calm her. "You're as strong as a horse! Nothing will go wrong with you or the baby. You're young and healthy."

"But, Brant—"

"Hush now," he told her quietly. "My mind is made up. In May I'll make the trip into Melbourne with you. I'll write Tan-

ner that we'll be coming in then. Honey, don't worry," he said, holding her close against him. "I'm counting on you to be brave about all this."

Caitlyn wished she could protest further, but she knew that continued objections would only irritate Brant and get her nowhere. The thought of Brant expecting Tanner to take care of her during her confinement was ridiculous. She wouldn't want Tanner to take time out of his life to do things for her. After all, he owed her no allegiance. It would be infinitely better if they weren't thrown together anymore. There was something between them that she couldn't define, that she didn't want to define. She realized, just before falling off to sleep, that it was as though she were in love with him in some unreasonable way. But that was too absurd! She loved Brant and they were going to have a child together. That was much more important to her than some silly infatuation with a man who seemed to invite those kinds of dangerous feelings.

36

CAITLYN STRAIGHTENED UP SLOWLY from leaning over the cookpot and put her hand to her aching back. She wiped a hand across her forehead and walked to where she had put the tin plates, stacked neatly and awaiting the arrival of the men this evening. She felt as awkward and round as a barrel, telling herself she was as big as a house. Why, she was probably twice as big as Marcella had been when she was expecting twins!

Resentfully, she pressed her hands to her bloated belly. Why had she been so excited about this baby? Now she wished she had never conceived. She was always uncomfortable, unable to sleep well at night, aware that Brant was unable to sleep because of her tossing and turning. She was nearly seven months along and every day he looked at her as though calculating how much longer until he would have to take her to Melbourne. He'd written Tanner already, and she suspected he'd already set the date for him to meet them.

Besides the bloating, she continued to have headaches which forced her to lie down during the day. It upset her because she would get so far behind in her duties that the men would have to go to the mine in the same filthy clothes they'd worn for the

last three or four days. Because of this baby, everyone was miserable, she thought indignantly. She remained quiet about her continuing bouts of nausea, hoping that Brant would not say anything about going to Melbourne. Despite her own misery, she dreaded being separated from Brant.

That evening when the men came home, Caitlyn could feel their eyes on her. She shied away from their gaze, pretending that if she didn't meet it, somehow they wouldn't see how very pregnant she was. When Brant took her aside to speak with her, her spirits fell. She knew what he was going to say.

"Caitlyn, I think it's time for you to go to Melbourne. I probably waited too long as it is. I know how uncomfortable it will be for you to travel. I've written Tanner and asked him to bring a wagon so that you can at least lie down."

"A wagon!" She felt like weeping. "I'll feel like a sack of potatoes you're sending to market."

He laughed gently. "Honey, you can't possibly ride a horse. It would be much too dangerous, not to mention how uncomfortable it would be."

"I can't do anything!" she complained tearfully. "I'm so useless!"

He caught her by her shoulders and drew her forward. "Don't say things like that. You mean so much to me, to all of us here. Why, if anything happened to you I don't know what Dan and Jimmy would do!"

"They'd have to learn to cook, wouldn't they?" Caitlyn said morosely.

Brant started to smile, but when she looked up at him, her eyes dim, he forced himself not to. "It won't be that long," he promised. "When the baby comes, you'll be busy being a new mother. You won't have time to miss me. And I'll come right away as soon as Tanner gets word to me. I wish I could be there when the baby is born, my dearest, but that will be impossible." He kissed the tip of her nose. "I promise to be there when the next one comes."

"The next one!" Her eyes widened as she thought of going through this misery again. She couldn't imagine how her mother had gone through four pregnancies. She thought morosely of how two of them had ended in stillbirths and shivered. All of that waiting, that sickness, for nothing!

"Tanner should be arriving next week," Brant informed her.

"Next week!" Caitlyn bit her lip. "Oh, Brant, I hate to leave

you!'' She laid her head against his chest, wishing it were possible for her to stay here and have the baby. But she knew it was far too dangerous. She told herself that in two months she would have the baby and then she could concentrate on regaining her figure. She wasn't sure what Brant would do if that should prove impossible. My God, she hadn't worn a corset since she left Melbourne—her waist was probably as wide as a cow's! She groaned inwardly and clung to Brant, wondering once more why she had wanted children so desperately.

Caitlyn sat in the wagon, feeling stupid. Brant had tucked blankets around and over her to make sure that she wouldn't be thrown against the boards if they hit any rough spots. It was bad enough to be sitting here like an invalid. It had been infinitely worse when Tanner Malone had arrived in town with the wagon, his blue eyes widening in surprise when he'd first beheld Caitlyn's increased size. Caitlyn had thought spitefully that at least he wouldn't be trying to kiss her on this trip! But the thought hadn't made her feel any better as Tanner had stared at her for a while.

"Well!" she finally had said crossly. "Have I grown two heads, or what?"

He shook his head and smiled at her. "You've definitely grown something, Caitlyn," he answered frankly.

"Tanner Malone, if you make any sarcastic remarks, I'll kill you!" she huffed, feeling as though she were an oddity on display. "If you continue with your rudeness, I'll make you sorry for it, I swear!"

He came closer to her and leaned over to kiss her briefly on the cheek, making her mad all over again when he made a to-do about the difficulty of getting close to her with her protuberant belly in the way.

Now, as she sat fuming in the wagon while Tanner mounted his horse and Brant sat on the wagon seat above her, she wished Brant had never asked Tanner to come. He was going to tease her about her girth constantly, she was sure of that.

"Well, are we going to move or must I sit here making a fool of myself for another hour?" she inquired crossly.

"My dear Caitlyn, you look quite regal sitting there in your robes," Tanner said with a grin. "Like a Buddha, I would say!"

She was relieved when Brant finally started the wagon. She looked back at Jimmy and Dan, who had already said their good-

byes, and her mouth softened automatically. She waved as gaily as she was able, not wanting them to see how disconsolate she felt at leaving them.

That evening as they made camp, Caitlyn tried to listen as the two men talked quietly around the fire. She was so tired, she found herself dozing off and missing most of the conversation. She knew part of their discussion had to do with the sacks of gold that had been cleverly concealed beneath the floor of the wagon as an added precaution against bushrangers.

The next morning Caitlyn awoke to the overpowering smell of bacon cooking in a skillet. She sat up quickly, feeling nauseous and dizzy. Getting to her feet, she moved a few yards away from the campsite and was sick, retching ineffectually as there was very little in her stomach. A few minutes later she emerged, pressing her handkerchief to her mouth and looking apologetically at the two men.

"Are you all right, Caitlyn?" Brant asked.

She nodded briskly. "The smell of the bacon made me a little nauseous."

Tanner was watching her, his dark blue eyes serious. "It's odd that you should still be nauseous so late in your pregnancy," he pointed out.

Caitlyn's brows arched upward. "And how would you know so much about how a woman feels during pregnancy?" she asked haughtily while at the same time feeling a stab of fear.

"You aren't the first woman who's been pregnant, Caitlyn," he reminded her.

"If you were a gentleman, Tanner Malone, you wouldn't even mention the word," Caitlyn reproved him. "In the South young men are brought up properly, and that means they never mention a lady's condition, especially not in her presence."

"Then how am I supposed to refer to it?" he inquired, looking mystified.

"You are just supposed to pretend not to see it," she told him, still in a haughty tone of voice.

"Whew! Now that *is* asking a lot!" he laughed.

Caitlyn whirled around to face him, her eyes stormy. It was bad enough that Tanner must make fun of her, but now her own husband was trying desperately not to show that he was laughing too. The thought galled her even more. "Well, gentlemen, I'm delighted to see how very entertaining you find me now. I can

only hope you'll find it as amusing when I borrow a pistol and shoot both of you between the eyes!'' she threatened wickedly.

''Brant, your wife badly needs to be put in her place,'' Tanner said in a teasing tone. ''I do believe she begrudges us having a little fun at her expense. I wasn't aware that she was so thin-skinned.''

''I'm afraid her condition seems to do that to her,'' Brant said, smiling. He walked over to his wife and put an affectionate arm about her, even though she tried to pull away. ''Honey, I'm sorry if you think we're tormenting you. We're not trying to be mean. It's just that you've been so touchy these past weeks, you're just begging to be teased about it!'' He kissed her fondly on the temple. ''I promise we won't do it anymore.'' He patted her belly proudly. ''After all, I did have quite a bit to do with this,'' he pointed out.

She nodded, sniffing a little.

''I think it might be a good time to ask Caitlyn what she thinks about my plan for her confinement,'' Tanner interjected, looking a bit awkward in the face of the tenderness displayed between husband and wife.

Brant nodded. ''Caitlyn, I know how worried you are about being alone in a hotel room during these last weeks,'' he began. ''Would you rather stay at the Wickhams' house in Sunbury?''

''You remember Deborah,'' Tanner added. ''She knows about your condition. She offered her hospitality if you'd rather stay with her.''

Caitlyn brightened considerably at the suggestion. ''Oh, yes, I'd like that very much!'' she said immediately.

''Then it's settled,'' Brant concluded, looking at Tanner. ''If you're sure Deborah and her father don't mind a guest—or two!'' He hugged his wife once more.

It was with considerable relief that Caitlyn beheld Wickham Station a few days later. The trip had been worse than she'd imagined and she was more than grateful when she realized that she would sleep in a real bed tonight. She gazed at the two-story clapboard house and smiled with genuine pleasure. Although she hadn't had much time to get close to Deborah Wickham on their last stop, she was sure they would get along. Deborah was a businesslike female who wouldn't tolerate laziness or sloppiness in her neat-as-a-pin house, but she was feminine enough to feel sympathy for Caitlyn's condition. Caitlyn folded her hands

over her burgeoning belly. She only hoped that Deborah would accept her without remembering the rather stuffy young lady she had been nearly a year ago.

A year ago! Caitlyn shook her head in amazement. Had it really been that long since she had come to Australia with such high hopes and dreams? How different the reality had been from the dreams she had nourished for such a long time. Yet she treasured her experiences in the bush, her times with Dan and Jimmy, and the times of closeness she had experienced with Brant.

As they neared the house, she saw Deborah Wickham come out to stand on the veranda, much as she had done the first time she had seen her. Caitlyn had forgotten what an imposing woman she was, how tall and regal she stood with her pale hair blowing slightly in the breeze and her capable hands shading her eyes. Caitlyn let her eyes wander over the twin-peaked roof, the gray-painted clapboards, and the long veranda, and she sighed with relief. She remembered Deborah telling her how she would much rather have four walls and a roof over her head than a canvas tent. Now Caitlyn understood what she meant.

When they reached the house, Deborah immediately came around to the side of the wagon, her light blue eyes showing her surprise at Caitlyn's transformation. Caitlyn was too exhausted to object and she smiled in friendly fashion.

Everyone filed into the kitchen where, with her usual brisk hospitality, Deborah set out food, apologizing that her father wasn't here, but explaining that he had business in Melbourne and wouldn't be back until the end of the week. Caitlyn marveled at how self-sufficient Deborah was. She'd never known a woman who expressed no fear at being alone in a house without male protection. It was quite refreshing, she decided.

When the meal was eaten, everyone retired to the drawing room to discuss Caitlyn's situation. Deborah informed the others that there was a physician within a few miles who had given up his practice in town to raise sheep. He would be willing to come to the house when it was time for the baby to be born. Brant was visibly relieved and Caitlyn realized he had been agonizing over Peg's fate in the mining camp. She felt her heart go out to him, realizing all over again how much she loved him.

Later that night, when they lay together in the same bedroom where Caitlyn had slept alone on her previous stay, she turned to him, letting her hand gently caress his cheek. He was looking

at her, his lazy dark eyes going over her face with a kind of wonder.

"I'll miss you so much, Brant," she sighed softly.

He reached over to run his fingers through the length of her coppery auburn hair, letting it fall around her shoulders like a gleaming cape. "I'll miss you too, Caitlyn," he returned. "But I feel much better knowing you'll be safe here. As the time gets closer to the baby's arrival, I would go crazy having to leave you alone to go to the mine every morning."

"I know," she said.

She couldn't control her weeping the next day as she waved good-bye to her husband. She pressed her belly wrathfully, wishing this baby would hurry and make its appearance. She didn't want to think of how it would change her life once it did come into the world. She only knew that it was keeping her from being with Brant.

Tanner had to leave, hoping to catch Seth Wickham while he was still in Melbourne. He kissed Deborah heartily before leaving and grinned a good-bye to Caitlyn. Caitlyn turned to Deborah, her shoulders sagging.

"I feel so blue," she admitted.

"It's just the baby," Deborah said. "You'll feel better in a few days."

"I won't feel better, not until this baby is born!" Caitlyn insisted.

Deborah clucked sympathetically. "In less than two months you'll have a beautiful baby in your arms and all this will seem like a distant memory," she told her.

37

THE NEXT WEEKS passed slowly for Caitlyn. She was used to being active. Now there was nothing for her to do but wait. She was plagued by stressful headaches that kept her from getting a decent night's sleep. Deborah watched her worriedly, especially when Caitlyn's appetite seemed to leave her altogether. But Deborah couldn't be with her constantly. Until her father returned, it was her duty to make sure that the shepherds they had hired were doing their jobs.

In the evenings, after the sun had set and the fire in the draw-

ing room had been lit, Deborah would have Caitlyn sit in the most comfortable chair with her feet up on a stool as she told her about Wickham Station. It was, she said, her entire life.

When Caitlyn would ask questions, Deborah would answer them eagerly, conveying her love for the land and for the animals that had always seemed such stupid creatures to Caitlyn.

"It takes nearly two thousand acres of land to feed two flocks of sheep," Deborah said, stirring the fire to bring it back to life. "That's about six hundred sheep."

"Won't you run out of land someday?" Caitlyn asked, stifling a yawn.

"We have thousands of acres here at Wickham Station," Deborah explained. "Australian sheep, which are the merino strain from Spain, require a great deal of country. Sometimes water holes are scarce and the natural pastures can be delicate and easily eaten out. That's why we have so much land. We're fortunate to have a stream running through our property. It can thin down to a trickle in the summer months when things get dry, but in the winter it provides plenty of water for the flocks."

Caitlyn was surprised to find out that Deborah loved this lonely outpost in the bush as much as she loved Mornhaven. It didn't matter that the Wickhams' house was modest, for the land was the source of their wealth. There was a growing market for wool, which meant that the Wickham fortunes were rising as swiftly as those of the gold miners who struck it rich.

"It has risen again because of the Southern embargo on exporting cotton," Deborah said. "Rumor has it that the South will lift the embargo soon in order to pay for its military imports, but it may be too late. Already imports of British and Australian wool have reached America, bringing prices of raw wool to reasonable levels. Since there's a shortage of cotton, the demand for wool has increased."

"But what happens when Southern cotton is brought back on the market?" Caitlyn questioned.

Deborah shrugged. "The British have developed alternative sources of cotton in India and Egypt. The quality is poorer than that of Southern cotton, but it's cheaper. It's ironic that the British are now exporting cotton to the States!"

Caitlyn tried to imagine what Winfield Cobb could say to justify this new turn of events. Everything seemed to have fallen through, she thought ironically. She remembered Winfield telling everyone that without cotton, Britain would be brought to its

knees and would be forced to join the war on the side of the Confederacy. His calculations had been wrong. By holding back its cotton, the South had lost its bargaining chip. Now it would be forced to bring its cotton back on the open market and prices had dropped because of foreign competition. The South's nightmare had come true. Southern cotton was no longer king!

When Seth Wickham returned from Melbourne, Caitlyn was a little afraid of him at first. Taller than his daughter, straight as a ramrod, and very bony, he seemed withdrawn and unfriendly. But as they grew used to each other, things became more comfortable between the taciturn old man and the pregnant young woman.

Several days later as she sat rocking quietly on the veranda, watching the sun beginning to rise in the east, Caitlyn was happy to see Tanner Malone come riding up. Deborah had already gone with her father to look into some problems they were having with one of the flocks, so Caitlyn was left alone and was glad to see that she would have some company. With her newfound serenity, she thought even Tanner Malone couldn't upset her.

"Good morning, little mother," he greeted her with his usual engaging smile.

"Good morning, Tanner," she returned with an answering smile. She indicated the chair beside her. "Sit down and tell me what brings you out here."

He took out three letters from his vest pocket. "From Mornhaven, Caitlyn," he said, seeing her eyes light up with sudden excitement. He sat down beside her and handed them to her. Her hands trembled as she pressed her fingers to each of them.

She looked up at him with a nervous laugh, pushing her hair out of her eyes self-consciously. "Don't look at me. I know I look terrible this morning."

"Don't worry about how you look," he told her seriously. "Read your letters. I don't want you to feel you have to see me first. I think we've gone beyond that stage," he added, his tone warming.

Gingerly, she opened the first letter. "It's from Papa," she cried in delight. She had so hoped to hear from him, especially after her long evening conversations with Seth Wickham. If only he were here, she thought.

She frowned as her eyes passed over the letter eagerly. "War news," she said at Tanner's upraised brows. "He says the Con-

federate Congress has passed the first conscription act, but many of the Southerners are angry about it.''

Caitlyn looked back at the letter and continued, "At least Mornhaven is safe. Papa let half the slaves go to dig breastworks for the Confederate Army near Vicksburg and he had to give up the chickens and pigs to help feed the soldiers. He says the Union army got to Mornhaven and made him emancipate the rest of the slaves.'' She stared at the letter, then looked up at Tanner, her eyes darker than usual. "I'm glad!'' she said fiercely.

"We'll have you converted to Yankee ideals in no time, my little rebel!'' Tanner said affectionately.

Caitlyn smiled. She had to admit that he looked particularly refreshing this morning in his buff-colored trousers and high brown riding boots. He wore a frock coat with a deeply notched collar, beneath which he sported a fine-looking light purple vest. She felt embarrassed in her plain calico frock, let out in the waist to accommodate her belly. She knew that her coppery auburn hair had lost much of its gleam, and she had taken to wearing it in two braids fitted around her head in a coronet. Her face had peeled and freckled many times in the sun and she doubted that it would ever be as creamy and fresh as it used to be. Mammy would probably throw up her hands in disgust if she saw her now. She wondered if Mammy had been taken away from Mornhaven too. She couldn't imagine her ever going of her own free will.

She opened the next letter, which was from her mother. She wrote that she hoped Caitlyn was happy in Australia and was finding married life agreeable.

"She must not have gotten the letter about my pregnancy yet,'' Caitlyn said wistfully, knowing how excited her mother would be at news of her first grandchild.

"There have been food riots in some of the Southern cities,'' Caitlyn continued, her brow wrinkling in anguish. "Food prices are exorbitant and rents are too. Mama says that at least they have plenty of food and their own roof over their heads.''

"I'm glad to hear it,'' Tanner said sincerely.

Caitlyn folded the letter thoughtfully. She opened the last letter, which was from her sister. Constance complained bitterly about the decline of the Southern standard of living. She wrote of wearing homespun clothes and how difficult it was to purchase manufactured items such as shoes, soap, and the better grades of textiles. Newspapers were now printed on wallpaper

or wrapping paper and books had become luxury items. Caitlyn suddenly felt guilty for living in relative comfort and told Tanner so.

He frowned. "Why should you feel guilty? You've endured worse hardships than your sister! You've had to live in a tent. Your hands are still cracked from all the washing you had to do for the men. You have no business feeling guilty, Caitlyn. I don't think your sister would want you to."

"Oh, Tanner," Caitlyn sighed. "Things get so mixed up, don't they? Here you and I can sit talking like old friends, yet back at home the North and the South can't seem to do anything but destroy each other. It's almost as though home doesn't exist for me anymore, and yet I know that someday Brant and I will return."

"We'll all go home someday, Caitlyn," Tanner said reflectively. "At least you can comfort yourself with the knowledge that you and Brant will go home with enough money to do whatever you want. You'll never be beholden to anyone again."

"I can tell whomever I please to go to the devil," she laughed. But as she laughed, she suddenly felt a sharp pain in her side that seemed to spread with alarming rapidity to her back. She placed a tentative hand on her belly.

Tanner saw her reaction and the look in his eyes immediately changed to one of deep concern. "What's the matter, Caitlyn?"

"I don't know, Tanner," she replied, a note of fear in her voice. "It was just a brief pain, nothing serious." But there *was* something different. She could feel it, sense it. Her back began to ache dully and she rubbed it with one hand, stretching it a little to help relieve it. "Perhaps I should go inside and lie down," she suggested, pushing back the rising tide of panic. After all, it wasn't as though she were alone. Tanner was here, and he could go for the doctor should the need arise.

Tanner nodded his agreement. "Let me help you to your room," he offered. "Do you think I should ride out to find Deborah?"

Caitlyn shook her head. "No, don't disturb her. I've heard babies can take quite a long time. I'm sure I'll be all right until she gets back." She stood up and a terrible pain seemed to cut across the small of her back, taking her breath away. "Oh!" She doubled over, squeezing her eyes shut.

"Caitlyn!" For the first time in his life, Tanner felt totally

incompetent. Reaching over, he cupped her shoulders with his hands and let her lean against him.

"Just let me catch my breath," Caitlyn whispered, leaning backwards with her head against his chest. "I'm—I'm sure I'll be all right." She breathed deeply for a few minutes.

"Caitlyn, let me carry you upstairs," Tanner suggested, beginning to think it would be best if he got her to lie down immediately.

She laughed breathlessly. "Carry me? Oh, Tanner, you don't know what you're saying!" she teased him, trying to bring a touch of normalcy to the situation. "*You* would be flat on your back and needing the doctor's attention!"

Leaning against him with his arm around her waist to help support her, Caitlyn went to the house and upstairs, negotiating the steps carefully. She sighed with genuine relief when she stumbled through the doorway to her bedroom and lowered herself onto the bed. Looking blankly at Tanner for a moment, she realized the deep concern he felt and tried to smile to reassure him. He smiled nervously in return, then tucked her beneath the covers as though it were an ordinary occurrence. She felt the panic begin to rise at the thought that he would be leaving her soon in order to fetch the doctor. The pain was insistent now and she was afraid to be left alone.

"You won't be gone long, will you?" she asked pleadingly, tears in her eyes.

Feeling his heart twisting in pain at the fear he could read so plainly in her eyes, Tanner shook his head. Leaning down, he kissed her gently on the lips and promised he would be back as soon as he could. He dashed out of the room, ran down the stairs, and sped outside to his horse, thanking God that he'd been here with her this morning.

Squeezing her eyes shut against the pain, Caitlyn held on tightly to the bedcovers, feeling the perspiration begin to dot her forehead. She felt terribly alone and scared. She waited tensely, twisting the covers and willing Tanner to hurry back.

It seemed hours later when she heard the sound of footsteps hurrying up the stairs. Breathing a heartfelt sigh of relief, she saw Tanner's familiar face, followed closely by that of the doctor, who looked quite competent and unruffled. Tanner took her hand in his, squeezing it gently when she smiled up at him.

"Mrs. Sinclair, I'm Dr. Morrison," the physician said, leaning over her on the other side. He signaled for Tanner to leave

the room while he made a thorough examination of her. "Have you been healthy throughout this pregnancy?" he questioned.

She nodded. "Yes, except that I did contract some sort of fever when I was about three months along. There was a doctor from the mining town who came and took care of me."

"Did the doctor know you were pregnant?"

She shook her head. "No, why? Is there—is there something wrong?"

He shrugged. "You seem healthy enough, but one can never tell what effect bouts of sickness will have on an unborn baby." He turned to call Tanner back in, telling him he was going downstairs to make a pot of coffee. "You sit here with Mrs. Sinclair," he told Tanner. "I'll be back in a moment."

Tanner pulled up a chair and took Caitlyn's hand in his. "Don't worry," he said soothingly. "Deborah should be home soon. She'll be a great help to the doctor, and once she gets here I'll be free to start out for the mining camp. By the time I get back here with Brant, the baby will have been born."

The doctor returned and handed Tanner a cup of steaming coffee. Caitlyn tried not to complain, but she was feeling more uncomfortable by the minute. She tightened her lips against another shock of pain in her back, arching her hips unconsciously as she squeezed her eyes shut once more.

"Ah-h!" she said thickly. "Doctor Morrison, I—I do think something is happening!"

Immediately the doctor hurried to the bed. Ushering Tanner out to get clean towels and water, he examined Caitlyn once more, pressing on the bulge of her abdomen and knitting his brow in consternation. "I'm not sure, but the baby may be in some distress," he said.

"What—what do you mean?" Caitlyn demanded, breathing in shallow gasps.

"I mean, Mrs. Sinclair, that I think it would be best if you had that baby as soon as possible," he told her bluntly.

It was hours later when Deborah returned, tired and dusty and looking forward to a hot bath and a chance to put her feet up. Nearly half the sheep in one area of the station had a disease, but neither she nor her father could identify it. She had had an exhausting day and was glad to be home. She was surprised to see Tanner sitting in the kitchen, slumped forward over the table with his head in his hands.

"Tanner? What's the matter? Are you all right?" Deborah went to him, tenderly putting a hand against his cheek. She was surprised to see the pain in those intensely blue eyes as he raised his head to look at her.

"Caitlyn—"

"She's had the baby?" Deborah interrupted. "Is—is something wrong, Tanner?" She started to rush up the stairs, but Tanner's hand on her arm stopped her. She turned back to look at him questioningly.

"The doctor is with her, Deborah," he said softly. "She's going to be all right."

"And the baby?"

Tanner's eyes revealed his own pain and Deborah could read the answer in them. She abruptly sat down in one of the kitchen chairs, staring at his face.

"Tanner, what happened?"

"The doctor doesn't really know. Maybe it was that bout of fever she had in the mining camp, maybe it was everything she's gone through. I don't know. Something affected the baby: either the medicine she took when she was sick, or the exhaustion from overwork. The labor was quite short. At first when the baby arrived, the doctor was hopeful that he would be all right. Caitlyn—ah, Christ!—she was so happy, so excited when she found out she'd given Brant a son," Tanner said numbly.

"The baby was born alive then?" Deborah murmured, her heart like lead in her breast. She couldn't even begin to imagine the devastation that Caitlyn must be feeling right now.

Tanner nodded. "But he only lived a little over an hour, Deborah. God, I don't think I could ever go through something like that again! That poor little baby fighting for his life, trying to fight for every breath! It was—it was a mercy when he was taken, Deborah. I could see Caitlyn suffering twice as hard, willing that baby to keep on breathing. But it was no use. The doctor thinks there was something wrong with his heart, something that didn't form right." He shook his head and rubbed his eyes tiredly. "When he died, Caitlyn just lay back in the bed and closed her eyes. For a moment I thought she was going to die too."

Deborah put her hand gently over Tanner's, seeing the intense pain he was feeling and wishing there was something she could do to alleviate it. "You do care a lot about her, don't you, Tanner?" she said softly.

He nodded. "When she first arrived here, I never thought she would do as well as she has. But she was determined. She proved that it was right for her to be here, proved that that damned letter that Brant sent wasn't just some terrible joke that fate had played on all of us. But after this blow, it's going to be difficult for her. I'm not sure how long it will take for her to recover. She's a damned strong woman, Deborah, but I think this may have beaten her."

Deborah shook her head fiercely. "It won't beat her, Tanner, it won't."

38

CAITLYN SAT QUIETLY on the veranda of the Wickhams' house, sipping tea and gazing out at the pastures as she had been doing for the last three months. It was spring again in Australia, mid-September, and little flowers were beginning to push through the moist earth and blossom into a carpet of color. Behind the house, Seth Wickham had started a small garden, where hedges of sweetbriar and hawthorn were beginning to turn green and the smell of lilacs permeated the air. He had planted roses too, and small oaks and elms. It was a beautiful garden, but Caitlyn had no interest in it.

She had very little interest in anything since her son had been born—been born and then died with barely an hour of life in this world. Many times, especially during the funeral, when the pitiful little coffin was laid to rest in the Wickham family plot next to the gravestone of Susan Wickham, Caitlyn had wished that she too would die.

She could not stop blaming herself, recalling with private horror how much she had resented that tiny life inside of her. She remembered with self-loathing how she had hated the loss of her trim figure. It was torture for her to recall those days at the mining camp when she'd wished she'd never conceived the baby. She had been so selfish.

When Brant had arrived, full of hurt and sympathy, she had turned him away, refusing to let him comfort her. Stiff and straight, she'd presented a closed face to him, brushing off his attempts to embrace her. After days of this behavior, Brant had finally given up, throwing up his hands and telling her that if

she didn't need him he'd go back to the mining camp. It was all she could do not to run after him, telling him that she did need him, she needed him desperately. Couldn't he see how much she needed him? She knew it was unfair, but she couldn't help blaming him for not being there earlier when she'd needed him most. He should have been there to see his son, if only for an hour.

Brant had gone back to the mining camp, leaving a silent and withdrawn wife who no longer had an interest in anything. Deborah's efforts to bring her out of her shell were met with equal lethargy. Even Seth, his gruff face crumpled with pity, had no luck in drawing Caitlyn out of her self-loathing.

Her thoughts revolved around memories of her family, of her home in Louisiana, and she felt a terrible yearning to be safe at home again. Safe at Mornhaven where nothing could hurt her, where her mother's arms would protect her from the hurts of the outside world, where Mammy's commanding voice would not allow anything to harm her lamb. Her eyes would touch on the green pastures surrounding Wickham Station and see Mornhaven's fields of upturned earth waiting hungrily for the cottonseeds to be sown. Her eyes would look at the Victorian architecture of the Wickhams' house and see the palatial lines of Mornhaven, with its white bricks dyed pink by the dawning sun. She wanted to go home, but she was silent about her wants, holding her memories deep inside her. She wasn't going to share anything with anyone. It was too dangerous, too hurtful.

When she thought of Brant, it was with a curious kind of detachment, as though he were but a passing stranger in her life. Her love for him was blocked as her heart struggled to make sense of what had happened to her. She had never imagined a pain so intense, a loss so deeply felt. She remembered the look on her mother's face whenever she would visit the graves of the two infant sons she had lost. It was a loss that a mother could never fully overcome.

Deborah had become concerned about Caitlyn's continued disinterest in life. One evening, as Caitlyn was about to retire to her room early, as was her usual routine, Deborah stopped her with a hand on her arm.

"Caitlyn, you can't go on like this," Deborah said kindly. "You've mourned long enough. It's time to let go now."

"What do you mean? Let go of my son!"

"There are other people who need you more. Brant—"

"I don't want to talk about Brant," Caitlyn said stubbornly.

"But you can't stay here at Wickham Station forever," Deborah pointed out.

Caitlyn's dark eyes burned as she looked at Deborah. "If you want me to leave, I'll go, Deborah."

"Caitlyn, for God's sake, it's not that I want you to leave! But Brant needs you! Caitlyn, you can't leave him out there in the mining camp, wondering why you haven't asked him to come back to you!"

"He should have come back without my asking!" Caitlyn burst out. "I shouldn't have to plead with him to come back to me. Doesn't he care how I feel? Doesn't he care about his son?"

"Caitlyn, you're being unfair! You know he cares deeply about what happened to the baby! But he cares about *you* even more! He can't understand what's happened to you. You've got to help him to understand."

"No! Do you know what he said, Deborah, when he came up to the room and looked at our poor dead baby? Do you know what he said?" Caitlyn demanded, her eyes fierce.

Deborah shook her head.

"He said, 'That's all right, my dear, there can be other babies'!"

"Caitlyn! Heavens, don't fault him for trying to make you feel better! Men never know what to say in terrible situations. You can't go on grieving for that baby for the rest of your life!"

For a moment Deborah had hoped she would be able to bring Caitlyn out of her dull apathy, but the curtain was already falling over Caitlyn's face, taking the fire out of her eyes. The numbness had returned and she was withdrawing from Deborah. Without a word, she got up and went upstairs, leaving Deborah watching her with a feeling of dread. If Caitlyn didn't bring herself out of this state soon, she would drive herself insane. No woman could hold on to her grief this long and not have it affect her mind.

Feeling her heart wrung with pity for Caitlyn, Deborah took pen to paper and wrote a letter to Tanner Malone. He was the only one she could turn to. Deborah knew that there was some kind of bond between the woman upstairs and the man for whom she herself held such deep affection.

A week later, as Caitlyn sat in the English garden that Seth so carefully tended, she heard the sound of someone walking through the house. Heavy boots strode purposefully across the

kitchen floor, and for a moment Caitlyn wondered if it were Brant. But as she half stood from her chair to greet him, she realized it was not Brant, but Tanner.

Letting herself fall back into her chair, Caitlyn turned away from him. "Deborah and Seth aren't at home," she informed him.

He strode forward and seated himself on an ornamental stone bench close to her. "I'm not here to see them, Caitlyn. I'm here to see you. Why aren't you up and about by now? Hasn't it been over two months since your pregnancy ended?"

"Since my pregnancy ended?" she repeated, her lips twisting. "What a sterile way of referring to the death of my son!" she added disdainfully.

"I'm sorry," he said gently, reaching for one of her hands, but she drew it away, refusing to let him touch her. "I suppose that was thoughtless of me. But, Caitlyn, it *has* been over two months since the death of your son. Don't you think it's time for you to pick up the threads of your life and continue? No one expects you to go on grieving forever, not even God!"

"Don't tell me what God expects of me!" she said, her voice hollow. "You don't know what He's done to me. He's taken away my son."

"Caitlyn, we all feel for your loss—Deborah, Seth, myself—and we want to comfort you during this time, but you won't let us. You drove Brant away because you wouldn't allow him to share your grief with you. It was cruel of you, Caitlyn."

"Cruel!" She looked at him and his heart twisted at the sight of those huge eyes in that pale, thin face. "Cruel of me! How dare you, Tanner Malone! He didn't stay long enough to share my grief. He waited until the funeral was over and then he couldn't wait any longer to get back to that precious gold mine!"

For a moment there were sparks in her eyes and he thought she was going to let loose with one of her old tirades, but then the sparks were gone as quickly as they had come. "I don't need his help," she said in a low voice. "I don't need *your* help, Tanner. Now will you please leave me alone?"

"No, Caitlyn, I'm not going to leave you alone," he said angrily.

"You don't understand," Caitlyn said, her voice rising a little.

"You're damned right I don't understand!" he said, standing up from the bench to pace in front of her. "I don't understand how you can sit there expecting life to pay you back for what

it's done to you. Life doesn't work that way, Caitlyn. Life is to be lived, not endured.''

"Shut up!'' she shouted suddenly, her cheeks coloring. "You think you know everything, don't you? Well, you're wrong, Tanner. You don't know me! You don't know how I pray every night that I won't have to think about my poor baby son fighting for his life, fighting for every breath. All I could do was lie there and watch him die.''

"But you can't blame yourself!'' Tanner said fiercely.

"Oh, can't I? You don't know how much I resented that baby, do you, Tanner? You don't know how unhappy I was when I thought I was losing my figure and getting fat. I *hated* the fact that I was pregnant! Don't you understand? I wished I wasn't having a baby and God punished me for it! He made my baby die!''

"You're talking nonsense! Caitlyn, look at me!'' He reached over to grab her arms and twist her around to face him. "All your feelings were normal. These things just happen sometimes and there's no one to blame. It doesn't mean that you won't have more children and that you won't be a wonderful mother to them.''

"I *won't* have more children!'' she shouted stubbornly. "You're—you're heartless, Tanner! How can you tell me I'll make a good mother when you know how much pain I've been through?'' She broke away from him and put her face in her hands. "I've failed! I've failed Brant and I've failed the baby!''

"Damn it, Caitlyn,'' Tanner returned, "you're failing them now because you refuse to look life in the face and say, No, I won't let you defeat me! You've got to be a fighter, Caitlyn! No one ever said growing up was going to be easy, but I thought you were going to make it. I thought you'd grown up from that little girl who thought her father would protect her forever.''

"Who are you to tell me about life? What have you done to enhance it for anyone but yourself? You're a selfish and greedy man, Tanner Malone! You use people! You've used Brant and you've used poor Deborah. And me—you've used me, haven't you? You've used me whenever you thought I might amuse you!''

His blue eyes darkened and his black eyebrows arched overbearingly. "In my life, Caitlyn, I've found that you can't use people for your own purposes unless they *want* to be used! Are you so weak and helpless that you would let me use you?''

"No, I'm not weak and helpless!'' she shouted, stamping her

foot and glaring at him angrily. Tears of outrage were forming in her eyes and her fists were clenched. "You get out of here, Tanner Malone! I don't want you here!"

"I'm not leaving, Caitlyn! Why should I listen to a poor little child who has given up on life, who has closed the door to happiness? You're not worth listening to, Caitlyn!"

"I said I want you out of here!" she shouted, bringing her hands up in front of her. "I didn't ask you to come here!"

"Well, that's just too bad, isn't it?" he said mockingly, stepping out of range when she lunged at him with her fist. "What do you think you're doing, little girl? I thought you were the poor grieving mother with one foot in the grave. Don't get angry, Caitlyn!" he said insultingly. "Getting angry means you still have life left inside of you!"

"Why, you overbearing bastard!" she shouted, stepping forward and missing him again with a sloppily aimed fist. "Do you think you're the man who can bring life back to me?"

She flailed at him again and this time hit a lucky punch to his jaw. For a moment the contact shocked her and she stepped back, her anger beginning to cool. But he wasn't about to let her return to her former mood. He rubbed the spot on his jaw and his eyes assessed her with a rudeness that shocked her even more than her punch to his jaw.

"You're damned right I'm the man who can bring life back to you, Caitlyn!" he said masterfully. "And I think you know it! I think you're scared of me, Caitlyn Sinclair, scared of the feelings I bring out in you!"

"You—you—pompous—" she sputtered, amazed at his limitless conceit. "I'm no more scared of you than I'd be of some fancy-dressed fop prowling on the levee in New Orleans! I know how you think, Tanner Malone! You think every woman in petticoats is just panting after you, don't you? You think you're God's gift to women!"

He smiled sardonically, aware that the conversation had taken a turn for the better and glad of it. He didn't mind if she called him the most ill-bred son of a bitch in the world. If it pulled her out of her former state of mind, it was worth it. "You protest too much, Caitlyn," he told her coolly. "Although I must say it has occurred to me that we could be very good together. As you say, I'm a man who thinks every woman in petticoats is panting after him, and you, my dear, are a woman who thinks every man in trousers is lusting after her!" He smiled, aggra-

vating her irritation to the point where she pushed him in frustration.

"Oh, Tanner Malone! And to think that I actually thought well of you just a few months ago! I thought I could overlook your pompousness, your arrogance, your *Yankee* breeding! I was foolish enough to think you were my friend!"

"Damn it, Caitlyn, I am your friend!" he said, the mockery gone.

"No!" she said, backing away from him. "You're too selfish to be anyone's friend!" She turned away from him, walking toward the house.

"Come back, Caitlyn!" he commanded, grabbing her arm to swing her toward him. "I won't let you go inside and start pitying yourself all over again."

"You can't stop me!" she spat.

He pulled her up against him with an abruptness that took her breath away. His dark blue eyes were blazing down into hers. She could feel his hands on her back, pressing her forward so that her breasts were pushed into his chest. "Damn it, Caitlyn, you're alive and healthy, but you're throwing happiness away with both hands! You're giving up on life and I won't let you do that!" he whispered fiercely into her ear.

And then he was kissing her, kissing her with a ferocity that she couldn't resist. His hands were pressing her closer, his lips were warm and demanding on hers. She felt dizzy as waves of sensation shot through her body and emotions tumbled about inside her head. This was wrong! But her body was hungry for him, her mouth trembled under his. She was afraid if he released her now, she would fall at his feet in a swoon. Life pumped back into her—life and a desire to go on living that transcended the deep valley she had allowed herself to sink into. He was right! She wouldn't give up on life, not when life had the power to make her blood pound through her veins like this! Not when life had the power to make her want to face it head on and embrace it as fiercely as she was embracing the man who held her—who held her so tightly that she knew instinctively that he would never let her fall into that deep valley again.

When he finally released her, she swayed against him, laying her head softly against his chest, her breath coming in deep sighs as she fought against the tears that were threatening to burst forth like a river from a broken dam. He had brought her back from the hell she had made for herself and she realized more than

ever how much he cared about her. And how deeply she cared for him.

As he reached down to tilt her chin up, her mouth trembled once more and with a startling suddenness the tears came forth, streaming down her cheeks, wetting her face and his shirt. She leaned against him and let the tears flow, feeling his hands rubbing her back gently.

When it was over she stepped back, disengaging herself and wiping her eyes with the sleeve of her dress. He laughed and pulled out the handkerchief from his coat pocket. "You seem to make a habit of forgetting your handkerchief at the most crucial moments of your life," he told her softly.

She nodded, wiping her eyes and nose and wondering why she didn't feel ashamed. "Tanner, I don't know what to say," she finally said. "You seem to have rescued me so many times that I suppose I've come to expect it. And yet," she added softly, "it should really be Brant who rescues me, shouldn't it?"

"You didn't let him," he reminded her gently.

"But *you*—you're just too damned stubborn to take no for an answer, aren't you?" She smiled.

He nodded. "Caitlyn, I care about you too much to let you hurt yourself." His eyes were serious as he searched her face. "What are you going to do now?"

She twisted the handkerchief in her hands for a moment. "I have to go back to Brant. You're right, Tanner. I did treat him terribly after the baby's death. I know all he wanted to do was comfort me and help me through the ordeal, but I wouldn't let him. I pushed him away and it was wrong of me."

"Are you going to go back to the mining camp?"

She thought for a few minutes about that. "No," she sighed. "I don't think I could ever go back there; things won't be the same as they were before. I still love Brant. After he forgives me I know he'll want me with him again. But I can't go through that again, Tanner. I'm going to tell him I want to live in Melbourne now. I want to be civilized again. I don't know if he'll understand, but I've got to try to make him understand."

"He loves you; he'll understand," Tanner told her.

She looked at him wistfully. "Do you think so, Tanner? I hope you're right. I can't lose the baby *and* him!"

"He'd be a damned fool to let you go, Caitlyn!" Tanner said. "A goddamned fool!"

39

IT WAS DECEMBER 1863, the beginning of summer in Australia. The acacias were in bloom and their heavy, sweet fragrance filled the air. Caitlyn looked around her new house in Melbourne with supreme pleasure. She had finally gotten her own home and a servant to go with it. Molly had been working for a pub, hauling beer on large trays and swabbing the tables after long nights of rowdy drinking. At the home of her new employer, she had very little to do other than keep the dust from collecting on the furniture. Molly's talents did not include cooking, but Caitlyn had told her it didn't matter. After using an iron cookpot over an open fire in the mining camp, Caitlyn found it a luxury to have a clean, bright kitchen in which to perfect her culinary skills.

Caitlyn leaned against the kitchen table and admired her well-stocked kitchen. Pots and pans sparkled overhead on an iron rack and the pantry was filled with smoked meats, vegetables, and seasonings. At the end of a short hall there was a wide foyer, on either side of which were several large rooms, newly decorated in the latest wallpapers, with thick rugs on the polished floors. Upstairs were three bedrooms: one for her and Brant, one for guests, and one for the baby she hoped to have someday. She still thought of her dead son, but there was no longer the deadening numbness that had overshadowed her life before. Now she realized that there would be time for more babies.

Of course, having babies required both a mother and father's cooperation, and it was difficult with Brant traveling back and forth between Melbourne and the mining camp. Sometimes he would be away from camp for days at a time, feeling guilty at leaving Dan and Jimmy to continue with the mining while he enjoyed the comforts of home in Melbourne. But Dan and Jimmy had agreed to the arrangement wholeheartedly, explaining that they were strictly bushmen now and wouldn't know what to do in Melbourne. It was better, they agreed, that Brant take Caitlyn to the city.

Besides, Dan said the gold was getting harder to mine now and they'd probably have to sell the rights to their claim to one

of the big mining companies that worked the goldfields with big machinery and large crews.

"And then you and Jimmy can come to Melbourne and stay with us," Caitlyn had said swiftly, letting them know how much they were welcome.

Dan had shaken his head. "No, Caitlyn, I'm afraid I'd get to itching for the bush again. I appreciate your offer, but I think I'll just have to start looking for another gold strike when this one's petered out."

As Caitlyn thought of her husband's good friends, she sighed wistfully. Last week when Brant was in the goldfields, Dan had told him that the easier gold was just about all gone. The tunnel had started to hit solid rock and it would be impossible for two or three men to dig into solid bluestone. The Beehive Mining Company had already moved into the area and had made them an attractive offer. Brant returned to Melbourne, tired but eager to discuss the deal with Caitlyn.

"Now why would you want to discuss financial matters with your wife?" Caitlyn teased him as they lay in bed together.

His restless dark eyes feigned surprise. "Can that be *my wife* talking?" he asked in amazement. "Why, I seem to remember the time when you would have fought me tooth and nail if I hadn't discussed financial matters with you. Aren't you the young woman who was determined to bring Riverhouse out of debt through her own resources?"

"Yes," she affirmed with a sigh. "I know you resented all of my well-intentioned interference at the time, Brant, but you must admit that I was only doing it for you." She giggled softly, pressing her cheek to his chest. "I remember how terrible I felt after I'd entertained Tanner Malone one morning only to find that you'd called while I was out. I was so jealous that you'd been talking with my sister all morning that I wanted to tear Connie's hair out and shoot Tanner!"

Brant recalled that time too, when he had thought it would be Constance who would grace Riverhouse as its mistress. How things had changed since those days! he thought to himself, realizing that he could no longer even imagine Constance as his wife. Caitlyn was his wife and, despite the rough times, despite the resentment in the beginning, he knew that he cared for her deeply and that she must be the woman whom fate had destined for him. He had seen her grow up, mature in front of his eyes, and it had been a remarkable process. A foolish mistake had

brought her to him. He smiled to himself to think that that little tart at Mrs. Wellington's would never know the favor she had done him.

Caitlyn brought her chin up to look at Brant's face. "I thought we were going to talk about business, Brant. What did you find out?"

He smiled to himself at her impatience to know everything, despite her earlier denials. "The Beehive Mining Company is anxious to take our claim off our hands," he informed her. "In fact, they've already put the offer on the table." He gave her the details and was gratified to see her eyes grow huge at the amount of money he named.

"Why, that's more money than I'd ever imagined!" she exclaimed incredulously. "Brant, are you sure they're serious?"

He nodded. "Dan and Jimmy let them in the tunnel to do some kind of tests and the results led to the offer. Apparently we hit on a site that's close to the principal lode. It's exciting to think about all the gold in there. Dan and I were wondering how much it would cost to put together our own company, buy the necessary equipment, and—"

"Let the Beehive Mining Company have it," Caitlyn urged softly. "You've done wonderfully with that mine already, and here's an opportunity to sell out to a bidder who's making you an incredible offer."

He kissed her tenderly on the tip of her nose. "I have to agree with you there, my dear. I'll see that the papers are drawn up here in Melbourne. Tanner has a good attorney who'll see to all the details."

"And speaking of Tanner," Caitlyn began slowly, "there's something else I want to discuss with you pertaining to business."

Brant looked at her curiously. "Don't tell me you've been hatching some scheme with Tanner?"

"Well, it's not really a scheme, darling," she interjected quickly. "It's more of an idea." She took a deep breath and faced him squarely. "Tanner wants you to join his import-export company. He has so much business now. Wool production is up and he's been talking to some winemakers who have vineyards near the Murray River."

"Hold it!" Brant put up his hand to stop her. "*Who* specifically came up with this idea, Caitlyn? Did *you* decide that I needed to go into business with Tanner, or did he suggest it?"

"Well," she said, coloring a little, "it was sort of a mutual thing, Brant. Tanner was visiting while you were away and we started talking about what you were going to do when the mine was sold."

"So you already had it in your head that I was going to sell the mine?" he questioned shrewdly.

She nodded, biting her lip. "Don't be angry, Brant. It's just that I thought you needed something to do, some way to deal with money and financial matters before we go back to Louisiana."

He laughed outright. "I've been making my fortune for the last three years, Caitlyn! Don't you think I've learned quite a bit about money?"

She pursed her lips, refusing to budge from her convictions. "You've learned how to *find* money," she said to him, "not how to do business with people."

"Well, I'll be damned!" Brant whistled, staring at her in surprise. "And so you and Tanner just hatched this great idea."

"Yes," she affirmed without a touch of shame.

He shook his head but said nothing. He reached over to put out the lamp, then relaxed next to her as he mulled the idea over in his mind. Caitlyn snuggled up against him. Brant hadn't given her a definite answer, but she felt sure she could convince him it was the best thing for him to do now. After all, her husband would soon be in possession of more money than most people knew what to do with; she wanted to make sure he would be able to deal with the New Orleans businessmen when they returned to Louisiana.

Tanner Malone was one of the shrewdest businessmen she'd ever known and she felt heartened by the prospect that Brant might find himself under his tutelage. Not that Brant really *liked* the business end of things. If it were up to him, he'd probably be happy to let someone else take care of his business interests when they returned home. But Tanner was different. He seemed to thrive on the daily trials and triumphs of running a business. Oddly enough, she'd never really thought of Tanner Malone in the mundane business of making money. He'd always seemed larger than life, a sort of adventurer who would find such matters too trivial.

Although he had been with her so many times when she needed him, sometimes Caitlyn felt she didn't really know Tanner Malone at all. There had been a time when she thought Tanner was

in love with her. He had been so kind, so attentive; she had never seen a man act that way unless he loved a woman deeply. Yet he had never said he loved her, only that he cared about her. Perhaps she had been conceited to think that he could be in love with her. The belle of the ball again, she thought with an ironic smile. How Tanner would have laughed at her had she admitted her thoughts to him!

She had loved and hungered for Brant for so long, there was no room in her heart for anyone else. Still, there were times when she would catch Tanner watching her with the oddest look on his face; it was as though he were waiting for something. But waiting for what? For her to make a fool out of herself?

Caitlyn told herself it was pointless to mull over her feelings for Tanner Malone. She loved Brant. That was her whole reason for being here. Still, she felt as though she were walking on thin ice whenever Tanner was around. As though every second she must be careful not to cross over a line—a line that she had certainly crossed over that afternoon outside the mining camp when she had given in to that crazy passion with Tanner. The thought of it still made her cheeks burn. But she pushed the unwelcome thought back into the recesses of her mind. Thank heaven Tanner had never brought up that interlude. Foolishly, she hoped he'd forgotten it altogether.

40

"MOTHER SENDS YOU her love!" Caitlyn called out to Brant as she sat in the drawing room, reading the latest letter from her family. "She says that your father has been doing quite well under the circumstances," she continued, looking up when Brant entered the room, dressed and ready to go to the office near Melbourne harbor. She smiled at how handsome he looked now that she'd convinced him to shave off that horrid beard and trim his mustache. He looked like the Brant she'd fallen in love with in Louisiana, with his merry dark eyes and his dark hair that never wanted to lie down properly. His years in the goldfields had given him a muscular physique that enhanced the look of his new clothes. She was bursting with pride whenever they walked together in the public gardens, especially when young women under their parasols would eye him with interest.

He smiled, although he pulled at the crisp new collar that seemed to be threatening to choke him. Sometimes he'd look back on those days at the mine when he wore no collar, even went without a shirt, and think how much better off he had been. "I'm not sure all these new duds are worth it," he admitted.

"But they do make you look like the proper businessman you are going to be," she reminded him with a twinkle in her eyes.

He shrugged. His eyes lit upon the letter in her lap. "What else does your mother say about my pa and Riverhouse?" he asked.

"She says the Union troops have used Riverhouse for their headquarters, so it's been spared any destruction. All the slaves are gone, freed by Lincoln's Emancipation Proclamation.

"Oh, Brant!" Caitlyn put down the letter and went to stand next to her husband. "When will we return to our real home?" she asked. "Must we wait until the war is over? It may go on forever!"

"Let me learn how to be a good businessman first," he said jokingly, putting his finger to her lips. "Give me a few more months of training and I promise I'll make you proud of me when we return."

She nodded, unable to hold back the sigh that escaped her. "I know you're right," she told him as she walked into the foyer with him to see him out the front door. "It's just that sometimes I'm so anxious to see my family again. And I want you to see your father, to show him how wonderfully you've done for yourself. I want to show you off to *everyone*, especially those businessmen in New Orleans who had no faith in you."

She watched as he went down the walk to the street, where a cab was waiting to take him to the office of the Malone Import-Export Company. Deep in her heart, Caitlyn knew that Brant would never be the businessman that Tanner was. His heart just wasn't in it. But she also knew that he would try his best for her sake. The thought warmed her even more than the summer temperatures and she waved to him as he rode away.

As the days passed, Brant found himself becoming more used to the daily routine of working in an office. He made valuable contacts through Tanner and learned how to juggle the intricacies of money and manners. But curiously, he longed for the times he'd shared with Dan and Jimmy out in the bush when there'd been no need for manners or fashionable clothing. He never let on to Caitlyn that he was unhappy with the new turn

his life had taken, but she could sense it. It saddened her to think that he didn't like his work, but she was selfish enough to keep him at it. She couldn't bear the thought of him leaving her for the bush again. Dan and Jimmy had moved north along the eastern coast of Australia to the colony of Queensland, where huge gold strikes were being made. She could tell that Brant had the itch to go with them, but his loyalty to her kept him in Melbourne.

As Brant became the well-dressed and well-respected businessman she had always ached for him to be, their life became orderly and routine. City life in Melbourne was not much different from city life in New Orleans. As their circle of acquaintances grew, so did their invitations to social events, balls, and the theater. Caitlyn reveled in the fashionable world of polite society once more. She pored over fashion magazines that came from England. Gowns now had overskirts and low-cut bodices that allowed a generous amount of bosom to be exposed. Coiffures had changed too and Caitlyn experimented with her own lustrous locks, parting her hair in the middle and torturing the back with a curling iron to make the long sausage curls that were so the rage.

One night as Brant watched her over the edge of his newspaper, she saw the restless look in his dark eyes. She pulled up a stool and sat next to him, laying her head artlessly on his knees. She felt his hand caressing the top of her head and she closed her eyes for a moment, wishing she could conceive another child.

"Darling, what's wrong?" she asked him.

"What do you mean?" he questioned a little defensively. "There's nothing wrong, Caitlyn. Do I seem distressed about something?"

She looked up at him, propping her chin on his knee. "I just feel you're not happy here in Melbourne," she sighed, unwilling to skirt the issue anymore. "If it weren't for me, you'd be off in Queensland with Dan and Jimmy, happily panning for gold."

He shrugged. "I'm happy here with you, Caitlyn. It takes some time to get adjusted to this life. Sometimes I look at Tanner when he's talking to some client and I'm truly amazed at how well he can handle business contacts. When it's my turn, I feel awkward, stiff, wondering what in the world I'm doing there and why I'm pretending to impress people with my nonexistent knowledge."

"Are you doing it to please me?" she asked, her dark blue eyes watching him closely.

He nodded. "Partly," he admitted. "But don't be upset, Caitlyn. I know you're simply doing what you think is right, what you think is necessary, just as you always have, just as you think it's right for us to return to Riverhouse someday."

"I've always pictured you and me sitting happily on the veranda at Riverhouse with all our children playing on the lawn," Caitlyn murmured softly. "Does that picture make you so unhappy, Brant?"

He shifted in his chair uneasily. "Let's just wait and see, shall we?" Knowing it wasn't a satisfactory answer, he leaned forward and kissed her. "I suppose it would be fine to settle down at Riverhouse for a time. Of course, even *you* might miss the adventure after a while, my dear."

He smiled. "Yesterday Tanner was talking about taking a trip to Queensland to see what business opportunities lay up there," he said, changing the subject. "Of course, just last week he was talking about going back to Boston. After checking on his business there, he might start something someplace else, maybe Canada or Mexico or California. He's full of ideas and energy. He's a lot like you in that respect, Caitlyn."

"I'm afraid I haven't been very energetic lately," she said ruefully. "I've grown complacent, Brant. I think I'm beginning to settle down at the ripe old age of twenty-one."

"You'll *never* settle down, Caitlyn!" he laughed. "You're just giving yourself a respite, waiting for the next adventure—like me!" He drew her up from the stool and folded her into his lap. "I'm glad you're here with me, my dear. Without you, I'd be as aimless as a ship without a rudder. You're my rudder, Caitlyn. Don't ever leave me!"

She looked at him in surprise. "Don't be silly, Brant! I wouldn't think of leaving you, not after it took so long to get you!" She lay against him happily, missing the restless look that came into his dark eyes at the thought that she would always be there to direct his future.

The days went by in a pleasant haze for Caitlyn, except for a tense visit from Deborah Wickham. Deborah had informed Caitlyn that she had told Tanner Malone she no longer wanted to see him. Deborah had finally realized that she wanted marriage, not a casual relationship, and Tanner had reiterated that he

wanted no part of the institution. Caitlyn had been troubled by the visit and by the fact that Deborah would no longer be coming to Melbourne for her weekly visits.

Brant had been introducing Caitlyn to the wives of business acquaintances, and she had cultivated a small circle of friends in Melbourne whose company she enjoyed and who helped her to forget about Deborah Wickham. She would preside over sewing parties where all the ladies would bring pieces of needlework as an excuse to gossip about whatever new and interesting things were going on in the city. Caitlyn decided to have a dinner party. It would be an important night for Brant as well as for herself and she wanted to make a good impression.

That evening she dressed with special care, recalling the days of the parish balls in Louisiana when every young girl would try to outdo the others. She wore a new gown made by one of the most respected dressmakers in Melbourne. It was of pale green satin with an overskirt of aqua silk that was draped on either side to resemble the panniers of the late eighteenth century. The bodice was stiffly boned and daringly low, pushing her breasts up so that they looked positively voluptuous. Brant had presented her with a pearl necklace and with pearl earrings that brushed the edge of her jaw.

When seven o'clock came she was standing next to Brant in the doorway, outwardly poised but inwardly as nervous as a cat.

As the guests began arriving, she tried to balance being a formal hostess and a warm friend. The husbands eyed her with interest, their eyes going over her décolletage with more than a casual fascination. But that was all right, she told herself defensively, for it only enhanced Brant's reputation to have an attractive wife.

It was nearly seven-thirty before the last of the couples arrived, including Tanner Malone and a young woman whom Caitlyn had never seen before.

"Welcome," she said softly, feeling Tanner's lips press themselves to her upraised hand. "Your partner is lovely, Tanner. Do I know her?"

"This is Lady Janet Penworthington," Tanner said as the young woman offered her hand to Brant, "the daughter of Lord David Penworthington, a high official at the British consulate here in Melbourne. He sends his regrets but told me I could bring his very beautiful daughter instead."

"How nicely put," Caitlyn smiled, reaching to take Janet's

hand to welcome her. Instead of shaking Caitlyn's hand warmly, the young woman let it slide limply in hers. Caitlyn looked into the sherry brown eyes that looked back at her with a combination of boredom and envy. "Welcome, my dear," she said.

"Thank you, Mrs. Sinclair. I must say I've had occasion to meet your husband already and you are a very lucky woman." Janet smiled and let her eyes slide over Brant in a predatory way.

"I'm well aware of that," Caitlyn returned, thinking all the while what a snob the young woman was.

"What did Lady Janet mean about having met you before?" Caitlyn asked Brant as they walked to the dining room together.

He seemed embarrassed. "Her father is very influential in the British consulate," he explained quickly. "She came to Tanner's office a couple of times and I was obliged to entertain her while her father was talking with Tanner. I think she's interested in Tanner."

"As long as she's not interested in *you*!" Caitlyn whispered in his ear.

After dinner had been eaten and everyone sat at the table talking, Caitlyn took a moment to reflect on how well the meal had turned out. Molly had improved her cooking skills, learning rapidly from Caitlyn's recipes. It wasn't like having Rachel back home at Mornhaven, but it was getting closer.

After a few more minutes of table conservation, the ladies adjourned to the drawing room in order to allow the gentlemen to enjoy their cigars. This arrangement would give Caitlyn time to collect her thoughts and talk individually to her female acquaintances.

As she moved about the small group, she was aware of Lady Janet Penworthington's eyes following her. She didn't like the feeling, but she had never shirked a battle before, so she made her way to where the girl sat.

"Are you enjoying yourself?" she asked pleasantly, seating herself next to the girl.

Janet sighed in an exaggerated way and looked toward the closed dining room doors as though hoping to be saved by her escort. "Dinner parties are always a strain," she said with another sigh. "I usually try to avoid the ones my father would have me attend with him. I have been accompanying him frequently since my mother's death. I suppose when one attends so many of these things, one gets—" She stopped as though remembering

her manners belatedly. "Well, let's just say they all tend to run together, Mrs. Sinclair."

"I didn't realize your father was a widower," Caitlyn said with sympathy.

The girl shrugged. "My mother's been dead for over two years." She sighed again. "And now I'm obliged to take her place at functions. I dread it."

"I'm sorry to hear that," Caitlyn returned smoothly. "This dinner party may be a bore for you, but it means a great deal to me and to my husband. The next time we have one, I will take great pains to see that Tanner does not bring you along!" She could hear the swift intake of Janet's breath as she delivered the insult. It was most satisfying to see the girl's cheeks turn red. With a murmured excuse, Caitlyn stood up and joined a group of ladies, quite pleased with her handling of the little snob.

When the gentlemen joined the ladies, Caitlyn hurried to Brant, latching herself firmly to his arm. She wished Tanner hadn't brought that young woman tonight. The party had lost some of its luster for her. On top of that, she was aware that her blatant insult to Lady Janet would not endear her to the girl, nor by extension to her father, who was oh so important. Still, she decided that she would not apologize, even though she spied Janet whispering furiously into Tanner's ear.

Caitlyn wasn't surprised when a few minutes later she found Tanner at her elbow, asking to speak privately with her. Caitlyn glanced over at Janet and saw the look of triumph on her face. Caitlyn couldn't imagine what Janet had to be so pleased about. Tanner certainly wasn't going to change her opinion of that little miss. Nevertheless she led Tanner out to the hall that led to the back of the house. Once in the kitchen, Caitlyn dismissed Molly and faced Tanner alone.

"What is so important that you must drag me away from my guests?" Caitlyn demanded immediately, leaping to attack first. "Is it about that arrogant little miss you brought to my house this evening?"

"Exactly so," he told her. "That arrogant little miss is the daughter of a very influential man at the British consulate, Caitlyn. I have been obliged to be nice to her because she has the ear of her father, who can be a useful ally to my business and also a great help to your husband. There is a post available as Lord Penworthington's assistant that would enhance Brant's career tremendously. I've been angling for it, trying to get Janet

to persuade her father that Brant would make a very good candidate for the post.''

''Why not angle for it for yourself?'' Caitlyn asked sulkily.

''Because I've got enough on my hands with my own business. Brant, on the other hand, has not been able to fit in as well as I'd hoped. I thought this position might prove more interesting to him.''

''Oh?'' Caitlyn tried not to let her anxiety show in her eyes as the truth of Brant's ineptitude for business stared her in the face. Then coming back to attack, she said, ''I don't think this Janet Penworthington is the right person to trust to help *anyone* get ahead. I don't like her, Tanner! I'm sorry, but she's not the type of woman I want around Brant. She's a spoiled brat!''

Tanner grinned, his blue eyes twinkling. ''Not so different from another spoiled brat who tried to run Brant's life in Louisiana,'' he pointed out, making her flush uncomfortably.

''Was I really like her?'' she asked.

He nodded. ''You weren't much different, Caitlyn. You were just as spoiled, just as haughty, just as sure that every man in the room was looking at *you*! I think Janet is out of joint because she didn't expect her hostess to be so lovely. It's annoying to find out that men are more interested in someone else, especially when you're used to them courting your favors. You were quite a shock to young Janet, Caitlyn.''

Her flush deepened. Why was she always embarrassed when Tanner paid her a compliment? She looked up, trying to meet his eyes, trying to read what was in them as they gazed at her.

''What do you suggest I do?'' she asked. She turned away to face the kitchen window and looked out at the starry night. ''Give Brant permission to do whatever he has to gain the girl's attention? I don't like that idea very much, Tanner.''

She felt him come up behind her so that he was nearly pressed against her. She felt his breath on the back of her head and on her nape, where it gave her gooseflesh. She could very easily have leaned backward a bit and felt his chest, hard and strong beneath his fashionable evening attire. She shivered and folded her arms in front of her, thinking that it was time she went back to join her other guests.

Just as she was about to speak, she felt his hands taking hold of her shoulders. His hands were warm and smooth as they exerted just enough pressure so that the sleeves of her gown were pushed down her arms a little. For a moment she had the absurd

notion that he was going to kiss the nape of her neck where the curls parted. She shivered again and felt the points of her breasts stand at attention beneath her bodice.

"I suppose I shouldn't have brought Janet," Tanner said, breaking the silence.

It wasn't what Caitlyn had wanted him to say. What *had* she wanted him to say? Turning around so that she had to take his hands off her shoulders, Caitlyn faced him uncertainly. But instead of stepping back when she turned, he stayed where he was so that she found herself almost touching him as she looked into his face. It was unnerving.

She could see the amusement in his eyes. "Caitlyn, what's the matter?"

She stepped back to a more comfortable distance and looked up at him again. "Nothing is the matter."

His eyes told her that he knew she was lying. "Ah, Caitlyn, that face of yours can be so transparent sometimes! I could have sworn you were expecting me to kiss you."

She laughed again, not very convincingly. "I don't know why you should think such a thing, Tanner. After all, you have Lady Penworthington out in the drawing room who deserves your kisses much more than I do. Who knows how much your kisses might do to further your cause and Brant's in her eyes?"

He chuckled. "Do you know how fast you talk when you're nervous, my dear? And how your beautiful breasts rise and fall so rapidly in your low-cut gown? I would venture to say that your heart is beating just as rapidly. You can be extremely intoxicating to a man when you're in such a state. But I would imagine that you're quite aware of that, aren't you?"

She backed away when he moved toward her. "Tanner Malone, you're teasing me! I hope you didn't bring me back here to the kitchen just to tell me that!"

"And what if I said I did?" he demanded insolently. "What if I said that the sight of you tonight inflamed my senses so much that I had to think of some excuse to get you alone?" He continued to stalk her, so that she involuntarily continued to back away. And then the wall of the kitchen was at her back and she couldn't move anymore.

Caitlyn looked up at Tanner, aware that her heart was indeed speeding up alarmingly. She tried to smile, but the look in his dark blue eyes stopped her. "Tanner, you—you're joking, I know."

"Tanner! Caitlyn!" Brant suddenly entered the kitchen. He looked harassed and was obviously too caught up in his own turmoil to notice their romantic tableau. "God, Tanner, you've got to come out to the drawing room! Janet is threatening to leave by herself. She's been telling me that my wife was horribly rude to her and that she's not about to take such an insult from a nobody. A *nobody*! That little snob! I'd like to tell her exactly what I think of her!"

Caitlyn was aware of the emotions flooding through her as she risked a last glance at Tanner's face. She could see her own emotions mirrored there and quickly pushed away from him, hurrying to Brant, who was running a nervous hand through his hair.

"Oh, dearest, I'm so glad to hear you say that!" she said fervently. "Does she really mean that much in the scheme of things? Do you really want to be appointed to that post by her father?"

"Don't you want me to gain some respect here?" he asked. "It's hard enough being an American among all these Britishers, but when they find out I made my fortune digging for gold, they close ranks. I'm the parvenu here just as I was in New Orleans."

She had noted his first sentence. "Don't *I* want you to gain respect, Brant? What about you? Don't you want the same thing?"

His dark eyes met hers. "I never have, Caitlyn. I've tried so hard to be a businessman because I knew you wanted me to, but I just can't seem to find happiness in it. I wish I could be what you want me to be, Caitlyn, but I just can't. I'd rather be in Queensland digging for gold with Dan and Jimmy or back home hunting with old friends while an overseer takes charge of the cottonfields."

"Perhaps I should excuse myself," Tanner interjected, clearing his throat.

Both Brant and Caitlyn turned to him, having forgotten his presence. Caitlyn was embarrassed that he had been a witness to her private discussion with Brant. Hadn't he told her one time that she could never change Brant into her idea of the perfect husband? She supposed that now he could tell her he had been right all along. But somehow she'd never realized that it was always *her* idea of what Brant should be that had stopped her from seeing who he really was.

"We have guests," Brant reminded her softly, taking her hands

in his. "I think we'd best continue this discussion later, Caitlyn."

Fortunately Tanner excused himself early, taking Lady Janet with him. Caitlyn blessed him silently and could almost forgive him the scare he'd given her earlier in the kitchen.

She watched him go, wondering how he might calm down the volatile Lady Janet. But then she realized that Janet Penworthington had only been the catalyst for the understanding she had come to with Brant. He wasn't really happy here. She had suspected it before, but she had never wanted to believe it. She had believed that she could change Brant's mind by means of sheer determination. She could *make* him into what she wanted.

But, she reminded herself, it was Brant that she wanted. Wasn't it? Had she fallen in love with Brant because of who he was, or because of who she thought he *should* be?

41

"IT WAS a lovely party, Caitlyn," Brant said casually as they undressed for bed later. "I heard several of the guests comment on how they enjoyed themselves. You were a bona fide hit, my dear, except with Janet Penworthington."

"Was I?" she asked nervously. She caught her nail on one of the hooks of her gown and tore the nail in frustration. For a moment she was caught between crying and cursing.

"Caitlyn, we need to talk," Brant said abruptly.

She let the gown fall to the floor as she stared at him, her eyes huge. Seeing her standing there in her petticoats, Brant found himself irresistibly drawn toward her. He knew why she was upset and it made him feel ashamed that she could love him so much.

"Caitlyn, I love you," he said, realizing that it was true.

She seemed to crumple, and if he hadn't caught her, she would have fallen to the floor. He held her tight against him, telling himself over and over that he didn't deserve her love. How could he hurt her? How could he tell her that he had always resented her pushing him, molding him, trying to make him into a replica of her idea of what the perfect husband should be.

"Oh, Brant, I'm sorry for being so demanding!" Caitlyn sobbed.

He pressed his lips to her forehead. "Don't apologize, Caitlyn," he told her. "It wasn't entirely your fault. I let you push me because I was too damned lazy to stand up for myself. I should have told you when we came to Melbourne that I didn't want to join Tanner's business. My poor Caitlyn! I let you believe that I was beginning to enjoy my work, that I wanted to succeed as much as you wanted me to. But I was lying to you and to myself. That's not the right way to have a marriage."

"Oh, Brant, I feel so terrible! I've been domineering and aggressive—just the things I told myself I wouldn't be when we got married. Tanner tried to tell me what I was doing to you, but I wouldn't listen to him."

He smiled. "Tanner knows you better than I do, Caitlyn. I sometimes wonder if he's not a little in love with you."

"Don't talk nonsense!" Caitlyn protested, pressing her face tightly against Brant's shoulder, afraid that if he looked into her eyes now, he might see that the thought had occurred to her too. "You're the man I married."

"You married me, but maybe it was for the wrong reasons, Caitlyn. Maybe you were just so determined—"

"Brant, don't!" she warned him. "It does no good now. I've made some mistakes and so have you. Instead of dwelling on them, let's see how we can avoid them in the future. I truly want you to be happy, even if it means you have to leave here and go to Queensland to dig for gold."

"No!" He shook his head. "I couldn't leave you here alone and I couldn't ask you to travel thousands of miles to endure the same kind of grueling experience you've already had. Truthfully, I don't know what to do. Lately I've been thinking of my father, of Riverhouse, of home."

Joy leapt up in her eyes at what he was suggesting. "Oh, darling, if you want to go home, I'll be happy to go!"

He'd suspected as much and smiled to hear her say it.

"When? When can we go?" she said, eager now to do what would please him. She had felt homesick herself, wondering what the war was doing to Louisiana. "It will please my family so much—and your father too, Brant. He'll be overjoyed to know that you're finally coming home. And so will Mama and Papa and Constance. We'll be with everyone who loves us."

Brant mentally shrank from the idea of Constance welcoming him home. He was ashamed of his cavalier attitude toward her *and* toward Caitlyn in that time long ago when he had assumed

that both of them could be his for the taking. Some of his earlier enthusiasm dwindled at the thought of actually facing Constance and his father. He'd proven himself a poor son. William, like Caitlyn, had expected things from him that he had never been prepared to give. Although he wanted to go home, wanted to vindicate himself by returning triumphant with his fortune, he was still concerned about his own emotions, his ties to that place where he was born.

Brant knew once he brought Caitlyn home, he would be expected to take over the running of Riverhouse, assuming that Riverhouse was still standing and still owned by his father. If it was, he was the heir apparent. It would be up to him to continue the tradition, and such a responsibility was a heavy one.

"We'll have to see about our journey to the States," he cautioned her, looking into her shining eyes and wondering why he couldn't quite share her enthusiasm. "I can't promise anything right away with the war going on."

He kissed Caitlyn again, thinking how lovely she was. As she returned his kiss, he could almost feel the invisible velvet chains of her love twining gently but strongly about him. His hands moved instinctively to her camisole, wanting to see her breasts, wanting to caress her body and kiss her wherever he desired.

Brant had seen the envy in the male guests' eyes tonight. It had made him proud that such a beauty was his, truly his. He was sure Caitlyn was blind to anyone else so long as he was beside her. It made him feel proud and incredibly virile now as he pushed Caitlyn onto the bed and began to undress her. Listening to the soft moans that his caresses elicited from her lips, Brant was foolish enough to think that no other man had the ability to extract the same response from her.

The next morning Brant went to work almost as though nothing had been discussed last night about returning home. It was frustrating to Caitlyn to observe his nonchalance, for she was the kind of woman who needed to exercise some control over the people and things in her life, if only so that she could count on certain things happening at certain times. But Brant seemed his usual self, kissing her on his way out the door after breakfast.

"Darling," she said softly, handing him his hat, "what are you going to tell Tanner this morning about our plans?"

His dark eyes shied away from hers. "I'm not going to tell him anything yet," he answered vaguely. "After all, we aren't

even sure when and how we'll be returning, Caitlyn. As I told you last night, we'll have to see how the war progresses. I'm not going to try to sail into hostile territory and risk losing my newfound fortune to a pack of Yankee soldiers.''

He patted her shoulder, then hurried out the door as though glad to get away from any unwanted discussion.

Caitlyn felt her temper rising. Brant was not being fair to her. Just last night he'd told her he hated what he was doing, that he wanted to return home. Now here he was blithely going off to his office as though nothing had changed, as though he still intended to make something of himself among the Melbourne businessmen.

Tanner came to call the following day in the late afternoon when Brant was still at the office. He found Caitlyn in the kitchen baking. She hastily dusted off her hands and face with her apron and went to greet him properly in the drawing room.

"Tanner, what brings you here this afternoon?" she asked, seeing him waiting for her by the fireplace and thinking how handsome he looked.

His dark blue eyes appraised her as he smiled. "You've got flour on your cheek, Caitlyn," he told her, striding over to brush it off with his thumb. "You looked quite the little domestic back there in the kitchen with rolling pin in hand."

"Did I?" she said saucily. "Well, I can assure you, it was all for the sheer pleasure of it. I've found I really enjoy baking."

"I would never have thought it of you," he admitted, taking both her hands in his and spreading them wide as he looked at her. "Hmm. Your dress is not as elegant as the daring ball gown you wore two days ago, but it'll do." His eyes roved over her face. "Your cheeks are pink from the heat of the oven. They look like ripe peaches and I want to bite into them!" He leaned forward as though to carry out his threat and Caitlyn turned her head, laughing at him.

"Tanner, you are positively too bold!" she told him. "You are the only man I know who always seems to get away with it."

His eyes twinkled wickedly. "I'm glad to hear it. It heartens me considerably."

"Now stop teasing me and tell me what brings you here today." Her eyes sobered. "It's nothing about Brant, is it? Has he mentioned anything to you about leaving Australia?"

"Leaving?" Tanner shook his head, his own eyes sobering. "He hasn't said a word. I wouldn't be surprised if he wanted to leave. His head is in the clouds half the time he's supposed to be working. I don't know if he still wants to try out for the post of Lord Penworthington's assistant or not. He's vague on his future plans whenever I ask him about them." His black brows drew down questioningly. "So you are thinking of leaving?"

She pulled her hands from his and clasped them together. "Tanner, I honestly don't know what Brant is thinking," she sighed, seating herself on the settee. "On the night of the dinner party he told me he wanted to go home. I told him I thought it was a fine idea." She looked up at Tanner. "I really do! I think he's done all he came here to do, short of going to Queensland to search for more gold with his cronies."

"So you're homesick, are you, Caitlyn?" he questioned, sitting down next to her on the settee.

She nodded. "Australia is beautiful, but it will never be home to me. Still, I've learned so much here," she admitted.

"Dare I hope that I've been a help in any way?" Tanner asked with a smile.

She met his gaze without flinching. "You *know* how much you've been a help to Brant and me," she told him. "If it hadn't been for you, I don't know what I would have done after I lost the baby. I owe you a great deal."

"All of which I intend to collect some day," he reminded her. "Really, Caitlyn, your debt to me is of amazing proportions!"

"Really?" she returned archly.

He nodded. "And I won't be paid in gold, my dear."

For a moment she was taken aback by his forthright boldness. "Tanner Malone, you are ever the villain, aren't you?" she observed. "You like to pretend you don't do anything without being paid, but I can see through the veneer to the man underneath. You're capable of tenderness and caring. It's the only thing that saves you in my eyes."

"My dearest Caitlyn, don't think I don't mean what I say. Someday when you're alone in this house and you begin to wonder if your marriage to Brant was the smartest thing you could have done, you'll think of me. And I'll come."

"Tanner!" Now he *was* being too bold. "You mustn't say such things! It's not right. Brant admires you so much."

"I like Brant too," Tanner admitted. "But that doesn't keep

me from wondering just what it is you see in him, what it is you've always seen in him. Sometimes I think you've seen what you wanted to see, Caitlyn. And when you find out that your picture of him isn't the real thing—"

"That will *never* happen, Tanner!" she assured him vehemently.

"Stubborn as always, aren't you, my dear?"

She looked away from him, wondering how they had managed to wander off the subject she wanted to discuss with him. Why was it that Tanner always asked questions that made her unsure of her own feelings, that made her question her own motivation? It was annoying that he was capable of hitting a nerve inside of her that responded exactly the way he wanted it to.

"Tanner, I don't want to discuss the possibility of my becoming disenchanted with my husband. I asked you, if you'll recall, what brought you here today."

He studied her through half-closed eyes as he leaned back in the settee. To her surprise, he said simply, "I wanted to apologize for the behavior of my companion at your dinner party. I'm sorry if it ruined the evening for you, or for anyone else."

As always, he had caught her off balance. How was it that he always said something that was totally opposite to what she was expecting? "So *that* is the reason you came here this afternoon!" she exclaimed.

He laughed out loud so that she leaned close to silence him, waving her finger in front of his face. "Hush! Molly will hear you and wonder what in the world we're doing!"

He caught her waving finger in his hand and pulled her forward with it so that she fell into his arms. "Why don't we give her something to wonder about, Caitlyn?" he said, his breath warm on her face. "Mmm, yes, I think this settee is large enough for what I had in mind. Unfortunately you've taken to wearing those damned corsets again. I can feel your stays with my hands."

"And it's a good thing too!" she whispered vehemently. "Tanner! Will you please behave! If Molly were to come in now—"

"She'd think that you and I were having a glorious affair!" Tanner replied, holding her head with his hands so that he could kiss her face without her squirming away. "Lord, you do taste good, Caitlyn!"

"It's the rolls I've been baking!" she told him angrily.

"I don't care about the rolls; I'll just eat the cook!" he whispered, rolling his eyes in dramatic fashion as he took her nose between his teeth and bit it gently.

Despite her irritation, Caitlyn couldn't help giggling. She wondered how it was that she could be tickled at his bold exploits instead of being angry and giving him the scolding he so richly deserved. But then she realized that Tanner would never take her scolding seriously. He could be such an adventurous, fun-loving mischief maker, she thought fondly. She wondered if that was the side of him that Deborah Wickham had fallen in love with. Thinking of Deborah sobered her and she pulled away from him suddenly, moving to her side of the settee while she smoothed her skirts and gave him an appropriately scathing stare.

"Now what have I done?" he inquired. "I can see by the look in your eyes that you've just remembered something. Oh, please don't purse your lips like that! You look like an old schoolteacher I had when I was a boy! She was the driest thing on earth, a bona fide old maid!"

She colored and unpursed her lips. Now that she had his attention, she wasn't quite sure how to approach the delicate subject of his relationship with Deborah. It really was none of her business and she felt sure he would tell her so. Still, she was curious enough to find out what he might say.

"Deborah Wickham came by about a month ago. I was quite distressed when she told me that you and she—"

Tanner interrupted her. "I told her that I was not a marrying man and that I was not in love with her. I cared very much about her, and if she'd been agreeable, I wouldn't have dissolved the attachment myself. But she wanted more from me, and I can't blame her for not wanting to see me again."

"She told me she'd concluded that *I* had something to do with your attitude towards her," Caitlyn resumed. "So I lost a good friend, though I felt that I'd done nothing to warrant it."

"What did she say to you?" he asked.

She looked away from his blue stare. "She said that you—you cared too much for me to care enough for her."

He was quiet for a moment, his eyes scanning her face as though gauging her reaction. After a while he said, "What do you think, Caitlyn?"

She looked up, flustered at his question. "Why, I don't know what to think. I told Deborah she was mistaken and that you and I were nothing more than very good friends, just as you are very

good friends with my husband. She didn't believe me." Caitlyn was suddenly very much aware of the locket Tanner had given her, hanging between her breasts beneath the bodice of her dress. The locket was warm against her flesh, almost as though his hands— She stopped herself abruptly, feeling frightened at the unforeseen direction her thoughts were taking.

"Well," he said slowly, "we *are* good friends, Caitlyn. And good friends have a tendency to care about each other, don't you agree?"

"Y-yes," she said, wishing her voice wouldn't tremble on the word. *Why* did she feel so awkward, so naked, in front of him?

"If Deborah misconstrued those feelings, then I'm sorry for her. It was wrong of her to make you feel guilty for caring about a friend."

"But you were *her* friend, too," Caitlyn said softly.

"She demanded too much of me, Caitlyn," he answered, reaching over to take her chin in his hand so that he could look into her eyes. "*You* never demand anything of me." The words sounded like a reproach and Caitlyn bit her lip.

"We're both selfish beasts, aren't we?" he said with a sardonic smile. "I was a cad to behave toward Deborah the way I did. And you—"

"Tanner, stop!" she protested, not wanting to hear any more.

They were both silent. With a slight sigh, he moved his hand away from her and leaned back in the settee. "What a coincidence that you and Brant have been thinking of going home!" he said softly. "As farfetched as it sounds, I've become homesick myself. I haven't seen my family for over four years. I've made more money down here than any man should be entitled to. Now that the situation with the Wickhams has become awkward, it might be a good time to sell my Australian interests to the highest bidder. One of the things that was holding me back was how to tell Brant. I knew he wouldn't continue in the business without me running things."

She nodded. "He's not happy anyway, Tanner. I don't really know what he wants to do," she admitted.

"I don't think Brant knows himself, Caitlyn," Tanner told her frankly. "Maybe going back to Lousiana would be the best thing for him. Riverhouse has always been a powerful magnet. Who knows? Maybe he'll find out something about himself once he goes back and is given the responsibility of taking over for his father."

"But he's so vague about it," Caitlyn said. "Tanner, I don't want to push him. I don't want him to think I'm trying to make him into something he's not."

"But *aren't* you?" Tanner intervened swiftly. "Haven't you always done just that, Caitlyn?"

She stood up and walked to the window. "I don't know. Maybe I *have* tried to push him and mold him and make him into this *hero* that I've always thought he could be. Maybe I should stop trying and just accept him as he is."

Tanner got up and walked over to stand behind her. "Accepting a man for what he is oftentimes helps him to grow beyond it."

She turned around to face him, her mouth trembling in a half-smile. "Just a few minutes ago, you said I reminded you of one of your old schoolteachers," she chided him. "Now it's *you* who's teaching me a lesson, Tanner."

"Ah, Caitlyn, if you only knew how much I'd like to teach you!" he murmured, reaching up with a soft finger to caress her jaw.

"Tanner, you mustn't talk that way!" she said in a low voice.

For a moment she could almost feel the raging emotions warring inside of him. His finger actually trembled against her skin, but then he drew it away, balling his hands into fists and sticking them into his trouser pockets.

"Well," he finally said after a short silence, "as always, Caitlyn, you've bested me again. It never fails to astonish me how you consistently avert my wickedest intentions." He smiled slightly. "I still haven't given up. I have every confidence of winning this war someday."

42

CAITLYN WAS SURE she'd never felt so happy, not even when she'd received Brant's letter asking her to come to Australia. Brant had finally agreed to go home. From the reports they'd been receiving for the last few months, the war was not going well for the South. No more letters had come from her family, but the newspapers from England were filled with details of the final death throes of the Confederacy. Inflation was running rampant throughout the South and President Jefferson Davis had sent

word to Britain and France by special envoy that he would emancipate all the slaves in the Confederacy in exchange for recognition of his dying government. But neither country took the bait—and thereby the South's fate was sealed.

Tearfully, Caitlyn had ridden outside Melbourne with Brant to say good-bye to this land that she still did not know after more than two years. She'd seen the eucalyptuses flower as well as the lovely acacias. She'd watched mobs of kangaroos scoot across the flat grasslands and endearing little koalas scurry up tree trunks. She'd seen the best and the worst that the country had to offer the new pioneers, but she hadn't seen it all. She understood Australia no better now than on the first day she'd stepped onto its shores. It was here that she'd conceived a child and buried that child in the earth. It was here that she'd found Brant. She had matured from a spoiled and willful brat, as ill-mannered as Lady Janet Penworthington, and had flowered into the self-assured twenty-one-year-old that she was now. She had survived the wilderness of this land and had grown stronger with the knowledge that it had not beaten her.

She and Brant would depart from this land so much the richer, not only for the fortune they would be bringing home with them, but also for the experiences they had undergone. It had been one of the hardest things she'd ever done to take leave of her dead son's grave on Seth Wickham's property.

The trip to England was a smooth one. Tanner was a good companion for Brant when Caitlyn experienced bouts of nausea that kept her in her cabin. She began to wonder if she were pregnant, trying to remember how many months it had been since she'd had her menses. It was already the end of November. Had it been four months since she had taken to her bed with her usual cramps? She kept her musings to herself for the time being, not wanting to alarm Brant.

As they neared port in England, she was positive that she was with child, a child that would arrive in April, she calculated. She fervently prayed that the child would be born when she was safe at Riverhouse with the people she loved. She wanted to tell Brant she was pregnant, but he had become sharp with her as his nervousness increased the closer they got to home. He was quarrelsome with Tanner too, even though he knew Tanner would be separating from them in Liverpool. Tanner would book passage on a ship bound for Boston, which would be a lot easier

than finding one bound for any Southern port. Most of the ports were too tightly blockaded by Northern gunboats for any foreign ship to break through. Caitlyn could only hope that the war would be over in time for the baby.

One evening only a week before arriving in Liverpool, Caitlyn stood on the main deck, glad for the brisk wind in her face that helped keep away the nausea that still plagued her. Brant had already gone below deck after dinner, but she had wanted to watch the sun setting behind the cool green waters to the west.

"Good evening, Caitlyn," Tanner said, coming up behind her as she leaned on the railing. "Has Brant already gone to his cabin?"

She nodded. "I know how fearful he is. He doesn't know what to expect when he gets home. What will his father say? What will his friends think of him? After all, most of them had to go off and serve in the army while Brant was safe in another world! We've heard such terrible news about the condition of the South. I feel guilty for having escaped it all. Everyone else had to endure the horrors of war. And we come home with a fortune. Will they ever forgive us?"

"Probably not," he answered thoughtfully. "It's hard to forgive someone who's wearing a new dress and fur cape when you haven't worn anything but mattress ticking for the last year. And it *will* be like that, Caitlyn. It doesn't matter how hard you try to win their hearts, they will always hold it against you."

He was silent, staring out at the reddish gold sun as it disappeared into the horizon. Then, shaking himself out of his melancholy mood, he smiled at her. "Of course there's always a new adventure to look forward to, isn't there?"

"Maybe for you, but I'm hoping never to set foot out of Louisiana again," she said quickly. "I want to sit on the veranda of Riverhouse with my children around me, waiting for Brant to come home from the cottonfields."

He laughed in disbelief. "Maybe that will hold you for a little while, Caitlyn, but you're too much like me. We've both got boundless energy inside of us that won't let us keep still for long. I just can't imagine you home with a baby all day."

"Well, you'd better start," she said with a laugh, patting her belly.

He stared at her in surprise.

She blushed, then added, "Brant doesn't know yet."

"When will you tell him, Caitlyn?" he asked bluntly.

"Soon," she said warily. "I was afraid it would be one more thing for him to worry about."

Tanner gazed at her with a look of genuine concern. He stepped forward and wrapped his arms around her so that she rested her head on his shoulder. Stroking her back softly, he murmured to her, "I know how frightened you must be about having this baby, yet you've kept the knowledge to yourself all this time! My brave girl, men can be such idiots!" he sighed.

Liverpool was all bustle and movement and shouting and jostling. Caitlyn had forgotten how lively it was. She wondered how she had ever handled it before without Brant and Tanner to push through the crowds and take care of the practical details. Her nose wrinkled at the acrid smells from the factories and industrial buildings that belched smoke into the sky. It was January, midwinter in England. Down in Australia, she couldn't help thinking, it was high summer. The acacias were blossoming there, and the roses were in bloom by her son's grave on Seth Wickham's property. She felt the burgeoning new life within her and silently prayed that all would go well with this child.

Finally Tanner was able to book passage for them on a merchant ship bound for New Orleans that was carrying supplies to the Union garrison there. It had taken plenty of money to get the ship to take on two extra passengers, but Tanner had refused Brant's offer of repayment, telling him to consider it a late wedding gift.

Tanner's own ship was scheduled to leave three days before theirs, and for Caitlyn the time approached far too quickly. She could sense the tension in Brant and felt sad that they would be separated from Tanner. He seemed so woven into the fabric of their lives that she could hardly imagine being so far away from him. Yet the morning finally came when it was time for him to leave.

They rode to the wharf with him, all three subdued, lost in their own private thoughts. When they arrived at the pier, Brant and Tanner stood together talking. Caitlyn watched them, thinking how her perception of this Yankee had changed over the years. She found it hard to believe she'd been so hateful and haughty to him the first time they'd met. How things had changed since then! Now she considered him one of her closest friends.

When Tanner finished talking with Brant and started walking toward her, Caitlyn found herself poised precariously on the

edge of tears. With an unexpected thoughtfulness, Brant had strolled a little distance away, ostensibly to help with the disposition of Tanner's luggage.

"I suppose this is good-bye," Caitlyn said, trying to smile.

Tanner nodded, his dark blue eyes searching her face. "It's hard to believe that I won't see you," he commented, reaching for her hands. When he realized she was wearing gloves, he took them off, slowly and deliberately, and tucked them into his vest pocket. Then he clasped her hands tenderly in his. "I wish you well, Caitlyn," he said softly.

"I know, Tanner," she murmured. His hands were squeezing hers and she was dangerously close to tears once more. Why did his leaving tear so at her heart? "You will come down to Louisiana and see us as soon as you can, won't you?" she asked him, wishing she'd thought to bring a handkerchief to staunch the flow in her eyes.

He saw her dilemma and produced his own handkerchief, tenderly wiping the corners of her eyes. "There was a time when you would have shouted hallelujah at the thought of sweeping me out of your life."

She sniffled and took his handkerchief to dab her nose. "You know I've changed, Tanner. I've come to realize what a good friend you've been to Brant and me. I'll never forget all you did for us in Australia."

"It's lucky for Brant that you've only recently found out what a gem I am," he teased her softly. "What a convenient time to tell a man how much he means to you—just as he's about to sail away!" He looked away and scanned the pier, his eyes picking out Brant. "Your husband must be wondering why it's taking us so long to say a simple good-bye," he commented. He looked at her again. "I suppose it really is time for me to go."

She clung to his hands. "Tanner! I—I will miss you!" she whispered.

"And I will miss you, Caitlyn," he returned earnestly.

For a few moments they stared at each other. Then with a careless smile, Tanner pulled her close, enfolding her in his arms and pressing her against him. "What the hell, my dear!" he whispered with a wicked grin. "I don't give a damn what your husband thinks!" And he leaned forward to kiss her, taking her lips and molding them fiercely with his own.

Despite her embarrassment at this public kiss in full view, not only of her husband, but also of the ship's passengers and the

longshoremen, Caitlyn clung to him, matching his kiss with her own fire. She felt his lips warming hers as they moved over them. She shivered in his arms.

And then he was pulling away, setting her gently back on her heels and touching her lips regretfully with the tip of his index finger. "What a woman you are, Caitlyn!" he murmured.

"You'd better go," she told him as at the corner of her eye she glimpsed Brant strolling toward them. "I'll miss you."

"I'll see you again, Caitlyn," he promised.

Rakishly, he blew her a kiss, then turned around and hurried toward the ship with a quick wave to Brant. Caitlyn watched him go, feeling a choking sensation in her throat that was unexpectedly intense. But she knew that Brant was approaching and she must compose herself.

"Darling, are you all right?" Brant asked suspiciously. He enfolded her in his arms possessively. "I was beginning to think Tanner might miss his boat," he said jokingly, hoping to lighten the atmosphere.

"It was hard to say good-bye to him, Brant," she admitted. "After all, he *has* been a good friend to us both."

"A good friend, Caitlyn," Brant repeated thoughtfully.

It was only later as they were driving back to their hotel that Caitlyn noticed she was still clutching Tanner's handkerchief. By extension, she realized he had forgotten to give her back her gloves. Or had he forgotten? She would never understand Tanner's motives. But it was good to know that he cared about her and that she would see him again. She pressed the handkerchief between her palms and a smile hovered about her lips.

43

IT WAS MIDMORNING of March 31, 1865, Caitlyn's twenty-second birthday, when they docked at the New Orleans levee. Surprisingly, the docks were filled with ships and the levee looked as bustling as ever, as though there had never been a war to interrupt commerce. But upon closer inspection, Caitlyn could see the remains of burned buildings that had not yet been cleared away. There was a plethora of blue-clad Yankee soldiers amidst the red-shirted longshoremen, as well as the surprising sight of black men lounging on the pier dressed in suits and hats.

But Caitlyn soon lost interest in these sights, for as she and Brant stepped onto the pier, she recognized her parents and her sister waiting for them. With a glad shout, she hurried towards them as fast as her bulk would allow. Crying and laughing, she hugged all three of them, the tears streaming down her cheeks. She was home again!

Her father cleared his throat several times before he could trust himself to speak. "Daughter, it's good to see you!" he finally got out, his eyes suspiciously moist as he looked proudly at his eldest.

"Caitlyn, how much I've missed you!" her mother said, her eyes streaming as she gazed at her daughter as though to reassure herself she wasn't dreaming. "And how wonderful you look!" she added, her eyes widening at the telltale bulge at the front of Caitlyn's cloak.

"Caitlyn, it's good to have you home again!" Constance said gently.

Then Brant came up and the welcomes were repeated. For his own part, Brant felt enormously relieved that Caitlyn's parents were welcoming him with open arms. As he moved forward to embrace his sister-in-law, he could see the momentary stiffening in her face. He held her awkwardly for a moment, then stepped back to look at the soft blue eyes and the strawberry blonde hair that he had almost forgotten. How different she seemed from his memories of her! he thought. They had each clung to something as insubstantial as a dream, but now Brant was much happier with the reality that was Caitlyn. He saw a look of slow-dawning realization on Constance's face. The indecision that had first clouded her eyes was replaced by a look that was part surprise and part relief. Then she smiled radiantly. "Welcome home, Brant!" she said softly.

"Thank you, Constance," he replied, realizing that the passion they had once had for each other had died away. Fate had seen to it that the right woman had gotten that letter after all! With enormous relief Brant stepped over to his wife and proudly put an arm around her.

They were all talking at once while the luggage was seen to and the carriage brought over. "I had to go to a great deal of trouble to procure this thing," Timothy informed Caitlyn with a wink. "All our carriages are gone, requisitioned by the Yankees early on. Although we've lost our livestock and most of the horses, we still have Mornhaven."

"So many others have suffered worse than we have," Margaret added as she helped Caitlyn get settled in the carriage. "Winfield Cobb lost his eldest in the fighting at Vicksburg. Poor, dear Marcella has those twin boys to raise alone now that Artemas is gone. Darby Howard lost a leg to gangrene while he was imprisoned."

"Mama, no more, please!" Caitlyn pleaded. She couldn't think of those friends of her youth right now. It was much too painful.

"Jesse Cobb made it home in one piece," Constance interjected softly.

Caitlyn looked at her. "I'm so glad, Connie!" she said fervently. As the carriage left the levee, she took a moment to look closely at her parents. Her father, who had always been robust, was much thinner now and his jowls sagged loosely. His red hair was nearly all silvered. Her mother had grayed too and was thinner, more delicate. But beneath the fragile outer shell, she seemed to be made of iron as she sat straight as a ramrod next to Connie. Even her sister had changed, Caitlyn noted. Gone was the plump roundness of her youth, but she still maintained that air of serenity that Caitlyn had always envied.

As they made their way down Canal Street, everywhere Caitlyn looked she saw blue Yankee uniforms. The flag of the United States was displayed prominently on the roofs of buildings where formerly the Confederate flag had waved. And all along the street were groups of blacks lounging against posts or squatting on the sidewalk to throw dice. Caitlyn wondered if her father had been able to find any laborers to work the cottonfields at Mornhaven.

When they finally arrived at the Savoys' house, there was another round of tears and backslapping so that Caitlyn felt buffeted by all the well-wishing. Uncle Paul and Aunt Helen seemed hardly to have changed. Pauline had two small children and seemed happy enough with Edward Winterby, although most of her father-in-law's land had been confiscated by Yankee troops. Patricia had married a young man who'd been wounded in the war, and even James had finally grown up and joined his father's law practice. He too was married, and his giggling young wife gazed shyly at the obviously pregnant Caitlyn.

And then there was William, Brant's father, his hair completely white, his hands shaking visibly as Brant came forward to greet him. As she embraced her father-in-law, Caitlyn could see the fierce joy in his eyes that not only was his son home at

last, but that soon he would be presented with his first grandchild. With a tacit understanding, William and Brant were left alone in Paul's office while everyone else trooped into the dining room for a splendid meal.

"It's not easy without Julia, my old cook," Aunt Helen said quickly, "but when she decided she didn't want to work for me anymore now that she was emancipated, I had to learn to cook for myself."

As she sat at the table and listened to the eager conversation, the retelling of Yankee misdeeds and Confederate heroics, Caitlyn felt a wonderful sense of home pervading her being. It was enough for now just to have her loved ones surrounding her. She gazed with affection at her mother, who was giving James's new wife instructions on the best way to cook squash, and at Connie, who was laughing and talking with Pauline as she held her little niece. Her father was caught up in a political discussion with Uncle Paul. It was almost as though she had never left them, as though her time in Australia was nothing more than a dream.

Tomorrow they would start the journey by carriage to Mornhaven, for Caitlyn was anxious to get to Riverhouse before the baby's birth. Along the way they would make a few brief stops. They would visit Aunt Caroline and her family; then Great-Aunt Marie, whose sister Eugenia had died last year of pneumonia; and finally Grandma and Grandpa Forrester. It was as though the threads of the past were reaching out to entwine her, Caitlyn thought. Was she dreaming? Was she still back in Australia with Brant and Tanner and the Wickhams? No. The Wickhams were the dream now, and the baby who had died, and Tanner who was safe in Boston. For a moment she felt a tugging at her heart as though she were loath to let go of them and accept the people who were with her now. In a curious way the people here seemed like the strangers.

She shook her head to clear it of invisible cobwebs. She was being silly. Something had changed. Maybe it was *she* who had changed. She recalled her petty squabbles with her cousins, the excitement she had once shared with Connie over the next party, her father's praise over how well she sat a horse. Those things seemed inconsequential to her now. She loved her family dearly, but now her real family was Brant and the baby who would soon be born. She had undergone a series of changes while she'd been away that these people had not. Despite the horrors of war and the devastation it had caused, everyone here was essentially the

same. It could have been five years ago, or ten years ago. For a moment Caitlyn felt lost, left out. She searched the room in a sudden panic, not knowing whose face she wanted to see.

"Caitlyn, are you all right?" Margaret asked her worriedly as she saw the strained look on her daughter's face. Caitlyn clasped her mother's hand in her own as though to reassure herself that she was really home.

"Just a little tired," Caitlyn whispered.

Margaret looked at her daughter wisely. "Does it all seem unchanged to you, my dear? We try to make it seem so at times, but in reality everything has changed. We are all making an effort on your behalf."

"I just feel so different," Caitlyn acknowledged, relieved that her mother knew her thoughts. "I feel as though I don't belong here anymore."

"You've been away, Caitlyn, on a grand adventure. Our lives must seem very trivial and mundane. While we continued here, trying to keep life unchanged in order to protect our own sanity amidst the insanity of war, you have been off seeing new things, experiencing new adventures. I'm proud of you for it, Caitlyn, more than you'll ever know. And so is your father."

Caitlyn felt tears welling in her eyes as she pressed her mother's hand. "Oh, Mama, I have learned so much while I've been gone!"

"I know, Caitlyn," Margaret smiled softly.

"But it's my first day back with all of you and I'm already wondering if I can be happy here as I once was," Caitlyn murmured fitfully. "What if this isn't what I really want?"

Her mother gazed at her for a while, then smiled bravely. "Then I suppose you will have to go off again and find yourself another adventure, my dear."

Two weeks later, only a few days after the Confederacy surrendered to the Union at Appomattox, Caitlyn was delivered of a healthy baby girl in the master bedroom of Riverhouse. As she lay exhausted and soaked with sweat, she smiled softly at her new daughter, who was squalling lustily.

"She's perfect," Margaret said, running a hand across her forehead wearily. It had seemed like hours to her, when in reality it had been a very short labor.

Caitlyn complied happily while the proud grandmother called for Brant to come in and see his new daughter. He practically

flew into the room. At first his eyes searched Caitlyn's face as if to assure himself that all was well with this child. When she smiled triumphantly back at him, he let out a great whoop of joy, startling the baby, who lost the nipple and screamed in frustration.

"I'm a father!" he cried. "And of a daughter, exactly what I was wishing for," he said tactfully, so that Margaret could have kissed him. "I'm so happy, my dearest," he murmured to Caitlyn. "She would have made a great little rebel with that yell of hers. Wait until Pa sees her!"

As it turned out, Margaret Christina Sinclair was the apple of both her grandfathers' eyes. Whenever visitors came to congratulate the proud parents, they were obliged to congratulate the grandfathers too, if they were around. For William, who had never had a daughter, she was nothing short of a miracle of perfection. Timothy claimed she was entirely Irish, with her lusty voice and her shock of red hair that stood straight up on the crown of her head. Caitlyn complained good-naturedly that the only time she got to spend alone with her daughter was when she was nursing her. But she was so happy that her daughter had been born perfect. Sometimes she would fall prey to the blues and think of her firstborn lying in a grave in a faraway land. At those times nothing would comfort her except to hold Maggie in her arms and rock her gently, telling her over and over how much she loved her.

44

IN THE SPACE of a few short weeks, life took on a comforting routine for Caitlyn, although outside of her safe haven the world seemed to have turned upside down. Abraham Lincoln had been assassinated and any plans he'd had for settling the differences between North and South had died with him. After a while the North's joyous celebrations of victory and the grim reports of Southern destitution purged the vengeance from the hearts of many Northerners, but this sentiment coexisted with the conviction that the South should be punished for rebelling. Northern politicians were calling it magnanimity tempered by justice.

At the end of May President Andrew Johnson signed a proc-

lamation offering amnesty and restitution of property to all Southerners, but it required taking an oath of allegiance to the United States. Less than two months after the war's end, the Southerners, who had fought and shed blood for the cause they believed in, were expected to turn around and pledge allegiance to their conquerors. It was a bitter pill to swallow. Many would not take the pledge and lost their plantations. Winfield Cobb had his plantation taken away by the federal government and was forced to live in a small house at the edge of the O'Rourke property. He hated having to take Timothy's charity, calling him a traitor to the cause for swearing allegiance to the United States, but Timothy was a realist. He had never been entirely convinced of the wisdom of secession and now he was not going to lose his beloved Mornhaven because of arrogant pride in a lost cause.

One day in early June Timothy was visiting Riverhouse, grumbling to Brant about the turn of events and wondering where it was going to lead. "It's a damned shame that all this political machinery has to get in the way of rebuilding our broken land," he said sadly. "Most of the planters and merchants aren't interested in politics; they just want to get to work repairing their buildings and equipment, planting the crops, and starting the wheels of commerce. At times it seems impossible. Much of the land is lying fallow, the slaves are freed but disorganized, and there is a need for credit to replace the capital destroyed by the ravages of war."

"If it's only a question of credit, sir, I've got all the money you'll need," Brant offered with a touch of pride. "There's quite a bit here in Louisiana, but most of it is drawing interest in a bank in Boston. Tanner persuaded me to let him deposit it there. You've helped my pa and me for so long at Riverhouse, and now I'm finally in a position to repay your generosity."

Timothy's eyes glowed. "Thank you, son," he said simply.

Caitlyn and William entered the drawing room. They'd been outside on the veranda playing chess while Maggie slept in her bassinet nearby. William was delighted to have so many people occupying Riverhouse. He loved his daughter-in-law dearly, and his granddaughter meant more to him than he could express in words. He told himself that now he could die happily when the Lord saw fit to take him to join his beloved Christina.

Either out of guilt, or because he imagined Caitlyn expected it of him, Brant had taken a renewed interest in Riverhouse, working with almost feverish determination to restore the once-

stately house and grounds. He was even able to plant a few acres of cotton with the help of forty freedmen he had hired for the season.

Timothy's face softened. "Enough of this business talk. Where's my granddaughter?"

"William and I just brought her in from the veranda where she was napping," Caitlyn said. William was holding the baby in the crook of his arm with as much naturalness as though he'd been doing it all his life. She laughed to see the look of consternation on Timothy's face.

"God's teeth, William! You'll drop her!" he cried half teasingly. "Give that child to me, you old codger! You get to see her enough as it is."

With a smile, William allowed Timothy to take her from his arms. "How goes it, Timothy?" he asked. "The word is that your Connie and Jesse Cobb are to be married."

"At long last!" Timothy exclaimed. "God, it took them long enough! Jesse asked Connie to marry him when he came home on furlough two years ago, but she refused him. She went about moping and sighing until I nearly tore my hair out. But when Caitlyn came back, it was like the old Connie had come back too. Poor Jesse Cobb didn't know what hit him. Our Connie marched straight over to his house, faced him and his tyrant of a father and declared that if the offer was still good, she'd damn well marry Jesse this summer!" He laughed outright. "Can you imagine little Connie facing up to that old curmudgeon?"

"Winfield's a curmudgeon, but he loves his family," Caitlyn interjected. "And it's certainly helped to smooth things out between the Cobbs and the O'Rourkes."

"I'm glad of it," Timothy sighed, tickling Maggie's chin with a gentle forefinger. "Jesse insists that Connie can live in that little house with him and his father. But I'll have none of that; they'll live in this house until Jesse gets enough money to build a decent house for the two of them." He winked at Caitlyn. "I'm giving your sister the same dowry I gave you: three hundred acres of good Mornhaven land."

In mid-June Constance had her wedding. It was held at Mornhaven for the convenience of the guests, some of whom had to travel many miles and would be obliged to spend the night. Everyone agreed that the bride looked positively radiant. Caitlyn's eyes were moist as she watched her sister look with open

love into the eyes of her groom, whose boyish face was still capable of blushing even after he'd witnessed the horrors of war.

Everyone had turned out. Friends and relatives came from New Orleans. Neighbors came from all over the parish, many of them attending the festivities as a relief from the hardships and boredom of everyday life. Mary and Darby Howard came with their three-year-old daughter. Caitlyn nearly cried aloud when she saw Darby refusing help and standing during the ceremony on his one leg with the aid of a cane. She remembered him as young and dashing; now he looked much older and his face had the permanently pained expression that came with the loss of a limb. Stephen Carter, wearing a rakish eyepatch to conceal the empty eye socket he'd earned in the war, escorted a girl from Mississippi, claiming he'd finally found the one he was going to marry.

Mornhaven had been decked out in its finest, helped liberally by Brant's money. Vases of fragrant blossoms filled every nook and cranny and the feast was magnificent, especially to people who'd eaten only plain fare for such a long time. Many of the men drank too much and many of the women ate too much, but it was the happiest event the parish had seen in a long time. Even old Winfield himself smiled at the thought of his son's good fortune in marrying Timothy O'Rourke's daughter.

Constance, looking radiant in her gown and veil, kept her hand firmly in that of her new husband as she received her guests in the ballroom of Mornhaven. As Brant bent to kiss her cheek, she gave him a radiant smile.

"I'm so happy," she said, glancing at Jesse with adoring eyes. "I only wish you and Caitlyn had had such a grand wedding."

Brant thought back to the dusty little town of Maldon and the rented room where they had spent their wedding night. "It doesn't matter," he assured her. "Each of us has been lucky enough to attain happiness with the right partner." He looked at her meaningfully.

Later when Constance had a moment to be alone with Caitlyn, she put an arm around Caitlyn's waist and hugged her. "Do you realize," Constance asked softly, "that when you went away to Australia to marry Brant, I thought I would never, ever marry?"

Caitlyn looked at her in surprise.

"I thought I had been robbed of the one man I could truly love," Constance admitted, her eyes looking straight into her sister's. "I thought that somehow something had gone terribly

wrong, that a terrible mistake had been made. I couldn't believe that Brant had sent for you and not for me."

"Connie, you don't have to tell me this," Caitlyn said quickly.

"But I want to," Constance said gently. "I hated you, Caitlyn. I hated you for a long time and I wished that you and Brant would never find love in that strange land you ran off to." She colored a little. "But then the hate went away and I sunk into dull apathy. I didn't care about anything for a while. And then Jesse came back and I still couldn't give him my love freely, although every instinct told me that I should. I was convinced that destiny had not played fair."

"Connie, no! Oh, my poor little sister!" Caitlyn said softly.

"It was my own fault," Constance admitted. "I was still a little girl; I hadn't grown up. And then when I heard you were coming back, I got this crazy notion that Brant would see me and realize what a terrible mistake he'd made marrying you." Her cheeks grew brighter at her confession, but she was determined to continue. "But then when I saw you and Brant, and you were so large with your baby, it just seemed right. And then I realized that destiny *had* played fair. When I looked at Brant, I realized that what I had thought was undying love was only girlish infatuation. That love had died out long ago, but I had been too stubborn to let go of it. I realized then that Jesse truly loved me, that he'd always loved me. Thank heaven he waited for me!"

"Oh, Connie!" Caitlyn hugged her sister tightly and they both wept. "I'm so sorry for all the pain I caused you! I was such a selfish monster in those days that I refused to see the hurt on your face."

"It's all right," Constance said gently, smiling through her tears. "Everything is all right now, Caitlyn. You're my sister and I'll always love you."

Caitlyn was overwhelmed. "And I love you, Connie," she whispered. "There's nothing I'd like to see more than you and Jesse happy together."

"Yes," Constance said softly, dreamily. "All the old ghosts are dead, Caitlyn, and I can give him my heart freely!"

A few days later Brant and Caitlyn received a telegram from Tanner Malone saying that he was planning a visit to New Orleans. Now that he'd spent some time with his family, he'd decided to make the trip to New Orleans to look into his business

interests there. Brant was excited at the thought of seeing his old friend again and hoped that by the time Tanner got to River-house, the cotton would be growing tall. He had hopes that Tanner would be able to help him with the marketing of this year's crop.

Caitlyn too was excited that Tanner was coming. She hadn't realized how much she'd missed him and his cocky humor. Still, she was a trifle anxious, recalling their farewell in Liverpool. For some reason she thought of her sister's words. "All the old ghosts are dead." Were they really dead? Caitlyn wondered.

45

IT WAS EARLY JULY; Maggie was nearly three months old and thriving. The cotton was thriving too, helped along by the forty laborers whom Brant had hired for eight dollars a month each plus room and board. Caitlyn was sitting on the veranda of River-house, rocking Maggie to sleep after her midmorning feeding. She felt drowsy herself in the warm air, hearing the buzzing of the bees nearby in the flower gardens that Brant had planted for her. Brant was out in the cottonfields and William was upstairs lying down, drained of energy by the summer heat.

A lone rider appeared far down the dusty drive, just turning in from the river road. Caitlyn shielded her eyes against the sun's glare and wondered who might be calling at this hour. Then she realized it was the only person it could be—Tanner Malone!

Standing up, she felt the heat flush her face. She put up a free hand to tuck away the stray tendrils of hair that had fallen out of the snood at the back of her head. Of all days to wear this old dress! she thought in dismay, glancing down fretfully at the printed cotton. There was nothing she could do about it now—he'd certainly seen her looking worse!

Tanner was smiling, doffing his hat and waving it at her as he urged his horse to a trot. He jumped off the steed before it stopped, then ran up the veranda steps. But the excitement in his blue eyes was replaced by curiosity as he realized that Caitlyn was not alone on the porch.

"Well, I'll be damned!" he swore softly. "You really did have a baby, didn't you, Caitlyn?" His smile turned merry as he tentatively touched the downy head in the crook of her arm.

"I certainly did," she laughed. And then she added proudly, "Isn't she beautiful?"

"Of course she's beautiful—just like her mother," he smiled.

They stared at one another for a moment, each so glad to see the other that words were not needed. "It's so good to have you here, Tanner!" she finally whispered.

"I'd like to show you just how happy I am to see you, Caitlyn, but I'm afraid I'll awaken your beautiful daughter."

She eyed him with studied impertinence. "You are such a devil, I'm surprised that would even stop you! But just a moment while I take her inside. I have a crib set up in the drawing room for her." She hurried inside to place her daughter in her crib, patting her bottom gently when she fussed for a moment at leaving her mother's arms.

When Caitlyn returned to the veranda, she had barely taken a step onto it when she was gathered up in Tanner's arms. Holding her tightly against him, he bent his head to kiss her thoroughly, taking the breath right out of her. When he finally released her, she stepped back and looked up at him, trying to keep her raging emotions from revealing themselves.

"You—" she began.

But before she could collect herself, he'd caught her again and was treating her to a repeat performance. She giggled as she felt his mustache tickle her mouth, but the giggle died quickly as the intensity of their embrace seemed to catch fire. His hands were pressed to her back, her breasts pressed against his chest as he embraced her with a passion that startled her. After releasing her, he led her to the chair she had recently vacated, then pulled up another to sit next to her.

"I love the way you kiss, Caitlyn," Tanner said, smiling into her eyes. "You always put your whole soul into it."

She didn't know whether to thank him or slap him. But he was watching her with such a merry expression in his eyes that she hadn't the heart to break his mood. "You are the most reprehensible villain, Tanner Malone!" she teased him. "Why I put up with you, I'll never know." She shook her head, but her eyes were laughing.

"I think it's because you like me more than you let on," he told her with a devil-may-care attitude. "It wouldn't be proper for the wife of one man to admit to a shameful desire for another, would it?"

"Tanner Malone!" Now she really was shocked at his boldness.

He laughed away her protests. "Don't worry, my sweet, I promise not to seduce you on the veranda of your husband's estate, although the idea is tempting. You look positively glowing with health, lovelier than when I saw you last. I'd say having babies agrees with you, Caitlyn."

She blushed, not quite knowing how to handle his glib talk. He could be such a puzzle. "Tanner, you must behave yourself," she pleaded. "After all, I *am* a mother now."

"And what is that supposed to mean?" he demanded, amused. "Does it mean you have been elevated beyond passion or desire? Does it mean I must put you in the same category as those pear-shaped matrons who talk endlessly of colic and wet nurses?"

"It means I'm entitled to some respect," she retorted, beginning to fume as she suspected he was making fun of her.

"Caitlyn, I respect your motherhood from the bottom of my heart," he assured her. "But what really holds my interest is your—"

"Enough!" she cried, standing up to exit. "If you insist on teasing me, I shall go inside and stay in my room until Brant comes home."

He looked contrite. "All right then, I'll behave," he said showing his white teeth in a grin that was anything but contrite. He took her hands in his and bade her be seated again. "Tell me what has been going on with you besides the new addition to the family."

She gazed at him suspiciously, but when he continued to sit quietly, she relented. She told him of their voyage home, of the changes since the end of the war, especially in the status of the former slaves. He listened gravely to her talk of William's poor health, her father's plantation problems, her sister's marriage to Jesse Cobb.

At that his black brows arched and he said sardonically, "So the little sister finally got married? I remember her being as besotted with your husband as you were."

"She confessed her infatuation for Brant," Caitlyn admitted. "But then she told me that when Brant and I returned, it was as though a curtain had been lifted from in front of her eyes. She realized it *had* only been an infatuation. When she saw Brant, she realized that he was not the white knight of her dreams."

"Then she has learned more than you have, my dear," he said softly.

Caitlyn stared at him. "What do you mean?"

"Nothing," he shrugged. "I'm just glad that everything was resolved so neatly. It would never do for the younger sister to lust after her sister's husband. But now she's safely married and no doubt head over heels in love with the long-suffering Jesse."

"Well, yes," Caitlyn returned, feeling a bit frustrated at the way he expressed his views. Why couldn't he be serious for once? "And what about you?" she asked, changing the subject. "Has some stiff-necked Boston miss worked her wiles on you yet?"

He shook his head. "You've heard me say I'm not too fond of the institution of marriage, Caitlyn. Of course I've always thought the right woman might be able to change my mind," he added, his eyes twinkling wickedly. "But at thirty I suppose I could be called a confirmed bachelor."

"That's too bad," she said with a playful pout. "Since the war there's been a terrible shortage of men around here. I daresay you'd find yourself deluged with females were you to put out the word that you're interested," she teased him.

"I never said I wasn't *interested*," he returned wickedly.

"You are quite impossible to talk with!" she laughed, throwing up her hands. "I try to be serious and you laugh at me, then I tease you and you start crowing about your masculinity! Honestly, Tanner, I just can't figure you out." She leaned down to pick up one of Maggie's toys that had fallen from the rocker. As she did so, the locket slipped out from beneath her bodice and dangled provocatively over her breasts.

Seeing it as she stood up, Tanner leaned over to grasp it. "So you found it?" he asked softly. "I never had the nerve to ask you after what happened that day."

She flushed at the memory. "Yes, you meant for me to find it, didn't you?"

For a moment his eyes were serious as they sought hers, but then he masked the seriousness with laughter. "Yes, I meant for you to find it and wear it to remind you of what you once were: the haughty, spoiled belle of the ball." He laid the locket back on her breasts, his fingers grazing the cloth of her bodice gently.

They were silent for a minute until Caitlyn heard Maggie beginning to fuss. "The baby's awake," she said, with relief. "I'd best go see to her."

Tanner stayed on the veranda, more moved than he wanted to let on that she had kept the locket for so long next to her heart.

When Brant returned from the cottonfields, he was more than pleased to see Tanner. William was up and playing a relaxing game of chess with Tanner while Caitlyn tended to the baby and helped the cook prepare supper. Brant strode into the house, his boots still muddy from the soil, and clasped Tanner about the shoulders with a warm welcome.

"God, it's good to see you, Tanner!" he boomed heartily.

They talked for a while as they waited for dinner to be ready. Coming from Boston, Tanner had his finger on the pulse of the North and Brant looked upon his news with interest. Likewise, Brant informed Tanner about new developments in the South.

"The hatred toward the federal government and the U.S. army is even more intense in the South than it was five years ago," Brant said seriously. "There's a group in New Orleans who are setting sail for Mexico. Emperor Maximilian has offered free land in Mexico for any ex-Confederate who wants to settle there." He looked thoughtful for a moment. "If it weren't for Caitlyn and the baby, I would risk a chance to start somewhere new again."

"It wouldn't be much of a chance," Tanner pointed out practically. "The so-called Mexican empire won't last long now that the war is over here in the States. Secretary of State Seward has been against the French intervention from the beginning, but with war in the States, there wasn't much he could do about it. Now I hear he's had General Sherman stationed at the Rio Grande just so the French know there is an American presence on the border."

"But I've heard the empire has become much stronger with the addition of well-trained Mexican soldiers to fight the Juárista forces," Brant interjected.

Tanner shook his head. "Juárez has the United States behind him. It's only a matter of time, Brant, before the French grow tired of losing men and money in a hopeless situation." He eyed his friend seriously. "Speaking of Mexico, though, I've been dabbling in the Mexican market for some time. Now I'm interested in selling arms to the Juáristas. When I leave Louisiana, I'll be heading down to Mexico to look into the possibilities."

"You're bound for Mexico!" Brant exclaimed. "Tanner, damn you! I wish to God I could come with you!"

"You're a happily married man, Brant, with a small daughter to take care of," Tanner reminded him abruptly. "You can't leave them to go off to Mexico with me. It could be dangerous with a war going on there. Besides, Caitlyn would have my hide if she thought I was putting notions into your head."

Brant looked away with an angry grimace. "Caitlyn would have me work these acres until I drop; she wants to mold me into a planter fashioned after her father. I've tried, God knows! But damn, it's just not in me! Truthfully, I hate this farming, Tanner." He looked at his friend and his dark eyes had the old restlessness in them. "I'll never be what she wants me to be."

If Tanner was taken aback by this admission, he said nothing. "Well, I won't be the one to take you away from Caitlyn again," he said firmly. "She'd never forgive me a second time."

Brant looked at him for a few moments, then snarled an oath and pushed a fist into his other hand. "I care deeply for Caitlyn, Tanner, and I love my Maggie to distraction, but I wish to God I didn't have Riverhouse chained to me! The fortune I made in Australia is nothing compared to what it would take to make this place great again. Everything here costs money—hired help, repairs, taxes, new equipment, maintaining the land. It's a damned drain on my resources, Tanner, and I can't help being angry at the cost of this plantation when my heart isn't in it."

"What about Caitlyn?" Tanner asked. "Are you sure this is what she wants?"

"Damn sure," Brant replied quickly. "Ever since Maggie arrived, getting Riverhouse back in shape is all she talks about. I can understand her wanting to give our daughter a legacy, but is it all worth it? Instead of spending so much money on Riverhouse, we could save it and give it to Maggie when she grows up. Hell, sometimes I think Caitlyn loves this land more than she loves me."

"Maybe it's all that she's got to hold on to right now," Tanner suggested thoughtfully. "She's sensitive enough to know that you're not happy, I'm sure, but she doesn't want to jeopardize her own security so that you can go out and explore new prospects. Caitlyn is a woman who needs to know she's wanted and loved all the time, Brant. I think you make her feel like she's on shaky ground," he ended bluntly.

Brant laughed bitterly. "It's not as if I say anything to her," he resumed. "What's the use? She won't listen to me anyway; I

don't think she ever has. She's too damned bullheaded to concede that someone else might be right."

Tanner watched the expression on Brant's face and wondered at the happy scene he'd witnessed when he'd first arrived. Caitlyn had looked so contented rocking her daughter on the veranda of Riverhouse. Had that all been a facade? Surely he could hear the frustration and bitterness in Brant's voice. What had happened here?

That evening at dinner, Tanner covertly watched the familial interactions around the dining table. William was too old and too oblivious to any undercurrents to play a role in the drama. Timothy and Margaret O'Rourke were too happy to have their daughter safe with them to worry about how stable her marriage to Brant was. Besides, Maggie was so important to them, they would have shrieked at the idea of anything disrupting her life. Constance was so obviously in love with her Jesse, it was a wonder she wasn't pregnant yet. That left Caitlyn and Brant. They were outwardly polite to each other, but without the warmth of love that shone in the eyes of Constance and Jesse. Tanner had heard that arrival of the first child often signalled the death of passion in a marriage, yet he knew there was passion in Caitlyn. The thought made him grasp his fork so hard he bent it. How ironic! he thought suddenly. Caitlyn had fought so long for Brant, had crossed so many obstacles to get to him. Now that the chase was over, had her ardor cooled? Was she finally finding out that he really wasn't her knight in shining armor? Tanner found it hard not to chuckle at the notion. Brant was certainly right about one thing: Caitlyn was damned bullheaded! Once she got a thought in her head, nothing would stop her from seeing it to fruition. Had she found out that being Brant's wife was not the adventure she had thought it would be? Leaning back in his chair, Tanner decided he was determined to find out.

46

ALTHOUGH CAITLYN tried to hide the condition of her marriage from Tanner, she was well aware that he was sensitive enough to know that everything was not as it should be between her and Brant. It wasn't as though Brant had begun ill-treating her, or

even that he was rude to her in any way, but they seemed to be growing apart in some subtle way that she could not quite put her finger on. She watched him come home from the cotton-fields tired and dusty, grumbling about the attitude of the work-ers or about some infestation of insects that had ruined a portion of the crop. She saw the defeated look come into his eyes when fifty acres of cotton were lost through unexpected flooding after a thunderstorm. He seemed eager to tell his troubles to Tanner, but when she expressed interest in them, the eagerness left him and he seemed to purposely shut her out. It hurt her not to be able to talk with him about his problems.

She had problems of her own and she would have welcomed sharing them with him if he had shown the least bit of interest in hearing about them. It was plain that William was slowly slipping away. Now that Riverhouse was thriving under his son's hands and Caitlyn had replaced Christina as mistress of the house he seemed content to let his life drift away. Most afternoons he napped for long periods of time, forgetting even to come down to dinner. There were times when he shook so badly as he held Maggie that Caitlyn was afraid her daughter would end up on the floor. Other times he would be in the middle of a chess game and would simply fall asleep in his chair. Caitlyn had asked the doctor to look at him, but the doctor had said that William was just old and that his heart was beginning to fail.

There were times when Caitlyn would watch Tanner covertly as he sat and talked with Brant and would envy Tanner's carefree life. He could go wherever and do whatever he pleased without the burden of responsibility that she and Brant had taken on. She knew that Brant felt the difference between himself and Tanner even more keenly than she did. At Tanner's talk of his plans to travel to Mexico and his hopes of using his business contacts there to sell arms to the Juáristas, Brant's eyes would light up in excitement and the longing in them was plain. Caitlyn hoped that Tanner's stay would end soon. His presence seemed to stir things up that she didn't want to contend with, and although she was fair enough not to blame Brant's sulks on Tanner, she knew that his talk of adventure did nothing to diminish them.

At night she was usually so exhausted that she could barely respond to Brant's sexual overtures. And those overtures were getting fewer and fewer. Brant himself was always tired from his day out in the cottonfields. Sometimes he would go into Baton Rouge with Tanner and would come home so drunk that his head

would barely hit the pillow before he began snoring. It seemed that their marriage was unraveling before her eyes and Caitlyn was powerless to stop it.

One evening Brant returned from the fields, grumbling loudly about what a rotten day it had been. Besides the July heat and humidity, he'd found that one of his workers had sneaked away the night before with one of the horses from the stable and was long gone by morning. This added one more bitter drop to Brant's already overfilled cauldron of resentment.

"What do they want?" he asked no one in particular as he flopped down in a chair in the drawing room, heedless of his muddy boots and dusty trousers. "God knows I've given them decent wages and a clean place to stay! What else can I do?"

Tanner, who'd ridden to the fields with him, had followed him in after dusting off his own trousers with his hat. "They're still not used to their freedom, Brant," he advised. "They think that being free means they don't have to work. It will take them a while to realize that they're no different from the workingmen in the North. With emancipation comes responsibility."

"You're right, Tanner," Caitlyn began, pushing a strand of wet hair out of her face as she came from the kitchen to meet them.

"Christ!" Brant suddenly exploded, interrupting her. "Is Tanner *always* right in your eyes, Caitlyn? *He's* not the one saddled with this damned plantation! He's not the one trying to make a respectable name for himself in this place! He's the Yankee and I'm the Southerner, but you'd think *I* was the outsider in this house!"

"Brant, I didn't mean—" Caitlyn started, but before she could finish he was speaking again.

"Damn it, Caitlyn, I just can't seem to do anything right, can I? Jesus, don't I do everything you want me to do? But it *still* isn't enough for you, is it? I can't complain or you think I'm ungrateful. If I get angry, you think I'm irresponsible. Well, damn it, I stood by you, didn't I?" His dark eyes were boring into hers, seeking a mastery over her that he had never really had.

She seemed taken aback and Tanner wished he could find some way to make them stop. But there was nothing he could do except to excuse himself from the room and walk out to the veranda, where he hoped to avoid being a witness to the marital quarrel.

"You make it sound as though you were doing me a favor, Brant!" Caitlyn cried after Tanner had made his exit. "I traveled thousands of miles to be with you! I didn't have to come, but you needed me; you said so in your letter."

"That damned letter!" Brant swore, his anger making him careless. "That damned letter! If it hadn't been for that letter, I'd still be in Australia with Dan and Jimmy, digging for gold instead of planting cotton. Damn, I wish to God I were with them now! At least then I didn't feel like I had a chain around my neck with Riverhouse attached to it!"

Caitlyn stepped backward, striving for calm. "I—I never realized you felt that way about it, Brant," she said in a quiet voice. "I suppose that *I'm* attached to that chain too, aren't I? And Maggie?"

"Oh, Christ, Caitlyn, I didn't mean it that way!" Brant said, becoming morose. He stared at his wife, seeing the tall, strong woman he had come to know so intimately. "I didn't mean it," he repeated.

Caitlyn turned on her heel, knowing she could not get through dinner with Tanner and William after this incident. "I'll go to my room and lie down, Brant," she said quickly. "I've developed a headache."

"Headache be damned!" he snarled, standing up from his chair. "I've heard that excuse enough lately," he added, his meaning quite clear to Caitlyn, who flushed to the roots of her hair. "Don't worry about dinner; I'll eat something in Baton Rouge."

She faced him, concern evident in her eyes. "You—you're going to Baton Rouge again? But weren't you just there two nights ago?"

"What if I was?" he questioned her sharply. "I work here all day. I've got a right to a little pleasure in the evenings." And he slammed on his hat and stalked out of the room, brushing past her with no more than a glance.

Caitlyn followed him out to the hall. She knew he was very angry, but she didn't understand what she had done to deserve to be his target. As she saw her husband striding quickly out the door and onto the veranda, she met Tanner's eyes. Flushing with embarrassment, she nevertheless pleaded silently with him to go with Brant. Tanner nodded and, without a word, mounted his horse.

* * *

It was very late when the two men returned from Baton Rouge. But Caitlyn was still wide awake. Maggie had been fussy tonight and it had taken a long time to get her settled for sleep. Now that the baby was finally asleep, Caitlyn hoped the two men wouldn't wake her up. She listened as they came inside. Brant was talking in a loud but unintelligible voice. He was dead drunk. She could hear Tanner's voice too, not quite as loud, but obviously under the influence of liquor. Sitting bolt upright in bed, she waited in dread for Brant to come through the door.

Disheveled and blinking in the lamplight, he was through the door before she was quite prepared for him. Knowing he didn't have the head for liquor, she was surprised he was still able to stand. Before Brant closed the door, she could see Tanner shuffling to his bedroom, looking tired but not nearly as drunk as her husband.

"I suppose I have Tanner to thank that you made it home in one piece," she finally got out.

He laughed drunkenly. "Tanner is my friend," he told her.

"Thank heaven for that!" she returned.

"Ah, Caitlyn, don't look so grim sitting there in bed!" he said sullenly, seating himself to pull off his boots. He nearly fell over, but he was finally able to get them off. "I won't get near you if you don't want me to." His dark eyes leered at her as he struggled with his coat and shirt. "Do you want me to, dear wife?"

"You are terribly drunk, Brant," she said pointedly, "and you smell like a saloon. If I weren't afraid you'd drown, I'd make you take a bath, but as it is, I would prefer if you slept on the chaise longue tonight."

He eyed that piece of furniture blearily. "You mean I am being forced out of my own bed!" he said with a hiccup. "Damn it, Caitlyn, I've not gotten such a good bargain in you, have I?"

"Bargain? Don't talk about me as though I were for sale, Brant Sinclair," she lectured crossly.

"You sold yourself to me!" he cried, standing up and hopping on one foot as he tried to extricate himself from his trousers. "Or did I sell myself to you? I can't remember now."

"No one sold themselves," Caitlyn interjected, hoping he would tire of conversation and go to sleep.

"And the price was—silence," he continued, following his own train of thought so that Caitlyn gave up in exasperation. "Marriage to Miss Caitlyn O'Rourke—that's what you were sell-

ing, wasn't it, my dear wife?'' He had finally succeeded in divesting himself of all his clothes and was now standing at the foot of the bed stark naked. "And I bought it all with a letter.''

"Heavens, Brant, will you stop talking about that letter!'' she pleaded. "I just want to go to sleep. I know how tired you must be and I—''

"The letter!'' he crowed. "The damned letter!'' He wove about the room for a moment, then scraped his shin on a chair and cursed roundly.

"Brant, please don't worry about the letter now," Caitlyn pleaded, wondering why in the world he kept harping on that in the middle of the night. "It is late and you have to get up early in the morning.''

"I'd be in Australia if it hadn't been for that letter," he mumbled, rubbing his shin and eyeing her as though it were her fault that he had stumbled.

"Stop it, Brant! Lord, you make it sound like some terrible mistake!'' Caitlyn said in utter exasperation.

"And so it was!'' he snapped at her, his dark eyes becoming angrier as they wandered over her. "That letter was a lie, Caitlyn, a damned lie! It was meant for Constance, not for you.''

Caitlyn's face went white and her eyes stared back at her husband in disbelief. "Brant, you don't know what you're saying. You're drunk and you need to go to sleep. I don't like you this way at all.''

"The letter was for Constance," he repeated, enjoying her discomfiture in his drunken state. He had put something over on her! he thought with glee. "You thought the letter was for you, but it was for your sister.'' He laughed and jumped on the bed next to her.

Caitlyn felt as cold as a marble statue, unable to move even when he pushed his face into hers. She could smell the reek of whiskey on his breath. Of course he didn't know what he was saying. Of course he was drunk. But why was she beginning to believe him? Oh God, don't let it be true! She felt his hand tangling itself in her unbound hair. He pulled her face back and kissed her mouth with moist lips. Feeling supremely powerful over her for the first time in his life, Brant was determined to make the most of it. His lips traced a slobbering trail down her throat, and when her nightgown barred his way, he reached up with his other hand and ripped it open.

Startled at the violence of his action, Caitlyn wondered why

her husband was suddenly treating her with a roughness that had always been alien to their marriage. "Brant, stop it!" she pleaded, trying to push him away with her hands. "Why did you say such a terrible thing?"

He hiccupped and eyed her in confusion. "What did I say?" he demanded.

"About the letter—that it was supposed to be for Constance, not for me," she told him.

His hands let go of her nightgown. "Sh," he said drunkenly. "That's a secret, Caitlyn; you mustn't know about it."

When he tried to resume his rough embraces, she leapt out of the bed, her bosom heaving as anger replaced fear in her heart. "I came to Australia to be your wife!" she flung at him. "I came to Australia, thinking I was the one you wanted to marry, when all the time—"

"Shut up, Caitlyn!" he commanded, his anger matching hers. "It all worked out, didn't it? I married you. You got what you wanted, didn't you? And Constance married Jesse. So there you are." He eyed her with increasing interest as her lovely coppery hair tumbled about her shoulders and her naked breasts trembled through the ripped opening of her nightgown. "Now I want you back in bed, wife!" he ordered her.

"Damn you, Brant Sinclair!" she cried, tears spilling down her cheeks at the news he had given her. "Why did you marry me?"

Brant sat back on his haunches and eyed her in exasperation. "For God's sake, Caitlyn, what difference does it make now?"

"Why did you marry me?" she asked again, her hands clenched into fists.

"Because Tanner persuaded me it was the only honorable thing to do!" he shouted at her. He jumped off the bed and came at her, intent on swiping the nightgown off her and burying himself in her soft, warm flesh.

But Caitlyn wanted none of that, not after the revelations of tonight. She felt as though her whole world had suddenly begun to spin around her. It was spinning faster and faster, out of control now, so that very soon she would find nothing to cling to. Brant had never wanted to marry her—it was Constance he had meant to send for! What a shock, what a terrible shock it must have been for him when he saw her that first time in Maldon! So many things were explained now, things she had been too stupid to see at first. How he must have hated being talked

into marrying her because it was the *honorable* thing to do! And then the unwelcome thought came to her: *Tanner knew!* All this time he knew! She wanted to weep in utter humiliation. The wicked talk, the forward manner, all those passionate kisses. He had taken them because he *knew* her husband didn't want them. The tears welled once again in her eyes.

But she was startled out of her weeping by her husband's hands grabbing her shoulders, then reaching down to strip off the rest of her nightgown. With a cry of rage at such effrontery after what he'd just revealed, she reached up to scratch his face, leaving two red weals on either cheek. Pulling back, Brant automatically brought a hand forward to slap her. Caitlyn staggered and fell to her knees, giving Brant an opportunity to fling himself over her, forcing her to the floor.

"Stop it, Brant, you're hurting me!" she said fiercely, squirming beneath him.

"You're a bitch, Caitlyn!" he returned angrily. "But you're my wife and when I want you in bed, you damn well better be there!"

Realizing it was no use fighting him, for he could really hurt her in his drunken state, Caitlyn stopped struggling and lay back on the floor, feeling his hands pulling away the rest of her nightgown. He fell over her, his mouth encompassing the flesh of her breasts as he alternately nipped and sucked the tender flesh. His hands were rough as they manipulated her breasts and Caitlyn cried out in pain and outrage, but he silenced her with a long, sloppy kiss that stifled her. Without much preamble, he sliced one knee between her thighs and nudged his body between them, but when he would have entered her, he suddenly realized that he couldn't—that part of him just would not work properly. Humiliated at his inability to perform and angry at the fact that his wife was not helping him at all with her cold eyes and unresponsive body, Brant let out a foul curse and flung himself away from her.

He looked sheepish for a moment, then blustered again, unwilling to let her have the victory. "If you were a more loving wife, I would have been able to overcome the drink."

"I have been a loving wife to you for three years, Brant," Caitlyn told him, still in a quiet voice, though she longed to scream at him for what he had revealed about the letter. "I thought that you loved me in return and that together we could bring Riverhouse back to its past glory. But now after what you've

told me, I don't know anymore.'' She realized it was true—she didn't know anymore. For so many years she had dreamed of being Brant Sinclair's wife, of being mistress of Riverhouse. But with the war, things had changed. No cotton plantation would ever rise to its former glory, at least not for many years. And besides the problems with Riverhouse, now Brant had told her he had never really wanted her for his wife. It hurt, it hurt terribly. Kneeling on the floor, clasping her torn nightgown with trembling hands, Caitlyn suddenly felt without purpose, without any clear idea of what the future held for her. She looked bleakly in Brant's eyes and saw her own expression mirrored in them.

47

THE DAYS THAT FOLLOWED were not easy for Caitlyn. She was still a mother with her duties to Maggie, still a concerned daughter-in-law with her worries over William's health, but she seemed unable to cope with much more. By pleading illness, she managed to escape from her husband and Tanner at dinner. She left the master bedroom to Brant and moved into one of the guestrooms, keeping the door locked against Brant, even when he pleaded with her to allow him in. If she saw Brant and Tanner about the house or lawn, she would quickly take her leave.

When she allowed herself to think about what Brant had revealed, Caitlyn could barely keep herself from screaming aloud in frustration. Her entire marriage had been a farce, a farce that had begun with a letter being written to the wrong woman, a farce that had been played out by two conspirators, Brant and Tanner, when she had come to Australia. If it had been up to Brant, would he have ever married her? she wondered. Perhaps he would have made her his mistress, she thought with irony, but he might well have kept her waiting for a wedding ring in the hope that he could find a way to send her back to Louisiana. The war had prevented that. Tanner had persuaded Brant to swallow his anger and give up his desire for another woman in order to marry Caitlyn. Oh God, it was too much to be borne! That she had been deceived by both of them goaded her unbelievably—and that she had been so stupid as to believe in Brant's love. What a fool she had made of herself!

She had been so much in love with Brant, so infatuated with

him, that she hadn't seen that he was using her. But she began to realize that she had used him too. Hadn't she been a young woman panicked by the thought that her twentieth birthday might find her an old maid? Hadn't she closed her eyes to the hurt and devastation on Connie's face the day they'd received the letter? In her pride and arrogance she had willfully ignored the signs of Brant's interest in her sister. She had always assumed that he loved *her*, that he wanted *her* for his wife.

Looking back, Caitlyn remembered how strangely Brant had acted when she'd found him in Maldon. If she hadn't been so conceited, she would have known that a young man in the full flush of love would never have treated his wife in such a manner. But she'd been so damned blind! She'd never seen anything but what she wanted to see. She'd even refused to see Brant's unhappiness in his role as master of Riverhouse. He had never wanted this kind of life; he had run away from it once before. Oh, what a fool she'd been to think she could change him, to think she could *make* him what she thought he should be! She remembered Tanner telling her how impossible it was to change anyone, but she hadn't listened to him. Instead she had congratulated herself that she had proved him wrong. She had told herself that she had molded her husband into as good a planter as her own father. God, how stupid she had been! She was as guilty as Brant.

But it was hard to admit her many mistakes. She was still hurt, still angry with Brant, still humiliated at the thought that Tanner had always known. Did she still love Brant? Yes, she thought, she still loved him, but that love had undergone a change. Gone was the blind, headstrong love of her youth; he had destroyed that. She wasn't even sure she could stand for him to touch her in passion again. What was left for her? Divorce? The humiliation was something she didn't think she could face, especially now that they had a daughter. So she was chained to him, bound to him as surely as he had been bound to her when he had first married her in Australia. Now she knew how he must have felt. She wept at the thought that she was bound forever to a man who had married her out of pity.

The next morning Caitlyn heard the usual soft tapping on her door. With a sigh, she wrapped herself in a dressing gown and went to open it. Wordlessly, she let Brant into the room, then closed the door behind him. They stared at each other for a while and she could see the tired look about his eyes and mouth. For

a moment she felt guilty that she had been the cause of his sleepless nights.

"You've decided to speak to me again," he murmured with a touch of childish resentment. "Are you still angry with me?"

Caitlyn shook her head and her dark blue eyes were watching him with a mixture of wonder and weariness. "I'm over my anger now," she said softly. "I realized that thinking about the mistakes of the past only keeps the wounds open and bleeding. I'm tired of hurting, Brant."

"Darling, let me help you," he said eagerly, glad to see that she wasn't going to reprimand him about the letter and his telling her about it. He reached out to take her in his arms, but she stepped backward. For a second she could see the surprised anger on his face, but then he let his arms fall and a fleeting look of understanding crossed his features. "You don't love me anymore, do you, Caitlyn?"

She turned away and walked toward the window, looking all the way across the lawn of Riverhouse and to the river road beyond. It seemed strange that Riverhouse no longer had the power to make her heart swell proudly in her breast. She was suddenly afraid, afraid of her dearth of feeling, of her lack of emotion. What was wrong with her? This was what she had wanted her whole life: to be mistress of a great plantation. This is what her upbringing had prepared her for. Somehow it was no longer enough, not when she felt so empty inside, not when she looked at her husband and realized she didn't care where he had spent his last four nights away from her. Had her love been so shallow that she would let the anger of a few days blow it away? Had there ever been any real substance to her feelings for Brant?

"Then you don't deny it," Brant said quietly. "You really don't love me anymore." And then he added in a fiercer voice, "How could our love have worn out so easily, Caitlyn, when we were doing so well together? All because of a stupid letter that's part of the past. You can't let that stand in the way of the future, our future at Riverhouse with Maggie and with our other children."

Caitlyn shivered. He was talking of their future, their future at Riverhouse. How like her husband to say what he thought she wanted to hear without really believing it himself! "I thought you hated Riverhouse," she said in a low voice. "I thought you wanted to free yourself of the responsibility of it."

He shrugged. "I was angry. It's been hard. This month of July has really taken its toll on everyone around here. You've heard your father talking; it's a tough time for all of us."

She felt slow tears welling in her eyes. He certainly knew the right words to make her want to erase the past few days from her mind, to forget they ever happened, to start over again, to be the way she was before. But could she ever *really* be the way she was before? It seemed impossible, and yet—

"Brant, I—you can't rush me into this," she told him, turning around to look at him, unaware of how lovely she looked in the morning light. The sun lit her coppery tresses to a deep glow, making Brant want desperately to bury his face in their warm lushness.

"Oh, Caitlyn, just let me hold you," he pleaded.

But the memory of his drunkenness, of his temporary impotence which had been all that had saved her from being raped by her own husband, made her wary of him still. Shaking her head, she brushed the tears from her cheeks. "No, Brant, I'm not ready for that yet. You must give me time."

His cheeks reddened with his frustration, but he was able to check his rising temper in the face of her firmness. "All right then," he said sulkily. He turned to go and then cast one last glance at her. "I'll be out in the fields if you need me."

After he left, Caitlyn sat down on a chair, shaking a little. She was glad that dreadful scene was behind them now. Her feelings were still a jumble, but at least she knew that she and Brant could converse together without raw emotions overtaking them. As to the future, she wasn't at all sure what to do about it. She had Maggie to think of, she reminded herself, hearing her faint cry from the nursery. Quickly, she left her own room to go to her small daughter, glad that her attention was drawn away from her own predicament for the moment.

Later that morning, after she'd dressed and breakfasted, Caitlyn felt better. She'd played with Maggie until the baby had grown fretful and then had instructed Lindy to watch over her carefully while she napped. She'd tapped on William's bedroom door and heard his fitful snoring. Then she'd gone downstairs to see to the menu for dinner that evening. Without her guiding hand in the kitchen, the cooking had been dreadful these past few days. She briskly went about her duties, glad to have something to occupy her mind.

By afternoon though, she was edgy again, having run out of

things to do. She considered dressing Maggie and taking her over to Mornhaven for a visit, but the baby was sleeping peacefully, so Caitlyn decided to go to Mornhaven alone.

Dressed in a soft blouse and skirt, she ordered one of the few remaining horses to be saddled for her, making a mental note to speak with Brant about purchasing more horses. It was ridiculous to have as much money as they had and not have a decent stable of horses.

Once out on the river road, Caitlyn felt the hot July sun on her shoulders and kept her horse to a sedate walk. She looked out lazily at the slow-moving Mississippi, remembering how she and her sister used to ride the packets in earlier days. Those days seemed so far distant, she thought sadly. Now the passengers on those riverboats were more than likely to be Northerners coming down to take advantage of the postwar confusion in the South. Adventurers and fortune hunters were beginning to pour into the South with the rapidity of a flash flood. They brought more confusion, more anger, and more resentment among the defeated.

So engrossed was she in her own thoughts, she didn't hear the sound of horse's hooves on the dusty road. It was not until the rider was nearly abreast of her that she realized she was not alone.

She turned her head and met the piercing blue eyes of Tanner Malone. In spite of herself, she felt her cheeks warming under his gaze. He was dressed in a spotless linen suit and panama hat that made him look cool and crisp despite the July heat. He was smiling at her, but there was a questioning look in his eyes that reminded her all over again that he had always known the truth about her marriage to Brant—that she had been an unwanted wife when Brant had married her in Australia.

She shivered despite the high heat. "I thought you'd gone already," she told him carelessly. "I know how eager you are to go to Mexico. I'm surprised you're still here." Her blue eyes gazed at him from beneath her long lashes, wondering what he was thinking.

"I am leaving, Caitlyn," he said in a gentle voice. "I'm glad to see you on the road today. I've already sent my things to New Orleans and I would have hated to leave without saying goodbye to you in person."

He really *was* going, she thought, suddenly feeling confused. With a shake of her head and an odd little laugh, she met his

gaze. "I've known you nearly as long as I've known Brant, Tanner. You know how much you mean to me."

"Do I?" he asked. "I was under the impression that you were pretty angry with me for the part I played in your marriage to Brant." His eyes bored into hers while the horses grew restive beneath them. "Would you walk with me just a little?" he suggested.

She nodded and he helped her dismount. They tied their horses to a tree and walked in the shade of the cypresses and willows, heading toward the bank of the mighty river. Both were silent, not sure how to handle this leave-taking. Caitlyn was only glad that fate had brought them together like this; she couldn't have borne him leaving without saying good-bye to her. The thought surprised her and she risked a quick glance at this man whom she had known for so long and yet hardly knew at all.

When they reached the riverbank, he finally spoke, gazing not at her but at the river before them. "I've already stayed too long, for I'm beginning to like it here in a way that will never do. Mexico seems far away and not very appealing at this moment."

She was surprised at his admission. "I'm sorry for my behavior this past week, Tanner," she told him quietly. "I should have been spending more time with you, knowing you didn't have much time left."

"Under the circumstances I don't blame you," he answered, turning to gaze into her eyes. "I'm truly sorry you found out about that damned letter from Brant. He blurted out the whole story to me."

"I was angry with you at first," she admitted, idly picking a green leaf from one of the willow branches. "But then I realized that without you there, Brant probably would never have married me. You kept me from being dishonored, Tanner, and I'm grateful for that."

"I should have married you myself," he burst out suddenly, almost angrily, surprising her. "But I knew how long you had waited to be Brant's wife. You wouldn't have accepted my proposal no matter how dire your predicament," he said with an ironic smile.

She too smiled ironically. "I wouldn't have had you on a silver platter, Tanner Malone. I was such a fool." She didn't know if she meant that she was a fool because she'd married Brant or because she wouldn't have married Tanner. "Well, I got what I

wanted all along, didn't I? I have Brant and I have Riverhouse."
She pulled viciously at the leaf and broke off the entire stalk.

"Yes," he said, "you're a tenacious woman, Caitlyn. You'll
always get what you want in the end."

"Will I, Tanner?" she asked wistfully. And then she added
with a brisk laugh, "I don't even know what it is I really want
anymore." She looked up at him, the tears shimmering in her
blue eyes.

Irresistibly drawn toward her in spite of himself, Tanner
reached to take her into his arms. He pressed her against him,
his hands rubbing her back with soothing strokes. "There, there,
Caitlyn," he murmured, "don't cry."

At his words of comfort, she sobbed all the harder. "Oh,
Tanner, I don't know anymore, I just don't know! I feel so lost
and alone!" She pressed her face into his shoulder, her tears
wetting the crisp linen of his suit coat.

"It's all right," he hushed her, one hand reaching to smooth
her hair. His fingers caught in the snood that was held only by
pins. She felt her hair freed, tumbling gently down her back to
be caught in his hands. He buried his face in its fragrance, wanting to commit to memory the very scent of her.

She was still sobbing but not as hard now, feeling his arms
holding her strongly. This should be her husband holding her so
closely, not Tanner with his knowing eyes and passionate mouth
that never failed to elicit a response from her, she thought guiltily. She pushed the guilty thought away. Her sobs lessened until
she was quiet, leaning her head against Tanner's shoulder and
taking deep breaths to calm herself. Shakily, she pulled away
from him, her eyes still moist as she looked up into that familiar
face with its piercing blue eyes and mobile mouth. She felt utterly devastated at the thought that he was leaving. How often
without realizing it had she relied on his strength? Tanner had
always been there when she needed him—on the pier in Melbourne, on the trail to Maldon, at the Wickhams' house when
her first child had come.

"Oh, Tanner!" she murmured as she had a flash of insight:
no man did those things for a woman without truly loving her.
But she had been so bullheaded, she had never seen any man
but Brant. "Tanner," she murmured again, feeling as though
all her dreams were shattered with her realization of this man's
love for her. She had been a blind fool not to have seen it. She
felt the warmth of the locket he'd given her dangling between

her breasts and pressed her hand unconsciously against her blouse.

He took her chin in his hand. "Yes, my dear, I love you," he said with a sigh. "I've loved you to distraction, but as I see it, there's no way out for me. You're married." He leaned down to gather her close so that her body arched against his like a drawn bow. With infinite gentleness, he touched his mouth to hers, feeling the moist tears on her face as he pressed harder. The kiss was slow, leisurely, as though he had all the time in the world. Caitlyn felt him molding her mouth to his, his lips warm and soft as their kiss lengthened.

Then he was parting her lips, seeking the interior of her mouth, fencing delicately with her tongue, until the delicacy turned to passion at the intimacy of the kiss. He kissed her harder then, with a sudden urgency that overwhelmed her. Leaving her mouth, his lips traveled toward her jaw and then down her neck to where her brooch fastened her blouse together. A sigh of frustration escaped him as he pressed his mouth to the tip of her breast, heating the cloth of her blouse. Caitlyn sighed aloud, feeling the glory of her passion fill her entire body and send tingling waves of pleasure throughout. If it had been up to her she would have willingly lain down on the grassy riverbank and given herself to Tanner Malone.

But he was already withdrawing, taming his emotions with the iron hand that he had used so many times before. He wanted this woman so badly, but he knew that she would grow to hate him if he seduced her. He knew that when she looked back on this moment, the passion and glory of it would be blanketed by a sense of shame.

He shook his head. "God knows how much I wish I could take you right here," he admitted with a shaky laugh. "But I won't add to your shame. You're still another man's wife," he ended slowly, his hand caressing her cheek regretfully.

She colored brightly and looked away for a moment. Then her eyes returned to meet his. "Tanner, I wanted you so much I was willing to forget I was Brant's wife, but then I was afraid, afraid that I was only using you to punish him. It wouldn't be fair to any of us, Tanner," she told him. Her eyes looked searchingly into his. "I've been such a blind idiot. All the time I was infatuated with Brant, all I could see was him, when you—you were always there when I needed you, weren't you, Tanner?" She smiled bitterly. "Beware of what you wish for—isn't that how

the old saying goes? I've saddled myself with a man who didn't want me for his wife. I've given him a child—''

"Hush now, don't say any more! Maggie's a beautiful child and a credit to you *and* Brant," he told her firmly. "Don't ever regret bringing her into the world." His old smile flickered. "Despite how you may feel now, Caitlyn, you are a survivor. Soon enough you'll realize that you've got to make your marriage work for Maggie's sake. Brant will resume the role of loving husband because he hates chaos in his private life."

"But I—I *can't* love Brant the way I used to," she said slowly.

"You're a strong woman, Caitlyn, and you can do anything you damn well want to do!" he told her, taking out his handkerchief to wipe her tear-stained cheeks.

"B-but you just told me that you loved me!" she blurted out. "How can you go away?"

"I've done it before," he pointed out. "You forget, my dear, I've loved you for a very long time and I'm getting used to these disappointments."

He reached over to touch her cheek, but she ducked away from him obstinately. Then he swung himself onto his horse, looking down at her a moment. "You'll do all right, Caitlyn O'Rourke," he said. "Besides, you're not getting rid of me forever. Remember what I said once: I'm letting you win the skirmishes, but I fully intend to win the war someday." He reached down from the horse and clasped the back of Caitlyn's head almost roughly, pulling her toward him so that her lips met his once more in a fiery encounter. Then he let her go, winking at her so that she felt caught between laughter and tears.

"Tanner Malone, you *are* a villain!" she cried as he turned his horse around.

"Yes I am, Caitlyn, and that's why I fascinate the hell out of you!" he laughed. "You won't forget me, my dear. You'll have my locket to remind you and you'll keep it right there between those proud breasts of yours," he mocked her, his blue eyes staring down into her very soul. And then he was off with one last jaunty wave of farewell. Caitlyn watched him for a long time, watched even as he was out of sight, the only evidence of his departure a cloud of dust in the humid air above the river road.

48

THE TERRIBLE HEAT OF JULY passed and gave way to a milder August. The cotton throve and Brant's frustration eased somewhat. William Sinclair continued to slip away, until one afternoon what Caitlyn dreaded finally came to pass. She left William sitting in a comfortable chair on the veranda, watching Maggie play with her baby toys on a blanket. She was only in the kitchen for ten minutes before hurrying back to the veranda to check on her daughter. Maggie was still playing, cooing and contented even in the mild heat. Caitlyn smiled lovingly at her before transferring her attention to William, who sat unnaturally motionless in the chair. Caitlyn's smile faded as she stepped over to him, her eyes widening at the pallor of his complexion. Hesitantly, she placed a hand on his shoulder to shake him. There was no response.

Two days later William Sinclair was buried next to his beloved wife, Christina. Caitlyn gazed at the coffin and thought kindly of the gentle old man who had never raised his voice in the whole time she had known him. She glanced at Brant, seeing the turmoil on his face—the guilt at having been away from his father for so long mingled with the guilt that he could never love Riverhouse the way his father had wanted him to. Her glance shifted to her own parents, both of them still quite hale despite the toll that the war had taken on them. Her mother caught her eye through the mist of Caitlyn's black mourning veil and the two women smiled at each other with understanding. In a protective gesture, Margaret O'Rourke put her hand on her husband's arm and kept him close beside her. Caitlyn's eyes moved to her sister, who was crying quietly next to her husband, Jesse, and she wondered what Constance would think if she ever found out that the marriage proposal from Brant had been meant for her. But then she realized that it would no longer matter. It was obvious how much Connie loved Jesse, and now with a new baby growing inside of her, there would be no chance of any nostalgic fantasies concerning Brant Sinclair.

As for herself, Caitlyn realized that she and Brant had grown closer again in the face of William's death. Brant had clung to her when he'd found out about his father, crying unashamedly

on her bosom. Their mutual comforting had turned into something more, and when it was over, Caitlyn had lain next to her sleeping husband, marveling at how right Tanner had been. He'd told her that she was a survivor and that she would find a way to make her life with Brant work. She was certainly not a woman who could make do with a cold and sterile marriage, and she still loved Brant enough to respond to him when he made love to her. Yet just before falling asleep, when she'd closed her eyes at the height of her union with Brant, it had not been her husband's face that she'd envisioned.

At the end of August 1865 a letter came from Vera Cruz, Mexico, to Brant Sinclair. Tearing it open in excitement, Brant read the contents rapidly while Caitlyn watched his expression anxiously.

"Jesus!" Brant muttered. "It seems that Tanner has finally gotten himself into some trouble he can't get out of."

"What happened? Is Tanner all right?" Caitlyn demanded, sick with worry. Her face was white against the pitch black of her mourning clothes.

"He's been caught red-handed," Brant said, standing up from his chair and pacing the drawing room. "The French have accused him of selling arms to the Juáristas. He's been imprisoned in Mexico."

"In prison!" Caitlyn's knees gave way as she imagined all sorts of terrible things. "We must get him out of there, Brant," she said firmly, her strength returning. "There must be a way we can help him!"

"There is," Brant replied quietly. "We can ransom him. The French military officers know enough about Tanner to know that he has a vast fortune in the United States. They'll be willing to forgo all charges, so long as we deliver the sum of two hundred fifty thousand dollars into the hands of a Marshal Bazaine in a city called San Luis Potosí."

"Ransom him!" Caitlyn cried. "But how do we know that he is all right?"

Brant looked at his wife. "My dear, I believe there is some honor in men, even in a French marshal. I'm sure he would not be demanding a ransom if something terrible had happened to Tanner."

"But why was the letter sent to you?" Caitlyn asked, her

thoughts running helter-skelter through her head. "Why wasn't it sent to his brother in Boston?"

"New Orleans is closer to Mexico and Tanner probably told them he has funds in a bank here. Obviously he trusts me to bring the ransom to him."

"You!" Caitlyn's eyes widened. "Brant, you can't mean that you're going down to Mexico alone with all that money. Why, that's utter nonsense! I'm sure Tanner didn't mean for you—"

"I'm going, Caitlyn," Brant interrupted her.

She stared at him. "Brant, you can't do this; it's far too dangerous! Surely there's someone else you can trust to do it." Her eyes pleaded with him not to do something so foolish. And then she saw the look in his restless dark eyes and she realized that he *wanted* to go.

"I'll leave for New Orleans tomorrow morning," he told her firmly. "Every minute counts. I'm sure you wouldn't want Tanner in that prison any longer than he has to be." He seemed brisk and self-assured now, more in control than he had been in a long time.

Suddenly Caitlyn's mouth turned down in anger. "You can't fool me, Brant Sinclair! You want to go! This is the chance you've been waiting for to escape from Riverhouse, isn't it?"

His dark brows drew downward. "Think what you like, Caitlyn, I'm leaving on the first packet in the morning. I'll be in New Orleans only long enough to make arrangements with Tanner's bank. He's already written his signature on this letter authorizing me to withdraw the money." Unconsciously, he pressed the gold signet ring that had been his father's and had been passed down to him upon William's death. He wore it on his ring finger and as it shone up at him, it reminded him of his father's legacy, Riverhouse. Striding quickly away from Caitlyn, Brant went upstairs to begin packing.

The next morning he was gone before Caitlyn awoke. She recalled the faint brush of his lips on her cheek while she had still been half-asleep and it irked her that she had not been fully awake when he'd left. She should have at least ridden down to the levee with him to wait for the packet. A sudden rush of sadness overcame her as she realized how different his leave-taking had been from Tanner's. Guilt flooded through her and she wished she had not picked a quarrel with him the day before, making their evening last night stiff and awkward.

She decided to take Maggie over to Mornhaven, feeling sad and lonely in the house without Brant and William around. Besides, it would be good to visit with her mother and with Constance. Talk about new babies was always cheering and Connie's was due in March.

Margaret hugged her daughter and then was allowed by Timothy to hold Maggie for a moment. Then Timothy took the baby again, admiring her red hair.

"And what brings you to Mornhaven?" he asked Caitlyn. "Anything wrong with the cotton?" As always, his concern was for the land and its bounty and Caitlyn had to smile at his fierce loyalty.

"No, Papa, nothing is wrong with the cotton. The workers will take care of it well enough until Brant returns."

"Returns!" Timothy blustered. "Returns from where? He shouldn't be leaving with the cotton nearing its harvesttime. By God, that boy will never make the planter his father was!" he continued indignantly.

"Papa, Brant had to go to Mexico," Caitlyn said slowly.

"Mexico!" Timothy nearly dropped the baby. Handing Maggie over to her grandmother, he eyed his daughter intently. "What the hell is he going to Mexico for? First he leaves to go to Australia and now he's decided to run off to Mexico!"

"Papa, we got a letter from Mexico saying that Tanner Malone was in trouble. He's been imprisoned by the French because he was selling guns to the Juáristas. The French asked for a ransom and Brant felt he was the only one who would make sure the money got there."

"What in hell—"

"Timothy, you'd better calm yourself or you'll burst an artery!" Everyone swung around to see the tall, hearty figure of Sean Flynn standing in the doorway. He seemed larger than life.

"Sean Flynn!" Timothy cried out happily. "God, it's good to see you, man! Where have you been keeping yourself since the war ended?"

"I've been keeping myself in a U.S. army hospital in New York," he told him, stepping into the room to hug both women before giving his hand to his friend. "I was wounded in the shoulder the last month of the war as luck would have it." He shook his head. "For a while I was laid up in Virginia in a Confederate army hospital. When the Yankees took it over, they

shipped some of us to New York, where there were better hospitals and more doctors. I guess I was lucky they did because I got good care while I was there. They saved my arm.''

''And never a letter from you, Sean,'' Margaret accused him, her eyes moist at the thought of him lying wounded and so far away without letting them know.

He looked at her apologetically. ''I'm sorry, Margaret, that's the truth of it, but in the shape I was in, I wasn't up to much writing. As soon as they released me, I made my way back here, hoping that Mornhaven would still be standing. By God, it's a sight for sore eyes!'' His own eyes were suspiciously moist as they lit upon the baby that Margaret was still holding in her arms. ''And by the looks of things, there've been some changes since my last visit three years ago. That red hair can only mean it's an O'Rourke,'' he observed, smiling.

''You're damned right she's an O'Rourke!'' Timothy roared loudly. ''She's our Caitlyn's daughter, but she's also a Sinclair, and right now I'm not feeling too kindly to that part of the babe's heritage.'' He eyed Caitlyn accusingly.

Sean laughed, sitting down next to Timothy to give his old friend a thump on the shoulder. ''What's all this I was hearing about Mexico?''

''My husband, Brant Sinclair, had to go down to Mexico to ransom his good friend,'' Caitlyn explained quickly. ''Papa's upset because—''

''Because he's going to get himself killed and leave my daughter a widow!'' Timothy interrupted.

''Is this the same Sinclair that you ran off to Australia to?'' Sean asked.

Caitlyn nodded. ''I really don't know why Papa's so mad. He'd do the same thing if you were being held in prison in Mexico. Tanner Malone's been our good friend for years. Brant only thought he was doing what was right.'' She was surprised to find herself defending Brant's actions so stoutly when only last night she'd wanted to wring his neck for running down to Mexico.

''There's a bloody war going on down there,'' Sean pointed out. ''Your father's right, Caitlyn, it's damned dangerous; your husband is taking a big risk, especially bringing money into the country.''

For a moment Caitlyn felt fear creeping up the back of her neck, but she suppressed the fear with an effort. ''Brant's only

doing what he feels he has to do to help his friend," she said firmly.

"Meanwhile," Sean said briskly with a smile at Caitlyn's wan face, "I can offer you my services, my dear. Although what I know about cotton would fit into a thimble, I can certainly help keep your field laborers in line and leave you free to take care of your household and your daughter."

"Thank you, Sean," Caitlyn murmured, relieved that he had offered her his help. She truly hadn't thought about being alone at Riverhouse.

As Caitlyn struggled to keep Riverhouse running in Brant's absence, Northerners continued to pour into the Deep South with schemes to get rich off the sufferings of the Southerners. Because New Orleans had fallen early, much of Louisiana had been spared the devastation experienced by the rest of the South.

Listening to the daily problems of the field laborers, Caitlyn began to see how frustrating it had been for Brant. She had her hands full despite Sean's help, and she realized that for a man like Brant, running the plantation had been an unending nightmare. His life as a planter made a bleak contrast to the freedom and camaraderie he had enjoyed in Australia with Dan and Jimmy. There he had been responsible only for himself; here he was responsible for his family, for his ancestral home, for all the workers who looked to him for their daily bread.

Caitlyn continued to fret, her worry broken only by the arrival of a letter from Brant. He wrote that he'd reached Vera Cruz safely and was beginning to make inquiries as to Tanner's whereabouts. The French military had proven themselves most helpful and Brant had every confidence that he would have Tanner out of prison within a few days, a week at most. He wrote that his health was fine and his spirits excellent, although he hoped to get out of Vera Cruz shortly because it was truly a dismal little town. With good fortune and the cooperation of the French military, he and Tanner should be in New Orleans by the beginning of November.

Caitlyn's hopes plummeted. The beginning of November! It seemed so far away. The cotton would be harvested by then, the crops sent downriver to be factored by Tanner's import-export company. Maggie would nearly be seven months old. Caitlyn gritted her teeth. She would get through the next four or five weeks somehow, but it wouldn't be easy.

November came and there was no word. As the days drifted slowly by, Caitlyn became more and more nervous. Why didn't she get another letter? Sean tried to comfort her by saying that with the war in Mexico, the mails were probably quite unpredictable. His words could no longer put her fears to rest when December came without word.

At Mornhaven Caitlyn paced the drawing room, nearly tripping over Maggie, who was beginning to crawl and was enjoying the new freedom it afforded her.

"Why haven't I heard anything? Where is he? What's happened with Tanner?" Caitlyn shot the questions out like bullets, striding back and forth in front of her parents. "I can't stand much more of this," she added.

"Dear, I know how worried you are; we all are," Margaret said kindly, her brow wrinkled with concern, "but it does very little good to get yourself into a state over it."

"If I don't hear from either of them soon, I'm going down there myself!" Caitlyn stared at her father with mutiny in her eyes, daring him to change her mind.

Timothy reddened. "You'll not be going off on another wild-goose chase, daughter," he said firmly. "I was crazy to let you go before, but I'll certainly not be giving my permission for you to go where there's a war going on."

"I'm Brant Sinclair's wife, Papa. I don't need your permission to go anywhere," she returned brazenly.

For a moment Timothy sputtered so that Margaret thought he might be about to have a stroke. When he finally regained his composure, he eyed his daughter with obvious irritation. "You're still a stubborn mule, Caitlyn. Despite everything you've learned, I'm wondering if you've learned the most important lesson: your responsibilities always come first. And you have responsibilities to Maggie and to Riverhouse in your husband's absence."

"I know that," Caitlyn said quietly, "but I can't go on without knowing what's happened to Brant. *Something* must have gone wrong or he would have written. I would have heard something by now."

"So you'd rush down there yourself," Timothy continued inexorably. "And what if something happened to you, Caitlyn? Would you want to leave Maggie an orphan?"

Caitlyn turned away, tears in her eyes at the thought that Maggie would be left alone.

"Then look before you leap, daughter," Timothy concluded.

49

A WEEK LATER Caitlyn received word from Tanner Malone that he was on his way back from Mexico. The note said only that he had been pardoned by Maximilian as a goodwill gesture toward the Americans. It had taken him a while to find a ship bound out of Vera Cruz for New Orleans, but he was writing the letter in hopes that he would be leaving in the next few days, enabling him to reach New Orleans before Christmas. Caitlyn wondered why there was no mention of Brant. Cold suspicion lurked at the back of her mind, but she refused to yield to it. It would be better not to leap to conclusions. The manner in which Brant had taken his leave of her after their quarrel weighed heavily on her mind.

Tanner Malone arrived on Christmas Eve, having been delayed an extra day in New Orleans. Caitlyn flew out from the veranda as he was dismounting his horse so that he just barely caught her in his arms as she flung herself at him.

"Oh, Tanner! You must tell me what has happened! Where is Brant? Didn't you see him? He set out for Mexico in August to ransom you from the French!" Her questions were fired in quick succession, her eyes huge and shadowed with deep concern. She clung to him, keeping a fragile hold on her tumbling emotions.

Clasping her close, Tanner smelled the fragrance of her hair, and felt the softness of her flesh, allowing himself a moment to enjoy her presence before beginning the painful task ahead of him. He wanted fiercely to kiss her mouth, but was well aware of the watchful eyes of the man who stood waiting for them in the doorway.

"Caitlyn, it's so good to see you!" he said finally, lifting her arms from his neck with infinite gentleness. "It seems like years since I last said good-bye to you."

Caitlyn looked at his face and hands and noted subtle changes since his sojourn in Mexico. There were lines around his eyes, some no doubt from squinting at the sun, but others from the hardships he must have endured in prison. A small scar on his left temple must have come from a blow and there were scars on his wrists, probably from manacles that had chained him to the walls of the prison. Wordlessly, she led him to the veranda

and bade him sit down while she hurried inside to get him something to drink.

"I'm Sean Flynn, a friend of Caitlyn's father." The big man Tanner had noticed came forward to introduce himself. He put his hand out and they shook hands tentatively at first, but then more forcefully as each took the other's measure and was pleased with what he saw.

"I'm glad there was someone here to help Caitlyn," Tanner said. "She means a great deal to me," he added, his dark blue eyes meeting Sean Flynn's level gaze without flinching.

Sean nodded but said nothing as Caitlyn fluttered out distractedly with a pitcher of cold lemonade which she hurriedly poured into glasses for all of them. She sat nervously in a chair, leaning forward a little as she waited for whatever news Tanner had. There was no need to fire questions at him now, for she knew he was getting ready to tell her everything that had transpired.

"I never got the ransom money from Brant, Caitlyn," Tanner began slowly. "I was imprisoned for nearly two months before I was finally released by the French on the promise that I wouldn't involve myself in trafficking weapons to the rebels. It's a whole different world down there, Caitlyn," he said quietly, "and they just don't play by the usual rules. I saw a man's tongue cut out because he refused to swear allegiance to Maximilian. On the road from Mexico City to Vera Cruz I saw men hanging, or what used to be men. They'd been hanged from trees until they bloated and grew black." For a moment his eyes were glazed remembering the horror of it. "It was foolish for me to think that I could deal with those people through the usual civilized channels."

"But what of Brant? Have you any news of him, Tanner?" she pleaded.

He took both her hands in his, ignoring any disapproval he might see in the eyes of Sean Flynn. "Through the French in charge of the prison, I did learn that someone had arrived in Vera Cruz with money for my ransom. After making more inquiries after my release, I found out it was indeed Brant who'd come to ransom me. Unfortunately, after making initial contact with the French, he disappeared on the road from Vera Cruz to Pueblo, where he was supposed to deliver the money. Later it was found that Juáristas had kidnapped his party and stolen all the money."

"But what about Brant?" Caitlyn demanded.

Tanner shook his head. "The French found some bodies later, but none were Brant's." He gazed at her. "I don't know if he's alive or dead, Caitlyn."

"Oh, my God, Tanner, if he should be dead, I—" Caitlyn brought her anguished eyes to his face. "I should never have let him go to Mexico."

Tanner frowned. "You couldn't have stopped him, Caitlyn; he's his own man. He wanted to rescue me and I would have done the same thing for him."

She stood up and pulled her hands from his grasp, then began pacing the veranda. "I can't help it, Tanner, I just feel so guilty about him going. I—I knew how much he resented me mapping out his life for him. His heart was never in Riverhouse, but I forced him to come back here when he would have been so much happier to have stayed in Australia." Her tears burned her eyes as she looked at Tanner. "None of this would have happened if I hadn't been so damned stubborn and willful!" Bursting into sobs, she ran from the veranda.

When Tanner would have gone after her, Sean's hand on his arm stopped him. "Let her go and have her cry," he advised quietly. "The girl's overwrought. She's been coiled as tense as a spring for the last few weeks. The tears will do her good."

Tanner sighed heavily and sat down again. "I just wish I could have brought her happier news."

Sean stared at the other man. "It appears to me you've brought her quite a bit of relief—*you* came back, didn't you?" He met Tanner's surprised look and there was a wealth of understanding there. "From what I've observed and from what I've been able to find out through my own poking, maybe destiny had a hand in bringing back the right man after all."

Caitlyn was still indisposed that evening, but the next day, Christmas Day, she made an effort to dispel her gloom and present a composed image for the sake of the holiday. Everyone at Mornhaven was infinitely glad to see that Tanner Malone had returned safely, although there was anxiety attached to thoughts of Brant's whereabouts. Various options were discussed and rejected over Christmas dinner. Timothy wondered about sending another ransom to obtain Brant's freedom, if he was still alive. Tanner vetoed that notion, holding that it was too dangerous to bring any large amount of money into the country. There were too many bandits and renegades roaming the country. Jesse

Cobb, in his usual quiet way, suggested sending a letter to the State Department in Washington and asking for its help since Brant was a U.S. citizen. Caitlyn looked at her brother-in-law gratefully, but Tanner told them that since diplomatic ties between the U.S. government and Maximilian's government were tenuous, he wasn't sure there was much pressure that the U.S. government could bring to bear.

Sean Flynn made the one suggestion that everyone else had carefully skirted. "The only way that we can ever really be sure what's happened to Brant Sinclair is for an interested party to go down to Mexico and find out."

There was silence at the table.

"I'll go," Sean offered after a minute. "I'm familiar with Mexico and the people. I've lived in Texas for quite a while and fought in the Mexican War. I can speak Spanish. I'm the logical one to go."

"I'll go with you," Tanner said quietly. "I'm responsible for what's happened to Brant."

Caitlyn looked from Sean to Tanner. "But you've just been talking of the danger," she stressed. "I don't want you to go—either of you."

Tanner leaned over the table and touched Caitlyn's hand with his own. "Caitlyn, my dear, when will you learn that you can't control men's lives?" he chided her, oblivious to the look of consternation that Timothy gave him at the use of the endearment to address his daughter.

Caitlyn flushed, aware of the several pairs of eyes that were directed at her and Tanner. But she was firm, her voice even as she announced, "If you both go, then I will be going with you."

There was chaos as everyone started talking at once. Timothy blustered, Margaret beseeched, Constance cried, and Jesse tried to bring some semblance of order to things. Sean said nothing as his eyes traveled from Caitlyn's stubborn face to Tanner's grim countenance.

"You won't be going, Caitlyn," Tanner said. "If you won't think of yourself, then you'd better think of your daughter. She already may be without a father. How can you leave her without a mother too?"

"I can't live with myself if I don't go with you," Caitlyn replied evenly. "Jesse and Connie can take charge of Riverhouse while I'm gone. Maggie can stay with my parents. They love her as much as I do."

"Caitlyn, I won't allow you to go," Tanner said, his voice rising just a little.

"I'm coming," she insisted, standing her ground.

"We shall see about that," Tanner retorted, his dark blue eyes giving her a measuring look. "If you'll recall, I've administered a spanking to you before, and I've a mind to give you another one, my dear."

Caitlyn completely disregarded the shocked look on her mother's face. Not even Timothy had ever laid a hand on Caitlyn. But Margaret was nearly as shocked to see Timothy chuckling next to her. "Timothy, this isn't a laughing matter!" she cried.

"Margaret, dear," he answered, "it's just that I've waited a long time to see a man best our Caitlyn in anything. It looks as though she may finally have met her match in this Yankee from Boston!"

Back at Riverhouse that evening, Sean excused himself to retire. It was past midnight and he wanted to get up early the next morning to go over accounts and procedures with Jesse, who had generously agreed to take over Riverhouse during his absence whether or not Caitlyn went to Mexico. It had been one hell of an evening! Sean thought with some pleasure. He was glad to see Caitlyn back to her old fighting spirit; she'd been going around in a daze ever since Brant had left. This Malone fellow was good for her, he thought as he climbed the stairs, leaving the two of them alone. He chuckled to himself, wondering which of them would be the winner in this confrontation.

In the small drawing room, Tanner and Caitlyn squared off, both determined to be the victor. Despite her black mourning gown, which was relieved only by a pristine white collar at her throat, Caitlyn looked dazzling. Her cheeks were flushed with excitement and her eyes were sparkling. She felt alive again, really *alive*, for the first time in many weeks. She'd be shot before she'd let Tanner leave her here while he went to look for Brant.

She folded her arms in front of her, standing with her back to the fireplace. "I'm going, Tanner Malone."

Her expression infuriated him and he strode from behind the chair to confront her. "Caitlyn, you are *not* going!"

"I *will* go!" she repeated, her blue eyes blazing.

"No!" he returned, his own eyes bright with mingled irritation and exasperation. He reached out and grasped her arms so

that she was forced to unfold them. Holding them just above the elbow, he shook her a little as though to shake some sense into her. "Damn it, that was no hollow threat at Mornhaven, Caitlyn!" he warned her. "I've spanked you before, I've a mind to do it again. For most women, once would be enough, but not for *you*!"

"Hah! Tanner Malone, do you think that's going to keep me at Riverhouse?" she inquired haughtily.

"It will show you that I mean what I say," he replied. "And I say that you are not going, Caitlyn."

"I'll not have you tell me what to do, Tanner. And I'm not going to stay up and argue with you about it. I have to get up early to start packing for the trip tomorrow."

He pulled her forward, still holding her arms. Without a word, he pulled her over to the chair where he'd been standing. He brought her down over his lap so suddenly that the breath left her.

"Tanner Malone, you let me up!" she cried. "I'll not let you humiliate me again. Let me up!"

"What's your answer?"

"All right, all right!" she snapped. "I won't leave tomorrow with you and Sean. Are you satisfied?"

He hesitated. "You give me your word on that?"

"Yes."

He picked her up before she could get to her feet and sat her down on his lap. "You don't know how tempted I was," he murmured.

She flushed to the roots of her hair. With a laugh, he reached down and smoothed her skirts, following the curve of her leg. His touch on her, even through the material of her clothing, caused a jagged bolt to skitter through Caitlyn's body.

He felt it and suddenly released her from his lap. Then they both stood up, staring at each other in confusion. After a moment he moved away from her, jamming his fists into the pockets of his trousers in a gesture she knew so well. It spoke of the frustration that she too was feeling. The tension in the air was so thick she could almost taste it.

"Tanner—"

"You see," he said slowly, his blue eyes seeming to burn through her, "you see why you can't come to Mexico with me, Caitlyn. I wouldn't be able to keep my hands off you, my dearest. There would come a time when we'd be alone together and

I—I wouldn't be able to keep a hold on my emotions." There was a blue fire in his eyes as they caressed her through the material of her gown. "I'd make passionate love to you, Caitlyn, and I wouldn't give a damn about Brant, or your family, or my honor or yours!"

She was silent in the face of his naked desire. Finally he turned away from her and his voice was harsh.

"Now, go to bed, for God's sake, Caitlyn! I'll see you in the morning."

50

CAITLYN WAVED to the two figures on the paddle wheeler, watching as it made its way down the Mississippi. When it was finally lost to sight, she sat down in the open carriage, opened her parasol, and directed the driver to take her to Mornhaven immediately. Smoothing the rustling taffeta skirts of her black day dress, she tried to think how to confront her mother and enlist her aid without alienating her from her cause. Caitlyn only knew one thing and that was that she was going to Mexico. She had slept very little last night, making plans, trying not to think of the look in Tanner's eyes when he had come so close to breaking all restraint last night. Yes, she knew he loved her, knew what a risk she was taking in placing herself so close to him. But she also knew she could no longer wait patiently at Riverhouse. At this point she wasn't even sure whose fate concerned her most. Loyalty to Brant made her worry for his safety, but a new and tender love for Tanner Malone seemed to have sprung up within her breast. It was a mixture of admiration, pride, and tenderness that she could barely keep hidden this morning as she had said good-bye to him on the levee. He'd searched her face with his dark blue eyes, expecting to see anger over the way he'd treated her last night.

"I'm glad you're not letting me go off in your bad graces," he had smiled.

She had shaken her head, wishing she had the right to clasp her arms around his neck and show him how much she cared about him. "I understand why you don't want me to come with you," she had answered in a low voice. "You will be careful, Tanner? I will be so worried about you."

He had nodded. "I promise to take extra care. After all, I've already been in prison in Mexico and I don't care to repeat the experience. At least I know that you'll be safe at Riverhouse."

She had smiled. "You won't need to worry about me," she had told him sweetly.

The paddle wheeler had blasted a sharp whistle, indicating it was time to board. Lingering another moment, Tanner had taken Caitlyn's hand and pressed it to his lips. "I would rather be kissing your lips," he'd whispered with a disarming grin, "but I'm not sure how Sean Flynn would take it."

"He would probably approve," she'd whispered back with impertinence. "But there does seem to be a gaggle of spectators on board the boat who might be shocked at such a liberty in broad daylight."

He'd laughed and touched her cheek with his hand before turning to board the boat. She'd gotten into the carriage to stand and wave while the boat pulled away, hugging her secret thoughts to herself.

Now as she made her busy plans on the way to Mornhaven, she felt the rising tide of excitement in her breast at the thought of the adventure ahead of her. It was crucial that she gain her mother's support. Already Jesse and Connie were making plans to move their things to Riverhouse in order to facilitate Jesse's running of the plantation. At least she was assured that Brant's ancestral home would be well taken care of, probably better than when Brant was here, for Jesse was a smarter planter than Brant would ever be. She was positive that her mother would be happy to take care of Maggie in her absence, although there would probably be some initial resistance. What she needed most was a promise of secrecy from her mother to enable her to get away before Timothy tried to stop her. He was well aware that neither Sean Flynn nor Tanner Malone wanted her to go to Mexico and he would try to do everything in his power to keep her at Riverhouse. Once she was away, she would have too much of a head start to allow him to bring her back.

As the carriage turned into the drive at Mornhaven, Caitlyn settled her face into placid lines. If she was lucky, her father would be out and she would be able to visit her mother alone.

As she suspected, Margaret was both happy and relieved to see her daughter. "Caitlyn, my dear, I'm glad you've come by to visit. I barely got to speak to you yesterday with all the excitement over Tanner Malone's return and the talk about Mexico.

Come into the sitting room and we can talk privately. Your father is in Baton Rouge today."

"Mama, I need to talk to you about something very important to me," she began, trying to gauge her mother's attitude by the expression in her eyes.

Margaret turned to her daughter, a look of wisdom written on her still-lovely features. "I thought perhaps you'd come about that," she said.

Caitlyn smiled with relief. This would make it so much easier. She was about to tell her of her plans to go to Mexico when her mother's next words halted her speech. "I could see it plainly at dinner last night," Margaret commented, her face composed though her fingers laced and relaced in her lap. "I'm not sure your father is aware of it, but I do know that everyone else at the table suspected it. My dear, I don't know what to tell you. You know that I want only your happiness, but I—I cannot condone a relationship with one man while you are married to another."

"Mama, what are you saying?" Caitlyn asked, her eyes wide.

Margaret stared at her daughter. "Why, I was talking about your relationship with Tanner Malone. I thought that's what you *wanted* to talk about."

Caitlyn leaned back in her chair. "My relationship with Tanner Malone," she mused softly. "Mama, that is such a complicated matter."

"My dear, it's very plain that he's in love with you," Margaret pointed out calmly. "I hesitate to speak to you about what is your own business, my dear, but I would hope that you haven't encouraged any physical display of that love."

"Mama, I haven't committed adultery with Tanner Malone, if that's what is worrying you," Caitlyn reassured her, blushing in spite of herself.

Margaret looked plainly relieved. "You've always been a headstrong young woman, Caitlyn, and I never know what to expect of you. I would hope that my teachings have had some effect on your stubborn nature. Tanner Malone is quite an attractive man and I have a feeling that it's not in his nature to refrain from taking what he wants." She had spoken plainly enough, so plainly that both women could not quite meet each other's eyes for a moment.

Caitlyn took a while to calm her emotions before speaking. She had never heard such talk from her mother. How Tanner

would have enjoyed *this* discussion! she thought suddenly. But then she realized that now was the time to speak about her plans, while her mother seemed open to plain talk.

"Mama, it wasn't Tanner's feelings for me that I wanted to talk with you about," she began. "I'm going to leave for New Orleans tomorrow morning and then go down to Vera Cruz to help Tanner and Sean look for Brant."

"What!" Margaret looked at her daughter as though she'd lost her mind. "You can't go to Mexico," she said firmly. "You know how dangerous it would be. And besides, you've got all your responsibilities here. Maggie and Riverhouse—"

"Jesse and Connie will do fine by Riverhouse during my absence, Mama," Caitlyn interrupted. "And I have no qualms at all about leaving Maggie with you and Papa."

"What about Tanner Malone?" Margaret asked.

"What Tanner thinks is his own business, Mama," Caitlyn retorted with a touch of defiance. "He has absolutely no control over my actions."

"But you'll be placing yourself in his hands when you go to Mexico," Margaret pointed out practically.

"Mama, I'm going and that's all there is to it!" Caitlyn exploded. "Just promise me that you won't tell Papa about this until after I've gone."

"I don't like you going to New Orleans on a paddle wheeler by yourself," Margaret said, used to her daughter's temper and unfazed by it. "You know what kind of people have been traveling on the river—adventurers from the North, newspapermen, riffraff from all over the South."

"Mama, I can take care of myself! I traveled thousands of miles to Australia alone, didn't I? I think I can survive the trip to New Orleans. If I need help getting a ship bound for Vera Cruz, there's always Uncle Paul to help me. Mama, I have to go!" Her blue eyes pleaded with her mother for understanding.

Finally Margaret sighed. "All right, I'll take good care of Maggie while you're gone. You're right about Jesse doing his best at Riverhouse. I'll think of something to tell your father if he asks about you." Margaret gave her daughter a level look. "But I don't really understand why you feel you must go, my dear. Are you so concerned about finding Brant, or are you running to Tanner?"

51

CAITLYN STRAINED for her first look at Mexico, trying to imagine how Brant had felt when he'd come to this land. She could see very little as there had been a heavy rain the night before and this morning there was fog obscuring the view. The captain had already informed the passengers that they would have to be taken ashore on lighters, smaller boats that would take them to the wharf in Vera Cruz.

Caitlyn had gathered her luggage from the large cabin where everyone's trunks had been set to be sorted out. She had parted with a few coins in order to have a boy bring her things to the railing so that she could be among the first of the passengers to be taken ashore. As she waited impatiently for the fog to lift, she hoped it would not be too difficult to find Tanner and Sean in Vera Cruz. She had assumed that the town was small, but from the talk on board ship, the town must be larger than she thought.

When the call came for the lighters, Caitlyn was first in line. In no time she was off the ship and aboard one of the smaller boats, feeling exhilaration speed through her as the fog gradually lifted so that she could see the city in front of her. As they drew closer to the land, she felt the heat and humidity more intensely than on the ship and she wished she could lift the heavy veil from her face. But common sense told her that it would be foolish to expose her face before she had the protection of Tanner and Sean. She would have to suffer through the discomfort.

By the time the lighters reached the port, Caitlyn was sweating profusely in her black bombazine gown and heavy shawl. Her large mourning hat with its heavy veil felt constricting on her head and she wondered if she was going to faint. It was hard to catch her breath in the heavy humidity. What kind of place had she come to? she wondered.

The moment she set foot in Vera Cruz, she realized exactly what kind of place it was: a tumbledown port with a peeling customhouse and row upon row of flat-topped white houses that made the city look like a giant cemetery. Any excitement she might have felt at this new adventure was effectively dampened by the dismal appearance of the city.

Steely fortitude made her straighten her slumping spine and she called sharply for a young boy of about fourteen to put her trunks in his cart. For a few American coins, he would gladly take her to the best hotel in the city, he assured her, and Caitlyn followed him through the dusty streets, wishing the heels on her shoes were not quite so high.

She was glad she remembered some of the Spanish that her teachers at the various schools she'd attended had drilled into her. Languages had always been her best subject, but Connie had been the one to really excel in them. What a pity she didn't have her sister with her now, she thought, and then laughed at the idea of her poor sister, seven months along with child, trudging through the foul streets of this disgusting city.

Her laughter died quickly when she beheld the dreary, run-down building that the young boy had brought her to. She questioned him anxiously and he nodded. This was the best hotel the city had to offer. She asked him to wait outside while she inquired about a room within. Once inside the double doors, she found it was blessedly cooler than outside under the sun, but the stink of the place came up to hit her full in the face. Pressing a handkerchief to her nose, she walked to the desk where a greasy fat man was thumbing distractedly through papers.

"Do you have a room for rent?" she asked in halting Spanish.

The fat man looked her up and down, trying to peer through the heavy gauze of her veil. Obligingly, Caitlyn raised the outer veil. He smiled at her, asking her if she were French. Caitlyn shook her head and told him she was an American. She asked him if there were any other Americans staying at this hotel.

To her extreme disappointment, the man shook his head. She had hoped to find Tanner right away. She asked him where she might inquire as to the whereabouts of a certain person and thought he told her to go to the French military office. When she couldn't follow his directions, she finally gave up and simply asked for a room. Perhaps after a brief rest she would have the energy to begin looking for Tanner and Sean. After quoting her a price, the man handed her a key with a number on it and pointed upstairs.

Caitlyn trudged wearily back outside in order to call in the boy who had brought her luggage here. Surprised that she did not see him in front of the hotel, she stepped around to the other side of the building and saw nothing but the bodies of slumbering peasants in the dust of the street. Nervously, she rushed back

to the front of the hotel, scanning the area in vain. The boy had disappeared—and with every bit of clothing she'd brought with her except for what she had on! Clutching her reticule and feeling infinitely glad that she had had the sense to put her money in it, Caitlyn marched back inside the hotel and demanded that the man behind the desk call a carriage to take her to the nearest police station.

Nearly an hour later, Caitlyn paced angrily in front of the unoccupied desk of the French officer in charge of the troops garrisoned at Vera Cruz. Tanner had been right, she thought furiously, the people in this city were uncouth, ill-mannered, and unfriendly. And that applied not only to the native inhabitants, but also to the French soldiers, who had grown slovenly and bad-tempered in this humid tropical hothouse.

"Madame Sinclair?"

Caitlyn turned to see a harassed-looking officer enter the small room, his face red and sweaty from the heat in the airless building. Caitlyn herself felt as though she were swimming in her clothes and tapped her foot impatiently while the officer bade her be seated while he shuffled through papers on his cluttered desk.

"My secretary said you were an American, just arrived," the officer said in imperfect English. "And already you have run into some trouble, eh?" He smiled in a falsely jocular manner that grated on Caitlyn's already strained nerves.

"My luggage has been stolen by some Indian boy," she said quickly, leaning forward in her chair and fixing the officer with an irritated stare.

The officer drew his hands together, steepling his fingers as he looked over them to return her stare. "Madame, might I suggest that it was most foolish of you to come to Vera Cruz without proper escort."

"I have traveled alone on more than one occasion and I have always managed quite well, thank you. But I must say that I was unprepared for the condition of this city as well as the lack of proper policing of the population."

"If I might interrupt, madame, you seem to think that you are still in the United States or some other *civilized* country," he half sneered. "This is not Paris or New York, madame. This is Vera Cruz and many of its inhabitants are nothing more than peasants, riffraff, and outcasts. What law and order there is is provided by the garrison under my supervision, but we cannot

police everywhere, madame. Perhaps it would be best for you to take the next ship back to your home, where things are more to your liking." His suggestion was made in a near insulting tone of voice that Caitlyn could not fail to notice.

"Lieutenant Legoix, I am to meet someone here," she explained quickly, realizing she would get nowhere by arguing with this man, who would just as soon throw her out of his office as listen to her complaints. "Since you seem to be telling me that you will be of no help to me in getting back my luggage, at least could you offer me your assistance in finding my friends?"

He too took a moment to get himself under control. "Madame Sinclair, perhaps I *can* help you in that respect," he said consideringly. "Who are you looking for?"

"Two Americans," Caitlyn answered. She described them in detail while the lieutenant wrote down her descriptions on a sheet of dirty paper. When he was finished, he called for a soldier to come in, gave him rapid instructions in French that Caitlyn found hard to follow, and handed him the paper. The soldier, after a considering look at Caitlyn, left the room, leaving Caitlyn to face the difficult task of relying on the lieutenant's help in providing her with a place to stay while she waited for news of Sean and Tanner.

Though it galled her to have to ask him for a favor, she cleared her throat and eyed him levelly. "Lieutenant, I'm afraid I must press you for one more favor," she began. "I was to take a room at one of the hotels in this city, but without luggage, I would rather wait until my friends are located. Is there a place you might suggest to house me until that time?"

"Madame, I'm afraid I cannot help you in that regard, although there are several establishments within the city where you might rent a room," he said.

Caitlyn's chin trembled at the thought of having to go back to that dismal hotel. "May I at least wait in the antechamber, Lieutenant Legoix? Perhaps your men will find out something within a short time."

"Madame, I cannot have you waiting outside my office."

"Please, Lieutenant, I promise not to be a bother. If my friends are not located by evening, I will go to a hotel and stay until the morning."

Lieutenant Legoix decided he most definitely did not want the lady to wait in his antechamber, but in the face of her pleas, he could do very little but nod stiffly, resenting the fact that she had

backed him into a corner. Heartily pleased, Caitlyn thanked him profusely and left the room to find a comfortable chair to sit in while she waited for news. None of the chairs were comfortable, so she made do with a wooden-backed chair and a stool upon which to rest her feet.

The day passed slowly and several times Caitlyn got up from her seat to pace the room, look out the small barred window, or stand in the doorway to catch any cool breeze that might blow by. But in Vera Cruz there were no cool breezes. The city was like a stagnant cesspool surrounded on one side by the ocean and on the other sides by sandhills which seemed to entrap miasmic odors that permeated the humid air. Behind her black veil, she continued to find it hard to breathe, but as the afternoon wore on and more soldiers crossed through the antechamber, she thought it best to keep it on.

With the coming of nightfall her spirits sank, for she knew that the lieutenant would not allow her to stay here. Already he had poked his head out of his office several times, wondering if she had left. He had eyed her with obvious irritation and she realized that she had been stupid to have made an enemy of him with her earlier haughty attitude. If only he would forget all about her.

But of course he didn't. Caitlyn saw him come out, frowning at the face of his pocket watch. "Madame, it is now past ten o'clock. I suggest you find a place to sleep immediately. I will be retiring soon myself and the orderly on the night watch cannot be expected to watch over you."

"Yes, Lieutenant, I know," Caitlyn said with a tired sigh. "I didn't realize it would be so hard to find two Americans."

"Are you sure that they are still in the city?" he asked her sternly. "Perhaps they traveled on to Pueblo or even Mexico City?"

At the thought, Caitlyn felt a moment's panic. What if they *had* gone on to some other city? Vera Cruz was not the most inviting of places; she wouldn't blame them for moving on. To her chagrin, she felt unwelcome tears trembling on her eyelashes. She thought seriously of taking the lieutenant's advice and finding a ship to take her back home.

Just then a soldier marched smartly through the door and said something to his commanding officer in French. Caitlyn was so tired she could barely make out any of it, but did hear the word *American*, which lifted her spirits considerably in the face of all

her recent disappointments. She saw the lieutenant glance once or twice at her, then whisper something in rapid French to his junior officer. The junior officer continued the conversation and Lieutenant Legoix suddenly burst out laughing. The two men enjoyed their private joke for a few more minutes before Lieutenant Legoix waved in Caitlyn's direction and disappeared once more into his office.

"Madame Sinclair?" The soldier clicked his boots in her direction and Caitlyn nodded, standing immediately as she hoped for good news. In heavily accented English, the soldier went on, "We have found your American friends, madame. If you will follow me?"

Caitlyn breathed a sigh of relief and followed the soldier into a small black carriage outside the military office. They rode for several minutes through the streets of Vera Cruz. In some places the silence was like death, in others she could pick out the strains of sad guitars and raucous singing. Obviously the saloons did a good business in this city, she thought.

It was in front of one of these establishments that the carriage rolled to a stop. Politely, the soldier opened the door for her and took her hand to help her to the slimy street. Pointing to the building from whence came music, laughter, and singing, the soldier explained as best he could that this was an establishment frequented by Americans and that she would find her two friends inside. As she thanked him, she suspiciously noted the parting grin he gave her.

Looking up at the sign which identified the saloon as EL LOBO NEGRO, Caitlyn turned back to ask the soldier a question, but found that he had already reentered the carriage and was giving the driver instructions to leave. Without a backward glance at the lone woman who stood in the street, the driver urged the horses on, leaving her to her own devices.

Perhaps the heat and humidity in this city made an uncivilized beast of any man who came to it. She only hoped that the soldier's information was correct and that Tanner and Sean were inside.

Taking a deep breath to steady herself and coughing a little at the odor she was forced to smell, Caitlyn picked up her skirts and stepped carefully over a suspicious-looking dark pile in front of the doorway. She had never in her life entered a saloon. She had thought the soldier would stay with her until she'd been reunited with her friends, but obviously Lieutenant Legoix had

thought she was independent enough to handle herself. Perhaps this was the little joke he had decided to play on her, she thought with some indignation. But her indignation gave way to shock as she stepped through the half-open slatted doors of the saloon and observed the scene of bedlam within.

Pressing herself against the wall and hoping that her black dress would make her inconspicuous in the half-light of the flickering candles, Caitlyn looked through her veil at the agglomeration of men and women in front of her.

Squeezed into every chair available were men of all types, some Mexican, with their fierce-looking mustaches and wide sombreros, and others French soldiers on their off-duty hours. Sprinkled among the rest were small pockets of Americans, whose loud, laughing voices intermingled with the elegant accents of the French and guttural responses of the Mexicans. The smoke-filled room was cluttered with food and drink, wine spilling from overturned glasses onto the wooden floor that looked like it hadn't seen a mop in years. On that floor lay several men in various stages of drunkenness. Some snored, oblivious to the danger of heavily booted feet; some tried to get to their knees to grab a glass of beer from a table; and others were staggering to their feet, looking for a place to sit down. Among all the men were a liberal number of women, frowsy, half-naked females who leaned against men or lay half sprawled at their feet while eager hands reached inside their open blouses to fondle their breasts.

Caitlyn felt as though she were nailed to the wall. So this was the cruel joke Lieutenant Legoix had played on her. He must have known what kind of establishment this was, and yet he had brought her here, leaving her without an escort to pick her way through the drunken mass of men to find her friends. A cold fear gripped her that perhaps Sean and Tanner were not even here. Would Lieutenant Legoix have gone that far to rid himself of her? Desperately she tried to see through her veil, but it was nearly impossible in the darkness of the room. Yet she was afraid to lift her veil and draw attention to herself.

A man fell at her feet, much the worse for drink, and he proceeded to empty his stomach of its contents. Sickened, Caitlyn stepped aside, bumping into another man who was weaving his way about the room. The sight of a black-shrouded figure seemed to frighten him in his drunken state and he backed away from her. Another man noticed the heavily veiled figure and

with an oath reached up to knock away the hat which held the veil over her face.

With a cry of alarm, Caitlyn reached for her hat, but it was already being trampled by booted feet while the men looked up at her white face and laughed insultingly. Whistles were directed at her and she held her shawl tightly about her shoulders, wishing she still had the protection of her hat and veil. Oh, God, where was Tanner? she wondered frantically. Please, please let him be here, she prayed, her eyes searching the room.

A man seated in a chair reached up to drag her down into his lap. Caitlyn lost the grip on her shawl and one of the saloon whores grabbed it possessively, covering her skinny shanks with it and prancing about the room, laughing wildly before being pulled down into rough arms and quieted with sloppy kisses. Caitlyn wrenched herself out of the drunk's hands and moved away, bouncing against another man before running solidly into a French soldier who caught her in his arms and leaned down to plant a sloppy kiss on her mouth. His hands were quicker than she would have believed as they pulled the collar of her dress, breaking two buttons so that the front of her dress hung at a crazy angle, exposing a tantalizing vee of soft flesh below her throat.

"Please, let me go!" she sobbed, really frightened now. Any knowledge of French or Spanish completely left her as she became mindless with fear. "Let me go!"

The French soldier laughed cruelly and reached to pull the rip in her dress lower, exposing the lace edging of her corset cover and the cleavage between her breasts. Guffaws and cries of encouragement egged him on as several other men noticed the struggle between the strangely garbed woman and the Frenchman. Many offered to help him, drunkenly creeping toward them. Caitlyn struck out with her hands, but her blows did little good. There were so many men and no one in the crowd seemed disposed to take her side.

Never in her life had Caitlyn found herself in a situation like this before. These men were not the gently flirtatious boys of her youth, nor were they the rough but courteous gold miners in Australia. They were different even from the Yankee soldiers, who had come as conquerors but still retained enough honor to keep from raping the women of their defeated antagonists. The men in this saloon had no regard for women. They were used to the whores who slaked their sexual desires during the occa-

sional respites from the skirmishes between the Juáristas and the imperial forces. Despite her black garb, this woman must be no different from any other prostitute who found her way in here to sell her favors. Any decent woman would be at home tending to her kitchen duties or taking care of her babies. Therefore this female was fair game to all.

A tall, wide-shouldered Mexican decided he wanted to taste the fair señorita for himself and worked his way through the crowd to seize her from the Frenchman's arms. Crushing her fiercely against his chest, he leaned down to mash his mouth against hers, pulling the pins out of her hair so that it tumbled down her back. Caitlyn felt tears in her eyes as the man yanked her hair, hurting her scalp with his roughness.

The French soldier, clearly upset at having his prize taken away, reached for Caitlyn's arm to pull her back to him. For a moment she thought the two of them would split her in half, but the Mexican won the battle, pulling on her with such force that she fell against him. Half fainting now, Caitlyn leaned to the side and tried to get away, but his arm was clamped firmly around her waist and he proceeded to half drag her back to his corner of the room, where things were still relatively quiet, most of the occupants paying very little attention to the brief display of excitement.

With a forlorn little cry, Caitlyn found herself pushed onto a bench behind a table. Oh God, now this terrible man would probably rape her and none of these crazy people would lift one finger to help! Caitlyn steeled herself to await the expected onslaught and when it did not come, she opened her eyes slowly to face the Mexican who had won her. He was grinning at her, his expression clearly interested for a moment before he shook his head and jerked it in the opposite direction.

Caitlyn turned her head around and came face to face with a very angry-looking Tanner Malone. The relief that flooded through her was so intense she almost fainted.

"Tanner! Oh, Tanner, thank heaven it's you!" she sighed, tears starting to run down her cheeks. "I was so afraid and I—"

"You're damn lucky I was here and saw you," he ground out, clearly keeping his anger in check with extreme difficulty. "If I hadn't sent Rafael to get you away from that French soldier, you might have found yourself outside in the alley on your back with your legs spread wide open."

His rough talk shocked her and she stared at him in confusion. "You—you sent this man to get me? But—but why didn't you come yourself?"

"Because, my dear, I'm an American and I didn't want to make myself conspicuous, especially with all these French soldiers about, considering the circumstances under which I left this country not too long ago." His dark blue eyes blazed at her even in the smoke-filled room, seeming like twin flames in the gloom. "*What* are you doing here? Why have you come to Mexico when you *promised* me you would stay at Riverhouse?"

"I—I can't talk to you when you're shouting at me like this!" she got out, feeling thoroughly miserable. She had just gone through the worst scare of her life and she wanted to be comforted and cosseted, not yelled at and accused by the man she thought cared for her. Her eyes flitted about the table, noting two men she didn't know, and then she saw Sean Flynn, his hand cupping the breast of a brazen woman who was staring at Caitlyn curiously. "Oh, Sean, at least you're not angry at me, are you?" she pleaded.

His eyes held out little hope for her. "You've done a very stupid thing, child," he returned stonily. "Tanner's right; you could have been raped, or worse. This is no place for you!"

"But I only came to help," she said. "I thought—"

"You think too much!" Tanner interrupted fiercely. "Now you'd better start thinking of how you're going to get back home, because that's exactly where you're going as soon as we can arrange it."

"I'll not go back now," she returned stiffly. "I've come this far and I'm not leaving until I find out what's happened to Brant."

For a moment she thought Tanner was going to strike her. He was so angry she could see the vein throbbing in his throat, but he calmed himself with an effort. "First things first, we'd best get ourselves out of here. If we continue asking for information about Brant Sinclair, someone might get suspicious. I'm afraid that I'm going to have to entrust you to Rafael's tender care once more, Caitlyn." He nodded toward the smiling Mexican. "It would look odd if he suddenly gave up his hard-won prize to me." He gave the man hurried instructions on where to bring Caitlyn after leaving the saloon. Then, without a backward glance, Tanner got up from the table and made his way out,

followed after a brief interval by Sean Flynn, who unceremoniously dumped the prostitute into the lap of the man beside him.

The Mexican, Rafael, draped a casual arm about Caitlyn's shoulders. He pinched her chin between his fingers and brought her around to face him. "You are in a world of trouble, little girl. My advice is to be quiet so we can make our departure with as little notice as possible. That French soldier might still be nursing a grudge against me. I can feel his eyes watching us." So saying, he abruptly brought his mouth down to hers, opening her lips in a wide-mouthed kiss that caught her by surprise. His mouth sheered away from hers, smearing the side of her face with saliva. "Just stay close to me," he ordered.

Despite her disgust, Caitlyn was obliged to paste herself against the big man as they walked past the table where the French soldier sat eyeing them darkly. Rafael even went so far as to place a fondling hand on her breast, outraging her so that she was tempted to slap him. But at least the pretense worked, for they got outside without any problems.

Quickly disengaging herself from him, Caitlyn wiped the side of her mouth with the back of her hand. She would have yelled curses at him, but he put a finger to his mouth and hugged her against him, drowning whatever words she would have said with another hearty kiss. Behind them she heard some French oaths and realized that a few of the French soldiers had come to the door to watch curiously the departure of the mystery woman and her conqueror.

Holding her tight against him, Rafael proceeded down the street, looking back often to see if they were being followed. After a few minutes he lengthened his stride, dragging Caitlyn along with him.

Within a few more minutes Rafael suddenly ducked inside a doorway and knocked loudly. A middle-aged woman opened the door and looked at the pair of them in surprise. "Rafael, you know damn well I don't allow no whores inside my boarding house!" the woman said with irritation. "You'll have to take her back to wherever she belongs." The woman was obviously an American, her tones the lazy drawl of the deep South.

"She's no whore, Liz," the Mexican laughed, his English liberally accented. "She belongs to Señor Malone."

"What?" The woman looked unconvinced, but at the pleading look in Caitlyn's eyes, she shrugged. "All right, then. But

if she's a whore she goes in an hour. I don't want her spending the night upstairs." She opened the door and let them through.

By the time Caitlyn got upstairs and was being steered in the direction of one of the bedroom doors she was nearly at the end of her rope. This whole country must be crazy!

"Here you are," Rafael said with a regretful look, opening a door and pushing her inside. He saluted her with a wry grin. "Good luck, little girl."

Caitlyn stared at him until he closed the door in her face. In a daze, she swung around and scanned the room. Her eyes lit upon the figure of Tanner Malone sitting comfortably in a chair, watching her from beneath dark brows that were like two slashes above his piercing blue eyes. He got up and stepped toward her. "So," he said softly, "now we are alone, Caitlyn."

52

HER FIRST INSTINCT was to throw herself in his arms, but she hesitated, watching him come toward her until he was within a few feet of where she stood. His eyes were watching her closely, the anger having receded for the moment.

Finally, when the silence grew too long, she cleared her throat and was the first to speak. "I—I know you're upset about me coming down to Mexico, Tanner," she began haltingly.

"Upset? I'm mad as hell at you!" he informed her, striving to keep a tight rein on his anger. "I can't imagine how you eluded your father and found a ship to bring you here. What I would like to know is how you managed to find Sean and me so quickly in this godforsaken stinkhole!"

She swallowed. "When I arrived, I had a young boy from the wharf bring my bags to one of the hotels—if you could call that flea-bitten place a hotel—but when I came back out of the hotel to have the bags brought in, he was gone."

"He probably had you pegged from the beginning," Tanner said.

"I went to the French military office here in the city and when the lieutenant refused to do anything to help me, I asked him if he could at least help me locate you and Sean."

"You asked a French officer! Good God, Caitlyn, didn't you think you might be putting me in danger? If you'll recall, I was

imprisoned not so long ago by the French because I was accused of selling arms to the Juáristas! Didn't you think they'd wonder why I had come back to Mexico? Damn it, Caitlyn!''

"I'm sorry, Tanner, I didn't think about that,'' she responded lamely, realizing now why he'd been so angry with her.

"Obviously you didn't think about a lot of things,'' he returned. "You've endangered yourself needlessly. There's no purpose served in your staying here in Mexico, Caitlyn. You'll return tomorrow on the first ship out of Vera Cruz.''

"But, Tanner, I want—''

"I don't give a damn what you want, Caitlyn,'' he interrupted her quickly. "You broke a promise to me—a promise I extracted from you for your own safety. You willfully followed Sean and me down here for God knows what reason. I suppose you think your being here can help in some way in finding Brant, but I think you're deluding yourself, Caitlyn.''

"What do you mean?'' she asked him. "Why else would I come?''

His blue eyes touched her face, noting the wide-set eyes, the graceful curve of her jaw, the lovely mouth that he had tasted more than once. "I told you before that I didn't want you coming down to Mexico with me, Caitlyn, because I couldn't be held responsible for my actions toward you. You came anyway, Caitlyn. *You came because you wanted me.*''

He heard her sharp intake of breath, saw the quickened pulse at the base of her throat. "I—I came—because of Brant,'' she whispered in a most unconvincing tone of voice.

He stepped forward and caught her swiftly in his arms, forcing her to lean her head back into the crook of his elbow as he stared down into her face. "You're only lying to yourself,'' he said in a soft voice. "You want me, Caitlyn, more than you've ever wanted Brant.''

"I—I came to Australia to find Brant,'' she reminded him weakly.

"You were a girl then, hardly a woman, but now you are a woman, Caitlyn,'' he reminded her. "And this time you've come to Mexico to find *me.*''

"No, you're wrong, you—''

He laughed softly. "Am I? Then why don't you scream, why don't you tell me that it's Brant you love? Sean is in the room across the hall; you could call for him to come and he would.'' His free hand came up and began to unbutton the remaining

buttons of her dress. "No, it's much too late, isn't it? We are finally alone and no one will come to your rescue this time, Caitlyn. There will be no interruptions, no graceful way for you to get away from me. If you want to get away, you will have to tell me that you don't want me, Caitlyn."

She was silent as she stared up at him, her huge eyes registering confusion, fear, but more than that an awakening realization that what he said was true. All the old arguments wouldn't work anymore. Any thought of her husband, her family, her moral upbringing were swept away. She trembled with her sudden need for this man and her face registered her desire.

"Caitlyn, I've wanted you for so long, and I've waited for this moment longer than I've ever waited for anyone or anything else." He brought his mouth down to hers, molding it with an exquisite mastery that took her breath away.

They kissed slowly, thoroughly, tasting the texture and scent of each others' mouths as they parted lips and sent their tongues inside to explore with delicate passion. As they kissed, his hand returned to the buttons of her gown so that when the last ones were undone, he could open her dress and slip the bodice from her shoulders, pushing it past her waist so that it pooled on the floor. Her petticoats were next and when she stepped out of them, she turned slightly in his arms so that he could untie the laces of her corset. Clad only in her thin chemise and stockings, she stood before him, her breath coming in gasps as though she'd run for miles. She was trembling so that she was afraid she might fall, but he came forward once more and held her against him, and she could feel that he was trembling too.

"You've made me wait too long for this moment," he whispered against the sweetness of her coppery curls, "and now I want you so badly I'm afraid I'll hurt you."

"You won't hurt me," she told him gently. "I love you, Tanner."

He groaned with the force of his passion and reached up abruptly to strip away her chemise, pulling it down and bringing the stockings with it so that she was naked. He stepped back and caressed her with his eyes as though memorizing every inch of her. Then he picked her up and laid her gently on the bed, standing away so that he could strip himself of his clothing.

A sudden shyness came over her as she watched him undress. But she realized that there was no need for shyness now. His body was beautiful, his chest wide and furred with dark springy

curls that tapered to his groin, his muscles corded and tense as he stood in front of her.

"Come to me, Tanner," she whispered with shy eagerness, holding out her arms to him.

Immediately he lay beside her, gathering her close against him as he rained tender kisses on her face and neck. His hands moved to caress her breasts while his tongue reached inside her mouth to taste its sweetness, running along the edge of her teeth and dancing with her own tongue so that she felt her passion running higher. His fingers brushed the sensitive peaks of her breasts, bringing the nipples to attention and then squeezing them gently between finger and thumb.

Caitlyn was reeling in this new world of sensual fantasy. Never had Brant taken such infinite care with her, never had he used foreplay to bring her to the edge of crazed desire. This man was a master at his art, using her body like a delicate instrument on which to play the music of love. She sensed he was holding back his own raging desire to give her time to be completely ready for him and for that she loved him even more. As his head followed his hands to her breasts, she arched forward, offering her flesh to him, sighing deeply when he took the turgid points into his mouth and suckled each of them with loving attention. His hands worked the flesh of her breasts into his mouth as his teeth nipped gently at the bursting peaks, making her squirm with building desire.

Not taking his mouth from her breasts, he let his hands wander downward to her belly, sliding delicately over it to reach the point of coiled passion that lay between her thighs. With a sigh, she opened her legs to his questing hand, feeling it begin its tentative exploration. As his fingers parted the swelling flesh to touch the sensitive bud inside, Caitlyn moaned softly, feeling desire begin to overwhelm her. Unconsciously her hips strained to meet his hand, demanding something more than the slow teasing torture he was performing. As he sucked at the flesh of her breasts, she felt as though there must be some invisible thread joining her nipples to that place between her thighs that he was so busily satisfying with his fingers.

With questing hand, he explored further, sliding his fingers gently into that part of her that was demanding satisfaction. With frenzied desire, Caitlyn pushed upward, her feet flat on the bed as he obeyed her silent command until she flopped downward, breathing rapidly, her head dizzy with the force of the tiny ex-

plosion inside of her. He withdrew his fingers and replaced them with his body, moving between her thighs so that she ached for the length of him deep within her.

Then he was kissing her again, with slow, hot kisses that fanned the flames of her raging desire so that she arched against him and cried aloud for him to oblige her passion by burying himself within her. She gasped as his body accepted him, clasping her knees around his ribs as he began to move. Smooth strokes drove her to the heights of frenzy as she felt the building inside of her, so different from her feelings with Brant. It felt as though she was going to stop breathing as she arched higher and higher to reach that pinnacle that she instinctively was striving for.

"Ah!" She held her breath and felt an explosion of feeling, desire, and passion that spread outward from her very core and made her throw her head back against the bed. "Tanner, oh, Tanner!" she breathed, overwhelmed by the force of her surrender to him.

His answer was to kiss her again, harder now as he reached for his own release. And then he was sending his warmth inside her, continuing to move sensually as he brought her back to another tiny explosion so that she clasped him hard about the neck and returned his kisses with equal passion.

When they had quieted, he lay next to her, brushing her hair back gently with his fingers and then tracing the lines of her face. She stared into his eyes and was surprised to see the look of pain in them. And then she knew what he was thinking.

"I wanted this," she told him fiercely, caressing the hair that curled against the nape of his neck. "Nothing will ever make this night shameful in my eyes."

He smiled gently. "Tomorrow you have to go back, Caitlyn. Tomorrow we may even find out where Brant is. If he's still alive, he will still be your husband." The pain seemed intensified in his eyes and he held her against him.

"No," she said tearfully. "I can't let you go, Tanner. I can't lose you now," she wept.

He held her face in his hands and kissed her tenderly, licking the tears from her cheeks. "I love you, Caitlyn," he told her. "I've loved you for so long, I can't remember the exact moment that I started." He sighed. "I want to tell you this now, so that you'll know that I'll never stop loving you no matter what happens."

She lay against him and wept soft tears that trickled down his chest. "Love shouldn't have to cause pain," she said thickly. "Why was I too stubborn to see your love, Tanner? I was such a fool."

"Hush, my darling. It does no one any good to blame themselves. Destiny plays tricks with us sometimes and somehow love gets tangled up with greed and selfishness and the very human desire to have things run in an orderly fashion in our lives. You've wanted to be mistress of a great plantation and the wife of a man—"

"No, no," she cried, holding him tightly. "I want no one but you, Tanner."

He kissed her hungrily and already she could feel the tingling tension inside of her that signaled desire beginning to spread. She wanted him again. She wanted as much of him as she could have in the time they had left. He sensed her passions and pushed her gently on her back, trailing kisses down her throat and to her breasts, going lower to caress the silken skin of her belly with his lips and tongue. Lower still, his mouth reached the juncture of her thighs and Caitlyn cried out with wonder and delight at this new sensation he was giving her. Her blood ran hotter in her veins as she tossed her head mindlessly with passion. As his hands reached beneath her to cup her buttocks and press her heated core to his eager mouth, Caitlyn arched passionately against him, blindly seeking blessed relief from this exquisite torture.

And when she was soaked with perspiration and his saliva and her own love moisture, he moved forward once more and slid the length of himself inside her aching passage, causing delightful twinges of satisfaction to run up inside her belly. Wild with her own need, she kissed him hungrily, greedily, as he moved inside her, bringing her again and again to the crest of some mysterious wave of feeling until finally that wave broke against the shore of her passion and she cried aloud at the wonder and depth of her body's reaction to him.

Slowly, she came back from the dizzying heights of sensual bliss to find him staring at her with a wry grin. "You, my darling, are one hell of a woman!" he informed her.

She smiled and kissed him. "Only with you, my love."

He smiled back, but his eyes were clouded. He was silent, not wanting to break the spell of their sensual cocoon. He gathered

her close against him, wondering how in the world he was going to let her go the next morning.

They were both awakened by a hard knocking on the door. As sleep left her, Caitlyn was aware of Tanner's strong arm holding her tightly against the length of his body and for a moment she gloried in their mutual possession. But the moment passed quickly with the sight of the early morning light and the sound of Sean Flynn's voice through the door.

"Tanner, for God's sake, wake up in there! Rafael's brought news of Sinclair's whereabouts!"

Caitlyn felt her lover's body stiffen against her and she knew what he was thinking. Already, in the light of the dawn, she felt the first signs of shock at what she had done the night before. She had committed adultery with another man when her own husband might be languishing in prison under the worst conditions. For a terrified moment shame invaded her whole being, but then she felt Tanner's lips gently kissing the back of her neck where he'd pushed her hair aside.

"It's all right, my dearest," he whispered. He kissed her neck again, then turned her around to kiss her mouth. "I love you."

"I love you," she whispered back, clinging to him for a moment.

Already he was withdrawing, swinging his legs around to pad naked to the door. "Let me get dressed, Sean, and I'll meet you downstairs for breakfast," he called out.

The sound of Sean's boots retreating down the hall brought a sigh of relief from Caitlyn as she sat up in bed clutching the sheet around her. "I—I have nothing to wear," she said rather forlornly. "My dress was ripped last night."

Tanner glanced at her with a grin. "I'll find something for you to wear, although I'd much rather keep you naked in that bed waiting for me," he answered. He surprised her with his light mood before she realized that he was doing it for her sake, and she loved him all the more for his thoughtfulness.

She watched him get dressed and couldn't resist teasing him a little. "Goodness, you're not even taking a wash, my love. Are you so anxious to leave me?"

He smiled wickedly. "I *hate* to leave you, darling, but at least I'll still have your scent on me to remind me of our hours of lovemaking." He chuckled. "I'll walk down to breakfast with the smell of sex on me and poor Sean will go crazy."

She couldn't help the blush that suffused her cheeks at such bold talk. "Well, *I* can't walk downstairs with the smell of sex on me," she replied with sudden boldness of her own. "You must ask your hostess to send up something for me to bathe in and some clothes for me to wear."

He donned his boots and came swiftly to her, pulling her out of the sheets so that he could plant a hungry kiss on her mouth while his fingers wandered downward to that part of her that he had loved so well through the night. Caitlyn gasped as he slid questing fingers to where the coil of heated passion was building again. On her knees, she clung to him, her legs turned to jelly as he worked his magic.

"Ah, you are a wicked villain, Tanner!" she cried as she found a quick release.

"Wicked or not, I love you," he said, pushing her gently back down to the bed. He walked to the door and blew her a kiss before leaving.

Caitlyn lay back in the bed, tingling all over as she reveled in the feelings that were running hotly through her body. Then she sobered. Sean had said that they knew where Brant was. She couldn't go back to Brant after her night of revelations with Tanner! Tanner loved her! a voice inside her head spoke. But Brant loves you too; he married you, he gave you a child. At the thought of Maggie, her innocent daughter, Caitlyn burst into tears. Her time with Tanner was like some fairy tale, a fantasy with no substance. Maggie was part of her *real* life. Maggie and her parents, Riverhouse—and Brant. She turned in the bed and punched the pillow in frustration. She had dreamed and manipulated and schemed her way to being Brant's wife, to returning him to Riverhouse so that she would reign as its mistress. She'd gotten what she'd wanted, hadn't she?

Tanner had been right in not wanting her to come to Mexico. He had known that this night would happen. Caitlyn curled herself into a tight ball. She hadn't wanted to listen to his warning. She had come anyway—come to him, knowing that she would give herself to him finally.

Then she straightened. "Yes!" she said aloud, fiercely. "Yes!" She'd given herself to Tanner for one night and she would not shame the memory of that night with useless mewlings now. If life was unfair to bring her such glorious love only to take it away again, at least she had had it once. And she knew that to be loved by a man like Tanner would never be a shameful thing.

Proudly she stood up on the floor, shaking back her hair and smiling. "I am starving," she said aloud to the empty room. "And I want a bath and some new clothes. Then we'll see what the morning brings."

53

DRESSED IN THE white skirt and camisa of the Indian women of Mexico, Caitlyn descended the stairs and hurried into the dining room, feeling as though she were barely covered enough for decency. The blouse was low-necked and designed to fall artlessly off one shoulder, leaving the whole of her collarbone revealed. Beneath the gathered ruffle of the neckline, Caitlyn felt her breasts caressed by the white cotton, standing high and pointed, unused to so much freedom. The skirt reached to her ankles and was held at the waist with a colorfully printed sash that was knotted at the side. The shoes were nothing more than strips of leather fashioned into sandals that tied around her stockingless legs.

"Holy mother, you look beautiful this morning, little girl!" Rafael cried enthusiastically, his black eyes resting on her mouth with fond memory. "With your hair flowing loose down your back, one might take you for a gypsy woman."

Caitlyn blushed, not quite sure if she should thank him for the compliment. Instinctively she sought Tanner's eyes and found them watching her with mingled pride and possessiveness. When he held the dining chair for her, she felt his hand touch the flesh above her shoulder with the merest caress as though assuring himself that last night hadn't been a dream.

After the morning greetings, Sean got down to business. "Rafael has brought us news of your husband, Caitlyn. It seems he was set upon by Juáristas on the road from Vera Cruz. The bandits relieved him of his money and gave him the choice of joining them or death." At her look of surprise, he continued, "It's not so unusual, their method of recruiting. There's so many deserters on both sides that they constantly have to replace missing men."

"He is with the Juáristas, fighting with them?"

"Yes, señora," Rafael broke in, his eyes still wandering over

her with attention. "There are many mercenaries on both sides of this war; most are Americans."

"Word has leaked out that Napoleon III has ordered his French soldiers home. It seems this war has cost him more than he bargained for," Tanner observed with a touch of sarcasm. "He's given the French twelve months to pull out and once they leave, everyone feels it's only a matter of time before the Juáristas recapture Mexico City."

"But what does all this have to do with Brant?" Caitlyn asked pointedly. "You know that he is still alive then?" She dared not look at Tanner as she asked this question.

Rafael nodded. "Yes."

"And do you know where he is?"

Next to her, Sean took her hand gently. "He's imprisoned somewhere near Puebla. During a skirmish with the French, Brant was captured with some of the other Juáristas. The French have no love for American mercenaries, Caitlyn," he said in a low voice.

"What will happen to him?" she asked in a strangled voice, pushing her plate away, her appetite gone.

"He will be executed—unless we can get him out before then," Tanner said, his voice hard.

"Oh, my God!" Caitlyn put her face in her hands, feeling the weight of her love for Tanner as heavy as lead in her heart. She had lost herself to him last night in passion and now this morning her worst fears were realized. While she had been loving Tanner, Brant had been suffering in some horrible place, awaiting the order to be executed. With haggard eyes, she looked at the men at the table. "What chance do we have to get him out?"

Sean shrugged. "Rafael is going to take us there. We leave immediately."

"You must stay here," Tanner said gently. "There is no sense in you risking your life when there is nothing you can do."

"But what if he needs me?" she pleaded, choosing not to see the pain in Tanner's eyes. "What if he's sick, wounded? He'll need care."

"If we can get him out, we'll bring him straight back to Vera Cruz," Sean promised. "Tanner's right, lass. The road is too dangerous and I'll not risk anything happening to you."

Caitlyn could see that it would be useless to protest further. Warily, she stood up from the table and made her way upstairs to Tanner's room. She looked around in a daze. Before long her

husband would be in this room with her, if he was still alive. At the thought of lying with him in that same bed where she had made love with Tanner, her heart shriveled. How could she ever look at Brant again? How could she live with him and not reveal what had transformed her last night? Tanner had been right, he had been right. She should not have come to Mexico.

His step in the room made her turn swiftly, her eyes frightened like those of a doe caught in a trap. Tanner saw the expressions flit across her face and his heart went out to her. She *was* caught in a trap—a trap that he had set for her with his love. And yet, he would not have wished away last night for the world. He loved her too much.

"We're leaving, Caitlyn," he said in a quiet voice that helped to steady her careening feelings.

"Tanner, you—you'll bring Brant back to me, won't you?" she asked flatly. "Despite your love for me, you'll bring him back, just as you forced him to marry me when it was *you* who really loved me!"

He nodded. "I won't have your love changed to hatred, Caitlyn."

She turned away. "But you know that last night—that we can never have that again."

"I know."

For a few moments they stood looking at each other, each reliving the passions of the night before. Then Tanner walked toward her and took her into his arms, pressing her yielding body against him so that he could feel the sweet length of her one last time. With infinite tenderness, his mouth caught hers and held it in one last, long kiss that held all the longing, the bittersweetness of their love for each other. And then, without a word, he turned and hurried out the door, leaving her to stand in the room, feeling as though she had lost her soul.

The days that followed seemed to lengthen beyond bearing for Caitlyn as she waited in the boarding house for word of her husband. There was very little to do beyond eating and sleeping and perhaps a little conversation with her American hostess when the latter was so inclined. Caitlyn found herself longing for her family, longing for home and Maggie. She hated this city of ill winds and tropical heat and could hardly wait to get out of it.

Sometimes, in desperation, she thought of running away with Tanner, leaving all that was dear to her in Louisiana and going

off to be with him. But she knew he would never allow her to do such a thing. She could never leave her daughter.

Pacing back and forth in the room, she wondered what would happen when she and Brant met again after so many months apart. Their marriage had already begun to crumble before he left. She wondered if this separation would strengthen it, or tear them even further apart. Surely if he had really tried to escape his Juárista captors, he could have. If he had really wanted to return to her and Maggie, he would have done anything to make it possible. Did Brant no longer love her? And what of that love for him that had held her heart for so long? Had she ever really loved him at all—had she ever even understood him? Their marriage had been a matter of honor because of the foolishness of a headstrong girl, the willfulness of a spoiled heart who had thought that any man she loved must love her in return. In her vanity, she had caused pain for so many—for Connie, for her parents, for Brant, and especially for Tanner who had watched her marry a man whom he knew did not want her.

There were moments when she felt tears gathering, tears of self-pity for her own stupidity. She had always thought she could make her own destiny, mold it to her will as though it were made of malleable clay. But always, fate had nudged and pushed her toward Tanner—so many times he had been the one to comfort her, even from the very first when he had come into the garden after a New Orleans ball to offer her his handkerchief. Still, she had been too stubborn to see, too certain of her own will to change her charted course. Now she would pay the price. She would remain wife to a man who didn't want her, mistress of a plantation that was haunted by the ghosts of an old man and his young wife. But she had no one to blame but herself. It had all been her own doing. She had thrown away the possibility of a happy future with both hands, laughing at fate, thumbing her nose at destiny. Fate had certainly gotten the last laugh, she thought ruefully.

Except, she *did* have Maggie, and for that she was grateful. Thoughts of her daughter made her loneliness even worse and she longed to hold her in her arms again. Each morning she waited hopefully for news, growing ever more anxious to leave this place behind and return to her own flesh and blood.

Finally, news came.

She had been in Vera Cruz more than two weeks, waiting in the boarding house, when a messenger came to the door with a

brief note for her. Eagerly, she opened the envelope, telling herself that any news was better than not knowing.

"Will return within a week," she read and then pressed her finger gently to Tanner's signature on the bottom of the paper.

Five days passed. Caitlyn was in the patio of the house, trying to escape from the heat and humidity, fanning herself next to the gay little fountain that bubbled in the center of the patio. Her landlady had found her some more clothes—some skirts and blouses which, Caitlyn had to admit, were much cooler than the black bombazine and corsets she had packed away in her stolen trunks. She almost laughed to think what the fourteen-year-old boy might have done with his stolen booty—certainly those things were of no use to anyone in this hot and sweaty climate.

She heard men's voices inside the house. The fan dropped from her suddenly nerveless fingers and she stood up, pressing her hands to the white material of her skirt and wondering what she would say to her husband. Trying to compose her face, she waited nervously, not knowing whether she should stay where she was or run inside to greet them.

And then she saw Tanner's tall figure, standing in the archway of the patio entrance. She tried frantically to push down the rush of emotions that made her want to run to him and throw her arms around him. He was not smiling and she hoped that he would not be there to witness her reunion with Brant.

"Caitlyn." His voice caressed her name for a moment.

"Tanner? You—you shouldn't be here when Brant comes," she said quietly, her eyes beseeching him to go.

And then Sean Flynn was standing next to Tanner and his kind eyes were filled with grief as he prepared himself to give her his news. "Caitlyn, my dear child," he said softly, "your husband—"

"Yes? Where is he?" Caitlyn asked with sudden fearful impatience.

"Brant is dead, Caitlyn," Tanner returned painfully.

Both men hurried toward her, afraid she might fall in a faint, but Caitlyn held her hands out in front of her as though to ward them off. "No!" She shook her head. Then she sat down in the seat she had just vacated, keeping a strong hold on her emotions as she stared at both men with bleak, suddenly hard eyes. "Tell me," she said.

Sean wiped a hand across his brow, shaking his head and

avoiding the hard stare she gave him. "There was an escape planned by the Juáristas who were imprisoned with Brant," he explained. "From what we were able to learn from the French officers inside the prison, dynamite was smuggled in some way and used to blow away part of the prison wall. A fire broke out and spread to the ammunition store causing a series of explosions. Brant must have been knocked unconscious during the initial explosion and then the fire . . ." He stopped, unwilling to continue, looking to Tanner for help.

"Dozens of bodies were burned by the fire," Tanner went on. He watched her struggling to hold on to the emotions that were tearing her apart. He wanted desperately to go to her, to hold her and let her cry against him. But he realized he couldn't do that as she stared back at him, stiff and wooden, looking through him as though he weren't there. "The captain in charge of the prison had all the bodies thrown into a communal grave. It—it would have been impossible to identify any one of them, he told us."

"Then, he might be alive still!" Caitlyn said hopefully. Oh, let him be alive, she prayed, to take this terrible burden of guilt away from me.

Tanner stepped closer and took something out of his pocket. She looked at it and gasped in horror. It was the signet ring that Brant had worn on his left finger, bequeathed to him when William had died. Trembling, Caitlyn took the ring and stared at it.

"This was the only piece of jewelry found on any of the bodies," Tanner explained. "The captain had kept it, but when I saw it—on his finger—I realized I had seen it somewhere before. It came to me that I had seen it on William's finger those times that we'd played chess together." The captain had been loathe to part with the piece, but had been "persuaded" after seeing the gold glinting in Tanner's palm.

"Then it must be true," Caitlyn said tonelessly, curling her fingers around the ring and holding it in her clenched fist. She stood up. She walked past both men as though they had suddenly become invisible. Then at the entrance to the house, she turned. "You . . . were not able to bring back his remains to be buried properly?" Her lip trembled noticeably and the tears had begun to gather in her eyes.

Tanner shook his head sadly. "It would have been difficult," he acknowledged, unable to meet her eyes.

She nodded with understanding, then disappeared from the

patio, leaving the two men to look mutely at each other, wondering what to do to help her.

54

IT HAD BEEN over a month since Caitlyn had returned home from Vera Cruz, returned with the sad news of Brant's death. Her parents had been incredulous. Timothy had blustered about the ferocity of the Mexicans and Margaret had tried to comfort her daughter who had looked so terribly sad, her dark blue eyes vacant with grief.

At Riverhouse, Connie and Jesse had been keenly aware of the change in Caitlyn. The old animation seemed to have been sucked dry by the heat of Mexico and they couldn't understand why Caitlyn's grief didn't abate after such a long time. Of course they missed Brant and they shared her grief, but both knew it was not like Caitlyn to become so disinterested in life.

They couldn't know the guilt she felt. Caitlyn could not stop hating herself for betraying her husband while he had been suffering in that prison. She tried to tell herself that she hated Tanner for forcing her to admit the love between them, but then she realized that she could never hate him. She loved him still—and that was why she hated herself all the more. Despite the realization that Brant had died in such awful circumstances, Caitlyn could not stop thinking about Tanner. At night, her dreams were filled with him and she would awaken, bathed in sweat, hating herself for her crude passions.

Only with Maggie did she feel secure. She showered all her love on the child, telling herself that without a father, Maggie must never feel deprived. She would love her enough for two people, she swore, and proceeded to spend most of her waking hours with her daughter, shutting out the other people who loved her.

Tanner had stopped in New Orleans on his way back to Boston. He had ridden up to Mornhaven to pay his respects to the O'Rourkes and then gone to Riverhouse to see Caitlyn, but she refused to see him. "Tell him I can't possibly see him, Connie," she told her sister. "I am still in deepest mourning for my husband."

It was hard for Connie to have to face the man that she instinc-

tively knew loved her older sister deeply. She'd given him the message and watched his eyes grow dark with some inner pain. Then he'd ridden away, staying only long enough to congratulate her and Jesse on the birth of their new son, James. Living with Caitlyn, Connie reflected sadly, was like living with a ghost these days. She would wander the house like some wraith, a pitiful shadow of the woman she used to be.

Summer came and went. Jesse struggled with the cotton fields, proving himself a much better farmer than either Brant or his father, but this only seemed to strengthen Caitlyn's grief and guilt. Brant, she remembered, had always thought of Riverhouse as hanging from some heavy chain around his neck. He hadn't gotten much joy from it, she reflected sadly, nor from her, she supposed. And the guilt would flood her until she could barely stand it, shutting herself in her room to weep her heart out. But the dreams of Tanner continued and she couldn't lie to herself about her love for him.

Days blended into weeks and then into months and Caitlyn struggled with her conscience and tried to give herself time to heal. The new year of 1867 came and on Maggie's second birthday, newspapers from New Orleans announced that there was a last-gasp battle being fought in Mexico between the Emperor Maximilian and his followers, and the superior forces of Juárez. Without quite knowing why, Caitlyn followed the news of the battle at Querétaro eagerly, until finally, two and a half months after it started, the battle was won by the Juáristas. She felt the icy hold on her heart begin to thaw at the news that those who had been behind Brant's death would finally be punished.

For the first time since she'd arrived back at Riverhouse from her brief trip to Mexico, Caitlyn began to take an interest in things around her. Jesse was flabbergasted when he looked up one morning from going over the accounts at Riverhouse to see Caitlyn staring at him, hands on hips, demanding to see what he'd been doing to Riverhouse finances while she'd been "indisposed." For a moment Jesse had thought she was really angry, but then, to his complete surprise, she'd winked at him conspiratorially and told him he was probably a much better manager than she'd ever be.

Dressed in a black gown, but without the suffocating veil she'd been used to wearing, Caitlyn asked one of the men in the stables to hitch up the light carriage for her so that she could take her daughter on a drive over to Mornhaven. Coming outside

quickly at Jesse's hurried suggestion, Connie had been surprised to see Caitlyn dressed in her riding gloves and one of her old bonnets, settling Maggie in the seat next to her in preparation of a drive.

"Caitlyn, are you sure you'll be all right?" Connie asked anxiously, wondering if the many months of guilt had finally caused her sister's mind to snap.

"I'm fine, Connie," Caitlyn returned with a brilliant smile. "Balls of fire!" she laughed upon seeing the nervous look in Connie's eyes. "I'm not going to run myself into the river, you goose. I'm just going over to see Mama. I'll be back by dinner."

And she had gone off jauntily, leaving Connie caught between tears and laughter at the realization that somehow her sister had finally healed herself of whatever it was that had been plaguing her.

Caitlyn looked around her with shining eyes as she guided the cart down the oyster shell drive of Riverhouse and onto the river road. Through the summer green of the cypress and willows along the river bank, she could see the mighty Mississippi flowing muddily down toward New Orleans. Ah, she thought, gazing down at her auburn-haired daughter who was clapping her hands in delight at getting to ride in the cart with her mother, she had forgotten what life really meant for too many months. She had been foolish to have shut herself off from the world and from those who loved her. She didn't think Brant would have wanted her to become an old widow, worn and shriveled inside who could no longer laugh at life and revel in its surprises. No, Brant had never been a farmer, but he had certainly appreciated a good adventure. He would never have wanted her to give up the adventure of life!

Upon arrival at Mornhaven, she swung herself down from the cart, brushing away the helping hands of the man her father employed to look after his horses. She picked up Maggie and set her on the ground, proud to see the chubby little legs beneath her short dress as they carried her unerringly to where her grandparents were seated on the veranda, watching the events with something like shock.

"Caitlyn, girl, what's got into you?" Timothy demanded, rising to pick up Maggie as she launched her small body straight at him.

"Mama's happy again!" Maggie lisped, beaming at her grandfather out of eyes the same color as his own.

Margaret rose to take her daughter in her arms. "Caitlyn, you look yourself again," she cried. "What has happened?"

"Nothing has happened," Caitlyn laughed, "except that I've decided I was being foolish to let life go by without a good fight. I suppose I've too much of Papa's blood in me to just twiddle my thumbs while there is so much to be enjoyed." Then she sobered as she looked into her mother's eyes. She turned to watch her father take Maggie down the veranda steps for a little walk to the vegetable garden, then faced her mother once more. "I was so confused, Mama. Confused about my marriage to Brant, his death—my feelings for Tanner Malone."

"Ah." Margaret nodded wisely and sat down in her chair, watching her daughter with fond expectation. "You know Tanner Malone came by to visit us here before he returned to Boston last year. It was written so plainly on his face when he spoke of you how much he loves you, my dear. He was in such terrible pain about your grief over Brant's death."

"I know," Caitlyn said quietly. "I was cruel to him, Mama, when he came to see me at Riverhouse. I refused even to see him. It was cowardly of me."

"Perhaps, but you needed time for yourself, Caitlyn," Margaret answered wisely. "When life deals us a terrible blow, I think the mind turns itself off to life for a little while to allow itself time to heal."

"But it—it wasn't just grief over Brant's death," Caitlyn said softly, looking into her mother's face. "It was guilt too. Guilt because Tanner and I—"

"Hush, no, don't tell me," Margaret interrupted gently. "There's no need. You've punished yourself enough, Caitlyn, and as you've already found out, it's time to go on with life."

"Oh, I'm so glad you understand," Caitlyn breathed, hugging her mother tightly. "I couldn't have borne it if you—"

"It doesn't matter what *I* think, my dear, but what *you* think—of yourself, of Tanner, of your plans for the future."

"The future," Caitlyn echoed, looking away for a moment. Then she turned back to Margaret's anxious face. "Do you think he would come if I wrote him?" She blushed painfully. "I mean, the way I've treated him—and without one letter to let him know how I feel. He might have given up on me."

Margaret laughed. "My poor darling, you still haven't learned much about men." She reached up to stroke her daughter's

cheek. "But I have an idea that Tanner Malone is the one to further your education."

55

FOR THE HUNDREDTH TIME, Caitlyn eyed herself in the mirror of her bedroom, gazing at her face, the hollows in her cheeks, the dark blue eyes beneath the slanting eyebrows that broke the creaminess of her complexion. She stepped back, feeling as nervous as a young debutante attending her first cotillion. Heavens, she had lost so much weight during her time of mourning over Brant, she thought, critically surveying the way her dress hung on her figure. She had taken off the deep black of the last eighteen months and permitted herself to wear moss green and lavender day dresses that were less severe—and certainly more fashionable. She hadn't seen Tanner in all that time, but today he was supposed to arrive at Riverhouse. She had written him a lengthy letter two months before, trying to explain all that had happened, although it had been terribly hard. She had felt clumsy writing her feelings on paper, but had told herself that if Tanner loved her as much as she hoped, he would see through the awkward lines to how she really felt.

His note back to her had been short, expressing his gladness that she was recovering and that all was well with her. Not exactly the note of a lover, Caitlyn had thought subjectively, trying desperately to keep her fears at bay. But at least he had written that he would come. And here it was, the appointed day. She rushed to the window to glance out at the cloudless, blue October sky. Her eyes narrowed as they followed the drive down to the river, hoping to see a rider.

"Caitlyn, dear, I thought I would take Maggie with me over to Mornhaven," Connie called from the hallway. Caitlyn turned around to see her sister with James on her hip, holding Maggie's little hand. "She's been begging to see her grandpa and since I'm going with James anyway, I thought you wouldn't mind."

"No, of course not. Perhaps it would be better," Caitlyn mused.

Connie smiled at her. "I can't remember ever seeing you so nervous," she admitted with a giggle. "Always you were the one in cool control of your emotions, Caitlyn. It seems you've

found someone who can reach behind that barrier.'' She came closer, her soft blue eyes teasing. ''Didn't I tell you such a long time ago that Tanner Malone was someone worthy of your interest?''

''Yes, you did, Connie,'' Caitlyn sighed. ''All I could see was a Boston Yankee, unfortunately.''

''Mmm, maybe so, but you weren't all that impervious to him even then,'' Connie went on with a touch of smugness.

''I could have saved so many people a lot of pain and heartache if I'd listened to your advice back then and taken more of an interest in Tanner,'' Caitlyn agreed. For a moment, regret touched her heart, but she shook it away firmly.

''We all don't get a second chance,'' Connie told her soberly. ''Destiny's been kind to you, Caitlyn, although I have no idea why,'' she added with another teasing giggle. ''Stubborn and willful, I used to think you'd never find true happiness. I'm praying that you'll find it with Tanner Malone.''

''Thank you, Connie,'' Caitlyn said, touched more than she would admit. She pressed her sister's hand, kissed Maggie and waved them out the door.

Then she rushed back to the window, disappointed that there was still no one on the road. She glanced back in the mirror, patting the soft coiffure that she'd done up with her sister's help, smoothing the moss green bodice of her dress. Well, it would do no good staring morosely into the mirror every five minutes, she thought practically. She might as well go downstairs to await Tanner's arrival.

She stood on the veranda and watched Connie and the children off, with Lindy keeping a close eye on them from the back of the cart. Jesse was out in the fields, for it was one of the busiest times of the year. For a moment, she spared a thought for the cotton crop, hoping that the yield would be higher this year, for Jesse's sake. He had toiled hard to bring about a good crop. She realized, with sudden inspiration, that Jesse loved this land more than Brant had ever loved it—as much as William had loved it. The thought came to her that she would not be foolish to leave this place to Jesse Cobb should Tanner come for her and want her to go back to Boston with him. Certainly there was plenty of gold left for Maggie's inheritance from her father and, somehow, the idea of burdening the little girl with the thought that all this responsibility would someday be hers was depressing to Caitlyn. She had fought so long and hard for Riverhouse that

she realized she no longer wanted that fight continued by her daughter. Reconstruction had finally come to the South with a vengeance and it was a burden she didn't want to pick up. Jesse seemed capable of handling it. Caitlyn smiled suddenly with soft irony. How funny that *she* had always envisioned *herself* as mistress of Riverhouse and yet, now she was proposing to make Connie its mistress, the very thing she had fought against so foolishly many years before.

She looked out toward the road once more and this time was rewarded by the sight of a lone rider coming at a slow trot toward the drive. Tanner! She felt herself trembling nervously. She had last seen him from one of the lighters off Vera Cruz as it rowed her to the American ship that stood in the harbor. Now he was coming toward her and she felt all the shyness, all the indecision of a schoolgirl. Feeling giddy, she pressed her damp hands to her skirt and licked her dry lips with a nervous tongue.

She stood there, waiting for him, letting her eyes grow used to him as he came ever closer. She could hear the quick thudding of her heart against her chest, wondering suddenly what she could possibly say to him after all these months. Panic seeped into her bones and she pushed it back with an effort as he stopped his horse in front of her and looked down at her from its height.

As she watched numbly, unable to say a word, he dismounted the horse and strode toward her, taking off his hat and flinging it carelessly to the chair beside her. In one fell swoop, he gathered her shaking body in his arms and proceeded to kiss her thoroughly, crushing her in his arms as though he would never let her go. His mouth demanded surrender from her and she opened her lips obediently, feeling his questing tongue plunge inside. They kissed so long Caitlyn felt as though her breath had been sucked from her body and she pushed her head away just a little in order to stop the world from tilting crazily around her.

"I think I'm going to faint," she protested, opening her eyes to see his blazing down into hers with a blue fire that spoke of his enduring love for her.

"Damn it, I'd like to make you faint," he grinned, "but more than that I'd like to make love to you, Caitlyn. You've made me wait for you too damn long, woman."

Everyone thought it seemed an indecent time before the widow, Caitlyn Sinclair, announced her engagement to that Yankee rogue, Tanner Malone. Many of the former plantation own-

ers remembered Mr. Malone from before the war and reconstruction, and some of the matrons whispered behind their hands that there had always been *something* between him and Caitlyn. It shocked them even more when the news became common knowledge that Caitlyn was deeding her dead husband's plantation to her sister and brother-in-law. Not that most of them didn't think it was a wonderful gesture since it was plain to see that Jesse had a way with cotton, and certainly no one wanted a Yankee trying to raise cotton in the Red River Valley. It was bad enough with those Yankee scalawags and carpetbaggers flowing down like the plague these days. No, it would be much better for Caitlyn Sinclair to take her Yankee husband and go back to Boston, or wherever it was they were going to go.

As the time for the wedding drew near, most of the neighbors relented enough to accept an invitation to the wedding. After all, it meant free food and drink and God knew that was hard enough to come by these days. By the week before the wedding which was scheduled for the first of April, cards had been flowing like fresh snow on the silver tray in the foyer of Riverhouse. Preparation went along briskly, for Caitlyn was anxious to have the formality of the ceremony over. It was hard enough, she thought with a giggle, to steal a few moments of love here and there with everyone always about. She knew how hard-pressed Tanner was to hide his desire for her and she went about with her cheeks flushed constantly, hoping Connie and Jesse didn't guess at the reason.

Sean Flynn had come up from New Orleans to stand as best man for Tanner, and with his presence in Riverhouse it became harder still to find a private place to express their love for each other.

"Are you truly happy, my love?" Caitlyn asked Tanner one evening as they rearranged their clothing after a love tryst beneath the willows by the river.

He laughed ruefully. "I'd be happier if we didn't have to make love out here by the water. The mosquitoes are terrible. God help me, it's hard to concentrate on your pleasure, my dear, when I've got a dozen of those bloodthirsty little varmints on my backside!"

"I'm jealous of them," she laughed brazenly.

He leaned down and kissed her hard. "I can't imagine why. You know damn good and well that every part of me is yours, my love."

It was the last day of March. The rider that came up the river road remembered that today was Caitlyn Sinclair's birthday. She would be—let's see—twenty-five today, he thought in some surprise. Had it really been ten years since he'd first met her so long ago, he wondered with a shake of his head. His face, beneath the hat he wore, boasted a new beard and a deep tan that spoke of hours in the sun. He was quite a handsome man with his dark hair and muscled body, but in the dark, restless eyes there was a deep sadness as he tried not to think of the woman and son he had left behind in Mexico.

Brant Sinclair halted his horse for a moment and stared at the river that ran alongside the road. Had it really been three years since he'd last looked out at the familiar waters that poured into the Gulf of Mexico? Time had become jumbled in his mind since he'd been imprisoned at Puebla, he realized. Or was it that he'd chosen not to think about the time flying so swiftly by? After all, he'd had Elena and most recently his son, William. He pressed a shaking hand to his face, trying not to see the tears staining Elena's dusky cheeks, the sadness in her dark eyes as she'd held their son against her breast. He had promised her he would be back but he had seen how the disbelief had crept into her beautiful eyes. He stared out at the river and wondered at the long road that had finally seen him back here, in the land he had been born to.

He no longer lied to himself about that time when he had gone off to ransom his friend Tanner Malone. He had looked forward to escaping this place, escaping the smothering feeling he had that he was tied forever to Riverhouse. He had not thought about Caitlyn's feelings—God knew, she had wanted the place more than he, he thought with irony.

After his initial fear when he'd been captured by the Juárista guerilla band, he had looked upon his initiation into Mexican banditry as something of an adventure. He had never known such freedom. He slept under the stars, rode under the blazing sun every day. He'd come to admire many of the others in the band as he slowly came to realize that they were fighting for their country's independence from a decadent European country that had had no place in trying to push an Austrian Emperor upon them. Francisco, the leader of the band, had become a friend. When he had tacitly given his approval for Brant to court

Elena, Brant had truly felt himself a brother-in-arms with the group.

Elena! Ah, she was such a beauty, he thought despairingly. From the beginning, when he had seen her cooking in front of her brother's campfire, he had wanted her. Black hair that reached to her waist, eyes as velvety-soft as midnight—she had captured his heart as easily as her brother had captured his money during the raid. And she had been drawn to him too—shyly at first because she had been a maiden, but then when their love had finally exploded in one passionate encounter she had not tried to hide her desire for him.

When he had been imprisoned with her brother and several others in Puebla, it had been Elena who had formulated the plan for their escape. Unfortunately, the plan had not been carried out as well as they had hoped. He had lost consciousness in the first explosion. There had been a terrible fire after that, but all he remembered was waking up much later to find Elena's lovely face hovering fearfully over him. She had told him that they had found him half-dead and naked, for one of the guards had thought him dead and had stripped him of all his possessions. He had regretted the loss of his father's ring, but had been happy to find that he had survived to come back to Elena.

In the months that followed, he'd grown stronger. His love for Elena had grown stronger too. She never badgered him to make something better of himself, like Caitlyn had always done. Elena accepted him for what he was and loved him for himself. All that she required was that he love her back. They had fought together for her cause and it had gradually become his cause too.

There had been the final battle at Querétaro where Maximilian had made his final stand. Brant had to admit that the man had fought bravely, holding out against vastly superior forces for longer than anyone would have guessed. When finally he had surrendered, Brant had cheered along with the rest of the forces loyal to Juárez.

Although he loved Elena deeply, after the days of battle and excitement, he had begun to think of Riverhouse and Caitlyn and Maggie. Guilt began to overwhelm him as he realized that he hadn't given a thought to his own daughter for so long. Not even a letter to Caitlyn to let her know that he was still alive. For all she knew, he was long dead. He tried to explain to Elena

that he must go back to see about his daughter, but she had told him happily that she was going to have his child, that their child would take the place of the child he had left in the United States. Reluctantly, Brant had given his promise not to leave until after the baby was born.

Upon the arrival of his son, Brant had been ecstatically happy. He'd kissed Elena proudly and proclaimed that he couldn't be more happy. And yet, he realized that he couldn't go on living this way. He had to go back to sort out his life. It was unfair to Elena and to Caitlyn.

Heartbroken, Elena had listened to his promise to come back, but the tears in her eyes had spoken of her disbelief. When he had finally gone, Brant had looked back at them and had felt a hard tug on his heart at the sight of them both. Fighting the urge to run back to them, he had turned his horse toward Vera Cruz where he would take ship for the port of New Orleans. The memory of Elena's sad, dark eyes burned in his memory and he found himself walking his horse more and more slowly.

As he came to the turn in the road that would bring him to Riverhouse, he hesitated. Something made him lead his horse through the oaks that edged the lawn. He needed more time before he could face Caitlyn, he realized. As he rode, his thoughts wandered, and he began to remember things that had been long buried. Running along the lawn when he'd been a child, learning how to climb a tree among these old oaks, kissing Caitlyn beneath an ancient elm. Although the memories had the power to make him smile, they could not pull at his heart like his more recent memories of Elena and his son.

As he moved his horse among the trees, he saw suddenly, in the distance, a man and a woman walking together. The woman looked up to the man whose entire body seemed to yearn toward her. She laughed softly and the sound floated over the still air to where Brant had stopped his horse to watch them. He could see that the man was tall and handsomely built, the woman slender, her coppery auburn hair catching a glint of sunshine through the leafy canopy over their heads. And then, as Brant watched closely, the two people came together in a sweet embrace, their mouths reaching hungrily, their arms clasping each other possessively.

Against all reason, Brant felt sudden, swift anger, for he recognized the two lovers now. His best friend and his wife, he

thought grimly. He watched them unclasp and walk farther on, back toward the house. He tensed to urge his horse forward.

But before he could do so, a rider surprised him from behind and he whirled around in his saddle to see a big man watching him with a mixture of curiosity and wariness.

"What are you doing here?" the man asked, his eyes narrowing slightly at the sight of this bearded stranger. "You're on private property and we don't take kindly to trespassers 'round here."

"Who are you?" Brant demanded suspiciously.

The big man seemed taken aback by such a pointed question. "The name's Sean Flynn and I'm a friend of Mrs. Sinclair and her betrothed, Tanner Malone. Why were you sitting here just now, watching them?"

"Her betrothed!" Brant looked back at the pair that was just disappearing around the side of the house. Then he sighed heavily, his anger leaving him as quickly as it had come. "I'm Mrs. Sinclair's husband," he said quietly.

Sean Flynn nearly fell from his horse. "What the hell? Mrs. Sinclair is a widow. Her husband was killed in Mexico."

Brant shook his head. "I wasn't killed in Mexico."

"But we looked for Sinclair. Found the prison he tried to escape from, but the French officer told us there'd been a fire. The bodies were too charred to identify," Sean rushed, somehow believing this tired-looking man whose eyes had burned so brilliantly for a moment when he'd seen the couple embrace. "You can't really be Brant Sinclair. We found his father's ring, on a body burned in the fire."

"Someone had stolen my ring," Brant explained wearily. Ah, he thought, how easily the pieces fell into place now. He looked at the other man and his eyes were bleak. "I *am* Brant Sinclair."

"Damn it, man, why didn't you let her know you were still alive!" Sean burst out. "She nearly died of her grief and guilt. She'd come to Mexico to help search for you and it took her more than a year to find happiness again."

"Happiness with Tanner Malone," Brant put in. He shook his head. "I think I knew all along that Tanner loved her."

"And she loves him," Sean put in with a challenge in his voice.

Brant looked at him, wondering at the protective note about him.

"They are to be married tomorrow," Sean put in grimly. "Lucky you came today to prevent her from committing bigamy." There was utter sadness in his voice now. Sadness for his friend, Tanner, whom he knew loved Caitlyn more than anything else in this world. And sadness for Caitlyn, herself, who had finally found the man she was destined for. What right, he wondered, did this man have to come now when all he could bring was unhappiness?

"*Why* did you come back?" Sean wondered curiously.

Brant laughed ironically. "I came back because I thought it was my duty."

"Then you don't love Caitlyn any more?"

Brant shrugged. "Yes, I love Caitlyn, but not in the way she needs. I could never love her as Tanner loves her." His thoughts turned to Elena again and he felt a swift and tender yearning to feel her soft arms around him. "Perhaps it is better this way," he murmured almost to himself. "Perhaps I can finally give Caitlyn the happiness she deserves."

"What are you talking about, Sinclair? Of course, you must ride and tell them both that you're alive. You have a daughter!"

"And a son in Mexico," Brant returned. "God, I don't even know my own daughter; I haven't seen her since she was an infant." Suddenly, he put his head in his hands and Sean saw his shoulders shaking. "I never cared about this place, never could be what she wanted me to be. Would it be so wrong to turn my horse around and go back to where I really want to be?" He looked at Sean with pleading eyes.

"Good God, man, you're not dead, you—"

"I *am* dead to them," Brant put in suddenly. "You saw them, Flynn—how happy they are. I should never have come back." His love for Elena and the wide openness of Mexico was calling him sharply and he almost wheeled his horse about in the direction of the river road.

But Sean's words stopped him. "Wait a moment," he said quickly. "Promise me, you'll wait." And then he urged his horse away, leaving Brant to watch him nervously. What was the man up to? He didn't want to see Caitlyn or Tanner. Let them think he was dead, he thought. It was the best way. Tanner was strong enough to be his own man; he would make Caitlyn a good husband. Tanner and Caitlyn, he mused—and realized that he felt no jealousy. He was fiercely happy for them instead, and relieved

that his conscience was clear and he could return to his Elena. At the thought of seeing her again, he felt a stab of pure joy and glanced backward, wondering if he could wait much longer.

And then he heard a horse making its way through the trees and looked up to see the big man coming toward him again, but this time he held a small child in front of him in the saddle. The little girl looked to be about three years old and Brant knew that he was looking at his daughter.

Tears came to his eyes and he let them run down his cheeks unashamedly as Sean came closer with the child who was looking at him curiously. She was, Brant could see, a beauty. Her hair was the exact color of Caitlyn's and her eyes were blue and vibrant, hinting at the strong will inside that robust little body. Sliding from his horse, he went to Sean and lifted his arms to hold his daughter.

"Who are you?" the little girl wondered, staring into his eyes with a direct gaze that reminded him sharply of Caitlyn.

"I'm an old friend of your mother's," he said thickly, glad that she did not try to pull away from him.

Maggie touched his beard and smiled. Then she traced one pudgy finger down his cheek wonderingly. "Why are you crying?"

He shook his head and felt his throat swelling so that he could barely speak. "I'm just sad, Maggie. Sad because I have to leave you."

"Don't be sad," she told him seriously. "Mama says everyone should be happy for her because she is going to marry Tanner tomorrow. I'm very happy."

"I'm glad of that," Brant whispered. He reached inside the neckline of his shirt and brought out a small crucifix done in mother-of-pearl. It had been given to him by Elena for good luck, but somehow, he knew she wouldn't mind him giving it to his daughter. "This is for you," he said and placed it around her neck.

Maggie squealed with delight. Then she looked at this stranger. "It is very pretty. I will wear it always," she announced solemnly with all the innocent sincerity that could only come from a three-year-old.

"That would make me very happy," Brant whispered and pressed his face into the softness of her hair for a moment. Then, fearing that if he lingered, he might risk discovery, he handed the child back to Sean quickly. Climbing his horse, he turned it

around. "Thank you," he said simply to the man who held his daughter. And then, without a farewell, he urged his horse away, keeping his eyes straight ahead on the river road through the sudden blur of tears that nearly blinded him.

Later that evening, Caitlyn found her daughter in her room, playing with her dolls. With a smile, she opened her arms and Maggie ran to be hugged. "Shall we take a walk outside, my darling, while it's still light enough?" She kissed the tip of her daughter's nose. "Tomorrow is a very important day, and so you must go to bed early. But we can take just a very short walk tonight if you wish."

Maggie nodded. She always loved this quiet time just before her bedtime when her mother gave her all her attention. She squeezed her mother's hand and happily followed her outside to the front of the house where the dark green carpet of the lawn was spread out before her. Thinking of the stranger she had met earlier, she brought the cross out by its chain and felt it with her little fingers.

"What do you have there?" Caitlyn asked curiously as they walked slowly.

For a moment Maggie closed her fingers around the new treasure. Then she reluctantly held it up for her mother to see.

"How beautiful!" Caitlyn said, smiling so that Maggie breathed a sigh of relief. "Where did you get such a beautiful thing, Maggie?" She wondered idly if she'd gotten into her grandmother's jewelry box again.

"Uncle Sean took me to see a man, Mama, a strange man. He was very nice and he gave me the cross."

"A strange man?" For a moment something stabbed at Caitlyn's heart, some inner sense that warned her not to question too closely. Once before, her curiosity and her stubbornness had led her to marry the wrong man. Now she was marrying the right man and nothing must come between them. Still, an old ache seemed to tear at her heart for a moment and she felt a tear sliding gently down her cheek.

"Mama, don't cry," Maggie chided her softly. "Remember, you said that everyone must be happy."

Caitlyn laughed shakily. "Yes, I did, didn't I?" she said softly. The old ache seemed to fade away and an inner peace filled her as she realized that the past was just the past, and her future was with Tanner Malone.

At the sound of a firm tred behind her, she smiled and turned around, her eyes meeting those of her beloved. Yes, she thought happily, Tanner had always been there when she needed him and now—now that she was ready—he was there again, just as he would be there forever, loving her and willing to share his life with her, as he had always been.